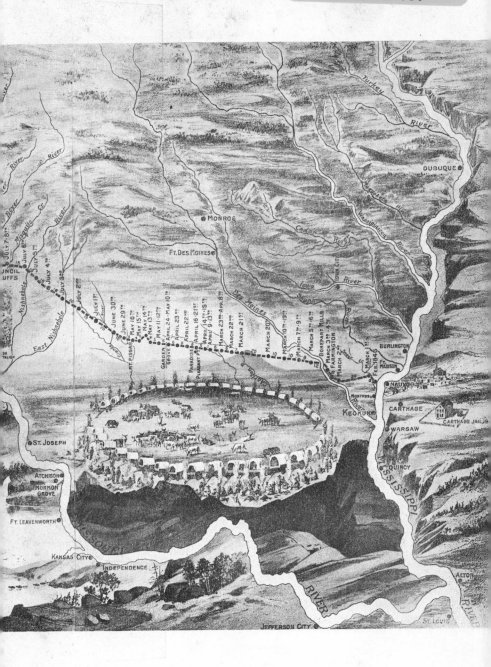

CHILDREN OF GOD

AN AMERICAN EPIC

CHILDREN OF GOD

AN AMERICAN EPIC

VARDIS FISHER

NEW YORK and LONDON

HARPER & BROTHERS

PUBLISHERS

CHILDREN OF GOD

THIRTEENTH EDITION

H–O

CONTENTS

PART ONE

MORNING

CHAPTER I

IN THE FRONTIERLAND OF WESTERN NEW YORK, PALMYRA WAS ONLY A SMALL town, but more itinerant evangelists had come to it than the pious Smiths could remember. Here, and in the thinly settled wilderness round-about, there had been in the early years of the nineteenth century one religious revival after another, with crusaders invoking all the terrors of hell upon an unbelieving world. Farther east, in such nests of infidelity as Yale and Bowdoin College, students were reading the French atheists, swearing by the memory of Tom Paine, and predicting that in another century Christianity would be as dead as Jonathan Edwards. Persons who pretended to be civilized went to church, if indeed they went at all, with caps drawn down to hide their cynical faces; and they sat in dark corners and smiled. God to them was a generic term for every Jehovah and Zeus who had lived as a dark and terrible myth in the minds of men.

Westward, upon the great sweep of the emigrant trails, religion was still a mighty force—from the Hill of Cumorah to the valleys of Tennessee; and prophets of all kinds declared new highways to salvation and God. Down in Kentucky, only a few years before, a Presbyterian preacher had awakened a whole countryside to frenzy: fifteen thousand persons writhed in the madness of the damned and then fell abject and hushed into a trance. Some, aghast at their sins, wild with anxieties and eager for purging, sat like hypnotized idiots, wagging their heads and chanting a dismal dirge to their lost souls; others fell to hands and knees and hopped about and ground their teeth and barked, as if they had returned to the ancient and terrifying jungles; and still others broke into solemn and terrible laughter that died away in chilling and inhuman overtones where the black shadows lay beyond the campfires. A few, beside themselves with ecstasy or woe, left the groups sotted with despair and wandered into the woods and the night, and with sexual orgies attempted to cleanse the disasters from their hearts and minds. The frantic preachers, as crazed and witless as any who heard them, built their thunderous sermons into such pictures of a race doomed and forgotten that an appalled listener, or sometimes two or three at once, fell into such utter lunacy they had to be taken away and roped to their beds or jailed in a woodhouse.

Young Joe Smith had seen the human soul bow low to the inferno of fire. He had seen whole groups converted after two hours of castigation and prophecy; and a week or a month later, he had seen another preacher convert the same group to another sect. For nobody knew which church led the way to heaven: one prophet, appearing suddenly out of the wilderness, offered one way, and a second crusader offered another way—until many persons swung in despair from sect to sect and sought immersion in all of them. One matter, nevertheless, none of them could doubt: every preacher who came to Palmyra declared the human race was lost in sin, and the day of judgment was close at hand. One month the Followers of Christ had the only road to salvation; next month it was the Methodists, in the next, the Presbyterians; and young Joseph, like his neighbors, knelt in prayer and asked God for a sign of the true church.

Though only fourteen in the spring of 1820, he was a tall and handsome youth. He wore patched trousers held by suspenders made of sheeting; a calico shirt that was almost as black as the rich soil in the forests northward; a ragged hat through the holes of which his uncombed flaxen hair thrust up in tiny golden sheaves; and shoes so worn that they barely kept to his feet. He had huge feet and incongruously small hands, and full blue eyes that were half-hidden by the longest and heaviest lashes in Palmyra. They were humorless eyes. Joe had never laughed, and his smile was rare, especially since he had seen priest fight against priest, and each claim, for himself alone, an intimate fellowship with God.

He was not smiling on this golden afternoon. For an hour he had listened to the most violent exhortation that had ever come to his ears, to the most graphic description of the torments of Hell, to the most impassioned plea for repentance. One statement stood in his mind italicized in words of flame: "Does it not say in the Epistle of James, first chapter, fifth verse, that if any of you lack wisdom you are to ask God who giveth unto all men liberally? Does it not say to ask God and it shall be given unto you? That is the message I bring you today!"

That was the message Joe was remembering when he slipped quietly away from the crowd and went to the old family Bible which he had read so many times that much of it he knew by heart. That is the verse he was saying over and over to himself as he went down a path and into the woods back of his home. Spring was upon the earth again. The violets were out; and the trailing arbutus, first sign of renascence to the early colonists, was hanging fragrant pink and white flowers against a prodigal background of green. The white baneberry would be blooming soon. He liked the mayflower best because of its fragrance, but the baneberry aroused his liveliest fancy: its berries, each with a purple spot like an eye, seemed to be looking in all directions, the eyes bulged out of their sockets and the pupils grotesquely dilated. He had often examined the fruit, wondering if there was vision in it and deciding that there might be; for God's world was curious and beyond the understanding of men.

Many a time he had prayed in this cathedral of red oaks, but today he did not kneel at once. He lay on his back in a pool of sunlight and reached out to the violets and thought of his sins. He had drunk beer, he had profaned, but it was not memory of these that troubled him now: he had been unclean with his own flesh and he was not sure that the God of Israel would ever forgive that. Unless he found the right way to salvation, he was lost, like his parents, his friends—like all the bewildered persons around him who had fled from one faith to a second and a third, and were still seeking a fourth that offered more certainty of refuge. It had been so with him and his kind as far back as memory went . . .

There was his maternal grandfather. Solomon Mack had been an adventurer by land and by sea, a wicked and headstrong and ungodly man who had not come home to the Lord until old age fell upon him. Then, like John Bunyan before him, he wrestled with a dark and invisible power and almost dropped dead in a fit. Convinced of his vileness, he had asked God for a sign, and he had seen such a holiness of light against the background of eternity that he had soaked his pillow with tears. Even before that, he fell one day on the Winchester Hills and came to his senses covered with blood and almost frightened out of his wits. When God spoke to him in the light, he found peace and lived in peace to the end. If the Lord spoke to old Solomon, Joe was thinking, He might also speak to him. And then he thought of his mother.

With Lucy the way had been less certain. The death of her sister Lovina had turned her to the Bible, and the great book she read faithfully and then knelt in prayer; but endlessly she asked, "How is a person to know which Church is the right one?" Joe had heard that question asked a thousand times in his home. His mother had asked it year after year but had remained aloof until a few weeks ago. Recently she had· been converted by a Presbyterian crusader, but she was still unhappy in her choice and she still asked the question that troubled her most. Her husband, about whose spiritual welfare she worried herself sick, was overcome by the same tormenting doubts. He had once been a Methodist.but in disgust he left that faith and now gazed at all evangelists with unhappy eyes. His son had heard him say many a time, "All churches look about alike to me. I think mebbe they're all wrong."

The anxieties of Joe's father impelled him to visions, two of which had left a deep impression on his son. In the first, the father had seen a great and spacious building which stood in the air, with the vast and unfathomable eternities above and beyond it; and in this vision he believed God had shown him the right church if he only had power to understand. "It was God's tabernacle," he said, and his·son pondered the statement. In the second vision, he saw a glorious tree burgeoned with fruit, and the fruit, he well knew, was intended to make a. man happy; but he did not know what it was. It looked like apples, he said, but it was not apples, nor was it plum or grape or pear, or any other fruit. he had ever seen. Joseph, the father, prayed too with his wife; and Joseph, the son, looked at them and pondered the dilemma and searched the Bible for a sign.

His parents, he was remembering now, had often been close to God. When the family lived in Randolph, Lucy suffered with fever and the doctors gave her up. Unwilling to die, she had cried out to God and she had heard a clear voice say, "Seek, and ye shall find; knock, and it shall be opened unto you." Thereupon she recovered quickly and sought instruction, going from one minister to another; but though these men knew much of the Bible they seemed to be strangers to God, and she turned away from them and brooded over her doubts. As a matter of fact, during their entire married life, while renting a farm in Tunbridge or going bankrupt in Randolph, or eking out a bare living in Sharon and Lebanon and Norwich, Lucy and Joseph had tirelessly asked of God a sign of the right church and had been given no sign. The son, more oppressed by doubts than his brothers Sam and Hy or his sister Sophronia, all of whom had become Presbyterians, was determined to learn which sect—if, indeed, there was any—God still smiled upon and approved.

There had been no sign in anything he could remember now: none in the way his giant of a father dropped humbly to his knees and prayed until sweat poured down his cheeks; none in the evenings when the father set his spectacles on his nose and looked around him and said, "Hyrum, Samuel, Joseph, get ready for your prayers"; none in the monotonous intoning of meaningless lines:

Another day has passed and gone,
We lay our garments by . . .

For the old doubts and questions lived again the next morning.

There had been no sign among the evangelists. The Methodist had cried, "Lo, here is the right church!" and the next month the Presbyterian had said, "Lo, the right church is over here!" and the Baptist had thundered: "They are all wrong! Here is the Church of God!" There was no sign in the way priest fought against priest, convert against convert, until God withdrew from the confusion of anger and spite, and the problem was more darkly unanswerable than before. There had been nothing, indeed, in all these years except that golden verse from the Epistle of James. This Joe murmured over and over, wondering if he should ask of God and if God would hear . . .

An hour later he had not moved. His hands still reached out to green leaf and blue flower, and his eyes still looked at the golden glory of the afternoon sun. For several minutes he had been feeling strange and lost, as if a great and nameless power had possessed the woods and hushed the song of birds. The sky had darkened. He sat up, feeling alarm, and gazed around him; and then softly, with his eyes on the blue vault above him, he moved to his knees and clasped hands to his breast. For a long moment he hardly realized that he was praying—for he had never prayed aloud before; nor did he quite understand what he said. He was obscurely aware of his trembling body and the strange deep passion of his voice; but his prayer, filled with biblical phrases and archaic terms, seemed not to be his at all. He listened as if to another voice and was moved to deep astonishment. He seemed almost to be standing apart and looking at himself, kneeling here in leaf-depth, and speaking in impassioned wonder to a great blue pasture with its solitary golden sun. After a little, he knew there were tears in his eyes and tears wet and running on his cheeks as the whole world listened to the anxious humble asking of his voice . . .

He stopped praying and for a long moment was still. His senses were swimming. All the meaning of his mind and body was withdrawing to a far and infinite meaning, as if a great power were sucking him dry, as if there would be left kneeling here only his flesh and his bones. The world had darkened. He felt sudden and awful terror. He strove to cry aloud but his hot tongue filled his mouth and throat; he tried to move but seemed to be roped to the earth. There was soft and unreal music in his ears as light and darkness fought to possess his mind. Without knowing what he did, he sank slowly to the earth, as if moved by a force not of his will, and lay on his back with his wide blue gaze on the sky. Without stirring a finger, without even blinking, he lay as one dead; and then very softly his eyelids closed upon the awful terror in his eyes . . .

He saw first an intimation of brightness far out in the universe: it grew like the softness of morning, like a gentle flowering out of utter darkness, as if heaven were overflowing the wastelands of night as brilliance spilled from God's robe as He walked. For a long moment the light spread and gathered strength and then suddenly fell downward in a broad beam of terrible splendor, in a great and blinding pillar that touched the earth and lay far out in a white column of eternity. Then, with startling swiftness, two persons appeared in this stupendous shaft of light, the Father and the Son; and they were exactly alike in countenance and in the incandescence of their glory. They walked down the beam as down a highway of light; and one called the prostrate lad by name and pointed to his companion and said, "This is my beloved Son. Hear Him!" The Son spoke. He declared in the voice of a great organ that all the creeds of earth were an abomination in His sight, and that those who professed them wore an aspect of godliness but were corrupt, drawing near to Him with their lips and mocking Him with alien hearts; and added that a new church would be established under the leadership of a new prophet. The voice died away in echoes that rolled in solemn music, and the highway of light slowly faded, with Father and Son standing as vanishing silhouettes against the infinite. The light closed like a shutter to a thin wraith of holiness and slowly withdrew to the lone glittering point of a star.

When Joe came to his senses he was still lying on his back. He strove to move but was so weak that for a moment he could stir neither arms nor legs, nor do more than blink his eyes; but presently he sat up, feeling as if all the blood had been let from his veins. He was amazed to find himself here, with birds singing around him and a fragrant breeze coming from the western hills. Remembering his vision of God and the Son, he looked around him, wondering about them and himself and trying to understand. After a little, he rose to his feet, weak and unnerved, and turned toward the log house which his father had built in a clearing. Upon approaching, he paused for a moment and gazed at the rough logs and hewn facings, and the roof of poles and earth, remembering that Jesus was born in a manger. Then he went inside. At once, sensing that all was not well with her son, his mother came to him anxiously and looked at his white face and troubled eyes. She carried a hand-painted oilcloth cover for a table; and across the room he saw a dozen more on which she had been working.

"What is the trouble, my boy?"

He resented her. Both God and the Son had talked to him, but as likely as not she would say, with the Baptist preacher, that nobody had visions in these days. He stared at her and his gaze was curious. She had a high forehead, a resolute thrust of chin; she was very wide between her pale eyes. Her eyes were so pale a blue, indeed, that it occurred to him, with a shrug of distaste, that she had washed them too much with tears. He remembered that she was and always had been the aggresisve manager of this household.

Lucy looked at her son, the strangest child who had been born to her.

"Tell me, boy. Something troubles you."

"Never mind me," he said, turning away. "I am well enough off."

"But something has happened. Tell me."

"Why should I?"

"Because I am your mother."

Choosing his words slowly, he said: "I have learned that Presbyterianism is not true."

Lucy stiffened. "My boy, how do you know that?"

"Would you believe me?"

"Of course."

Joseph drew himself to his fullest height. "Because," he said proudly, "I have just talked with God."

"You have— What is this you're saying!"

"I have had a vision. I have talked with the Son. But you," he said, staring at her with reproachful blue eyes, "would never believe that. A sinful world will never believe. But I swear it is true."

"My boy, of course I believe. What wonderful thing are you telling me?" She was trembling and gazing at him with anxious eyes. "The blessed Lord Himself talked to you? Tell me."

"Yes, He spoke to me," said Joseph, and he trembled also.

"What did He say?"

"I went out," he said, looking away, "to pray and to ask advice." He considered a moment and then fell into the biblical manner of speaking which, since early childhood, he had used when alone. "It says in the Epistle of James that whoso lacketh vision, he shall seek of God who giveth liberally. I prayed, and lo, it came to pass that God and the Son appeared to me in glory that was brighter than the noonday sun; and, verily, they did say unto me that all churches are an abomination in their sight." He paused, breathing heavily and remembering. "And it came to pass that I did behold God and the Son in a great light, and the Son spake unto me, saying, 'Verily, verily, I say unto you, my servant Joseph, that a new church will be established in these latter days and you will be my prophet.'" He stopped again, not knowing with certainty whether the Lord had said that; not knowing, indeed, what had or had not been said. "He said I would be held as evil by all men and in all tongues. He said, 'Verily, the Church of God will be established among all tongues and kindreds. Behold, I, the Lord, will establish my church through you, even unto all men who have cursed me and brought shame upon me. And so let it be.' That," said Joseph, turning strange blue eyes on his mother, "is what the Lord said unto me."

"My boy, my boy!" she cried, touching him reverently. He looked at her face and saw that she believed, and in his own heart he pronounced it good. "I must go tell your father," she said, her voice shaking like her body. "Oh, my boy!"

"I warn you," he said solemnly, "that scoffers and unbelievers and sinners will say I lie."

"But you don't lie! Oh, it is true, true! God has made Himself manifest with a sign."

"Verily," said Joseph, "it is so."

Beside herself with joy she went to find her husband; and Joseph left the house, walking with new pride in his dirty ragged clothes. He wanted to be alone again. There could be no lie in this that he had told but he wanted to be alone to examine his heart and his conscience and learn if God were still speaking through them. He went into the woods and sat under a great oak; the softness of early dusk was upon the western hills. In all directions, he reflected, there were millions of persons, living in evil ways, praising God with their lips but with their hearts turned against Him; fighting priest against priest and sect against sect, with the church that Christ founded as dead as last year's leaf. Westward in Buffalo, south in Waterloo and Fayette, east in Utica and Pittsfield and Tunbridge, ministers were crying, "Lo, here is the true church!" and every one of them was an abomination in the sight of God. They were hypocrites and Pharisees all. They wore the vestments of holiness, but their minds were unclean and their hearts were turned to the Devil. As he sat here, telling the vision over and over, giving to it the meaning which he was certain it must have had, he believed deeply that God had spoken and called him to prophethood. He wondered if his father would doubt.

Joseph Smith, the elder, did not doubt. A man six feet two in height and of great bulk, he was sober of mein, and impatient of the light heart and the careless tongue. He also had had visions, though he had never talked with God, and he saw no reason at all why he should question the tale of his son. After hearing it, he was thoughtful a long while, solemnly pondering what had been told. At last he said:

"When are you to start this new church?"

"I don't know," said his son. "I'm to wait until the Lord speaks again."

Joseph looked at the other members of his family, gathered around. His older brothers, Sam and Hy, gazed at him with earnest belief; and his sister trembled and bit her lip.

"What size was God?" asked Sam.

"The size of man," said Joseph. "God is like us, only He is pure and glorified."

"And you say the Lord looked like Him?"

"They were just alike but more beautiful and holy than I could tell you."

"Did the Lord," asked Lucy, "say when He would come again?"

"No. He told me to prepare myself. He said He would establish a church through me and it would be the true church."

Joseph did not welcome questions. There were uncertainties in his mind, too, and he wished to be alone with them and inquire into the doubts. In this night he did not sleep well. He tossed in his dreams and awoke often, believing that God was near. Sitting up, he would search the attic room for a sign, a light, and he would listen; and then he would lie down again, knowing well that God would not speak to him for many days. Now and then he wondered unhappily if the Lord had spoken to him at all; but after remembering, after saying over and over the words he had told his parents, unconsciously adding little by little to what had been said, he knew that he was a prophet with a great mission on earth.

In the days that followed, nevertheless, he struggled with doubts and despair, until the thought came suddenly that he was being tempted, as prophets had been tempted of old. He felt better then. God was placing burdens upon his belief and his will. "Verily," he said to himself, walking in the woods, "it is so." He resolved to cleanse his heart of all evil and be ready for the next vision. So certain after a while became his belief in himself as a prophet that he sought the Methodist minister and told of what he had seen and heard. That large man, with his heavy face and his small eyes, was speechless with amazement.

"What lie are you telling? You say God talked to you, a mere child!"

"I do say that God and the Son talked to me. Verily, it is true."

"What blasphemy! My boy, you will be struck dead for that!"

"I expect to be persecuted, even as Jesus was."

The man turned red with fury. He laid a heavy hand on Joseph's shoulder and shook him and admonished him with a thick finger. "You go home and take a physic! This is the most horrible blasphemy I ever listened to. God does not reveal Himself any more, or speak in person to mankind. There are no prophets today. And certainly," he added, shaking the lad again, "if there was a prophet, he wouldn't be no beardless ragamuffin like you. You cease this terrible abomination before lightning blasts you!"

"But I tell you God did manifest Himself unto me and speak unto me, even as He spake unto Moses. If I lie about that——"

"Stop! You're a child of the Devil, I say. You are fevered and need some blood-letting and you go home now and take a physic."

Joseph shook the hand off and stepped back. "Priests of all churches will persecute me and say evil things against me. Nobody believed Paul when he was brought before King Agrippa. They said he was mad. But Paul knew he had heard God, and I know I heard and saw God; and if I denied that——"

"You abominable upstart!"

"You can persecute me. All the priests with evil hearts can say evil things against me, lo, even as they were said of Jesus. But if I was to be crucified for it, I would not deny the Lord."

"I tell you, boy, a devil is in you!"

"I expect many priests to say that."

"You run home and take a physic. And don't tell this blasphemous story to anyone else. Go home now!"

When Joseph entered the log house, the other members of his family were there. His mother was working on another oilcloth cover for a stand; his father was searching the Bible; his brother Hyrum was standing by a broken window and looking out. Joseph crossed the slabs of the floor and sat on a block of wood that was used for a chair. Already persons were saying he was mad or possessed of devils; there was ribald laughter when he walked the streets. Upon entering the town, he saw persons come from store and harness shop, from tavern and trading post and barn to stare at him, or to snicker softly and jeer. But when he looked at the members of his family and knew that they believed in his mission, he felt better; and quietly he climbed a ladder to the attic and sought his barren room, knowing that God had spoken to him and would speak again.

CHAPTER II

Two and a half years passed before his next vision but he was not idle. He labored on his father's farm, cutting cordwood, gathering materials for baskets and birch brooms, and sap for maple syrup. Lucy said he ought to give himself wholly to the work to which God had called him; and he did give much time to it, spending many days in solitary walks and meditation, reading the Bible, and preparing his heart and mind for the stern duties of a prophet. His doubt of himself diminished as persecutions became more severe. After a group of men and boys set upon him and drubbed him soundly, he felt that he did not doubt at all; for had not punishment and evil jeers been the lot of every prophet since the days of Adam? No matter where he went, he ran into taunts and abuse.

"Hi, Joe! Has God Amighty been showun hisself to you lately?"

"Why, by gum, there's the new prophet again! What's new, Joe? Don't you think you'd better grow some chin whiskers and look like Moses?"

"Deacon my calf! There's that gallinipper of a prophet. Hey, you and God trading chin music these days, or did you go and get slewed again?"

But sometimes it was a rebuke.

"For the shame of you, boy! To go a-tellun you seen the blessed Jesus! You'll roast in hell for that, my foolish lad."

But not everyone on this frontier regarded him with amusement or scorn. The Rockwells and Whitmers—and other families, too—came to the Smith home and talked of the vision and stared at Joseph with awe; and one day Porter Rockwell, a rugged boy with a scowling face, gazed at him gravely and said: "When I get big I'll help you. I'll jounce your enemies to hell and across lots." Joe looked at the lad and smiled, little realizing with what zeal that promise would be fulfilled.

He did not allow awe to turn his head, or spite and hatred to deflect him. Before God would speak again, he told himself, he must understand what was intended; and he thought often of Moses, of the ancient Joseph, of Elijah and Isaiah and Jeremiah, of John the Baptist and Peter and Paul.

Religion had impelled these men to noble thoughts and phenomenal deeds —for God was a God of power. It was nonsense to say He was an idea: He was a person, a glorified man, and all the peoples of earth were His actual children. Religion was a force that energized, that gave faith and strength and purpose, sending apostles from their wives and children, as it had sent Paul over the civilized world.

There was another matter, too, that occupied his thought. He had heard speculation on the origin of Indians; and there came to him the notion, faintly at first, but more and more insistently, that God would reveal the origin to him. From this conviction sprang the idea that he must write a book, and often as he walked in the woods, he phrased sentences and whole paragraphs, wondering again and again if God was speaking through him when he talked. "I must purify my heart," he said alone one day. "Lo, I must cast all evil thoughts from me and the Lord will speak again." He liked to think of the book and to plot it, summoning from his resourceful fancy the figures of destiny in legends of his own making, letting them talk to one another, each narrating a part of his ancient story, until the book assumed enormous proportions and threaded its fables back almost to the beginning of time.

But casting evil thoughts from him was not easy. When, on Palmyra or Manchester streets, he saw lovely girls, his mind turned to them in conjecture, his hunger seeking their youth; and he was abashed and saddened and groaned under the temptings. A sweet voice or laugh, a colorful face, a trim ankle or a bower of hair would fetch him up with a start and scatter his pious phrases to the four winds. Now and then when alone, and unable to endure the torment, he yielded to his carnal appetites; and guilt thereupon became such a burden on his conscience that he felt abandoned to the Devil. In morning and evening, and often during the long nights, he knelt in prayer, confessing his sins and promising to be pure of heart and worthy of his calling.

In one of these nights, after an hour of anguished prayer, he fell asleep and saw a vision. The world around him was flooded with brilliant light and in the splendor was a person in a gown as white as snow, with a face like an image out of lightning, yet full of gentleness and goodwill. Joseph saw that the naked feet did not touch the floor but stood in the light, as if the person were softly suspended in radiant atmosphere, with the holiness of heaven upon his body and robe. He knew next that the visitor had been speaking: never in his life had a voice come with sharper clarity, yet gently, like the far mellow sound of a great church bell. The voice said to him that God had work to do, but, lo, it would require vast courage and boldness, for the name of him, the new Joseph and the last of the prophets, would be called evil among all nations, and his sufferings would be many and great. Then, to his happy amazement, the voice declared that the Indians were from the Twelve Tribes of Israel and had left upon golden plates a record of their past; and that these plates contained also the full-ness of the everlasting gospel, soon to be made known to men. . . . And suddenly the vision was gone, and Joseph found himself sitting up in bed and staring into darkness.

Deeply shaken, he lay down and reflected on what he had heard; and after a long while he slept and dreamed. Again, as before, he was awakened as if a bugle had sounded his name. Looking to the left, he beheld the awful unearthly brilliance and saw in its depth the image of a hill and a cave in the hill that was like an oval of still fire; and in the cave the paler glow of gold. Out of the far darkness of the room came a voice. "Verily, these are the plates of gold upon which is recorded the everlasting gospel." And, as before, the light faded, though slowly this time, as if a great lamp had been withdrawn. Joseph put a hand to his brow and closed his eyes. He was now shaking as with chills and he was afraid. He thought of calling to his brothers who slept in an adjoining attic room or of tip-toeing downstairs to seek the strong bulk of his father; but he dared not leave his bed, and so pulled a quilt over his eyes and pondered. Whether he had seen an angel or had dreamed, he could not be sure: in memory he called back, word by word, what had been said, and saw again the awful majesty of the clothed visitor. Turning over, he buried his face in a pillow and shook with terrified prayer.

He did not in the next morning tell his parents of these visions. Enter-ing a forest, he lay on his back and gazed at the sky, no longer doubting that an angel had come to him, and knowing more certainly now the kind of emotional receptivity he needed to put himself in touch with God. He could induce it by thinking only of holy matters and by fixing his mind on the thought that he was a prophet. When he did so, in this hour as formerly, he could feel the earth withdraw with its burden of sin, could feel himself move, as by a guiding arm at his waist, to the serene glory where Jehovah dwelt. All immediate things were drowned in consciousness and lost, including the trees, the earth on which he lay, the song of birds; and the sun and the sky expanded into eternity and were neither sun nor sky, but a vast realm softer than clouds and whiter than new snow. His breathing became an enormous wonder that filled the immensity of space. He left the tabernacle of his flesh and was clothed with eternity.

His vision now, after lying for two hours in the warm sun, was only of a voice, though he seemed to be far away from his own body, with his emotion embracing all the wonder of heaven. It was the voice, he well knew, of the angel Moroni, who had spoken to him the night before. The voice said he would go to the Hill of Cumorah and there look upon the plates; but it warned him that the time for bringing them forth was four years hence. Whereupon, quite out of himself in the transporting intensity of the vision, he went in a pilgrimage as swift as light to the hill and lifted the plates out of their ancient stone box and gazed at them, with his soul triumphant for the church which God would establish through him. He returned as swiftly as he had gone; and when he came to his mortal senses, he found himself again in the tabernacle of his flesh, staring at a pale sky. Feeling a little like a person who had awakened to find himself lying in a coffin, he rose to his knees and moved his white lips in prayer. "Our Father," he whispered, with bowed head, "I will do thy bidding!"

Then he went home, remembering that his parents and their friends had been impatient for another vision. Well, he would tell them now. He knew now what he was to do and when he was to do it. In four years he would begin to translate the everlasting gospel, as well as the records of the lost tribes; for then, the angel had said, the secrets of the golden history would be given to him. Meanwhile . . .

"You say," asked his father, "there's a history of the Indians?"

"Yes," said Joseph, for he already knew the answers to many questions. He knew, indeed, that for two and a half years, God had been guiding him when he plotted the genealogies of ancient peoples, or wrote one paragraph and another of the many chapters. And now he announced gravely: "The Indians are the Lamanites. Laman was one of the sons of Lehi."

"Who," asked his mother, "was Lehi?"

"Lehi was a man who built a boat and led the pilgrims to South America."

For a long moment there was silence while father and mother looked at their son. Hyrum, the brother, gazed too; and at last he said:

"And you really saw golden plates?"

"Yes."

"With your mortal eyes?"

Joseph hesitated. The incredulity in his brother's voice impelled him to make one of the gravest mistakes of his life. He knew well that he had seen the plates only in a vision, but he felt nobody would believe that. If he had said he saw them in a vision and if he had added that he would translate them while the power of God was upon him, but without ever actually seeing them or holding them in his mortal hands, he would have avoided what was to become his most serious problem. But he did not in this moment foresee the difficulties. The only thought in his mind was this, that nobody would believe in golden plates if they were not tangible objects that could be measured and weighed . . .

"With your own eyes?" Hyrum asked again.

"Yes."

"How big are they? I mean the plates?"

"Not very big. About like this—and this," said Joseph, measuring with his hands.

"And you say there was a Urim and Thummim?"

"Yes."

"What is it for?"

"To translate them with."

"Oh," said Hyrum, abashed by his ignorance.

"And they're out in a hill?" asked Sam.

"Yes, in the Hill of Cumorah."

"I don't think," said the cautious father, "I'd tell anyone. People might go diggun around to find them."

"Of course they would," said Lucy. "No, my boy, tell no one."

"They're probably worth a lot," said Sam.

"Samuel!" his father said.

"I just meant— Well, they're made out of gold, ain't they?"

"Did you see the writing on them?" asked Sophronia.

"Yes, of course."

"Could you read it?"

"I didn't try," said Joseph sternly. "I'm not to read it for four years."

"And you'll be persecuted?" asked Hyrum. "Did God say that?"

"It was not God," said Joseph with dignity. "It was an angel. The angel said my fame would go around the world and I would be known for good and for evil among all nations and tongues, even as Jesus was before me. Lo, that is what the angel said. And he said I am to look at the records once each year for four years and then translate."

"You best be careful," said his father. "Someone might follow you and dig them up. It would be a nice mess if the records was stolen."

Joseph could have explained that he would visit the records only in a vision; but he let the opportunity pass, and it came to be known that he would visit a hill and open a vault and look with mortal eyes upon plates of gold. Though only a youth of seventeen, his knowledge of human beings was canny; and he knew there would be persons—scoffers of every color and breed—who would demand to see the plates and the writing on them. Whether he could match his cunning against incredulity, he did not know: perhaps he could find some objects that would be accepted as the holy ones he had seen in a dream. In many of the hills in this area, there had been digging for gold, or for ancient treasure which legends declared the Spaniards had buried and left. He could do a little exploring of his own and possibly God would direct his search. Perhaps, indeed, the plates *were* real; for in this, as in many other matters, he was still uncertain and proceeded cautiously on his way. That he was now a prophet, even as Moses and Isaiah were, he no longer doubted. He girded his loins and prepared for his huge task.

In Palmyra was a debating club for younger persons, and this he joined. As he became more confident of his power and destiny, he developed a fluency of speech, of homely metaphor, of mystic elusiveness that astonished those who heard him. Until recently he had been a quiet and melancholy lad who haunted the forests; and now, with his flaxen hair wild and his blue eyes flashing, he spoke in bold language, and silenced hecklers with a gesture of his small white hand. "Behold and hearken, O ye children of evil, for the eye of God is upon ye and the God of Israel is displeased! Verily I say unto you that righteousness cometh down from above, from the Father of light; and evil cometh from the unclean devils in your hearts! Behold and lo, ye must humble yourselves so that you can see God with your spiritual and not your carnal minds. When ye are worthy, then God in His own due time will confer blessings upon you.

But now ye are all lost in vile wickedness and your hearts do turn to the sins of the flesh, and the Almighty is wroth with you! . . ."

After he had become at ease before the awed and the insolent who came to hear him, he went boldly to the matter nearest his heart. One Sunday afternoon, he left no doubt of what he meant. At two hundred persons he shook a clenched hand and cried: "Behold, I do say to you that all churches today are an abomination in the sight of God! Ye worship with your lips, yea, verily, but your hearts are far from·Him!"

"Hey, Joe, where do you get all those yea verilies and lo and beholds?"

"Silence!" Joseph thundered. "Ye are speaking to a prophet, not to the dust of a common man. I say to you that a new church will be established, and that all who seek godliness may be saved. Repent ye!" he roared, his eyes flashing at a lout who snickered with hands to his face. "Purify yourselves, ye and ye, for the new dispensation, lest God smite ye for denouncing the only true gospel! Lo——"

"I tell ye, cut out all that loing at us!"

"You back there, Silas Cashart, with carnal lusts in your heart and the abominations of Satan making a bulging wickedness of your mind! Listen to me, ye infidel with the mark of eternal hell upon ye! I do tell you I am a prophet sent by the Almighty to show the way to salvation, and if you don't humble your heart before the only true gospel, then forever and ever to the last eternity of time you will fry in torment and agonies in the deepest and darkest pits of the Devil! You, Silas Cashart, and you, Paul Waldman, and you, Frankie Stoal, with your souls scarred and pockmarked with your lecherous ways, and your minds choked and overflowing with the sins of Satan and the damnable doted wood of a wicked world! . . ."

His fame spread far ·beyond these hills of his home. Some, awed by thought of him, said a new prophet had risen; and some with an oath cried that he was a hellhound and a dowser, and ought to be taken out and hanged. A few gathered to his leadership while hundreds plotted his ruin. Those who threatened him, or shadowed him on dark nights, did not know that young Joe Smith, for all his dirt and rags and quaint stories, had the soul of a poet and the heart of a lion. He placed himself in the blood brotherhood of the ancient Joseph and the apostolic fellowship of Jeremiah and went fearlessly ahead.

CHAPTER III

HE SPENT TWO MORE YEARS IN LONELY MEDITATION AND GREW TO MAN-hood. Standing over six feet without his shoes and weighing almost two hundred pounds, he was the handsomest giant in western New York. Matured by reflection and public speaking, he had his plans clearly in mind but he refused to divulge them. On the contrary, he withdrew to solitude in the woods, taking the family Bible with him, and read aloud to himself the magnificent prose, memorizing much that he had not already learned and cultivating a biblical manner of speaking, even to his relatives and friends. He felt now that he was so receptive to the will of God that God was with him at all times. But he was not ready to undertake his bold career until he had foreseen all the perplexing problems which would arise. He had to formulate the outlines of his history, determine the tenets of his new gospel, and look around him for converts who would be both fearless and meek. One question he had forever settled in his mind: he was a direct descendant of the great Joseph of Israel, and he now frowned with displeasure when his family called him Joe.

While he thoughtfully marked time in his twentieth year, there came to Palmyra a man named Josiah Stoal, a dark and dirty fellow with the fever of gold in his eyes. He was from Harmony, a frontier village just over the border in Pennsylvania; and he came to find laborers to help him dig in the hills for a legendary mine. Joseph was interested. He needed money to found a church: if he went with Stoal, perhaps God would guide him to a treasure-trove.

But his soft white hands were not for a pick and shovel. It was un-seemly, he reflected, for a prophet to be engaged in physical toil; and on the second afternoon he left Stoal's rocky hillside and wandered far afield. He came to a tiny lake between two green hills and espied upon the water a bed of beautiful lotus, with larger leaves and flowers than he had ever seen. Removing his clothes, he waded out and stood waist deep in the garden upon the water, remembering that this plant was called water-chinquapin or duck acorn. The pale yellow flowers were sweetly fragrant. He was breathing of them and admiring the great broad leaves, afloat like the beds of water sprites, when, looking shoreward, he saw a young woman. Too surprised to speak, he wondered if she were real or a vision.

"Hello!" she called. "What are you doing?"

"Exploring," he said.

"Bring me a bouquet," said the girl.

"I'm naked!" he cried, feeling very foolish. "My clothes are there on the bank. You run and hide and I'll wade out and dress."

She lost no time in fleeing. Almost before he knew it, she had vanished; whereupon he gathered a handful of flowers, and then a large leaf which he held in front of him like a shield as he waded out. He sat in grass and hastily clothed himself.

"All right!" he called, getting to his feet. "Where are you?"

Very slowly she came in sight. She was tall and queenly, with black hair and black searching eyes: a stately and austere and lovely madonna in a calico dress. She came up and looked at him and smiled.

"Did you bring my flowers?"

"Here," he said, and gave her a handful of yellow blossoms. "Who are you?"

"I'm Emma Hale."

"Oh," he said, observing that her lips were too thin for passionate kissing. "Is your home nearby?"

"Just yonder—about a half a mile. Who are you?"

He looked down the path but could not see her home. "I'm Joseph Smith."

"What!" she cried. She could not have shown more alarm if he had said he was the Devil. Slowly she walked backward, step by step, her frightened eyes on his face.

"Don't be afraid," he said. "I guess evil tongues have been busy over here."

"Are you the Joe Smith who talks with God?" There was scorn in her voice.

"I'm Joseph Smith, the prophet. But I'm also a man, and women need not be afraid of me."

She caught her breath. Her gaze went up and down him and again studied his face. "You're the man who looks into peepstones!"

"I know not," he said with dignity, "what you mean by peepstones. You have been listening to evil men."

"I must go now. Here—here are your flowers." And she tossed the yellow handful toward him.

Swiftly he moved around her and stood in the path. "Not yet. Tell me: does your father take in boarders?"

"As to that," she said severely, "you'd better ask him."

"What is his name?"

"Isaac Hale."

"Oh, yes, I've heard of him. A very worthy gentleman. You are not very kind," he said, annoyed by her haughtiness. "Do I look like the Devil?"

"You look like a very crazy man. And now, if you please——"

"I'm going to live at your home," Joseph announced. He smiled. "Don't you want the flowers?"

"No."

"Shall I wade out and get you a big armful?"

"No."

"All right, I'll go with you now." He stepped aside and she fled down the path, gathering her dress in one hand and going like the wind; and Joseph strode after her, smiling to see such haste.

Isaac Hale was a huge man, bronzed and wind-burnt, with great tough hands that could have held both of Joseph's in either palm. Known as a two-gun man and a dead shot, he was perhaps the most pigheaded hulk of fearlessness in western Pennsylvania. He could throw a young deer in shot-pouch hold over a shoulder and tramp all day with the burden, or swing a heavy axe for twelve hours without pause. For his wife, and for Emma, his only unmarried daughter, he was a titan of iron and blasphemy whom all men feared and few dared approach.

It was little wonder that Joseph was abashed when he saw the man. In Isaac's big face that looked like reddened granite were the coldest eyes Joseph had ever seen. His voice matched his bulk.

"You say you want a-board with me? Who are you?"

"I'm Joseph Smith."

"That peepstone spoops who talks with God?" Isaac's baked face broke into a grin.

"I'm no spoops. I'm a prophet."

"Well, you see the missus. If she'n stand to have a prophet around, I guess I can."

Mrs. Hale said it would be all right; but Emma, standing by a window in pensive scorn, turned angrily and said no. "He thinks he's a prophet or something. I don't like him."

"But you don't know me," said Joseph, meeting her contempt with his most winning smile. "You might like me after a while."

"I'll never like pretenders."

"Hush," said Mrs. Hale. "Don't judge, daughter, lest ye be judged. If Mr. Smith is as nice as he seems——"

"Anyone can *seem* nice. That's how the Devil is."

"What," asked the mother, "might your business be over in these parts?"

"Oh," said Emma, "he's peeping around in holes, looking for gold plates or something. Or taking his clothes off and wading out after wankapin. Or maybe he's looking for the lost tribes."

"Daughter, for shame." Mrs. Hale smiled at Joseph. He was handsome and she liked him. "I think it will be all right. We'll have supper about seven."

The supper was of cold venison and milk and wild fruits. Isaac looked from time to time at his strange visitor; and at last he said:

"A prophet, you say. What by the tarred and blackened face of the Devil do you mean?"

"God has called me to establish the true gospel on earth."

"I thought that old fool Peter was supposed to a-done that." Isaac grunted and drank his milk. "You mean the Almighty has got His dander up and wants to try it again?"

"All churches today," said Joseph quietly, "are an abomination in His sight."

"Well, holy Jesus, I don't blame Him. They're a 'bomination in my sight too. What new fancy sickle-hammed doctrine you got in your mind?"

"Just the simple honest principles necessary to salvation."

Isaac grunted again and wolfed his fruit. Emma looked at Joseph, her opaquely black eyes full of contempt.

But Joseph did not mind. He had set his heart on winning her and he was not a man who set his heart lightly. Nevertheless, one day passed, a second and a third, and she refused to speak. At breakfast and again at supper he strove to meet her gaze but she kept her graceful head turned from him and her thoughts darkly to herself. At mealtime, indeed, less and less was said: Isaac fed his great appetite in silence, and Mrs. Hale, perplexed and ill at ease, only now and then ventured a swift glance at their guest. One morning, seeing how matters stood, she followed Joseph to the yard and touched his arm.

"I think Emma likes you some now. She's got so she watches you leave."

He smiled. "Maybe she'll walk with me this evening."

She walked with him this evening and many evenings thereafter. He told her, with overwhelming pride, that he was a prophet of God, the first in centuries; that he received visions—and these he so graphically described that she almost held her breath; and that many sinful persons were vilifying him and speaking evil of his name. Her incredulity softened a little, less because of the biblical precedents he cited than because of the sensuous ardor she felt in the man. That he believed in his divine gift, she could not doubt; and if he received such visions as he told of, then perhaps his incredible story was true. But whether true or not, she did not care: he was both handsome and eloquent, and men of his kingly bearing were not common in this backwoods area. It was in a beautiful evening that he spoke of love.

"It is best for us to be married soon," he declared, speaking as if the matter had been settled. "I'll ask your father tonight."

"Married!" she cried, turning upon him black eyes full of amazement. "What makes you think I'd marry you?"

"You must. God has ordained it."

"I can't see that God has anything to do with it. Marrying is my business, not God's."

"Everything is God's business," he said. "It is His will for us to marry soon. This summer—or not later than this fall."

"But I don't love you."

"Yes, Emma, you do. It is in the plan of things for you to be my wife and assist me. I must establish the true church——"

"You seem to take me for granted," said Emma, amused by his solemn presumption. "Because I have been kind to you, that is no reason——"

"It is God's will," he said, cutting her short. For a moment he was annoyed by the laughter in her eyes; but then, noting how red her lips were, he grasped her arms and moved to kiss her.

"No!" she cried, and put a hand to his mouth. He kissed her hand. She liked the kiss and wondered if it would not be nice to let him kiss her lips. When she strove to free herself, his hands closed on her flesh until she cried with pain and fought against him, kicking at his legs, and exclaiming in a voice that was half-angry and half-amused. Crushing her resistance, he drew her close and sought her lips. When she felt his warm eager mouth, she stopped fighting and closed her eyes, yielding with a sigh to his strength; and he kissed her mouth and cheeks and throat, his hands moving up and down her back and then holding her close to him, curve to curve. After a long impassioned kiss, she cried: "Don't, Joe! No more now!"

But he was aroused by her youth and only pressed her closer, his hungry lips exploring her throat. Again she yielded, her soft lips opening to his and her hands rising to his shoulders and then to his hair.

"You see you do love me," he said, drawing away to look at her. "It is God's will that you shall not resist me."

"I should think my will has something to do with it."

"No. Emma, we must be married soon."

"Don't I have anything to say about that?"

"Emma, God has ordained you to help me. You must marry me."

He moved to kiss her again but she turned away, her laugh mocking him. "And is it God's will that you should kiss me right now?"

"Yes," he said. "The spirit of God guides me in everything I do. We were fated to meet. I am fated to kiss you—now."

"What a strange man you are!" she cried, but she closed her eyes and yielded to his mouth. After a long moment she drew back and stared at his lips, as if to see how sensuous and warm they were; and then moved toward him and offered her kiss.

"I will see your father."

"But he doesn't like you. He will never say yes."

"Then we'll elope. Your father cannot oppose God."

"You don't know him. He'd oppose the Devil."

"God," said Joseph calmly, "will make him understand."

But Isaac Hale could not see that God had anything to do with it. He stared at Joseph with eyes as coldly pale as clear ice and bit off a quid of tobacco half as large as his thumb. "Marry my daughter. Is that what you said?"

"It is God's will for your daughter to marry me."

"God, my foot. What has that old pumblechook got to do with it? I say no. You think I'd* let my girl marry a lollygag who squints at peepstones? A man who digs around in dirt piles lookun for gold plates? No, not me."

"But I love your daughter."

"I don't give a tinker's dam about* that. I still say no."

"Beware," said Joseph sternly. "I'm a prophet of the Lord——"

"I don't care if you're all the prophets this side of Adam."

"Mr. Hale, I'm going to marry Emma."

"And I say you ain't. And I don't want you in my home any longer. Pack up and hit the grit."

Joseph was not a coward—and certainly not when he felt the will of God moving him. His eyes turned cold too; his face was as unrelenting as that of the man who opposed him and his jaws were as hard in their muscular set. He squared his shoulders.

"It is the Lord's will for me to marry Emma and I will marry her."

"If you do I'll break your neck. You'll not be lookun in no peepstone when I get through with you. And now, get out of my sight."

"All right, I'll go. But I must speak with Emma first."

"Clear off!" cried Isaac, losing his temper.

Turning to the house, Joseph shouted, "Emma, come here!" and Emma came. She looked at the two men who had squared off as if for a fight. "Emma, your father says no. But I'll come back and you're to marry me. Do you understand that?"

"Yes," she said, but her voice was low.

"Here!" Isaac roared. "Get your damned peepstones and skin. And don't come back."

"I'll come back," said Joseph, undaunted. "I expect worse persecution than yours. I expect my name to be reviled among all kindred and tongues—but your daughter will be my wife."

Isaac turned to his daughter. "Do you love this scatterbrain?"

"I—I think so."

"You know what he is? A lazy loafer who peeps at a hunk of rock. I tell you never to lay eyes on him again."

"Yes, father."

"Now you hit the grit and don't leave no tracks behind you."

Joseph turned away but he was not at all daunted by this man's gray contempt. With a small pack on his shoulder, he went up a hill and turned but he could see no sign of the girl on whom he had set his heart. It did not matter. He would return and Isaac Hale would meet his superior in brain or brawn.

CHAPTER IV

HE FOUND PALMYRA AND ITS COUNTRYSIDE ON THE WARPATH AGAINST him. Everywhere in the Manchester Hills, men had dug for the plates of gold; and failing to find them, had gone to his home and threatened to hang the whole Smith family.

"Your life isn't safe!" cried his anxious mother. Her pale blue eyes looked as if they had wept incessantly for days. "You must go back to Pennsylvania."

"No," said Joseph calmly. "The Lord will watch over me until His work is done."

"Yes, my boy, but the Lord helps those who help themselves. The men are crazy mad, hunting for the golden plates. They've dug everywhere. Joseph, you sure the plates are safe?"

"Yes, they're safe."

"Some of the men plan to kill you," said his father. "They don't mean any monkey business. They're as mad as hornets."

"They intend to hang you," said Hyrum. "They showed me the rope."

"Trust in the Lord," said Joseph. "Everything will be all right."

But when he entered the town, he learned that everything was not all right. A big dirty man roared, "There he is, by God! There's Joe Smith come back!" In a few moments a crowd of men had gathered around him, their faces ugly with suspicion and their eyes lusting for gold.

"Where's them plates?" asked one. "We want a-see that gold bible you got hid away."

"Where you been all these weeks? You take the gold with you?"

"By Jesus, yes, where is that gold you found in them hills?"

A brawny fellow stepped forth and thrust his chin out as if inviting a blow. "If you found gold we want a-see it, and if you lied, we intend to make you eat dirt."

A little angered, Joseph looked at the men. "I don't have any golden plates. They belong to the Lord."

"You lie!" a man cried; and another said: "You found gold, all right.

It's that old treasure the Spaniards left and we want it. Where'd you hide it?"

"I tell you I found nothing."

"Mebbe if we strung him up to a tree he'd remember."

"Beware," said Joseph, "of what you do. If you molest me the Lord will strike in vengeance. I tell you I have no gold."

The men were baffled. They looked at one another and a bolder one said: "Mebbe you have and mebbe you haven't. But if you have, we'll find it."

"All right. Dig up every foot of earth in New York."

"Oh, dig, huh! You hear that, men? I guess he's hid it in a house or a tree. I'll bet his old pap knows where it is."

"My father has nothing in his house. And lo, I say to you, beware, lest the wrath of God strike you dead."

This solemn warning sobered them. One man tried to laugh but only snickered; and another, slowly withdrawing, with his gaze on Joseph's face, spoke out of sudden awe. "Look at his eyes! Men, look at his eyes!"

"He ain't no prophet," said another, but he was not sure. There was something about this blond giant that baffled them: a strange purpose in his bold blue eyes, an unearthly pallor in his smooth cheeks, and a manner of standing and looking at them that sapped their courage. One by one they withdrew, with Joseph's unwavering gaze upon them. Two remained.

"Are you really a prophet?" asked one of them.

"I am."

"Maybe he is," the man said, and looked at his companion. Together they stared at Joseph, as two boys might have done, their eyes grave with wonder and fear. Then they turned and went away and Joseph was left alone, a man courageous and fearless, whose eyes, whose strange intense directness, had abashed his enemies.

Tongues still wagged and feverish men still dug in the hillsides. From Palmyra and Manchester, and from other hamlets east and south, came threats of violence; and when Joseph withdrew to the forest to meditate he was followed by spies. He saw skulking men dodging from tree to tree or hiding in underbrush and peering, but he gave little heed to them, having no fear. The spirit of revelation was upon him now, and part by part he saw the outlines of the book he was to write.

On a Saturday afternoon, after hours of praying, he knew he was to receive another vision; and after gazing at the sun until he had induced a trancelike state, he saw an angel appear. He heard a divine voice that was a deeper voice in his own soul. The voice said he must now translate the ancient records but ought first to find an able assistant, a man of learning and of great fortitude. After recovering and going his way, Joseph thought it a little strange that the angel should have urged what had already been in his own mind; for he had been wondering if he did not need scholarly aid.

To Oliver Cowdery, a young school teacher in Palmyra, he went with his mission. Oliver was not only formally educated; he was a sensitive person, with soft hair curling over his ears, with earnest eyes and a thin straight mouth, with a gentle ministerial air. Joseph had always liked him. He was a dreamer—and Joseph needed dreamers and poets.

The two young men left Oliver's home and entered the woods and sat under a tree to talk. "The God of Israel," Joseph said, going straight to the point, "is going to establish the true gospel and I am His prophet. You have been chosen to help me. You are to leave family and friends, as the apostles did of old, and follow me."

"But what," asked the astonished Oliver, "am I to do?"

"I have a task. The angel Moroni has commanded me to translate the records of the people of the new world and the gospel of the new dispensation. I need you to act as scribe and to set down what I say when God speaks through me."

"You say the Lord has commanded me? How do you know that?"

"I had a vision yesterday. You are to write as I dictate. When the records are translated we will print the book and it will be the new bible. All churches today are an abomination. My church will be the only true one."

Oliver looked far away at a scarf of cloud. "If I assist you, I will be persecuted too."

"Yes. But verily, I say unto you, if ye are faithful, great will be your reward in the fullness of glory. If ye are faithless, awful will be your punishment therefor. Oliver, you will need much courage."

"Joseph, I do not doubt it."

"Your name will be had for good and evil among all peoples. But," added Joseph earnestly, "your fame will go around the world. Do you accept the command of God?"

"If it is God's command, I must." He had turned a little pale. "Am I to see the records also?"

"If it is God's will."

For a long moment Oliver gazed at the sky. "When do we begin?"

"Soon. I'll go to Harmony over in Pennsylvania and you are to follow."

"How long will the translating take us?"

"Only the Lord can answer that."

Oliver turned to look at his strange companion. "Do you know Martin Harris?"

"Yes."

"I was thinking. Martin is interested. Besides," added Oliver humbly, "he is wealthy. He beats his wife but he might be of service in getting the—the bible printed."

"I had him in mind," said the wise Joseph. "He is a vain man. He would spend a lot of money to be famous." Joseph rose to his feet. When Oliver rose, Joseph placed hands on the man's thin shoulders. "Are you afraid?"

"No, I think not."

"Do you believe in me as a prophet?"

"If God speaks to you, you must be a prophet. When I hear the new bible I will know."

"I am not educated like you," said Joseph. "What God says to me I will say to you, but it will be your task to put it in good English for I am only mortal man."

"Yes," Oliver said, looking as if he wanted to flee.

"I will go to Harmony soon and you will come. It is best to travel apart." For several minutes, Joseph had seen a man watching him from behind a far tree. He now said: "Oliver, behind yonder tree—the big oak with the blazed trunk—is a spy and an enemy. Are you sure you are not afraid?"

"If it is God's commandment, I will obey."

"That is good. Do not tarry long."

Joseph's return to Harmony was not welcomed. Blunt old Isaac Hale had spread the peepstone story and before Joseph had been there a week he was approached by two men who looked like the most barbarous scoundrels he had ever laid eyes on. They hailed him when he was alone upon a path in the woods.

"Are you," asked the larger man, "Joe Smith?"

"I am Joseph Smith."

"Well, the likes of you ain't wanted in these-here parts. Take my advice and skin out."

"I take my orders," said Joseph quietly, "from God, not from men."

"Oh, hear him! You're in partnership, you and God, I guess. Well, listen to me, you peepstone loonytick. You come back here to marry Emma Hale but she is my woman. Besides, Bill and me, we're prospectun these hills hereabouts and we don't want nobody findun our gold. So I say hit the high trails."

"It is true. I do intend to marry Emma Hale."

The bearded giant slapped his companion a blow that staggered him and burst into profane laughter. "Listen to him! He plans to marry my woman!"

Bill's face was sober. "Jess here," he said gravely, "is as tough as a buck's horn. I wouldn't try to make him mad."

"I know," said Jess. "We'll fight for the gal, best man to take all, including the hide and taller. What do you say to that?"

"We'll let Emma decide it."

"No, we won't. I don't let a woman decide things for Jess Miller. So get yourself ready for I aim to make you roll like a wagon wheel." He clenched his big hands and thrust his hairy chin out. "Poke me, boy. Let's see if you'n make me blink."

Joseph withdrew a few steps and looked around him. There was nobody within a mile of this spot. He was not afraid, he knew that the Lord would give him great strength, but he did not want to engage in a vulgar fight. "I think—" he began, but Jess cut him short with an oath.

"God blast you and your peepstones, I don't care what you think! I'll give you two jerks of a dead skunk's tail to skin out of here!"

"I'll stay here until I'm ready to go."

"Hear him, Bill! I'm going to send this guy in a wagon box for a coffin. Stand back while I whang him in two like a maple twig." And without further ado, Jess plowed forward, his fists mowing the air and his tongue cursing. He misjudged the strength and nimbleness of his foe.

Joseph was a powerful man. In a moment like this, feeling that God was with him, and believing that faith would make him invincible, his might drew not only from every great muscle in his body but also from the calm singleness of purpose in his mind. Ducking under the wild fists, he seized the hulk of his enemy and lifted the man as he would have lifted a child. He brought him down with crushing power. Leaping back then, he waited until Jess rose to his feet, slobbering with profanity and blind with rage. Again Joseph ducked and laid hold of him; but this time with all his strength he pitched the braggart over his head, and Jess came down on head and shoulders, stunned. Coming to his senses, he pawed leaves and roared, acting more like a maddened bull than a man. Finding his legs he advanced again, but more cautiously this time, his yellow teeth bared and his eyes lighted with murder. He crouched, his palms spread and his huge shoulders weaving from side to side; and when he sprang forward suddenly, his hands clutching, Joseph stepped quickly to the right and swung with all his strength. The blow fell on the man's jaw and he went down like an ox under a maul. He kicked and rolled over, his eyes staring up in bloodshot astonishment; and Bill backed away. When Joseph turned to him, he cried:

"It ain't none of my business! I don't care who marries the gal!"

Jess was trying to sit up now but his wits had left him and after an effort he fell back and groaned. Joseph went over and looked down at him.

"I like peace," he said.

"By God," said Bill, "it's the first time I ever see him knocked flat."

"I'm a peaceful man," said Joseph. "I'll go now."

A legend went abroad that Joseph Smith, for all his peepstone gazing, was the mightiest man in the western hills. No other bully came from this region, seeking a fight. He was still shadowed but he did not mind: persecution was part of his destiny and he expected to have to smite his enemies from time to time.

He lived in an abandoned miner's cabin, across the single room of which he built a crude partition; and after Oliver came, he sat on one side of the cabin, with Oliver hidden beyond him, and translated from the ancient records. When translating, as when receiving revelations, he was awful to behold; for he was aware of nothing except a voice, his voice, that spoke for God. All blood left his face until its pallor was ghastly; all consciousness of the world left his eyes. For Oliver, sitting at a crude table with paper and pencil, there was only a voice in the cabin, the sound of which chilled and shook him as he wrote down the lines. Day after day in a wild windy autumn, the two men labored here in a lonely cabin on the edge of a forest; and page by page the new bible came to life. After Joseph's voice had died away in the sound of wind outside, he would come forth, so white and terrible of mien that Oliver was afraid to speak to him; and later, after he had eaten of a simple meal which Oliver prepared, he would prowl in the woods, hoping to see Emma.

Twice he had gone to her home but Isaac had threatened to blow him to pieces with powder and ball. Thereafter, he lingered in the woodlands near the house. It was not until a cold clear day in January that he saw her fleeing like a specter among the frozen trees.

"Emma!" he cried, and leapt to overtake her.

"Oh!" she cried, turning. "Joseph, it's you!"

"I told you I'd come back."

"But you must go," she said, looking around anxiously. "Father will kill you."

"I've come to marry you." He took her resisting body to his breast. "Emma, we must elope." He raised her alarmed face and pressed his mouth to her cold lips.

"Go, please, please!"

"Never. You must be my wife."

"No. I tell you father will kill you."

"I'm not afraid of him or any man. We must elope at once."

"Joseph, please go." She struggled to free herself and then looked homeward; but the woods were cold and silent and with a sigh she yielded to his arms and mouth.

"Emma, you do love me?"

"Yes."

"Will you elope with me? . . . Will you?"

"No, no. My father——"

"The Lord will soften his heart."

"Nothing will—or could. He'll kill both of us."

"Emma, you have no faith. Ye of little faith, beware, lest the wrath——"

"It's my father's wrath. You've never seen him good and mad."

"You must have faith, for faith conquers all things. You will go with me now—tonight.'

"No, not tonight!"

"Tonight," he said, crushing the breath out of her. He kissed her until her lips parted helplessly and her hands trembled on his back. "Then tomorrow night."

"No, no!"

"Yes," he said, shaking her. "God will be angry——"

"Oh, it's my father's anger I'm thinking of!"

"We'll come back and live with your father."

"Joseph, you must be mad."

"We'll elope tomorrow and then come back and live with your father. I'm translating the records now and no mortal hand can stop my labors. Emma, tomorrow meet me here and do not fail."

"No, I don't dare."

"I dare for both of us. Promise me." She did not promise and again he shook her, and looked down with solemn rebuke. "Promise," he said sternly.

"Yes."

"Here."

"Yes. Oh, I must go now!"

"Tomorrow noon, Emma. God help you if you fail."

"I—I won't." She withdrew from his arms and stared apprehensively at his face. He was, she decided, either God or devil, but she hardly knew which. He was a terrible man who plundered her being until she had no will left.

"Awful things will happen if you do not come."

"Or if I do. I don't know which will be worst." He looked very kingly against the white earth and the evergreens.

Emma came at noon. She was pale and anxious, but when his arms closed around her and she felt the mighty will of the man, she sighed like a child. He led her up the path over frozen snow, saying a sleigh waited and they would flee to New York. In the sleigh was a thin young man who was introduced to her as Oliver Cowdery; and in a few moments they set off over white landscape, with Joseph sitting in the bed and holding her in his arms to shield her against blinding sunlight.

Over at Palmyra, in the same hour, Martin Harris was beating his wife. For more than a year he had been shouting his belief in "Joe Smith's golden bible," and his wife had done no more than pooh-pooh him and look bored; but when he said he was going to print the book at his expense, she called him a blockhead and a fool. That was too much for the superstitious Martin who had been in turn a Quaker, a Universalist, a Restorationer, a Baptist and a Presbyterian.

"By the holy angels," he thundered, "I'll beat your head off!" And he seized a long whip that he used on oxen and waded in. His wife screamed and ran from room to room, with Martin in earnest pursuit, cursing and yelling and striking with the bull-lash. She fell to her knees and implored him not to murder her, but he struck a mad blow across her shoulders and then kicked her, with rage frothing at his mouth. "You'n go to hell if you want to," he howled, "but I aim to save my soul and go to heaven!" And with that he drubbed her soundly and hurled her to the floor. She lay there, terrified, gazing up at him, and Martin dropped to a chair and mopped his brow.

"I know Joe Smith has talked with God!" he shouted. "He aims to begin the right church and by the holy angel I aim to help him. I made the money, didn't I? Ain't it my farm?" He breathed heavily and stared at her, wondering if he had trounced her enough. "Besides, ain't I talked with Jesus myself, and the angels? And even with the Devil. Didn't I see the Devil with my own naked eyes and didn't he look like a jackass with hair all over him like a mouse? Didn't I see Jesus and wasn't He the best-lookun man in all creation just like Joe says he is?"

"Do as you please," said his wife, gasping with pain. "But if you beat me again I'll leave you."

"All right, if you want a-go to hell——"

"I guess you think a wife-beater will go to heaven!"

"I never beat you," he said gravely, "except when you get plumb full of the devil. Then I have to knock the devils out of you. I say to you, repent ye, for the kingdom of God is at hand."

"You're awful mouth-almighty today," she said, looking at him with contempt.

"I aim to save my soul," said Martin, and left the house.

When he learned that Joseph had come to Palmyra with a wife and then returned to Harmony, he said he would pack up his daisy kickers and follow; and riding one horse and leading another he set out for the Pennsylvania hills. Along the way he heard only vilification of Joseph, and this argued in his mind that he was on no fool's errand; for it seemed to him, if his memory served, that all prophets had been kicked from pillar to post. He hoped, to be sure, to make a fortune by printing the new bible; but he hoped also that it would lead him to heaven.

He was surprised to find Joseph living right in the home of an unbelieving father-in-law. "I come over to help you," he said bluntly. "Is that-there new bible about ready to print?"

Emma smiled, and Isaac lifted shaggy brows. Joseph was annoyed. "The records—" he began, but Martin cut him short.

"I tell you what I want. I want a-take a part of the bible over and show my wife. She don't believe it, not a single word."

"What I want," said Isaac, "is a squint at them plates."

"Sure," said Martin. "Couldn't you let us have a peek? Then we could say to unbelievers, verily, I seen the plates and Joseph is sure a prophet."

"The first person to see the records," said Joseph, "will be a son born to my wife."

All eyes turned to Emma who looked rosily foolish.

"But if I could see them," Martin persisted, "then I could go out and preach."

"Ye of little faith! The Lord is displeased with you, Martin Harris. You had better go back to Palmyra."

"Not at all," said Martin. "Let me see the book and show it to my unbelieving missus. After I convert her, then I'll convert all my neighbors."

Day after day he begged Joseph to let him take the completed pages to Palmyra. He would show them only to his wife, he said solemnly, and to his parents and brother, and to his wife's sister; and when at last Joseph gave to him a hundred and sixteen pages of manuscript, Martin held them as if they were a part of heaven. He also asked Joseph to copy some characters from the plates, for he wanted to show them to learned men in New York City. Joseph yielded again and drew some characters on a sheet of paper. He felt dismay and loss when he saw Martin set off as happily as a child, promising to return soon and bring the manuscript with him. He felt deep in his bones that he had been unwise.

And he was right.

CHAPTER V

ONVINCED THAT HE HAD BLUNDERED, HE WAITED IMPATIENTLY FOR Martin's return, unable to translate and oppressed by the cold contempt of Isaac Hale. For Isaac, after listening to his son-in-law's jeremiads, his castigation of a sinful world, and a few of the tenets of the new gospel, decided that the man was an addlepated fool. Nevertheless, when he observed Joseph's anxiety, his loss of appetite, his daily watching of the road for Martin's coming, he told him he could take a horse if he wished to go to Palmyra. "You'd best see what that gallows-faced gump done with your book."

"Thanks," Joseph said, and set out at once.

Upon reaching the home of his parents, he sent a messenger for Martin; and when that stocky farmer appeared, looking as if he had been caught stealing sheep, Joseph thundered: "What have you done with my manuscript?"

"Well," said Martin, looking around guiltily, "I ——"

"You what? Where is it?"

"Now don't go off your ear. You see ——"

"Have you lost it?"

"Don't look at me that way," said Martin, wiggling around like a scolded lad.

"Have you lost it? Answer me!"

"Yes."

"O my God!" Joseph cried, and clutched his face. Then he marched over and laid violent hands on Martin and shook him. "Where is the manuscript? The wrath of God is upon you!"

"Don't," said Martin petulantly, and shook the hands off.

"Have you searched for it?"

"Dodrot it, yes. I plumb tore the house up. I ripped the bed open and tore the pillows open. I even looked in the well."

"My God, my God!" said Joseph, beside himself with grief and anger. "All is lost! God will punish me for this—and you, you bilker!" He began to weep. He paced the room, groaning and wringing his hands; and Martin blinked at him in astonishment. "You go hunt again!" Joseph roared. "Hurry, before the Lord strikes you down!"

"But I tell you I looked everywhere. I even looked in the barn and under the bed and down the well."

"Did your wife steal it?"

"No. I shook her till she felt like she was being measured for a funeral but she swore to God she don't know anything about it."

"My God!" cried Joseph again, tears running down his cheeks. His frightened mother wept too, and his father sat like a man of stone, his lips twitching with woe. For several moments Joseph paced like a madman up and down the room. "Martin Harris," he roared suddenly, "prepare ye for the punishment of God!"

That was too much for Martin. He sank to a chair and began to groan as if devils were already in possession of his soul. He rubbed at his eyes and looked imploringly at Joseph, but when he saw no compassion in that anguished face, he redoubled his grief and made most lamentable sounds. "I hunted everywhere," he vouchsafed feebly, staring at Lucy. He rocked back and forth, digging fretfully at his eyes; but now and then he glanced cunningly at Joseph to learn how matters stood with him, and then nodded his heavy skull in solemn thought.

Lucy went to the door and looked out and saw that the sky had darkened as if for a great storm. Clouds with black bellies were rolling up from the southern hills, and thunder like wrath out of heaven was shaking the earth. "God is angry," she said, and her husband went to the door to look out. Joseph was still pacing the room, with large tears rolling down his pale face. Martin, hearing the thunder, shook with dread.

Joseph left Palmyra as unexpectedly as he had come. A few minutes later he mounted his horse, and the picture of him as he rode away was one that his parents and Martin never forgot. There was no rain, but there was terrific thunder, and there was lightning flung upon the darkness in great blinding sheets. He looked terribly alone, but every inch of him a prophet and a conqueror, as he turned from the yard and rode down into the darkness of the sky.

When he told his wife of the catastrophe, she angered him by saying that it was well, for now he could come to his senses and get a farm and till the soil. It was, she declared, a sign from God, if indeed it was any-thing at all: he was now to go about his business in the way of other men.

"What blasphemy!" he cried. "I have sinned and this is my punishment."

"If that gump of a Martin Harris——"

"Silence! You'll do well to prepare yourself for the coming of God."

"And you'd do a lot better if you'd support your wife."

"The Lord will provide."

His appalling blunder in giving the manuscript to a bench-babbler like Martin Harris left him for weeks without certainty of purpose; and it added nothing to his attempt to recover from the loss when he learned that Martin had slipped away to New York City to show the ancient characters to scholars. After many days of solitary reflection, he realized that he must not try to translate the hundred and sixteen pages again. Evil persons might discover the lost pages and make odious comparisons, finding that the two translations did not in all matters agree. No: he would have to begin where page one hundred and sixteen stopped, and proceed from there to the end.

A few days later Oliver joined him, but that shy and melancholy young man was now beset by doubts. If, he reasoned, God allowed more than a hundred pages to be lost, and if the prophet himself had no power to find them, then perhaps he was a fraud. Perceiving the misgivings, Joseph invited him to the woods. He would inquire of God, he said, and Oliver could hear the Lord speak through His prophet.

Today, as in former times, Oliver was overwhelmed by the change in the fair young giant as he bared his head in sunlight and gazed at the sky. The blood left his face until it was whiter than death, and an unearthly light shone in the full blue eyes. With hands to his bosom, Joseph prayed silently for a long while; and then very deliberately he spoke. The words were sharp and vibrant and evenly spaced.

"Verily, I say unto you, that there are records which contain my gospel which have been kept back because of the wickedness of the people. I command you that if you have good desires—a desire to lay up treasures for yourself in heaven—then shall you assist in bringing to light with your gifts those parts of my scriptures which have been hidden by iniquity. And now, behold, I give unto you, and also unto my servant Joseph, the keys of this gift which shall bring to light this ministry; and in the mouth of two or three witnesses shall every word be established . . ."

Joseph said much more, but the statement that broke like a light in Oliver's mind was the declaration that God was giving to him, as well as to the prophet, the keys of the gift. The gift he understood to be that of translation. So eager was he to try that in the next afternoon he asked Joseph for permission.

"Maybe," he said, "I'm a prophet too. God said so."

"If you have the light of God in you, you can translate."

"Let me try," Oliver said. He took his position in darkness and Joseph sat at the table with pencil and paper. There was a long silence. Then Oliver declared solemnly: "I am placing myself in communion with God. I begin to feel the light." Another long silence followed; whereupon he came forth, looking shamefaced, wagging his head like a foolish fellow. "I could *feel* words," he said. "I—I couldn't understand them. It was thousands of words swarming in the universe."

"Yes," said Joseph, not at all surprised. "Your bosom did not burn within you. You had a stupor of thought and that is why you could not translate. Verily, Oliver, I say unto you, if you feel light opening out of darkness, that *is* God; but confusion of your senses, that *is* the Devil."

"But," persisted Oliver, looking very unhappy, "I'm to be a prophet too. The revelation said so."

"When the Holy Ghost fills you, then shall you be a prophet."

"Well," said Oliver, distressed by his ignominious failure, "I'll try again sometime. I could feel the light but I couldn't understand the words. Tell me: how do you know when God is speaking through you?"

"When everything is clear, that is God. When everything is dark, that is the Devil. Verily, Oliver, the way of God is the way of light."

"If I feel a light in me, is that God?"

"Yea, it is so."

Oliver did not ask to try again. Chastened, he was content to be the scribe, believing again that the voice beyond the partition was the voice of God through Joseph. For six weeks the two men labored here; and then with Emma they went to the village of Fayette in New York and lived in the Whitmer home. For the Whitmers, parents and children, had embraced the faith; and when David, John and Peter Whitmer inquired how they could assist, Joseph went off alone to ask of God, and then baptized the men in Seneca Lake.

Joseph was translating rapidly now. The vast story had taken shape in his mind and he had only to place himself in a receptive mood and speak slowly and distinctly to Oliver who sat out of sight in another room. It was a dramatic story of plot and counterplot which God revealed hour by hour. . . .

Six hundred years before Christ, twenty men and women left Jerusalem, led by Lehi, and by Nephi, his fourth son. After eight years of wandering in a great wilderness, they built a boat and set sail, and landed after a heroic voyage on the shore of South America. A thousand years earlier, the Jaredites from the neighborhood of the Tower of Babel, had also sailed and landed in this far country and built a kingdom; but these adventurers were almost exterminated by a bloody war soon after the Lehites arrived.

The colony under Lehi prospered; but upon his death, it split into two factions, led by his sons, Nephi and Laman. The Nephites pushed into the huge forests of the region, taking with them on plates the record of Hebrew scripture down to Jeremiah. The Lamanites, forebears of the Indians, had no literature to quiet their savage natures, and so degenerated, becoming a wild and nomadic clan. After a while the Nephites came upon another tribe, the Mulekites, whose departure from Jerusalem had preceded that of the Lehites. The Nephites and Mulekites united forces and lived for eight hundred and fifty years in prosperity and peace. Jesus visited them in person and taught them in socialistic government, whereupon for two centuries these people shared all things in common.

After a long while dissensions disturbed their quiet as envious and ungodly leaders strove for power; and among these warring bands none was more terrible than the Gadianton Robbers who pillaged and murdered with extraordinary zest. By the end of the fourth century after Christ, the Nephites were exterminated. Outstanding among them had been a military prophet named Mormon who wrote on plates of gold a history of his people, and then gave the plates into the care of his son Moroni, asking him to add to the record during his lifetime and bury the plates before his death.

Such was the story which Joseph translated and Oliver wrote down. There were many subplots. In one of them the villainous Amalickiah, a Nephite, resolved to be king, and escaped to the Lamanites where he maneuvered his fortunes through one bloody deed after another until he was crowned. He then set out with his barbarous hordes against the

Nephites but was slain one night while asleep in his tent. There was also record of famines and plagues; many pertinent verses from the Old and New Testaments; and a prediction of the coming of Jesus to the Jews. The history was ungrammatical, poorly written, often redundant and sometimes pompously rhetorical; but all this Moroni himself realized, and declared that more literate readers in ages hence would doubtless mock the faulty style and say the Nephites were unskilled in composition.

During long evenings in the Whitmer home, after a day of translation, Joseph would sit among his devout disciples, including members of his own family, and tell of the ancient inhabitants of North America: of their dress, their ways of travel, their buildings and cities and warfare, and their forms of religious worship. He liked especially to dwell on the long and successful experiment in socialism.

"They held everything in common, as we should. There was no poor man, no rich man. Nobody was hungry or went in rags, for everyone shared with his neighbor and everyone was happy then."

"Mebbe," said old Pete Whitmer, "we should try that."

"I ain't so sure," said Martin Harris, the wealthiest man who listened to these discussions. "I've worked dodrotted hard for what I have. Some of the hog-in-togs don't work at all."

All eyes turned to Joseph. "For shame," he said. "It is God's will for us to share everything. Rebuke the greed in your heart, Martin Harris, lest ye be damned."

"Just the same," said Martin stubbornly, "I've worked plumb hard."

"Some," said Joseph, "labor in the fields, and some in the vineyards of God. Those who have must give to those who have not."

"All right," said Martin, mopping his brow. "If the Lord says so, I guess I will. But I don't relish helping these devil-dodgers who never done a lick of work in their lives. It just don't seem fair, no matter what the Almighty says."

"You are greedy," said Joseph, and there the matter ended.

Not in every day was Joseph able to translate. Sometimes he quarreled with his wife, for Emma had been growing more and more restive, with her pride suffering under the charity of the Whitmer home. One morning, finding herself alone with her husband, her black eyes flashed with scorn and her tongue lashed out.

"I'm sick of living this way! What we eat, other folks give us. We sleep on their beds, live in their houses, just like a couple of bilkers."

"Your tongue is evil this morning."

"I won't go on like this. If you didn't plan to support your wife, you should not have married."

"I have the Lord's work to do," he said, speaking with patience that maddened her. "The food we eat here is a small matter."

"Oh, the Lord's work! I listen to that day in and day out. I guess the Lord wouldn't mind so much if you got out and earned a dollar now and then."

"Silence!" he cried. "There's a devil in you."

"And we have a child coming," she persisted, her eyes hating him. "I guess someone is going to support it too. Look at us. What do we have? We're as fat as a hen's forehead!"

"The Lord will provide," he said.

"You mean the Whitmers. Call them the Lord if you want to."

He gave no answer to that. He felt very unhappy when he took his position to translate, and after a little while he realized that God was not with him. "Oliver," he said, "what is the matter? Everything is dark today."

"Let me try," said Oliver.

"Wait. Perhaps the Lord will speak in a moment."

"God said I was a prophet too. Let me try again."

"The Lord," said Joseph a little angrily, "said you're to be my scribe. Don't tempt His wrath." After a long moment of silence: "Everything is dark—dark. There is a vast gloom on the earth this day and I cannot tell what I do. Oliver, tell me: is it not true that John the Baptist appeared to us and ordained us into the Aaronic priesthood?"

"It is true," said Oliver, speaking into the next room.

"Did not Peter, James, and John give us the Melchizedek priesthood?"

"Yes."

"Did they not command us to establish the true church?"

"They did."

"Then why this darkness? God is angry with me this day." He left the room and went to walk, saying to Oliver as he passed: "I'm going to learn why the Lord is displeased."

There were other matters troubling Joseph besides the scorn of his wife. Among his followers, several were having visions, including old Mother Whitmer who babbled one morning as if out of her wits. On her way to the barn, she had been accosted by a strange man with a knapsack on his shoulders. She fled to the house, pale and agitated, and told deliriously of what she had seen.

"It was an angel! I know, I know! He had glory in his face like the light of heaven, and his voice was like music! He spoke to me," she wailed, becoming hysterical. "He said I had been complaining about feeding and caring for the prophet Joseph and his wife! He said I should be ashamed of myself. I am, I am! O Lord, Lord, forgive me, forgive a poor old woman and her sinful ways!" Tears were now washing out of her tired old eyes. Work-worn hands clutched her breast. "Forgive me, O Lord, our God!" She prostrated herself in abject grief while her husband and sons, Joseph and Emma and Oliver looked at her.

Unexpectedly she started to her feet. Clasping her hands, she gazed at the ceiling and moaned out of penitent shame. "Oh," she cried, lost to everything now, "the angel opened the knapsack and showed me the golden plates! Glory be praised! O merciful God, forgive a sinful old woman!" Turning to Joseph, she knelt and clasped his legs with trembling arms. She looked up at him, with tears running down her withered old cheeks. "The Lord told me you're a prophet. Oh, in the name of a just God, have mercy on a complaining old woman! Forgive me, forgive me!"

"You are forgiven," declared Joseph, and laid a hand on the gray head.

He was remembering the scene as he walked now. He was remembering also the growing skepticism among a few who believed in him, and among many who did not. Martin wanted to see the plates. In Joseph's new bible it said, "The Lord God will proceed to bring forth the words of the book; and in the mouth of as many witnesses as seemeth him good, will be established his word; and woe be unto him that rejecteth." Joseph believed he must show the plates to three witnesses; but inasmuch as they were only spiritual plates, witnesses would have to gaze at them with spiritual eyes; and he was not at all sure that unimaginative Martin could do so.

Of the persons who asked to bear witness, he decided to choose Oliver because he was very receptive to visions; Dave Whitmer, most religious of the Whitmer sons, who had been searching in his father's stable for the plates; and Martin. He had to include the stubborn Martin or that impatient man would withdraw his financial support. So he called him in one morning and addressed him in a voice that made him quake in his shoes.

"Martin Harris, humble yourself before God this day and ask forgiveness of your sins! Cast all evil out of your heart and you will see the plates!"

"Glory be," said Martin, looking pompous and pleased. He was grinning when Joseph rebuked him in a voice of thunder.

"Martin Harris, this is no time for light thoughts! Your grin is an abomination!"

"What?" asked Martin, sobering at once. "I didn't know the Almighty didn't like to see me grin."

"Come," said Joseph.

With the three men he went into the woods near the Whitmer home. There, with bared head, he stood motionless, gazing at the sky, his eyes so bright and hypnotic that Dave looked anxiously at Oliver, and Martin looked at all three and smirked. Glancing around him, he reflected that a thousand cords of excellent wood were waiting here to be cut. But he was not grinning and he made no sound. Suddenly, in a terrible voice that made Dave jump as if he had been prodded, Joseph addressed the blue universe.

"O God, our Father, look down upon us this day and make thy will manifest!" Clasping hands and gazing at the sky, he sank slowly to his knees; and Dave and Oliver, as if moved by his will, did likewise. Martin looked around him first and then reluctantly obeyed. Joseph resumed his praying in a voice so solemn that Oliver felt the blood leaving his cheeks. "O God, grant to us humbly kneeling here a sign of thy presence, that we may purify our hearts. Grant to us, O Almighty Ruler, a vision of the plates, so that thy children may bear witness of the truth of thy gospel. . . ." When his long prayer was done, he said simply, without turning: "Oliver, pray."

"O God, our heavenly Father," said Oliver, his hands shaking on his breast, "grant to us a vision of the plates that I may bear witness of their truth to all kindred and tongues of earth. Grant to us, O divine Father, an everlasting sign of thy gospel, that we may go forth among men, proclaiming its truth and laboring for thee in the vineyards. . . ." When Oliver had finished, Joseph said:

"David."

And David prayed too, with his soul in his throat; but when Martin was called, he made a sound like a sneeze and choked. "O God," he began, "I—let me look at the plates so I——"

"Our heavenly Father," Joseph resumed; and when he had finished, Oliver and David followed in turn. Martin rose to his feet and shook his head as if he had water in his ears.

"I guess I'm too blamed sinful," he said. "I don't think God will show Hisself while I'm around." He stared at the kneeling figures. "I think I best go away." He went off through the woods, stumbling in his stride and from time to time glancing back.

Again Joseph prayed, with his two disciples following him in turn; and the fervent prayer became a solemn ritual, with a oneness of thought and emotion possessing all three until they were conscious only of their voices, crying here in a wilderness. It was Oliver who cried, "I see, I see!" for there was a light above him. He said he saw a great glory and in a moment David said in a voice of awe, "I can see heaven!" Then Joseph spoke.

"God is manifesting Himself. Lo, he is sending an angel. Lo, an angel appears." And David said, "Lo, an angel," and Oliver said, "Behold, I can see the plates!" "Lo, an angel," said Joseph, "is showing the plates." "He is in a beautiful light," said David. "I can see him standing in the light and he has the plates in his hands." A voice said, the voice of God speaking through Joseph: "The translation of these plates is correct and I command you, my servants David and Oliver, to bear witness of what you now see and hear." "I will, I will," said David, almost whispering. Oliver said: "Behold, we will all bear witness." Said Joseph:

"Lo, the angel is withdrawing and I can see the plates dimly in his hands."

"He is going," said David. "I can see the light going—the beautiful white light—and an angel in the light, and the plates in the angel's hands."

"Oh!" Oliver gasped, as if in sudden pain; and he sank with a hand to his brow and lay on his face. Joseph and David rose and looked down at Oliver; and Joseph said:

"He is overcome by the glory of God."

David's face showed astonishment. Feeling that he had come back from a far journey, he gazed at Joseph and then at Oliver, surprised to find them here. He saw that Joseph's face was very white and strange.

"I must seek Martin Harris," Joseph said.

He found that obstinate skeptic kneeling behind a tree and praying for all he was worth. He was muttering with earnest entreaty and clasping and unclasping his hands and blinking solemnly with unbelieving eyes. Joseph approached softly and listened to the man. After a bit, Martin momentarily abandoned hope and seemed to be meditating. He dug thoughtfully at one ear, still gazing meanwhile at the sky; and then resumed with renewed ardor.

"Ye of little faith," said Joseph.

Surprised, Martin staggered to his feet and looked very ashamed. "It ain't no use," he said. "God won't show no plates to me. Just the same, I did think I saw a light once." He gazed skyward, as if to be sure.

"Kneel with me," said Joseph. "Pray with me."

Martin knelt; and while Joseph prayed, Martin muttered in his breath, trying to follow the prayer. He repeated a few of the words, making of them a fervent monotony; or now and then he glanced slyly at the prophet. Whereupon, abashed by his godlessness, he applied himself with more desperate effort. Joseph began to speak, gently, insistently, of what he saw.

"Lo, the angel comes again, bringing the records. There is a light of surpassing brilliance, and an angel is in the light; and the angel is speaking to Martin Harris. 'Lo, Martin Harris, here I am, an angel, sent from heaven to rebuke your sinful heart and your doubts, and show to you the golden plates; for you are to bear witness unto all nations and men.' Behold, the light grows in brilliance, and the angel draws near. . . ."

Suddenly, with an astonishing yell of triumph, Martin leapt to his feet and fairly danced with joy. "I saw!" he cried. "Lo, my eyes beheld! I saw the angel and I saw the gold in his hands! Hosannah, blessed be God, blessed be God! Glory and halleluiah, blessed be me!" And then, like a man out of his mind, he danced back and forth and suddenly fell to his knees in a torrent of thanksgiving. "O God, I thank you, I thank you for this blessed vision! I will tell the whole world about this blessed day and I will bear witness that Joseph is a prophet! Blessed Jesus, blessed Virgin, blessed everlasting gospel! Lord God, your sinful servant kneels here in blessed thankfulness. . . ."

When the four returned to the Whitmer house, Joseph and Oliver and

David looked pale and undone, but Martin acted like a man who had been to a circus. He mopped his brow and blew his nose. He looked at the earnest faces of the Whitmers and Smiths.

"It's true," he said, as if he alone had power to settle the matter. "Joseph is a prophet of God."

CHAPTER VI

THE 26TH OF MARCH, 1830, WAS A DAY THAT SEEMED TO FORETELL THE crack of doom: a dismal rain soaked the earth, deep ominous thunder shook the windows of houses, and clouds hung in a black and unbroken pall from horizon to zenith. Persons in Palmyra and in hamlets roundabout expected something to happen; and when, within the shuttered gloom of their homes, they read that the Book of Mormon had been published and was on sale, they gave way to rage as dark as the storm. A few bought the book and many gathered around to read. From one of these gatherings, a man broke away, cursing horribly, and said he would ride Joe Smith out of New York on a rail. He prepared a statement which declared that Joseph was a loafer, a coward, a braggart, a drunkard and a thief, and before the sun had set he had a hundred signers.

Another man resolved on a bolder attack. With a gang of ruffians he went to the Smith home; and when Lucy opened the door, he shouted: "Send out that prophet son of yourn! If he likes to have visions, he'll have plenty when I darken his daylights!"

"Go on away!" cried Lucy; but she was frightened and over her shoulder she called to her husband. "Tell Joseph to run out the back way!" To the man she said: "My son isn't home."

"You're a liar! Send him out here or we'll come in and get him."

"We'll make him see God good and plenty," said another, and laughed. "If he's a prophet, he'n make a miracle to protect hisself."

"Let's get him," said a third, and the crowd surged forward. At the door the leader gave Lucy an evil grin and told her to begone.

"Joe," she said, turning, "get your gun."

A moment later the father appeared with a rifle in his hands. "Go on, you fellows. Our son is not here."

"Where is the gallows-gawk?"

"I do not know."

"Where is that gold he found? You got it hid in there?"

"There is no gold in here. Now get off of my farm." When the men did not move, Smith raised the gun. "Move—and make it quick."

Two miles away, Martin Harris had worked himself into a fine frenzy. Having invested a part of his earnings in the new bible, he was eager to sell it, and approached first one of his neighbors. "Bill," he said, "here is the new religion I told you about."

"What?" asked Bill.

"The new bible! Here it is all down in black and white. How many you want a-buy?"

"Take it away," Bill said.

"You'll never get to heaven without you read it. This-here is God's word to us in the latter days. Look——"

"No. I wouldn't have the thing on my farm. I wouldn't even let my cows sleep in the same shed with it."

"You've always been a wicked man, Bill. Lo, I say to you——"

"Martin, leave me be. I don't want none of your new bible. The old one is good enough."

"Bill Jessup, you'll be damned with hellfire and brimstone without you buy this book. It's two dollars and a half——"

"To hell with it!" Bill roared. "Take the dodgasted thing out of my sight."

"Bill, let me read to you——"

"No! Listen, Martin, you'll make me lose my temper." He struck Martin a blow on his shoulder. "Go on, before I knock you down."

"Listen what it says on page 481. 'Whosoever shall smite thee on the right cheek, turn to him the other also.' Don't that sound like God said it?"

"It sounds like the bible I always been used to. Anyhow, I don't want the dadbinged thing. Now scat."

"Bill, you'll burn in hell forever and ever. Lo, I tell you that, for I seen an angel and I heard God speak. This book will show you how to save your soul. Besides——"

"Do you want me to hit you over the head with this shovel?"

"You're so plumb wicked," said Martin, "you make me scringe. I'll sell you a copy for two dollars."

"No!"

"A dollar and a half. That's because you're my neighbor."

"I wouldn't have the damn thing if you give it to me. Now leave me be."

With a sigh, Martin went into town and saw a crowd gathered on a corner. He rolled up the hind wheels of an old cart and mounted, believing it was time to learn whether or not he was a public speaker. His statements, if not his eloquence, made some of his listeners gape with astonishment.

"Verily, I say unto ye, the government of the United States will come to an end mighty soon now, and the new religion of Joe Smith will rule the world. That's a fact. God Almighty told me so Hisself. And if that ain't true, I'll tell you, by cracky: you'n cut my head off and roll it down the road from here to Fayette. Yes, you'n roll it from here to London." Looking over the heads, he saw Oliver Cowdery. "Hi there, Oliver! You'n speak to them when I get done.

"And I'll tell you something else. Joe Smith has an unmarried sister, hasn't he? Yes, that's right. She's big with child, ain't she? Sure, we all admit that. But here's something you don't know. The father of her child ain't any mortal man like you or me. Not by the cut of your jib he ain't. Listen to me, you men! The father of that child is God Almighty up in heaven. Verily, and do you think that is so strange? No, and this book, this new bible, tells you why. It's two dollars and fifty cents.

"There is still miracles to be performed. Joseph, the new prophet, will perform miracles any day now. You mark my word. And if you don't buy this book and read it, I would not give a tinker's hoot for your soul. Not a hoot. I'll tell you another thing. There's men around here who want the blood of Joe Smith. There's men who say they aim to kill him. They aim to hang him to a tree or shoot him or throw him in a well and blow it up with hell and high powder. But let me tell you: there ain't a man who can yank one whisker from the prophet's face and live. I seen the plates myself. An angel talked to me. That's the truth and I wouldn't deny it if you tied me up and poured hot oil all over me—not if you skinned me and filled my hide with pin cushions and cockleburs. I was a sinful man like you once. I beat my wife and raised merry Cain all over the place but I know the true way to heaven now. Just step up and I'll read you things from this new bible will make your old eyes bug like the clevis on a neckyoke. Then you'n buy your books . . ."

Oliver had been listening with a sinking heart. He went to Joseph and said: "Martin Harris is a fool. He's doing you a lot of harm."

"What is he saying?"

"He's telling about your sister. He says she's with child by God."

"What!" cried Joseph. It was seldom that Oliver saw Joseph step out of his role as prophet and seer and act fallible and human. He was surprised now to see how completely Joseph forgot himself. "Another holy birth! Is that what the madman is saying?"

"That and much more. He is predicting the downfall of our government."

"The fool! Oliver, I'll have to ask God what to do with him. He brings me nothing but trouble."

"My advice is to shut up his jabber."

"Not even the Lord could shut up a man like that."

"As you say, I guess nobody can shut up Martin Harris. He loves to hear himself talk."

"I need men strong and wise, but they must be humble men. Oliver, talk to him. Try to shut him up."

"There's something else," said Oliver, no less distressed by another matter. "It's Hy Page over in Fayette. He says he's having revelations."

"He's a fraud," said Joseph angrily.

"Yes, of course. Still, he has a stone and he peeps into it and he says he's going to translate a book. Joseph," he said earnestly, "it seems to me there will be false prophets everywhere. Dozens of persons will be having visions. There's Newel Knight——"

"Yes, Newel. But he's very religious."

"Too religious, I say. You can't ever establish a church with false prophets in every town. If a lot of your disciples begin to have visions —or pretend to—then after a while nobody will take you seriously."

"There's truth in what you say."

"Joseph, don't you think it would be a good thing to perform a miracle?"

"Why?" asked Joseph suspiciously.

"So persons would know you're the true prophet."

"Yes," Joseph admitted, seeing a point in that. "But not yet. Faith is weak if it needs miracles."

"But right now," Oliver persisted, "when you're getting things started.

I tell you to watch out or Hy Page will have more disciples than you have."

"I'll have to go over and see him."

"And Newel Knight——"

"I think Newel has a devil in him. I'll see him too. Oliver, I think we'd better organize the church."

Sensing the danger of false prophets all around him, Joseph did not delay, but called a few of his followers to the Whitmer home. He asked those assembled if they were willing for him to be the first elder, and Oliver the second, in the organization; and when they said yes, he and Oliver ordained one another, with wafers and wine consecrating the sacrament. "Receive ye the Holy Ghost," Joseph said simply, and ordained his brothers and the Whitmers.

"Today," he announced, looking around him, "we are organizing the Church of Jesus Christ of Latter-day Saints. It's a mistake to say there are no saints today. There are, just as there were in olden times; for every man is a saint who keeps the commandments of God. I want you to understand that this is not my church. It is God's, organized through me. I am His instrument." He looked from face to face. "Do you have any questions?"

"Then," said his brother Hyrum, "we are all saints who belong to this church?"

"As long as you keep the Lord's commandments."

Hyrum swallowed with difficulty and looked at his mother. "Am I a saint now?"

"You are."

Looking even more solemn than was his custom, Hyrum swallowed again. "If I can have a bible, I'll go out and make some converts."

"One thing I don't like," said Oliver, speaking with the boldness of the one second in power. "Our new bible says on the title-page it is by Joseph Smith, Jr., author and proprietor. It seems to me God is the author."

"Let's see a book," said Joseph, frowning, and one was brought forth. "You're right. I authorize you to correct that in the next printing. Any more questions? . . . Then I command my disciples to preach the new gospel and make converts."

The eager disciples went forth to preach, and into Palmyra from all directions poured converts, as well as curious persons who came to ask for miracles or to jeer. Among them was a tall and sickly man named Newel Knight. Newel had a lean and sallow face, diseased teeth, and morbid eyes. For many years he had been troubled in his soul; and when he sought the prophet's advice, he was told to go off alone and pray and ask of God. He went off to pray but he was unable to make a sound. During a whole afternoon he knelt in the woods, moving his bloodless lips and trying to speak; but not for the life of him could he utter a word. Terrified, he returned to his wife who, upon seeing his ghastly face, sent a messenger for Joseph.

The prophet was amazed by what he saw. Newel was on the floor of a house, rolling in agony and twisting his limbs; kicking out at imaginary foes and smiting with both frenzied hands; and rolling his eyes and frothing at his lips. His white mouth was full of spasms as if the tortured man were trying vainly to speak; his awful gaze turned on Joseph, mutely imploring his aid. Word had gone out that Newel was in a fit, and now the neighbors came and gathered around him, some staring as if their eyes would leave their skulls and others swooning with dread. Newel was writhing now as if an invisible and malign power were tying every muscle of his body into knots.

In a stricken voice a woman whispered: "There's a devil in him!"

This notion was taken up and whispered from tongue to tongue until it came to Joseph. A voice said: "You're a prophet. Let's see you cast the devil out."

Joseph was distressed. He saw an opportunity here if God would assist him but he was reluctant to rest the whole future of his church upon one effort. If he failed . . .

"Hurry!" a woman cried. Newel rolled his suffering eyes and looked at Joseph. Then he fell into a more extreme convulsion and slobbered, and dug at his own flesh with his hands. Joseph gazed at him and hesitated. Newel now began to bounce as if full of springs, hopping up and down and then kicking over and knocking his head on the floor. Deciding to try, Joseph bent over the tortured man and grasped one of his arms. In a loud voice he said:

"Newel Knight, there is a devil in you!" He jerked Newel to his haunches, and with both hands clasped the flesh of the man's arms so powerfully that the body stiffened. Then, gazing into Newel's eyes with hypnotic intensity, and speaking in the most awful voice at his command, he thundered: "Newel Knight, in the name of the power invested in me by the Almighty God, I cast the devil out of you! Arise and walk!"

The crowd fell back as from a leper. Newel lay for a moment, with shudders running through him as if he were coming to life; and then slowly, quietly, he rose to his feet. The convulsions in his body ceased. His face, though yellow in its pallor, looked untroubled and serene. He stood for a moment as if experimentally finding his legs; whereupon, in a voice that electrified everyone who heard him, he cried: "Glory be to God!"

His wife came forward and assisted him to a bed. He lay on the bed, looking very exhausted but also very calm. Smiling faintly at Joseph, he said: "It was a devil all right. I saw him leave."

"I saw him too!" cried a woman, her voice almost screaming. She seized one of Joseph's hands and kissed it again and again. "Glory be! God be praised!"

Newel, meanwhile, was speaking again, but very quietly. "I can see God. I am looking into heaven and I can see God. He is smiling at me. The glory blinds my eyes, it is so bright, but I can see God on one throne and Jesus on another—and Mary just behind them." His voice was very weak. "They are all smiling at me," he said, and smiled. "I feel full of peace. There was a devil in me but he is gone and I am all right. I can pray now." And his white lips moved in silent prayer.

The woman was still clasping Joseph's hand. She kissed it again and looked up at him with earnest entreaty. "I want to be baptized. I want to belong to your church."

"And me," said a man, coming forward.

"And me," said a second. "I want a-be baptized in the Holy Ghost."

Word of this miracle spread like fire under a wind. Scores of persons, some bringing all their belongings with them, came to Palmyra, seeking the new prophet, asking for the man who could cast devils out, and make the sick rise and walk.

Joseph was deeply pleased. The fury and desperation of his enemies were growing, but his church was growing too, with new converts added to it almost every day. Some of his disciples were so wildly happy that he was afraid for them, lest they get beyond control and go mad; and in the first conference of his church he had his hands full. After the sacrament of the Lord's Supper had been given, a number of men were ordained and appointed to various offices—for Joseph shrewdly realized that if his followers were to be faithful they would also have to be distinguished. Oliver preached another of his earnest sermons, relating again for the new members, as well as for curious onlookers present, the revelations he had received; and after he was done, the congregation broke into song.

> Come, Holy Ghost, for moved by Thee
> The prophets moved and spoke!
> Unlock the truth, Thyself the key;
> Unseal the sacred book!

Standing in a wagon box and using a shaft of maple as a baton, Joseph led the singers, his deep baritone rolling like the sound of a drum above the other voices.

> How blessed are thy eyes
> That see this heavenly light,
> So long desired by ancient seers
> Who died without the sight,
> Who died without the sight . . .

The occasion was so solemn and the singing so earnest, the forested fields so hushed and the sun so golden and still, that a few persons in the crowd began to behave strangely. Beset by overwhelming emotion, they fled from song into ecstatic prayer and prophecy; and some saw visions. A woman cried shrilly, "I can see God!" and another, gazing earnestly at the sky, exclaimed in a high lost voice that she was looking into heaven. Persons gazed at her rapt face and starry eyes, and then across treetops at the sky; and one saïd, "Look, I can see what she sees!" Another shouted, "Behold, an angel comes!"

Soon the crowd was wild with excitement and moved in a surging tide from spot to spot, trying to see the visions in the sky. A man climbed to the rear wheel of a wagon and balanced himself. "Hear, O ye sinners!" he howled, and lost his balance and fell. Recovering his position, he waved his arms frantically and asked for silence, but the crowd had gone wild with religious joy. Groups gathered around those who were seeing visions; and others, meanwhile, shouted that they were full of the Holy Ghost and ready to predict the future of all things.

"Hear ye!" bellowed the man on the wagon wheel. "God has poured the Holy Ghost on me and I can see the future! Hear ye, hear ye! I will now prophesy of things to come!"

Hearing him, other persons felt impelled to predictions, and climbed to any vantage point they could find. One, a man with a large red face, looked as if he was furious or drunk. "You sinners!" he roared. "I predict you'll all go to hell if you don't jine the new church! I intend to jine myself just as soon as anyone will baptize me!" He wiped his forehead with a piece of cotton sack and looked around him. Dave Whitmer went to him and said:

"I will baptize you now."

"Fine. I been lettun my finger ride my thumb too long."

Another man, gentler of voice and appearance, was uttering less violent prophecy. "Friends!" he cried, and waved his hands. "God is speaking through me and he says all you who don't belong to the new church should get baptized at once!"

"I want to," said a woman, looking at him.

"Here," said Dave. "All who want to be saved, follow me." He headed for Seneca Lake with a dozen persons trailing him. The man on the wagon wheel was now shouting thunderous predictions.

"The world is lost in sin and God is plumb angry! Lo, I say, repent ye and be baptized, or ye will burn in brimstone as long as water runs downhill! Hearken ye, I prophesy the doom and ruin of every person in the world who doesn't follow the new prophet! Hearken, ye sinners out of hell——"

An agitated woman ran to him, crying: "How can I be saved? Be kind to a sinful woman!"

"Get ye baptized!" the man thundered. "Go wash your sins away!"

Fifty yards distant, a man was seeing visions and telling a group of what he saw. He was a pale thin man who swayed as if he might fall, and who now and then put a hand to his brow and closed his eyes as if thinking. He always opened his eyes before he spoke. "I can see heaven and its streets are paved with gold, and the throne of God is bright with diamonds. I can see God on the throne. I can see Jesus . . ."

Joseph was distressed. Though he liked the way persons followed Dave to baptism, there were seers and prophets everywhere, and he was not sure that so many visions would help his cause. Still, the spirit of the Holy

Ghost seemed to have been poured out in abundance. To the man on the wagon wheel he said:

"Brother, come down here." The man left his perch, but sheepishly as if he expected a spanking. "Don't you think you've prophesied enough today?"

"Mebbe," he said. "But the Holy Ghost is sure in me."

"The people are getting too excited. You'd better help them to quiet down."

"Glory be!" cried the man, and blew his nose into a big yellow handkerchief. "Ye are the only real prophet around," he added humbly. "I'll do as ye say."

"Then find Hiram Page and bring him here."

When, after a few minutes, the man returned with Hiram, Joseph saw before him one who had about him the sulking craftiness of a person whose plotting had always been frustrated. His eyes were small and gray and much too close together; his beard was reddish and thin. He gazed at the prophet with obvious unfriendliness.

"Brother Hiram, I'm told you say you've received revelations."

"I have. The Lord——"

"You have been looking at a piece of rock. You have received no revelations. I am the only prophet of the new dispensation."

"Now see here," said Hiram, glancing around him craftily, "I don't see why you're the only one. The Lord sure told me——"

"Beware, Hiram! You are trifling with holy matters."

"But I can look in that peepstone of mine——"

"A common piece of rock!" Joseph cried.

"No it ain't, by cracky. When I look in it——"

"Brother Hiram, you're a member of the new church. You've been baptized in the Holy Ghost. If you are a pretender, God will smite you hip and thigh."

"All right," said Hiram, scowling. "If that's how you feel, then I'd best throw my stone away. I don't want a-cause trouble." He drew from a pocket a shining piece of rock.

"Let's see it," Joseph said. He gazed at the stone. "All you can see in this, Hiram Page, is your own face. Throw it away."

Hiram took the stone and fondled it. "I'm sure it's a peepstone," he said. "Ain't it all right for me to keep it?"

"No. Throw it away."

Hiram shrugged and hurled the stone from him. "That," he said, "is the best stone I ever did see."

"The Devil has been working in you."

Troubled by disciples who pretended to be seers, Joseph went to Oliver and asked him to withdraw with him to the woods; and they entered a grove of hemlock. The gloom of the forest was strangely illumined by the pale underlinings of the leaves, so that the delicate ceilings above seemed to have caught and imprisoned a part of the sunlight. Joseph walked until he found a sky-window framed by treetops. "I am going to ask of God," he said, "and I want you to hear." What Oliver heard did not surprise him at all.

"Verily, verily, I say unto thee, no one shall be appointed to receive commandments and revelations in this church excepting my servant Joseph Smith, Junior, for he receiveth them even as Moses. For I have given him the keys of the mysteries, and the revelations which are sealed, until I shall appoint unto them another in his stead. And I say unto you that you shall go unto the Lamanites and preach my gospel unto them . . ."

Joseph turned. "Oliver, you heard God speak unto you. You will bear witness that I am the only one to receive revelations."

"Yes," said Oliver, uneasy and perplexed.

"Now go, Brother Oliver. I want to sit here and commune with God."

Joseph wanted to reflect on the false prophets and devise a plan to silence their tongues; for if they were allowed to thrive, he knew that his church would disintegrate. He also wanted to think of the enemies who were seeking his life. He had expected to be persecuted, but he had not foreseen vindictive hatred. Why so many wanted to murder him he did not know: his father said it was because men believed Joseph had found old Spanish treasures in the hills; Oliver said it was because Joseph declared all other churches to be abominations in the sight of God; but Dave Whitmer said it was only because all prophets had been persecuted, and many of them stoned or hanged.

Joseph did not know. For a long while he sat under the hemlocks and thought of the matter.

CHAPTER VII

EARNING THAT A MISSIONARY HAD CONVERTED SEVERAL PERSONS IN THE village of Colesville and that they were impatiently awaiting baptism, Joseph sent two of the Whitmer sons to dam a small creek and so form a pond for immersion; and on the next day he set out with his wife and Oliver. It was a beautiful day in late June, with birds singing like heavenly choirs, with wild flowers making lovely gardens of the open meadows and the hills. The dogberry was a glory of sweetness and color: each slender stem, sheathed with great oval leaves, supported an umbel of greenish yellow flowers; and upon a hillside he saw a thousand of these bouquets nodding in a breeze. Sitting with Emma in the wagon box and gazing around him, he saw other favorites: a spider lily whose blue blossoms, veined with purple and tinted with orchid, were surpassingly lovely on their long slender pedicels; the wake-robin whose broad rhombic leaves framed a solitary lily; and the white baneberry, one of the most unusual plants he had ever beheld. He was fond of it. He looked for symbolism in every beautiful thing that God set on a fragrant earth; and the white fruit of the baneberry had a purple spot like an eye. A dozen of these berries on a brown stem, thrust out from the main stalk, seemed to him to be a dozen eyes, with pupils grotesquely dilated, gazing in all directions as if to see everything to be seen.

"Emma," he said, "are you happy? Let us sing." And without waiting for her, his voice rolled in organ tones over the hills.

Come, we that love the Lord,
And let our joys be known!
Join in a song with sweet accord,
Join in a song with sweet accord,
And worship at His throne!

"Why don't you sing with me?"

"I can't sing with enemies all around us."

"The Lord watches over all."

"You won't think so some day when you get your head poked into a bucket of tar."

"Ye of little faith. Emma, smell the hills. God loves all growing things."

Emma sighed. "I have a feeling we'll both be dead soon."

"Not till our work is done."

"Oh, our work! Did you know a mob came to the house when you were away yesterday?"

"Mobs will come to kill me and stay to be converted."

"They'll come with a bucket of tar and soak your old head in it."

"Listen, Oliver. My wife hasn't much faith."

Oliver was driving the team. "It's true," he said, "that you're hated. They say you're guilty of awful blasphemy, saying you talked with God. Besides, they think you've found a lot of old Spanish treasures. They want to kill you, Joseph."

"The Devil is in them. Faith will conquer."

"The way it conquered my father!" said Emma.

"Your father will be a saint yet."

"He's about as saintly as the Whitmer bull. He'll die with a curse on his mouth."

"You'll see," said Joseph, and sang again.

> Happy the man who finds the grace,
> The blessings of God's chosen race,
> The wisdom coming from above,
> The faith that sweetly works by love. . . .

He did not sing when he came within sight of the dam. As a matter of fact, there was no dam: an angry crowd of men had torn it out; and now, upon seeing Joseph, they surged forward like a herd of beasts. Their profanity was so terrible that Emma thought she would swoon. They were calling Joseph every vile name they could think of, and shouting that they would hang him to a tree. Surrounding the wagon, they began to clamber up to seize him but he stopped them in their tracks.

"Back, you sinners out of hell! If you lay a hand on us, the Almighty will strike you down!"

"You lie!" a man yelled, but his voice croaked with uncertainty. All eyes were now on Joseph's angry face.

"What sinners you are!" he shouted. "You know the world is sinful and

God is angry and the day of judgment is close at hand! You know we are all born in sin and have to be saved! You want salvation, don't you? If there is a man among you who doesn't want glory in the world to come, let him speak!"

There was silence. The men looked as if they had turned to stone. One started after a moment toward Joseph but another seized him and drew him back.

"You believe in God, even as I. What is the way to salvation? By immersion for the remission of sins! We all have to be baptized or we are forever damned. You know that. I have come here to baptize a few persons who do not want to go to hell and suffer the everlasting torments of the sinful; and look at you! You come like fiends out of the infernal pit. Shame upon you! You want to see souls saved, and so do I. We are all of us fighting against the Devil. I say to you, in the name of the Almighty God in heaven, go back to your work, back to your homes! Cast evil and anger from your hearts or God will visit His terrible wrath upon your heads and you will suffer the agonies of hell to the end of time!" Like a picture of divinity, Joseph stood with clenched hands and blazing eyes, with his angry gaze meeting the gaze of every man who dared to look upon him. "Back to your homes!"

The men withdrew, baffled and muttering and frightened. With astonishment and admiration, Oliver looked at his leader: a few minutes ago, he would not have given a fig for his own life; but now the men who had come to lynch, who had fetched a rope, were withdrawing one by one or in pairs, their abashed gaze upon the blond giant in the wagon box who had given them a thundering rebuke. This, Oliver reflected, was a miracle. This man beyond all question was a prophet of God.

This night Joseph slept in the home of a convert; and early the next morning he slipped out and baptized a dozen persons, including his wife. He was wondering where he could confirm his followers when a man approached him in great haste.

"Are you Joe Smith?" he asked anxiously.

"I am Joseph Smith."

"Well, I guess that's about the same thing. Listen, a mob is coming to lynch you. Come with me."

"Where to?"

"To jail, by God. Then you'll be safe."

"Never!" cried Joseph; but Emma and Oliver seized his arms and implored him to flee.

"If you don't," said Emma, "they'll kill all of us!"

"I won't run from my enemies." He turned to the man. "Who are you?"

"I'm the constable hereabouts, and if you don't want a bunch of jacknasties putting a rope around your neck, you better come. Besides, I got a warrant for your arrest."

"They wouldn't dare lynch me," said Joseph, but his face had paled. He was trembling.

"Hurry," the constable said, and took his arm. Joseph allowed himself to be led away.

He soon found himself in a small jail, and for twenty-four hours he was guarded by four men as savage of countenance as any he had ever beheld. They not only stared at him as if they would enjoy putting a noose around his neck but came close and blew their alcoholic breath in his face and bared teeth in evil grins.

"So," said one, "you cast out a devil, did you? Well, mebbe you'n fix up a little miracle to get out of here."

"What I'd like," said another, "is to take you out in the jailyard and knock that dodrotted snout off of your face. I bet you wouldn't darst to touch me."

"Hell amighty, no. Look at his hands. Hi, Joe! You ever done any work in your life? Hey: you tell us where you found that-there gold and we'll sneak you out."

Joseph resolved to preach to them; but as soon as he began to tell them how sinful and hellbent they were, he was silenced by lewd laughter and profane jeers. They said he would hang from a cucumber tree tomorrow. His heels, they said, would be only a foot from the earth but there might as well be a mile of depth under him; and his tongue would hang down his belly like a wagon-reach. His eyes would pop out and lie upon his cheeks. Sickened by their gloating, Joseph lay on an iron cot but he did not sleep: all night his jailers cursed him or told him obscene tales or urged him to perform a miracle and free himself.

When he went before a justice of the peace the next morning, he saw thirty persons who were ready to testify against him. But Oliver and other friends had been busy during the night, and two farmers who sometimes practiced law were ready to defend him. The small courtroom was crowded to the doors and a hundred persons outside struggled to gain entrance when the prosecuting attorney opened the case. The charges, he said, were disorderly · conduct, setting the country in an uproar, stealing horses, abducting a girl and marrying her against her will, hunting for treasure on private lands, and blasphemy against God.

"Your honor," he said, looking at Joseph as if he would like personally to hang him, "I will prove that this Joe Smith is a wife stealer and a horse thief, a public nuisance, a blasphemer in league with the Devil, a dangerous character, a lazy loafer, a drunkard and a gold robber. I want to call Josiah Stoal." After the dirty shaggy Stoal had taken the stand and been sworn, the prosecutor thrust a finger at him and cried: "Did Joe Smith go to you and say an angel told him to take some of your horses?"

"No."

"Then how did he get the horse from you?"

"He bought it."

"Oh, he bought it! Has he ever paid you for it?"

"That's none of your business."

"But you admit he has never paid for it. Isn't that so?"

"He gave me his personal note. I'd sell him another horse on the same terms."

"And he didn't tell you an angel authorized him to go into the business of horse stealing?"

"He never stole any horses from me."

The prosecutor gazed at Stoal for a long moment and turned to the justice. "Call the next witness." A man came forward. He was a large man who smelled of the soil. "Mr. Witness, isn't it true that the defendant got a yoke of oxen from you?"

"Yes."

"And isn't it true that he got them by saying he had had a revelation to get them?"

"No. He bought them, just like any other man."

"Didn't he say God told him to go steal a yoke of your oxen?"

"He did not."

"Then," roared the prosecutor, "what did he say?"

"He said he wanted to buy a yoke of oxen."

"Did he pay for them?"

"He gave me his note."

"Do you think you'll ever get your pay?"

"I do."

"I wouldn't give you ten cents for your note."

A third witness was called. His hair and his whiskers, black, dense and shortly cropped, framed only a strip of forehead, his eyes, and a nose with a small patch of cheek on either side.

"Isn't it true to your personal knowledge that the defendant stole Miss Emma Hale and ran off and forced her to marry him?"

"He didn't force her, not that I know."

"You admit he ran off with her?"

"I've heard he did."

"Isn't it true that he tied her down in the bottom of a sleigh and abducted her into another State?"

"Not that I know."

"Isn't it true that she never wanted to marry him?"

"You'd better ask her," said the man. "She's here."

The prosecutor mopped his brow and stared at his other witnesses. They were, he reflected, a fine bunch of Judases; and after looking them over, he decided to call Jess Miller, the huge rowdy whom Joseph knocked down. Jess came forward like an ox.

"Mr. Miller, is it true you were engaged to marry Emma Hale when the defendant kidnaped her?"

"Well, no," said Jess, looking at Emma. "I wanted to marry her, that's true."

"Didn't the defendant abduct her?"

"I· don't know what you mean by that-there word."

"Didn't the defendant force her to go with him?"

"Not as I know. I think she just went. I guess she wanted to."

"Didn't Joe Smith steal her right in the middle of the night?"

"I don't know as to that. I wasn't anywheres around."

The trial ran from middle forenoon until midnight. Almost thirty witnesses were called by the prosecutor; and though most of them were unfriendly to Joseph, none accused him of wrongdoing, and some so flatly contradicted the testimony of one another that Justice Chamberlain yawned. Some said the prophet gazed into peepstones; others said he had behaved queerly since childhood. After the evidence was in and the prosecutor had asked for conviction on six different counts, one of

Joseph's lawyers rose to his feet. He was a bearded man who spent more time behind a plow than in a courtroom; but he was nobody's fool and he went straight to the point.

"Your Honor, we have heard witness after witness today, but not one of them has proved a single allegation against my client. Not one of them has sworn he stole a horse or an ox or a woman. Not one has proved he was ever drunk or disorderly or a public nuisance. A lot of them have said he pretends to talk with God.

"The constitution of this great country allows every man to worship God in his own way and to believe what he wants to. This isn't Europe, from which our forefathers fled. This is a nation founded on principles of freedom. It guarantees freedom to every man as long as he keeps the laws of the land. No evidence has been presented to show that my client has broken any law. . . ."

The tired and sleepy justice leaned forward. For hours his boredom had been declaring itself in great gaping yawns.

"The evidence," he said tartly, "is insufficient to convict. The prisoner is free."

Joseph rejoiced. He set out for home with Oliver and his wife, saying to them that God watched over him and would protect him. He had not gone far when a lone rider ordered him to halt.

"Who are you?" asked Joseph, rising in the wagon box.

"I'm an officer of the law. You're under arrest."

"What for?"

"A lot of things," said the constable, riding close to the wagon. "And a mob is on your trail and if you don't want to hang from a rope, you'd better come with me."

"He was just tried and acquitted," said Emma angrily. "We're going home."

"No, ma'am, you're not. That is, he's not, for I got a warrant here from Colesville. You'd all better hurry if you want to save your lives. Follow me!"

"Brother Oliver, turn around and follow."

Oliver turned the team and whipped the horses to a galloping trot; and jouncing madly in a reeling wagon, they pursued the horseman to Colesville. There was no jail here, the constable said. Dismounting and taking Joseph's arm, he left Emma and Oliver with the wagon, and set off for a grog shop, saying as he went: "I'll take you to Hank's and guard you there. We ain't ever got around to building a jail here."

Hank's grog shop was full of tobacco smoke and harlots and half-drunken rowdies. As soon as Joseph entered, they gathered around him, staggering and mocking and thrusting at him with unclean fingers. "Hey you, Joe Smith, where is all that-there gold you found?"

"God gives him gold and he sends it to a mint and has it turned into eagles."

"Eagles, hell! Buzzards, you mean."

A harlot pushed through the crowd and tried to put her arms to Joseph's neck. "Nice big man," she said. "Honey, you're sure good-lookun." The constable was at the bar, sipping grog and watching.

"Don't bother the prisoner!" he cried, and waved his gun.

"What this devil-dodger needs," said a big man, swaggering, "is a rope around his gullet!"

"Shut up your jabber!" cried the lugubrious constable, menacing with his grog in one hand and his pistol in the other. "Let the prisoner be."

"I want a-fight this prophet," the big man said. "I'll black his day-lights in a jiffy. Shoot me for a pair of berkeleys if I don't."

"Leave him be," said the constable.

"You horse thief," said the braggart.

"He's a woman thief," said the harlot. "Honey, don't you like me?"

Joseph pushed her away. These persons were the worst assortment of hellhounds he had ever seen—all of them headed for the Devil at a double shuffle. He went over to the stove and sat on a packing box. The big man followed.

"If you stole my daughter," he said, "I'd cut you open from your chin to your crotch."

"Here!" said the constable, leaving his stool and marching over. "Leave the prisoner alone, you hear? You want a-be arrested?"

"We ought a-take him out and string him up like a hind quarter of beef."

"Back," said the constable, and prodded the big fellow with his pistol. "I'm the law around here."

"Who you think you are?" asked another man, peering at Joseph. "Moses or someone?"

"Moses! He's a plain horse thief."

"But he wrote a new bible. Hi you, where's that-there new gospel book?"

"For a nickel," said the big man, "I'd hit the pop-squirt so hard he'd wizzle right up."

"Hey, there!" said the annoyed constable, and set his glass down. "Leave the prisoner alone."

The brawlers left one by one and Joseph was alone with his jailer. He sat on the box, his face in his hands, and wondered whether, if he stayed in New York, God would protect him against the ruffians who lusted for his life. Perhaps he should gather his disciples and leave. Westward was an enormous wilderness from Palmyra to the Pacific Ocean, and possibly he could find a fertile valley where he could build his church and his kingdom and live in peace. He had expected persecution; but he had not expected under the flag and constitution of the United States to be tried on false charges, or threatened with violence and death. Looking up, he saw that the grogkeeper was dozing, and his jailer was quaffing a huge beaker of ale.

"You want to crook the elbow with me?"

"No," Joseph said, "I don't drink the stuff."

"It's a bad habit," the jailer admitted, and gulped greedily. "I get ashamed now and then and whip the Devil around the stump and then go right out and get slewed. I guess I'll go to hell all right."

At his trial the next morning, Joseph found himself before three justices of the peace, as well as another assortment of witnesses who had been gathered from the hills and valleys and grogshops. The witnesses all looked to him as if they had come from hell after being whipped by the soot-boy. Among them was Newel Knight. A man named Seymour, prosecutor of the day before, was on duty again, looking angry and very determined. In presenting his case, he said it was no matter today of horse and wife stealing, but of rabble-rousing and witch-baiting and consorting with the Devil. . . .

"Your name is Newel Knight?"

"Yes, sir."

"You know the defendant, Joseph Smith?"

"Yes, sir."

"How long have you known him?"

"Oh, quite a long time."

"Mr. Knight, did the prisoner cast a devil out of you?"

"No, sir."

"You mean you haven't had a devil cast out of you?"

"Yes, sir."

"Didn't Joe Smith have some hand in it?"

"Joseph Smith was the instrument in God's hands on that occasion."

"Are you sure it was a devil?"

"Yes, sir."

"Pray, what did he look like?"

"It would be no use to tell you what the devil looked like. It was a spiritual sight and you don't understand things of the spirit."

"Never mind what I don't understand. Mr. Knight, is it true you had a fit or something?"

"I was possessed by a devil."

"And did you bounce around on the floor?"

"My soul was in extreme torment."

"Answer my question! Did you hop around on the floor like a madman?"

"I was in great torment."

"Is it true that once you bounced clear up to the ceiling?"

"I levitated," said Newel with dignity.

"You did what?" asked Seymour, flabbergasted. "You mean you ascended through the air to the ceiling?"

"Yes, sir, I did."

"Listen to that!" cried Seymour, addressing the solemn justices. "He says he floated on air. Like a feather, I suppose," he said witheringly to Knight. "So you floated around against the ceiling, did you?"

"Levitation," said Knight, "has happened before. It says in Second Kings that Elijah ascended into heaven. Then there is the case of the axehead which fell into the Jordan River. Elisha made it swim to the surface and it was lifted out. And Jesus the Christ, He was a person of flesh and bone but He ascended."

"As I understand you," said the harassed prosecutor, looking as if he were addressing the Devil himself, "you had a fit and bounced on the floor and after a while you just—just levitated. I suppose you lay against the ceiling without a single thing under you. Don't you call that a miracle?"

"It was a miracle," said Knight gravely.

"And the prisoner cast a devil out of you, did he?"

"He was God's instrument."

"But a devil was in you, was he?"

"Yes, sir."

"And when the devil was cast out, you saw him leaving, didn't you?"

"I did."

"Did the devil walk away or fly away?"

"He went off in the air."

"Oh, off in the air!" cried Seymour, his patience almost exhausted. "You saw him float off in the air. What did he look like?"

"I've told you, sir, that you would not understand."

"Mr. Knight, how did you feel when the devil got out of you?"

"I felt very peaceful and happy."

"How long had this devil been in you?"

"Oh, quite a long while, I think. He wouldn't let me pray."

"Oh, the devil wouldn't let you pray." Seymour stared at the witness as if trying to decide whether the man was stupid or mad. "Have you been able to pray since the devil left you?"

"Yes, sir, a great deal."

"What do you pray for?"

"To ask God to help me be worthy."

"Is God helping you?"

"Yes, sir, He is."

"Mr. Knight, do you think the prisoner is a prophet of God?"

"I do."

"You think he talks with God?"

"I think God is using him as an instrument to show sinful people the way to salvation."

"Do you believe in this new bible he has printed?"

"I do."

"Mr. Knight, do you think you'll go to heaven when you die?"

"I hope so," said Newel humbly.

Seymour mopped his incredulous brow and looked around him. "That is all. Call the next witness."

This trial, like the other, was long and tedious; it was past midnight before Seymour summed up his case. "The evidence presented," he said, scowling at the sleepy justices, "convicts the prisoner of consorting with the Devil. He is preying on unsuspecting persons and making them think they are headed for hell. He is getting them so wrought up that they fall into fits and think they are floating on air; and nobody in his right senses could believe God had a hand in that. It is the work of Satan, and Joe Smith is Satan's instrument, not God's. If allowed to continue, he will drive everybody crazy in western New York, and then he will go to another state and drive everybody crazy there. By his own admission he talks with God. He digs golden plates out of a hillside. He translates what he calls a new bible. He says all churches are an abomination in the sight of the Lord, and he is making decent law-abiding citizens go mad by telling them they are doomed if they don't follow him. This Moses in a wilderness wants people to think he is a prophet. The court, please, I don't have to point out the evil he will accomplish if he is not punished and restrained. . . ."

When the plea was done, Joseph's attorney rose and rested his argument upon the constitution of a free nation. Nothing, he declared, had been proved against his client. Witness contradicted witness, lied shamelessly, and were motivated by prejudice and hatred. Not a single bit of evidence had been brought forth to show that Joseph was not a law-abiding citizen, living within his constitutional rights. "If he's to be convicted for worshiping God according to the dictates of his own conscience, then our forefathers fought and died in vain, and the principles they died for died with them. . . ."

The three justices retired behind a locked door and pondered. A half-hour later they returned and one of them arraigned the prisoner and said:

"Mr. Smith, we have had your case under consideration, examined the testimony and find nothing to condemn you, and therefore you are discharged. But I wish to give you a solemn warning. Though nothing is proved against your character to justify a verdict of guilty, just the same the testimony does show that you seem to be having a malicious influence with a lot of people. The laws of the nation let every man worship God in his own way; but my advice to you is to leave this state and take your bible with you because we are peaceable here and we don't want our citizens having fits and seeing devils. It is the opinion of the court that you are not a desirable person to have in our community. If you are to escape mob vengeance, you had better leave."

That solemn pronouncement so amazed Joseph that for a long moment he was speechless. He had been acquitted but he had been warned to flee for his life: that was it, and when he grasped the full import of the matter, he felt furious. Rising to his full height, he spoke.

"This court," he said, his voice shaking with anger, "reminds me of a trial held before Felix of old, when the enemies of Paul hailed him before a judge. There was nothing for which they could hang Paul or put him in bonds. Just the same, to please the Jews who were persecuting him, they left him bound, so evil people could taunt him and heap abuse upon him. You find me innocent, but warn me to flee from mob vengeance. I shall long remember the regard of this court for the rights of a free and peaceful citizen under the American flag!"

Joseph turned to leave the building and seek his friends but at the door he stopped, appalled by what he saw. A huge mob was waiting for him. Out of darkness came the constable, smelling of alcohol and stuttering with alarm.

"Listen, they intend to hang you! Let me help you get away."

"All right," said Joseph. "God will bless you."

"You slip out the back way and you'll find a horse there. I'll wait here like I expected you to come out. I'n hold them a few minutes."

"God will bless you," said Joseph again, and went swiftly to the back door. He softly left the building and found a horse hitched to a railing close by. Leaping to the bare back, he dug heels into the beast's flesh and set off at full speed through moonless darkness. He heard angry yelling as the clattering hoofs smote the courtyard, but the horse under him was fast and eager. Soon he had left Colesville far behind.

CHAPTER VIII

H E KNEW HIS LIFE WAS NO LONGER SAFE IN NEW YORK. THE TWO TRIALS had advertised him far and wide, and from friends came stories of organized mobs determined to lynch him, and to tar and feather his family and every disciple he had. He did not know where to go. He needed men of iron in his church instead of so many Newel Knights and Oliver Cowderys and Dave Whitmers: these were faithful followers but they shook with dread. He wanted two-fisted leaders with wrath and courage in their hearts, and while hiding in his father's house, he prayed to God for such men. As if in answer to his prayer, a stranger appeared at his door.

"Come in," Joseph said, and a powerful young man entered, high of forehead and strong of mouth and jaw and limb. He had aggressive eagerness written all over him.

"I'm Parley Pratt," he said. "I'm a member of your church. I've been baptized and confirmed and I'm ready to go to work." He had been, he added, a Campbellite preacher but he had doubted that faith; and after a missionary had shown him the new bible and told of the new prophet, he read the book and decided that God was again speaking to the hearts of men. "I'm a good preacher," he declared, speaking not as a braggart but as one who knew his own power. "I can get a lot of converts."

Joseph had been studying the man. He liked the mighty heart and the iron will. He liked the directness of Pratt's gaze and the wide determined set of his jaws. "Brother Parley, the Lord needs men like you. I'm glad you came."

"How are things going?"

"Not very well. Mobsters are after my life."

"I know that. Why don't you go westward?"

"I've thought of that. But where?"

"Ohio. It's a fine country with rich soil and plenty of water and timber. We can build a church there."

"No matter where we go," said Joseph sadly, "we'll be persecuted. The Lord has told me that. Brother Parley, I'm a hunted man."

"We need boldness—bold leaders, eloquent preachers, more converts. My brother Orson, he is only nineteen but he converted eighty persons last week."

"That is good." Joseph pondered and said: "I'd like you to go and preach to the Lamanites."

"You mean the Indians?"

"We must carry the gospel to those wild people. If we can convert all of them ——"

"They'll be tough," said Parley, frowning. "An Indian ——"

"Nothing is impossible with the Lord's help."

"Nothing," said Parley, and squared his heavy shoulders. "When shall I go?"

"Soon, but not alone. I'll send Brother Oliver Cowdery with you."

Joseph called Oliver because that impatient and ambitious man had been giving him trouble. When Emma complained that she was living like a parasite off her neighbors, God addressed her through Joseph, saying, "Thou needst not fear, for thy husband shall support thee from the church." Oliver had snorted at that. But it was a revelation in regard to baptism that impelled him to act; for Joseph had said that after baptism by water, there must be baptism by fire and the Holy Ghost. Oliver persuaded the Whitmers that baptism by fire was not from God but from Joseph's ghoulish fancy; and then boldly declared that God had revealed to him, Oliver Cowdery, and to no other, the true nature of baptism.

When Joseph heard of the matter he was angry. His energy and patience were again and again exhausted by disciples who disputed and argued, and sometimes called him a false prophet to his face. It would be best to send them on missions and get them out of sight.

"You mean I'm to go to a wilderness of Indians and wild beasts!" cried Oliver, aghast. "You're plotting to get me killed?"

"The Lord will watch over you."

"The Lord helps those who help themselves. A man doesn't have any chance to help himself out there among Indians."

"Brother Oliver," said Joseph sternly, "it is God's commandment."

"You forget that God said I'm to receive revelations too. If He wants me to go, He will tell me, not you."

"God reveals Himself only through me."

"I don't believe it. I think I'm as much of a prophet as you are."

"Oliver Cowdery, you have aroused God's wrath before! In the name of the Lord, I command you to carry the gospel to the Lamanites."

"All right," said Oliver impatiently. "But you just want me out of the way."

"We are to build Zion in the West. You and Parley must prepare for our coming."

"When do we leave?"

"At once. You will preach the gospel on the way out."

Joseph now summoned Parley and introduced the two men. Oliver stared at Pratt with dubious interest; but upon sensing the man's great energy and resourcefulness, he felt relieved. He felt almost happy a little later when he saw Parley eat. The rugged fellow had the appetite of a wolf: after the others had finished, he devoured everything on the table and gazed around him for more. His laughter was loud and genuine. His eyes twinkled for the good sensuous things of life.

"We won't fare this well among the Indians," he said, and laughed at the thought.

"We'll probably eat tree roots."

"Don't you worry," said Parley, and laid a hand on his full belly. "We'll eat a haunch of buffalo at a sitting, and a hind quarter of venison for dessert. We'll say our prayers under the stars and all will be well."

"I hope so," said Oliver, glad to be going with so zestful a man.

The next day, with knapsacks on their shoulders, they turned their faces toward the great wilderness. They would enter Ohio first, where towns stood on the lake shore, and small settlements inland looked like villages hewn out of a great forest. Beyond Illinois, they would enter a vast territory of Indians and beasts, and a few trappers who had pushed adventurously westward. But Parley was singing as they went, afoot, and side by side, down the road and over a hill.

Joseph turned to Emma. "I wish I had a thousand disciples like Parley."

"You have one."

Yes, he had only one, and his mind was full of anxiety. In Colesville, one of his missionaries had been flogged within an inch of his life; south of Fayette, another had been soaked with feathers and tar and thrown into a thicket to die. Reports from scouts came to him daily, telling of barbarous treatment and blasphemous threats. Excited men still searched the hills for the golden plates. Mobs posted runners in all directions from the prophet's home with instructions to kidnap him and drag him to Manchester, where three copies of the new bible had been burned in a public bonfire. One ardent preacher, a lad of eighteen, had been bound in the rear of a grog shop and anointed with evil-smelling drugs and told to get out of New York by noon of the next day.

It was little wonder that Joseph remained in hiding or gave way to despair. He would have to flee soon but he did not know where to go and day by day he waited. In December two men knocked on his door.

One of them, huge of frame, had a stern ministerial face that shone in yellowish pallor out of a heavy beard. He had a great nose, bushy brows, and a wide drooping mouth full of cunning and cruelty. The other, also middle-aged, was of a different sort: his eyes were sad, and his mouth looked as if it had been shaped by years of grief.

"I'm Sidney Rigdon," said the big man. "This is Edward Partridge."

"Come in," said Joseph, knowing he would never like this bearded giant. The man was pompous and oracular. He had a way of lifting his shaggy brows as if astonished when he was not astonished at all.

"We have come from Ohio to join your church."

"Ohio? Has word of me traveled so far?"

"My friend, Parley Pratt, stopped at my house and told us about you. I have been a minister in the Church of the Disciples."

"He is," said Partridge gently, "the best orator west of Boston."

Rigdon liked that. "It is true," he said.

"That's good," said Joseph, but he distrusted the man. He saw in Rigdon a man who looked too ambitious and headstrong. He was saying:

"Some of us sent Ed back to investigate you and see what was going on. From what he came back and told us, I judge you have the only true religion."

"I have," Joseph said. He was aware that Rigdon looked at him as if measuring a foe. "Did Oliver and Parley make many converts?"

"A few. I intend to go back and convert every person in Ohio."

"Very good," said Joseph.

"I intend to make more converts than all your other preachers put together." For a long moment his cold eyes studied Joseph's face. "How are things going here?"

"Not very well. The persecution is bitter."

"Then why," asked Rigdon, "don't you move to Ohio? It's a good country and I can convert every last man, woman and child there."

"Such matters," said Joseph, gently rebuking the man, "God decides. I've been told that Zion will be established in this nation—but I don't know where. It might be Ohio and it might not."

"I see," said Rigdon, and caressed his beard with a large hand. "What you doing now?"

"Translating the Bible."

"You mean the Old and New Testaments?" asked Rigdon, astonished.

"Yes. You see," said Joseph, his dislike growing, "many precious truths are missing from the Bible—and even some entire books. The Lord has commanded me to revise both Testaments."

"Indeed," said Rigdon. He turned to his companion and said: "Edward, it's almost unbelievable. Joseph is *revising* the Bible." He gazed solemnly at the prophet and pulled his beard. "Is it true that God gives you revelations, saying what the new members of your church should do?"

"If I ask Him."

"Well, you think He'll give you one about me?"

"If you wish it."

"Of course I do," said Rigdon with a show of impatience. "God gave you one about Parley and Orson. I'm as important as they are. When can I have my revelation?"

Joseph considered. He did not like this man's impatience or the lusting in his eyes or the thin hard cruelty of his mouth. "Any time I ask for it."

"I'm a fine orator," said Rigdon, as if offering suggestions to God. "I could convert a stone image to anything. Couldn't I, Ed?"

"I believe you could."

"It is not difficult," said Joseph, a little annoyed, "to convert persons to the new gospel."

After the two men had left, Joseph remembered them unhappily. "There's no guile in Partridge," he told his wife. "He's like Nathaniel of old. But I don't like Rigdon. I think he will cause me a lot of trouble."

"Why?" asked Emma, looking with tired eyes at her husband.

"He's too ambitious. He'll want to run everything."

"Joseph?" she said.

"What?" he asked, thinking gloomily of Rigdon.

"Do you realize you never pay me any attention? Are you tired of me?"

"For shame!"

"I think you are. Ever since our child died, I think you've wanted another wife."

"Silence," he said.

"It's true. I noticed yesterday how you looked at another woman. You once looked at me that way."

"Emma, you sound foolish. 'Ye of little faith.'"

"It's not a matter of faith. You said you loved me."

"Verily, I do."

"Verily fiddlesticks. You love your new bible and your revelations. Must you give all your time to God?"

"Emma, you're blasphemous."

"No, I'm a woman. I get lonesome. I left all my people for you, and you—well, you spend all your time with your religion."

"I have my work to do."

"All your time," she added bitterly, "except when you're looking at other women."

"Some women are beautiful. I like to look at them. But every time I look at one I pray for grace."

"I should think so! Your thoughts about them would make you pray for something. Joseph, when are we leaving this awful place?"

"When God commands me."

"Do we have to wait for God on everything?"

"Emma, you're a very godless woman sometimes."

"I'm lonely. You married me, not God. I've a right to a husband."

But Joseph was lost in thought. He expected soon to be told the site of Zion; and now he sat with elbows on his knees, face in his hands, and sank into spiritual meditation. Emma spoke to him but he did not hear, and with contempt in her dark eyes she left the room.

Rigdon came early the next morning, eager to learn what the Lord had in store for him. Joseph said they would enter the woods; and in a grove of magnificent trees, his temple and cathedral in these weeks, he looked at the sky and prayed silently. Rigdon watched him with a skeptical stare. When he saw the pallor in Joseph's face and the far-seeing hypnotic brightness of his eyes, he was convinced, and he listened attentively when the prophet spoke.

"Listen to the voice of the Lord your God, even Alpha and Omega, the beginning and the end, whose course is one eternal round, the same today as yesterday, and forever! I am Jesus Christ, the Son of God, who was crucified for the sins of the world, even as many as will believe on my name, that they may become the sons of God, even one in me as I am one in the Father, as the Father is one in me, that we may be one. Behold, verily, verily, I say unto my servant Sidney, I have looked upon thee and thy works. I have heard thy prayers and prepared thee for a greater work. Thou art blessed, for thou shalt do great things. Behold thou wast sent forth, even as John, to prepare the way before me, and before Elijah which should come, and thou knowest it not. . . ."

It was a long revelation, but Rigdon did not for a moment take his gaze off Joseph's face. He had, indeed, turned pale, for he did not doubt at all that the voice of the Almighty was speaking to him, and calling him to His service. When Joseph finished and said simply, "You have heard the commandment of God," Rigdon was almost overcome.

"Yes," he said. "I am to baptize in the spirit of the Holy Ghost."

"It is so."

"And I am commanded to watch over you and protect you and preach your gospel."

"The Lord's gospel," said Joseph severely.

"Yes. Well, I'm a good orator. I'll make a lot of converts."

"God knoweth all things. He calls each to the office that best befits him."

"I understand that. It would be strange if He did not command an orator to preach."

For two weeks Joseph pondered. His enemies were still plotting to kidnap him and he remained in hiding, with his father and brothers and the Whitmers guarding him, their rifles always within reach. He waited for God to tell him what to do and where to go. One morning, after a night of troubled dreams, he knew that the Lord would speak, and he summoned Rigdon and went to a small grove near the house. Today the prophet did not spend much time in prayer: the urge to reveal was upon him and after a few minutes he spoke.

"Behold, I say unto you that it is not expedient in me that ye should translate any more until ye shall go to the Ohio, and this because of the enemy and for your sakes. I say unto you that ye shall not go until ye have preached my gospel in those parts, and have strengthened up the church whithersoever it is found, and more especially in Colesville. . . ."

"You heard the Lord speak," he said, turning to Rigdon.

"Yes. It seems God is troubled about Colesville. Maybe I'd better go there."

"It is a wicked place. I was tried there like any common hoodlum. Your life will not be safe there."

"I'm not afraid," said Rigdon. "I've talked myself out of tight places."

"Colesville needs you. It is full of the devil."

Matters were settled now, but Joseph did not leave for Ohio at once. Converts were still coming to him, and many of them sought a revelation for their guidance, having heard that God called each disciple to the work that suited him best. Joseph had no time to ask divine counsel for each of them, but a man named Jim Covill was insistent.

"I'll do what God says but I want to hear Him say it."

"Your faith seems weak."

"No, my faith is as strong as steel bands. But if the Almighty tells others what to do, then He'n take a little time off and tell me."

"Come," said Joseph impatiently.

He went to the grove with Covill and prayed and then spoke; and God commanded Covill to go to Ohio at once and help build the church there. Covill was amazed.

"You mean to tell me that was a revelation?"

"Verily, it was."

"You mean God was speaking to me?" asked the astounded man.

"God spoke to you through me."

"I'm not so sure about that," said Jim. "Besides, I don't want to go to Ohio."

"God has commanded you to go."

"I guess I'll decide that. I aim to stay right here."

And Covill stayed. He told his friends that Joseph was a fraud and a fool. "Why, he went out on a hill and ranted away and said it was God speaking. If that was the Almighty I heard, then my old jackass is the voice of the Devil!"

Covill's story, as well as the malicious gossip of others, caused a score of converts to repudiate the new faith. Learning that schisms were imminent, Joseph decided to hasten his departure and take the faithful with him; and in January, messengers carried his call through the countryside and from town to town. Like Paul Reveres they rode from home to home, crying, "Assemble together at the Ohio against the time that Oliver Cowdery shall return!" Three hundred followers sprang to their feet and packed their belongings as if God Himself had thundered the message from heaven.

CHAPTER IX

IN MIDWINTER JOSEPH SET OUT IN A SLEIGH WITH EMMA, RIGDON AND Partridge for the frontiers of Ohio; and day after day they jingled merrily over the white rolling hills or down the valleys and along the streams. Partridge drove and Rigdon talked endlessly of his ability as an orator and a leader; but Joseph, wrapped in blankets with his wife, was lost in thought. He was busy planning his kingdom, and during this long ride he settled many matters that had been troubling him.

There would be no odious priestcraft in his church. Every man would be his own priest and would spend part of his life declaring the new gospel. Missionaries would go over the world to preach, not to the heathen tribes but to the priest-ridden civilized nations that had forgotten their God. There would be no trained and paid ministers, no useless sermons on obscure biblical verses, no caste and pomp and elaborate rituals. Soon he must have, it seemed to him, twelve apostles, as Jesus had; for the church needed to be restored to the simple pattern of eighteen centuries ago. Missionaries would travel two by two, because in the mouth of two witnesses, Jesus said, every word could be established.

Another dream, more important than those, he considered during the journey. During the time of Jesus there had been a society that shared all things in common: no one amassed great wealth or power: all were brothers and neighbors in the fellowship of God. So too, he resolved, it would be in his church: goods would belong to a community of members; each village, and every great city as they were founded, one by one, would be an experiment in socialism. There would be a vast empire without avarice, without the empty distinctions of social position, and without the disintegrations which private fortunes introduced. This was God's will, as he understood it; this was his dream.

There was to be a land of Zion, flowing with milk and honey and governed by kindness and mercy. It would belong to the saints, to be held in this world and in the next, forever and ever; and within it there would be a great and beautiful city, wisely governed and full of goodwill.

There would be no harlots in it, no gamblers and drunkards and rogues, no greedy ambitions and no vulgar display of wealth.

Each night he spent at the home of a new disciple; for Oliver and Parley had converted nearly every person along the road. Some of the settlers wept with joy to see the prophet; all of them said they would follow him to Ohio. They gave him the best of what they had, urging upon him the juiciest portions of venison, the choicest of wild fruits, beaded jackets and buckskin gloves. While journeying in Ohio he gazed around him curiously: the hills were softer of contour, more beautifully wooded than those back home, but the streams were more sluggish. The forests were of red spruce, black walnut and hickory; and upon bottomlands along streams he saw beech and sycamore, and the lovely yellow twigs of the golden osier willow. Ohio looked like a fertile land. The hardy frontiersmen who had come here looked prosperous: every one of them seemed to have cleared a great many acres, to have a rugged cabin, luxuriant crops. Upon the walls of nearly every house he saw, pelts were spread and spiked; and piled in the yards or hanging from trees were the antlered heads of deer.

His journey was slow because the road lay among stumps and fallen timber; but on a cold afternoon in early February the sleigh drew up in the village of Kirtland. This, Rigdon said, was the place. Joseph looked at a sign:

GILBERT AND WHITNEY
General Merchandise

Joseph looked around him. This village, with its rough log buildings and muddy street, seemed to be inhabited chiefly by trappers; for no matter where he gazed, he saw men who looked like trappers, as well as signs of their trading posts. When he entered the store he was momentarily confused: though used to frontier stores, he perceived in this one the most tumbled and scattered assortment of goods he had ever beheld. Bags of flour and dried pelts, guns and traps and garments, wagon wheels and sleigh runners, lamps and candles and snowshoes were everywhere heaped in piles or stacked on a rude counter of logs or hung from the walls. It was a gloomy and dimly lighted store and for a few moments Joseph could see nothing except the bewildering confusion of goods. Then a fat, jolly, apple-cheeked man came out of the gloom.

"Are you Newel Whitney?"

"Yes."

"Newel Whitney, thou art the man!"

"What man?" asked Newel, astonished. "I'm sorry, sir, but I don't know you."

"I'm Joseph, the prophet. You prayed for me to come. Now what do you want?"

Newel's whole face smiled. "By heaven, I sure have been praying for you to come. We need you."

"First," said Joseph, "come and meet my friends."

They went to the sleigh. "What you all need," said Newel, shaking Emma's cold hand, "is a hot meal and a warm fire." He turned to Joseph. "Parley said you looked like a prophet. By heaven, he's right."

"How are things going here?"

"Awful," said Newel, and lost his sunny smile. Looking around as if for spies, he added: "Some of the converts certainly kick the wind. I think they're crazy."

"Well, let's eat, Brother Newel, and you tell me about it."

The story which Newel had to tell did not please Joseph at all. Nearly all the persons in this town and countryside had been converted, with one baptizing a second, a second a third, until half the men fancied themselves as John the Baptist, and several of the unmarried women dreamed of giving birth to a Son of God. Matters had gone so far, indeed, that there had been drunken revelry and sexual orgies. "But only," said Newel, a kindly man, "because they're so dadburned happy." Just the same, it was shameful of young women to behave so, and for young men to take advantage of their foolishness. There had been religious frenzy, wildly extravagant enthusiasm, predictions and exhortations and visions. Some believed themselves to be reincarnations of Isaiah or the Virgin, of Martha or Moses. Newel shook his head. "It's awful tragic or awful funny," he declared, "depending on what you had to eat for supper."

Joseph was troubled. "If matters are as bad as you say, I'd better go at once."

"They're worse. I don't have the words to tell you."

"Come with me."

They went down the main street. News of the prophet's coming had spread through the village, and persons had gathered in stores and grog shops or on corners, and now stared wide-eyed as he and Newel went past. They had not gone far when a woman dashed screaming out of a building and clutched Joseph's arms. He did not know whether she wanted to embrace him or tear him limb from limb. Her eyes were insane.

"God gives me revelations!" she howled. "He said you wasn't to come here, you're to stay in New York! I'm the prophet in Ohio!"

"Silence!" Joseph said.

"God told me that!" She stepped back and spit at him and shook her clenched fists. "You go on back!" she hissed. "I'm the prophet out here!"

A group of persons had drawn near and now listened. This creature, Joseph decided, had a devil in her but he was in no mood today to cast out devils. "Let's go," he said to Newel, and they went down the street; but the woman followed, screaming at him and spitting. After a few moments she stopped and began to harangue the crowd.

"She has a devil in her. Are there many here that bad?"

"Several think they're prophets but she's the worst. She has revelations every day."

"She's full of the buffetings of Satan. Where are these sinful women who think they are going to have a Son of God?"

"There must be a dozen of them. Mary Alden, do you want to see her?"

"Any of them. She will do."

They went to the Alden home. When Newel introduced the prophet, the whole family rose and stared as if they were looking at God; and Mary, with heaven in her eyes, came timidly forward. She was a tall unlovely girl with a dull red birthmark across her left cheek. Slowly, as if acting a part, she clasped hands upon her flat bosom and advanced step by step until she stood before Joseph.

"Sister Mary, what is the trouble?"

"I'm happy," she said. "I'm very happy."

"How old are you?"

"Twenty-six."

"Mary, are you with child?"

"I'm with child by the Holy Ghost," she said, and smiled. "My son will be a prophet."

Joseph shuddered. For a moment he had the horrible thought that all his followers were madmen or fools. He looked at her sternly and asked: "Who is the father of your child?"

"God," she said.

"That is blasphemy!" he thundered. He turned to the parents, a bearded solemn farmer and a woman who looked almost as insane as her daughter. "What man has been with your girl?"

"Why—" said the mother.

"Wasn't it a man named Jim?" asked Newel.

"Not as I know."

"Who is the man?" asked Joseph of the girl.

"I'm Mary," she said, still smiling sweetly.

"Isn't one of your sisters having a prophet?" asked the father, bewildered by this turn of events.

"No. That's an abominable lie. Mary, God is angry with you."

"With me? Why?"

"Because you have sinned."

"I haven't sinned," she said, speaking like a child. "God told me in a dream——"

"Never mind that. Who is the man?"

The parents were alarmed, but an older brother was wagging his head solemnly, as if putting two and two together.

"I haven't sinned," said Mary with such stupid sweetness that Joseph wanted to slap her cheeks. "I'm to have a prophet."

"Newel," said Joseph, "let's go." Outside he added: "I think there's a devil in her."

"That," said Newel, "or she sure has experienced religion up to the hub."

"A conniption fit," said Joseph. "Satan shows himself in cunning ways."

"The whole family has always been as crazy as a bedbug. But they're no worse than some others here. If it's the Devil, as you say, then he has homesteaded right here in Kirtland. I think Mary got full of blackstrap in a grog shop. Jim Overton is the man."

"Does he belong to our church?"

"He pretends to but he doesn't know beans about it."

Newel gave his bedroom to Joseph and Emma, and Joseph sat by a window, gazing at the frozen landscape and wondering why God made his problems so difficult. He was full of woe, he said, like the prophets of old, but Emma said he had eaten too much gumbo and flannel cake.

"How many women around here have been sleeping with the Holy Ghost?"

Her tone was so caustic that Joseph did not answer. Newel said there were more women than men in some of these communities and Joseph wondered what to do with them. They were harlots or spinsters, he supposed, and he hated both for their barrenness. In the cities of his kingdom he did not intend to tolerate barren women.

"It seems to me," said Emma, "we've got in a worse mess than the one we left."

"Satan is working here. Tomorrow I'll ask God what to do."

The next day he went off alone with Rigdon and Partridge and knelt in prayer and asked for wisdom and comfort; and God delivered a rebuke so violent that Rigdon was amazed. This, he reflected, writing down the words, was the thunderous wrath of Jehovah of old. "And ye that hear me not will I curse, that have professed my name, with the heaviest of all cursings! For it is not meet that the things which belong to the children of the kingdom should be given to them that are not worthy, or to dogs, or the pearls to be cast before swine!" A few days later, divine wrath again burst forth in rebuke and warnings and commandments; and when Rigdon made the matter known to the saints here, the sinners shook with fear. The woman who believed herself to be a prophet locked herself in her cabin and wept endlessly; and Mary Alden confessed in wild grief that she had lain with a man in a grog shop, and was thereupon booted out by her enraged father. Some came to Joseph, seeking his forgiveness; and others, afraid of his intense blue eyes, went to Rigdon.

Revelation followed revelation in the next few days. In one, God commanded the saints to build Joseph a house and to provide for him whatever he needed; and men at once entered the forests with axe and ox team to gather the logs. Persons came to him, bearing food and money and gifts. A second revelation called all the saints to Ohio, and commanded those already there to go forth and preach; and the men left, two by two, for the frontier villages. Joseph went from outpost to outpost, seeking men who were bold and fearless; saying, "Brother Amasa, the Lord requires your labor in the vineyards. Go preach the gospel."

In March, Parley Pratt suddenly returned and told a tale of incredible hardship. He and Cowdery had traveled a thousand miles afoot in the dead of winter, wading in snow to their knees, facing bitter winds that froze their faces, eating raw flesh when they could find no wood to make a fire, and suffering the derision of every Indian agent whom they met.

"Oliver was always coming out of the little end of the horn," he said. "Plowing through snow all day and sleeping on the hard earth wore him out. He got weak. Raw wild turkey didn't suit his taste, or ashcake either. One night he froze almost as stiff as a wagon tire and I had to thaw him out. He hung on like grim death but he was as homesick as a kitten in a well."

"The Lord is pleased with you," said Joseph. "How many Lamanites did you convert?"

"Not many. You can't argue with an Indian. While I preached the gospel, they looked at their knives and thought how nice it would be to scalp me and have a war dance. Besides, the agents told them we were devils and a devil scares an Indian plumb out of his mind." Parley grinned. He was wind-beaten and bronzed to the color of an Indian and looked cheerfully invincible. "There are millions of acres of fine land in Missouri. I think we should go there."

"I don't know," said Joseph. "We are to build Zion somewhere but the Lord has not told me the place." After a moment of thought he added: "Brother Parley, our city is to be four-square like the new Jersualem in the Apocalypse. The streets will be wide and every home will have room for a lawn and gardens and shade and fruit trees. There won't be any barns or coops or outhouses in it. In the center of the city is to be a magnificent temple."

"It sounds fine," said Parley. "When will the Almighty tell us where to build it?"

"I don't know. We have to build up the church here in Ohio. Where is Oliver?"

"I left him in Missouri. He's going to look the country over. Besides, he was plumb tuckered out."

The notion of a great and beautiful city took hold of Joseph's imagination; and often, when not translating or watching the workmen build his house, he went off alone to think and build his dream. Every day persons came to him to ask questions. Marriage, he told them, was a sanctified law which God had given unto men; complete abstinence from meat was not demanded; Zion was to be established before the second coming of the Lord; evil spirits had been turned loose on the earth to confuse the minds and hearts of men. God not only revealed these answers, but He now designated symbolic names for his leaders. Joseph He sometimes called Enoch or Gazelam; Rigdon was Horah or Olihah; Martin Harris was Shalemanasseh or Mahemson; and the village of Kirtland was Shinehah. The saints were so impressed by these distinctions that some of them saw visions or were possessed of the gift of tongues.

In a religious meeting one afternoon, an excited woman leapt to her feet and cried: "Mela, meli, melee!" For a long moment there was silence as all eyes turned to Joseph. He was still too astonished to speak when a boy sprang up as if released like a jack-in-a-box.

"I know what she said!" he cried, waving his arms at Joseph. "She said, 'My leg, my thigh, my knee!'"

Joseph frowned at that. If God were to speak in tongues, He certainly would not make a senseless remark about a woman's leg. "Say some more!" the lad was shouting at the woman. "I'll interpret it!" But the woman was too abashed to say any more. She sank to a chair and hid her crimson face in her hands. Another woman rose.

"That interpretation," she said gravely, "was false. The words mean, 'Blessed be God, blessed be the Son, blessed be the Holy Ghost.'"

Joseph marched over to the boy and led him outside. "My son," he said sternly, "don't you realize that God doesn't talk about a woman's leg?"

"But that's what the words meant," said the lad stoutly. "I knew just as quick as a fiddle."

"You were confused. Satan was working in you. You must learn to distinguish between what God says and what the Devil says."

"How?" asked the boy, solemnly round-eyed.

"When you feel a light in you, that is God. When you feel darkness, that is the Devil."

"Oh," said the lad. "Well, I did feel a light."

"No. And after this, don't interrupt our meetings."

These cunning confusions, these dark and malicious betrayals by Satan, distressed the prophet, but no more than the insolent skeptics who came to mock. He was accosted one morning by a Campbellite preacher with a bold and disturbing grin.

"If you can perform a miracle, I'll join your church. I'll bring my whole flock."

"My dear man, I don't go around performing miracles. I am God's instrument——"

"Yes, yes, I've heard all that. But I want a miracle. If you don't show me a miracle I'll be the worst enemy you have."

"Do you want me to strike you blind or dumb? Do you want to be paralyzed or have a withered hand? Take your choice, and in the name of the Lord Jesus Christ, you shall have it."

"I don't want that kind. I want a good miracle."

"Sir, I'm not going to bring trouble on anyone just to please you. If you want to be stricken blind ——"

"I don't believe you can perform miracles. I think you're a fraud."

"When it pleases God to have me perform a miracle, I will—but not just to please a curious unbeliever."

"Then I'm your enemy."

"I have many enemies. Jesus had many, too."

"Listen! I suppose you think you're Jesus come again!"

"No," said Joseph, gazing at the malicious eyes. "I'm only a humble person doing God's will. And now, if you'll excuse me, I'll attend to my labors."

"You're a fake and a mouth-almighty boaster! And by the blessed heaven, you'll be hung to a tree before you get out of here."

As soon as Joseph dismissed one trouble he was overtaken by another. The unpredictable Newel Knight had come to Ohio, upon the death of his wife, and fallen in love with a woman and asked her to be his mistress. Because she already had a husband, even though a deserter, she was insulted and furious and dismissed Newel from her home. "And don't show your sinful face again or I'll throw a kettle of scalding water in it!"

Overcome by grief, Newel sought Joseph's advice; and the prophet, as was his custom when perplexed, went to the woods to inquire of God. God said the woman was free of her husband and should marry Newel; and when Joseph in person conveyed this message to her, she fell to her knees in joy and clasped his legs and wept.

"For I do love him!" she cried, gazing up at Joseph with streaming eyes. "But I thought he was sinful!" A few days later she learned that her husband was dead.

Many came to the house where Joseph lived to spy on him. They peered through a window and saw him, in one hour, translating the Old Testament; and in another they saw him on the floor, playing like a child with a neighbor's children. There was, they declared, no sense in such grotesque conduct. He did not behave like a prophet and he did not dress like one.

"Why," demanded a woman angrily, "does he wear them old trousers and that old ragged shirt? That's no way for a prophet to be. Why, he even chops wood!"

"Yes, and romps around on the floor like a kid. Imagine Moses or Abraham doing a thing like that!"

"I tell you he ain't a prophet. A prophet walks kingly all the time and acts like a king. He don't wear rags and make toys out of billstead and willow twigs."

"He isn't a prophet," said a man named Simonds Ryder. "I can prove it."

"How?" asked the angry woman.

"I'll tell you how. He asked me to go out and preach, didn't he? And how did he spell my name? R-i-d-e-r!" said Ryder contemptuously. "I guess if the Almighty talks to him He could tell him how to spell my name right."

"I'd think so," the woman said. "Well, and the way he goes around. In shirt sleeves and with his hair uncombed! He should be in his best bib and tucker all the time."

"But he ain't no prophet. A prophet would know how to spell a man's name."

"Still," said another, "he sure predicts correct. He told that woman to marry Newel Knight. He must have known her husband was dead."

"Guesswork," said Ryder. "Could you imagine Moses or Paul misspelling my name?"

Joseph was learning that the role of prophethood was an almost intolerable burden. He was expected in all hours to stand and walk like a king and to speak with the tongue of heaven. Never was he to sit or kneel to the plain homely things of life or show simple joys or sorrows; for spies watched him constantly, waiting for him to sneeze or stumble or belch. And as annoying as the skeptics were some of his frenzied disciples: they wanted dramatic spectacles, visions of healings, casting out of devils—as if inexplicable phenomena were as necessary as their food and drink. They came in from outlying regions, agog with excitement, eager for a miracle that would darken the sky and shake the earth. He wondered if it would not be best to move to a wild frontier where his followers would have to spend their energy conquering Indians and beasts, clearing forests and breaking the sod. But he was a dreamer and not a man of aggressive action, and day by day he put the matter off while the forces of ruin closed in upon him and gathered to his door.

AFTER EMMA'S INFANT DIED IN NEW YORK SHE BROODED OVER THE LOSS AND became increasingly bitter toward her husband's devotion to the new gospel. When he was with her she nagged him, and when he was away she wept. Seeing how distressed she was, Joseph prayed for another child; but the months passed and Emma was still barren. "It's strange," she had said, "that you talk with God and yet I cannot have another child!" After arriving in Ohio he was gravely concerned; and when a woman died in giving birth to twins, he at once adopted them. Children, he told his wife, were precious; and if they could have no more of their own, they would love and cherish another's. Emma was happier then, even though the infants were sickly and a great burden: at first they howled day and night with colic, and then came down with measles. By turns Joseph and Emma sat by the babes and nursed them through the long nights.

After a week of such vigilant care, they were ill too, and very tired. One evening, seeing how white Emma was, Joseph said: "You rest. I'll watch tonight." Emma lay and slept; but at midnight she came to Joseph and urged him to lie down also. The children were asleep. He kissed their tiny sick faces and knelt by them in prayer; whereupon he stretched out upon a trundle bed to sleep.

He was soon awakened by violent screams. He sprang up, full of sleep and weariness, and ran to another room where Emma, like a ghost in her nightgown, was shrinking against a wall and staring at several men.

"Joseph, they're going to murder us! O my God!"

In the next moment the mob surged forward out of darkness and Joseph found himself in a desperate struggle. One man had both hands in his hair, another seized his drawers and tore them off, and a third tried to choke him. With all his strength he broke free and struck a blow that knocked one of the men down.

"God damn you!" a man howled. "Stop that or we'll kill you!"

"String him up!" cried a voice.

"No," said a man who seemed to be the leader. "Listen, Joe Smith, we know all about your bible and the gold you found. We know about your blasphemy in pretending to talk with God. We know they tried you back home and now you come out here. Well, we don't want any devils around here. So come along or your life won't be worth a tinker's hoot."

Joseph had withdrawn to a wall and was standing by his terrified wife. "What do you want?"

"We want you to come along. And no more fighting back or we'll gut you open."

"Never!" said Joseph. "Get out of my house!"

The mob howled again and surged forward; and though Joseph fought like a wild beast, there were too many hands on his throat and too much strength dragging him down. He was stretched naked on the floor, and men stood or knelt on his legs and groin and belly while hands choked him into senselessness. Darkness and agony filled his mind. For a moment again he heard Emma's screams and then blackness engulfed him. Two men seized his feet and dragged him across the floor and outside and across the yard. The rough frozen earth brought him little by little to his senses, and he struggled and rolled over and strove to sit up.

"Don't you wiggle a finger!" a man roared, and struck him a blow on his mouth.

The blow helped. He shook his head a moment; and then, realizing what had happened, he leapt to his feet. At once he was seized by a dozen hands. Looking around him over the heads of the men, he saw Sidney Rigdon: that man, stark naked, bloody and unconscious, was stretched out like a dead person.

"You're not going to kill me, are you?" Joseph asked the men who held him.

"Call on God for help! We'll show you no mercy."

Other men were coming now from all directions. One man had a plank: upon that, Joseph decided, they intended to bear him away after they had murdered him.

"Let's go!" the leader said.

With two men on either side, clutching his arms, Joseph was led away over the cold earth. They took him to a small meadow. One said:

"Hey, put some drawers on him or he'll take cold!"

"Sure, we don't want him to get sick. God wouldn't like His little prophet to get the sneezes."

"Let the bastard get cold. He'll be dead in a jiffy anyhow."

A man came up out of darkness and peered at Joseph. "Well," he said impatiently, "we going to kill him or ain't we? Let's get it over with."

Most of the men had gathered in council a few yards away and were talking earnestly. Wondering if he could make a dash for freedom, Joseph moved a little; and at once a dozen hands tightened on his flesh. One of the men smote him in his groin and cried: "Don't try none of your catty-cornered tricks or I'll make a steer out of you!"

"That's an idea I like," said the man who came up to look. "Why don't we cut him?"

A third man now edged through and stared at Joseph who, stark naked, was shivering from the cold. "Why don't you call on God?" the man asked. He squared off; and before Joseph could guess his intent or dodge, the man struck him a vicious blow on his nose. Blood ran across Joseph's upper lip and made a red line of his mouth and trickled to his chin.

"If you'll let me go," he said, his teeth chattering, "I'll leave Ohio."

"Oh, will you! You lousy bastard, you'll leave in a coffin."

"Hey!" roared a man to those in council. "Make up your minds!"

Another now came up out of darkness with a rope. He rubbed the rope across the blood on Joseph's mouth. "Well, why don't we hang him? What's all the waiting for?"

"Mebbe we're going to castrate him. They ain't decided yet."

"How you like the smell of that?" asked the man, pushing the hard rope against Joseph's lips. "You'll look fine, hanging from a tree. You'n kick the wind like all wrath and call on God then."

"Please let me go," said Joseph. "I'll leave Ohio tonight."

"Shut up, before I smash that big nose as flat as a hoecake."

"Hey, over there! For Christ sake, hurry it up!"

"That's his trouble," said the man who struck the blow. "It's that long snoopy nose." He peered solemnly at Joseph and said: "You jimber-jawed swag-belly!"

A heavy bearded rowdy left the group and came over. "Hold him solid," he said. He squared off but suddenly he looked at Joseph with curious interest. "Why, dodrot me, where's that blood from?"

"Gus poked him," said one of the men holding Joseph. "Hey, why in hell don't they stop their chin music and do something?"

"They can't decide if to hang him or tar and feather him."

The council now broke up and a man called: "Simonds, where's the tar bucket?"

"I don't know. Ask Eli."

"Hey, ain't we going to hang the son-of-a-bitch?"

"No," said Simonds. "Just hold him fast. We're going to soak him with tar."

"But he'll wash the tar off and preach louder than ever!"

"Shut your head. Just hold him, I tell you."

"Let's fill his belly with tar."

"And his eyes and his ears."

"No, let's castrate the bastard or hang him!"

Simonds came over. "Throw him down," he said. A half-dozen men forced Joseph to the frozen earth and knelt or sat on him. A man fetched a bucket of tar and the mob gathered round. One man drew a dripping ladle from the pail and tried to shove it into Joseph's mouth; and when Joseph threw his head from side to side, the man roared: "God damn you, this is how the Holy Ghost falls on folks! Hold your head up and eat your supper."

"Where's the bottle?" asked Simonds.

A man stepped forward and knelt and tried to force a liquid down Joseph's throat. The glass of the bottle broke against his teeth and the liquid spilled. "Look, he bit it in two!"

"Get away!" Simonds roared. "Here, Eli, poke that ladle in his mouth. Dope him full of tar."

A man now burst through the inner circle and threw himself on Joseph's body and dug with his nails like a madman. "God damn you," he cried, "I'll give you some Holy Ghost!" Drawing a piece of wire from a pocket, he dug at Joseph's flesh until blood ran. Other men fell to their knees and prodded with sharp sticks. One of them had a steel spike and with this he jabbed viciously at Joseph's genitals until Simonds reached down with an oath and seized him and dragged him away.

"Make him bleed all over," said a man, quietly observing, "and then fill the wounds with tar."

And while Joseph fought to keep the ladle out of his mouth and eyes, flinging his head from side to side, hands were busy over his naked flesh, gouging small wounds and pouring tar into them. He groaned from the agony and beat his head on the frozen ground. Simonds called for more tar; and when it came, men poured it over Joseph from his head to his feet, and then rolled him over and poured it over his hair and down his back and legs. While the tar was being poured, a man with a ladle smeared it and thrust into armpits and between thighs.

"Fill his hair good," said Simonds.

Two men lifted Joseph's head a little, and a third brought a bucket down over it like a bonnet, and tar flooded him in a black tide.

"Bring the feathers."

Men sprang forward, bringing with them great bags of feathers. These were poured in a pile on the earth; whereupon, men grasped Joseph by his head and his feet and lifted him and laid him on the pile. They rolled him over and over in the pile; and while they worked, other men seized handfuls and thrust them against his face and ears and hair.

Joseph was so nearly unconscious that when the men left him he did not hear them go; and for an hour he lay here like a dead man. When he stirred he could feel only dark pain or a vast heaviness as if he were imprisoned in liquid earth. After a while he strove to sit up but fell back, groaning; and later, realizing dimly what had happened and where he was, he put hands to his mouth and eyes and tried to scrape the tar away. When he freed his lips he could breathe more deeply and regained a part of his strength. Lying quietly, with his eyes still sealed, he breathed slowly and deeply until he felt strong enough to move. Sitting up then, he rubbed his hands in snow and old leaves to get the tar off them and then dug a part of the tar off his eyes. But he dared open his eyes only a little, only enough barely to see his way.

Getting to his feet, and feeling as if sheathed in heavy rubber, he staggered homeward, and then leaned, numb and frozen and weak, against the door. When at last he knocked, an excited woman answered and screamed. She looked once at this appalling black giant and screamed again and slammed the door in his face. When a man answered the knocking, he, too, was aghast. "Fetch a blanket," Joseph whispered. A blanket was thrown out to him and he wrapped it around his body and staggered inside.

After learning of his abduction, several persons had gathered in Joseph's home; and now, when he staggered into the room, they all fell back in horror—for this was the strangest sight they were ever to see. The blanket was around him only from his waist to his feet. His torso seemed to be all blood and wounds—for blood had mixed with the tar and streaked it red. And there were the feathers that appeared to be growing out of his body and hair, out of his ears and nostrils, out of the wounds. Emma stared at him and fainted. Women screamed, and men jabbered like astonished monkeys in a jungle.

"I want some brothers," said Joseph, speaking feebly, "to scrape me off."

Four men went with him into another room and spent the remainder of the night trying to remove the tar and feathers. While one washed his hair in one hot suds after another, a second gently dug tar out of his ears, and the third and fourth busied themselves over his body. With warm water they bathed the wounds. If he groaned in agony, the busy hands ceased; whereupon he cried: "Go on! I must be ready to preach tomorrow." When the lower part of his body had been scraped and bathed and dressed, the women came in and assisted; and as he lay on his back or his belly, the men and women knelt around him, and a dozen gentle hands moved over his flesh. "I must preach tomorrow," he said, again and again. "Don't mind my groans. Get it all off."

And he did preach on the morrow (which was Sunday) to the largest audience he had ever faced. Though his body was lacerated and bandaged, though he felt pale and weak and smelled of tar, he was still the undaunted prophet with divine wrath in his soul. When in the audience he recognized three of his brutal tormentors, he summoned all his strength and delivered a rebuke so thunderous that it abashed even his enemies.

"Our forebears," he cried, "left the shores of Europe to escape persecution for their beliefs! They came here to build a free nation. They came here to worship God according to their own conscience. They fled from priests and kings and tyrants; fought a bloody war to throw off the yoke of oppression; and wrote the democratic principles for a great and free land. I say to my friends here today, and to my enemies, that we are unworthy of the sacrifices of our forefathers if we allow mobs to beat free men, to tar them, to drag them over the frozen ground, to break into their homes! We are a shame to the pilgrim fathers if we persecute law-abiding citizens! Only the corrupt heart, only one who turns his back on God, can set the heel of tyranny on a free man! Only cowards and boasters break like thieves into a peaceful home! Only the instruments of Satan express their degraded hearts in the cudgel and the tar bucket!

"And I say to you who are for me and to you who are against me, the Almighty God will not long tolerate such brutal treatment of His children. I and those with me came to Ohio to live in peace; and I say to our enemies here this morning that we will not forever yield to barbarous treatment and invasion of our rights. The time will come when we will no longer turn the other cheek. We will take up arms like free men and fight for those rights which the constitution of this country grants to us! And verily, I do deliver this warning unto my enemies here today: we are a peaceable people but we will not rest under the tyrant's heel! . . ."

In the next few days, Joseph was sick at heart. Rigdon had been so savagely abused, had been dragged by his heels for so great a distance over frozen ground, that he was delirious, and night and day raved like a madman. One of the adopted babies had died. Emma, beside herself with despair, wept incessantly, and Joseph had to be nurse and mother to the sick child that lived. A score of persons left the new church, declaring that no real prophet would allow himself to be tarred and feathered. It was a dark and critical time. A few of his disciples came to him to offer comfort or advice but they came under cover of darkness and looked around anxiously as if expecting attack. Only Porter Rockwell was bold enough to come in broad daylight.

"Joseph," he said, "I guess you need me now. Remember when we was kids? I said when I growed up I'd fight your enemies for you. I'm ready."

Joseph looked at the hairy young fellow. "What for, Porter?"

"To fight. I'm as good a shot as there is in this country. With my fists, I ain't so bad."

"But I want peace."

"By God, the best way to get peace is to fight for it. Any man is peaceable after he's licked."

"I don't want fighting, Porter. Not yet."

"I learnt the names of two of the men who beat you. I caught them out in the woods the other day and—well," said Port, his bearded face parting in a grin, "they won't bother you for a while. I sure dusted their jackets for them."

"I don't want you doing that. You'll have the whole country up in arms."

"Not them," said Port, still grinning. "I'll tell you what I think. We need a secret order. Let me choose ten men and I'll take care of your enemies."

"How do you mean?"

"Leave that to me. You ain't going to establish no church if you let them pour tar all over you. Besides, they lose faith in you."

"Yes, I know that."

"Why don't you do a miracle and smite all your enemies blind? That would be the quickest way. But if you don't like that, let me pick ten men and I'll lick the whole Ohio country."

"No, Porter. I don't want fighting."

"Then what are we to do?" asked Port impatiently. "Set around until we're all skinned alive?"

"I think we'll have to move again."

"Where to?"

"Missouri."

"The worst hellhounds in creation live there. They're all thieves and murderers and niggers."

"We'll go," said Joseph wearily, "where nobody lives. We'll settle a new region."

"Joseph, you're too dodgasted gentle. God Almighty, didn't He raise Cain now and then? He sure did if I'n read the Bible. He never let them slap Him on both cheeks. If you'll let me clean the jack-nasties out of here ——"

"No, Porter. We must live in peace. We'll find a new land."

"No matter where you go," said Port, shaking his head, "you'll be persecuted. It's human nature. You'n go to the ends of the earth but your enemies will follow. If you ain't going to perform a miracle and bust them plumb out of their senses, then let me handle them. I won't murder nobody without he kicks the wind too much. I'll just darken his all-fired daylights for him."

"No," said Joseph, and patted Rockwell's arm. "Porter, I can count on you, and God will bless you; but we must live in peace."

"You said in your sermon we wouldn't turn the other cheek no longer."

"I know I did. But we must live in peace as long as we can."

"We can't here. Dog on it, I tell you your life ain't worth a nickel."

"We'll go to Missouri."

"Joseph, where you go, I go. But I tell you the worst scum out of hell lives down there. They'll cut your throat backwards and forwards and up and down."

"Porter, watch my baby while I go see how Rigdon is."

"He was yelling bloody murder when I come by." Port went to the bed and gazed at the sick child. "I'll watch right careful, the poor little tike." Softly he touched the babe's face. "You just run along. He'll be all right."

CHAPTER XI

IF, JOSEPH REFLECTED, LISTENING TO RIGDON'S INSANE GIBBERISH, OHIO WAS so lawless that the lives of peaceful men were in danger, then he would have to move again and push farther into the West. He told Emma he had chosen Missouri. If God founded Zion on this continent, He would doubtless place it midway between the oceans; and the reckoning of distance sent back by far-western fur traders indicated that Missouri was the center of the country. When Joseph said in meeting that the saints would move again, the excitement was unbounded. The Colesville group, which had come in a body from New York, packed their belongings and set out at once; and others, no less eager, gathered in streets and homes and talked of the beautiful city that was to be built on the frontier, with a great temple, with broad streets flanked by lawns and flowers and trees.

Joseph told his disciples to go in pairs and to preach on the way; and in June he chose three leaders and set forth to explore the new land. It was a long and difficult journey by wagon, by canal boat and afoot. From St. Louis to Independence, he and his disciples walked, and Joseph studied the soil and the flora and speculated on the climate. The Missouri country, he perceived, was a huge landscape of rolling prairie, with few trees but with lush vegetation and with more wild flowers than he had ever seen. He was interested especially in thickets of coral honeysuckle, a high-climbing vine with corollas in large clusters of scarlet so bright and vital that they symbolized for him the fertility of the region.

Every day while the men walked, Martin Harris dug into the earth and examined the soil; whereupon, gazing across a great sweep of country, he would say that a man could get wealthy here. Ed Partridge, melancholy and fearful, said nothing; and Rigdon, still half-crazed from his beating at the hands of thugs, muttered in his breath and declared he would be murdered no matter where he went. "Be of good cheer," said Joseph, looking at a lovely unfamiliar flower. He had been arrested by a garden of it in a swamp and had gone out of his way to examine it while

Rigdon declared that flowers were of no use, and Martin wondered why God had made swamps and bogs. The flower, several feet tall, had ribbed green leaves and an elongated white spike of tiny fragrant blossoms. The long stem reached upward in an arc and curved downward at the tip: it reminded him, Martin said, of the spined and flowering tail of a reptile.

"It smells sweet," said Joseph, and gathered a handful of blossoms to breathe of as he walked. "Not everything is for money, Martin. God made some things to look at and smell and touch."

"He made too many useless things, I say."

"Not this," said Joseph, and went to a shaded bank to gaze at the red baneberry. It was in full bloom. The flowers in a dense raceme were a tinted handful of white loveliness. The red berries looked luscious and full of wine. "That, Martin, is only to look at. God put it here to soften savage hearts."

"Yes, all these wild flowers have softened the Indians' hearts, all right! Ain't this the land of slaves?"

"I guess there's some slavery in Missouri."

"What does the Almighty say about that?"

"Slavery, Martin, is an abomination in His sight."

"Well, it's a good way to get rich. If I had a flock of them-there niggers on land like this, I'd be wealthy in a jiffy."

"Spiritual richness is what you should seek."

"We need money too. I lost about all I had printing the new bible."

"God," said Joseph, now gazing at a gorgeous steeplebush, "will reward you."

"He don't put food in my belly. I'll have me the biggest ranch in Missouri."

Joseph liked the country but not the people. They seemed to him to be lean of intellect, spiritually impoverished, ferocious of heart, and in some instances degraded. It seemed to be true that Missouri was a refuge for escaped robbers and murderers: some of the men looked as if they had been trained in all the villainies known to humankind. Joseph felt better after he had met his people here—those in Ohio who had gone ahead of him and those old settlers who had been converted. When he met Oliver Cowdery he broke and wept.

"Brother Oliver, I'm happy to—to ——"

"It has been a long time, Joseph. Only a few months but it seems—it seems like eternities." Oliver's eyes filled with tears. "I have suffered since you saw me."

"And I, Oliver." Joseph bowed his head. "Can you smell tar in my hair?"

"Did the scoundrels tar you?"

"They almost murdered me. And Brother Sidney, too. He was delirious for days."

"I've been beaten," said Oliver, and shook his head, remembering. "Every day here I expect to be mobbed. We should settle somewhere else."

"No. God has chosen this spot."

"But I tell you these people are the dregs of earth: cutthroats and brigands and counterfeiters and niggers."

"No matter where we go," said Joseph, looking around him with tears filming his blue eyes, "we'll be persecuted. That is certain."

"But you're choosing the worst spot on earth. I tell you, Joseph, we'll all be murdered here."

"We'll see," Joseph said.

In his first Sunday meeting, Joseph gazed at the strange audience and reflected that before him were nearly all the families of earth: there was Ham in the Negro, Shem in the Indian, and Japheth in the white man. The unbelievers in the audience scowled and fingered their guns but they did not jeer, for they were uncertain of the purpose of these invaders and had come to learn. Joseph spoke quietly and briefly, saying that he and his people wished to live as neighbors and friends; but while he talked he decided that before him was the worst breed out of hell that he had ever faced.

In the afternoon he chose a site a few miles west of Independence, and a log in the first cabin was laid by twelve men, representing the Twelve Tribes. Assisting Joseph was a handful of saints; and closing in upon them were a hundred men who rested hands on their guns and scowled. Standing on a mound, Rigdon faced the saints and said he would now consecrate this land to the children of God.

"Do you receive this land for the land of your inheritance with thankful hearts from the Lord?"

A score of voices said: "We do!"

"Do you pledge yourselves to keep the law of God on this land which you have kept in your own lands?"

"We do!"

"Do you pledge yourselves to see that others of your brethren who shall come hither keep the laws of God?"

"We do!"

"Then I pronounce this land consecrated and dedicated unto the Lord for a possession and inheritance for the saints, and for all the faithful servants of the Lord to the remotest ages of time, in the name of Jesus Christ, having authority from Him. Amen." Rigdon looked around him like a great shaggy goat. "Joseph, we need a site for the temple."

"Of course. I have chosen it. Follow me." The site he had chosen was a small hill just west of the town. They could all walk to it in an hour or two, he said, and set forth, his stride measuring the distance in yards. The saints fell in behind him, and behind them, on horse or afoot, came the horde of unbelievers, solemnly armed and implacably curious. It was a strange caravan across the hills. Hatless, with his flaxen hair shining in the sun, Joseph strode like a conquering giant at the head of his people; and his dirty bearded enemies marched gravely over the miles, determined not to let him out of their sight. On the hill he had chosen as the site of a great temple, he turned and faced the crowd, and his voice boomed through the eighty-seventh psalm.

His foundation is the holy mountains! The Lord loveth the gates of Zion more than all the dwellings of Jacob. Glorious things are spoken of thee, O city of God! I will make mention of Rahab and Babylon to them that know me: behold Philistia, and Tyre, with Ethiopia: this man was born there. And of Zion it shall be said, this and that man was born in her: and the Highest himself shall establish her. The Lord shall count, when He writeth up the people, that this man was born there. As well the singers as the players on instruments shall be there: all my springs are in thee.

Overcome by curiosity, one of the bolder men now pressed forward. "What in the name of God," he asked, "do you kallate you're doing here? Has your dodrotted mind gone dickey?"

"I am dedicating the site for a temple of God."

"A temple on this hill!" The man and his companions gazed around them.

"The true church of God," said Joseph quietly, "is to be established here in Missouri. This is holy land."

"Holy hell, I say. Listen, you better build your temple somewheres else.

This is our country down here. We don't want no long-faced temple builders puttering around."

"This is God's country. Brother Partridge is appointed the judge here to divide the lands of the heritage of God unto His children, and to judge with the assistance of his counselors, according to the laws of the kingdom. God's law must be kept in this land. Let no man think he is ruler. You are to be peaceful and respect the rights of others and be obedient to the laws here——"

"Hold on!" the man cried impatiently; but one of the saints grasped his arm.

"Hush," he said. "The prophet is having a revelation."

"We will found here," Joseph continued, "the new Jerusalem, with Zion its beautiful capital in the empire of Christ. But beware of wrong-doing, lest the blessings of God be taken from you."

"Amen," said the man, and there was ribald laughter. "Imagine the all-fired gall to come right here among us to build a temple!"

"We are a peaceful people," said Joseph, looking at the man's grinning face. "We keep the laws of God and man."

"We don't have no laws down here. No, I'll tell you, Joe Smith: you'd best build your little holy house somewheres else. Ain't that true, men?"

"Yes," said a half-dozen men; and one added: "Down here we're all blacker than a funeral of niggers in a thunderstorm. We don't want none of your white purity."

Joseph went to another hill and sat down with his chief disciples. Partridge, he said, would establish a United Order here in which the saints would share all things in common, with special privileges to none. In Ohio the Order had been a disgraceful failure but only because of un-godliness: here, where the land was holy, where eventually all the people of earth would gather to worship their Father, the Order must not fail.

"But what," asked Partridge, staring at the armed men on the other hill, "what are we to do if attacked? Shall we resist?"

"If you obey the laws of the land, God will watch over you."

"That isn't always true," said Oliver. "Besides, there are no laws down here."

"You must be faithful and law-abiding." Joseph looked away over the prairie, dreaming of the golden city which he would build. "In Ohio, many of the saints consort with the Devil. That is why God allowed our enemies to mob us. If you are righteous ——"

"But why does God allow the innocent to be punished for the guilty?"

"Because we are the leaders. We must keep the saints pure in heart."

"I see trouble ahead of us," said Oliver. "Look at that gang over there. They're plotting even now to mob us."

"Your faith, Brother Oliver, has always been weak."

But when, ready to leave for Ohio to learn what was happening there, Joseph gazed at his handful of people who were remaining here and thought of the dark lusts in this frontier land, he too felt premonition of tragedy ahead. The eyes of gentle Edward Partridge were blind with tears when he grasped the prophet's hand. He tried to say good-bye but faltered and turned away.

With ten men, Joseph set out by canoe down the Missouri; and as they paddled along, drawing other canoes loaded with provisions, he wondered what lay ahead of him. The time was August. The river was low and clear; and the vegetation along its shores, tropical in its luxuriant wealth, was so beautiful that often Joseph paused to examine a bush or a flower or to gaze at a tree. Most of the plants were unfamiliar to him but he knew the steeplebush and loved it: the white and pink clusters seemed to climb up the long stem as if reaching for the sky. All the leaves pointed upward too; and for him this erect shrub was a symbol of all lowly things that aspired to heaven. He recognized the elegantly groomed beech, the sycamore, stately and solitary, and the scarlet haw. The blind gentian distressed him. The blue corollas, set in bracts of leaves and closed at the summit, with the larger leaves drooping loosely away, reminded him of the dark and unseeing life of the Missourians. Letting one hand trail in cool water, and gazing at a deep blue sky, he said:

"Brother Sidney, there are troubled days ahead of us."

"Yes," said Rigdon, also idly afloat. "There'll probably be a mob waiting at Kirtland."

A man heard the remark and became so excited that he almost overturned his canoe. "A mob?" he said. "Then why go back there?"

"Be prepared," said Rigdon. "We'll all be skinned alive."

"Then why not stay in Missouri?"

"Because," said Joseph, "we have work to do in Ohio."

"I think we should all go to Oregon."

"Oregon," said Joseph, and was lost in thought. He had dreamed of the Oregon country: Lewis and Clark, and others since, had told of its forests, its mountains and lakes, its immense gardens of wild flowers, its fish and game and rich soil. Perhaps, Joseph reflected, he ought to lead his small band to the western shore; but the distance was nearly two thousand miles and none but the most reckless dared undertake such a journey. Nevertheless . . .

The excited disciple was thinking too. He was thinking of mob vengeance, of the tar bucket and the hawthorn cudgel and the awful blasphemy of his foes. He wondered if he should not fall behind and turn back to Missouri; but when he gazed at the jungle banks and realized that both Indians and wild beasts might be lurking there, he was afraid and kept his canoe close to Joseph's. Day by day his agitation increased. He could think only of mobs waiting, of women ravished, of men beaten or hanged.

And one evening, while the small party was encamped on the river bank, he leapt to his feet with an insane cry; for he had heard a great and terrible sound. The other men had heard it and they all rose and listened. Rigdon thought it was a buffalo stampede; Harris said it was Indians; and a third declared it was only thunder across the gloomy hills. One of the men, gazing at the sky, turned as white as death.

"I can see it!" he shouted. "I can see the Destroyer riding upon the face of the waters! In all his horrible power I can see him!" His voice fell to a whisper. The other men looked at him or the sky and waited. "I can see the Destroyer upon the face of the deep! He is riding a whirlwind and in his hand he has a sword of lightning and his voice is like thunder!" And then, with a mad cry that chilled them, he sank shuddering to the earth and covered his eyes.

"Did you see it?" Rigdon asked of Joseph.

"No, but I heard the sound."

"I thought it was buffalo."

"Or Indians," Martin Harris said.

"No," said Joseph. "Our Brother has had a vision."

Together they stared at the sky and listened, or looked down at the one who was moaning and hiding his face. They had prepared supper but they were now too distressed to eat. The man shuddered and cried aloud and kept his face hidden; and the others gazed out into darkness, thinking of the wilderness and the Destroyer upon the deep. When

Rigdon asked what the vision had meant, Joseph looked at the supine man and said:

"God is angry with him. He has committed some sin."

Most of them slept fitfully but Joseph spent most of the night in prayer; and when morning came, he knelt on the bank of the stream and offered his soul to God. He rose and stood like a king and the ten men looked at him. After a long moment he spoke. God spoke through him, saying that in the beginning He had blessed the waters, but in the last days and by the mouth of John He had cursed them; and that travel upon the waters was now dangerous and not to be undertaken by Joseph and Sidney and Oliver. Henceforth, except on canals where travel was safe, they should go always by land.

"And now, verily, I say unto you, and what I say unto one I say unto all, be of good cheer, little children; for I am in your midst and have not forsaken you!"

That declaration comforted the men but they made haste in their journey, nevertheless; and Rigdon said God was not pleased by their tarrying to look at trees and flowers, but Martin said God was angry because they had been laughing and jesting too much.

"He called us little children," said one of the men.

"We are all His children," said Joseph.

"And He is watching over us all the time. Mebbe He will not let the mobs hurt us in Kirtland."

Oliver had been silent. "I think the sound was a warning to us not to go back. We'll be killed in Kirtland."

"No," said Joseph. "We'll build the church up in Kirtland and all of Ohio."

But the men looked at Oliver and thought of what he had said, and in the anxious eyes of nine men was the belief that he was right.

CHAPTER XII

WHEN JOSEPH RETURNED TO KIRTLAND AND LEARNED WHAT HAD HAP-
pened during his absence he was amazed. "It seems," he cried
to Emma, "that as soon as my back is turned, the saints think they have a
license to wickedness! They act like a bunch of abominable griddle-
greasers and pukes!"

"I'd hate to tell you everything that's going on around here. I'm sick
of it. It's not a true religion that makes people sinful."

"The sin is in their hearts."

"No matter where it is, it is everywhere. Wait till you see. Wait till
you hear Ezra Booth."

Ezra Booth, a former Methodist preacher, was an impatient and hot-
tempered man who flung himself around like a lunatic when he was
unable to convert an unbeliever. When his temper was gone, he called
upon God to strike the sinners down. "O God," he would howl, "smite
these infidels and make them believe! Put the fear of hell in their hearts!
Show thy wrath for I can't convert them without your help!" But God
remained aloof to Ezra's pleas, and day by day the man waxed more
furious until at last he roared: "To hell with this new church! It's the
work of the Devil and I'll have no more to do with it!" Whereupon,
feeling at peace, he wrote letters to the newspapers, declaring Joseph was
given to jesting and false faces and a short temper. Those things, he said,
argued that Joseph was no more a prophet than he was. "If Smith was
really a prophet, then he'd call on God and God would scare everyone
into the church. For if God wants people converted, He can do it in a
hurry. I prayed till I was black in the face and He never converted anyone for me."

Joseph was still wondering what to do with Ezra when he heard that
Rigdon was again cutting monkeyshines. Rigdon, indeed, learning one
day that Joseph was absent from Kirtland, had a revelation of his own
and published it abroad. It declared that the keys of heaven had been
taken from the saints and would not be restored until the people had built

for Sidney Rigdon a house. Hyrum Smith was dubious, but several alarmed men set out for the woods to gather the logs.

"How," asked Hyrum, staring at Rigdon and despising his huge nose and oracular air, "do you know it was a revelation?"

"Know!" snorted Rigdon, trying to look like a prophet. "Didn't the saints build a house for Joseph? Why don't they build one for me? I'm tired of working like a dog and having no place to lay my head!"

"Let us go to Joseph. We'll learn what he says."

Rigdon went but he sulked darkly and muttered in his breath. When he saw Joseph flush with anger, he felt enraged and badly done by and began to tell of the neglect and abuses heaped upon him. Joseph cut him short.

"God will deliver you to the buffetings of Satan!"

"But I did receive a revelation. God told the saints to build me a house."

"God told them nothing of the sort. Haven't I said that God reveals Himself only through me? . . . Answer!"

"Yes, Joseph."

"Now the Lord is angry with you——"

"But why can't I have a house? I'm third in command."

"If God wishes you to have a house, He will tell me. Now repent and seek forgiveness in prayer or you are eternally damned."

Joseph watched him turn away, looking old and defeated, looking shabbily gaunt and stooped. Ever since the mobbing, Rigdon had, it seemed to Joseph, behaved queerly; and he was not surprised therefore to learn that the man went home and suffered incredible agonies. He fell out of bed first and cracked his nose; whereupon he writhed as Newel Knight had, with devils tearing him limb from limb. Then, said Newel Whitney, who reported the matter to Joseph, the man sat on the floor a while like a huge meditative fly and rubbed his whiskers; but after a little, he gave off terrible yells and bounced around in unbelievable torment. Sweat poured out of him. He went to bed then and was quiet and Newel thought the ordeal was over; but suddenly with a maddened yell Rigdon crashed again to the floor as if he had been thrown from the bed and doubled up in horrible convulsions. He frothed at the mouth and screamed like a great vulture.

"At last," said Newel, his apple-cheeked face sober with woe, "I got him to pray with me. We prayed a long time, and Rigdon told God he wouldn't pretend to have revelations any more. Then I got him in bed and now he's sleeping."

"I told him," said Joseph, "he would be delivered to the buffetings of Satan."

"Well, he was. He stood right up to the rack and Satan went after him. It was awful."

"Perhaps he will come to his senses now."

"If Satan larrups him again, there won't be much left of Sidney. I thought he was a goner this time. Will you come over and see him?"

"No, Newel. I have to go deliver Jim Brewster to Satan now. He has been wicked too."

Jim Brewster, a youth of sixteen, had received revelations, and thereupon had converted his family and most of his neighbors to his gospel. He was a sallow, pimpled boy with a lean ungainly body and large sunken eyes. Having begun his own church, he set to work writing a manuscript which he called the Book of Esdras: with his mother as amanuensis, he sat in a bedroom while with paper and pen she sat in the kitchen, and he dictated to her the new gospel.

When Joseph appeared at the home, he looked through the open door and saw the mother writing. Upon seeing Joseph, she leapt up like an infuriated cat and slammed the door in his face but he pushed it open and entered.

"Get out!" she cried. "You false prophet!"

"My dear woman, it is your son who is a false prophet."

"You lie! God talks to my son and he is laying down the true principles."

"Ohio is full of false prophets."

"I know it!" she said, staring at him with murderous eyes. "You're one of them!"

"Mrs. Brewster, if you keep on this way, God will be very angry with you."

"Look out for your own soul!"

The son now looked in anxiously from a bedroom. Joseph bade him enter and he shuffled in as if he were all incoherence and feet.

"My boy, you are wicked."

"I'm a prophet," said the lad, standing gawkily proud with his mother's arm around him. "I'm restoring the lost books of the Bible."

"You're doing nothing of the kind. You're playing with the Devil."

"You lie!" said the mother shrilly. "You make a poor mouth and get yourself a house built but you ain't no prophet. My son's as smart as a steel trap."

Joseph turned away from the thin tightness of her mouth, the madness in her eyes.

"Unless your son repents, I'll have God deliver him to the buffetings of Satan."

That brought wild laughter from the mother. She rocked with insane mirth and gazed up at her son; but suddenly her face changed to murderous fury. "Get out of my house! You puke, scrouging up to God!"

Joseph left the house and shuddered at the vile abuse which followed him. He wondered gloomily what was getting into his people: there were so many false prophets, so many deluded fools or deliberate frauds, that his church was disintegrating for want of ruthless leadership. He was not a ruthless leader: his heart was too gentle and his patience too great.

"Satan is busy here," he said to Emma. "Most of the saints have devils in them."

"It's just plain ornery human nature, I say. Like Martin Harris. You heard what he's shining up to?"

"Martin?" said Joseph wearily. "Is he sinful again?"

"Well, he's telling plenty of stuff about you. He says you're a bigot and a tyrant and a drunkard."

"A drunkard!" cried Joseph, raising his head.

"He says when he helped you translate the bible you were drunk all the time. He says you were so rip-snorting drunk you fell off your chair."

"Martin says that?"

"That isn't half of it. He says you were a mouth-almighty person who bilked him out of his money and left him bankrupt. He says you promised to make him second in power in the church and then put in Oliver and Rigdon and Partridge."

"Martin Harris is a fool."

"Just the same, he's told everyone you got drunk and made hell's delight and then fell in a fit and pretended you were talking with God. He's told that story all over here."

Joseph rose to his feet, trembling with rage. Emma said later that he seemed to swell with fury: the veins in his forehead rose in purple ridges, and his eyes looked like glittering blue glass. "Tell Newel Whitney to send Martin here!"

"Yes," said Emma, appalled by this picture of her husband.

Martin, the sly skeptic, came like a hulking fox, his eyes fearful but agleam with spite, his mouth fixed in an alarmed but resolute grin.

"Martin Harris, what are you telling?"

"The truth, Joseph."

"Truth! May God have mercy on you! Have you said I was drunk?"

"You got drunk when you was translating the bible."

"Liar! You abomination out of hell!" Joseph stepped forward as if to grasp the man and break his spine; and Martin withdrew, still grinning.

"You sounded drunk to me."

"When? What are you saying?"

"When you translated. One day you sounded dead drunk. Your tongue was thick——"

"Satan is in you, Martin!" Remembering, then, that he had established a High Council of judges to handle apostates and troublemakers, Joseph turned to Newel. "Have the High Council call this sinner before it. He will be excommunicated."

"Yes, Joseph."

But excommunicating Martin and driving him from the church as if he were half-wolf and half-fox did not chasten others whose ambitions or delusions were driving Joseph mad. They heaped scorn on the language of his revelations, saying that God would not utter such phrases, such idle or childish or trivial matter. Loudest of these critics was Bill McLellin, a huge obtuse man who took his notions from his wife. His wife told him he could do better as a prophet; and Bill was so taken by the thought that he could not sleep for dreaming of his new importance. One day he harangued a crowd, saying that if he was not a better prophet than Joseph, he would eat the shadbelly coat of every Quaker west of Boston.

When Newel reported the matter to Joseph, that weary man had no anger left in him. False prophets were everywhere: when he rebuked one, a dozen others sprang up, each with revelations and a bible and a shortcut to heaven.

"Bill says he's the wisest man in the whole church. He says your revelations are silly and he can do miles better. Why don't you let him try?"

Joseph considered. "I will," he said at last. "Tell him he is to have a revelation and if it's better than mine, then he can be the prophet."

"That," said Newel, "ought to make him pull his stakes."

When word of this was carried to Bill, he was so pleased that he cut capers. "Tell everyone to come," he said. Then he knelt in prayer, with his wife at his side, and rose to his feet. "I feel ready," he declared, and left the house to look at the sky. "This will be the biggest revelation God ever give to man. Let's go." With a crowd following him, he set off for Joseph's home and boldly announced himself at the door.

"Do you feel the spirit of God in you?" asked Joseph.

"By gum, yes. I prayed and I'm ready."

"All right," said Joseph, and went with McLellin to a hill. A score of persons went with them.

Clasping hands to his breast, Bill gazed at the sky and began to pray. For a full minute he prayed earnestly and then paused to reflect; whereupon, with a sigh, he prayed again. "I'm ready," he said. "Write it down." There was a long pause before he spoke. "Hearken and lo and—and behold, I am the Omagga and—and Delpha, and I say unto you, verily, verily, you are sinful and I am wroth with ye. I am the one and only God who is everlasting to everlasting, forever and ever, the beginning and the end. I say—" He paused, his gaze on the sky. Then: "Behold, I say unto ye, hearken to the words of my servant William E. McLellin who is pleasing in mine eyes. Hearken, ye sinners! Verily, thus saith the Lord . . ."

This was too much for Joseph: he was smiling, and men around him were ready to explode with laughter. They stared at the round solemn face of Bill who was clasping and unclasping his hands and trying to think of more to say. Turning to the group, he said simply: "Just wait. I ain't done yet."

In spite of himself, Newel snorted with mirth and then choked until his round plump face was red and strangled.

"Hearken!" cried Bill. "Verily, this is my servant William E. McLellin and from now on he will be the prophet in the new church."

Newel burst with unholy joy and sank to the earth, clutching his belly. Other men roared, and one advanced and slapped Bill on his shoulder. "Bill, I reckon you ain't no prophet!"

"Why?" asked Bill angrily.

"You just ain't got enough holiness in you. You better go back to your farm."

"Listen, ye unbelievers! I'll ask God——"

"No, Bill, you go back to the farm. We could all have a revelation as good as yours. We can all say hearken and behold but that don't mean anything."

Throughout eastern Ohio, from town to village and valley to hill, spread the story of Bill's revelation; and laughter for a little while restrained others who fancied themselves as prophets. McLellin, completely abashed, went back to his farm and his plow. His wife ranted up and down the countryside, preaching to neighbors and abusing friends, and declaring that if her husband hadn't the salt in him to stand up to the rack and hear what God had to say, then she would do it herself. Her zeal encouraged others; and again reports came to Joseph of men impelled to prophecy, of sexual orgies, and of women who were determined to give birth to a savior.

One morning, feeling that God had deserted him, he went alone to a large thicket of wild crab apple. The flat matted tops were a great burst of rose-colored bloom, and the exquisite spiced fragrance drenched the air. When he gazed on such loveliness as this, he knew there was a divine plan in the universe and a God who watched over His people. Hidden in a forest of blossoms, he knelt for a long while in prayer and then rose and walked among the trees, breathing the clean sweet depth and softly touching the flowers. Once before, when his followers turned to sinful doings, he rebuked and terrified them with thunderous revelations; and today he knew that he must do so again. He would explain to them the three degrees of glory in the next life: the telestial for those who, in their earthly pilgrimage, were so negligent or sinful that they barely missed hell; and the terrestial for those who, though more pious and zealous, fell far short, nevertheless, of the task assigned them; and the celestial for the few who obeyed all the commandments of God. Those in the highest degree of glory would dwell forever with God and the Son.

When he announced this revelation, he learned that it appealed strongly to the imaginations of his people. On another matter, too, they came to seek explanation and advice.

"You mean we all lived in a life before this one?"

"We did. After we die in one life, we start in the next where we left off."

"You mean in heaven we'll all begin where we stop here?"

"Yes. The more we accomplish here, the farther along we'll be in heaven. God is constantly changing and growing. He was once a man like us but now He is a god. There are gods many, and they vary in glory as the brightness of the stars."

"And you say we can all be gods?"

"If we are worthy. The most righteous will be gods first."

"But how about me?" asked a woman. "Will I be a goddess?"

"Never mind," said her husband impatiently. "You say every god rules over a kingdom?"

"Verily. There are gods many and kingdoms many."

The man looked at his wife and considered. "Then I'll rule over a kingdom some day."

"Not," she said scathingly, "without you stop your sinful habits."

"But Joseph says we'll all get there in time. And you say God is the father of us like we're the fathers of our children?"

"It is so. God is our father and we are His children. He is a glorified father now, but what God is, we may become."

This dramatic doctrine was breath-taking, yet very simple and reasonable too; and persons gazed solemnly at one another, speculating on what their chances would be.

"I'd think," said one, "we'd stand a better chance the more children we have."

Joseph was startled. He had had the same thought. "That," he said, "is true."

"What about me?" asked a man with a barren wife. "I'll never have no children. Is that fair?"

Another man spoke. "But he says in the next world we'll have children. We'll take up our bodies as we laid them down."

"What of that?" asked the other impatiently. "If I live with my wife forever and ever without no children, how can I be a god? Why don't God let me have two wives?"

Joseph looked far away. That also was a thought which had been in his mind.

This revelation did much to chasten the sinful, but it also excited loud scorn among his enemies. They had hardly recovered from their amazement when they heard that Joseph was boldly revising the Old and New Testaments; and before another week passed, mobs were organizing everywhere. Port Rockwell kept Joseph advised. Some of the men, he said, wanted to hang the prophet, some wanted to castrate him, and a few wanted to give him another soaking with tar.

"They call us the Mormons now. They say we'll soon rape their wives and daughters and burn their homes."

"Who is the leader now?" asked Joseph wearily.

"Ezra Booth is worst. But there's mobs everywhere, Joseph. You got to quit translating the Bible and get out and fight and lead us. If you'd let me handle Ezra Booth——"

"No, Porter. I don't want any violence."

"But you'll be in a peck of misery soon. Stick a pin there and don't forget it. Without you stand up to the rack and make the fur fly, you'll be hanging to a tree before a month is out. And down in Missouri now, they're beating the living daylights out of the saints. They're beating them with black snakes. Joseph, why don't you let me pick a dozen men and I'll whip all the paddies and pukes and griddle-greasers in Ohio."

"No, Porter. We must live in peace."

"By the Almighty Christ, there won't be no peace! Your revelation about us all being a god in the next world has made them as savage as a meat axe."

Joseph rose and paced the floor. "God is angry with us, Porter. I don't know what to do. I must revise the Bible and do the spiritual work and I need some strong leaders to take care of other matters."

"Let me go down to Missouri and take care of them."

"No."

"Then we'll all be hung as high as the top of a tulip tree. I don't have to be no prophet to know that. Next time a mob gets aholt of you——"

"I know!" Joseph cried, and sank to a chair and buried his face in his hands. After a few moments he raised a desolate face. "Porter, I need strong men. I'll ask God to send me some leaders."

"I'n whip my weight in wildcats," said Porter, wagging his bearded head. "Why don't you let me brush-whip the whole stinking murderous tribe?"

"No, Porter. You leave me now and I'll seek God."

CHAPTER XIII

BRIGHAM YOUNG'S EARLY LIFE HAD BEEN MUCH LIKE THAT OF THE PROPHET. His parents had moved from farm to farm in western New York, suffering under poverty and a stern moral code. Brigham spent only twelve days in school: during the remainder of his boyhood, he chopped cord-wood, plowed and planted and reaped, going barefoot most of the time and in rags, but keeping his will unbroken and his mind serene. His father often punished him, giving a blow first and a warning afterward, because his son often walked on Sunday, not for exercise but for pleasure. Brigham's mother died when he was fourteen; whereupon, in spite of his father's angry rebukes, the lad went his headstrong way, refusing to sign a temperance pledge because he was set on a free life, and learning to profane with the best of them. By turn he was joiner, painter, glazier, typesetter, carpenter and farmhand. When twenty-three he married Miriam, daughter of Asa and Jerusha Works, and soon found himself with two daughters to support. He was still without anchor or goal when he fell upon a copy of Joseph's new bible.

During his childhood, Brigham had pondered religious matters but had never worried about them. One of his solemn brothers prayed most of the time, and another saw visions and tried to cure ailing young women by laying his hands upon them. A third brother also had visions, and in them God said He was gravely concerned about Brigham's wel-fare. But Brigham was not concerned. Once he went to hear Lorenzo Dow, famous throughout the backwoods country as a fire-eating preacher; but that loud gentleman bored Brigham to tears. After hearing other preachers, he decided to become a Methodist, not because he believed in this faith, but because persons were rolling and bawling and thumping all around him, and he was weary of being told what a sinner he was.

When a copy of Joseph's book was shoved into his hands, he looked at it curiously and read a few pages; but after a few minutes he hurled it at a wall. "To hell with it," he said. "It's like all the other damned religions." But later he read it again, and again; learned that his father and brothers had been baptized into this sect; and resolved to go with his good friend, Heber Kimball, to see the new church in action. After several days of alert study he said:

"Heber, what do you think about it?"

"Well, Brig, it don't look so bad to me. It's different."

"By damn," said Brigham, "I guess I'll get baptized."

But he did not act in haste. He went to the colonies and watched what was done and talked with the members. There was none of the mystic in Brigham: he was a hardheaded man of thirty with shrewd knowledge of men and what men were made of. The new religion, it seemed to him, would probably get a man to heaven as quickly as any other; and it would offer greater opportunity to leadership. The saints told him that out in Ohio and Missouri, persons were being converted by hundreds; that a great city was to be built in the land of Zion and all the peoples of earth were to be gathered into this church. That, Brigham reflected, was something a practical man could get hold of.

"Heber," he said, "let's go to Ohio and meet the prophet."

In Kirtland they asked for Joseph and were told that he had gone to a forest to chop wood.

"To chop wood!" cried Brigham, astounded. While walking with Heber he added: "Don't it sound funny for a prophet to be out swinging an axe?"

"It don't seem just right," Heber said.

"Damn it, no. A prophet should act like a prophet. He can't expect to build a church if he acts like a farmhand."

"It sounds funny to me."

"By God, Heber, he needs men like us."

"That's why we're here, Brig."

"Yes. . . . Well, there he is."

The two men stopped to look at the scene. In shirt sleeves Joseph was driving an axe with powerful blows into a tree; two other men were hauling cordwood. Brigham guessed that the man in shirt sleeves was the prophet; and as he advanced now he studied him curiously, noting his size and strength, his fair skin and flaxen hair. When Joseph saw them coming he rested his axe and waited. The men approached, smiling, and offered their hands.

"I'm Brigham Young. This is my friend, Heber Kimball."

"I'm glad to meet you," said Joseph. He mopped sweat from his brow and looked at them. Brigham, he observed, was perhaps two inches under six feet, but he had a deep and powerful frame and the most unwavering gray eyes he had ever seen. Kimball was a large man, and darker, with black sideburns to the bottom of his ears. His eyes were quizzical but steady and searching. They were, Joseph realized, men of quality—two natural leaders looking for a job. He set the axe by a tree.

"Come," he said, and took them to his home.

He entered the house and sat with them but he was not at ease. Men of the spirit he knew and could handle; but rugged giants of the kind who built physical empires made him feel transparent and insecure. He had been praying for leaders and two had come. Nevertheless, he felt, while studying their strong bodies and bold eyes, that they would probably throw him out of the church and take control. As if reading Joseph's mind, Brigham said:

"How are things going here?"

"The persecution is bitter."

"Why?"

"Right now it seems to be chiefly because I'm translating the Old and New Testaments."

"I heard you got tarred and feathered."

"Yes. I was almost murdered."

"Why don't you build up an army?"

"An army! What for?"

"To take care of the scoundrels. I hear the saints in Missouri are being driven out. In my opinion, you can't build up a strong church by turning the other cheek all the time. You must fight."

"I want to live at peace with all men."

"Nobody can live at peace with all men," said Brigham, and Heber nodded approval. "If you don't make a stand you'll be run off the planet. The earlier you fight, the better."

Joseph did not like such bold words. He said he thought it would be well to call in some of his assistants. They came—but Brigham was not impressed. John Whitmer he sized up as a humorless man who did not see anything far, and nothing clearly; Newel Whitney as too fat and dimpled and boyish; Rigdon as too overbearing and obstinately stupid; and the others as romantic mystics and not leaders of men. They were not the kind who could build a kingdom in spite of hell and high water and all the emissaries of the Devil.

For two hours Joseph spoke of church doctrine. He explained to the newcomers the three degrees of glory in the next life; dwelt for a few moments on the commandment to send missionaries over the entire world; and then came to a matter that was close to his heart. In several revelations, he said, and for a period of more than a year, God had been laying down the principles of a huge United Order to govern His people. It would be socialism of the kind under which a group long ago prospered in South America for centuries. There would be storehouses of the Lord; and in these large granaries, supplies would be kept for the poor, the sick and the old; for in Zion, no saint was to suffer want. There would be great community enterprises which would be shared in common by all the people, in regard both to ownership and management; there would be pride in achievement and growth; and there would be pride in labor.

Nobody, he said, growing a little uneasy under Brigham's gaze, would be allowed to grow wealthy and accumulate goods as an instrument of power over his fellows. There would be no social distinctions, no caste and snobbery, no special privileges; because all men were to be equal in property, in management, and in consumption. There would be a small Order, a unit, in each village, town and city; and there would be a large centralized integration and control of the countless units. "Because," said Joseph, "we must all be equal in earthly things or we cannot be in heavenly things."

Brigham's dubiety was clear in his face. "If the Lord says it's to be that way, then it must be that way, but I don't see how it will work. There'll always be lazy people and ambitious people, honest people and dishonest people. Some will have a lot and some won't have anything."

"What I'm telling you," said Joseph quietly, "is a revelation from God."

"Yes, I understand that. I'm just saying it all sounds too good to work. But anything is possible with the Lord's help."

Joseph had decided that Brigham needed more humility, and unexpectedly he astonished everyone present by commanding Brigham to pray. It seemed to Brigham a strange request. Nevertheless, when Joseph and others sank to their knees, Brigham did so, and soon astounded himself by speaking in an unfamiliar tongue. He spoke for a full minute; and when Joseph rose, the men gathered around him, eager to know what Brigham had said.

"He was speaking," said Joseph, "in the Adamic tongue."

"You mean," asked John, "the tongue Adam and Eve spoke?"

"Yes."

Surprised by his fluency, yet pleased to find himself speaking in the language of the ancient Adam, Brigham slapped Heber on the back and grinned. "We're in the right church. I know it now. You know," he said to Joseph, "I've always wanted to speak in tongues. What did I say?"

"I don't know. The Lord does not make it known to me."

"It might have been important," said John Whitmer.

"If," said Joseph, his voice so gently caustic that they all missed the edge, "if it was important, God will tell me." And later he said to Emma: "I have a feeling that Brigham will rule this church."

"Why?" she asked, looking at her husband.

"I have that feeling."

"I should think you'd boss it yourself. It's yours, isn't it?"

"It belongs to God."

"Well, if you don't like the man, throw him out. You threw Martin Harris out. It seems your say-so who can go to heaven and who can't. And why do you let everybody run over you? That's what I want to know. Why don't you fight? You're the strongest man in Ohio but you sneak around and get your head poked in a tar bucket."

"Emma, I don't believe in fighting."

"Oh, no, you big baby! You'll let them come and murder your wife and you'll be out behind the woodshed correcting God's Old Testament. You'll hang around here until you get knocked into a cocked hat."

Joseph gazed at his wife, wishing gently, persistently that she was like some other women whom he knew. They were lovely girls with fresh lips and bright eyes. He hungered for them with his strong loins aching and then asked God for forgiveness and grace. "I feel old tonight," he said, thinking of Brigham.

"Old! You're twenty-six as I calculate it. How old is this Brigham Young?"

"About thirty, I guess."

"Take my advice and throw him out. Then you'n be the boss."

But Brigham had no wish, nor even any thought, of being the boss.

He wished only to be Joseph's most vigorous defender and to learn what was going on; and soon he knew more of what was happening in Ohio than Joseph would have known in ten years. Hypocrites and liars and frauds did not fool Brigham: for thirty years he had been knocked from pillar to post and he knew men and how to handle men. He looked at a man's eyes and if he could not read his soul there, he looked at his mouth.

He had not been here a week before he learned that some of the members who professed loyalty to Joseph were plotting to depose him. They wanted to put Dave Whitmer in his place, that man who, in Brigham's opinion, was an addlepated simpleton and a superstitious bench-babbler. Brigham waited until the next secret meeting was in full swing and then suddenly strode in and roared to the man talking to sit down and keep his mouth shut. "I'll see about this," he said, striding to the front of the big woodshed and facing the group. "I know what you damned cowardly scoundrels are up to! You intend to throw the prophet out. You intend to put Dave Whitmer in his place and have things the way you like them. I'm here to tell you that I'll knock the living daylights out of the first mouth-almighty hypocrite who opens his jib!"

"Hey!" roared a man, for in the audience was a pugilist named Jake Bump. Jake was now so furious he could not sit still: he clenched his big hands and howled with curses and said he was the worst ringtail roarer west of Boston. "How," he shouted, "can I keep my fists out of that feller's face?"

Brigham looked at the man a moment and then walked over to him and pulled off his coat. "What did you say?"

"I said," cried Bump, losing most of his ferocity, "I can't keep my fists off of you!"

"Then don't try. Stand up."

"Why?" asked Jake, beginning to look very foolish.

"Because I aim to hit you so hard you'll roll from here to Jerusalem."

Jake gazed around him and leered. "I guess I won't do him no harm today."

"Now," said Brigham to the plotters, "this meeting is adjourned. I don't want to hear any more nonsense about kicking the prophet out. Get back to your homes."

The men left the shed, looking fearfully at Brigham, for this kind of leader was new to them. Joseph asked for peace or invoked the wrath of God; but this man argued with his fists. And this man, they learned, seemed to know every secret plot and conspiracy in the whole region. He knew about Job Hawley almost as soon as that ragged, barefooted lunatic entered Kirtland.

Back in New York, while following his plow one day, the thought came to Job that he must go to Ohio at once and tell Joseph that God had rejected him as a prophet. Leaving his team in the field, and without even saying good-bye to his family, he set off on bare feet and in great haste; and when he arrived in Kirtland, half-starved and in rags, he looked like a wild man from a jungle. He said Joseph let the men wear caps, the women wear cushions on their coat sleeves, and God was very angry about it. Brigham heard the man's rantings, looked at his lacerated feet, his dirty bearded face and matted hair, and decided that Job was a pathetic fool who would probably go back home soon. But Job did not return home. He nodded his shaggy head and shook his unclean fists and shouted denunciations almost day and night. "Woe unto ye!" he bellowed. "You will suffer in everlasting hellfire!"

Brigham kept his eye on the man. In a few days, Job began to fancy himself as John the Baptist out of a wilderness; and tirelessly he went through the town and countryside, crying woe upon the people. He was an intolerable nuisance who was driving everybody out of his wits. Brigham hardly knew what to do with so tattered and persistent a specter; for the man looked like something out of bedlam and was more to be pitied than cursed. Nevertheless, when he was awakened in the dead of the night by the fellow's loud shouting, he swore a great oath and left his bed and dressed. "I'm going out," he said, "and beat the living hell out of that man."

He took a cowhide whip and left the house. Job was out in the street, pacing up and down and shouting at the top of his voice. "Woe unto the inhabitants of this sinful place! Woe—woe—woe!"

Brigham listened and watched the man wave his ragged arms and then went out to him. He grasped Job and shook him so violently that the man's teeth chattered and his eyes rolled wildly in his skull. "Shut up your damned infernal racket!" Brigham cried, and shook the fellow again. "How do you think the saints can sleep with you bellering down the streets? You prophet out of hell!" Brigham shook him again and kicked him soundly on his buttocks. He grasped the man's throat and choked him until Job's eyes rolled in terror. "Listen to me, you damned yelping fool! We have the prophet of God in Joseph Smith and we don't want to hear no prophet of the Devil running around in his bare feet and waking the dead! If I hear another croak out of you I'll cowhide you until your skin hangs in shoelaces! You understand? . . . You understand!" he roared, shaking the man again. Job shook his head drunkenly. "Now get the high lonesome out of here and don't ever show your fool face in Ohio again!"

He released the man who now staggered away from him and trembled as if he were looking at the Devil. "Get back to New York!" Brigham thundered. "Hit the grit and hit it hard!" He seized the whip and struck the man; and Job, with a yell of horror, turned and fled, with his naked feet showing their soles to Brigham down the road. That was the end of Job Hawley. He vanished and was never heard of again.

In rebuking the foolish, in intimidating the ambitious and headstrong, in supporting a tottering church that was disintegrating into schisms and sin, Brigham had the kind of task he liked. But Joseph was afraid of him. Joseph was a philosopher with the soul of a monk; and when he saw this man of iron striking terror into the hearts of plotters and fanatics, he wanted to get him out of his sight.

"Brother Brigham, God has called you to a mission to the eastern states."

"Brother Joseph, you need me here."

"God commands and we obey."

"But you need someone to put down treason and plots and fools. If you send me away, what will happen here? You'll be murdered."

"God," said Joseph calmly, "will watch over me."

"All right, if you want me to go, I'll go." Brigham gazed at him for a long moment. "I can't help the feeling, Joseph, that I should be right here."

"No, Brother Brigham. You must go at once."

As soon as Brigham left, Joseph sighed like a great boy and turned to his dreams. He liked to study Hebrew and Greek and other languages; he liked the metaphysics and theology of the new gospel; he liked to give revelations bearing upon abstruse points. He still believed, indeed, that rebukes from the Almighty were better than Brigham's two-fisted chastisements; and he felt that with thunder from heaven he could discipline and control his people. And so, as soon as Brigham disappeared, Joseph withdrew to the forests to receive revelations, and gave daily or weekly announcements of what he had been told. He traced the priesthood from Moses back to Adam, defined the various blessings to be conferred, predicted wickedness and plagues, and declared that those who received the Holy Ghost could cast out devils and heal the sick, open the eyes of the blind and unstop the ears of the deaf and make the dumb speak.

Now and then he withdrew from spiritual meditation and speculated upon matters in the national news. In the spring of 1832, there was threat of rebellion in South Carolina, for the fight over slavery was becoming implacably bitter; and one day Joseph predicted a war between the northern and southern states. The time was coming, he said, when war would be poured out upon all nations: with the sword and by bloodshed, the inhabitants of the earth should mourn; with famine and plague and earthquake, with the thunder and lightning of heaven, the people of the world would be made to feel the wrath and the chastening hand of an Almighty God, until the consumption decreed had made a full end of all nations. This prophecy so terrified some of the saints that Joseph was alarmed by their behavior; and after considering the matter for two days, he withdrew again and received a message of peace. "Those who obey the commandments," he declared, speaking to a gathering of his people, "will rise from the dead, body and soul, to live forever in the kingdom of glory. The earth rolls upon her wings, and the sun giveth his light by day, and the moon giveth her light by night, and the stars also give their light, as they roll upon their wings in their glory, in the midst of the power of God. The Lord commands you to cast away all idle thoughts and excess of laughter and seek truth through study and prayer; and then you will understand things both in heaven and in the earth, and under the earth; things which have been, things which are, things which must shortly come to pass; things which are at home, things which are abroad; the wars and the perplexities of the nations, and the judgments which are on the land; and a knowledge also of countries and of kingdoms.

"In this manner will the Lord come. Angels will fly through heaven, crying with a loud voice, sounding the trump of God, saying, 'Prepare ye, prepare ye, O inhabitants of the earth, for the judgment of our God is come!' Then another angel will say, 'That great church, the mother of abominations, that made all nations drink of the wine of the wrath of her fornication, that persecuteth the saints of God, that shed their blood— therefore, she is ready to be burned.' There will then be silence in heaven for half an hour. Lo, then the curtain of heaven will be unfolded and the face of the Lord will be unveiled, and both the living and the dead will be caught up to meet Him in the midst of the pillar of heaven. An angel will sound a trumpet for the redemption of those who are Christ's at His coming; and a trumpet for those who must wait in their graves for another thousand years; and a trumpet for those who shall remain filthy still . . ."

Some of the saints were overwhelmed, many were confused, by the prophet's poetry and rhetoric; and a few were bored. His language declared him to be a prophet of no mean skill, but they were at wits' end to know what he meant. They argued endlessly over one point and another as the revelations were given to them, and sometimes fought with fists and curses when words failed them.

One afternoon, Joseph heard loud argument in a grog shop and stepped softly inside. He sat unobserved in a dark corner behind a pile of casks and listened—for a dozen men, smoking pipes or chewing tobacco, were almost at one another's throats.

"God damn you!" a man yelled, and spit halfway across the floor. "You'n argue like that till the crack of doom but I say you're wrong. It don't make sense to me. It ain't no open and shut proposition to say we'll have flesh and blood in the next world."

"Why, you fat-brained bastard," said a bearded man, smoking a pipe, "of course it's true. Didn't God tell Joseph that's the how of it?"

"It's all catty-cornered to my mind. How in hell can we have flesh and blood? Why, we'll be plumb used up when we die."

"Don't you think the Almighty can make a man feel like new? He'n give us new bodies and blood. We'n tough it out here and foot the bill but in the next life we'll shine like a new booby-hut."

"That ain't how I understood the revelation."

"Just the same, that's how it was. And I aim to be Charlie on the spot when that first trumpet blows. Why lay there in the ground another thousand years? I'll just hop up in my go-to-meeting clothes and go right into heaven."

"Dog on it," said the man with the pipe, "you won't ever get up.

Didn't the prophet say in the Word of Wisdom we ain't to use tobacco or drink any more bald-face?"

"Word of Wisdom: ain't that the revelation what told us how to eat and drink?"

"That's it. It says strong drink is to wash the body, and tobacco is not for the belly but is for sick cattle. It says hot drinks ain't for the belly neither."

"I can't figger what good tobacco would do sick cattle. For poultices, I guess it means."

"Anyhow, if strong drink ain't for the belly, then you fellers are all damned clear to the hub. You'n talk like a Dutch uncle but you won't be no nearer to heaven than right now. You just as well drink your blackstrap and go to hell."

"A curse on you! We'n repent, I guess."

"Not by a jugful, you can't. Didn't the prophet say a angel will blow a horn for them as is still filthy? That's you. You'll lay in the ground till hell freezes over and never get up."

The man addressed rose to his feet and looked around him. "Dodgast it, I aim to find out what the prophet meant. I ain't had enough learnun to understand him."

"Well, for me," said one who had been silent, "if I can't never have a little whiskey or a puff of the old pipe, I'd just as soon never hear them angels' trumpets. I don't want a-be a god nohow. If I'n read the Bible right, God has always been up to the hub in trouble. Put your finger on a single time when He ever had any peace."

"That's right," said another, and thoughtfully spit between his knees.

"It ain't so much fun to be a god as some might think. Is it fun to be a parent? Why, wizzle my hide, my family is enough to make me as crazy as Job Hawley. Just think what it would be like to be the daddy of millions."

"Yeah, just think."

"Well, mebbe we don't understand the prophet. I tell you his revelations have me all slewed. Dodgast it! Why can't the Almighty talk so we'n understand Him? Is it true we ain't to eat meat in the summertime?"

"The prophet didn't say that. He said just a little."

"He said in winter we'n eat more than in summer. That's how I sensed it."

"And never smoke a pipe! Never crook the elbow and get slewed!"

"Well, you heard him, you pot-sopper. He said if you don't swig it, then you'n run and never get tired."

"I tell you I figger I don't understand him. I'm going to wait and see what the next revelation says."

"It will tell us to get busy and build that temple. Thus saith son Ahman; or, in other words, Alphus; or, in other words, Omegus. What does all that Ahman and Alphus and Omegus have to do with it? Sometimes I think the prophet is just trying to show off his learning."

"You jimber-jawed deadhead," said another. "What do you understand about things of the spirit?"

"I don't understand all that Alphus and Omegus stuff and if I have to to be a god, then I guess I'll just have to lay down there with the filthy until the last angel blows his trump. And even then I think I'll just lay quiet and pretend not to hear."

Joseph left as softly as he had entered. The revelations, for some godless reason, confused his people and sent them hellbent to seek wilder orgies; and down in Missouri the appalling conditions could no longer be ignored. When Brigham returned from his mission, he went to Joseph and declared that something must be done or every saint in Missouri would be scalped and quartered.

"They're living in sin," said Joseph impatiently. "I sent a messenger with a warning and I have written letters. I told them to hearken to the warning or Zion would fall."

"They probably need help and leadership."

"They are sinful. They need to repent."

For a long moment Brigham looked at Joseph; and again he reflected that the prophet's eyes had a faraway dreaminess that boded no good for Zion. He needed to come to his senses and look around him.

"What they need," said Brigham quietly, "is not repentance. My guess is that they need a few more guns."

CHAPTER XIV

WHEN THE FIRST COLONY OF SAINTS MOVED TO MISSOURI IN 1832, THEY were overjoyed by the beauty of the country and by the realization that they were in Zion upon which a temple and a great city were to rise. Liking their zeal and industry, many of the non-Mormons there welcomed them at first; but after a year had passed they distrusted them and resolved to drive them out. For so many Mormons had come into Jackson County and begun so many settlements that it needed no prophet to foretell their eventual control of every public office in the county. Not only that: they were sending missionaries all over the county to preach their gospel; and the more zealous ones boasted that they would fill Missouri and possibly the entire world. Because they were a chosen people, they said God had set Missouri aside as the land of their inheritance. Parley Pratt said so. Lyman Wight said so, that powerful and fearless man who with all his might had been preaching in the very homes of his enemies.

"And by God, they're right!" said Jim Dunk, as black a rogue as ever fled from the law. "They'll own every stick and stone in Missouri!"

Spring opened early in 1833. The backs of streams, frozen solid, broke under the sun and poured into the great Missouri River; flowers came in such profusion that the baldest prairies looked like gardens; and thousands of birds filled the mornings. Most of the early Missourians cared little enough for flowers and birds. Living along streams in small windowless cabins, floored with earth, they were an independent clan who felt contempt for the refinements of life. They liked horse racing, profanity and strong drink. They admired men like Jim Dunk.

In the previous autumn he had gathered a handful of thugs and attacked a Mormon settlement, stoning the houses and smashing all the windows and doors, setting fire to a haystack and a few buildings, and then getting drunk and cursing all night. Looking around for a henchman, he chose one Finis Ewing, a preacher; for Ewing had said that all Mormons ought to be destroyed. He and Dunk drew up a petition that set forth the grievances. Mormons, it declared, were the dregs of society; they were lazy and vicious; they invited Negroes to settle in Missouri; they pretended to cast devils out and to talk with God. "We must," the petition said, "rid ourselves of the Mormons, peaceably if we can, forcibly if we must."

Mormons were already using the word *gentile* to designate all non-Mormons. Dunk accepted the term, and forthwith sent a call to all "gentiles" to assemble at the Jackson courthouse, and five hundred of them answered the call. A colonel named Dick Simpson was appointed chairman and he addressed the meeting.

"My friends, we all know that these people who call themselves Mormons are the dregs of society, lazy, vicious and deluded. We have resolved that in the future no Mormon can settle in this county; and we have resolved that the Mormons here now will have to get out as soon as they can sell their property and move. If they refuse to move, then we'll inform them of the lot that awaits them."

"Let's move them now!" Dunk roared, and set off at the head of a great mob. Yelling like Indians, the men went first to the Mormon printing office, and with axe and pike and mauls, they razed it to the ground. "That's fine!" Dunk cried. "Follow me!"

He next led the horde to the nearest Mormon house, and it fell under the assault like a stack of chips in a wind. A man yelled, "Let's get the leaders!" and the cry was taken up and shouted from four hundred throats. Pouring in a blaspheming tide through the town, with women and children fleeing like rabbits before it, the mob surged up one street and down another; and when it saw Ed Partridge, bishop of the saints, and Charles Allen, his friend, it sent up a mighty roar. The men were seized and hurled to the earth, and Dunk came forth to strike the face of Partridge and spit at him.

"You dirty Mormon bastard!" he cried. Turning to the mob, he said: "Take them to the public square!"

The mob closed in. A dozen hands grasped Partridge and Allen by their heels and dragged them down the street. At the square they were spread-eagled and sat upon while Dunk roared for silence.

"Lynch them!" voices were yelling. And others shouted: "Tar and feather the sons-of-bitches!"

"Shut up!" Dunk roared. He waved his arms and bellowed for silence.

When he could be heard he said: "We'll give them their choice. They'n get out of Jackson County or say their new bible is a pack of lies. If they say it's a pack of lies——"

"Sure it's a pack of lies!"

"Make them eat it! Stuff their bellies full of the lousy stinking thing!"

"Shut up! Listen, you men——"

"Shove their bible down their throats!"

"Shut up!" Dunk howled. "They got a-do one or the other!" He turned to the prisoners who lay at his feet. "Will you disown your bible?"

"Let me speak," said Partridge, trying to sit up and wiping blood from his face.

"Hey, he wants to speak! Shall we let the bastard speak?"

"Sure, stand him on his legs and let's hear him."

Hands grasped Partridge and set him on his feet and he faced the mob. Blood was running from a cut above one eye and from a gash in one cheek. "Friends——"

"Don't call us your friends!"

"Shut up!" Dunk roared, and waved his arms.

"Friends, let me speak. Let me say to you that the saints expect persecution. The saints have suffered persecution in all ages, and I am willing to suffer for the sake of the Christ——"

"By God, you will in just a minute!"

"I am willing to suffer for my belief," Partridge went on. "I will not be a Judas and I will not leave this county——"

"Tar and feather the son-of-a-bitch!"

"No, lynch him! String him up!"

"Silence!"

"I have harmed no one. I have been a God-fearing man and a good neighbor."

"Yeah, by converting my wife to your mouth-almighty religion!"

"I wish to live in peace with all men. If you injure me, you will injure an innocent man. I plead with you——"

His voice was lost in a sudden bellowing rage. Above the din was a shrill voice, crying: "Call upon God now, damn you!" Then a big man stepped forward and shouted, "Let's fix him!" and the mob surged in. Dunk and Ewing were shoved aside as eager hands reached for the prisoners and hurled them to the ground.

"Fetch the tar!"

Hands were busy now, tearing the clothes off the men, ripping it off garment by garment.

"Brother Charles," said Partridge to the man gasping at his side, "put your trust in God and be not afraid."

Out in the mob, hundreds of men were struggling to push in and see what was going on. They surged in a tide, and the men working over the prisoners were knocked down and piled in heaps. A giant of a man got to his feet, slobbering with rage. "Back, you fools! You want a-kill all of us?"

"We want to see!"

"Back, before I break your skulls!"

The inner circle howled and shoved, and the mob fell back a little; and then through it, traveling from hand to hand, came a pail of tar, with lime mixed in it to sear the flesh. Men knelt by the prisoners and poured tar over them; and one asked: "Why don't you call on your God now?"

"You still believe in your bible?" another asked.

"I do," Partridge said.

"Fill his mouth!"

A ring of men were now holding the crowd back while others poured the tar. Then from hand to hand came a great sack of feathers. These were dumped on the earth, and the prisoners were rolled over and over in them. Partridge was still conscious. The mob sounded to him like a thousand blasphemous demons: he was pained more by their oaths than by the lime burning into his skin. In that mob he had seen the county judge, the constable, the justice of the peace, and Boggs, the lieutenant-governor. Boggs now came forward, with the mob giving way for him. He looked down at the two men.

"Well, you know now what our Jackson boys can do. Why didn't you stay in your own villages? Why did hundreds of you have to settle in Independence? You'd better get out of our towns and out of Missouri."

Partridge turned like a segment of a huge black serpent. "Never," he said. "Murder me, but you'll never force me to leave."

"We'll see about that."

The mob now fell back, seeing that their work was done. Darkness had come now, and some went away quickly, either from shame or fear;

but others stood a little way off and watched. Partridge and Allen did not move. They lay in the square like two gleaming black corpses, with feathers standing grotesquely as if growing out of their bodies. After a while, Partridge spoke but Allen gave no answer; and he moved little by little until he could reach out with a hand. His hand found the body and moved over it and upward to the eyes. They were closed . . .

Every saint in town, meanwhile, had fled for his life. Men, women and children had run like hunted animals into the country and hidden in thickets or under the banks of streams. After nightfall, some of them returned, slinking back to search for relatives or friends or to learn if their homes had been destroyed. Long after midnight, a few men went to the square and carried the two men away.

For two days Independence was very quiet. On the third day, five hundred men rode into it suddenly, armed with rifles and pistols, daggers and whips and clubs. They carried a red flag. Almost at once there was wild hubbub everywhere. Some of the riders, recklessly drunk, fired their guns and dashed madly up and down the streets, shooting at the sky and cursing with all their might. Now and then one would stop and announce to spectators the purpose of the vigilantes. "We aim to whip all the damned Mormons with five hundred blows apiece! Then we'll let the niggers burn their crops and houses! If that don't make them hit the grit, we'll kill the men and rape the women!" And with a whoop and an oath, the speaker rode pell-mell down the street, firing at the tops of buildings or entering a tavern for another drink.

As before, the saints fled. Singly or in twos or in small groups, they ran from the town and hid under banks, the women clutching infants to their breasts and the men gathering in secret council.

"What does Joseph do about this?" asked one bitterly. "I guess he's having another revelation to tell us how sinful we are!"

"Hush," said Partridge. From head to feet he was covered with burns from the lime. "Brother Corrill, we're all going to be killed."

"Yes," said Corrill, a man of few words.

"This is my plan. Let's all us leaders offer our lives to the mob if they'll promise not to murder anyone else and leave our women alone." This bold statement was followed by silence, but Partridge was speaking to bold men.

"I'm willing," John Whitmer said.

"And me," said Isaac Morley.

"Brother Gilbert?"

"Yes, I will."

"Then let's go."

Leaving their hiding place they entered the town and walked six abreast up the street. A great yell went up and from all directions riders dashed in until the six men were prisoners, ringed by horses and men. To Finis Ewing, Partridge said: "We've come to make a bargain with you——"

"Listen to him!" a man howled. "I thought we killed this bastard!"

"We will give up our lives," Partridge went on, "if you promise to leave the rest of the saints alone. Take us and murder us if you agree to that."

"God deacon me!" roared Jim Dunk. "Who are ye to say what we'll do or won't do?"

"We are offering our lives——"

"A crummy-doss on your lives! You dust out of this county, you paddies and hawkeyes!"

"Give them five hundred with a bullwhip and see what they say."

"Dry up," said Dunk. He grinned at the six men and considered. "So ye want a-be killed, do you? Judas priest now, ain't that a far piece of spunk!" He leaned down from his horse. "Listen to me! If you pot-soppers don't hit the grit, we'll take the soles off of your shoes. Then—" He paused and looked at his men. "How about their women?"

"May God have mercy on you if you touch our women!"

"Never mind about us and God. Do you aim to leave this county?"

"Let us talk it over," Partridge said. On command from Dunk, the horsemen fell back, and Partridge and his companions sat in the street.

"If we let them kill us," said Morley, "what guarantee do we have that they won't kill the rest of the saints?"

"That's right. I think they would."

Partridge looked around at the horsemen who were watching him. "It looks like we must leave. If we don't, blood will run like water. Let's ask Dunk to choose a committee to meet us and see if we can arrange plans." Partridge rose and went to Dunk and said: "Choose a committee to talk with us. Let's try to settle this peaceably."

"All right," said Dunk, grinning broadly. In a few moments he came over with five men.

"What are your demands?" asked Partridge.

"That all you Mormon bastards leave Jackson County."

"Is that final?"

"As final as hell."

"If we refuse, then what?"

"We'll answer that later."

"We'll go," Partridge said. "But you must give us time to sell our belongings and arrange things."

"We want all you leaders to skin out right away. And we want you to tell no more Mormons to come in here. We'll hold back like all wrath for a time but don't let no grass grow under you."

"We'll go as soon as we can."

Partridge did not intend to go. He sent a messenger posthaste to Joseph to ask for help but Joseph had more worries in Ohio than he could take care of. He sent the messenger back with advice and rebuke. "He said, if we'll give up our sinful ways, God will protect us."

Partridge and his people then petitioned the governor of Missouri and that distressed gentleman wrote a long answer, declaring that no citizens had a right to take matters into their own hands. "I am not willing," he wrote, "to persuade myself that any portion of the citizens of the state of Missouri are so lost to a sense of these truths as to require the exercise of force in order to insure respect for them."

"Listen to that!" Morley cried. "And he says to take the matter into the courts!"

"We will," said Partridge. "We'll get lawyers from the next county and we'll see if the American flag is for brigands or law-abiding men."

But when he engaged lawyers from an adjoining county the storm broke. It had been gathering for weeks. Dunk and Ewing and others had been trying to restrain the mob. After the petition to the governor, after lawyers were hired, furious men swore they would wait no longer, even if the governor sent an army into the town.

"That's what he'll do," said Dunk. "He's mad as all hell."

"I swan now, ain't he! He don't like the Mormons no better than we do."

"Let's wait a while," Ewing said.

"No, by God! They give us a lick and a promise and now out they go."

The time was October. Fifty men gathered in secret and resolved to exterminate a new settlement on Big Blue Creek. They chose as leader a tall rawboned fellow named Andy Pitcher.

"Now we ain't to kill nobody," Andy said. "We'll just beat the livun Jesus out of them and burn their homes."

"How about the women?" asked one.

"You leave the women be. Don't you lay a finger on them."

They lay concealed until midnight and then mounted and rode into the settlement, firing their guns and howling at the shrillest pitch of their breath. Believing they were attacked by Indians, the settlers ran from their beds to the doorways and were there seized by Andy's men as fast as they appeared. "Search the houses!" he said. "Bring all the yellow dogs out!"

The mobsters vanished into the homes. One of them was intent not on capture but rape. He knew where a young girl lived and crept through a window into the dark house. He saw her mother first. The mother screamed and the man felled her with a blow. He was binding and gagging her when the terrified daughter entered the room; and at once he sprang upon her like a beast and forced her backward into the bedroom. He gagged her and roped her to the bed and searched the house to be sure nobody would surprise him. Returning to the girl, he bandaged her eyes, ripped the clothes from her body and then for a long moment gazed at her in moonlight, his wet tongue moving meditatively across his lower lip. Bending over her, he touched her warm flesh and cupped her two firm breasts in his big hands. He went to a window and looked out and listened and then returned softly to the bed. . . .

Meanwhile, Andy and his gang had taken a dozen men up the creek to a grove of trees. "Strip them naked," Andy said, and the men were stripped. "Tie them to the trees with their hinders out." Each prisoner was shoved belly forward against a tree and his arms were drawn around the tree and his hands were roped together. Then the man's legs were drawn around likewise and tied: he looked like a strange naked beast trying to climb and resting in his labors.

"Fetch the black snakes," Andy said. The whips were brought and Andy gave them to a dozen of his most powerful men. "Take your places and do as I tell you." The twelve men took their places, each standing behind a prisoner, his whip ready, his face turned to Andy. "When I say go, give them twenty whacks and then wait till I say go again. You ready?"

"Yes!"

"All right, ready. Go!"

The twelve whips were drawn back by twelve powerful arms, and fell in twelve mighty blows. The white and gleaming flesh roped to the trees writhed in agony. A man screamed. After a few blows, blood came out on the backs and ran in bright crimson drops; and roped men bit their lips until blood ran on them, or knocked their heads against the trees. After twenty lashes, every back was bloody from the necks to the rumps.

"Halt!" Andy roared. He went from prisoner to prisoner, looking at the flesh or now and then prodding with a finger to learn how deep the wounds were. "You sons-of-bitches, do you deny your new bible or don't you?" There was no answer. Andy seized a man's hair and drubbed his face against the tree. "Speak, or I'll cut all the flesh off of you! Do you?"

"No. Kill me but I never will." This man, one of the strongest, heard the man on his right groaning out of terrible pain. "Brother John," he said, "be comforted. The Lord is watching tonight."

"You mouth-almighty bastard!" Andy cried. "If the Lord is watchun, He's going to see the fur fly. Men, lay it on their hinders this time. Twenty whacks. Ready. Go!"

Again the bitter lashes stung like wires dipped in acid. As the quivering flesh was laid open on the buttocks, the man addressed as John began to scream; and another beat his face so madly against the tree that his cheeks were bruised and his lips torn.

"Nine—ten—eleven!" Andy was calling, standing back with arms folded and alertly observing his men. Suddenly there was a ghastly yell. One of the tortured men had thrown his head backward and seemed to have broken his neck; for his head now hung back and to one side and did not move as the blows fell. "—nineteen—twenty! Halt!" As before, Andy went from man to man to see how deeply the blows had cut. Swinging, he wrenched the whip from a man's grasp. "God-damn you! You ain't been layun it on this fellow a-tall!" He peered at the man from whom he had taken the black snake. "For a red cent I'd tie you up and give you some. Ike, come here!" A man left the group and came forward. "Give this bastard twenty and we'll go again."

Ike laid on with all his power; and while the man screamed, others, except the one whose neck seemed broken, drooled blood from their bruised lips or knocked their heads on the hard trunks. "All right," said Andy when Ike had finished. "Now twenty more on their backs—and if any of you tries to go easy on it, we'll tie you up and give you some. Ready. One—two—three— Hey, wait! What's the matter that bastard with his head back? Hank, what's the matter with him?"

"I don't know," said Hank, looking at the man he had been flogging.

"By God," said Andy, peering at the man's face and then pushing his head from side to side, "I guess he's dead. Cut him down!" They cut the man down and stretched him out. Andy experimented by putting a toe under the body and rolling it over. "He's dead, all right. Well, get ready. Four—five—six ——"

One hundred lashes were given. Every prisoner's back was furrowed in long bloody wounds or corrugated with swollen flesh. From their rumps some of the flesh had been cut away. None of them had screamed during the last blows. When Andy ordered the ropes cut, the bodies fell backward like dead meat and the bleeding backs lay in autumn leaves. Five of the men were unconscious. Only one seemed to have strength to sit up and look around him with bloodshot eyes; and after a moment he groaned and toppled over and lay still. Andy went from man to man, prodding them with a toe and looking at their faces or rolling them over to look at their backs.

"Mebbe they'll leave now," he said. "Let's be off."

"Ain't we going to bury this dead one?"

"Hell, no. Let them bury him."

They mounted and returned to the settlement and Andy told his men to enter the houses and drive the women and children out. And they were driven out, the children crying and the mothers cowering like cattle herded in a rain. They were forced in a group to a path leading into the woods; and Andy told a dozen men to drive them two miles out and leave them.

"And now down with the buildings, every God-damned one!"

Yelling like devils, the men set to, some smashing windows and doors, some slipping inside to loot, and others building fires. After half an hour they rode away and turned to watch. The settlement was a great bonfire under the stars, with long manes of flame riding up into the darkness and with smoke flowing out in a gray prairie to hide the moon.

In the next night a dozen mobs prowled. One went to Independence and smashed the doors of homes, thrust long poles through windows and then hurled stones inside; and destroyed the Mormon store. Another mob went to the Colesville settlement twelve miles west. It was here that the indomitable Parley Pratt lived. When he heard a racket and left his house, a man leapt from shadow and laid the breech of his gun across Parley's skull. He staggered back, with blood running in streams down his face. Then he roared and fought like a demon and a dozen men came to his aid; and when two of the mobsters were captured and bound, the others fled.

This was Andy's gang. He and his followers fled this scene and rode over to the Big Blue settlement to see if anyone had returned to the outlying buildings which had not been fired. In one of them a very sick man lay alone on a bed.

"You sick?" asked Andy, putting a hand on the man's brow. "Well, I understand you Mormons cure sickness by laying hands on. Lay them on, boys!"

Three men came forward and dragged the sick man from the bed and flogged him with long pieces of stovewood. While two held him, a third smote the man's rump until it was a welter of bruises and blood. They then rolled him over and gouged the man's stomach until, unable to catch his breath, he doubled up, convulsed with agony, with his eyes rolling so horribly that the irises turned out of sight.

"Set him on the bed!" one cried. "I want a-try my aim."

The three who had flogged the man laid him on the bed and propped him up with chunks of wood; and while he shuddered there, with his head falling forward, the man with the pistol took deliberate aim and fired. Instead of entering the skull the ball struck high on the forehead and was deflected, and plowed a furrow through the hair from forehead to crown.

"That'll do for him," said Andy. "If he gets well now, the son-of-a-bitch ought a-live."

"By God, yes," said the other man, and put his pistol away.

CHAPTER XV

NOT ALL THE SAINTS WERE TURNING THE OTHER CHEEK. AMONG THEM were hot-blooded men who lusted for vengeance; and so many small volunteer armies were organized that a part of Missouri seemed to be only men in flight or men stealthily stalking their foe. Word went abroad that the Mormons were armed to the teeth. They were armed but the weapons of many of them were only cudgels or a pocketful of stones or a useless musket or pistol that an enemy had thrown away. And usually when a dozen or a score of the marching men espied a mob, they found themselves so greatly outnumbered that they scattered and fled into the cornfields and thickets.

One afternoon two armed bands came within sight of one another, and after a swift appraisal both mobs scurried into hiding behind brush and trees. There were thirty Mormons but they had only seventeen guns. There were at least three times that many gentiles.

"We're outnumbered," said the Mormon leader. "Shall we fight?"

"Sure!" a man cried. "I'm tired of running like a coyote."

One of the enemy thrust his head in view. "Shoot, God damn you, shoot!" Several of the gentile rifles belched flame; and one of the saints who was standing boldly in sight fell with three pieces of lead in his bowels.

The Mormons opened fire and dropped two men and six horses. That was enough for the mob: with wild halloos they rode away pell-mell, and the saints gathered around their fallen comrade. One said they could cure him by the laying on of hands; whereupon a half-dozen men knelt by him in prayer and asked God to cure the wounds. But another said:

"We can't expect God to cure bullet holes. Fevers and miseries He can cure but not lead in a man's belly."

"He can cure anything if He wants to."

"Go over," said the leader, "and see if the men are dead—and the horses. If the horses are still alive, shoot them."

Several men went over to the enemy position and fired several rounds. They returned, saying the men were dead and they had killed the wounded beasts. "We'd best take him along," said one. "He needs a doctor more than prayer."

"Brother Parley Pratt might save him."

The men looked down at the unconscious man and the gaping wounds in his stomach. The man looked dead but his heart was still beating. "Let's make a stretcher," one said, and they made a stretcher and carried the sick man away.

This part of Missouri was in wild uproar. Word went abroad that the Mormons were on the warpath and had been joined by hundreds of Indians. Mobs on both sides were busy organizing and gathering ammunition and guns. Among the gentiles, the sheriff, more level-headed than those who urged him to massacre, sought Morley and Corrill and begged them to lead the saints out of Missouri.

"You ask me," Corrill said, "to do what no man can do. My people are scattered all over the country. They are hiding in cornfields and along ditch banks and out in the forests. How can I get them together as long as mobs are horsewhipping and murdering them? Besides, some of them have their blood up and refuse to leave."

"If they don't leave they'll all be killed."

"There'll be killing on both sides," Morley said.

"Yes," said the sheriff, shaking his head sadly. "There'll be hell to pay. We'll have civil war."

"Why don't you call the mobs off?"

"Now, Corrill, you're asking me to do what I can't do. The whole thing is out of my control."

"Mine, too. I guess we'll just have to fight it out."

The next day the lieutenant-governor ordered out the militia. The Mormons west of Independence, hearing that some of their fellows were imprisoned and threatened with death, gathered an army of a hundred men to march upon the town; but when a mile out they halted and sent scouts. The scouts returned to say that Independence was full of State troops.

"The hell it is," said Lyman Wight, most fearless of all the Mormon leaders. "Well, we can't fight Missouri."

"Why can't we?" demanded a man whose brother had been horsewhipped and whose sister had been raped. "I'll wade in blood to my knees before I'll turn back."

"No," said Lyman. "We'n fight bandits but not the government."

"What's the difference? They're all bandits. And why in hell doesn't Joseph get down here and see about things?"

"For shame to speak that way of the prophet!"

"A fine prophet he is!"

"We must go back to our homes," Lyman said.

"Oh, my home! What is my home but a pile of ashes?"

Lyman stood on the back of his horse and looked at his ragged army. "Men, we are going back. The troops have been called out." There were yells of protest. Men cried that they would rather die fighting than to die while being hunted through a cornfield. "Silence!" Lyman roared. "Am I your leader?"

"Yes!"

"All right. I'm ordering you back to your homes."

But the colonel commanding the troops had been told of Lyman's advance and in great fury he now came at a gallop.

"Who's the leader here?" he demanded.

"I am," Lyman said.

"What in hell do you mean? You trying to start a civil war?"

"No. We are going back to our homes."

"I'll have something to say about that. Who are you?"

"Lyman Wight."

The colonel looked at him and sneered. "A major or general or what is your rank?"

"Just a common man, Colonel, fighting for my life. What do you want us to do? Stand in line so you can shoot us down?"

"I want the leaders of the mob who murdered two of our men."

"What for, Colonel?"

"To stand trial for murder." The colonel pulled at his moustaches and looked around him. "And I command you to deliver up your arms and ammunition now."

"No, Colonel, we'll not do that."

"By God, you will do it! Don't tell the state of Missouri what you'll do."

"You mean," asked Lyman, restraining his anger, "you intend to disarm us?"

"That's what I mean."

"You want us to be defenseless so the mobs can butcher all of us?"

"I want your arms right now and I want no more of your chin music."

Lyman rode close to the colonel and drew a deep breath. "Colonel, we'll see you in hell first."

"What!" The furious man dismounted. "Do you intend to fight the state of Missouri?"

"I mean this: we'll deliver our arms if you'll disarm all the mobs that are horsewhipping us and burning our homes and raping our wives."

"Raping your wives! What in hell do you mean by that?"

"That's what we mean!" cried a young man. "Mebbe you'd like to see my sister."

"Be still," Lyman said. "Well, Colonel, how about it?"

"Of course I intend to disarm the mobs. That's why I'm here."

"You promise that?"

"I do."

"Let's understand one another. If we give up our arms, you pledge your honor as an army man to disarm the mobs?"

"I pledge it on my honor and on the honor of Lieutenant-Governor Boggs."

"All right, Colonel. Men, fetch your guns here."

But one of them drew Lyman aside. "You're a fool! You don't think he'll keep that promise?"

"I do."

"Then you're a fool. I know God-damned well he won't."

"Men," said Lyman, "hurry! Fetch your guns. The Colonel has promised to disarm every mob in Missouri."

The men stepped forth, but reluctantly, to lay forty-nine rifles and one pistol at the Colonel's feet.

"Now," said the Colonel, walking among the men to look for undelivered guns, "I want the leaders of those murders."

"Colonel, do you pledge them a fair and honest trial?"

"On my honor I do."

Lyman called six men by name. They came forth and stood before the Colonel with folded arms.

"Colonel," said Lyman, "we have met all your demands. If you break your promises, may the Almighty God have mercy on you. I will have none."

"Don't worry," said the Colonel, smiling now. "Everything will be all right." He summoned soldiers who had waited in the background and rode away with the arms and the prisoners.

It was not long before Lyman Wight learned what a credulous fool he had been. The mobs were not disarmed. Not only that: even State troops were sent in gangs through the countryside to search for hidden weapons; and again and again they overtook fleeing Mormons and flogged them within an inch of their lives. Nor was that all: the six men whom Lyman delivered to the Colonel were brutally beaten during their first night in jail. Within three days after the surrender, women and children were fleeing in all directions; and one company of two hundred, including several old men, were driven for thirty miles across a frozen prairie and abandoned to a wilderness, with their feet leaving blood in their tracks.

No man was more hotly pursued than Lyman Wight himself. He was chased across three counties and into Indian territory; and for three weeks he remained in a forest, eating what he could find and sleeping under trees.

Leaderless now, and hunted like wild beasts, the saints left Jackson County singly or in small groups, some going to the adjoining county south from which they were again driven, but most of them assembling on the bank of the Missouri. Here, without shelter in November, and almost without food, they waited for their prophet; but Joseph did not come. He sent by messenger another revelation, saying that God had allowed affliction to fall on the saints because of their wickedness; but that He would, in His own time, permit the pure in heart to return to their inheritance.

"Some prophet!" cried a man bitterly. "To hell with his God-damned church! I'm leaving it now."

"Wait," said another. "I'll go with you."

"And me," said a third.

On the bank of the river one night the cold weather softened and rain fell in a deluge. Persons sought protection under the bank or under trees and bushes, or tried to crowd into the few tents. A woman, sick with fever and big with child, lay on her back in a gully, helpless and unprotected, and groaned all night in the pangs of childbirth, with the storm driving in her face. When murky morning came, a man in passing saw an infant at her breast and stopped in pity to look at the woman; but she was dead. Her hair was a wet mat around her face and over her breast; her clothes outlined her thin and wasted frame. Wondering if others had died, the man sent a woman to the infant and then searched up and down the stream, peering under bushes and logs or lifting the flaps of fallen tents. It was in a thicket that he heard a whimpering sound. He looked in and saw a small lad, rain-soaked and curled up, half-asleep and half-dead. The man crawled through with rain showering upon him and gathered the boy in his arms and carried him to a fire. All day he went among the tents or those sitting by open fires, seeking someone who knew this boy or his people; but no one knew him, and in the next night the lad died.

Several persons, sick from exposure or want of food, died and were buried among the trees. Some of the hardier men felled cottonwoods and began to erect small cabins; and after a few days the settlement looked like a wigwam village. Other men foraged in the country, some buying or borrowing food and some stealing it; and all the while, the hundreds of persons huddled in the wet cold on the bank of the river waited for their prophet to come. Their leaders were all scattered now. Lyman Wight was hiding; Parley Pratt had gone nobody knew where; and others were in jail.

On a night in November a strange thing happened. The sky was lighted by the incandescent brightness of a meteoric shower, with flame bursting like rockets and streaking in blinding paths down the sky, until the earth was as bright as day and the saints looked in awe at one another and marveled. One of them remembered that the coming of Jesus would be attended by falling stars; and when he spoke of the matter, all eyes turned heavenward, expecting the redeemer of man to come.

"But it don't mean Jesus is coming," a man said. "It means God is watching over us."

"Of course that's what it means. Glory be to God!"

"Yes, glory be to God!"

Then a voice said: "Let us pray."

Three hundred persons sank to their knees in prayer. It was less prayer than a lamentation of joy and pain, with a deep voice leading off and other voices taking up the refrain, while others, sick and feeble or old, wailed in monotone. Some laughed and some wept. Children stared solemnly at their parents or up at the sky.

A voice began to sing and was joined by a hundred voices.

> Jesus, lover of my soul,
> Let me to thy bosom fly,
> While the nearer waters roll,
> While the tempest still is high! . . .

There was a pause. Another meteor had come down in a thin channel of flame.

> Other refuge have I none,
> Hangs my helpless soul on thee.
> Leave, O leave me not alone!
> Still support and comfort me.

Again they waited and looked at the sky but the whole wide expanse was a desert of darkness. The strong voice took up the chant.

> Thou, O Christ, art all I want;
> More than all in thee I find.
> Raise the fallen, cheer the faint;
> Heal the sick and lead the blind! . . .

After singing, they all looked again at the sky. A man said: "Let's dance. We must be happy and brave."

"Yes," said voices, "let's dance."

And under the night sky they danced, some barefooted, all of them in ragged clothes. Others stood apart and watched them and tended the fires.

"Brother Harry," a man said, "God promised Zion to us and Zion is in Missouri. We will all live there yet."

"I hope so," Harry said. But he looked away to a hillside where sticks and stones marked the coffinless resting places of those who had died.

CHAPTER XVI

JOSEPH, MEANWHILE, THOUGH WORRIED ABOUT THE SAINTS IN MISSOURI, still believed, nevertheless, that their sufferings were a punishment for their sins. Man after man had come to beg his advice and aid. Oliver came and reported the first acts of violence. Orson Hyde came, a level-headed man who had a clear grasp of the difficulties.

"It's not," he said, "because we've been sinful. Of course, some have misbehaved. There are wicked persons in every church ——"

"That's the reason, Brother Orson."

"No, it isn't. The reasons are political and economic. Remember that the early settlers in Missouri are mostly from the south and have different ways from ours. They hate the Negro. You told us to convert and baptize the Negro, and so we did, but the old settlers won't stand for that. We shouldn't have accepted the Negro as our equal—or the Indian. And then, some of the saints have boasted that God will give Missouri to us and that Independence is the Garden of Eden and that in time we'll own the whole United States. That's all true but it isn't necessary to boast about it. Boasting about it has helped to cause a civil war down there. Also, we grew too fast. So many saints moved into Jackson County that it began to look as if we'd control it soon, and those old settlers won't let outsiders come in and control anything. And there's the question of slavery ——"

"The chief reason, Orson, is the transgressions. God is angry with the saints in Missouri because they have sinned."

"Fiddlesticks!" cried Orson impatiently. "We admit there has been some sin. There are some hotheaded rowdies among us who like to fight. But the reasons are the ones I've named—and the problem of slavery. We don't believe in slaves and a lot of the old settlers do. And I don't see how we can ever live at peace down there."

"It's the transgressions," said Joseph, unshaken in his belief.

He admitted to Emma that he did not understand why God had punished so severely, or how long the time of affliction would endure. The saints would eventually be restored to their homes. Just the same, he received a revelation commanding the saints in Ohio to build a temple in Kirtland, and it was begun at once. When other messengers came to tell of horsewhipping and arson, rape and murder, of wholesale expulsions from the county, of hundreds freezing and starving on the bank of the river, Joseph sent word to appeal the matter to the courts, to the governor, and if necessary to the President. But he felt that appeal was useless and for many days he brooded over the problem. His face was so grave that Emma said:

"Why don't you raise an army and go down and fight it out?"

"An army!" he cried, appalled. "We believe in peace."

"Just the same, it's like Brigham says. The only way to make a man peaceable is to whale the living daylights out of him."

"No," he said, but the notion took hold of him. He went off alone and asked God what to do and God told him the wealthy men of the church should go to Missouri and buy all the land, and Joseph should go and curse the gentiles. "And whomsoever ye curse, I will curse, and ye shall avenge me of mine enemies!" God also said that His prophet was to raise an army. "If you cannot obtain five hundred, seek diligently that peradventure you may obtain three hundred. And if ye cannot obtain three hundred, seek diligently that peradventure you may obtain one hundred. . . ."

Joseph called his leaders to him and told them to raise an army to march upon Missouri.

"Is this," asked Brigham in amazement, "a commandment from God?"

"It is."

"Then it shall be done, though it seems to me like suicide." And Brigham went away, shaking his wise head in doubt; for the marching of an untrained body of men against a State seemed to him to be an instance of stupidity without precedent. Nevertheless, he set to work, assisted by others, to recruit men and buy guns; and Joseph went to New York to enlist volunteers there.

When word went abroad that the saints were to march upon Missouri and restore Zion to its people, the rejoicing was great. Gentiles, learning of the plan, sent news of it to Missouri; and a saint came in haste to say that in retaliation, two hundred homes had been burned. That was what Missouri thought of the plan.

"How many armed men are there?" asked Brigham.

"I don't know. There are hundreds in the mobs, and hundreds of State troopers."

"And Joseph is going against them with two hundred greenhorns!" He shook his head and considered. "I'm afraid the Missouri will be red with the blood of the saints. Still, I guess we can win if God wants us to."

"They say if we start with an army, they'll kill all the Mormons down there."

"God," said Brigham wearily, "will have to protect them. Don't they have any guns left?"

"No, they surrendered all their arms."

When Joseph returned, he was sidetracked by another problem. His United Order, his dream of a communal society in which all property would be shared equally, had degenerated into bickering and thefts and lies. One man, hailed before the High Council for pilfering, countered with the charge that while he was supposed to have been stealing, his accuser was lying in adultery with his wife. Another said he had taken only what he needed, believing that God would replenish the granaries; and a third, in towering wrath, declared that he was tired of working like a dog to support drunkards and loafers.

Brigham had never known what to think of the United Order. His knowledge of human nature did not support utopian dreams; nor did he believe that drones should feed off the workers, even though the old and sick should be cared for. He was not surprised when the Order in Kirtland was dissolved, but he was distressed by Joseph's grief. Nothing was closer to the prophet's heart than his dream of a society without avarice, poverty or wealth, distinctions of caste and position, meanness and bigotry and greed.

"Cheer up," Brigham said. "When we get through with Missouri, mebbe we can start the Order again."

"It is sin," said Joseph, his blue eyes haunted. "God is angry with all of us." And with renewed energy he worked day and night to get his army on the march.

In May of 1834, twenty men and four supply wagons left for Missouri; and five days later, Joseph set out at the head of his army of twenty baggage wagons and a hundred and fifty men. He called his army Zion's Camp. If he had put it under the command of Brigham, or even Parley Pratt or Lyman Wight, he might have avoided humiliating disaster; but he was eager to prove himself a great general and he set out with colors flying gaily and a feeling of triumph in his heart. After three days, Lyman joined with a company he had recruited; and Joseph's army was two hundred and five men, eager to fight for Zion and God.

Still, that was not quite true. Some of the men, even from the first, were truculent and ill-tempered and unwilling to leave their homes. They marched with mutinous faces and said they were on a fool's errand.

"Why," demanded one, "should I risk my neck for people in Missouri?"

"It is God's will," Joseph said.

"How do I know that? I have a wife and babies back home. Is it God's will for me to desert them and get murdered?"

"Your faith is weak. Go back to your wagon."

Another said, "By hell, I'm sick of this!"—for this amazing journey was enough to make any man sick. With insufficient provisions, with overburdened beasts, the caravan dragged slowly day by day under withering heat, in rolling clouds of dust; day by day over a thousand miles of poor road, with the men footsore and limping and sweating and cursing; with enemies on all sides, including wild beasts and Indians and sharpshooting Missourians who were out scouting the advancing horde; with mutinous blasphemy, sickness and death. Day by day the train moved, covering fifteen or twenty miles and camping by a stream under the stars; rising at daybreak and packing and marching again—endlessly, day after day, week after week—this untrained and poorly equipped and weary and desperate caravan, headed for Missouri to avenge in the name of God.

One evening, having unpacked and eaten and then gathered, dirty and weary, around campfires, the men discovered that the land was infected with rattlesnakes. One who had gone to bed leapt up with a terrific yell and dashed off, with his drawers falling to his knees and hobbling him; whereupon he fell headlong and rolled, howling as if he had been stabbed. Men everywhere sprang to their feet. When the frightened man was set upright and asked the cause of his racket, he pointed a finger at his bed and declared it was full of devils. Brigham turned the cover back. There, within, was a large coiled snake, his forked tongue like tiny black lightning, his tail like small castanets. Calling a man to him, Brigham said:

"Carry this snake away and tell him not to come back. Advise him to tell all his neighbors to stay out of our camp." Uncertain whether Brigham spoke in earnest or in jest, the man got a forked stick and captured the rattlesnake and bore it away. "Don't kill him!" Brigham called. "A scared enemy is of more value than a dead one."

Other men looked around fearfully and explored; and some of them, hearing sounds, jumped as if shot. One man climbed a tree and said he would sit on a branch all night, and others left their tents and sought open ground. The hours that followed were a nightmare. After the camp was quiet, a man leapt up with a frantic yell that brought two hundred men to their guns.

"What's the matter with you?" asked Brigham.

"It's a snake!"

"All right, give him a part of your bed. Mebbe he wants to share your pillow."

"Put your arm around him," said Parley. "He's cold."

"He'll be all right," Lyman Wight called, "if you don't hog all the covers! Lay down and go to sleep."

The man left his bed and gazed back at it as if he were looking into hell. Again and again, during the night, men yelled or cursed until nobody could sleep; and when Joseph was asked for advice, he said it was presumption to provoke a snake, but if a man was unwittingly bitten and had faith, he would be healed. If a man provoked a snake and was bitten, then he would die. The men pondered this pronouncement.

"Just the same," one said, "I'd rather not count on God in the matter." He left his bed, followed by others, and spent the remainder of the night on the bank of a stream.

On the next day the caravan passed a tumulus and Joseph ordered a halt. There were bones on the mound. The prophet asked several men to dig and in a few minutes they unearthed the skeleton of a human being. Joseph examined the bones and then mounted a wagon to address his army. This, he said, was the skeleton of a Lamanite, a large thick-set fellow and a man of God. He had been a warrior under the great prophet Omandagus, who was once famous from the Hill of Cumorah to the Rocky Mountains. The man's name was Zelph. He was killed in battle in the last great struggle between the Lamanites and Nephites.

"The camp will now proceed."

While tramping behind a wagon, Brigham marveled at the way God revealed all things to Joseph. Sometimes, as in business matters, or in expeditions of this kind, he questioned the prophet's judgment; but never in anything relating to the spiritual realms. He thought too, while walking, of a prediction Joseph had made two days ago. Dissensions and petty ambitions in the camp had aroused the prophet's wrath, and he solemnly announced that a plague would overtake the men and they would die like sheep with rot. If this were so, Brigham reflected, then the camp ought to turn homeward instead of marching day by day to inevitable ruin.

After four weeks the prophecy was fulfilled. Cholera struck the camp and the men fell sick one by one and raved in delirium; but still the army forged ahead, slowly, persistently, with the sick men lying in wagons and raving out of madness, and with the well men trudging behind them and feeling defeated and lost. The journey now lay across prairie, treeless and without water; and after marching for twelve hours in intolerable thirst and heat, the men pitched camp on a wide and burning plain under a gray sky. They were unable to eat, unable to endure much longer the wild rantings of their sick companions. No matter which way the men looked across the prairie, they saw a mirage of water, lovely and cool in the suffocating heat.

Brigham and Lyman and Parley went to Joseph. Brigham moved his hot tongue in his dry swollen mouth and said, "We must do something. Our beasts can't move without water. Our men can't march."

Joseph looked up at the sky, wondering if God would support him in this crisis. "Fetch me a spade," he said.

Brigham brought a shovel and Joseph took it and went two hundred yards across the burned landscape. In sight of everyone he knelt and prayed. Then he began to dig; and though he paused from time to time, overcome by heat and exhaustion, he drove himself to the last ounce of his strength. For an hour he dug while his men watched him and prayed or doubted, or looked at the mirages shimmering upon distance. After a while, Brigham and Lyman licked their parched lips and went over to the prophet.

"Let me help," said Lyman.

Joseph had a hole three feet deep; and by turns now the men spaded and rested, their blood feeling as if it were drying in their veins. When the depth was five feet, Joseph knelt in the hole and took earth in his hands and then held it up for the men to see. It was damp. With a cry, Lyman seized the shovel and dug with all his might. In another foot, water came into view and gurgled, and the men leapt into the hole and cupped their hands and drank of water that was half mud. Color returned to their cheeks. In a few moments they were standing in water to their knees; and they climbed out and watched the miracle of rising water, for it slowly filled the hole until it was level with the earth. A hundred men now came limping and staggering and fell like beasts around the hole and drank until their bellies were full.

No woe, it seemed to them, could be more severe than the agony of thirst, but in that they changed their minds. In June they camped in Missouri between two branches of Fishing River, unaware that a mob of three hundred men had marched out to meet them and were now across the river, preparing to attack. They would have attacked if a great storm had not intervened. A mighty wind came out of the southwest, driving clouds of dust and rain before it, and increasing in velocity until it uprooted small trees and carried them on its breast, and splintered large cottonwoods into scattered boughs. It came so suddenly that the tents were leveled, and the river was so convulsed that long waves rolled upward and broke against the current—so suddenly that men were caught unprotected and hurled to the ground before they realized that a storm had come. The storm, Joseph said, was a warning to their enemies.

But a more terrible enemy than mobs struck three days later when cholera laid the army low. Such wild deliriums and heart-rending agonies Brigham had never before seen. Without doctor or nurse or medicine, and with only a few well men to give aid, the weary wanderers lay sprawled in their tents or on the earth or in wagons, or they crawled to the river to cool their fever or to die. Some, trying to walk, swooned and fell face downward and did not move for a long while. Some fell into convulsions and writhed in hideous pain and then staggered to their feet and went blindly, not knowing what they did. Others were overwhelmed by religious ecstasy and had visions. One such man whom suffering had maddened stood in a wagon and stretched a hand to the sky.

"Hear ye!" he cried. "I can see God! Look, God is reaching down to touch me!"

Brigham went over to the man. "Brother Pete, stop this nonsense. You don't see God any more than I do." Then Brigham looked at the man's eyes and shrank back, horrified, and walked over to gaze at another man who was dying.

Some gathered in groups and set up a wild and blood-chilling dirge, or laughed with such grisly demented abandon that men in their right minds could not bear to look upon them or hear their sounds. In the beginning, Joseph had tried to cure his sick brethren by praying and putting his hands on them; but soon he was sick also and lost faith in his efforts. When the bewildered Parley asked him why he did not cure the men, Joseph gave him a pale smile.

"When God decrees destruction, we must not attempt to stay His hand."

"Well, we'll all die like rats. Simmons died an hour ago. Hargreave will be dead in a minute. Are we all to perish like beasts in a foul pen?"

"God is angry. He is punishing us."

"But you're not sinful, yet you're sick."

"I have offended in some way."

Brigham had another notion. It was a damned fool undertaking, he said to Lyman, and they would all die like a bunch of poisoned mice in a stone crock.

"What can we do?"

"Nothing. Just grin and bear it."

"But a dozen are dead now. The rest of us will soon be too weak to bury them. Then we'll die with the dead all around us."

"Has Jenson died yet?"

"I think so."

"Then we must bury him. We must keep the dead underground."

Lyman went to Jenson and gazed at the awful face. The limbs were drawn up to the body, convulsed and rigid; the hands were clenched. He got a piece of stout canvas and rolled the body upon it and then grasped two corners and dragged the dead man away. He dug a grave and rolled the body into it and knelt in prayer before shoveling in the sod.

When he returned, he saw a man who had mounted to a stump and was preaching wildly. A dozen men listened and from time to time clapped hands like children or howled like Indians. Out in a field of grass and low bushes, a man was chasing another with a cudgel which, Lyman supposed, he took to be a tomahawk. Others were howling in unintelligible jargon. Nearly the whole camp, it seemed to Lyman, had gone mad, though Brigham was still sound and sane and went from wagon to tent, from tent to mound, to look at the sick and bring water to their hot lips. The man with the cudgel had now overtaken the luckless one and knocked him down with a terrific blow on his skull. The victor then set up an awful cry and danced around his victim like an Indian. Lyman watched but he did not greatly care: nothing could move a man now—for what did it matter if a person was slain by a club or died of fever and rot?

Only sixteen of the men died. All the survivors except a handful were left weak and unnerved; and Joseph himself was so bewildered and shaken that for days he went around like a man moving in a dream. He ordered the feeble and ragged men to march again and drew close to Independence; whereupon he sent scouts to learn the purpose and number of the enemy. They declared it would be madness to continue. The saints had all been driven out of Jackson County, their homes had been burned, and great mobs were waiting, ready to attack.

"If we march on," said Lyman, "not a one of us will return alive."

"How many are there?"

"At least a thousand well-armed. They want us to go away."

"We must go back," Brigham said.

"Parley, what do you say?"

"We're whipped. We don't stand any more chance than a snowball in hell."

"We've offered," said Joseph, "to live in peace. Equal rights are all we ask for, yet the governor won't use the militia to reinstate us."

"He's afraid to."

Joseph looked at his advisers. They wanted to return to their homes but he delayed, hoping for arbitration of the matter; and not until hope was utterly dead did he climb to a wagon to address his army.

"Brothers," he said, looking down at their emaciated faces, "we are disbanding. You are to go back to Ohio—but go in pairs and preach the gospel on the way. Zion will be saved and returned to us but God is not yet ready. Be on your way now—and God will bless and protect you."

With a few of his leaders as bodyguard, he retraced the thousand miles to Kirtland. Three months ago, he had set out at the head of an army, with a bright banner flying as his soldiers sang.

> Their horses white, their armor bright,
> With courage bold they stand,
> Enlisting soldiers for their king
> To march on Zion's land!

To see our armies on parade,
How martial they appear!
All armed and dressed in uniform
They look like men of war! . . .

But now, barefooted and in rags, they came two by two back to their homes, with no banner flying and no song in their hearts. None more deeply than Joseph himself felt the galling defeat, or looked more chastened; but for one thing he was happy: he could now return to his translations and his dreams.

CHAPTER XVII

H E HAD PLANNED FOR A LONG WHILE TO HAVE TWELVE APOSTLES, AND TO these high offices he called his strongest men: Brigham and Heber Kimball, Parley Pratt and his brother Orson, Luke and Lyman Johnson, Orson Hyde and five others; and after sending them on missions to preach, he returned to his work. A man had come to Kirtland with a roll of papyrus covered with ancient characters. It was, Joseph decided, a part of the writings of Abraham, and of Joseph while in Egypt; and after buying the papyrus, he joyfully set to work to translate the symbols.

He found himself disturbed, as he had been formerly, by the number of Abraham's wives. The more he thought of the matter, the clearer it seemed that any devout man should have many wives; because in the next life, the men with the greatest number of children would, if equal with competitors in other glories, proceed most rapidly toward godhood. God Himself was the father of all the people on earth, and had become a god largely because of the great number of His offspring. Great leaders among the Jews multiplied abundantly. That God would give him a revelation in the matter, he did not doubt; but not yet—not until the church was firmly established and the building of Zion had begun. He liked to think of himself as a prophet with many wives, and with interest he looked at the more attractive women in Kirtland.

He was happy in his work. He studied Greek and Hebrew, translated the papyrus, and received reports on the progress of his missionaries. The summer was quiet. The autumn would have been peaceful if it had not been for his brother William. When Joseph started his church, William had been too young to be interested; and after moving to Kirtland with his parents, he looked around him and found women more attractive than Joseph's doctrines. Bill, it was rumored, was the only man in Ohio of whom Joseph was afraid; for Bill wanted to be a prophet too, or at least to have many privileges, and his demands he backed with his fists. When he started a debating society to promote his ambitions, Joseph said it would breed dissension and asked him to dissolve it.

"To hell with you," Bill said, speaking in the home of his father. "It's my business, ain't it? And listen, Joe: the next time you try to have me excommunicated, I'll knock the daylights out of you."

"Stop that talk," the father said.

Bill walked over and faced his brother and squared off. "Who are you to give orders to me?"

"I'm the leader in the church."

"Yes, a damned fine leader! You march down to whip the pukes and come sneaking back in the night. Last summer you said I was spending too much time with women. Well, I'll tell you this much: I do my lolly-gagging in the open and not the way you do yours."

"That's enough!" Joseph cried. "You're full of the Devil. You're as ugly as Satan."

"What's that?" asked Bill, clenching his big hands. "Say that again."

"You boys stop that talk!"

Ignoring his father, Bill thrust a snarling face at his brother. "You coward, say that again. I'm what?"

"I said you act as ugly as Satan himself."

That was enough for Bill. Suddenly and with all his might he struck, and Joseph went down as if he had been hit by a pile driver. Bill leapt upon his prostrate brother and drove fists into his face and belly, and then seized his throat to choke him; but the father in rage greater than his son's grasped Bill by his hair and hurled him backward.

"Stop it!" he bellowed, aghast at this picture of a son who was beating a prophet.

Joseph rose to his feet, with blood running from his nose and mouth. What to do with such a man, he did not know: he was torn between loyalty to a brother and loyalty to God. Twice he had driven Bill from the church and twice he had forgiven him.

"You're a fine one!" Emma cried. "You set there with blood running down your face and all because your brother wants to be the boss. Why didn't you jounce him?"

"My own brother?"

"Your brother! You ought to hit him with a wagon tongue."

"No. I'll write him a letter." Joseph wiped blood from his face and sat at his desk. "I undertook to reason with you," he wrote, "but you manifested an inconsiderate and stubborn spirit. I then despaired of benefiting you, which drew from me the expression that you were as ugly as the devil . . ."

"What good," asked Emma, reading over his shoulder, "will that do?"

"I think it will chasten him."

"Chasten him! Two fists right in his face might. Joseph, sometimes I wonder if you're a man or a monkey. Your brother knocks you down and beats you and you write him a love letter!"

Joseph turned to her and smiled. "Emma, did you hear the story Heber Kimball told? One day he and his wife went on a visit and told their little daughter Helen not to touch the dishes; for if she broke any, she would get a whipping. Helen let a table leaf fall and broke several dishes and then she went out and prayed that her mother would not whip her. Mrs. Kimball always keeps her promises and she took Helen into a room to whip her. You know what happened then?"

"She wrote her a letter!" said Emma scornfully.

"She was unable to raise her hand. She did not know that Helen had prayed, but she had, and God had answered her prayer. When I heard Heber tell that story I wept like a boy."

"I don't doubt it at all. You always could weep easier than a woman."

"The glory of God, Emma, is a wonderful thing. Prayer is more powerful than blows."

"Well, you might try blows once in a while."

"We need the faith of little children. Then we could build a beautiful world."

"Yes, you marched off to Missouri with the faith of a little child! And you escaped by the skin of your teeth. Go on: pray and have the faith of a little child, and when you come to your senses, other men will be running the church for you. If it isn't Bill, it will be Parley or Brigham or Heber or someone."

"It is faith that conquers all things."

"Oh, good Lord! Plague and famine, I guess. How about the men buried down on Fishing River?"

Distasteful to Joseph was the memory of his warlike march to Missouri. He was not a Brigham Young or a Lyman Wight: he preferred peace and gentleness. He leaned on faith and not on the fist or the sword. He realized, nevertheless, that many ambitious men were eager to depose him;

and when he saw plotting and greed in their eyes, he rebuked them as the spokesman of God.

Remembering Emma's scorn, he delivered a rebuke on the following Sunday. He looked so much the prophet and the king, with his blue eyes flashing and his biblical reprimands echoing like thunder, that many in the audience began to weep or pray. Before Joseph had finished, nearly the whole congregation was weeping, some blubbering in uncontrollable shame and others bowing their heads as they sobbed in prayer. Some of the apostles had returned from missions; and among them sat Brigham, marveling at the power of this man to sway an audience and move it to enthusiasm or grief. He was an unsentimental fellow himself but his eyes were moist now. After the last of Joseph's ringing words, the audience rose as if by command and followed their prophet in prayer.

Then a strange thing happened. First one, then two or three, and soon a dozen or more were talking in the gift of tongues; for as Joseph said later, the spirit of the Holy Ghost came upon them like the rushing of a mighty wind and they were forced to speak. A tall thin woman was shouting, "Dib ulonthi melakeethun clabrum!" but a short fat man was saying simply, "Loodoog, loodoog!" Those not impelled to speak turned to those who were speaking, eager to interpret what they said. Some, despairing of one tongue, moved from person to person, seeking a language they could understand; and then persons spoke and translated, and the building was full of strange babbling and of shouting voices.

"Mormon! Mormon!" a man was yelling. A woman, remembering Joseph's translation of this ancient name, cried ecstatically: "It means more good! *Mor* is English for *more*, and *mon* is Egyptian for *good*! The Latin is bonus, the Dutch is goed, the Greed is kalos, the Goth is goda, the Hebrew is tob! Mormon means more good!"

Another woman was saying: "Kulos, kados, onos tobadam!" and a nervous young man, almost beside himself with frenzy, was translating for her. "She is saying, 'God is blessing us in the spirit of the Holy Ghost for confessing our sins!'" "Algemani wilgememi astar!" The young man cried: "She says Jesus and God are smiling down upon us!"

More than twenty persons were speaking in tongues, each with an interpreter standing by. Brigham felt impelled to speak but his tongue was thick today, and after experimentally uttering a few sounds he withdrew to silence and watched the others. Oliver, he observed, was talking in tongues, and two of the Whitmers; and then he saw Emma Smith standing apart, her black eyes alive with scorn. Why there was so little of the spirit of the Lord in her, Brigham had never understood. Parley's wife, Thankful, a tall slender woman with a heart-shaped face and a pile of soft hair, was weeping and wringing her hands; but Parley, looking handsome today under his brown curls and in a flowered double-breasted waistcoat, stood calmly aloof and gazed at his fellows. His brother Orson, small and effeminate and visionary, was translating for Oliver Cowdery who was putting on the dog today with fair-top boots and a black vest and a white bang-up.

Observing how the Holy Ghost was poured on his people, Joseph decided the next day to dedicate the new temple, a large stone structure that had cost forty thousand dollars and excited a great deal of wonder. It had drawn editorials from eastern papers and visitors from far away. Joseph called it the Lord's House. It had been built with donations and free labor, all the best masons and carpenters among the saints having pitched in and worked like men driven until the temple was done. Though it was the most impressive building in a vast area, with its tower rising a hundred and ten feet into the sky, for the prophet it was only a modest harbinger of the magnificent temples which he intended to build.

On this day of dedication he and his leaders donned their best clothes. Joseph looked very handsome in his black coat with its tails falling away from his hips and to his knees behind, the collar rolled into a peak at the back of his neck, and the sloping revers curving away to show a broad expanse of frilled lawn shirt. His neckwear was a blue stock wrapped about the high collar and tied in a wide front bow. His trousers, loose at the hips but snugly fitting the legs, vanished into polished boots. His light hair was done in a high pompadour that lay in a kind of bang across his forehead and ran in side whiskers in front of his ears. His leaders were also fashionably dressed—and especially Rigdon who had a rich waistcoat, and the tallest chimney-pot hat Joseph had ever seen.

The glories attending the dedication were greater than the prophet had hoped for. Many of his more spiritual brethren had visions and revelations; and Joseph himself beheld the splendor of the celestial kingdom, the beautiful door leading thereto, and the throne upon which sat the Father and the Son. He saw both Adam and Abraham, as well as his own brother Alvin who had died before the church was founded. Jesus appeared and said He accepted the temple as a House of the Lord, and the saints as His people; Moses came and restored the keys of the gathering of Israel; and Elias and Elijah made themselves known.

After the visions, there were various rites in the upper chambers. Women, denied entrance to these rooms, sputtered with anger and said the whole matter was very strange indeed. But there was nothing strange. There was anointing with oil and washing of feet—the latter, Joseph explained, to show that they were all servants and not masters. Oliver, a rather fastidious man, reflected, while washing the feet of others, that some of the saints seemed to have forgotten that cleanliness was next to godliness. He was offended especially by the odor of Sidney Rigdon, the smell of whom he had never liked anyway. Save for a few unkind thoughts, the rituals were graciously performed, with one kneeling to wash the feet of a brother and then rising to anoint him with oil and bless him in the spirit of the Holy Ghost.

There was also sacramental wine. Some of the saints who had never drunk strong liquors, as well as some who had, imbibed too freely and staggered around as if they were as drunk as lords. Joseph himself, whose taste for the stuff he had always regarded as one of his worst vices, drank until he was dizzy, though he did not know whether his senses swam from wine or joy. The dedication of this temple marked the supreme triumph of his thirty-one years; but he remembered, after a glad outburst, that Emma was waiting for him, and this thought was more sobering than cold water would have been.

"Brother Sidney," he said to his ministerial righthand man, "I think you'd better walk me around awhile. The blessings of God have overcome me."

Rigdon took his arm and led him into the dark night where a cool breeze fanned Joseph and partially restored his wits. "I'm full of joy too," Rigdon said.

"I'm afraid," said Joseph, "Emma will be very angry with me."

Rigdon grunted. He had never liked this black-eyed, sharp-tongued woman. "You'll be all right," he said, and left Joseph at his door.

Emma was very angry. Joseph had hardly entered the bedroom where they slept before she was at him like a great hornet. "You're drunk!" she cried, sniffing his breath. "You big lazy ox! You make poor people dig up money to build a temple so you'n get slewed in it!"

"I'm just full of the spirit of the Lord," he said. "I'm dizzy with joy."

"You're dizzy with wine, you woman-chaser! If you were so plumb drunk you couldn't lift your head, you'd still say it was God in you!" She sniffed again and peered at his blue eyes, fogged with wine and visions.

"It was glorious," he said. "God showed me the celestial kingdom."

"You mean somebody showed you a wine barrel!"

"God let me see Alvin," he said, his blue eyes rebuking her. "God told me Alvin can be saved."

"I wouldn't worry about Alvin. He's dead. I'd worry about myself."

"Don't be blasphemous. God revealed marvelous things today."

"Get your clothes off and come to bed. I suppose you saw all the beautiful women in heaven."

"All the angels are beautiful." He considered a moment and added: "Things are going well. With our temple——"

"I thought God told you to build the temple in Missouri."

"We'll build one in Zion later."

He knelt by the bed and bowed his head in prayer. In a low deep voice, he thanked God that the priesthoods were established, that a House of the Lord could now serve as the core of a vast spiritual organization. Converts would soon come in from all points of the earth, enemies would embrace the new faith, and the gospel would fill the country from ocean to ocean, and then the world.

When he looked up, Emma was startled, as she had been many times, by the intense faraway expression in his eyes. He rose and stood calm and imperturbable. She peered at him sharply for a long moment; and then lay back, wondering about him, and reflecting that after all he probably had been drunk with visions instead of wine.

CHAPTER XVIII

IN JUNE, A MESSENGER CAME TO TELL JOSEPH THAT THE ENRAGED CITIZENS OF Clay County in Missouri had decided in mass meeting to drive all the saints out of their area. They had resorted to violence. Remembering the bitter lessons in Jackson County, the saints had packed their belongings and set out for the wilderness of western Missouri in which there were only trappers, Indians and wild beasts. Joseph listened gravely. Zion was a tremendous worry and he hardly knew what to do with it. Perhaps, he decided at last, the saints down there were still sinful and would have to be punished further; and meanwhile the church could be strengthened in Ohio and other regions.

Brigham said the church needed money if it was ever to be powerful; and he persuaded Joseph to establish a banking institution in Kirtland.

"We can buy land around here," said the shrewd Brigham, "for a little or nothing. As converts come in from all over the world, we can sell it at a big price. We can make the church wealthy—and we must have money if we are to build cities and temples."

"I never think much about money," Joseph said.

"We have to. We should build printing shops and sawmills and tanneries. We can make a million dollars right here in no time. You say Kirtland is to be a big city?"

"Yes, a large city."

"Then we should get started. We must have money if we are to survive."

The bank was founded. It was called the Kirtland Safety Society, a name, Brigham said, that would appeal to investors; and the saints were called upon to hand over their savings. They were told not only that the bank was safe, but that it was their duty to invest in it; and with eagerness many of them did. They dreamed of becoming rich men in a short while.

The founding of a bank, capitalized at four millions of dollars, was a reckless undertaking for a man as cautious as Brigham. But he believed Joseph when he said that Kirtland would be a large city and that converts would come to it by the thousands. He was caught in the spirit of the wild speculation that was rampant throughout the United States; and he went aggressively ahead, building shops and mills and urging the saints to dig up every dollar they had. After a while he boldly issued paper money on the new bank, and the church invested right and left in everything that looked profitable.

"Money is power," said Brigham. "If we are wealthy, our enemies will eat out of our hands. If we are poor, they will tar and feather us."

But he had believed Joseph too when the prophet said that many of the new converts would be wealthy. On the contrary, they had no more than the clothes they came in and the ox team and wagon with which they journeyed to the new land. Brigham looked at them and was aghast.

"We'll go broke," he cried to Joseph, "if we don't find some rich converts! Why, the men who come in are as poor as church rats. I thought you said they'd be rich."

"They're rich in faith," said Joseph.

"Faith and be damned! They come with rags on their backs. We planned to sell them land and we have to feed them."

"Rags on human bodies are no disgrace, Brigham, if God is in their hearts."

"I tell you we'll go broke. We can't support all these paupers."

Joseph looked at Brigham and pondered. "Do things look bad?"

"Damned bad. If we don't get some rich converts we're headed for bankruptcy. Where are the wealthy men you said would come in?"

"I guess they haven't seen the light yet."

Brigham shrugged. "I advise you to send word to the missionaries in the field to send no more paupers here. And do it at once."

"Do you think that is necessary?" asked Joseph, pained by the thought.

"Joseph," said Brigham impatiently, "can you realize that a crash is coming? We are overcapitalized. Our paper money soon won't be worth a nickel to the yard of it. We can't pay our hired help. If we should get a run on the bank ——"

"All right," said Joseph, "I will." And to every missionary in the field he sent a letter. "It is improper and unchristian to send the poor from among you to this place, without necessary means of subsistence. It becomes the duty henceforth of all the churches abroad to provide for those who are objects of charity, and not send them to burden the church here. We are feeding hundreds of them now . . ."

But it was too late. Financial panic swept the nation in 1837, and the safety bank went down like a stack of cards, with its paper money and its stock worth less than the engraving alone had cost. Because it had no charter, the bank's money was rejected in New York City, Pittsburgh and Cleveland; and for huge stores of supplies bought on credit, the saints were now unable to pay. Like a trapped beast, Brigham looked around for a way out.

When the disaster became known in Kirtland, the town went mad. Leaders accused leaders of malpractice; friend turned against friend; and the gentile enemies looked on and rejoiced. Mobs gathered and plotted lynchings. Even some of the highest officials, including apostles, bitterly denounced Joseph and said he was no prophet at all. He was a swindler, a thief and a hellhound in league with the Devil. Some, insane with rage, pronounced judgments even more severe: they said Joseph and other leaders had been living in luxurious harems. Even Oliver Cowdery, for so many years obedient and faithful, swore by everything holy in heaven that Joseph had seduced an orphan who had been living in his home.

"You sure of that?" asked a horrified saint.

"Of course I'm sure. In fact, Joseph admitted to me it was true."

"You mean Joseph, the prophet of God, admitted he seduced this poor girl?"

"That's what I mean."

"Then he isn't any prophet."

"He never was!" said Oliver hotly. "I've doubted him for a long time. He's a seducing fraud who squandered other peoples' money while he lived like an Oriental polygamist in a harem."

"I can't believe it," the other said.

"Look around you. You will."

Men gathered in angry groups and discussed not only the bankruptcy of the church, but also the stories of polygamy, of riotous living, of drunkenness and debauchery, and even of rape. Throwing commonsense to the winds, they believed everything they heard; and if what they heard was not scandalous enough, they invented tales and spread them through the town.

"That orphan girl," said a man, "ain't the only one he raped. But he ain't no worse than Brigham or Sidney or a dozen others. They're all liars and thieves and devils."

"That's true. Great Jesus, what fools we've been!"

"Well, I'm leaving the church. It stinks to high heaven and I wouldn't believe Joe Smith again if he swore to it with his hand right in God's face. The mouth-almighty hog-in-togs with his bedroom full of women!"

"Not his bedroom. Emma wouldn't stand for that."

"What about Emma? She must a-known all the time."

"I guess he fooled her too."

"Well, it's a fine mess. Every cent I owned has gone up in smoke."

"What we ought to do," said a man who had been listening, "is take him out and horsewhip him."

"Lynch him, you mean. You know some of the apostles have left the church? Luke and Lyman Johnson have."

"The hell! Well, I'm leaving it too. If I have to go to heaven by believing in Joe Smith, then I'll go the other way."

A few days later a group of men were talking in a tavern. "Did you know," asked one, "that Brig Young has hit the high lonesome?"

"You mean he has skinned out?"

"Like greased lightning. He's gone."

"How you know that?"

"I'll tell you how I know. A bunch of us last night decided to knock the ripsnorting hell out of him and roll him in tar. But we couldn't find hide or hair. He's gone."

"That shows how guilty he was. If he wasn't guilty he wouldn't run away."

"No, by God. Why didn't he stand up to the rack?"

"Joseph and Sidney are here. Why don't we fix them?"

"No, let's wait. There's to be a conference tomorrow and they're going to defend themselves."

"Like as how they could!"

"Where's the meeting to be?"

"In the temple."

"In the temple! They got drunk in the temple and now they're going to defend themselves in the temple. God will like that, won't He!"

Called by the dissenters, the meeting in the temple was for the purpose of investigating Joseph and Sidney; but Sidney was too ill to walk and was half-carried and half-dragged into the building. Joseph followed him. The prophet looked as if he had neither eaten nor slept for days, and when he was greeted with boos and hisses, his face paled to the whiteness of death. To those guarding him, Sidney said he wished to speak first.

"Rigdon wants to speak!" a man cried. "Will you hear him?"

Some shouted "No," but a strong voice rose above the din. "Let him whip the Devil around the stump! Let him speak!"

Famed as one of the greatest orators in the church, Rigdon now faced the audience, with hands on a chair to support himself. He looked as near death as he could. "Brothers—" he began.

"Never mind that brother lingo. Let's have your say-so."

"Defend yourself, you guilty sneak!"

"Brothers in the church of God——"

"Church of thieves, you mean."

"Let him speak!" a man roared. "Shut up your heads!"

"—I am a sick man, a very sick man. My health has never been good; and now, seeing the ill-will and hatred in your faces, in you whom I have loved and served and fought for, I feel it would be just as well if I was dead. If I were dead, brothers, perhaps then you would think of me with a little kindness. Perhaps you would remember that I have always worked hard for justice and right, no matter what you have thought of me. It bows me with grief to see you looking at me without love." He straightened a little; and when he spoke again, his voice rang with some of its old fire.

"I am guilty of nothing! Our bank failed, that is true; but hundreds of banks throughout the nation have failed. That was not my fault, nor Brother Joseph's, nor Brother Brigham's. We acted with all the wisdom we had. We cannot control the whole economic structure of the country.

"And now I am a sick and a brokenhearted man. I am beyond the reach of your abuse: my conscience must settle with God, and my conscience is clear. . . ."

After he finished there was silence. In silence he left the building, supported by a man on either side; and when he had disappeared, the audience turned to Joseph who had been waiting.

"All right, Joe, let's hear your bilking chin music."

"I suppose you're a sick man too!"

"You ought to be, you drunken adulterous——"

"Silence!" the chairman thundered. "Let him speak."

Joseph faced them. He had not come here to apologize: he had come here to fight, for he was a prophet of God and God was with him.

"Brothers, you have been told many stories about me. You have heard that I am a seducer and adulterer and drunkard. Those stories are lies!" He advanced a step and clenched his hands. "This church was established by God through me and I am still its leader and prophet. Without me, there is no church, no salvation. Don't be deceived by liars and false prophets——"

"What about your bank?" a man shouted. "You said it was God's bank! You said it wouldn't fail no matter what happened."

"I made no such statement! If anyone told you that, he was speaking for the Devil. I said if the bank was conducted on righteous principles it would not fail——"

"Then you admit it wasn't conducted on righteous principles."

"I do not. There are dishonest persons in all churches. Your leaders are not dishonest——"

"But your damned bank failed!" a man yelled.

A leader of the dissenters now stepped forth. "We have our side to present. We have lost our money, our homes. We are bankrupt. We——"

Joseph interrupted him with a wave of his hand. "Let me say that the church will first excommunicate those opposing me and hear them afterward."

That astounding declaration brought the storm. The audience rose, howling like madmen. Every voice was shouting jeers or threats or was offering suggestions.

"We'll excommunicate you and then hear you!"

"You take our money and then excommunicate us because we don't like it! I suppose God agrees to that, don't He?"

"To hell with you, Joe Smith! We'll hang you to a tree and then hear you!"

The dissenting leaders gathered and talked among themselves while the mob roared. They decided to postpone the meeting a few days. "Silence! We're going to take a few days to talk it over and prepare charges! Then——"

But the outraged and bankrupted saints were not willing to wait at all. After leaving the temple and considering the matter, they were so furious that they organized in gangs, some determined to tar and feather the church leaders, and some to lynch them. Scores became apostates to their faith and swore they would have vengeance if it took them the rest of their lives. Kirtland fell under pillage and drunkenness and mob rule, with the more sober gentiles standing aside and marveling at the wild mutiny that had demoralized the new religion.

Joseph and Sidney hid among friends, knowing well that mobs were bent on their death.

"Well," said Emma, "what do you think of yourself now as a prophet?"

Joseph looked at her with sad and haunted eyes. "The prophets of old had to flee for their lives. Did not Jesus say that when they persecute you in one city, flee to another?"

"So you're going to run again, are you?"

Joseph did not answer. He was thinking of the inflamed mobs in this, his city, the stronghold of his church and his faith. He had been driven out of New York, his people had been driven out of eastern Missouri, and now it looked as if he would have to run for his life. There were warrants out for him. If found guilty of half the charges, he would spend the remainder of his life in jail.

"Where did Brigham hit off to?" asked the caustic Emma.

"I don't know."

"If you hadn't listened to him you wouldn't be in this mess. But he isn't here to face the rack. The sly old fox hit the grit when he heard the first yell." She stared at her husband. "Is it true polygamy has been practiced here?"

"Not by the leaders. There are sinful persons in any church."

"Is it true you've been seducing other women?"

"No."

"Then Oliver Cowdery is a liar?"

"Oliver," said Joseph, shaking his head woefully, "is a sinful man."

"Well, what are you going to do? If you stay around here you'll be lynched—or put in jail the rest of your life."

"I'll have to go to Missouri."

"You mean desert your wife and family?"

"No, Emma. I'll leave and wait for you a few miles out."

"I suppose I'm to load the furnishings on a horse and ride out to meet you!"

"We have friends. They'll bring you to me. But I must go, for there are men here lusting for my life."

"Even some of your leaders!"

"Yes."

"I must say you show a lot of sense in choosing leaders. The Johnsons and Oliver and Sidney and Martin Harris. And that what's-his-name who was caught in adultery."

"He confessed and was forgiven."

"God, yes, and then stole twenty-five thousand dollars from the bank! And Dave Whitmer wants to be prophet again. I told you all along he was a snake in the grass. What men you choose to help you!"

"Some of them," Joseph admitted sadly, "are full of Satan."

Joseph did not leave at once. He hoped that God would intervene and rebuke the sinners; but matters went from bad to worse until all the property was foreclosed and the church was completely bankrupt. A mob burned the printing shop. A mob controlled the temple.

On a cold, dark night in January, Joseph and Sidney slipped out of hiding and mounted horses and set out for Missouri. The next day their enemies learned that they had flown and went in furious pursuit; and for two hundred miles they tracked the fugitives, once even sleeping in the same house. There was only a thin partition between, and for three hours Joseph and Sidney sat almost without breathing and listened in the darkness to what was said.

"Where do you think they went to?"

"Damned if I know. I don't think they're far from here."

"Wait till we get our hands on them. But I ain't in favor of a quick hanging. We should set candles under their feet awhile."

"We'n settle all that when we get them."

"The dirty crooks! By God, if Joe Smith's a prophet, I'm the Holy Ghost."

"Every dollar I had was in that bank."

"Served you right to put your money in a Mormon bank."

"You think we'n hang them and go scot free?"

"Free! The Federal government will give us a pension."

Joseph looked at Sidney. The man was shaking with fear. Joseph reached out to touch him reassuringly and Sidney whispered: "We need guns."

"The Lord will protect us. Have faith in Him."

They slipped out long before daylight and resumed their journey. After they entered Missouri, Joseph felt safe and he sang hymns as they rode day by day or he talked of Zion and the city and the temple which were to be.

"We'll build the Lord's kingdom down here," he said.

CHAPTER XIX

THIS WAS NOT THE MISSOURI HE HAD SEEN ON FORMER JOURNEYS. THE country then was prairies of lush grass, of flowering or wooded hills, of lovely streams between burgeoned banks; but now in early March it was a desolate and frozen landscape. It did not look like the ancient Garden of Eden. It did not look like Zion. The saints had been driven out of the eastern counties; and some had deserted the church and returned to the land they came from, and others had pushed into the west. Here they had built homes and villages under the resourceful leadership of Lyman Wight; but gentiles followed them and soon they had as many enemies as they had had in Jackson and Clay counties. Even before Joseph arrived, there had been violence, sporadic attacks by mobs, and two murders. For the Mormons had again boasted that Zion would be established in Missouri and that no power under heaven could wrest the land from them. The pioneers under Wight were the boldest of those who had been expelled: the weaklings and those of little faith had fled. Among the saints now were desperate and dangerous men who were ready to fight.

And Joseph himself, after understanding more clearly what had happened to his people, was in no mood to turn the other cheek. A hundred and twenty miles from Far West, the chief settlement, he was met by a delegation who greeted him with wild joy and led him to the new home. While riding along he heard in detail what had happened: how the saints had petitioned the governor, the President; had been advised to move to Wisconsin, an area recently taken from Black Hawk; and had been driven westward into wilderness. Besides Far West, they had Diahman, Gallatin, DeWitt and Haun's Mill, all thriving settlements. Converts had poured in from all parts of the nation.

"How many saints are there here?" asked Joseph.

"At least ten thousand."

"In that case," said Rigdon, "we can protect ourselves."

"And by God, we will," said one of the men.

Sidney looked fiercely around him; and soon after arriving, he preached a sermon that was cheered by a thousand men. "Our cheeks," he shouted, "have been given to the smiters—our heads to those who have plucked off the hair! But from this day and this hour we will suffer it no more. We take God and all holy angels to witness that we warn all men to come on us no more forever. That mob that comes on us to disturb us, it shall be between us and them a war of extermination! . . ."

Joseph, too, was emphatic.

"Brother Sidney's speech is a declaration of independence from all mobs and persecutions which have been inflicted upon us time after time, until we can bear it no longer. In the name of Jesus Christ, the Son of the living God, we will endure it no longer, if the great God will arm us with courage, with strength and with power to resist them in their persecutions! We will not act on the offensive but always on the defensive; but our rights and our liberties shall not be taken from us, and we peaceably submit to it, as we have done heretofore! . . ."

Men threw their hats into the air and yelled, and women wept for joy. This, they said, was a fighting prophet, and they would follow him to the ends of earth.

"You're right, Brother Joseph! By the Holy God, we'll fight them right in their teeth!"

"Lead us, Joseph, and we'll follow you to hell!"

"Yes, by the holy angels. Let's give three cheers to our fighting prophet!"

The great crowd gave three cheers so mighty that Joseph's heart was lifted to his throat. He had been driven like a thief out of Kirtland, he had been trailed by lynchers, he had been deserted by many of his leaders; but here, more than a thousand miles away, were bold men ready to die for him. Here were Lyman Wight and Parley Pratt, Orson Hyde and Brigham Young: a prophet could build a kingdom out of material like that.

Feeling his old confidence, he gave a revelation the next day, declaring that Far West and another temple should be built speedily, and that a settlement named Spring Hill should be called Adam-ondi-Ahman; for this was the spot where Adam would visit his people, or the Ancient of Days should sit, as spoken of by Daniel of Old. He excommunicated Oliver, Lyman Johnson and Dave Whitmer, all of whom stank in his nostrils; and was overjoyed upon learning that five hundred saints in Ohio had set out in a body for Far West, and that his own family was on the way.

"Brother Sidney," he said, "the Lord smiles upon us again. Our troubles are over."

"I don't know about that," said Sidney, for he had heard rumors.

He had heard that all the gentiles in this area were sending out spies and secretly organizing mobs. They had heard that the prophet had come. A few had seen him and had heard his fiery speech. They had heard Sidney declare: "We will follow our enemies until the last drop of their blood is spilled, or else they will have to exterminate us; for we will carry the seat of war to their own houses and their own families!" That was a challenge and a threat. It drew privately from Brigham an angry retort.

"The damn fool! If he doesn't keep his mouth shut there'll be civil war."

Sidney did not intend to keep his mouth shut. He was second in power and he felt his position mightily. Smarting under his desperate flight from Kirtland, and hurt by Emma's saying upon arriving that mobs declared Joseph and Sidney to be the biggest cowards in the nation, he went from one hot-blooded statement to another. "If our enemies come against us, I say woe unto them! We're resolved to be a free people and that determination can never be broken! No, never! NO, NEVER!" Hotheaded young men applauded him, but those older and wiser wished that Sidney had remained in Ohio.

"He's a bigger problem than our enemies," Brigham said.

Joseph, serenely unaware of the gathering storm, went out daily with guides to look over the surrounding country and to find new sites. He smiled and was happy. He gazed at the sky, feeling that God's wrath had been appeased, believing that here in western wilderness he could build his kingdom. There was abundance of land, water, timber, and his people were arriving almost daily.

The storm broke in a settlement named Gallatin. There was an election, and the saints had been told to come armed if they intended to vote. They went unarmed and found themselves facing a mob. The village was divided into two factions that for an hour stared at one another like enraged cocks. Among the gentiles were men who swaggered and jeered and cursed, or squared off and invited their opponents to fight.

"Come on," a big man said. "I'n whip any Mormon from here to hell." He was drunk. He went from group to group, singling out one and another for his abuse. "You're all a bunch of cowards! Send out your David to oppose me!" Gazing around him, he spotted a Mormon who looked as if he lusted for battle. Marching up, he laughed in the man's face. "You believe in visions, do you? Well now, by God, ain't that a kick in the wind!" He turned to eager henchmen who had followed him. "Hey, look at this fool standing here. By God, he thinks Joe Smith is a prophet. Let's see now what kingdom of glory you going to be in: the pigestial or the bestial?"

"Go on about your business," said the Mormon.

"My business is to see you don't vote. You'd better go back to the place you came from."

"We saints don't want trouble but we don't aim to turn the other cheek."

"Oh, you don't! Then I'll turn it for you." The man aimed a blow but another caught his arm and hurled him back.

The gentiles set up a great howl. All the drunken bullies who had been lusting for a fight now fell upon the Mormons nearest them; and in a few minutes both factions were warring like savages. Some of the men on both sides slipped up behind lone enemies and knocked them senseless with a single blow; and others went in pairs, with one man dropping swiftly to hands and knees and the other knocking an opponent end over end across the man who knelt. For the most part they fought in groups, striking so blindly that sometimes they hit friend instead of foe, or leaping to a fallen man and drubbing him soundly before learning who he was.

"By God," cried an astonished saint who had been sitting astride a man and threshing him. "Is it you?" He assisted a comrade to his feet; and while looking at him, unable to believe his eyes, he was felled by a blow from the rear that laid him out.

The saints were too many. The gentiles, bruised and bleeding, withdrew from the scene, but not without shaking their fists and cursing.

"You Mormons, we'll finish you yet!"

"All we want is to vote."

"You'll never vote!" a man roared. His face looked slaughtered. "Cut my belly open if you ever do!"

One of the Mormons called his companions to him. "Brothers, we are American citizens. Our fathers fought for liberty and we will fight, but we'd better go and get our guns. They'll all be back in a minute—" He broke off. A sheriff was approaching with several men.

"Hit for the brush," said the sheriff, riding up. "They'll come back armed."

"We're not running. We intend to fight."

"Looks like you been fighting." The sheriff gazed around him at the bloody faces. "They don't intend for you to vote. You'd better go. I can't control them and I don't want murder."

"We'll go back to our homes."

"No, hide out for a while."

"Hide out!" cried one. "Why should we?"

"It's the only thing to do," said the sheriff patiently; and the county officers with him nodded approval. "I can't handle them when their blood's up."

The Mormon leader considered. "All right, we'll hide. But I'm sending word to our prophet and he'll march over here with an army. We're free men and we are going to fight for our liberties."

"Yes, but I don't want any murders around here. You men understand that I ain't against you but there's nothing I can do."

"All we ask for is our rights as citizens."

The saints returned to their homes and then went with their families to hide in a hazel thicket. They sent a rider to Joseph. "Tell him to bring an army. Tell him to hurry."

More than a score of families hid in the jungle. Soon after dark it began to rain, and before midnight there was a terrific storm riding on a strong wind. The women sat under bushes, trying to keep their children dry; and the men stood guard. When morning came, they all looked as if they had come out of a river.

The man who carried the news to Joseph dramatized the story until the fight sounded like a massacre. He said men had been killed, women had been attacked. He said some of the saints had limbs and jaws broken, some had all their teeth knocked out, and others had been scalped.

"You say they want an army?"

"A thousand men armed to the teeth."

Joseph went to his leaders to ask advice. Rigdon said they should march over and wipe them off the face of the earth; but Brigham said no. "We don't want civil war."

"We must fight," Rigdon said. "We've been driven out of Palmyra, out of Kirtland, out of Independence. Are we going to wait for the slaughter?"

"We might whip them," said Brigham impatiently. "But then we'd be fighting Missouri and then the Federal government. We'd lose in the long run."

"What do you say?" Joseph asked Lyman.

"I say I'n whip half of them myself. Besides, are we going to let them persecute us forever? We go to a new country and build a city and they run us out of it. They'll run us right out of the nation next."

Joseph turned to his leaders assembled around him. "Get an army ready with plenty of ammunition. We'll leave in two hours."

And two hours later, Joseph set out at the head of a hundred armed men. When he learned that the report had been grossly exaggerated, he listened to Brigham's counsel and resolved to seek peace. Choosing a committee to go with him, he rode to the home of Adam Black, the justice for this area. Black was a mild and illiterate man and not at all unfriendly; but his huge wife hissed and spit like a great cat, her tongue pouring venomous abuse on the meeting. When Joseph asked Black if he would administer justice impartially, Mrs. Black stepped forward and made a hideous face.

"You sinner out of hell! You black devil from the infernal pits!"

"Will you?" asked Joseph, trying to ignore her.

"Yes," Black said.

"Will you give us a statement to that effect?"

"You polygamous skunk!" cried the woman, thrusting a wet tongue at Joseph. "You blood-sucking weasel!"

"I guess so," said Black, staring with distaste at his wife. He got a sheet of paper and a pen and for several minutes was busy. Then he handed the statement to Joseph and this is what Joseph read:

I, Adam Black, a justice of the peace of Davies county, do here by Sertify to the people, colen Mormin, that he is bound to suport the Constitution of this State, and of the United States, and he is not attached to any mob, nor will he attach himselff to any such people, and so long as they will not molest me, I will not molest them, This the 8th day of August, 1838.

Adam Black, J.P.

Pained by the man's illiteracy, Joseph looked curiously at Adam. "We'll take this document with us." He turned to Mrs. Black. "Madam, why are you so bitter toward the saints?"

"Saints!" she said, and cackled like a witless hag. "You adulterous murderer!"

"I have murdered no one." He turned to Adam who was gazing at him uneasily from under shaggy brows. "Mr. Justice, we wish to live in peace but we will fight for our rights. Good day, sir."

Knowing how impotent his document was, Joseph went to see Joe Morin and Jack Williams, two men of the county who had been elected to the legislature. They seemed to him to be kind and intelligent. He showed them the statement from Black.

"We wish to live in peace, but we've been driven out of New York, Ohio and parts of Missouri. We are sick of running like criminals."

"I don't see," said Morin, "why we should have trouble. If we all mind our business we shouldn't have. Of course, there are rowdies who like to fight for the fun of it."

"I know that. But why not turn the rowdies over to the law? If my people offend, I want them punished. Why not agree to protect one another's rights?"

"Of course. Jack, doesn't that sound reasonable?"

"Yes," said Jack. "If the Mormons live within the Constitution ——"

"We always have," said Joseph.

"Then there shouldn't be any trouble."

"Do you promise to see we are protected in our rights?"

"Certainly," Morin said.

Joseph grasped his hand. "I feel," he said, "that our troubles are ended."

But he did not know the temper of the men in this county. He did not know the man who was now governor of Missouri. Boggs sent out an army of five hundred men to protect Missourians, he said, from Mormons and Indians; and General Dave Atchinson marched in to learn that there were mobs everywhere, including a hundred armed men under Lyman Wight. Wight, he reported to the governor, was a bold and brave and desperate man; but he added that there seemed to be no cause for alarm. His report had hardly been sent when another general publicly declared that the Mormons were base and degraded, and should be exterminated from the face of the earth.

That statement angered Joseph, but in human beings he still had the faith of a child. When he learned that a mob had laid DeWitt under siege and cut off the food supply, he was distressed, but he believed in the integrity of the local officers, the legislators and the governor. Upon hearing, a little later, that Governor Boggs himself declared the quarrel to be between armed mobs and the Mormons, and added that the two factions could fight it out, Joseph was amazed. He could not believe that a governor in a free land could have so little regard for civil rights.

Some of his leaders wanted peace and some wanted war, and between the two groups Joseph was helpless. He could not make up his mind when he heard that the saints had been driven out of DeWitt, or when he learned that Millport had been sacked and burned, or when he was told of a battle on Crooked River. One leader advised him to flee to the Rocky Mountains, another to Illinois or Iowa, and a third urged him to put on his sword and fight. But Joseph wanted a life of peace and study and reflection.

It did not matter. The feud was beyond his control now: Governor Boggs had spoken and the war was on.

CHAPTER XX

IN AN EARLY MORNING OF SEPTEMBER JOSEPH LEFT EMMA AND HIS CHILDREN asleep in their cabin in Far West and went to the bank of a stream to watch the rising sun make magic of the water. The air was sweet and the woods were full of song; but the prophet's heart was heavy with woe. Not for the life of him could he tell what to do—for mobs were everywhere and all roads of escape were closed. He watched the sun rise and turn the stream into golden dimples, or gazed at a scarlet haw, remembering the heavenly loveliness of its bloom three months ago. It seemed strange to him that God's children, to whom He had given so beautiful a world, should be so intolerant and hateful and murderous.

While Joseph sat here, a young man slowly advanced, trying to make no sound with his feet. Tim McBride had never seen the prophet before. He stood a little way off, solemnly gazing at him; and when Joseph looked up and saw the intruder he leapt to his feet, not knowing whether he faced an enemy or a friend.

"Who are you?"

"Sir, are you Joseph Smith?"

"I am."

"I'd like to speak to you." Tim drew near and stared at the prophet, not daring to sit in the presence of one so mighty.

"Sit down," Joseph said.

Tim was so solemn that he looked a little owlish; but he had honest Irish eyes and a straight firm mouth. "Sir, I want to ask you some things."

"What is it?"

"Well," said Tim, almost tongue-tied, "I—you see, I live over at Haun's Mill. I'm one of the saints."

"Yes," said Joseph, remembering that he had never seen many of his people.

"I— Sir, do you know Dr. Sampson Avard?"

"Avard?" asked Joseph, frowning. "I think I've heard the name."

"Did you—have you—" Tim swallowed hard and then blurted: "Do you know what he's doing?"

"No, I don't."

"That's what I come to see you about. Do you know about his secret society?"

"Secret society? What do you mean?"

"Well, sir, I thought you didn't. So I come to tell you. He says you told him to form this society ——"

"What society?" asked Joseph impatiently.

"The Danites."

"I've never heard of it. Tell me."

Tim breathed more freely now. "Sir, if I tell you I'll be breaking an oath. I'll be killed if—do you promise not to tell on me?"

"I'm the leader of the church. It's your duty to tell me."

"That's what I thought." For a long moment, Tim gazed at the stream, remembering. "Well," he said at last, "Dr. Avard said you told him to form a secret society called the Danites. It's also called the Destroying Angels. He says it's a very ancient order. Well, I joined it. But honest, sir, I didn't know what it was like—not until after I was in it."

"Yes," said Joseph softly. "Go on."

"Well, a lot of the saints have joined."

"You say you took an oath? What oath?"

"A horrible oath," said Tim, and shuddered. "It—well, it makes you swear by God and the Son and the Holy Ghost to murder our enemies. It says there will be blood from the Rocky Mountains to the Atlantic Ocean and we will walk over the bodies of our enemies until—" Tim broke off, abashed by the way Joseph was looking at him.

"Go on," said Joseph sternly.

"Well," said Tim, as if swallowing his tongue, "it says if we are false to the order—that is, I mean if we tell any secrets, then we'll be gutted alive and burned with fire." Tim paused again. Almost in a whisper he added: "Bert Mann, he told, and I seen him afterwards."

"You mean ——"

"Sir, I wouldn't want to tell you what they done to him. And if Dr. Avard finds out I told you ——"

"Don't worry about that. Go on."

Tim was silent again, looking at the stream and remembering the gutted body of Bert Mann. "Well, that's about all, except Dr. Avard says we're to protect one another. He says we're to lie and murder and if anyone stands in our way, we'll put him under the sand like Moses did the Egyptian. He said if I ever told he'd put me where the dogs wouldn't bite me."

"How many Danites are there?"

"Several bands. In each band there's about ten or twenty men. When I went out I was with Dr. Avard."

"When you went out where?"

"Sir, that's another thing I wanted to tell you. After the battle on Crooked River—well, you knew Brother Patten was killed. That is, the gentiles just shot all his guts out. And Gideon Carter, he got his face blowed off. Then ——"

"Then what?" asked Joseph. He had seen something swift and strange in Tim's eyes.

"You see, Dr. Avard said the Destroying Angels should go out and get vengeance. So we went. There was twenty of us. It was a black night and there was a little rain and we all had fast horses and good guns. Dr. Avard, he said he knew the leaders, and so we went to their places." Tim broke off again. He was trembling.

"Did Avard find the leaders?"

"I can't say about that. He said they was the leaders."

"What did you do with them?"

Tim sprang to his feet. He gazed down at Joseph and after a long moment he said: "It makes me sick to think. We—we killed them."

"Killed them!" Joseph cried.

"Yes, sir. Dr. Avard, he says we're to murder all our enemies. I'n see how we should protect ourselves but it seemed to me— My father was beat by a mob; and my uncle—Uncle John, that is—he starved to death over in Jackson County a year ago. It ain't that I don't want to fight. I'll fight with the next man and I ain't afraid. But it seemed to me ——"

Joseph rose and grasped Tim's shoulders. "What did you do?"

"We—we tortured them."

Joseph turned away. There was no peace or beauty left in this morning. His people, the chosen of God, were torturing their enemies: no wonder the Lord was wreaking His anger in pestilence and murder. He turned to face Tim again and looked into the youth's haunted eyes. "How did you torture them?"

"With fire."

"O my God!"

Tears came to Tim's frank gray eyes. "We—we held fire against them. We burned the flesh off of their feet—almost. Then—" Sinking to the earth, he bowed his head and shook with grief. Joseph knelt by him.

"Pray with me."

But Tim could not pray. He sobbed while Joseph prayed; and then Joseph rose and laid a hand on Tim's head. "Go back to your home. Leave this abominable society. Do you hear me?"

"Yes," said Tim, sobbing like a child.

"This Avard will be driven out of the church. But don't tell him that. Never see him again."

"Yes, sir."

Tim rose without looking at Joseph and went away, and with his heart sinking, the prophet watched him go. His people would fight for their rights, yes; but to sink to the level of savages, to torture and maim—that he would never forgive. When he left the stream he walked like an old man, for he could see no way out of this darkness, this hell of persecution and death. He entered a thicket and knelt in prayer; but he rose from prayer without strength, feeling that God had deserted him in this bitter time.

In another week he knew he was helpless. Reports came to him daily of guerrilla warfare in a score of places, of barbarous torture on both sides, of arson and blood and ruin. Lyman Wight came. There was not a more fearless man among the saints than this rugged hotheaded man who believed that the argument should follow the blow. He was angry; and when Lyman was angry he was almost terrifying: he snapped his jaws as if he were biting off spikes, and rolled his eyes as if wrath had blinded them.

"We are facing extermination!" he roared. "We must fight and fight now! By the holy angels, do you know our people are being butchered? Atchinson disarmed my men and promised to disarm the mobs—but did he? You know he didn't! He's a dirty accursed Judas. I don't trust men like Atchinson with his long nose and his hoglike hair. And Governor Boggs is nothing but a rabble-rousing pot-sopper!"

"What," asked Joseph, "is happening now?"

"In the name of the most high God, don't you know? They're murdering our men, raping our women, burning our homes! Are we to sit back and pray while they butcher all of us? Are we to wait for the Almighty to act?—And if we do, we'll all be bleaching bones along the river banks. There are nine different armed mobs in Daviess County alone——"

"Brother Lyman, do you know anything about the Danites?"

For a long moment Lyman looked searchingly at the prophet as if trying to read his mind. "What," he asked at last, "do you expect? If you don't lead the saints, they'll take matters in their own hands. Yes, I know about the Danites. I know Sampson Avard has several bands of night raiders. Their blood is up and they don't intend to wait for you to make up your mind."

"Lyman, you know the church doesn't approve of such methods. They're torturing——"

"Yes! In the name of the Almighty God, they are, but so are our enemies. Have I forgotten Independence and Colesville and Big Blue? I don't belong to the Danites but I'm telling you there'll be worse than Danites before long. There'll be five thousand of us avenging the murder of our comrades and the rape of our wives! And something else: the mobs will be over here soon and then what will you do?"

"I don't know," said Joseph gloomily. "God is still angry with us."

"He ought to be, the way we sit around like a pack of sheep and wait for the wolves. Didn't God say to you He would curse our enemies? Didn't He say we are to fight?"

"Yes."

"Then why in hell don't we fight?"

"As Brigham says, we can't fight the state of Missouri."

"No, we'n let the state of Missouri watch us get butchered! Didn't the governor say the mobs and us had to fight it out?"

"But the governor is helping the mobs."

"All right, that's why the Danites went into action. I'm not in favor of them any more than you but something has to be done."

"I'm going," said Joseph with sudden spirit, "to ask the High Council to excommunicate Avard."

Lyman's anger burned afresh. "So you want to punish those who are fighting for their rights! Is that what you mean?"

"The church won't consent to torture."

"How about torture on the other side—raping women, beating old men to death, shooting little children? You know what a mob leader said? He said nits grow into lice and ordered a brute to kill John Wilbur's little son. By the Almighty God, Joseph, you can drive the Danites out if you want to, but if you do you'll be a dead man in a month."

"Avard must be driven out," said Joseph, but he did not look at Lyman. "You'd better talk with Sidney and Brigham and Parley. Learn how they feel."

"I know how they feel. Didn't Sidney say we'd walk on the dead bodies of our enemies? Parley and Brigham aren't cowards. But you're our leader. It's not time to pray now, Joseph. It's time to fight."

"Go, Brother Lyman, and leave me to ask of God."

After Lyman had gone, Joseph left the cabin and entered the woods. He wanted to place himself close to God and feel His will in the matter; but even while he knelt in prayer, a terrible thing was happening a few miles away.

Tim McBride left Joseph, feeling very guilty and determined to leave the Danites at once. If he did so, he well knew that he would have to flee for his life; but this he was prepared to do, having had enough of torture and bloodshed. Upon entering the settlement at Haun's Mill where his family lived, he observed that several immigrant families had moved in during his absence, and had pitched their tents behind the blacksmith shop. Two hundred yards beyond was the Decker home, and there lived Lucy Ann, the lass of sixteen whom he loved. He wanted to tell her that he was leaving the Danites and would never again torture a human being by burning the hair off his body and pressing burning embers into his flesh. When he knocked on the door, it was Lucy Ann who opened it.

"Hello," he said bashfully, for he was only nineteen.

"Hello, Tim," she said, and smiled to show the dimples in her cheeks.

"I want to talk to you. Can I?"

"Why, I guess so, Tim. You in trouble?"

"Sort of. Would you walk out to the creek with me?"

"Wait till I get my hat." She got a straw hat and put it on and tied two blue ribbons under her chin.

Out by the stream he told her what he had done. He told how he had gone with the Destroying Angels to wreak vengeance on his enemies; of his talk with Joseph; his shame. He saw horror in her eyes.

"It's awful," said Lucy Ann, "but no worse than they do. Did you know Governor Boggs has just given another order?"

"What now?"

"He says all us saints has to leave Missouri or be killed."

"When did he say that?"

"While you were away. Father told me."

"I guess we'll all be killed," Tim said. He gazed at her fair young face. "Lucy Ann, if we ain't killed will you marry me?"

"It isn't any time to talk about marriage."

"I know," he said. "But I'd like to kiss you once before we're killed."

Lucy Ann looked at his sober face and smiled. "Here, kiss the dimple." Holding his breath, he pressed his lips to her dimpled cheek and then gazed at her lips. "Could I kiss your mouth?"

"Just one little kiss, Tim. This isn't any time to be kissing." She pouted her lips and he had barely touched them with his own when she drew away and began to weep. "I'm so unhappy," she said. After a moment she dried her tears and asked brightly: "What is Joseph like?"

Tim was troubled by the question. "He's tall and kingly. His eyes are blue."

"Blue? They should be black." She wept again.

He put an arm around her and drew her to his breast, and for a long while she lay against him with her eyes closed. He looked at her face and sighed or gently touched the long braids of her hair. He wondered if they would be killed and if Lucy Ann would ever marry him. She had not promised but had said she might.

Hours later he was in her home. He had said good night and was hesitating at the door when he heard galloping horsemen. Leaping to a window and looking out, he saw men running from all directions to the blacksmith shop and vanishing into it like squirrels into burrows. Beyond these fleeing men were a hundred horsemen, thundering into the village. Tim saw all this in one flash and then swung and seized Lucy Ann and disappeared with her through a rear door and headed for the woods. As he ran, half-dragging the girl, he heard shots behind him and the shouts of the mob. Grasping one of Lucy's hands, he plowed through a thicket and dropped face downward, with his arms around her and his voice crying to her to be still.

She was weeping. "My father and mother!" she wailed and started up; but he jerked her fiercely to the earth.

"Be quiet! Please!"

He was only three hundred yards from the shop and could clearly hear the shouting and cursing and the firing of guns. For several minutes there was steady bombardment. Then there was a high thin scream, followed by silence. In a few moments there was sudden galloping, with the feet of horses loud and terrible in the streets. Struggling to be free, Lucy implored him to go back and find her parents; but he crushed her under him and put a hand to her mouth. Her parents, he whispered, were dead now or had escaped. And besides, he had forgotten his gun.

Telling her to be very quiet, he crawled on hands and knees until he could see more clearly. The mob had fired a home and it was a bursting bonfire in a wall of darkness. The horses were nowhere in sight but he could see several men prowling like shadows around the blacksmith shop or from house to house. Softly he crawled back to Lucy and told her to follow him; and they went deeper into the thicket until the leafy ceiling shut out the golden radiance of the bonfire. They would have to remain here, he told her, and be very quiet until the mob had gone; and he reflected grimly, bitterly, that it would be best for him to return to his Danite gang. There was no other way: not with a leader like Joseph who prayed when he should have been marching at the head of his men.

Exhausted now, Lucy was lying face downward with hands to her mouth and moaning in her breath. Tim lay at her side and put an arm around her. A few moments ago he had heard a lone shot but the firing had stopped now and there was no sound of riders. The settlement was as quiet as a graveyard but he knew that men were prowling stealthily, looking for those who had escaped. A little later, when he heard a prowler coming through the thicket, he rose to his hands and knees.

"Lucy Ann," he whispered in her ear, "don't move! In God's name, don't move!"

He rose quietly to his feet and listened. The prowler was coming his way: for one swift moment above the bushes he had seen the glint of a gun barrel and the pale moon of a face. As softly as a cat, Tim moved away from Lucy and stood behind a clump of bushes and waited. The intruder was coming softly too, stopping from time to time as if to look around him and explore. Rigid, with clenched fists, Tim waited; and when the man stepped within reach, Tim struck a blow that felled him. He leapt to the fallen man and clutched his throat; and his desperate strength was such that the man did no more than to kick out with his legs and in a little while he did not kick at all. Then Tim moved off the body and knelt for a moment to gaze at the bulging eyes.

He returned to Lucy and patted her gently. "I got one of them," he whispered, and showed her the man's gun.

Lucy sat up to look at him. "I didn't hear you shoot."

"I just used my hands. I choked him to death."

"Oh, Tim!"

She burst into grief and frantically he clapped a palm to her mouth. "Shut up!" he whispered. "He was an enemy!" He removed his hand.

"Tim," she gasped, "it's horrible!" She gazed at his big hands as if she were looking at a snake. "You—choked him?"

"What difference does it make how I done it?"

Shuddering, she drew away from him and bowed to her lap in silent grief.

It was long after midnight before Tim ventured forth, with Lucy Ann trailing him. He had nerves of iron but they were not iron enough for what he saw now. It was not the terrified women and children who had come out of hiding to seek husbands and fathers; it was not their strangled efforts to keep their grief soundless, lest their enemies might hear. It was first the dead body of his grandfather, old Tom McBride who had fought gallantly in the War of Independence; for the old man had been hacked with a corn cutter that now lay near him, rimmed with hair and blood. His skull had been laid open. His white hair was a dark and clotted mass; his nose and a part of his lower jaw had been chopped away. And there was a lad of twelve, lying in the street with the entire top of his head blown off. There was an old woman with her back broken, dragging herself fearfully over the earth and looking around her, not knowing whether the two persons who watched her were enemies or friends.

But most of all it was the slaughter of men and boys in the blacksmith shop. The mob had thrust rifle barrels through the cracks of the wall and had fired until every person in the shop had been wounded or killed. When Tim wrested the door open and looked in, he recoiled: it was not the dead piled in heaps: it was the wounded with arms and legs and backs broken, or a part of their faces shot away. A few of them, supposing the enemy had returned, now struggled in terror; and one horribly mutilated man rose to his knees and begged for his life.

When morning came, Tim found his parents hiding in a maple thicket. "I talked to the prophet," he said to Moroni, his father.

Moroni came out of hiding and his wife Kate followed him. He went down· a path and stood for a long moment gazing at the ruins of the settlement before turning to his son.

"What did Joseph say?"

"He said for me to leave the Danites. He says he doesn't want no such organization in the church and will kick the leaders out."

"Did he say what he expects us to do? Are we to stay and be chopped to pieces?"

"He didn't say. You should see **what the mob** done."

"I don't have to see. I heard the shooting."

Tim clenched his big hands. "By God, I think I should go to the Danites right now! We should kill this mob!"

"No," said Moroni, taking his son's arm. "What Joseph says is best, that we will do. Right now we must bury the dead."

They went over to bury the dead of whom there were nineteen. Nearby was an old well; and to this they dragged the corpses and dropped them into the cool dark depth, putting the men in first and the boys on top of them, and then shoveling sod to hide them from sight. Between the blacksmith shop and the well was a path of blood when the labor was done. The old woman with the broken back had died but they did not bury her with the men and boys. They put her on a wagon with the wounded to take her to Far West.

When Tim returned to Lucy Ann, he found her unconscious at his mother's feet. She had fainted, Kate said, and they had not been able to fetch her to. Tim gathered Lucy in his arms and carried her to the wagons, and the survivors set out over the prairie, with two wagons in the lead upon which lay the dead and dying.

"I still think," said Tim angrily, "that I should go back to the Danites. By God, are we to let them kill all of us?"

"They won't," Moroni said. "Just do as the prophet tells you."

"But he might not always know the best thing to do."

"God talks to him," said Tim's mother. "He should know."

"Yes," Tim admitted gloomily, "he should."

It was late afternoon when the caravan pulled into Far West. Joseph came out and looked at the persons in the first wagons, and then broke into tears and covered his face with his hands.

CHAPTER XXI

EARLY THE NEXT MORNING, RIDERS CAME TO TELL JOSEPH THAT LARGE bodies of armed men under Generals Lucas and Doniphan were marching on Far West; and other scouts reported butcheries besides the one at Haun's Mill. Joseph withdrew to pray, but Lyman and Parley got their indomitable heads together.

"Now we have to fight," said Lyman. "By the holy God, we should have fought months ago!"

"Yes," Parley said. "Lyman, what's your plan?"

"To fight. To fight until we are all in our graves."

"Yes, I know. But we might not be in our graves. Shall we fortify Far West or march out?"

"Fortify it. What chance would we stand marching out? Make them come up to us behind our breastworks."

"I think that's the best plan. Shall we consult Joseph?"

"To hell with Joseph. He's off somewhere praying. I want every able-bodied man to work with me all night getting our defense up. You see to the guns and ammunition."

"Did you know," asked Parley, "that the mobs are joining the soldiers, dressed up like Indians, red with warpaint?"

"God, yes, I know it."

"Two thousand men will march upon us tomorrow."

Lyman swung impatiently. "Parley, we have to fight. There's nothing else to do."

"But after we're killed, they'll attack our women and murder our children. Don't you think we might arrange peace?"

"Twice I've arranged peace. Twice they've betrayed me. You do as you think best but I'm fighting from now on if I wade in blood to my waist."

Parley looked at him. He liked the man. He liked his courage and will, and he wished Joseph had in him the steel of Lyman and the cunning of Brigham. "I'll take care of the guns and ammunition," he said, and went away.

During this evening, Lyman was talking with the prophet when a rider approached.

"What is it now?" asked Joseph anxiously.

"General Doniphan sends a message."

"The dirty dog!" roared Lyman. "What message does he send?"

"He says to send out the three leaders or he'll kill everyone in the city."

"What leaders?" asked Joseph.

"I don't know, sir."

"Tell him," said Lyman, "that if he sends any more messages we'll cut his black heart out!"

"Brother Lyman," said Joseph reprovingly. "Perhaps if we——"

"Perhaps hell! Tell Doniphan I'm fortifying this city tonight. Tell him to march in and we'll blow a hole in him a skunk can crawl through."

"Yes, sir."

"How far out is the damned mob?"

"About two miles. On Goose Creek."

"We'll be ready in the morning. Tell him that."

"Yes, sir."

And all night the saints labored with feverish energy, building crude fortifications to protect the town. Lyman went from spot to spot, encouraging, commanding, and working with the men; but he was worried about a saint named Hinkle. Hinkle, taking the title of colonel, had organized a small army and was marching toward Far West. Lyman did not like the man. He did not like his eyes, for they had the cowardly alertness of the eyes of a coyote; and he did not like the weak mouth that hid in a well-trimmed beard. But when he suggested to Parley that Hinkle might betray them, Parley laughed at the notion.

"He's a fine man, Lyman. He'll be here in the morning to help us."

"I wouldn't trust him as far as I'n see the leg of a gnat. Do we have enough ammunition?"

"I think so. Enough to kill ten thousand men if we shoot straight."

"But we're short of guns."

"Yes," said Parley, and looked around him at the labor of a thousand men. They were building parapets, digging trenches and piling bags of sand, with women and a few children assisting. There was no moon tonight, and only a few stars. Joseph was working too, but where the wily Brigham was, nobody knew. Brigham never put himself where the trouble was hottest. He was never arrested or pursued or shot at, because he was never close enough to danger zones.

Rigdon was here, though he was too terrified to do much; and Tim McBride labored like a beaver and cursed himself for leaving the Danites. Nightlong, Lyman moved from group to group, directing the labor, urging the men to greater efforts, or waking those who, exhausted, had fallen asleep. "Up, Ben! We'll all be shot tomorrow and then you'll have time to sleep." Or to a weary woman: "Sister Emily, you'd better go home now and rest." Or to a lad: "Here, my boy, you run on to bed now. You'll be a fine soldier when you grow up."

"Brother Lyman, could I have a rifle tomorrow?"

"No, my lad. You stay back out of sight."

When morning came, gray and cool and ominous, the saints were behind their breastworks and their guns, ready for attack. A thousand of them lay prone in a wide arc and gazed into the east. Lyman stood on a lookout spot and waited too; and when he saw Hinkle riding in alone, he called to Parley and Joseph and went out to meet him. Hinkle came up.

"General Lucas sends word he wants to meet the leaders and see what is to be done."

"Meet us?" said Lyman suspiciously. "You mean it's a truce?"

"Yes. He says everything can be settled peaceably."

"Who brought this about?"

"I did," said Hinkle proudly. "I talked him into it."

Lyman turned to Parley and Joseph. "Do you believe him?"

"I do," said Parley; and Joseph said: "God be praised!"

"Listen, Hinkle, do you swear by your own soul that this is true?"

"Of course I do. General Lucas says there's no sense in fighting. He wants to talk things over."

"We are ready to fight. We're not afraid of the whole damned army." Lyman stepped closer to the man and looked at him intently. "Where's the forces you were bringing?"

"Back there. They're waiting for us. They've made friends with the army."

Lyman was still unconvinced. "Shall we go?" he asked Joseph.

"Yes, Brother Lyman. God is protecting us this day."

"All right," said Lyman. "We'll go."

The three men rode with Hinkle out to Goose Creek. As soon as Lyman observed the way General Lucas and his men sat their horses, he had an impulse to turn and flee; but he rode up and said: "General, we understand you wish to confer with us." He had hardly finished before Hinkle cut in.

"General Lucas, here are the prisoners I agreed to deliver to you."

Astounded by the perfidy, Lyman turned his horse sharply, but he saw a hundred rifles aimed at his head; and a moment later a thousand men yelled like a horde of Indians. Many of them were dressed and painted like savages, and now brandished their arms and howled. Lyman looked at Joseph and Parley who were speechless and then addressed Lucas.

"General, what is the meaning of this?"

"You are my prisoners," said Lucas, grinning.

"Colonel Hinkle said——"

"That was a trap," said Hinkle blandly. "You walked right into it."

"You scurvy Judas!" cried Lyman. "You dog of a Benedict Arnold!"

"Be careful," said Hinkle, and his bearded face grinned. "There's a hundred cocked rifles aimed at you."

"Let them fire!" said Lyman furiously. To Lucas: "How many pieces of silver did this dog of a Judas receive?"

"He's defending his country's flag against treason. Come with me." He waved his sword and marched off with the prisoners.

They were taken to open ground and guarded by a dozen armed men. Rigdon had been captured too and now was thrust among them; and all night they sat or stood in a drizzling rain, with the guards jeering and telling foul stories, or boasting how they would rape the women in Far West.

"Hey, Joe, show us an angel!"

"Which one is Joe Smith?" asked another guard, drawing nearer.

"Him there. Him with the big nose."

"So you're Joe Smith, are you? Well, by God, let's have a revelation."

"Or a miracle. Tell the Lord to strike me dead."

"You sons-of-bitches, you know what we aim to do with you all?"

Lyman looked at Sidney. The man had been behaving strangely for an hour and now fell forward as if he had been struck a blow and vomited between his knees. A few moments later he was possessed by a fit. He bellowed horribly and rolled his big solemn eyes around and around in his skull, seeing nothing, knowing nothing except his agony of soul. He lay on his side in the wet and turned over and over convulsively, kicking and striking as if tortured with hot irons. The guards were filled with loud and obscene joy. They pushed forward to stare in amazement and then slap one another and yell wildly with mirth.

"By God, he's got a devil in him!"

"Yeh, if you're a prophet, cast that-there devil out."

"Holy Jesus, look at him! He's bleeding at the mouth. By the mouth-almighty Christ, if that ain't a Mormon for you!"

A guard moved in and kicked at Rigdon. "You ripsnorting snag you, what kind of a monkeyshine is this?"

"Back!" Lyman roared.

The guards leapt back and cocked their rifles. "What's that?" asked the leader, aiming at Lyman's head. "You want me to blow your skull off?"

"Shoot and be damned! This man is sick. Haven't you any respect for a sick man?"

"Sick, hell. He's in a fit, by Jesus."

Lyman and Parley looked at Rigdon who was still in the throes of a convulsion, his eyes bulging, his mouth drooling. Joseph gazed straight ahead at the drizzling sky.

"Sidney's afraid," Lyman said to Parley, not knowing whether to feel pity or contempt. He was soaked to his hide now, and the others also; and all night they sat here in the rain, rarely speaking for there was nothing to be said. After a while Sidney lay quietly, with water running off his white face or into the furrow of his closed white mouth. Joseph had not spoken since the betrayal. Hour after hour he sat like a man of stone, his gaze on the gray wetness of the sky; and he neither stirred nor looked around him when guards prodded him with a long stick to make him speak.

When morning came rain was still falling; the wide world was bleak and wet. Sidney now aroused himself and sat up, his ghastly pallor enhanced by his long matted hair and his clinging clothes. The guards stood off a little way, silenced at last, and stared thoughtfully at their woebegone prisoners. When the four men were told they would be taken into Far

West to change their clothes and thence to Jackson County to stand trial, Lyman shrugged in his wet garments and spoke in a low voice to Parley.

"I hope our men are ready with their rifles."

"Yes," Parley said.

They did not know the extent of the treachery.

Tim McBride was soon to learn. After the prisoners had been allowed to change their clothes they were taken to a wagon and there looked beyond the army surrounding them to the village they had helped to build. Tim saw that Joseph was weeping, that Sidney was humped over as if sick; but Lyman and Parley were defiant. He watched the wagon roll away into the east, surrounded on all sides by the soldiers, and then turned back to the town, wondering when and where the next blow would fall. He did not wonder long.

The wagon had hardly disappeared when a general named Clark rode in and arrested fifty-six of the men and sent them posthaste under military guard. Then Clark sent criers to assemble the saints in the public square and spoke to them while sitting on his horse.

"I am General Clark," he said. "Colonel Hinkle, your military leader, agreed to four terms to save you from destruction. The first was that you surrender your leaders and this you have done. The second was that you give up your arms. The third was that you sign over your property to pay for the cost of this war." Clark paused and turned on his horse to look around him.

"Another article yet remains for you to comply with, and that is that you leave the State forthwith; and whatever may be your feelings concerning this, or whatever your innocence, it is nothing to me. I am here to see that the terms of the treaty are fulfilled. The character of this State has suffered almost beyond redemption from the character, conduct and influence that you have exerted. And we deem it an act of justice to restore her character to its former standing among the States by every proper means." He paused again. A thousand men, women and children were listening to him, but in the vast crowd not a person spoke or made a sound.

"The orders of the governor to me were that you should be exterminated, and not allowed to remain in the State; and had your leaders not been given up and the terms of the treaty complied with, before this you and your families would have been destroyed and your homes in ashes. You must not think of staying here another season or of putting in crops, for the moment you do this the citizens will be upon you. If I am called here again in case of a non-compliance of a treaty made, do not think I shall act any more as I have done, you need not expect any mercy, but extermination, for I am determined the governor's order shall be executed.

"As for your leaders do not once think—do not imagine for a moment—do not let it enter your mind that they will be delivered or that you will see their faces again, for their fate is fixed—their die is cast. Their doom is sealed. I am sorry, gentlemen, to see so great a number of apparently intelligent men found in the situation you are; and oh, that I could invoke the Great Spirit, the unknown God, to rest upon you and make you sufficiently intelligent to break that chain of superstition and liberate you from those fetters of fanaticism, with which you are bound, that you no longer worship a man!

"I would advise you to scatter abroad and never again organize yourselves with bishops, presidents and so forth, lest you excite the jealousies of the people and subject yourselves to the same calamities that have now come upon you. You have always been the aggressors; you have brought upon yourselves these difficulties by being disaffected and not being subject to rule; and my advice is that you become as other citizens, lest by a recurrence of these events you bring upon yourselves irretrievable ruin.

"You will appoint a committee of twelve to make arrangements for your removal; and these men will wear white badges on their hats so that in going from place to place their mission will be known. And now, though your leaders have surrendered their arms, it is necessary to search your homes for hidden weapons." He turned to his soldiers. "Search every home and find every weapon of every kind in this town."

Well, Tim reflected, it could have been worse: they were to be disarmed and driven out with only the clothes on their backs but they were to go in peace. They would never see their leaders again, and those who were not shot or jailed for life would be wanderers on the face of the earth, homeless like the Jews, and with no land to call their own. But they would not be beaten or murdered on their way out of Missouri.

He turned away to search for Lucy Ann when he was stopped dead in his tracks by blood-curdling yells; for a thousand men painted like savages were riding down upon the village. At once there was complete pandemonium. No matter which way Tim looked, he could see his people fleeing, with horsemen in mad pursuit, brandishing their guns and knives and clubs, and almost running the women and children down. Some vanished into homes, and others poured out of homes and fled, carrying infants or a few household goods or nothing at all. Such mad confusion Tim had never seen before; and even so, what he saw was only a small part of what might have been seen in the holocaust of looting and flogging and raping that overwhelmed the village.

He ran first to the shack in which Lucy and her people had been living but it was deserted, with a window smashed and a door almost torn from its hinges; and in rage and fear he went from street to street, looking at the persons fleeing all around him, seeing the mob pour into buildings and stagger out with their arms full of goods, or into homes to steal or destroy what they found there. Nobody paid any attention to him. He was only an unarmed man who ran wildly as if scared out of his wits; and the mobsters, looking in their war paint like Indians, drunk with whiskey or triumph, yelling and fighting among themselves to possess the loot, cared nothing about a man who dashed anxiously from street to street, looking for a face. Now and then he paused to stare at men laden with the goods they had filched. If he saw a fleeing girl he pursued her until close enough to learn that she was not Lucy Ann; and then set off again, racing like a madman, with sweat pouring down his face and breath scalding his lungs. He had searched for an hour when upon the threshold of a house he stopped in amazement.

There were several men in the room and a woman; and in one swift glance, Tim grasped the whole scene and realized what was being done. He saw the naked woman bound to a bed and the men around her; and in this moment Tim went mad. Springing forward he struck with all his might at the man embracing the woman. A few moments later he was senseless on the floor.

He came out of darkness and pain, groping for light and meaning and trying to sit up and look around him. There was a sudden thrust of pain in his skull like the entrance of a knife; and when he raised a hand to his hair he felt the blood in it and moved his fingers around an open wound. With horror and rage he remembered now, but when he strove to rise he fell back and darkness closed around him again. A little later he was dimly aware of men bending over him and tearing his shirt off; and still later, when the blows of a whip fell, he was hardly conscious of the pain. How long they flogged him he could never have told, nor did he know when they left. How long he lay here naked in his own blood he never knew. When again he could see and think, there was darkness around him, though whether of his pain or the night he could not be sure until he crawled to the door and looked out. He could see stars. After a while he could hear voices and feet; but the effort to learn if they were of friend or enemy overcame him and he fainted and lay still.

In the days that followed he was in a strange house and Lucy Ann was his nurse. He lay on his stomach because his back was a welter of wounds and bruises. He wanted to talk. He wanted to know what had happened and if the prophet was dead; but when he strove to speak, Lucy closed his mouth for him and told him to hush. "Don't talk yet." she said. He reached out to touch her and she gave him one of her hands. He looked at her face and thought she was thinner and whiter than she had been.

One day he said: "Lucy Ann, you must tell me what happened. Is Joseph dead?"

"I don't know. I guess he is."

"Did they shoot him?"

"I don't know. All we know is that Lucas sent an order to General Doniphan."

"An order to what?"

"To take Joseph and the others in the public square and shoot them. But General Doniphan said it was cold-blooded murder and he wouldn't."

"God bless him. What did they do then?"

"They took Joseph away."

"Where am I? In Far West?"

"Yes. You mustn't talk any more now."

"I guess they beat me, didn't they?"

"I shouldn't think you'd need to ask that."

"Did they beat all our men?"

"No, just a few. Don't talk any more now."

"What are the saints doing?"

"Oh, getting ready to leave."

He turned a little to gaze at her. "Did they—" He hardly knew how to ask the question. He looked down at her body, wondering if she had been ravished. "Did they treat you rough?"

"No, I hid out in a field. While I was hiding, some men they came out and shot all the horses and cows. They just shot them and rode away."

"Did they shoot all the cattle we have?"

"No, just some of it."

"Lucy Ann, who is our leader now?"

"We don't have any, Tim. They arrested all the leaders and took them away."

"But not Brigham Young. Did they find him?"

"I don't think so. But we don't know where Brigham is."

Tim was thoughtful a long while. "I must get well," he said. "We must find Brigham Young."

CHAPTER XXII

WHEN JOSEPH WAS HAULED AWAY UNDER GUARD WITH HIS COMPANIONS he was so depressed that he did not speak at all during the first day's journey; but in the camp on Crooked River he slept well and felt new hope and strength when morning came. After they set forth again, going none of them knew where, he spoke cheerfully, saying the Lord had made Himself known during the night. "The Lord told me our lives will be saved."

"He did?" cried Rigdon.

Parley said: "That makes me feel all right. I can face anything now."

Lyman believed too that the Lord had spoken but it was his way to depend on his own prowess. He was hatching plots.

"Did the Lord say," Rigdon asked, "where they're taking us?"

"No. He only said our lives will be spared."

Over Rigdon's large bloodless face came a smile of joy and peace. "Glory be to God!" he said, and looked around him at the guards, and at General Wilson who was in charge. Seeing his stare, Wilson rode up to the wagon.

"How are you? All right?"

"I guess so," Parley said.

Wilson looked kind and jolly but he was inordinately proud to have these men in his custody; for he had helped to drive the saints out of Independence four years ago. He gazed at them now as if they were a small menagerie of unusual beasts. "Why did you come back to Missouri anyhow?"

"Because," said Joseph, "the Lord commanded it."

"Oh, the Lord did! He seems to want to keep you in a peck of misery all the time."

"Righteousness," said Rigdon, feeling bolder because his life was to be spared, "has always been persecuted. The Savior was crucified."

Wilson grinned at that. What sort of men these prisoners were he could not for the life of him tell. "Why didn't you go to some State where you could live in peace?"

"In peace!" Lyman roared. He was annoyed by this paunched fellow who not long ago had been only a storekeeper. "Where have the righteous ever found peace in all the years of man?"

Wilson sighed and considered. "What makes you think you're more righteous than other folks?"

Rigdon's big face looked full of indignation and sermon. Had he not predicted on the last Fourth of July that the saints would so completely exterminate their enemies that blood would dye mountain and prairie from ocean to ocean? Yet here he was, being hauled in a wagon under heavy guard as if he were a common scoundrel! "Sir," he said, "people everywhere are lost in sin. It is a thieving, lying, blasphemous world. Our church is the right church, the only true church, the only church through which souls can be saved. If we are more righteous than other people, it is by God's will."

Wilson threw a leg over his horse's neck and grinned at Rigdon. "You seem to be mighty sure of yourself."

"We are. We'd be fools not to be when we have a prophet who talks with God."

Joseph did not like Sidney's loud and pompous declarations. He lay back in the wagon and closed his eyes. Lyman turned to the general.

"I suppose you're taking us somewhere to hang us."

"Oh, no. I'm taking you to stand trial."

"Trial for what?"

"Probably for treason."

"Treason!" Rigdon bellowed. "Sir, treason for what?"

"For rebellion," said Wilson, still gazing curiously at the men. "You've thrown half of Missouri into civil war."

"Because we defend our rights you call it civil war. What about the mobs who beat our men and attacked our women?" It was Lyman speaking. He was angry.

Before Wilson could answer, Joseph said: "Brother Lyman, don't speak with so hot a temper. It does no good."

"Women," said Wilson, "were attacked by Mormon mobsters. Your Danites tortured and murdered and raped."

"It's a lie!" Rigdon cried.

Joseph sat up and looked at the general. "The Danites were no part of my church. They were brigands who pretended to be saints. They have been expelled."

"It's high time." After a moment Wilson added: "Where's your leader named Brigham Young?"

"Oh," cried Lyman witheringly, "hasn't the state of Missouri with its thousands of armed bandits been able to catch him? Brigham is too smart to be betrayed by a Judas like Hinkle—or to be captured by all the hellhounds you can muster."

"We'll find him," said Wilson calmly. "We'll hang him."

"I predict," said Rigdon, half-rising and looking as leonine as he could, "I predict that you'll hang none of us. God is guarding us, not your bandits."

"We'll see about that," said Wilson. "As for Brigham Young, I predict we'll have him in twenty-four hours."

"If you catch Brigham," said Lyman, "you can take me out to a public square and shoot me without trial."

"Oh, we'll shoot you. And the trial won't take long. Just be patient." And Wilson grinned at them and rode to the head of his troops.

Long before they saw the town, the prisoners knew they were going to Independence. Lyman said they were taking them back to the mobs that once chased him from hell to breakfast; but Joseph told him to be comforted, that God would protect them day and night. Lyman said he preferred to protect himself, and wished he had the army of desperate men whom he was leading a few days ago.

The prisoners were not delivered to a mob. They were hauled up and down the streets of Independence as if they were strange animals brought from a jungle; and hundreds of persons fell into line to stare at them. Though a few jeered, the saints were surprised to see so many friendly and sympathetic faces. Indeed, after spending two days and nights in a dirty cell with only a floor for a bed, the men were housed in the best hotel and allowed to move freely, with only a few guards to watch them.

Most of the persons with whom they talked were friendly. Some, like an old, gray woman, wanted to know if Joseph pretended to be the Lord.

"No," he said, "I am only mortal man."

"You don't think you're God?"

"I am a man sent here by God to preach the gospel."

She was disappointed. All sorts of men preached all sorts of gospel. "But don't you cast out devils?"

"I have cast out a few," said Joseph.

"If," said Rigdon, "he cast all the devils out of human beings he'd have to work twenty-four hours a day and be ten thousand men."

She looked at Rigdon. "Are you a prophet too?"

"Well," he said uneasily, "I've done a little predicting. But Joseph is the only real prophet among us."

"And what do you do?" she asked, turning to Parley.

"Oh," he said, grinning broadly, "I just preach some and try to mind my own business."

She gazed from one to another of the four men, disappointed in all of them. "I thought," she said at last, "you Mormons had horns."

"We did have," said Lyman scathingly. "The bandits knocked them off."

"We are," said Joseph, "only ordinary men."

She decided they were, and so did others who talked with them. The townspeople, as a matter of fact, were so friendly that Wilson with difficulty found three men who would volunteer to take the prisoners to Richmond for trial; and these, more interested in whiskey than in guardianship, got dead drunk the first night out and gave their arms to the prisoners.

"This is our chance," said Lyman, looking at the drunken guards sprawled on the earth.

"No," said Joseph. "God is protecting us. I'll not run."

"Mebbe," said Lyman impatiently, "this is the Almighty's way of helping us. He let the guards get drunk so we can escape."

But Joseph would not budge, and Sidney and Parley could not prevail against him. The next day they resumed the journey, and the guards looked at them with sly astonishment, as if wondering why they had not fled. In Richmond they were thrust into a deserted house and padlocked ankle to ankle with a huge chain. The charges against them, they were told, were treason, murder, arson, larceny, theft and stealing.

Early one morning General Clark came to them with several men. He pointed to the chained prisoners and said: "Gentlemen, you shall have the honor of shooting the Mormon leaders on Monday morning at eight o'clock."

"Fine!" said one of the men; and they all loaded their rifles with two balls each.

After the men had gone, Lyman gazed at the chain on his leg. "God gave us a chance to escape. Now we'll be shot."

"No," said Joseph, "we'll not be shot."

Sitting on a rude bench, chained ankle to ankle, the four men were silent until Lyman became aware that all was not right with Sidney. He turned to look at him and was appalled; for beyond all doubt the man was insane. Since the night when he writhed in convulsions, Sidney had behaved queerly, his lucid intervals alternating with slobbering madness; and now, after hearing that he was to be shot on Monday, he broke again and rolled his eyes and drooled. Lyman was chained next to him and tried to move away; but unexpectedly Rigdon threw his long arms around Lyman and gave a terrible yell that brought the guards on the run.

Seeing one of the prisoners behaving so, a guard cried by the holy angels that there was a devil in the man, and forthwith procured a long stick and thrust at Rigdon. When gouged, Sidney roared like a goaded beast and smote his own flesh. The guards liked this scene. They entered the dungeon and sat on their heels and howled with laughter.

"Look at him!" cried one. "He's as crazy as a bat!" He thrust again with the stick and Sidney gave a roar of insanity and grief.

Laughing until tears washed their cheeks, the guards rocked shoulder to shoulder or leaned forward to gaze at Rigdon and poke him again. His eyes luminous with hate, Lyman stared at the tormentors; but Joseph and Parley looked beyond them, trying not to see or hear. One of the men was annoyed by Lyman's contempt.

"You know what we done?" he asked. "I'll tell you. You know how many of your babies' brains we knocked out against trees?"

"And what we done to your women!"

"I'n preach that lick-spittle a sermon," said one of the guards, rising to his feet. "Listen, you paddies and wolverines, you snags and griddle-greasers and buckeyes, you pot-soppers and hard-heads and hawkeyes, greenhorns and Whigs, rackensacks and masons, you call us Missourians pukes! Well, I'll tell you. We drink brandy-rovers and gin-jumpers and tickle-me-in-the-gaslight whiskey punches; but we don't fall into fits!"

"Shut your jib," said one of his companions and dragged the man down. "I want a-tell these pot-soppers what we done to their women. You know Mary Kenyon?"

"Let's tell them some dirty stories to cheer them up. You want a-hear some dirty stories, you Mormon snags?"

Lyman was gazing with such vindictive hatred that one of the guards, momentarily abashed, seized the stick and thrust at him. "Don't look at me that way or I'll poke your eyes out!"

"Poke that ringtail roarer again. I like to hear him yell."

"No, let's tell them some dirty stories."

"Let's tell what we done to Mary Kenyon. How many of us was there?"

Joseph could endure this no longer. He rose with his chains clanking and shook his clenched hands at the guards. "Silence!" he thundered. "Ye fiends out of the infernal pit! In the name of Jesus Christ I rebuke you and command you to be still! Stop this vile talk or you or I will die this instant!"

Astounded by the wrathful majesty of the man, the guards rose hastily to their feet. They looked at one another and then retreated to the door and looked at Joseph; and then step by step they withdrew from the dungeon until only one face was visible. This face peered in but after a moment it disappeared.

Joseph sank slowly to the bench.

Two days later the prisoners were brought to trial. Joseph had hoped to appear before an impartial court but as soon as he saw the face of Judge King, of Tom Birch, the prosecuting attorney, and of the assembled witnesses, he knew he could expect no justice here. Both judge and attorney looked triumphant.

But this was not a trial, the prisoners soon learned. It was an investigation. The charges were murder, larceny, arson, theft and treason; and day after day for two weeks, witnesses testified against them. The first to appear was Ike Gibbs, a tall gaunt farmer from the Crooked River area.

"Mr. Gibbs, do you know the prisoners?"

"I kallate I do."

"Do you know any good about them?"

"Dog on it, no, not a thing."

"Were you present during the murders on Crooked River?"

"I was there but I was a-runnun for my life most of the time."

"Were any of the prisoners on the scene of the murders?"

"One," said Gibbs, peering in turn at the prisoners.

"Which one?"

"Him there." He pointed at Parley.

"Any others?"

"Not as I'n be sure about."

"Was this man there?" asked Birch, indicating Joseph.

"I can't say. I don't know as he was." He stared at Joseph long and earnestly. "But him, mebbe he was." He pointed at Rigdon who, white and drooping, looked as if he lived between vomiting and prayer.

Now and then the judge interrupted to say, "You prisoners will have to get your witnesses here to testify for you—if you have any." After the statement was made a fourth time, Lyman rose in fury.

"Witnesses! You throw our witnesses in jail as fast as they show up!"

"Silence!" The judge turned to the clerk. "Write that down. It's a strong point for treason."

General Doniphan, the man who had refused to execute the prisoners, had volunteered to represent them. He now rose. "What good will witnesses do my clients? If a cohort of angels were to come down and declare these men innocent, you would jail them anyway."

Judge King reddened and thumped his desk.

Hyrum Smith had been arrested and jailed separately from Joseph and the others but had been brought in with them for the investigation. When one forenoon he saw a Mormon brother peering into the courtroom, Hyrum beckoned to the man to enter, and then addressed the judge.

"Your honor, we have a witness here and he is ready to be sworn."

"Where?"

"Here," said Hyrum, and pushed the man forward.

"I object," said the prosecutor. "This is not a trial. We are investigating the prisoners to see if evidence will sustain the charges. There is no point——"

Doniphan rose and cut him short. "I'll be damned if the witness is not sworn! It's a shame to treat these defendants in this manner. They are not allowed to put a single witness on the stand. The witnesses they have sent for have been captured by force of arms and thrown into the bull pen. Is this an investigation or a farce?"

"An investigation," said Birch calmly.

"Well, by God, this man will be sworn and he will testify."

"Very well," said the judge.

The man was sworn but he had answered only one question when a huge rowdy leapt forward and grasped him by the nape of the neck and the seat of the trousers and kicked him bodily out of the courtroom. In towering rage, Doniphan was on his feet again; but the witness was fleeing for his life before the amazed general fully realized what had happened.

"Your honor," he bellowed, "what kind of a God damned farce is this? I demand the expulsion of this scoundrel from the room!"

"You'd better leave," said the judge.

The big fellow left but he looked back through the doorway and grinned.

Doniphan mopped his brow. "What's the use of my calling witnesses if they're to be thrown out on their faces?"

"The investigation will proceed," said the judge, addressing Birch.

The prosecution called a man who was once a Mormon but now an apostate. King looked at him with interest and decided to question the man himself. "Mr. Witness, is it true that Mormons send missionaries to foreign countries?"

"Yes, sir."

"Do the Mormons profess a belief in the seventh chapter of Daniel, the twenty-seventh verse?"

"They do."

The judge turned to the clerk. "Put that down. That is a strong point for treason."

And day after day the investigation proceeded. Most of the witnesses were apostates or members of the gangs in Daviess County; and when the evidence was all in, the prisoners stood guilty of every major crime except rape. But the most amazing incident came a little later. In summing up, Birch was so violent that he made himself sick with rage and eloquence. Suddenly breaking off in his harangue, he looked for a moment as if he would scream, and then vomited almost at the feet of the horrified judge. The distressed man doubled over and heaved out of convulsed sickness and straightened and wiped his mouth. "Your honor," he said, pale and apologetic, and was stricken again. Parley Pratt could not restrain a chuckle; but the other prisoners, used to anything now, looked very solemn and waited. "Your honor," said Birch, gazing with appalled eyes at the floor, "I need a few moments to recover."

After Birch had finished, the bold Doniphan rose again to his feet. He was being assisted by Pete Burnett who wore a pistol; and before Doniphan rose, Burnett said to him: "Let yourself go. I'll shoot the first man who attacks you."

And while Burnett sat with a cocked pistol, Doniphan let himself go. "Your honor," he said, "this court has spent two weeks trying to fasten every crime in the calendar upon the prisoners. You have called apostates and mobsters, scoundrels and thieves, horsewhippers and house-burners. You have called only persons who hate the Mormons and all that they stand for. You have tried to show that they are guilty of pillage and arson, larceny and murder and treason. You have made no attempt to show that they were law-abiding citizens who were protecting their property and defending their rights." Doniphan observed that Judge King had turned pale. He observed that persons crowded into the courtroom looked as if they were ready to mob him; and he heard their low hisses and jeers. But Pete Burnett was sitting with his pistol cocked.

Doniphan spoke again; and his hot temper got the best of him and rode in withering sarcasm upon his words. "You have proved nothing except a wish to have the lives of these men. You have proved nothing except that the Constitution of the United States has no place in this courtroom or in the judge who presides over it. First, last and all the time, you have sniffed hungrily at every lie, every false charge, every abominable heresy that tends to fasten the crime of treason upon Joseph Smith and his followers. That is justice, that is impartial investigation, that is the honor of Missouri as you represent them!"

He stepped past Birch who was still pale and sick. He drew close to Judge King and shook a fist at him; and when a man in the crowd moved forward, Burnett turned to him and showed his cocked pistol.

"Go on!" Burnett said.

"Your honor, my forefathers and yours came to this country two centuries ago to escape injustice and tyranny. They came to build a great and free nation. They fought a bloody war in defense of their principles, and drew up a charter to govern free men, and that charter is today the noblest document in history's annals. But you—you, forgetting why our grandfathers fought and died, forgetting why and by whom this great nation was founded, forgetting everything but prejudice and tyranny and injustice—you, sir, have chained these men in dungeons and refused them bail! You have planted spies in the dungeon with them! You have allowed guards to torture them, taunt them, tell them foul stories, insult them, and heap upon them every abuse that degraded men can think of. You have sent for witnesses and you have had them thrown into dungeons. You have allowed men to testify against them who have openly boasted of murdering their children and raping their wives; men who have told of taking Negresses out into the woods and of what they did to them there; men who have burned their homes and stolen their property, men who have sworn to neither eat nor drink until Joseph Smith is dead! That is the kind of justice found in this courtroom in Richmond in Missouri! That is the kind of farce you have allowed while newspapers all over this nation are crying out indignantly against what you have done!"

"Stop him!" a man cried, and in an instant, fifty men had risen to their feet.

Pete Burnett swung to face them. "Stay where you are! I'll drop the first man who moves!" He turned to Doniphan. "Go on, General."

"Your honor," said Doniphan, again speaking quietly, "when General Lucas commanded me to shoot these men in the public square in Far West, I refused. I said it would be cold-blooded murder. I risked court martial. But I'll dare court martial again before I see men shot down like rats in a free country. I'll give my life before I'll see you make a travesty of the principles our forefathers died for. These men, these prisoners before you, are not guilty of larceny or murder or treason. They are guilty of nothing except an effort to protect the homes they built. There has been no treason. There has been no killing except in self-defense. And I say to you before Almighty God that if you do not free them, if you do not let them go back to their wives and children, if you do not allow them to go peacefully out of this state, then your name will go down in history with that of Benedict Arnold as a traitor to the principles which Americans love! Your name will stink in the records, and be a shameful thing on the tongue of every child in our schools! Free these men, your honor: in the name of a just God, let justice be done!"

After this denunciation, the judge was as pale as the prosecutor who had sat throughout with his gaze on Doniphan's angry face. The spectators stirred, ready for attack; but Judge King saw their eagerness and rose to his feet.

"The evidence," he said, speaking thickly, "is sufficient to hold the prisoners for trial for treason. The guards will take them back to the jail."

CHAPTER XXIII

PARLEY WAS KEPT IN THE RICHMOND JAIL, BUT JOSEPH, SIDNEY AND Lyman, together with Joseph's brother Hyrum and a man named McRae, were taken to the Liberty jail in Clay County. This small stone building, with two tiny windows set high in the thick wall, seemed to Joseph more like a tomb than a prison; and he smiled bitterly when he looked around him and remembered its name. He still believed that God would set them free, but Lyman decided that if they were ever to get out of Missouri, they would have to help themselves. He became convinced of this after Sidney was allowed to escape. For Rigdon, since his arrest, had been violently insane so many times that he had wasted to skin and bone.

"They let him escape," said Lyman. "That means they don't think they'n convict us and would be glad to get rid of all of us."

"No. They were afraid Sidney would die in jail."

"We can get out if we set our minds to it. Hyrum, what do you think?"

Hyrum was a gentler image of his brother, a fair and superstitious young man given to visions and dreams. He now turned his haunted blue eyes on Joseph. "If the prophet says we'll be freed, then we will be."

"I imagine," said Lyman scornfully, "God would like to have us help a bit. Alex," he said, speaking to McRae, "what do you think? Are we going to sit here like hogs in a pen and eat this stinking food until we are too weak to crawl? We'll have leprosy next. I feel as if I'd been born in a stable and fed with the pigs."

Joseph looked up at a small square of light. "I wish," he said, "that all the mobocrats of the nineteenth century were in the middle of the sea, in a stone canoe, with an iron paddle; and that a shark would swallow the canoe and then be thrust into the bottom of hell, and the door locked and the key lost, with a blind man hunting for it."

That outburst made Lyman grin. "We'n get out of here. In fact, if we just dash out and run I don't think anyone would stop us."

"We could try it," said McRae. "They might shoot us but they intend to anyhow."

"For shame!" said Joseph. "God has told me our lives will be spared."

"Yes," said Lyman impatiently. "But He'll like it better if we help ourselves."

Lyman so persistently urged flight that the other men resolved to run with him for their lives; and one evening, when the meal was brought, they all bolted through the door. A half-dozen guards aimed cocked rifles at their heads and ordered them back; and back they went, scampering like wild beasts from a yard to a kennel.

"You want your heads blowed off?" asked a guard, looking in.

"We don't like this mansion," said McRae dryly. "The rug is too thick and the chairs are too soft and the food is making us fat."

The guard grinned. "The food is some of your Mormon beef."

Another guard stepped up. "Which one of you bastards killed my brother on Crooked River?"

McRae's long face broke into a sardonic grin. "A hundred men have asked us who killed their brothers and sons and fathers on Crooked River. I'm sorry to have to tell you that only one man was killed."

"Some mouth-almighty Mormon shot my brother. Was it you?"

"If it was, I suppose that's the reason I'm in a jail called liberty. I think I'll stretch out on my soft couch and take a nap."

"Oh, your soft couch!" The guard peered in at the unclean floor of stone. "How would you like a nice feather pillow?"

"And some strawberries and cream!"

"Or a bunch of roses to smell the place up nice."

"If we had any more comfort we'd get lazy. Take this mattress out and let me sleep on the floor."

"Your mattress!" cried the guard, looking again at the cold stone. He looked at McRae and grinned. "You ain't so damned bad. You'n joke about it." He stared at Lyman. "Hey, you the one who told General Wilson to shoot and be damned?"

"He's the one," said another guard.

"If he ever gets out of here," said McRae, "you'd better leave the country. He'll roast your thick skull in a bake oven."

"Listen, you snags and griddle-greasers! When you leave here it will be for the firing squad. You're all as good as dead."

"Fine!" McRae cried. "I'd rather sleep in a coffin than in a jail called liberty."

The guards liked that. They gazed at McRae and pondered. "Mebbe," said one, "it won't be a coffin. Just a hole in the ground."

"At least it will be clean."

"This does smell rotten," said a guard, sniffing. "Here, hand your pots out and I'll scrub them up for you."

Plotting escape, Lyman spent a part of his time quietly tunneling through the deep foundation of a wall. He used his hands to dig, or with a piece of stone he chipped mortar off and broke the rock, flake by flake. Though McRae encouraged him, nobody assisted in the labor. Nobody paid much attention except Hyrum whose fair face was constantly alive with fear.

Joseph believed God would deliver him; and though he weakened day by day under the foul air, the stone he slept on, the unclean food he ate, he gave his mind, nevertheless, to plans for rebuilding his church. Now and then one of the saints outside was allowed to talk with him. Tim McBride came.

"Don't you want me to get you out of here?" he asked, peering into the dungeon.

"How?" Lyman said.

"I'll raise an army."

"With cornstalks for guns!" cried McRae.

Tim had forgotten that all the rifles had been confiscated. He scratched his dirty head and considered. "I could try."

"No," said Joseph. "Brother Timothy, what are my people doing?"

"Freezing and starving to death—and getting ready to leave Missouri."

"Who is leading them?"

"Brigham Young."

"That is well. Brigham is a great man."

"At least," said Tim, "he never gets arrested."

"Was all our livestock killed?"

"No, just some of it."

"Where is Brigham moving to?"

"I don't know. He has some place in mind."

"Did Sidney Rigdon get back alive?"

"Yes, but he sure acts queer. And, dodgast it, was he mad! He says all our enemies will be murdered yet."

"He talks too much," said Lyman. "Tell him to shut up."

"Take," said Joseph, "this message to my people." The message was an exhortation to peace and patience. "Tell them the prophet and his companions are compelled to hear nothing but blasphemous oaths, and witness a scene of blasphemy, and drunkenness and hypocrisy, and debaucheries of every description. But tell them we will be freed in God's own time."

But the patience which Joseph commanded, he himself after a few weeks could no longer assume; and one night he rose suddenly and cried out in agony of soul. "O God, where art thou? And where is the pavilion that covereth thy hiding place? How long shall thy hand be stayed, and thine eye, yea thy pure eye, behold from the eternal heavens the wrongs of thy people, and of thy servants, and thine ear be penetrated with their cries? Yea, O Lord, how long!"

The other prisoners sat up to look at him and to listen; and after a few moments, Hyrum moved over to Lyman and put a trembling arm around him. Joseph was speaking again.

"My son, peace be unto thy soul; thine adversity and thine afflictions shall be but a small moment; and then, if thou endure it well, God shall exalt thee on high; thou shalt triumph over all thy foes." He was silent, his gaze on the dark roof of the jail. Then: "If thou shouldst be cast into the pit, or into the hands of murderers, and the sentence of death be passed upon thee, if thou be cast into the deep, if the billowing surge conspire against thee, if fierce winds become thine enemy, if the heavens gather blackness, and all the elements combine to hedge up the way; and above all, if the very jaws of hell shall gape open the mouth wide after thee, know thou, my son, that all these things shall give thee experience, and shall be for thy good! The Son of man hath descended below them all: art thou greater than He?"

After waiting as if to learn if God would speak again, Joseph slowly sank to the stone floor and bowed his head. A half-hour passed before Lyman spoke.

"I thought God told you He would set us free."

"He did. Just now He spoke like we might all be condemned to death."

"That's the way it sounded to me."

"You know as much as I do. You heard Him."

"In that case," said Lyman angrily, "I might as well get back to my digging!"

And a few days later, he had the tunnel ready for the removal of the last stone. Tonight, he said, they would run for their lives; for they might as well be shot running as standing against a stone wall. McRae crawled over on hands and knees to look at the hole: it was, he decided, large enough for Joseph to worm through, and Joseph was the largest man here.

"How long will it take to finish it?"

"Just a minute. I just have to move that one rock."

The men sat close to the tunnel and waited. When they heard persons moving around the jail outside, they thought the tunnel had been discovered; but in a few moments the feet went away and there was silence.

"About two in the morning will be best. The guards will be asleep."

"Or drunk."

"You think we can escape?" asked Hyrum anxiously.

"We'n try," said Lyman. "There's no use to stay here till they shoot us."

McRae moved over to Joseph who was leaning against a wall as if asleep. "Joseph, shall we try it?"

"Yes," said Joseph wearily. "Perhaps it is God's will."

McRae crawled back to Lyman and whispered: "He is willing."

The men waited. Now and then they could hear a drunken guard cursing, but except for outbursts of profanity, the world beyond was as silent as the dungeon in which they sat.

"I wonder what time it is."

"Not midnight yet."

"If I could see the big dipper," said McRae, rising and trying to look through one of the small windows. He was peering out when, with suddenness so sharp it was like thunder, there was a terrific yowl of astonishment and rage. There seemed to be a hundred men cursing their lungs out.

"Good God!" said Lyman, staggering to his feet. "They've discovered it!"

"Sounds like it," said McRae.

Joseph and Hyrum rose and the four men stood together in the cell, listening to the howls of fury outside. In a moment the door was opened and a dozen gleaming musket barrels were thrust inside.

"You sons-of-bitches!" a man roared. "What you been doing in there?"

"Don't shoot!" Joseph cried.

Lyman stepped forward. "Shoot and be damned!" He looked down the barrels at angry faces. "We're only rats in a hole. We've been here for months so go ahead and murder us."

"Back!" said a man, and waved the guns aside. "So you intended to escape, you dodrotted Mormon pot-soppers! Watch them, men, while I go inside." The guard entered and went over to the wall to examine it. Without speaking, he left the dungeon and turned to peer in. "Who done that?"

"I did," Lyman said.

"For a cent I'd blow your skull off."

"Do it!" cried Lyman furiously. "You think I want to live like a rat in this stinking place all my life? Why in hell don't we have a trial? If we are to be cooped up until we rot, then shoot us!"

The guard looked at him and considered. "I don't blame you a hell of a lot. Here, men, get busy and fix that hole." The other guards went away but the leader remained, rifle in hand, peering into the cell. "Don't you try any more of them tricks. I won't shoot you this time but I will next time."

"If," said McRae, "you want to shoot us standing you'll have to do it pretty soon. In another week you'll have to prop us up."

The guard turned away to spit tobacco juice and grin. "Oh, we'n prop you, all right. Or we'n shoot you in the back of your head while you lay on your bellies."

"That's about the way you'll do it," said Lyman scornfully. "Give me a gun and I'll come out and fight the whole drunken bunch of you."

"Don't get impatient. You'll be shot soon enough and I'll be there to see it."

"You pack of gin-jumping blasphemers!" Hearing a sound behind him, Lyman turned. He saw Hyrum on hands and knees, doubled over and vomiting.

The tunnel was filled with huge stones and a guard was posted there day and night; but Joseph did not yield his faith and hope. During the next weeks, while the others sat like dead men, their spirits almost broken and their hope gone, he gave the long hours to thought, reflecting on the way his people had been scattered, wondering if he could rebuild his kingdom. Word had come to him of hundreds who had become apostates, including many of the leaders; and of others who cursed him for a false prophet and said they would lynch him if he ever got out. Oliver Cowdery and Dave Whitmer and Martin Harris had denounced him and been excommunicated—and John Whitmer and Orson Hyde had gone, and even the gentle Edward Partridge. They could all desert, but he would remain steadfast and God would be with him. He still believed in the beauty of the human body, the dignity of the human personality, the power of the human mind. Every person was a child of God, no matter how sinful or weak or degraded; and God had given to him the simple truths with which an erring humanity could be saved. That was his message; that was his church.

He thought too, while sitting day after day in this dark dungeon, of the millions of souls waiting for birth—waiting on the evils that produced barren women and harlots; or waiting on the selfishness of those who wished to have only one or two children or none at all. He abhorred the sterile wicked waste of prostitution in which women sold their beauty and youth and did nothing to hasten the millennium. The pilgrimage of spirits through birth and their earthly journey, and then through death and resurrection, needed quickening, needed larger families; and again he thought of Abraham and the other ancients and wondered how long it would be until he received a revelation on this matter.

That a revelation would come he did not doubt. It was absurd for a man of his vitality and health and genius to have only one wife, or to have only a few children when there could be a hundred bearing his name. . . .

"Brother Lyman," he said unexpectedly one day, "we shall soon be free."

"How do you know that?"

"God is making His will known."

"I wish the Almighty would hurry. We're wasting time."

"Are you sure?" asked Hyrum, raising his white emaciated face.

"Yes, Hyrum. The time will come soon."

"We're certainly a bunch of fine patriarchs," said McRae, fingering his long dirty beard. He gazed at the other men and grinned. Lyman had a dense crop of whiskers that almost covered his face, but Joseph's and Hyrum's were a thin growth, and looked more like fair foliage of silk. The hair of all the men fell upon their shoulders.

A week later the time came, but not in the way Joseph had expected. The men were removed from the dungeon and told that they were to be sent to another jail in Richmond.

"What for?" asked McRae.

"To stand trial for murder and treason."

"To be ambushed and shot, you mean."

Stiffly, blinking in the strong light, and looking like wild men out of a jungle, the prisoners mounted horses and rode away, with guards ahead of them and behind them. The time was early April. All winter they had lain on a floor of stone. Their hair and beards were full of lice; their clothes hung to them in foul rags; and their bodies had wasted away until they were only grotesque skeletons of what they had been. Joseph looked around him at the beauty of earth and filled his lungs. He heard birds and saw wild flowers; gazed at the limpid loveliness of streams and breathed the fragrant April air until he felt drunk; and felt so happy that he began to sing.

Lyman gave little attention to the glory of the world. He was plotting to escape; but on the journey to Richmond, he found no chance to flee or to get hold of a gun; nor later when the prisoners were arraigned before Tom Birch, the prosecutor at the first trial who was now a judge. The witnesses against them by day were the men who guarded them by night. The grand jury returned indictments for treason, murder, arson, theft and stealing; and when Joseph asked for a change of venue to Marion County, he was granted one to Boone.

When, with a sheriff and three guards, they set out for the county seat, Lyman believed their opportunity had come. Joseph, he reflected, angered by the man's patience, seemed willing to stand trial, believing that God would set him free. Lyman resolved that there would be no trial for him: he would escape or be shot now.

The sheriff and his assistants had several flasks of whiskey with them and drank freely and sang as they took their way over the rolling hills. One of the guards, a red-faced bewhiskered man named John Hogarth, seemed very friendly. Now and then he rode up to the wagon to jest with the prisoners.

"How you feeling? You ready to be shot?"

"Shot, hell!" Lyman cried.

The sardonic McRae added: "There's nothing in us to shoot. We've dried up so in dungeons that bullets would go right through us and never bother us at all."

"We'll take care of that," said Hogarth, still grinning. "We'll blow you to pieces with a cannon."

While encamped at noon, Hogarth took Lyman aside. "Why," he asked, "don't you fellows escape?"

"How?" asked Lyman suspiciously.

"Well, tonight we might all get as slewed as owls. How would that be?"

"You mean you want us to run so you'n have an excuse to shoot us."

"By God, no. I think you've been punished enough."

"Maybe you're another damned Judas like Hinkle."

"I don't know Hinkle from Adam. Well, you do as you like. I'm just saying what I'd do if I was in your shoes."

"All right, we'll see."

John Hogarth was not a Judas. During this evening, he encouraged the sheriff and the two guards to drink lustily, and pretended to drink with them. He told Lyman and the other prisoners to pretend to drink also and to act as drunk as lords; and Lyman did. He affected such drunkenness that he staggered and fell on his face.

"By the holy mother of Christ!" the sheriff roared, waving a bottle. "You're all drunkern I be!"

The other prisoners, accepting the flasks when offered and making gurgling sounds in their throats, also pretended to be as drunk as pirates. Lyman and McRae staggered arm in arm around the camp and then crawled on hands and knees, swearing by all the angels that they were unable to stand; and the sheriff and the two guards laughed at them until they wept. Hogarth sat a little way off, nodding stupidly as if falling asleep; but his alert eyes were watching the sheriff. Lyman crawled over to the sheriff and begged for a bottle but the sheriff swore by all the devils in hell that he hadn't more than enough for himself.

"You don't need no more. You'll be dead soon."

"Thash," said Lyman, wagging his head owlishly, "ish why. Pleash give a drink to a dying man!"

The sheriff doubled over and howled. He looked around, with tears streaming from his drunken eyes, and saw Joseph who lay prone on the earth as if dead. "Look at your old prophet!" he yelled. "By God, ain't he in a pickle now!"

Lyman was gazing with sly covetousness at the pistols hanging from the sheriff's waist.

The sheriff turned and slapped a guard on his back. "Holy Jesus!" he howled. "Look!" He pointed at McRae who was solemnly trying to drink whiskey from an empty tin can. Then he saw Joseph crawling over to a blanket and fumbling with it. When Joseph stretched out, with the blanket over nothing but his feet, the sheriff almost burst with joy and staggered over to a saddlebag for another flask.

McRae crawled over to Joseph, taking the can with him, and lay on his back; and soon the two men were snoring as if sound asleep. In a few moments Hyrum went over and lay by them. John Hogarth was still sitting with his chin on his breast, his half-closed eyes alert to everything that was done. A little later, too drunk to stand, the sheriff sank to the earth, clutching a flask; and the two guards staggered over and sat by him and the three men drank until none of them could sit up.

Lyman looked over at Hogarth and waited. At a moment when he thought the time had come, the sheriff waved his flask unexpectedly and howled.

"Don't you fellows try to escape!" he bellowed. He struggled to sit up and then fell back and grunted. "You hear me?" he asked. Nobody answered him and in a few minutes he was dead to the world.

Hogarth rose and came over. "Now's your chance," he said softly.

"Can we take their guns?"

"Sure. You'll need them."

Lyman went quietly to the sheriff and the two guards and looked down at them. He stooped and drew the pistols from the holsters. Hogarth had gone with Joseph and McRae to catch and saddle the horses, and Hyrum had moved out into darkness.

When the prisoners were mounted and armed, Hogarth turned up to them his red and friendly face. "Good luck. Mebbe I'll see you again some day."

Joseph leaned down to clasp his hand. "God will bless you," he said.

"I don't know about that. I just figgered you'd suffered enough."

"You're true blue," said Lyman. "If you ever get over our way, we'd like to have you in our church."

"Thanks," said Hogarth, grinning. "I ain't much for religion."

Joseph straightened and looked over at the sheriff and the guards. "Come," he said, and the men rode into the night.

CHAPTER XXIV

UPON THAT DAY IN FAR WEST WHEN JOSEPH AND THE OTHERS WERE marched off to jail, Brigham Young was in hiding. During the weeks that followed, he knew that efforts were being made to capture him; but he outsmarted his enemies at every turn. Stealthily, swiftly, he moved over the frozen prairies, rebuking the apostates, instructing and cheering the faithful, and preparing for a great migration to another land. Only his energy and resourcefulness saved the church from ruin.

Tim McBride went with him often and saw what was done. The saints were scattered in a thousand places, some hiding in abandoned shacks, some in hazel or cottonwood thickets, and some in tents far out in the wilderness. Others moved by wagon or horse or afoot from place to place, going fearfully, going none knew where, but afraid to remain long in one spot. Day after day Brigham rode over the huge area around Far West, seeking the refugees and wanderers and bringing them to new life and hope.

"Cheer up!" he would say. "Damn it, we're not whipped yet. All the gentiles in hell can't whip us."

"I don't know," said a half-starved man one day. With a wife and six children he had crowded into a tent in a thicket of maple. They had a little frozen beef and a little corn meal.

"Where's your cattle?"

"I don't know."

"Where's your wagon and oxen?"

"Somebody stole them."

"Go find them. Get ready. We're moving to Illinois." He turned to the gaunt wife. "Can't you smile any more?"

"All the smiles has gone out of me."

"Smile! God doesn't love a coward. How are the children?"

"All about half-sick."

Brigham looked at six children shivering in rags. "Tim, ride over and fetch some food and clothes."

After Brigham had found all the saints in the villages and open places, he rode up and down the streams and through the forests, seeking those who had fled; commanding them to find a team and wagon to make the journey; telling them where to go for clothes and food. He was first among the twelve apostles now. With Joseph in prison, with Rigdon terrified or insane by turns, he was the leader of the scattered people. He called the High Council, his body of advisers, and had apostles chosen to replace the apostates who had fled; had hundreds excommunicated and cast out; and rebuked with vigorous and profane words those who were weak and afraid.

"By the living God of Israel," he roared to a multitude, "we ain't whipped yet! We'll build our kingdom somewhere, and the damned gentiles can froth at the mouth and bite their own unclean flesh but they will not prevail against us! We have power in us and I want you to feel it. God is on our side. This is no time for your damned infernal whining and puling! Let your beards grow, get dirt under your fingernails, get calluses on you as big as hoecakes; but never say you're whipped! Let the weaklings flee: we don't want them. Let the cowards go back to Ohio or New York or England. We'll move to a new frontier; and I give you my word by the living God that I'll never rest until our kingdom is built and our enemies come crawling on hands and knees to lick our hands and ask for peace! . . ."

Nobody could resist a leader like that. Nobody could hear him without cheering, or grasp his strong hand without feeling new strength. And one by one or family by family, the saints began to move and gather their belongings and prepare for a long journey to another home. Brigham appointed men to assist him with the exodus; sent agents to store granaries of corn along the route; and made contracts for ferrying the thousands across the Mississippi near Quincy. In December the first train of wagons set out, and from then until early spring there was a continuous caravan of emigrants, some in wagons, some on horses or afoot, herding a few beasts along with them or leading small children by the hand.

Many fell sick and some died of hunger or cold weather; but Brigham kept the ragged line moving across the frozen earth. Nights passed when he did not sleep at all but kept riding to cheer the stragglers, to help the sick, to bury the dead, and to keep hope burning like a fire in ten thousand hearts.

Early one cold morning, when the sky looked like chilled slate and the marshes steamed, Tim rode furiously up to the shack where Brigham had slept.

"Run!" he howled, tumbling from his horse.

"Now what's the matter?"

"They're coming to murder you!"

"Who? Calm yourself."

"Get on my horse!" cried Tim, agog with excitement. He grasped Brigham and shoved him toward the nag. "God Almighty, hurry! A mob is on the way to murder you!"

"You sure?" asked Brigham, gazing across frozen prairie and seeing no one.

"One of them told me. My God, be quick!"

Brigham looked back at the hut. "Go get my gun," he said, and mounted the horse. "Tim, you keep your eyes peeled and let me know. I'll head for Quincy."

Brigham rode away at a stiff gallop and Tim ducked for cover. Within a few minutes a dozen horsemen came over the skyline and bore down on the shack; and Tim, peering from a snow-covered bush, saw that they were well-armed. They dismounted and entered the shack and then came out and gazed around them. One of them saw hoof prints in the thin snow and pointed in the direction Brigham had taken; and they all mounted and set off in pursuit.

Brigham had never been outwitted yet and did not intend to be now. He hid by day and rode by night until he came to the river; whereupon, suspecting that enemies would be waiting at the ferry, he went several miles downstream and hired a lad to take him across in a canoe. In Quincy he was safe. In Quincy, indeed, he was an honored stranger; for he had been here many times, arranging for the migration and establishing goodwill. The citizens of Illinois, outraged by the treatment of the Mormons in Missouri, had appointed committees here and elsewhere to relieve the destitute and homeless and provide work for those who sought it. The Democratic Association recommended to the residents of Quincy that in all intercourse with the strangers they should be careful not to wound their feelings, or "in any way reflect upon those who, by every law of humanity, are entitled to our sympathy and commiseration."

The rebuke to a neighboring state was vigorous. "The inhabitants upon the western frontier of the state of Missouri, in their late persecution of the people denominated Mormons, have violated the sacred rights of conscience and every law of justice and humanity. The governor of Missouri, in refusing protection to this class of people, when pressed upon by a heartless mob, and turning upon them a band of unprincipled militia, with orders encouraging their extermination, has brought a lasting disgrace upon the state over which he presides."

It was with sympathy and aid that the saints were met as they poured into the city. A few who had means went out and purchased small farms; others sought employment in the town; but hundreds lived in shacks and tents on the outskirts, awaiting the next move. Both the governor and Stephen Douglas spoke boldly against the brutalities in Missouri and welcomed the Mormons, but the wise Brigham knew there was trouble ahead.

He foresaw, as the citizens of Quincy did not, that among the endless horde pouring in there would be adventurers and shysters who would take advantage of charity or seek to loot. And when he arrived now, he was not surprised to learn that matters were not as he had left them a month ago. There was growing anger because of the insolence and thefts of some of the invaders. Knowing that he must act at once, he published in the Quincy newspaper a statement, declaring that in so great an influx of strangers there were rascals, pretending to belong to the church, who had come only to exploit human kindness. There were blasphemers and drunkards and thieves who had been expelled from fellowship. He called upon the citizens to scorn these persons and drive them out.

But that, he realized, was not enough. He was appalled when he saw how his hordes had given to an attractive city the aspect of a migratory camp. The homes of generous citizens had been filled to overflowing. The edges of the town, east, north and west, looked as if beggars and nomads had laid siege; for there were temporary shacks, tents on every vacant lot and roadside, livestock breaking into every pasture and field, hogs and dogs and sheep and chickens running wild, as well as hundreds of families who had less than a shack or a tent and lived in a wagon or nothing at all. And even now, the ferry was busy all day long as a steady stream of weary and hungry and ragged persons marched in. Here was a situation that demanded the utmost of tact.

"By God," said Brigham to an assistant, "we'll have civil war if we don't get out. We must move in a hurry."

"Yes," said John Taylor, a tall, intellectual and dignified man. Though quiet and unassuming, he was morbidly sensitive about his person and his rights. In Missouri he had once turned purple with rage and bellowed: "I wouldn't be a slave to God Almighty Himself!" He now added: "I suggest you see Dr. Galland. He has a lot of land up north and says he will sell it to us cheap."

"Is it good land?"

"No, it's a swamp but we could drain it."

"You watch things here and I'll see about it."

"The governor of Iowa has invited us to move over there."

"All right, get a bunch of them moving. I'll see Galland."

Galland's bog dismayed Brigham almost as much as the condition of his people in Quincy. It was a timbered swamp on the bank of the Mississippi River—a sunken area of mosquitoes and fever; and when Brigham set out to explore it, he fell headlong into a quagmire and thought for a moment he had reached his end. After threshing around like a mired ox, he crawled out, dripping with stinking slime and mud.

"No wonder," he said, after returning to Quincy, "Galland wants to sell it. Neither land nor water animal could get across his damned property. You can't walk, wade or swim."

"There's nothing else," said Taylor. "I've searched everywhere."

"The Oregon country. That's where we belong."

"Reports say California has good soil."

Brigham looked around him and considered. He missed the spiritual leadership of Joseph: that indefinable power in the man that could arouse a multitude to feverish industry and unite them in a common crusade. Without the prophet, he himself was only an organizer who gathered the thousands into a group and wondered what to do with them; for God did not speak to him or announce revelation by revelation what was to be done next.

So when, two days later, Brigham learned that Joseph had escaped, he was overjoyed. A messenger came through to declare that half the state of Missouri was chasing the prophet to the Mississippi River, but that Joseph was far in the lead and was safe.

"God be praised! Will he soon be here?"

"Any day now."

"Did the others escape too?"

"All of them, I think."

Brigham was glad. He was deeply pleased until he gave earnest thought to the matter. He was president of the Twelve. For months he had been the leader of the church. He had ignored the pompously ambitious Rigdon as well as every other man who had stood in his way. But Joseph was another matter: he would be the leader again if he outwitted the mobs and got across the river. Joseph was a good prophet and seer; he was invincible in the spiritual realms, but he was no leader of men. Three times now he had almost wrecked the church with his impractical notion that God would take care of things when Joseph could no longer do so. He had even got himself thrown into a dungeon and it was a wonder that he was alive at all; and while in jail he had sent epistles of hope and patience and prayer, as if these had anything to do with moving ten thousand freezing and starving persons beyond reach of their enemies.

Yes, he was a great prophet: Brigham never doubted that; but he was no man to take a ragged and embittered people and build them into a kingdom. Nevertheless, when Joseph suddenly appeared one afternoon, bearded and pale and dirty, and looking like a John the Baptist just emerged from a jungle, even the hard-headed Brigham wept. He threw his arms around Joseph and gave him a mighty hug, and then turned away to hide tears. Everyone wept. Everyone rejoiced, including the astonished gentiles who had never seen him before. Word of his coming went like fire on a wind, and Mormons left their shacks and tents and work and followed him in a great mob as he went down a street. Hundreds of voices broke into jubilant song.

> We thank thee, O God, for a prophet
> To guide us in these latter days!
> We thank thee for sending the gospel
> To lighten our minds with its rays! . . .

Children wept, seeing their parents weep; women, wild with joy, pressed in to touch him; and men whose eyes had never before been wet marched with blurred vision. In his triumphant pilgrimage down the street, Joseph was overwhelmed by the welcome and walked with tears running down his cheeks. These were his people, this was his church! Behind him a thousand voices rang high and clear in thankfulness to God.

> There is hope shining brightly before us,
> And we know that deliverance is nigh! . . .

Brigham marveled at the power of this man to arouse wild enthusiasm. For nearly six months he had been chained in a dungeon; and now he was here, walking like a ragged king, and greeted by the most thunderous welcome Brigham was ever to hear. Looking to his right, he saw the pale ambitious face of Sidney Rigdon, and he did not like what he saw in the man's cold eyes. He did not like the way the tall gaunt bigot was looking at Joseph.

Joseph, the prophet, was again with his people and he was again the leader. His heart was a bugle within him. There had been times when he doubted himself but those times were gone: God had delivered him from his enemies and he was never to doubt again that he could be as mighty as he wished to be. His confidence was so great that it overwhelmed those who grasped his hand or looked into his blue eyes. He walked like a king and he felt like a king; and he was fully determined to be a powerful ruler before his days were done. His first act was so dramatic that it left Brigham speechless.

For Joseph went to look at the Galland bog; and while standing on an eminence, gazing over the area of fevers and pestilence, he extended an arm and spoke.

"Right on this spot we will build a great and beautiful city. We will call it Nauvoo which is from the Hebrew and means a beautiful place."

"Confound it," said Parley Pratt, who had also escaped from jail, "this is a malaria bog! It's no spot for us."

Joseph smiled. A man who had escaped from chains and a dungeon was not to be afraid of a swamp. Besides, he liked to think of doing what no other man would dare undertake. "Here," he said, "we will build Nauvoo, the city beautiful. In three years it will be the largest city in Illinois."

"Damn it," said Brigham, recovering from his amazement, "why choose a bog? Why not go west?"

Joseph was seeing in a vision the city that would soon be here. "Make arrangements to buy all this land. This will be our home." He turned to the men with him. "Come, I will show you something." With them he descended from the eminence and entered the swampy meadows. He stooped and pointed to a wild calla in the grass. It was a cone of dense perfect flowers surrounded by a large white lily that turned over and downward like a piece of white velvet. Framing it were enormous green leaves on slender tubular stalks. "If," he said, "God chooses such a spot for such loveliness, we can build a city here."

He walked with the men and came next to a small garden of wild yellow lilies. Countless flowers nodded on long peduncles, with lovely leaves forming a vase. The blossoms, yellow and red and orange, were thickly spotted with dark brown dots as if they had been sprayed with flakes of tobacco leaf. "This flower," said Joseph, "was abundant in New York. Do you remember it? And the grass pinks?" he said, moving to another garden. He pointed to loose racemes of pink sepals and petals, bearded with yellow and rose-colored hairs. "I say to you that where God places such loveliness, there can we build a city. Make arrangements to buy this land."

And arrangements were made. Land was purchased and the hardier saints began to move in and build.

"We'll all die of fever," Brigham said to Parley, "or fall into bogs and disappear."

"It looks bad, but where Joseph leads, we follow."

"You," said Brigham slyly, "followed him to jail but I didn't."

"I'll follow Joseph anywhere."

The saints followed with such energy and eagerness that the gentiles were astounded. Hundreds of families loaded their belongings on wagons and moved to the new site; and within a week there was the clear hard sound of axes in the adjacent forests, the smell of lumber and sawdust, the fragrance of broken sod. Even many of the leaders were in rags. Parley went into the timber barefooted and bareheaded and felled trees and recited florid Popean couplets to the men who labored with him. Brigham went in worn-out shoes that were laced to his feet with twine.

The proud John Taylor, in tattered shirt and patched trousers, looked like a scarecrow.

Almost overnight the swamp became a settlement of tents, and then one by one houses appeared and the city began to grow. Some pushed farther north or east, buying land or leasing it; some went across the river to Montrose, a village in Iowa, and others pushed westward from there. The whole country in all directions was alive with the industry of thousands; and saints in New York and Ohio, hearing of this new and mighty effort, packed up and moved to the new Zion. Brigham had been the Moses who led the hordes out of Egypt, but Joseph was the prophet and king who directed their labor now. All day long he was busy, riding among his people on a white horse and cheering and commanding.

"Sister Betsy, your child is sick? You've been drinking polluted water. Have your husband dig a well."

One day he met Lyman Wight. "Lyman, you give us too much trouble. Why did you say the Democratic party was responsible for our troubles in Missouri? That is not true."

"It is true. The damned Democrats ——"

"I say it is not true. Watch your tongue. Here in Illinois are two parties, the Democrats and Whigs. Soon we'll control the elections but we don't want to make enemies."

"I despise the damned Democrats!"

"For shame, Lyman. You have too hot a temper. Learn to control it."

One and another he instructed or advised or rebuked. "Parley, haven't you any shoes? Ask Brigham for some. He always has money, though I sometimes wonder where he gets it." Or to Rigdon:

"Brother Sidney, you're too proud. Get an axe and cut logs and build you a house."

"I?" asked Rigdon, still looking half-crazed. "I'm second in command. Why should I do common labor?"

"We must all labor in the vineyard of God. Find an axe and get to work."

"Why don't you chop logs? Are you better than the rest of us?"

"Brother Sidney, I have spoken. Go build a house."

And so matters went for two months, with the prophet giving strength to weary bodies, putting faith in weak souls. But Parley and Brigham had been right: the new site was a swamp of fevers, and suddenly the dreaded malaria swept the encampment. In cabins, in tents, or along the river bank or in brush upon the sand, persons lay by scores. Remembering the scourge of cholera in Zion's Camp, Joseph was frightened, not knowing what to do in the face of this new catastrophe. He went from tent to hut, from hut to river bank, laying his hands on fevered brows and speaking words of cheer to persons who were dying. He sent riders for doctors, but doctors upon this frontier were busy and none of them would come. One evening in the tent where he lived with Emma he bowed his head.

Emma had been dragged from place to place so long, had suffered so many indignities, had hated and despaired and hoped so often that she now looked like a gaunt spinster of fifty. Her mind was full of malice and her tongue was sharp.

"A fine mess you got us into this time! You dragged us off to Missouri where bandits chased us, and then you took us into a bog to die of rot. And you call yourself a prophet!"

"God is very angry again," said Joseph, and raised a haggard face. "Too many of the saints are living in sin."

"You're no gilded lily yourself."

"The Almighty is angry with His people."

"I can't see what the Almighty has to do with it. It looks like mosquitoes and stinking water to me."

Leaping to his feet, Joseph thundered: "Silence!"

"Don't tell me to shut up. I say you took us into a swamp to die."

"I'll make that swamp the most beautiful city in the world."

"The biggest graveyard in the world. Just plow sod over them when they're all dead."

"Silence, I told you!"

"And I thought," Emma went on remorselessly, "you said the United States would pay for our losses in Missouri."

"They will."

"You make a poor mouth! Why, in a few days you'll be sick too or Governor Boggs will have you extradited and throw you in a dungeon again. It's sixes either way."

"You drive me insane!" he cried, glaring at her. "You're no wife for a prophet."

"You're no prophet. Why don't you go out and heal the sick?"

For a long moment he gazed at her. "You don't think I can?"

"If you're a prophet you can."

"I can," he said.

"Then do it. It's quicker than medicine."

He went out and looked at the sky but after a moment he peered into the tent. "I'll go and heal the sick," he said.

"Do!" she said scornfully. "And why didn't God get you out of jail sooner? There's no sense for a prophet to sit in a dungeon for six months."

He went away and called Parley and John Taylor and Heber Kimball and said he was going forth to heal the sick. "Come," he said, his face gray with determination. "We'll go to Montrose first."

They crossed the river in canoes and climbed the bluff to the village. Of the first man he met Joseph asked: "What saint over here is nearest death?"

"Why—well, by gum, I guess Elijah Fordham is."

"Take me to his house."

While going to the house, Joseph silently prayed for strength. When he looked at Elijah he was dismayed. The man was very ill. His face had a leprous pallor, his eyes were yellowish, his mouth looked as if it had been dead for a week. Joseph stooped and laid a hand on the moist brow.

"Brother Elijah, do you know me?"

Elijah rolled his dying eyes upward. His dry lips moved but uttered no sound. Then, with an effort, he nodded his head faintly in assent and gave Joseph a wan smile.

"Do you believe I am a prophet of God?"

Elijah nodded.

"Do you believe that as a prophet I have power to heal?"

"Yes," said Elijah in a whisper barely audible.

"Do you understand that I have come to heal you?"

"Yes."

Joseph rose to his fullest height. He took one of Elijah's limp hands and for a moment gazed at the man with hypnotic directness; and then, in a voice that would have startled the dead, he thundered: "Brother Elijah, in the name of Jesus Christ, the living God, I command you to rise and walk!"

A tremor ran through Elijah's gaunt body as if new life were being poured into his veins. He stiffened, as from shock; and then, slowly, deliberately, he rose from the bed and stood erect, sheathed in bandages and plasters from head to feet. With amazing strength he tore a plaster from him; shuddered again as if he had been raised from the dead; and turned and clasped Joseph's hand.

"Bring me food!" he cried. "I'm as hungry as a horned owl."

He tore other plasters from his body and wrapped a blanket around him. His wife went for food and returned with a bowl of bread and milk; and Elijah sat at a table and ate as if he had been starved for months. "Just as soon as I dress," he said, speaking out of bread and milk, "I'll go with you. I am a well man."

He did go, and other persons too; and in a little while Joseph was followed by a crowd of saints and gentiles. Word of the healing went before him. Persons came to meet him and to beg his presence next in this shack or that tent; and all day he marched up and down healing the sick. Over some he had no power: if a person failed to rise to his thundering command, Joseph told his leaders that the sick one had been very sinful or had no faith in his soul, and that God probably wished his death. But many, including children, left their sick beds and dressed and followed him; and a few amazed gentiles, watching the miracles, asked to be baptized at once and accepted into the church. With awed eyes they stared at Elijah Fordham as if doubting that he was real. He looked, it is true, more like a cadaver than a human being; but he walked all afternoon and found himself strengthened when evening came.

Confident of his power, Joseph sent his leaders forth to heal, and their success was hardly less miraculous than his own. For days they labored in faith and prayer. Some of the saints died and were buried in wagon boxes in the forest or along the stream; but the magnetism of Joseph had filled the settlement from end to end. In two weeks the plague abated and the building of Nauvoo was resumed.

"Do you think now," Joseph asked his wife, "that I am a prophet?"

Emma's black eyes still shone with contempt. "If you are, why did you let so many die?"

"They had no faith in them. They were too sinful."

"That's a handy excuse. If a person lives it's because you healed him, but if he dies it's because God wanted him to die."

"I healed dozens," he said proudly. "They would have died without me."

"I don't believe it. Some people always get well."

"You have no faith. If you get sick you'll probably die."

"I won't count on you."

"Ye of little faith," he said, and left her to look at the town and plan its growth.

Fully restored to leadership and to confidence in his power, he received revelations again. God asked the saints to build a temple here, and a large boardinghouse for Joseph. Some came with tools to work; some came in rags and laid their last dollar at the prophet's feet. Some fetched trinkets. "We want gold and silver," Joseph said in meeting, "but we don't want your old nose rings and finger rings and brass kettles. If you have watches or guns, go sell them and bring us the hard metal. If any of you are hungry or naked, come to me and I will divide my last morsel. If you are not content then I will kick your backside."

"You're getting mighty bold," said Emma that evening, "to be telling persons you'll kick their hinders. You might get your own kicked."

"I?" said Joseph, smiling. "Emma dear, I can whip any man from here to Boston. From now on I am a fighting prophet. If my enemies bother me any more, I'll use them for dung in my garden."

"Lord, but you're getting bold. You didn't talk so mouth-almighty in Missouri."

"I'm building a kingdom. In two years I'll control Illinois. Then I'll run for President."

"You'll run, all right, but it won't be for President. You'll be running from the sheriff."

Joseph turned to look at his gaunt and bitter wife. For fifteen years he had tolerated her contempt and her scorn. He thought of women here who were young and lovely, and he sighed. "Only the Almighty can whip me now. You see how Nauvoo is growing? Can you imagine what a city I will have here? But no: you hate me whom everyone else loves."

"Oh, Lord! I guess Sidney Rigdon loves you. He'd cut your throat if he could."

"Sidney is too ambitious."

"So are you."

"I am only a humble prophet who is building a kingdom for God."

Emma's spinsterish eyes looked at him. "When do I move into this big boardinghouse you're building?"

"Within a year. I have much to do and I'm going to do it myself. I have too many ambitious men around me. I'm going to send them all on missions. We need more converts."

"You'll send them away so you can sleep with their wives."

"Emma!"

"Oh, to hell with your pious stuff! Don't you think I know what you've been doing? Because you're a prophet, does that mean you can be adulterous?"

"You're blasphemous!" he cried. "The spirit of God has never been in you."

"I've seen too much of it in you."

"Yes?" he said, wondering what she meant by that.

"I saw you shining up to Orson Pratt's wife."

"For shame," he said, thinking of Abraham and Solomon. "I'm going to build a kingdom right here on the bank of the Mississippi. I'll have my own city, my private army, my own judges and courts——"

"You'll have nothing of the sort. As soon as he gets around to it, Boggs will have you extradited and throw you in a dungeon again."

"I'll take care of Boggs."

"Why didn't you long ago? Why didn't you set Port Rockwell on him?"

Joseph looked at her sharply. "You talk too much," he said.

Joseph not only wanted more converts; he wanted some of his head-strong leaders out of the way. He called the twelve apostles to missions in England and ordered them to go even when some of them were ill. Brigham was so weak that he had to be assisted from Montrose to the ferry; and upon arriving in Nauvoo he sank with a groan and had to be nursed for days before he was able to stir.

"Brother Brigham," said Joseph, looking in on him one day, "you must be off."

"Yes," said Brigham.

"You are to go with Heber."

"But Heber's wife and all his children are sick."

"The Lord will watch over them." Joseph entered the shack and laid a hand on Brigham's forehead. "You're not very ill. Your faith is weak."

"By the living God, if I'm not sick I never want to be."

"You are strong enough to go now."

With a great effort Brigham left his bed and sought Heber, and the two men hitched a team to a wagon and set out for the East. Heber's wife was shaking with ague; all his children were in bed. Heber himself was very ill. A crowd gathered to watch the men depart and to cheer them; and after the wagon had gone fifty yards, Heber rose to his feet, his eyes blind with tears, and looked back.

"Brigham, this is damned tough but let's give them a cheer."

"All right," Brigham said, and staggered to his feet.

Supporting one another, the two sick apostles waved their hats and feebly shouted a hurrah for Israel. The multitude answered. "I feel," said Heber, "like we'll never see them again."

Other men, sick in body and soul, left when Joseph called. Three of them set out in a wagon which overturned; and two of them were too sick to rise and had to be assisted by the third. In pairs, or three by three, the sick men were called and said good-bye to their families and set out, with no money and in ragged clothes, for a strange country four thousand miles away. To those who protested, Joseph always gave the same answer.

"He that loveth father or mother, houses or lands, wives or children more than he loveth me is not worthy of me. Come, you must go."

And the apostles went.

For Joseph had a mighty dream in his heart now and he was being driven by impassioned eagerness that gave him no rest. While his leaders were gone, he would build a great and beautiful city here; and when they returned, they would stare in amazement at what he had done. Needing money, he resolved to go to Washington and try to collect for the losses in Missouri; and one morning, not long after he had sent the apostles forth, he set out in a carriage with Rigdon and Porter Rockwell to see the President. Day after day as he traveled he sang hymns. Enemies, he knew, were all around him, for Governor Boggs had sent spies out; but he was unafraid of enemies now.

In Springfield, Rigdon fell ill and Joseph left Rockwell with him and went on alone. It was a long and tiresome journey. Sometimes he ate and slept in the homes of his people, and sometimes with strangers. All the gentiles seemed friendly. They had read of the persecutions in Missouri, and they denounced Governor Boggs and encouraged Joseph in his mission. Joseph was convinced, long before he reached Washington, that President Van Buren would listen to him and redress his wrongs. He did not know what a fat and pompous little politician he would have to deal with.

As soon as Joseph presented his letters of introduction his heart sank. Van Buren read them and looked up and scowled.

"What do you expect of me, Mr. Smith?"

"Justice, Mr. President."

"Justice?"

"Yes, sir."

"Well, possibly your cause is just. I can't say. But I can do nothing for you."

"Why not, Mr. President?"

"That's a stupid question. If I did anything I'd lose the vote of Missouri."

Joseph stared at the sandy little man and felt wrathful. "Mr. President, mobs in Missouri not only murdered us and ravished our women. They also stole or destroyed nearly all our property——"

"Yes, yes, but there's nothing I can do."

"You mean that the Constitution of this great nation——"

"I cannot afford to arouse the anger of Missouri."

"Under the Constitution——"

"Yes, Mr. Smith, I know all about the Constitution. But I am helpless."

"Then we'll petition Congress."

"That is your privilege."

"Mr. President, out in Illinois, prominent persons have been outraged by our treatment in Missouri."

"What prominent persons?" asked the President, scowling.

"Abraham Lincoln for one. Stephen Douglas for another."

"Abraham Lincoln? I don't think I've ever heard of him."

"He is well liked out there. Some day I think he will be a very powerful person."

"That may all be true," said the President impatiently. "I can do nothing for you. And now, if you don't mind, I am very busy." The plump little cherub rose behind his huge desk and bowed. "Good morning, Mr. Smith."

"Good morning, Mr. President. Permit me to say that this matter is not settled yet."

Joseph went out in great fury, noting the vulgar elegance of this mansion in which lived the president of a democratic nation. He went to Senators and jurists and arranged to have a petition presented to the Congress; but he knew his cause was lost. Feeling bitter and vindictive, he ordered his carriage and set out on the long homeward journey.

If he could not win in one way, he would win in another. If, under the charter of a free land, there was no protection for human conscience and human rights, then he would build a kingdom of his own. He would control the elections in the province he governed; and year by year he would push his boundaries out, add converts by the thousands, recruit to his cause the wisest of leadership, and become the most powerful man in the United States. Then there would be no smug little egoist sitting on a nation's throne.

Such was his dream during the long journey homeward; and when he arrived, he was ready to fight as he had never fought before.

CHAPTER XXV

A FEW MONTHS LATER, THE NAUVOO HOUSE WAS DONE. A TWO-STORY structure of red brick in the form of an L, with a frontage of a hundred and twenty feet on two streets, and a depth of forty, it had cost a hundred thousand dollars. It stood on the bank of the river, with Nauvoo behind it in the north and northeast, and Montrose in clear view across the river in the southwest. North of it, Joseph planned to build another house in which to live, and some day to use this big structure chiefly for entertaining and for church offices.

He could stand at the window of his study and gaze at a thriving city. The swamps had been conquered, and upon them stood homes, stores and shops. A temple was rising on a hill in the north, and it was to be much handsomer than the one in Kirtland. Of white limestone, eighty-three by a hundred and twenty-eight feet in breadth and depth, and sixty feet in height, it would have an upper story and a basement. In the latter would be a baptismal font, wrought after the manner of King Solomon's brazen sea. The huge tank would have panels upon which would be painted scenes both biblical and Mormon; and the stairway to it would be supported by twelve great oxen, overlaid with gold. The temple would be crowned by a high steeple surrounded by angels and trumpets. It would cost a million dollars.

It made Joseph happy to think of it, but he was happy for other reasons also. Emma was going to have another child and he hoped she would nag him less after the infant came. The apostles in England were converting persons by the hundreds. One of them indeed, a kindly blue-eyed gentleman named Wilford Woodruff, had converted so many that Parliament was alarmed and in a mood to do something about it. A few of the English converts were wealthy and had come to Nauvoo. Missionaries in the United States were also successful, and were establishing colonies from the Atlantic Ocean to the Mississippi.

And there were still other reasons why Joseph was happy. By promising the Mormon vote to the Whigs, he had exacted from the legislature a charter for a university, a military organization, and for his city; and with those, his power in his small kingdom would be absolute. Abraham Lincoln had voted for the charters. So had Stephen Douglas. Influential men in Illinois smiled upon him and his people. Soon he would have an army of several thousand well-trained and fully armed men.

"Then," he thought, gazing at Nauvoo, "let my enemies dare come against me!" Suddenly he saw Louisa Bemen and raised a window to smile at her. "Good morning, Sister Louisa."

"Good morning," she said, returning his smile.

His gaze roved down her handsome body and then rested on her saucy face. "I want to see you in a few days—when I'm not so busy."

"All right, Brother Joseph."

He liked this girl. She was healthy and vivacious and—yes, so sensible; and besides, she had been smiling at him for weeks as if to show how white her teeth were.

He hardly knew why he wished to see her in a few days. Still, he did know. Month by month, as he came into power and peace, as he saw his city grow and his military organization take form, he thought of the advantage in the next life for those who had many offspring. He needed many wives—and many children if in the next world he was to advance rapidly toward godhood; because power there was determined by the number of progeny, as well as by righteous living in this world. He remembered again that God had peopled this planet and was still siring the millions of souls that came to human birth. There were other reasons no less urgent. In Nauvoo were more women than men, and Joseph abhorred prostitutes. If a woman had no husband, she would probably seek a lover and fall into abominable adultery; or she would sell herself in the brothels. He wanted no harlots in this city. Another reason, he admitted, with a wry smile for himself, was his appetite: he had never looked at a beautiful woman without wishing to touch her. This he had formerly regarded as a weakness of his flesh; but now he felt that God had planned for him to have many wives, and the more he considered the matter, the more certain his conviction became.

Whether he should take wives and keep the matter secret, he did not know. Perhaps there was no need to worry: he was king in this tiny empire: his word was law. If he were caught, he could inquire of God and receive a revelation; because he had known for a long while that

God would speak to him on the subject before his years were done. It was first a matter of making himself secure and his people happy.

A few days later, he saw Louisa passing his window and called her in. It was a beautiful morning, he said. It was, she admitted, and gave him a roguish smile. She said the woods were full of wild flowers.

"Yes," he said, looking at her. He added: "Louisa, I wish to speak of a very important matter. You believe I am a prophet, don't you?"

"Yes, Brother Joseph."

"You believe that what I do is sanctioned by the Lord?"

"Yes, of course."

He took her hands and gazed at her fair face. "Louisa, you are to be my wife."

"Your wife!" she cried, astonished. "But you have a wife."

"Yes, but I'm to have another wife. It is God's will."

"I don't understand," she said, but her voice was gentle.

He drew her to him and held her close. He stooped and kissed her soft mouth and looked at the pleased astonishment in her eyes. "I'm a prophet and not like other men. Besides, in our church, the duty of the sisters is to marry and have children and assist their husbands toward godhood. That is their earthly function. If they do not serve that function, then they are damnable in the sight of heaven. They will have only the lowest degree of glory or none at all. You must understand and remember one very important thing in salvation: in this church, a woman cannot reach glory in the next world if she has no husband in this one."

"But I can get a husband," she said pertly, looking up at him.

"A husband like me?"

"Well, no."

"I've watched you for months. You're in love with me."

"With you?" she asked, pouting at him. "I've admired you. All the sisters admire you. I wouldn't have dared to touch you, yet you have kissed me."

"I'm kissing you again," he said, and put his lips to her throat. "Will you be my wife?"

Her blood was racing. He was so large and handsome and self-assured. "Are you sure," she asked, feeling weak, "that it would be all right?"

"In Nauvoo, anything I do is all right."

"But Emma, what will she say?"

"I'll not tell her about it."

"Oh," said Louisa, wondering about that. "But if you don't tell her ——"

"You'll move into the Nauvoo House and have a room. I'll say you have no money and I'm taking care of you."

"But—" she said, troubled. She gazed up at him, thinking of his handsome head on the same pillow with hers. "You sure it's all right with God?"

"Of course. Am I not His prophet? Was He angry with Abraham because he had many wives?"

"Many!" she cried. "How many wives do you want?"

"The more wives I have, the sooner I'll be a god in the next life. You'll be one of my wives there, forever and ever."

That thought pleased her. It would be sweet to be the wife of a prophet in this world, and of a god in the next. "When," she added breathlessly, "am I to come?"

"As soon as we are married."

"Who will marry us?"

"Someone I can trust."

"But Emma—you know we're all afraid of her."

"Don't worry about Emma. We must keep it a secret. You'll have a room all your own and you'll eat at our table; but you'll be only a destitute sister I'm providing for. You will treat me like any other brother except when you are alone with me."

Louisa moved into Nauvoo House and was given a room on the second floor. Joseph intended to have more than two wives; but he learned that not all the women of his choice would yield with Louisa's impulsive candor. He had set his heart on several, among whom were Fanny Alger, Lucinda Harris, and the Huntington sisters—as well as the beautiful wife of Orson Pratt who was away on a mission. There was Sidney Rigdon's daughter, Nancy, a charming lass of sixteen. There was Helen Kimball, tall and dark and dignified. There were the Lawrence sisters. . . .

He saw Fanny one evening out on the river bank; and after watching her gaze out of loneliness at the mighty stream, he resolved to make her his third wife. He drew near and spoke, and then sat by her. Fanny was not a sensuous girl like Louisa: she seemed full of melancholy and strange buried fire. He saw the fire after he told her what was on his mind.

She leapt to her feet, horrified, and gazed down at him as if she were looking at a monster. "You must be crazy!" she said.

"Sister Fanny, don't offend the Almighty. Sit down."

"I won't sit down!"

"Then," he said, rising, "I'll set you down." He lifted her as he might have a child, his gaze meeting the amazement in her eyes. Then, without warning, he kissed her throat and held her against him while she fought like a cat. Setting her on the bank, he dropped at her side and smiled. "There's no use opposing a prophet. God will punish you if you do."

"Oh, God! What does He have to do with it? Besides, you have a wife, haven't you?"

"I need many wives. In the next world ——"

"There won't be any next world for me if I sin in this one!"

"It's not sin," he said sternly. "Do you think I, a prophet of God, would lead women into sin?"

"It looks that way." Her gaze fell to his mouth: she was remembering how he had kissed her; and she was annoyed because she remembered with pleasure. She started to rise but he grasped her arm and drew her to him.

"Fanny, you must be my wife."

"No!"

"I say yes. It is God's will for you to marry me. If you do not, you will go to hell and be damned."

"Oh, will I!" Her mouth was scornful but her eyes were troubled. After all, he was a prophet who wrought miracles; and who was she to say he was wrong! "I'll have to think about it. I must go now."

"Tell no one. If you tell, your punishment will be terrible."

She rose and drew her breath sharply. "I'll probably tell."

"No," he said, facing her. "I command silence."

She held his gaze for a long moment. "All right, but I must think about it. I must be sure it is not sin."

Fanny thought about it for many days and the days grew into weeks. She came to his study and he talked persuasively, eloquently, explaining to her that he was taking wives, not to satisfy carnal desires but because God willed it. He reminded her of the ancient prophets who had had wives many. Little by little, week by week, she yielded, until one day she allowed him to kiss her lips.

"I can't feel right about it," she said, her eyes dark with grief.

"Fanny, if it was sinful, think what my punishment would be. You don't think I'd send myself to hell, do you?"

"No."

"You don't think God would allow our church to prosper, do you?"

"I'm not sure it will. What will the gentiles say when they find it out?"

"They won't find out."

"In time they will. Then they'll persecute us again."

"I have an army now."

"But you can't fight the whole country."

"Fanny, leave those worries to me."

She looked at him again. "Has God told you this is not sinful?"

"God will give me a revelation when I ask for it."

"All right," she said and sighed, and let him draw her to his strong arms.

For Lucinda Harris, a buxom and unimaginative lass, Joseph was almost as mighty and infallible as the Lord. She did not argue. She did not protest at all. It was her duty: that was clear, and she came to him willingly, cheerfully, glad to be the wife of so great a man. But before approaching the Huntington sisters, Joseph thought it would be wise to talk with their brother. He summoned Dimmick and walked with him down Mulholland Street to the river and sat with him on the bank.

Dimmick was so astounded after the proposal that he acted as if he were a water animal, thrown to the bank and fighting for breath. He rolled his eyes and gasped. "You mean," he gurgled at last, "you want a-marry both my sisters?"

"Yes," Joseph said calmly.

"But you got a wife!"

"I explained all that to you. You see, Dimmick, a long time ago, when there were prophets on the earth they had many wives. You have read the Bible?"

"Some," he said.

"Today, we must keep the matter a secret or a sinful world will persecute us again. Under pain of death you must never breathe a word of it."

"But you got a wife," said Dimmick again, as if he could think of nothing else.

"I need many wives. Besides, your sisters are about thirty, aren't they? Are they never to have a husband?"

"That's what they've been wondering. They're too dodgasted homely." Thinking of their homeliness, he turned his wondering gaze on Joseph. "Why should you want a-marry homely women?"

"It's my duty," said Joseph modestly. "If I married for lust, then I'd choose young and beautiful wives. I want children."

"I see," said Dimmick, who saw nothing at all.

"Call Precinda out here and we'll ask her."

The flabbergasted Dimmick went to find his sister, and Joseph sat on the bank, gazing at the stars and wondering which one would warm the planet over which as a god he would eventually rule. He thought of Eliza Snow: he must have her for a wife, too, for she was a poet, and very intelligent and able. . . .

"Here she is," said Dimmick. Joseph looked up to see the tired patient face of Precinda. "I told her all about it."

"That's good," said Joseph. He rose and faced the woman. "Precinda, I want you and Zina to be my wives."

Precinda was as speechless as her red-faced brother: to have a prophet propose marriage to her, a spinster, was as miraculous as the healings. "But—" she said. After staring open-mouthed she added: "It's so unusual, Brother Joseph."

"Yes, perhaps." He looked at her and knew she would yield. She needed a little time. "You think about it, Precinda. Then let me know."

A week later, Dimmick burst into the study, crying that his sisters had made up their minds. They had prayed and prayed and God had answered them. "But they want to tell you themselves!"

"All right. Have them meet me on the river."

Joseph went without haste, knowing what the answer would be. It did not seem strange to him that he was choosing women less attractive than Louisa. It was a duty to marry these unlovely women and save them from the abominable barrenness of the old maid. He took one of Zina's hands, one of Precinda's, and looked from face to face.

"What is your answer, sisters?"

"We will," said Precinda, still feeling that she dreamed.

"Very well." He turned to Dimmick who had followed and now stood gaping. "This is a secret. Watch your tongue and God will reward you."

"If you say it's all right," said Dimmick, wagging his head, "then it must be. But me—could I—would God care if I got me another wife?"

"Brother Dimmick, many wives are only for prophets and other high leaders. If you are faithful, if you become a leader— But not now."

"I see," said Dimmick, almost swallowing his tongue.

"Brother Dimmick, you leave us now. I wish to walk with your sisters."

Joseph now had six wives, but six, he reflected, were less than a handful in comparison with Solomon's; and in the next world, Solomon's offspring would vastly outnumber his own. There were other women in Nauvoo whom he had his eye on, though he was content for a little while to devote himself to the five he had recently chosen. He strove to be impartial with them and to visit them in turn; but he had to confess to himself that some women were more adorable than others and more pleasurable to be with.

One morning Emma said: "Seems to me you're getting a lot of charity cases on your hands. Do you intend to board and room all the women who come here?"

"Charity," he said, "is a part of my service."

"But do you intend to have a whole houseful?"

"I don't intend to turn needy persons away."

"What is it some of them need, that's what I don't understand. I don't like the way Louisa Bemen looks at you."

"Louisa is a nice woman."

"I don't like it," said Emma. "And if I'm not mistaken I saw you coming out of Fanny Alger's room the other morning. Tuesday, it was."

"Sister Fanny was in trouble and called for me."

"What kind of trouble?"

"She had a dream about the Devil."

"About you," said Emma witheringly. "It wouldn't surprise me they all dream about you, because you're Charlie on the spot when they call." She stared at him, wondering what was going on in this huge house.

"I think," he said, keeping his gaze away from her, "that you will have to go to St. Louis to buy supplies."

"Why me? Why not you go?"

"Because you're a better buyer. You always get the bargains."

"That's true," she said, gazing at him suspiciously. "You never did have any nose for bargains. But if I go, I guess you intend to fill this house with women before I get back."

"If," he said gravely, "any needy sisters come to me, I'll see that they are taken care of. I won't allow anyone to go hungry or unclothed."

Her black eyes were so alive with suspicion that he decided to be more discreet. Nevertheless, the thought of skulking around was distasteful to him; for was he not a direct descendant of the ancient Joseph and a prophet of God? Why should anyone dare to question his motives or impute to him unworthiness or carnal desires? He was moved by the will of the Lord in everything he did; and if that were not so, then he would not be a prophet.

So convinced was he of his godliness in taking many wives that he approached Sarah Pratt, the beautiful and fiery wife of Orson who had been sent to Jerusalem. He liked her. If she were his wife, she would share a higher glory in the next life; and with this thought in mind he went to see her one morning.

"Sister Sarah, how are you today?"

"Very well, Brother Joseph. How are you?"

"I think you must get lonely, with your husband so far away."

"Yes, of course. But as long as he is doing the Lord's work I must be content."

"I've been thinking about you," he said, sitting in her small cabin. "You are one of the most remarkable women among the saints."

"It is kind of you to say so, Brother Joseph."

"Sister Sarah, in the next world, persons will not be equal in glory. Take women, for instance. To share the celestial glory, a woman must be married to a man who will inherit it. That means——"

"Yes?" she said, wondering what he was driving at.

"It means that women married to me will enjoy celestial glory."

"Oh—and don't you think Orson will have that glory?"

"I'm afraid not. Brother Orson is a good man but only the highest in the church will inherit the celestial degree. If you were one of my wives——"

"Brother Joseph, what in heaven's name are you talking about?"

"Celestial marriage. We saints must marry for time and eternity, as well as for this life. If Brother Orson reaches only the celestial glory in the next world, then that is all you will have. A wife cannot rise above her husband. If you were married to me ——"

"But you have a wife. And I," she added, remembering, "have a husband."

"I know, Sister. But God has made it known that I am to have many wives. In the next world," he added hastily. "I want you to be one of my celestial wives in the life hereafter."

"Brother Joseph, are you mad?"

"No, Sarah." His smile was patient. "My days on this earth are numbered. I do not want to die without providing for wives in the next world."

"But I am a married woman."

"Not for the celestial life."

"In the hereafter I want to be where my husband is."

"Your celestial husband?"

"My earthly husband. I will be with Orson."

"But think of the greater glory if you are my wife hereafter. You can't afford——"

"Nonsense!" she cried angrily. "If I have to be a sinful woman I don't want any glory."

"You are unreasonable, Sister. You had better think it over."

"If I thought about it until the crack of doom, I'd say what I say now."

"You think it over," he said gently, and left her.

He returned again and again to argue with her. He tried to reason with her. At last, very softly, he threatened her; and beside herself with fury, she ordered him out of her house.

"I'm sick and tired of this talk about celestial glory with you! I don't want to be with you! Now leave my house."

"What did you say?"

"I said to get out and never darken my door again!"

"Sister Sarah, you are speaking to a prophet."

"I don't care if I'm speaking to God Himself! You leave my house and never come back! You send my husband clear to Jerusalem and then you sneak in and try to seduce me. And you call yourself a prophet!"

A little pale and shaken, Joseph rose to his feet and gazed at her angry face. "Sarah, you have misunderstood. I am not trying to seduce anyone. I offered you the privilege of a higher glory in the next life. That is all."

"I don't want it! I'll be with my husband, and if he goes to hell, I'll go there too."

"You'll be sorry for this."

"Oh, will I! I suppose you intend to cut me off from the church. Is that it?"

"You are very unreasonable. You will be sorry. I only want to be sealed to you, not to live with you now."

"What do you mean by that?"

"Under the ordinances of our church, a man can marry a woman for the next life but she can be married to someone else in this life. Then in the next world, she would be the wife of the man she was sealed to."

"Oh," she said, flabbergasted. "I suppose you expect to get sealed—as you call it—to every wife in Nauvoo so you can have thousands in the next life."

"No, not thousands, Sister—but a great many. If you marry me for the next life, your glory ——"

"Oh, shut up about glory! Leave my house!"

"Very well, Sister. But I solemnly charge you to say nothing of this matter to anyone. It is to be a secret until God tells me to make it public."

"A secret? I should think it would be!"

"So please say nothing about it."

Pained by her stubborn spirit, Joseph left the cabin. It seemed to him very stupid of her to imagine she would be content, during all of eternity without end, in a lower degree of glory than she could have. She might be satisfied now but she would be sorry then.

CHAPTER XXVI

JOSEPH HAD HEARD OF JOHN BENNETT. THAT SHREWD OPPORTUNIST, REPREsenting himself as a soldier of fortune, a politician, and a favorite of the great, had been writing flattering letters for months, extolling the new church, praising Joseph to the skies, and offering his services. When Nauvoo prospered, Bennett added that he was a doctor, had been a general in the Illinois militia, and had the ear of men who could be of great assistance in the growth of Mormonism. Joseph smelled the insincerity in the urbane letters. He distrusted the man's handwriting, his rhetorical flourishes, his boasting and the sweeping curves of his signature. Nevertheless, he invited Bennett to come to Nauvoo.

And when John Bennett walked into the study, Joseph looked up to behold a handsome man whose gracious bearing and soft voice declared him to be as worldly an adventurer as any person between Nauvoo and the Hill of Cumorah. Joseph eyed him closely and wondered if he had made a mistake.

"The time will come," Bennett was saying, after the inanities of greeting were done with, "when enemies will again be at your throat. That is where I can serve. I have spent most of my life in politics and war. You can use me. You need a man of broad experience to advise you. Besides," he added, without even the shadow of a smile, "I have been converted to your religion. I believe yours to be the only true church on earth."

"It is," said Joseph.

"On that," said Bennett gravely, "we fully agree. If by any chance you have a man of my experience already in your service——"

"No, Brother John, I need you."

John liked the familiarity. He rubbed his soft white palms and proceeded to other matters. "You are so busy with spiritual problems that you need a man to take care of the temporal ones. You need someone to take off your mind all the petty worries and details of government and city management. I could be your righthand man. As mayor of Nauvoo, for instance? With your assistance and approval, of course."

Joseph was still studying the man. Whether John Bennett was a rascal or only a man of extreme zeal, he could not tell. No matter: he believed he could handle him. Had he not put the ambitious Sidney Rigdon in his place, and sent the ambitious apostles on missions?

Bennett had been speaking. He now added graciously: "If I have erred——"

"No. Let's go out and look things over."

They looked things over, and almost before Joseph realized it, John Bennett was mayor of Nauvoo and a powerful man in the city. But he was an obedient, almost an obsequious, lieutenant and Joseph was not alarmed. He took Bennett into his confidence and told him of plural marriage, and said Bennett could have as many wives as he wished. Bennett rubbed his hands again and smiled serenely upon the privilege. As a handsome man and the mayor of the city, he had an advantage over all other men but Joseph; and he was quick to see it. Besides, he was tired of his wife.

"I can understand," he said softly, "that God finds it wise to restore the divine right of polygamy."

"I do not use that word," said Joseph. "I think of it as celestial marriage."

"Of course," said John. "How many celestial marriages have you—consummated?"

"I do not choose to tell. You are privileged to take as many wives as you please."

"Are any of the other saints taking more than one?"

"Not yet. All the leaders but Brother Sidney are on missions—and Sidney is too old. When the apostles return, I expect to tell them of God's will in the matter."

"They'll probably be astounded," said John, with his soft sly smile. "Does your wife, Sister Emma, know of this?"

"No. Telling Emma is a problem I have postponed."

"I can understand that too," said John; but his voice said he intended no offense. "And speaking of Brother Sidney reminds me of his daughter. Nancy is very lovely."

"Yes," said Joseph a little sharply. He had been thinking of her.

"How old is she?"

"Sixteen, I think."

"Well," said John, composing his face, "I'll think it over. I'm not at all sure," he added, lying with the calmness of thirty years, "that I want more wives. Even, I mean, celestial ones."

"It is your duty. It is God's will."

"Yes, I can appreciate that."

Foreseeing that John might want Nancy for a wife, Joseph asked her to his study; and after she had visited him twice and had listened to the glory of celestial marriage, Joseph rose one afternoon and went around his desk to her.

"Sister Nancy," he said, "I want to kiss you."

"Kiss me!" she cried, starting up.

"Yes," he said, and reached for her hands.

Dodging him, she ran to the door, only to find it locked. Trembling with fear and anger she turned to face him, with her head high and her throat crimson with shame. "Let me out of here!"

"No, Nancy. God intends for you to be one of my wives."

"Wives! Then it's true you have a lot of wives!"

"I have only the wives God has commanded me to have. You are to be——"

"Unlock this door!"

"No."

"Then I'll scream. I'll tell the whole city about you."

"You wouldn't risk God's anger, would you?"

"God's anger!" she cried scornfully. "Isn't my father second in command? Why should God be angry with Sidney Rigdon's daughter?"

"I, not your father, am the prophet."

"If you don't open," she said, stamping her foot, "I'll scream! I swear it by everything in heaven!"

Distressed, Joseph went over and unlocked the door, and watched Nancy flee like a wild thing. He returned to his desk, wondering what to do. Perhaps it would be best to write her a letter; for after she had cooled off she would see the wisdom of his purpose and return to him in remorse. He wrote a long letter. He explained to her that what God commanded was right, no matter how much it offended tradition or prejudice; and asked her to pray and to consider the proposal calmly, not as a willful girl but as a saint resolved to do her duty.

After he had dispatched the letter he was still worried: she was headstrong and violent like her father and as likely as not would try to set the whole city upon his head. Going alone to the river, Joseph knelt in prayer and asked God to reveal to Nancy the folly of her stubbornness. The next day he waited—and the next.

It was not Nancy but her father who came on the third day. Sidney Rigdon was furious, and when furious, his huge ministerial face, with its great thrust of nose, its grotesquely wide upper lip and high forehead, his cold humorless eyes, made a picture that was terrifying.

"Joseph," he roared, "what is this I hear?"

"Brother Sidney, you're agitated. Sit down."

"I don't want to sit down! What have you been trying to do with my daughter?"

"Your daughter? You mean Nancy?"

"Of course I mean Nancy! What did you mean by that letter you wrote?"

Joseph frowned thoughtfully. "As I remember it, Sidney, I was trying to explain to her some matters of church doctrine. She came to me ——"

"Yes, and you locked the door and tried to seduce her!"

"Seduce her! Brother Sidney, you're out of your mind again."

"I'm in my mind all right. Do you deny you tried to kiss her?"

"I do. I asked her to kiss me. I was testing her virtue. Some of the sisters are getting careless."

"Yes, by God, they are! Is it true you're living in adultery with a flock of them?"

"Adultery!" cried Joseph, horrified. "Sidney, you don't seem to know what adultery is."

"Is it true," Rigdon went on, almost slobbering with rage, "that you have several mistresses in this house?"

"I have several wives."

"Wives! Do you think you're Solomon?"

"I'm a descendant of Joseph. It is God's will."

"And you wanted Nancy for a mistress, did you? It's true, then, that you were seducing girls in Kirtland! What Oliver Cowdery said ——"

"I'm doing only what God commanded me to do."

"Such as kiss my daughter who's only a child!"

"Sister Nancy is a very attractive young woman."

"You adulterous fraud!" Rigdon howled, now beside himself. "I'll have the church on you for this! I'll have you thrown out!"

"Brother Sidney," said Joseph, his voice soft but dangerous, "you tried that once before. I forgave you and asked God to forgive you. Henceforth, you had better understand your position."

"Then I'll leave the damned church!"

"Do as you please. Your faith has been weak for a long time. What you know about me is a secret and I advise you to say nothing to anyone."

"What will the apostles say?"

"I'll explain celestial marriage to them when they return. If you want several wives ——"

"One wife is enough for a God-fearing man!"

"—you may have them. You are a leader. The leaders are privileged because they will inherit a higher degree of glory."

"Other wives!" cried Rigdon, aghast. He remembered that he was a much older man than Joseph. "One wife is all I care to have."

"That is for you to decide."

"How many concubines do you have in this building?"

"I resent that. These ladies are my wives, not concubines."

"Well, you leave my daughter alone. You understand that?"

"I have no wish to marry your daughter."

"I tell you, Joseph, that when the other leaders hear about this, there will be hell to pay. And what about the gentiles? Are you trying to get us in jail again?"

"I am not afraid of our enemies. I have an army now."

Rigdon turned away, shaking his huge gloomy head. "I don't like it. I think I'll go to Pittsburgh."

After Rigdon left, Joseph thought the distressing episode was closed. He had forgotten John Bennett. And when, an hour later, that cunning man strode in, he was angry too, though anger with him was never more than tightness in his mouth and a sharper alertness in his eyes.

"Joe," he said insolently, "what is this I hear? Have you been cutting shines around Nancy Rigdon?"

"My name is Joseph, not Joe."

"Joe or Joseph, it's all the same to me. Didn't I tell you I want Nancy for one of my wives?"

"I don't remember. But what if you did?"

"I intend to have her. I'm a worldly man, Joe, and it takes sly skulduggery to fool me. I've been watching your monkeyshines."

Joseph smiled faintly. "I'll wrestle you for her."

"No, I'm not fool enough to wrestle you. There are better ways in love and war. I told you a week ago I wanted Nancy. Why do you try to hog all the best women?"

Joseph was distressed by the man's vulgar way of putting it. He was annoyed. The faint smile left his face. "I am the prophet," he said.

"Yes," said Bennett softly, "but I'm the mayor of Nauvoo."

"With my permission."

"Your permission! If Nauvoo knew you have a harem, what would happen to your power?"

"You trying to threaten me?"

"No—not quite. We are both playing a game. You're wise enough to know we're in the same boat. If you start rocking it, I'll tip it over."

"So you're threatening me," said Joseph, looking at Bennett's immaculate whiskers.

"I'm just saying I want Nancy Rigdon."

"Take her then. I don't want her."

"But you tried to seduce her."

"That's a lie!" Joseph rose from his desk. He was angry now. "Don't try to intimidate me. Any power you have in this city is the power I give you. I am the ruler here. If you can persuade Sister Nancy to marry you, do so. But don't try to cause me any trouble——"

"Sit down!" cried Bennett impatiently. "Your high and mighty righteousness has never fooled me, Joseph. We are two of a kind."

"What do you mean?"

"I mean you don't believe in Mormonism any more than I do. Like me, you saw in it an instrument of power."

"You're blasphemous! Do you mean——"

"I mean we should understand one another. We had better play the game together or we will both sink. But if we sink, you'll sink deeper. I can run but you'll have to stand up to the rack."

Joseph looked at Bennett, astonished by his perfidy. "Do you mean to tell me, Brother John, that when you joined my church you did so for your own worldly advantage?"

"My motive," said Bennett blandly, "was about the same as yours."

"You Judas! I'll have you thrown out of the church and out of Illinois!"

"I wouldn't try any ringtail stuff, Joseph. It is an open and shut proposition. We are in the same boat and you're rocking it."

"You'll be lucky," said Joseph, narrowing his gaze, "if you get out alive."

"Oh, indeed! You mean Porter Rockwell, I suppose."

"I mean there are ways to handle a Judas."

Bennett rose to his feet, deciding that he had overplayed his hand. "I'm sorry," he said gently, "if I angered you. I was jesting. I wanted to test your emotional convictions in the matter."

"Now," said Joseph, still gazing at the man, "you are adding lies to apostasy."

"No, my faith is firm. I just lost my head, Joseph. I wanted Nancy and I thought you were after her."

For a long moment the two men looked at one another. Joseph said: "If your heart is with God, you will remain in the church. If it is not, the sooner you get out of Illinois, the better."

"My heart," said Bennett, simulating anger, "is where yours is. You can count on me." He went to the door and turned. "I shouldn't have jested about holy matters but I wanted to learn how strong your faith is."

Joseph did not have Brigham's canny power to read human hearts, but he knew now beyond all doubt that he had made a mistake in this man. Bennett had not been jesting at all; and he had gone away, not in shame, but to plot more cunningly. That Bennett could ruin him, Joseph knew well—unless the apostles stood behind their prophet. They were sailing home now. They would be here soon and they would find another crisis impending. They would come home to learn that the mayor of Nauvoo was a stealthy and cold-blooded rascal who had slipped like a Judas into Zion. Joseph knew that he would have to convince the apostles that plural marriage was approved by God; he would have to enlist their support. Without it, he could not hope to survive this new storm that was gathering.

Whether he could convince them, he did not know: he had worried about the matter, realizing that all of them would be appalled, that some of them would be very obstinate. He could not decide which to approach first: Brigham perhaps, or Parley, or one of his own brothers. In any case, he had to convince the twelve of the godliness of plural marriage, and persuade them to take other wives to themselves.

For many days he considered the problem. He could turn to no one for counsel, nor did he wish to: he was not the frightened man who had been chased out of New York, out of Ohio, out of Missouri: he was thirty-seven now and confident of his power. He was the absolute dictator in this city. He had a well-trained army that would soon reach its quota of five thousand men. Both the Whigs and the Democrats fought for his favor. The ambitious Abraham Lincoln, the wily Stephen Douglas, and the governor of Illinois were glad to call him friend. His apostles had converted thousands in England, and whole boatloads were embarking for Nauvoo; and missionaries between Nauvoo and the Atlantic seaboard had converted other thousands and were establishing strong branches of the church.

What had he to be afraid of? He was the general of an army, the ruler of a free city, the political balance of a state and the prophet of God. There was nothing, it seemed to him, to be afraid of and he was not afraid.

He waited confidently for the apostles to come home.

CHAPTER XXVII

H E DECIDED TO APPROACH HYRUM FIRST, HIS ONLY BROTHER WHO HAD risen to power in the church. Unlike William, who had trounced Joseph, Hyrum had always been loyal, never doubting the prophet's wisdom or integrity; but after hearing of plural marriage he was shocked speechless. His fair face turned ghastly pale and his blue eyes grew wide with horror.

"What," he gasped, "are you telling me!"

"The truth. I always speak the truth, Hyrum, when I speak as a prophet."

"Then you're not speaking as a prophet now! This is blasphemy!"

"No, Hyrum. It is God's commandment to us."

"I can't believe it!" Hyrum paced the floor, trembling and sick and horrified. "Do you have more wives than Emma?"

"I do."

"Great God! Joseph, this abominable doctrine will break up the church!"

"Nothing can break a church that God has founded."

"It will cost you your life! It will be the death of all of us!"

"My life, Hyrum? I've always believed that I would pay for my ministry with my blood. But didn't Jesus? And did you ever think that Jesus was crucified perhaps because He had many wives?"

"Jesus had many wives! Joseph, are you insane?"

"I think Jesus had many wives. At least, several women loved Him."

"I tell you you'll ruin the church with this doctrine!"

"It's the Lord's commandment, not mine. If you don't believe, ask the Lord yourself and He will make the truth known to you."

"I will!" Hyrum cried, still pacing the room.

"Then I'll want you to help me convince some others—including Emma."

"Emma! Nobody could convince Emma of anything. She can't pray."

"She must be convinced. If she isn't, she'll raise Cain. She'll blow the roof right off this building when she learns about me."

"I don't doubt it. She'll kill you."

"Kill me?" said Joseph. He had not thought of that. "You argue with her, Hyrum, but we must convince the other apostles first."

"I'm not convinced yet!" cried Hyrum angrily.

"You will be. You must pray. Go off alone and ask the Lord."

"Yes." When he turned, his eyes were filled with tears. "Joseph, I've never doubted you; but God Himself must tell me before I can believe this. I'll go away and humble myself in prayer."

Joseph put an arm around his brother. "Do so. Then come back. I will need your help with those whose faith is not so strong."

Brigham's faith Joseph had never doubted. He summoned him next. He was not prepared for his response; for after listening to Joseph, after learning that God had commanded all the leaders to take other wives, the practical hard-headed Brigham bowed his face and wept. He did not shed tears. He shook with great dry sobs and hid his face in his hands. When he raised his face, it was haggard with anxiety and doubt.

"Joseph, have you gone crazy?"

"No, Brigham. You have not studied your Bible well or you would know that plural marriage has always been commanded of God's chosen people."

Like Hyrum, Brigham rose and paced the floor, his strong and unsentimental face twitching with anguish. "I can't believe it!" he cried again and again.

"You will, Brigham, after you have humbled yourself in prayer."

"Damn it, I think you're out of your wits! Do you have several wives now?"

"Yes."

Brigham shook his head sadly and pondered. "I'm not a man to shrink from duty. I will do what God wants me to do. But this—damn it, this makes me want to—to be dead! Never in my life before have I wanted to be dead; but now I want to be in my grave and never get up, not even for the last bugle. I want a ton of sod piled on me and earth in my eyes."

"After you have humbled yourself and prayed and asked of God, you will know that I am right."

"I can't believe it. I wish I had never been born." After pacing a few moments, he turned. "Who else has been taking a lot of wives?"

"Only John Bennett yet."

"I don't like that man. Have you talked to any of the other apostles?"

"Only Hyrum. He humbled himself and God gave him a revelation."

"He did! Does Hyrum believe now?"

"Yes."

Brigham had never doubted Joseph as a prophet. He had questioned his wisdom in temporal but not in spiritual matters. Nevertheless, this was astounding doctrine, this notion that a man in this day and age could have many wives. He rubbed his perplexed brow and considered.

"Listen well to this," said Joseph. "We must keep this matter an absolute secret among the leaders until God tells me to reveal it to the world. If we don't keep it secret——"

"Why," said Brigham, "we'll be run out of here. You talked with Heber?"

"No."

"Talk to him. If you can convince him—but damn it to hell, you can't!"

Joseph was not prepared for the response of the tall dignified Heber Kimball. Heber looked as if he had heard a sermon by the Devil. He was so amazed that he could not speak, but only stared at Joseph, his incredulous eyes full of terrible pain. His whole face twitched from his hair to his chin, with his beard behaving as if minute invisible animals were running through it. Joseph rose and patted Heber's shoulder but the man did not speak. He only gazed ahead of him, his eyes fixed in immutable horror.

"Great God!" he cried at last, as if he had seen the end of everything he had loved and fought for. Then, like Brigham, he bowed to his hands and shook with grief.

Joseph looked at the bowed head and talked quietly, patiently, reminding Heber of ancient leaders who had many wives; and pointing out that a saint's pilgrimage to godhood depended largely on the number of his offspring. He told Heber the whole matter must be guarded as a secret for months and perhaps for years. Then he used an argument that was to be used again and again by him and the apostles.

"Heber, if a man marries and his wife dies, it is all right to marry again. It is all right to marry a third, a fourth, a fifth time. When this man rises in the next world, he will have five wives, won't he?"

"I had never thought of that."

"Does it matter," Joseph went on, "whether he has five wives one at a time or five all at the same time? They'll all be with him in the next life. If many wives are all right with God in the next life, why are they not all right in this one?"

"I hadn't thought of it," said Heber.

"Think of it and you will understand the beauty and wisdom and necessity. Celestial marriage is only for the pure in heart who are also leaders. It is not for every man, Brother Heber. It is for those who will inherit celestial glory. It is your duty."

Heber rose. "I must think about it," he said. "I will go and humble myself in prayer."

A few days later Heber's daughter Helen came to Joseph's study. She was agitated. Her eyes showed that she had been spending sleepless nights.

"It's about my father," she said. "He is going insane. He can't eat, he can't sleep. He walks the floor all night. He won't tell Mama what the trouble is. He just wrings his hands and weeps, or he prays and then lies on the bed for hours and moans. He's sick. But we don't know what to do."

While she talked, Joseph studied her. He had been intending for some while to ask Helen to be one of his wives. He had nine now. Since marrying the Huntington sisters, he had taken Eliza Snow, Sarah Whitney and Desdemona Fullmer.

"I'll tell you what is troubling your father," he said. While he explained, she gazed at him with dark eyes that steadily filled with amazement. Then came horror and she began to weep. "There now," he said, reaching over to pat her hands. "There are many things we must do that may not seem for the best; but God in His infinite wisdom is working for our salvation and happiness and glory. We must try to understand His purpose. When we understand, then we realize how ignorant we have been." He assisted her to her feet and placed hands on her shoulders. "Helen, I want you to be one of my wives."

"I!" she cried, shrinking from him.

"I know you feel shocked. Your father did. I want you to go home and explain everything to your mother. Tell her to pray to God to show her what is right. And you pray, Helen. God will reveal the truth to you if you humble yourself."

Helen was backing away from him. "No wonder my father can't sleep! No wonder he is losing his mind!"

"You do as I say. Tell your mother and then both of you pray for light."

"My poor father!" The loathing in her eyes, Joseph realized, was not for him but for what he had told her.

"You must go home and pray, Helen. God will reveal to you the wisdom and glory of celestial marriage."

Slowly she had been backing away from him. When she reached the door she opened it and backed out, her gaze still on Joseph's face.

To his surprise, Helen returned within a week. She was radiant. Her mother, she said, had suffered terribly but she had prayed day and night; and at last she had a vision in which the glory and truth of celestial marriage had been opened to her. She understood now how it would exalt her above most women in this life and in the next, what honor it would bring to her, and the greater glory that would come to her husband in a world without end. Her father was overjoyed too.

"He knows it is right now," said Helen. "We all know. We are very happy."

"Then you will be my wife?"

"Yes, Brother Joseph, if you want me."

Joseph rose without haste and came to her side. In her eyes he saw such happiness as he had never seen in human eyes before. "Come," he said.

One by one he convinced the apostles and a few other leaders and pledged them to secrecy; and they began to take wives, though none took so many as the prophet himself. After marrying Helen, Joseph wedded the Partridge sisters, Emily and Eliza; and then set his fancy on a lass of sixteen named Lucy Walker. He was bolder now. He called Lucy to his study and went straight to the point.

"I have a message for you," he said, looking at the question in her clear gray eyes. "God has commanded me to take another wife and you are the woman." He had seen surprise in women before but never such amazement as now left Lucy speechless. Her eyes opened wide and round; her mouth opened and her shoulders sagged, as if his statement had relaxed every muscle of her body. "Do you consent?"

Lucy was too astounded to answer. She gaped helplessly while he explained. When he asked, "Do you believe I am a prophet?" she gasped and looked more bewildered than ever. "What have you to say?"

Coming a little to her senses, she moistened her lips and made an effort to speak. Failing, she drew away from him, her eyes still wide and round, her mouth helplessly open. With a great effort she gasped: "Nothing!"

"You go home and pray," he said gently. "You will receive a testimony from the Lord."

She continued to look at him as if hypnotized. When he opened the door for her, she suddenly came to life and fled.

The next day Joseph called at the cabin where she lived alone. She had no parents. She had no one to turn to for advice; but for hours she had been praying frantically, desperately, and looked now like a girl who was losing her mind. She was haggard because she had not slept. She was worn out from prayer and weeping and anguish of soul.

"How are you?" asked Joseph, smiling. "Will you marry me?"

"No."

"Have you prayed?"

"Yes."

"Have you received a testimony?"

"No."

"Haven't you received any answer to your prayers?"

"No."

"Then you must pray again. I warn you, Lucy: if you reject this commandment, heaven will be closed to you forever."

That statement did something to Lucy. She had been standing like a woman of stone, giving a yes or a no to everything he said; but now she came to furious life. The astonishment left her eyes. They flashed with fire; her lovely lips curled in bitter scorn.

"Listen to me!" she cried. "You're a prophet but you can't make me marry you unless I know God wants me to!"

"I told you to pray."

"I did! I prayed for hours. I don't want you to speak to me about it. I won't marry you unless God commands me. I won't!"

Joseph was smiling. He looked very handsome today. "May God bless you," he said. "You will receive a testimony. I'll tell you what it will be. You will feel deeper joy and peace than you have ever felt. But you must first humble yourself in prayer."

"I did humble myself!" she cried wildly. "I tell you I did!"

"Not enough. When you really humble yourself, God will make His will known to you."

"I don't believe it!"

"Yes, it is so. You pray more earnestly. Then God will give you a testimony." He smiled and bowed and left her.

He almost forgot her in the days that followed. He was wooing several other girls, including Almera Johnson, Malissa Lott, Fanny Young and Maria and Sarah Lawrence. Early one morning Lucy unexpectedly entered his study. She had been walking in the fresh air and looked very radiant.

"Have you received a testimony?"

"Yes!" she cried happily. "Night after night," she went on, her words pouring out in almost breathless joy, "I prayed and prayed. I couldn't sleep. I thought I would go mad. Then, just before daylight this morning, my room was all lit up. It was so bright I thought the sun had come up and I jumped out of bed but it was still dark outside. Then I knew what had happened. Oh, I was so full of holy peace! I was so happy I went out to walk, just to be sure it was all true." She advanced with hands on her breast, her gaze worshiping him.

"You have received the testimony," he said softly. "Sit here, Lucy, and I will bless you." She sank to the chair and Joseph laid his hands on her head. He blessed her with every blessing he could think of and then drew her to him. "We'll be married now," he said.

He had nearly twenty wives now, all living in the big house as his nieces or adopted sisters. He had foreseen that the gaunt and embittered Emma would smell the deception eventually and demand to know where all these nieces and sisters were coming from. Nevertheless, he might have gone on for many years, cunningly deceiving her if his enemies had not loosed their tongues. John Bennett had been ousted from his position as mayor, and was now vindictively bent on Joseph's ruin, telling all over Nauvoo that the prophet was a lecherous scoundrel. He said Joseph was seducing every girl he could get his carnal hands on. He even said that Joseph had been a lascivious villain from the beginning, and a fraud and a Judas as well.

Other persons began to talk. When the stories came to Emma, she aroused herself one morning like a tigress coming out of a long sleep and went into her husband's office. He heard her coming. He knew by her stride that she boded thunder and cyclone. When she strode in he rose and faced her, but he was not so calm as he seemed.

"What's this I hear about you?" asked the embattled Emma. "I mean all these women! All these nieces and adopted sisters and charity cases! So you've been sleeping with them, have you? You long-nosed fraud! You low, scurvy hypocrite!"

"Watch your tongue," he said.

"You lustful devil out of hell! So you're a prophet, are you? A prophet! You mouth-almighty stinking rascal, that's what you are! Right in my house, right under my nose, you have a whole damned harem! I could murder you!"

"Will you listen to reason?"

"You deceitful two-faced lying Judas! Do you think I'm a fool? Why, the whole city is talking about you and saying how you pulled the wool over my eyes! The whole city——"

"If you'll listen to me——"

"Shut up!" she yelled, her black eyes loathing him. "You clean the whole adulterous mess out of here or I'll climb to a roof and tell the world about you! You and your celestial wives! You and your concubines! I suppose the Lord gave you a revelation about this, didn't He?"

"He did."

"You liar!" She advanced and breathed up into his pale face, her mouth snarling at him, her eyes black liquid contempt. "You adulterous sneaking skunk! God never gave you a revelation in all your life! You've fooled others, you demon of lust, but you never fooled me! I would have put up with it if you hadn't moved your harem right into my house."

"Will you listen to reason?"

"I'll listen to nothing! You get these prostitutes out of here or I'll raise a scandal that will blow you over the moon! You hear me? Get the filthy wenches out of here!"

Joseph was a little angered. "If you try to ruin me, I'll throw you out of the church. You'll be damned forever."

"I want to be damned forever if I have to live with a houseful of bawds! And don't threaten me, Joe." Her lips drew back in thin mockery. "You threaten others but I'm up to your tricks. Throw me out of the church and I'll tell everything I know about you. I'll publish it all over the world."

Joseph sank to a chair. This violent woman had been a thorn in his side ever since he married her. He hardly knew what to do.

"You were run out of New York," she was saying, hissing at him. "You got in a big swindle and were chased out of Ohio. You got stuck in a dungeon in Missouri. You'll get worse than that if you don't get these wenches out."

"Don't speak that way of my wives."

"Your wives!" she said, snorting with mad wicked laughter.

"They are all good pure women."

"God, yes! Do the hypocrites want me to know about them? Haven't they all been liars and pretenders right under my nose? Nieces and sisters! Good pure women, are they? Since when have hypocrites been good pure women? Listen, you lustful dog of a man, I don't intend to argue with you. Get them out of here."

"All right," said Joseph, mopping his brow, "I will. But I want to keep those who don't have any place to live."

"They had a place before you smuggled them in here, didn't they?"

"They have no place now."

"Which ones?"

"Emily and Eliza for two. Let them stay and I'll move the others."

"In God's name, just how many do you have?"

"Why—" he said, trying to remember.

"You can't tell how many!" Her mad laugh rang again. "You mean you have so damned many concubines you've forgotten the number? Well, I guess Solomon forgot too! And what are you going to do with all the babies? Unless my eyes lie like you do, a lot of these nieces and sisters—or," she asked witheringly, "are they just getting fat?"

"Emma, I wish you'd think it over. I can't move them out into the street."

"That's where prostitutes belong."

"Silence!" Joseph roared. "I'll not allow you to speak that way of good women."

"Shut up. Get them out of here."

"You think it over. You are very uncharitable."

Emma thought it over and returned to say that Eliza and Emily could remain if he took the others out at once.

"All right," he said, and went to find his wives. Some, like Lucy and Helen, smilingly assented and others protested; but they all yielded to his will and gathered their few belongings and went to the homes of relatives or friends. It was absurd, Joseph reflected, to allow the hard-bitten Emma to drive his wives out.

He had other worries. The unscrupulous John Bennett was trying to split the church wide open and to become the leader of a dominant faction. Stories of celestial wives had reached the gentiles; there were angry mutterings throughout Illinois. There was unrest among the saints, too, and some of them in disgust were leaving the church. Others were furious because the privilege of plural marriage had not been given to all members. In every day now, angry men came to Joseph's study to argue with him, or to heap abuse and threaten. There was Tim McBride.

He stalked in with his honest red face full of woe and wrath. Scowling at Joseph, he asked: "You remember me?"

"I don't think so. I meet so many persons."

"I'm Timothy McBride. I talked with you just before you went to jail."

"Yes, I remember now. Will you sit down?"

"I'n say what I have to say just as well standing up."

"What is the trouble?"

"All this polygamy is the trouble. I didn't believe it until last week. I mean I thought it was a wagonload of lies."

"It is, Brother Timothy."

"It isn't! You know Lucy Ann Decker?"

"I think I've met Sister Lucy."

"Well, Lucy Ann and me, we've been engaged. We was to be married when I got a house built."

"That's very good. Do you have the house built?"

"Built, hell!" cried Tim, almost purple with disgust. "Yes, damn it, I got it built. And then what happened?"

"What?" asked Joseph softly.

"Why, Brigham Young comes along and says Lucy is to be one of his wives! He tells her she'll have more glory in the next world if she marries him. So what does she do? She shines right up and marries him!"

"Well, there are other girls——"

"Why didn't he marry them? Lucy was mine. Didn't I save her life one night? Didn't I help her out of Missouri?"

"Brother Brigham is right. Sister Lucy will share more glory in the next life as one of his wives."

"To hell with glory! What about me? What about Jack Daggett? He had a girl and along comes Heber Kimball and marries her. What about

Jonas Littleton? Ain't Parley Pratt marrying his girl? It's all mighty nice for you and the apostles but what about us?" Tim drew a long handkerchief and snorted into it furiously. He looked up. "What about me?" he said.

"You must understand that it is God's commandment, not mine. Would you oppose the Almighty?"

"No, I wouldn't. But I don't think the Almighty ever meant me to lose my girl. If He did, then I don't think a hell of a lot of the Almighty."

"You are being blasphemous."

"By God, I should a-stayed with the Danites who became apostates, I guess. I should a-knowed there was something crooked about the whole business."

"Silence!" Joseph rose and faced the man and Timothy was overwhelmed by his bearing. "Do you believe I am a prophet?"

"I guess I do."

"I say to you it is God's will for Brigham to marry Lucy Ann and for you to marry some other woman."

"It don't look right to me," said Tim stubbornly.

"Many things may not look right to you or to all of us. I advise you to go off by yourself and pray."

"I'd rather fight," said Tim.

"I command you to pray. You will see the light and you will understand."

"I'll try," Tim said, "but I don't think it will do a damn bit of good. My father don't either."

"Who is your father?"

"Moroni McBride. You saw him in Far West."

"Brother Timothy, you should not have told your father about this. Celestial marriage is a secret ——"

"The whole city is talking about it!"

"I know that. But it is a secret, just the same."

"Are you lying about it? If persons ask you if it's true, do you say no?"

Joseph hesitated. "Yes, Brother Timothy. We must not tell the truth until God reveals to me that I am to make celestial marriage known. Tell your father to say nothing about it."

"You mean to tell me," asked Tim, amazed, "that a prophet of God tells lies?

"Brother Timothy, you do not understand all things. I tell you again to pray and God will make His will known to you."

"I don't think so. And I don't think God intends His prophet to be a liar."

"Brother Timothy, that will do. You may go now." Joseph followed him to the door. "Say nothing about this to anyone. If your father would like to take another wife——"

"He wouldn't! My mother is his wife."

"If he should, tell him to come to me."

Joseph soon forgot such trivial matters. He had bigger worries. Bennett was telling that licentiousness was rampant in the Mormon city, and was inciting men to organize and march on the town. More serious still, at least for the moment, was an attempt to assassinate Governor Boggs in Missouri. While sitting by his window one night he was shot by an unknown man outside; and the Missouri newspapers declared in great black headlines that Porter Rockwell had been the skulking would-be assassin, and Joseph Smith had been the instigator. Rewards were placed on the heads of both men, and posses came from Missouri to Nauvoo to capture the prophet.

"Missouri is demanding your extradition!" cried Brigham, bursting into the study. "You'd better hide."

"Hide, when I have an army of several thousand men?"

"Right now it's better to hide than to fight. If we fight, Illinois will be up in arms too. If we hide, the matter might blow over."

"I'm tired of running. I've been running from place to place for twenty years." He led Brigham to a west window and looked out. "We should have gone yonder."

"Yes, to the Rocky Mountains or Oregon."

"Somewhere."

"We're headed for trouble again, Joseph. Celestial marriage is going to be our downfall."

"Brigham, is your faith weak? What God commands, we do."

"But we can't keep it a secret. How long are we going to lie about it?"

"Until God tells us to stop lying."

"It would have been better to go west. It's plural marriage causing the mobs to form again. We can lie and lie but they don't believe us."

"We have an army."

"An army would be all right in the Rocky Mountains. Here it will just bring the government down on us. Besides, you can't fight bandits with an army."

"Too many of the brethren talk too much."

"It's the women. Don't you know that women can't keep a secret—especially when they learn their husband has another wife?"

"We must rebuke the sisters."

"Yes, and they'll gossip all the harder."

"Brigham, I do not intend to run again."

"But hide, Joseph. Let's see if it won't blow over."

For a month Joseph hid, going stealthily from home to home; moving under cover of night when one place was discovered, and crawling like a hunted thing into the next. It seemed stupid to him for a prophet of God, with a trained army at his call, to sneak around like a thief—and all because bandits from Missouri had come here to get him. He felt great wrath and now and then resolved to march forth and defy the world; but always one of his leaders slipped in to counsel him, to argue, to implore secrecy, and to report what was happening.

Porter Rockwell had escaped from Missouri and had fled to the East. Here in Nauvoo were sheriffs with warrants: they were offering a huge sum of money to anyone who would betray Joseph and point out his hiding place; but every saint approached told them to go to hell and be damned. These reports brought tears to Joseph's eyes.

"Thank God for their loyalty! But why should I hide like a fox? I'd rather march out at the head of my army."

"No." It was Parley speaking. "There'll be trouble soon enough—and plenty of it. It's celestial marriage that has brought our enemies down on us. I'm afraid it was a mistake."

"A revelation from God cannot be a mistake."

"Just the same, I'm having an awful time myself. When my wife finds out I have other wives I think she will murder me. Anyhow, I can see no way out of this mess."

"We'll fight our way out."

"But we can't fight the government. Joseph, don't you think it would be best to sell our property and go to the Rocky Mountains?"

"No. I'm sick of running. I'm going to fight it out right here."

"But we can't fight mobs with an army. They're already beginning to burn our haystacks out in the country. They'll sneak in here and burn our homes. It will be Missouri all over again."

"I won't run," said Joseph. "The Constitution of this nation protects us in our conscience and form of worship and in our rights. If the United States won't defend free men, we'll defend ourselves."

"But we can't, Joseph. We can't fight mobs except with mobs."

"Don't argue with me, Parley. I tell you I am going to fight."

"If we had kept celestial marriage a secret, we'd be all right. John Bennett betrayed us."

"He's a Judas. He will burn in hell forever."

"Well, you stay in hiding a while longer. We'll wait and see what happens."

But Joseph did not stay in hiding. Unexpectedly one day he marched boldly forth and summoned his people in a huge meeting. He had donned his uniform of lieutenant-general in the Legion and looked very regal in his tight breeches and swallow-tail coat, ornamented with glittering braid. He mounted a platform; and those closest to him saw that he was very angry, that his eyes were like cold blue flame.

"My people," he said, lifting a hand to still the cheering, "I am tired of arrests and writs and trials and dungeons. I'm tired of hiding out like a coyote. And to you I say this: if any citizens of Illinois say we shall not have our rights, treat them as strangers and not friends, and let them go to hell and be damned! If we have to give up our chartered rights, privileges, and freedom, which our fathers fought, bled and died for, and which the Constitution of the United States and of this state guarantees unto us, we will do it only at the point of the sword and the bayonet!

"I tell you before I will bear this unhallowed persecution any longer— before I will be dragged away again among my enemies for trial, I will spill the last drop of blood in my veins, and will see all my enemies in hell! To bear it any longer would be a sin, and I will not bear it any longer! Shall we bear it any longer?"

He waited. For a moment there was silence. Then a voice shouted. "No!" and "NO!" rolled in thunder from eight thousand throats.

"I say in the name of Jesus Christ by the authority of the holy priesthood, I this day turn the key that opens the heavens to restrain you no longer from this time forth! I will lead you to the battle; and if you are not afraid to die, and feel disposed to spill your blood in your own defense, you will not offend me. Be not the aggressor: bear until they strike you on the one cheek; then offer the other, and they will be sure to strike that. Then defend yourselves and God will bear you off, and you shall stand forth clear before His tribunal. If mobs come upon you any more here, dung your gardens with them! . . ."

It was the boldest speech they had ever heard from their prophet. Some thought he looked like a larger Napoleon in his brilliant uniform; others compared him with the Caesars or with prophets of old; and all of them, after his fiery words had been spoken, sent up a shout that rocked the city. Here at last was the fighter. Here was no academic man who sat in a study translating ancient records or studying Hebrew and Greek. No: here, they told themselves, pressing forward to touch him or to swear allegiance, was a fighting prophet, ready to lead his people and shed his blood.

"Glory be!" the great throng roared; and for a day and a night the city went mad with joy.

CHAPTER XXVIII

THERE WERE CALMER AND WISER HEADS THAN JOSEPH'S. BRIGHAM SAW DIS-aster ahead and wished the saints had gone out of the United States and into the Rocky Mountain wilderness. Parley had a sense of the ironic; and often he was amused, while walking the streets in dark nights, to see the other apostles, or sometimes Joseph, skulking along fearfully to visit their wives. Often now, because of mob threats, the leaders took bodyguards to protect them on their nocturnal prowls; and often Parley grinned, while himself on his way to visit a bride, to see Joseph or Brigham or Heber darting among shadows in the company of armed men. But Parley did not grin when his brother Orson returned from Jerusalem and looked around him.

Orson was as angry as a man could be. He had spent a weary time in the Holy Land, learning a strange language and trying to convert a strange people; and he came home to learn that his wife had almost been driven out of the church, and that she and her children had nearly starved. When he strode into Joseph's study, he was the most furious man Joseph had ever seen.

"Brother Orson," he said, rising, "you seem disturbed."

"Disturbed!" roared Orson, choking with wrath and insult. "By the living God, for a cent I'd tear your heart out!"

"It would take a better man than you to do that."

Orson glared, too infuriated to speak. "So," he howled at last, "you tried to seduce my wife while I was gone, did you? You black-hearted villain!"

"You are out of your mind."

"And when she kicked you out of the house, you tried to starve her to death! You let my wife and children starve and freeze! That's why you sent me on a mission, you devil out of hell!"

"Calm yourself," said Joseph impatiently. "You are talking like a lunatic."

"You long-nosed hypocrite! Do you deny that you tried to seduce my wife?"

"Of course I deny it."

"You add lying to seduction, do you?"

"I made no attempt on your wife or any other wife."

"You liar!"

"Be careful with your tongue. Your wife has inflamed your mind with falsehoods."

"My wife never lies. What she has told me is true."

"I say it is false."

"And I say again you're a liar!"

"If you doubt me," said Joseph, trying to control his temper, "ask Parley. Your brother will tell you what is true."

"Oh, Parley! Parley thinks you're the Almighty Himself. He believes you in everything."

"He knows that I am a prophet."

"You're an infernal scoundrel!"

"Brother Orson, beware. If you insist on being foolish, you will be excommunicated."

"Excommunicate me and be damned! The church stinks anyway. You've ruined it. From its high purpose you've turned it into a whorehouse."

"Brother Orson," said Joseph advancing, "close your blasphemous mouth before I shut it for you. This is no time for petty strife. Our enemies are closing in around us. I came here today and expect to be arrested any minute. We have bigger worries than the trivial delusions of your wife."

For a long moment the two men faced one another. Then Orson faltered and turned away. There came to him overwhelmingly for a moment his old belief in the goodness of this prophet and king.

"I still believe my wife," he said.

After Orson had gone, Joseph looked through a window at this city which his genius had built in a swamp. He felt frightened and a little sick: he could endure the persecution of his enemies but not the faithlessness of his friends. He sent for Parley.

When Parley entered, he came in quietly, looking as if he were ready to weep or to laugh. He sat and mopped his brow.

"Did you convince Orson?"

"No, Parley. See if you can reason with him."

"I can't. I've tried."

"Try again. It's enough to have John Bennett raising Cain. We don't want Orson going over to our enemies."

"He believes his wife. I don't think anybody can change his mind."

"Try again."

"No, Joseph. Not even the Almighty could reason with him."

"I wish he'd go to Pittsburgh and stay there. We should throw him out of the church."

"It might be just as well. Maybe it would bring him to his senses." For a long moment Parley gazed at Joseph and then broke into hearty laughter. "Dodgast it," he said, "we have to laugh once in a while. It's the only way to get rid of trouble."

"Parley, I'm going to run for President of the United States."

"You?" asked Parley, astounded.

"Yes. Why not?"

"But why? You wouldn't carry a single state."

"I might be elected."

Whether Joseph spoke slyly, Parley did not know. "You could try. It seems to me, though, there's enough trouble here to keep you busy."

"If I run for President, it might get our enemies off the track."

"It might," said Parley, recognizing shrewd statesmanship in that. "But what are you going to do about our troubles here? We're headed for another downfall. The Masons are getting up in arms. They say we stole their ritual for our temple services. And our celestial wives——"

"It's that cur of a Bennett. He's causing all the trouble."

"Not all of it. Rigdon is misbehaving again."

"He wants to be the prophet."

"He told me you tried to seduce his daughter."

"The church is full of liars, Parley. As for Rigdon, I've washed my hands of him. If the rest of you want to put up with him, do it, but I won't."

Joseph went to a window and looked out. His kingdom here was only a small one: he was lord of a city and an army and twenty thousand persons but he had dreamed of a vast empire. He was hungry for a greater destiny than any he had found.

Parley was saying: "We've worn out our welcome in Illinois. What are we going to do? Celestial marriage has ruined us."

"It's not that. It's the wickedness of the people."

"It's envy. They're saying you have a thousand wives." Parley waited a moment; and when Joseph did not speak, he asked: "How many do you have?"

"Only twenty-four—or maybe it's twenty-five."

Parley grinned. He had only a half-dozen and was not sure that he wanted more. He wondered what he would do with twenty-five and how he could support them. He sighed. It made him shiver a little to think what his first wife would say when she learned of the others.

"We should have gone west."

"Yes," said Joseph, gazing outside and remembering the cowardice of Calhoun and Clay, or thinking with scorn of the pusillanimous little man who sat in the White House.

"Let's go now," Parley said.

"No. I'm going to run for President."

"We should go now," said Parley, folding arms over a belly that was growing plump. "In Oregon we can live as we please."

"We'll go to Oregon in a few years."

"In a few years, Joseph, we won't be alive to go anywhere. I'm no prophet. I've never been able to get close to the Lord like you. But in my old bones I know that what we've been through is just a sip from the pot of vinegar we'll be drinking soon."

"Are you losing your faith?" asked Joseph, turning to look at his apostle.

"No. But we can't fight Missouri and Illinois and the Masons and all the mobs. Not even with an army. Brigham thinks we should go now. So do Heber and others. Brigham says if we don't go now, we should use strong-arm methods."

"What kind?"

"Well, in Missouri the Danites are the only ones of us who got anywhere. The rest of us landed in jail. I like peace but Brigham says the time has come to flee or to fight."

"We'll fight," said Joseph, still gazing at the city.

"But not in the open. We'd be whipped before we got started."

"You mean Brigham thinks we should use guerrilla tactics?"

"Yes. That's how I understood him."

Joseph turned from the window to look at Parley. "Go find Brigham," he said.

Whether or not he really liked Brigham Young, Joseph had never decided. He envied the man. He envied Brigham's shrewd appraisal of human beings, his statesmanship, his hard commonsense: while the other leaders sat in dungeons, waiting for the firing squads, Brigham had been a Moses to a fleeing people. He had said (but not to Joseph): "I'll just set around and wait, and when you all get dumped into jail I'll patch things up again." He was that kind of man. He made friends of men whose friendship was needed. It was rumored that he made short work of skulking enemies who stood in his way. Yes, Joseph envied and admired the man but he had always been a little afraid of him.

When Brigham entered, Joseph looked at him curiously. "How are you today?"

"I could feel a damn sight better. We can't keep plural marriage a secret. We can lie about it and fool most of the saints—but not all of them. One by one they'll find out."

"What is the trouble?"

"Is there anything anywhere that isn't trouble?"

Joseph gazed at Brigham's strong determined face, convinced that he was the greatest statesman in the clan. "I've talked with Parley. He thinks we're headed for disaster."

"I know it. We should have gone west."

"We've been driven out of three states. Are we going to let them drive us out of here?" Joseph laid clenched hands on his desk. "Brigham, I prefer to fight, to lead my people, to shed my blood."

"You'll be shedding it soon enough."

"I'm tired of running."

"I'n understand that. But even with an army of five thousand men, we'd be whipped before we could say absquatulate. There are mobs all around us. We can't fight bandits and brigands with an army. Besides," he added, lowering his voice, "there are traitors in our midst."

"Yes, I know that."

"And the number is growing."

"God save me!" cried Joseph. "Even my counselors turn against me. One by one, they all plot my downfall. Perhaps," he said, looking intently at Brigham, "even you."

"No, Joseph. You can count on me and Heber and Parley and John Taylor—and many more. I never liked some of the men you put in high places. I knew John Bennett was a villain the moment I saw him. I never trusted Rigdon as far as I could walk on greased lightning."

"They all betray me."

"You shouldn't put ambitious men in high places. And since I'm being plain-spoken, I want to say this: you can't build a kingdom with gentleness. Even the Almighty couldn't do that. He didn't show much mercy to His enemies—so why should we?"

"What," asked Joseph, "do you mean?"

"I mean we have some bold men we could use to sock away these mob leaders."

"You mean——?"

"This is how I see it. God has commanded you to build up the only true church. Are you going to let ungodly brigands undo everything? Do you think the Lord wants you to let these hellhounds destroy His church? I don't. I think it would be all right with God if we used up the damned scoundrels."

"How?" asked Joseph, gazing intently at Brigham.

"There are ways," said Brigham, his eyes turning cold. "Take Porter Rockwell: we have a lot of men like him. And where is Bill Hickman?"

"I haven't seen him since we left Missouri."

"We need him. Let's find him. He did some good work over in Missouri. He's as brave a man as ever fired a gun, and he can keep his mouth shut. I don't know whether he was with the Danites or not but I know he can be counted on to do a tough job. If we put some of these mob leaders out of the fight——"

"But what's the matter with my army? I have soldiers, armed and ready, and I am ready to lead them."

"Yes," said Brigham impatiently. "But you can't fight coyotes with an army. Besides, the State militia would march in, just like it did in Missouri. Damn it, Joseph, the United States would send an army out here and then what would we do? We can't go to war against our country."

"We could fight until we were all killed. That would be better than to hide out like wicked sinners."

"But our job is to build the Lord's church. As long as the Almighty is on our side, we must build it in any way we can."

"But my army!" For a moment Joseph was lost in thought, seeing himself in his splendid uniform at the head of his troops. "I think," he said at last, "I should flee to the west."

"Not now. If you went now the church would go to pieces."

"If I am not to flee or lead my army, I see nothing else to be done."

"We must fight our enemies with their own methods. Choose forty of our bravest men to patrol Nauvoo day and night. If they find any murderous Missouri pukes around here, use them up and give them a free grave in the Mississippi. Send Porter and some other scouts into the country to give daily reports of movements there." Brigham paused, reflecting on what he would do if he were in Joseph's place. "If worst comes to worst, use up the mob leaders and dung our gardens with them as you said we would."

Joseph turned. "I'll put Nauvoo under martial law. Send Brother Porter in to see me." After hesitating a long moment, he walked over and faced Brigham. "I feel that my end is near. If I am murdered, I want my brother Hyrum to succeed me. Will you remember that?"

"Yes."

"I'm going to send Hyrum back east where he will be safe. I think you and the other apostles should go, too. It's my blood they want. When I am dead, perhaps they will leave my people in peace."

"They want more than you, Brother Joseph. They want all of us. So let us fight while we can—and fight in the only way we can."

Joseph rose to his fullest height. "Send Porter Rockwell to me."

Porter's entrance a little later was enough to startle anyone: it brought Joseph to his feet with a greeting that was almost a cry of alarm. Because Porter, with his black-bearded face, his tangled uncut hair, and his way of moving as if he had been propelled by a cannon, presented the most terrifying aspect of any saint in Nauvoo.

"How are you?" he asked, his voice booming in welcome.

"Full of grief, Brother Porter."

"That's too dodrotted bad," said Porter, who always softened his oaths around the prophet. He sank to a chair, looking like a wild man out of a jungle, and spread his whiskered face in a grin. "All these damn bilks and swag-bellies and blowhards and Missouri pukes hangun around Nauvoo, I guess. All our enemies is on the warpath again. They ain't dressun up like Indians this time, but they're as slick as greased lightning on a banana peel. It looks like we got a-fight."

"Tell me, Porter, what's happening."

"Well, it's plenty. The whole gallows-faced pack is just a-holdun back like all wrath right now, a-waitun for a chance to draw a bead. They're all as mad as a settun hen yanked off of her nest and throwed out into a rainstorm. There's big mobs and little mobs, just like there was in Missouri. They swear by hell and high principles that all the saints is dark-culls with as many concubines apiece as Solomon had. You can't tell them no different."

"About how many men are there in the mobs?"

"I don't know but there's thousands. And they're armed to the teeth. Some of them have so blasted many smoke-pistols that they fall down under the load. But the worst thing is the Judases right here in Zion. If you had let me use up John Bennett when I wanted to, then we might not a-got in all this trouble."

"Brother Porter, is it true that you went down in Missouri and shot Governor Boggs?"

Porter's hands dropped to his pistols. "Don't you ask me no questions and I'll tell you no lies. Mebbe I did and mebbe I didn't. But if I did, I'm plumb ashamed of myself that my aim wasn't no better. I hear that the bastard got well."

"For shame, Brother Porter. We saints are not murderers."

"Well," said Porter, turning in his chair, "I don't figger it's murder to use up a skunk. Them-there pukes down there should ought to be put away. They ain't no earthly good to anyone. And right now they're sneakun around in Nauvoo and they'll grab you the first chance they get. You won't never get out of jail alive this time. I don't think you'll be alive when you get to jail."

"I should go west. Would you go with me?"

"Hell amighty, yes. I'd go with you right into the barrel of a cannon."

Joseph considered. Here was a man, he reflected, in whom he could place absolute trust. He did not want to be mayor of Nauvoo or general in the Nauvoo Legion or prophet of God.

"I want you to act as scout outside of the city and learn what is going on."

"I know already. The mobs is ready to move in and burn the city. Ever since that what's-his-name started his dirty newspaper and you junked his press, well, that give outsiders an excuse to have you arrested. That's what they want. They want to get their hands on you. Then they'n say you tried to escape and they'n shoot you and you won't get no trial this time. I thought it all out and I just about got my mind made up the best thing you'n do is hit the grit."

Joseph rose and paced his study. He went to a window and looked at the temple which stood northward upon a hill. "I don't want to run away," he said. "We came here and took a worthless swamp and built a city on it. How can I give up everything here that I have worked for?"

"Well, if you fight, you could count on me to use up a lot of them before they knowed what it was all about."

"Porter, I think I'll send all the apostles back east where they'll be safe. Then I don't know what I'll do. But I want you to find out every day what's going on and come and tell me. If officers come with warrants from Missouri or anywhere else, you let me know in time."

"I will." Porter rose and then hesitated. "You wouldn't care, I guess, if I socked John Bennett away."

"Don't do that. It would only give our enemies an excuse."

"Yes," said Porter, shaking his shaggy head, "I guess it would. Well, I'll keep my eyes peeled and let you know."

Joseph sent the apostles eastward—or at least those who would go; and the sleepless days and nights that followed he spent alone, alternating between anger and despair. The city was under martial law. At the door of the house in which he was hiding, he had a heavy guard posted. When he felt premonition of impending doom, he strove to shake it off by remembering his loyal army; but in the next hour he would think of all the known and unknown traitors in his midst, of every Judas who was trying to dethrone him and usurp his power. Night after night he sat and pondered, or rose to gaze at the dusky and beautiful city which his genius had built. Perhaps it would soon be laid in flaming waste; his wives would be raped and his children murdered; and his people would be scattered leaderless to the ends of earth. For there was no courage in those governing Illinois or the nation.

He sat at his desk and looked through various papers, wondering which to leave and which to destroy; and, while searching, he came upon copies of letters he had written to Calhoun and Clay. He had asked what their course would be in regard to the Mormons if they were elected to the presidency. Calhoun had written:

"But as you refer to the case of Missouri, candor compels me to repeat what I said to you at Washington, that, according to my views, the case does not come within the jurisdiction of the federal government, which is one of limited and specific powers." To that Joseph had answered scathingly: "Before you let your candor compel you again to write upon a subject as great as the salvation of man, I would admonish you to read in the eighth section and first article of the Constitution, the first, fourteenth and seventeenth 'specific' and not very 'limited powers' of the federal government, what can be done to protect the lives, property and rights of a virtuous people, when the administrators of the law are unbought by bribes, uncorrupted by patronage, untempted by gold!"

Henry Clay had written: "Should I be a candidate, I can enter into no engagements, make no promises, give no pledges to any particular portion of the people. I must go into that high office with no guarantees but such as are to be drawn from my whole life, character and conduct." To that, Joseph had sent the most violent letter of his life. "Your whole life, character and conduct have been spotted with deeds that cause a blush upon the face of a virtuous patriot. So you must be contented in your lot, while crime, cowardice, cupidity or low cunning have handed you down from the high office of a statesman to the blackhole of a gambler!"

In reading his answers now, he was distressed by their bitterness; but just the same, there was no courage left in the leadership of a nation which had been founded by courage and dedicated to freedom. For more than fifteen years, he and his people had been driven from place to place, raped and murdered, persecuted and destroyed. The Constitution had become a document that political demagogues praised and paid no attention to; and presidents like Van Buren, statesmen like Clay and Calhoun, exploited prejudice and hatred and mocked the founders of a great republic. There was no haven in the States more than there had been in the Old World for a people who chose to worship God according to their conscience.

Joseph knelt in prayer and rose after an hour feeling strengthened. Then he went to the window and looked across at the magnificent temple which his people were building; and there came to him the feeling that he must march at the head of his army and die at the point of a sword. Having resolved on this desperate course, he lay clothed on a couch and slept.

In the morning he put on his uniform of lieutenant-general of the Legion and summoned the army and all the saints in Nauvoo and climbed to the roof of a building. There, in full view, he looked down at the thousands of faces that gazed up at him and waited.

"My brothers and sisters, we are American citizens. We live upon a soil for the liberties of which our fathers periled their lives and spilled their blood upon the battlefield. Will you stand by me to the death, and sustain at the peril of our lives the laws of our country, and the liberties and privileges which our fathers have transmitted unto us, sealed with their sacred blood?"

The multitude roared a mighty assent.

"I call upon all men from Maine to the Rocky Mountains, and from Mexico to British America, whose hearts thrill with horror to behold the rights of free men trampled under foot, to come to the deliverance of this people from the cruel hand of oppression, cruelty, anarchy and misrule! I call upon God and angels to witness that I have unsheathed my sword with a firm and unalterable determination that this people shall have their legal rights and shall be protected from mob violence, or my blood shall be spilled upon the ground like water, and my body be consigned to the silent tomb! . . ."

When his ringing challenge was done, there was a stupendous roar of approval; and then the band broke into martial music and the multitude into song. The great Legion, uniformed and armed and ready, stood at attention while their leader came down from the roof.

The prophet was ready to lead his people. The saints were going to war.

CHAPTER XXIX

JOSEPH DID NOT KNOW THAT EVEN WHILE HE WAS SPEAKING TO HIS PEOPLE, the timid and academic governor of Illinois was hurrying to Carthage where the prophet's bitterest enemies had gathered. Petitions and committees and threats had driven Governor Ford to action; and at once he dispatched messengers to Nauvoo, demanding Joseph's surrender, as well as the surrender of every other man "who has committed gross outrage upon the law and liberties of the people, and violated the Constitution."

When Joseph read that, he took his brother Hyrum aside. "You go to Cincinnati. I am lost."

"No, I won't leave you."

"Hyrum, you must go. You must live to avenge my blood and lead the people."

"I tell you I won't leave. I'll die with you."

"There's no wisdom in that. As your leader I must command you to go."

"I'm sorry," said Hyrum stubbornly, "but this time I can't obey you."

"Do you realize," asked Joseph impatiently, "that I am going to be murdered? You are to be my successor. Your life is not safe here. You must go where it will be safe and leave me to my enemies."

"I'm sorry," said Hyrum again, "but I refuse to leave you. If you are to die, we will die together."

Joseph turned to the messenger. "How soon will the posse be over after me?"

"Today, I think."

Joseph picked up a letter from Governor Ford and turned to several of his leaders present. "He pledges his honor and the honor of Illinois to protect me if I will go to Carthage and stand trial for treason. But that," he said bitterly, "is a lie. I'll soon be a dead man. Brother William, fetch me paper and pen." When these were brought, Joseph wrote a letter to Governor Ford. In it he said:

"We are left to the mercy of the merciless. Sir, we dare not come, for our lives would be in danger, and we are guilty of no crime." He read the letter aloud. "William, is it not so?"

"Yes," said William Clayton.

Joseph asked the messenger to leave. Then he said: "Brother William, what do you think I should do?"

"I think," said Clayton, observing that Joseph's hands were trembling, "that you should go west with Hyrum. The rest of us could follow later."

"Porter, what do you think?"

"That's what I think. Get away from these-here pukes and bandits."

"Will you go with me?"

"By God, yes. I'll go with you anywhere."

Joseph went to a window to gaze at the city he had built. "And leave all that? We have spent five years building our homes here."

"If you stay," said Clayton, "our homes will be in ashes. What happened in Missouri will happen again."

"Has word been sent to the apostles to come home?"

"Yes. But not to Sidney Rigdon."

"Oh, let him stay in Pittsburgh and save his precious hide! Porter, are you sure the mobs are ready to move in?"

"There ain't no doubt about it."

"And Governor Ford is waiting in Carthage to grab me. I won't get a fair trial any more than I did in Missouri. I'll be killed, or thrown into a dungeon for the rest of my life."

"The Lord protected you before," said Clayton.

"God did not save Jesus when His time had come. I've always felt I would have to pay for my ministry with my blood." Joseph placed hands on his desk and considered. They trembled so that he removed them from sight of the men watching him. "I will give myself up," he said at last, "and Hyrum will go with me. Porter will be our guide. Get everything ready." He turned again to the window. He was now trembling from head to feet. "Yes, I'll go. I'd rather march at the head of my army than sneak off to let my enemies kill me. But when I am dead, perhaps they will spare the rest of you."

"But why," asked Clayton, "don't you go west?"

"They would overtake me. They'd have a good excuse to murder me then."

"By God, no," said Porter. "They'll never find us. I promise you that."

"If Brigham was here, he'd tell you to go west."

"Yes, Brother Brigham would."

"Then go west. It's your only chance."

Joseph hesitated. "All right," he said, "I will. Get the horses ready at once." He went to Emma's room. "I'm leaving for the west today."

"That doesn't surprise me. I always thought you'd run away and leave me to be murdered."

"You won't be murdered."

"Of course I will. We'll all be killed. All except you—you'll save your own skin all right! You're a coward. If you aren't, then why are you shaking all over?"

"Shaking?" he said, and held up his hands. "Yes, it's true. But I'm not afraid."

"If you hadn't got a whole lot of concubines we wouldn't be in this trouble."

"It was the Lord's will. And they're not concubines. They're my wives."

"I guess it's the Lord's will for us all to be slaughtered!"

"It's me and Hyrum the mob wants. If we leave——"

"Then they'll butcher the rest of us. Why don't you stay and face the music? Why do you run away like a coward?"

He sank to a chair and looked at her with haunted eyes. "We'll go, Emma, and the saints can sell their property and follow. We'll build our kingdom in the West."

"You're a coward," said Emma scornfully.

"You're unfair. I want to lead my army but others think I should leave. Governor Ford is in Carthage now and is sending a posse over to get me."

"If you aren't here he'll hang me in your place."

"Not a hair of your head will be touched. I promise you that."

Emma rocked in her chair like an embittered grandmother. She gazed at him, her thin lips curling, her black eyes hating him. "Just run along and leave us all to be killed. I'd as soon be dead anyhow as to sit around and see you marry every woman in Nauvoo. You have twenty-seven wives. Did you have to have so many?"

"You will join me later," he said quietly, and entered another room to change his clothes.

Long after dark, Joseph and Hyrum and Porter were rowed swiftly across the river and on the far bank mounted horses and set out for the

Rocky Mountains. They had provisions for a few days, and after that expected to forage in any way they could. They had no map but Porter said he could find the way. Only once, while riding through the night, did Joseph speak.

"In the morning, Ford's posse will be hunting for us in Nauvoo."

"Yes," said Porter. "Let the sons-a-bitches hunt. If they come out west I'll blow their brains out."

After riding until the first signs of dawn, the men fetched up at the house of a saint who had homesteaded in Iowa. Joseph said they would hide their horses and sleep here until evening; but Porter said he needed no sleep.

"I'll keep watch. They'll be on our trail."

He took a position behind a tree, his pistols ready, and watched the road down which they had come. Joseph awakened after a little while and came out with Hyrum and said he thought they had better be off; and they mounted and rode again. They had not gone far when they heard the pounding of a horse behind them. Porter swung and raised his rifle but Joseph cried:

"Don't shoot! It's Reynolds Cahoon."

Cahoon came up at a gallop. He had been riding for hours in desperate chase, having used three mounts; and now looked red-eyed from fatigue and loss of sleep.

"What in hell," asked Porter, "are you here for?"

"I have some messages," said Cahoon, and dug into a saddlebag.

"A pardon from the governor, I suppose!"

"Brother Joseph," said Cahoon, "they want you to come back."

"Who?"

"The saints. Here's a letter from Sister Emma."

Joseph opened it and the men watched him while he read. "She asks me to come back. She wants me to give myself up for trial."

"Don't go," said Porter.

"You must," said Cahoon. "The Governor has promised to protect you."

"Protect me!" said Joseph bitterly. "The way I was protected in Missouri."

"You must come back. They all feel you're a coward to run away. They say you're sneaking off and leaving them without a leader. If you don't come back, they will always say you were a coward."

"A coward!" said Joseph, looking back across the green landscape of Iowa. "Hyrum, what do you say?"

"I don't know, Joseph, what to say."

"I say to hell with them!" cried Porter. "It's some of the Judases who want you used up."

"Who are the ones who want me to return?"

"All of them, I guess. Brother Kimball, he called the meeting."

"Oh, he did!"

"I don't trust him," said Porter. "We're off to the Rocky Mountains and we won't turn back for hell or high water. Tell them——"

"No, Porter, wait a minute. You sure they want me back?"

"You'n see what the letters say. Even your wife——"

"Emma never did care if I live or die. Do John Taylor and Orson Hyde and William Clayton want me to come?"

"I can't say how that is. I never talked with all of them. I was just sent to say you are a coward if you run away."

"It's the Judases," said Porter. "They want you dead so they can rule."

Joseph gazed into the west. "Well," he said at last, "if my life is of no value to my friends, it is of none to me."

"Don't go!" Porter cried. "Damn it to hell, you'll be murdered."

"If that is what they want, then I'll be murdered. My mind is made up. If they are calling me a coward, I'll go back."

"Please don't. Joe, let's go on."

"No, Porter. We are going back. Come!"

On the long ride back, Joseph did not speak. He rode in advance of the others, silent with the bitterness of his thoughts; reflecting, "If my life means nothing to them, it means nothing to me!"; thinking, "They trust Ford to protect me: that is stupidity or cunning and I'll die without knowing which"; and looking at the loveliness of this country in June and believing that he would never look upon it again. It was after dark when they came to the river. Quietly they rowed across it and quietly they entered the hushed city. To his companions he said:

"I'll send a message to the governor that I'll go to Carthage in the morning. I'll ask him to furnish a bodyguard. I'll ask for a fair trial but I won't get it. I'm a doomed man."

"If they touch a hair of your head," said Porter, "I'll spend the rest of my life using them up. You want me to take the message?"

"No, you stay with me. Fetch Brother Jedediah."

When Hyrum returned with Jedediah Grant, Joseph ask him to ride over to Carthage and tell Governor Ford he would surrender in the morning. "And tell him I want a bodyguard to protect me and a fair trial."

Jedediah's long lean face was very grave. "I'll tell him," he said.

After Jedediah had gone, Joseph turned to Porter. "I want to go off alone and pray. I'm like Jesus in Gethsemane."

He went down to the broad dark river and knelt in prayer, and Porter stood close by with his hands on his pistols. Down the river a little way, Hyrum was also kneeling. The two brothers prayed a long while and Porter watched them or looked around him for prowling enemies. There were Missourians in Nauvoo, as well as leaders of waiting mobs; but the darkened city seemed asleep. Nevertheless, Porter knew that spies were searching and he did not for a moment relax his vigilance. When Joseph rose from prayer and came to him, Porter saw that the prophet's eyes were clouded with tears.

"Hyrum and I will wait here. You fetch Jedediah when he returns."

"You take my smoke-poles."

"No, we'll be safe. We'll hide under the bank."

When Jedediah returned, his face was graver than before. "The governor won't promise anything. He won't offer protection or pledge a fair trial. He says you're to come to Carthage without any bodyguard. If you don't, he said to tell you Nauvoo will be sacked and burned."

"I have been betrayed."

"And he won't let him have a bodyguard to protect him from the bandits?"

"No, Brother Porter. Governor Ford says he must come alone."

"The coward! I'll go with him."

"No, you must remain here. Am I the only one he wants?"

"He wants Hyrum too, and John Taylor and Willard Richards."

"Very well, Brother Jedediah. We'll set out in the morning." Joseph turned to Porter. "Hyrum and I want to be alone again. You keep watch."

Porter took a position where he could command all approaches, and Joseph and Hyrum went into a thicket by the river. The prophet did not try to sleep. Most of the time he spent in prayer, asking God for wisdom to guide him and courage to meet his death; for that it was

God's will for him to die, and seal his ministry with his blood, he did not doubt. He did not ask for deliverance. He asked only for the strength to go without faltering and to die without complaint.

And early in the next morning he set out with Hyrum and a few others for Carthage. Upon coming abreast of the temple, he paused.

"Hyrum, we've built a beautiful city and the saints are the best people in the world. Little do they know the troubles just ahead of them."

"They will all be murdered."

"No. After the mobs have our blood, they will leave most of the saints in peace."

"I doubt that," John Taylor said.

"It is so. It's only the leaders they want."

"There can be no church without leaders."

"Others, Brother John, will take our place."

They rode on, but again and again Joseph turned on his horse to look back at the city, shining gloriously in the morning sun. Very few persons were astir. The saints did not know that their prophet was going forth to a town filled with his enemies. Smoke rose from a few chimneys, but Nauvoo was still asleep.

"I'll never see it again," declared Joseph, looking back from a far hill.

"We mustn't be discouraged. God is with us."

"God was with Jesus, too, on the cross."

"Jesus was not taken," said John Taylor, "until His work was finished."

"We never know when our work is finished. No, John, I'm going like a lamb to the slaughter. This is true: my conscience is clear toward God and all men. I shall die innocent and it shall be said of me that I was murdered in cold blood."

"All of us," Hyrum said.

The plump boyish face of Willard Richards was twitching with grief. "But why, Brother Joseph, do you feel we will be murdered?"

"I know it. All night I prayed. I knew it then."

"Why don't we go back?"

"God has ordained it otherwise."

The men rode in silence. Four miles out of Carthage they were met by sixty soldiers; and when Joseph saw them he rose in his stirrups. "Let us be unafraid. Let us die like brave men."

The soldiers rode up to meet them; and without saying a word they swung around in a cordon and marched in with their prisoners. En-camped in the public square of the town were the Carthage Grays, a company of militia, every man of whom, legend declared, had sworn to have the prophet's life. They now laid hands on their guns and pressed forward as the prisoners rode past.

"There he is!"

"Which one?"

"The tall one with the big nose."

"Yeh, that's him all right! The God-damned Mormon!"

"Hey, Joe Smith, we got you now!"

"Yes, by God, and you won't get away this time!"

"Hey, Joe!" cried a less vindictive Gray. "You got any nice little brunette in your bunch of concubines?"

"How many wives has he got?"

"The holy Christ knows! About a thousand, I guess."

"Joe, you got a nice little brunette?"

"A thousand concubines! We ought to fry the son-of-a-bitch in oil!"

"We'll fry him, all right. He won't get away like he done in Missouri."

"Hey, how much do you want for a nice little brunette?"

As the prisoners were marched down the street to the Hamilton Hotel, the Carthage Grays followed, together with scores of angry and cursing men who had heard of Joseph's coming. They raised such a blasphemous din that Governor Ford pushed up a hotel window and thrust his head out.

"What's the matter with you men out here?"

"We want to see the prophet!"

"Damn it to hell, Governor, we want to see the son-of-a-bitch!"

"Silence!"

"To hell with you, Governor! We want to see the man with all the concubines!"

"Listen to me a moment!"

"Shut your jib, you griddle-greasers! Let's hear what Tom Ford has to say."

"Gentlemen, I know how eager you are to see Mr. Smith. Tomorrow morning I'll have him out on the public square and you can see him. Now behave yourselves."

"Is that a promise, Governor?"

"That's a promise. You'll see Mr. Smith tomorrow."

"Hurrah for Tom Ford!"

"If you break your promise we'll come in and get him!"

"I tell you," shouted the exasperated governor, "you will see him tomorrow! Now act like gentlemen!"

"Hurrah for Tom Ford!"

The crowd fell away, though many remained close by the hotel, hoping to see the prophet. Early the next morning, Tom Ford set out to fulfill his promise; but when he marched Joseph and Hyrum, arm in arm, to the public square for the inspection of the curious, the Carthage Grays closed in, howling like demons. One of the officers drew his sword and yelled:

"Listen to him! He's introducing the adulterous hoodlum as a general!"

Other officers drew their swords and cursed, and at once there was great confusion. Alarmed by their vehemence, Ford turned to argue with them.

But an officer cried: "What do you mean by calling him a general?"

"That's his title in Nauvoo."

"This isn't Nauvoo."

"He is lieutenant-general of the Nauvoo Legion."

"Nauvoo Legion! He wouldn't even be a corporal in a decent army!"

"Listen," said another, "are we going to take this insolence?"

"No, by God! Nobody can call him a general around real officers."

"I've told you before," said the exasperated governor, "that you will get full satisfaction. These men are to be tried for their lives."

"That doesn't give you license to insult us by calling them generals!"

"General Deming, come here."

General Miner Deming came over. "These officers," said Ford, "persist in insubordination."

"Sir," a captain said, "we resent anyone who calls these hoodlums generals."

"Silence, Captain, or I'll have you placed under arrest!"

"Men," said the captain angrily, "will you let yourselves be arrested for so trifling an offense?"

"No!" they roared. "By God, no!"

Deming flushed and turned to an aide. "Major Beems, place all these men under arrest."

Joseph had overheard the altercation. If, he reflected, the governor had the courage of Deming, the prisoners would not be in danger of their lives. But the governor was no such man. Flabbergasted by this turn of events, he hustled the men back to the hotel; and a few moments later, a constable entered to arrest Joseph and Hyrum and take them to jail.

"Sir," said Joseph, stepping forward, "let me see your mittimus. You cannot arrest me until I have had a hearing before a justice."

"Oh, I have a mittimus." Gazing at Joseph with a sly smile, he dug into a pocket and fetched out a document. "There," he said triumphantly, "read it."

Joseph took the paper. "This," he said, "is a falsehood. It says I am arrested for treason but I have never appeared before a justice."

"I don't know about that. The justice said to arrest you and that's what I'm here for."

"You can't arrest me until I have had a hearing. Treason? Where were the witnesses? Where is the evidence? Call the justice over here."

The nonplussed constable looked around him. "I'll have to see Governor Ford," he said.

Joseph went to a window and looked at the street. It was filled with angry men who were gazing up at the windows and cursing; and even while Joseph stared at them, a dozen Carthage Grays entered his room. They said he was to be taken to jail, and they seized the arms of the prisoners and led them out. They led them up the street, with a howling mob following, and placed them in the debtors' chamber, a large room with a bedstead and mattresses. When the door was closed, Joseph said:

"We are doomed."

"If," said Willard Richards, "it is only your death they want, let me die in your place."

"No, Willard. If I must die, then I must."

"Why?" asked John Taylor. "I could go to Nauvoo and march back with an army. We could get out of here and go west."

"No, it is too late for that."

"John, sing again. Sing the song about the poor wayfaring man of grief."

"No, Hyrum. I don't feel like singing now." John went to a window and looked out. Suddenly he cried, "Great God, see!"

The other prisoners ran to the window. A huge mob was coming, a howling horde with blackened faces, with cudgels and knives and guns in their hands. They poured down the street in a great tide. A moment later, there was a sound of profaning men on the stairway outside the cell; and remembering that there was no lock on the door, Joseph sprang to it and the other men followed. They hurled their combined weight to the door and fought with all their strength to keep it closed. Joseph had hidden a small pistol in his clothes. While shouldering against the door, he slipped a hand down to the gun and cocked it. Under the pressure from without, the door shook on its hinges, and four men fought desperately against it with the strength of giants.

A voice yelled: "Come out of there, you Mormon sons-of-bitches!"

For a moment there was silence. Then a man cried with an oath: "I'll shoot them through the door!"

In the next instant a ball splintered a panel of the door and buried itself in the opposite wall. Joseph and John leapt to one side. Hyrum started across the room but had taken only two steps when a second bullet struck his nose. He spun and fell with a cry; and as he fell, a third ball plowed through his flesh and lodged deep in his side. He struck the floor and turned convulsively. After a swift glance at his brother, Joseph sprang to the door and opened it far enough to thrust the muzzle of his pistol through. He fired blindly at the howling mob; and while he was desperately pulling the trigger, another bullet crashed through the door and made a gaping wound in Hyrum's throat. A half-dozen barrels were shoved through. These John wildly beat down with a club.

The next few moments were nightmare for everyone but Joseph. John ran to a window to look out. A ball tore through one of his legs and turned him half-around, and a second bullet smashed his watch. As he fell, a third struck his thigh and blew off a piece of flesh as large as a man's palm. Willard was insanely clubbing the musket barrels as they were shoved through.

Suddenly, while John and Willard were fighting like wild men, Joseph felt deep peace. Like lightning the thoughts came to him that he had known, for many long years, that he must eventually seal his ministry with his blood; that this was the end. He drew to his fullest height for a moment, no longer expecting to escape, no longer afraid. Then slowly he walked to the window. At the moment when he looked out, two bullets entered his breast. They spun him around and left him reeling over the sill.

"O Lord, my God!" he said. His hands sought something to grasp and found nothing; and in the next instant he pitched headlong to the street. Seeing him fall, a Carthage Gray ran up with fixed bayonet. With the point at Joseph's throat, he leaned forward to look at the face. He stepped back.

There was no need to drive with the bayonet. The prophet was dead.

PART TWO

NOON

CHAPTER I

O N AN AUGUST MORNING IN THE YEAR OF 1844, A YOUNG MAN OF twenty-nine rode across the green hills of western Illinois. Powerfully built but quick and light in moving, he looked like an adventurer seeking a new land as he turned right or left in his saddle to gaze around him. His forehead was broad and full under soft brown hair that curled over his ears and down his neck; his mouth was wide and straight above a firm chin; his eyes were coldly gray. He was a handsome but not a vain man.

Already he had more daredevil experiences behind him than most men twice his age. His boyhood had been spent on a wild frontier: in almost every night he had heard the screams of panthers or the howling of wolves, and had become so accustomed to the sound and sight of danger that he made pursuit of it his pastime. To save a pet dog, he had thrown himself, knife in hand, upon a panther and plunged the dagger into the beast's heart. Singlehanded he had gutted an enraged wild boar.

He had grown up with danger always at the doorstep of his life. Death in some form had been for him almost a daily experience; blood for him had been as common as water; a desperate struggle to survive was the only law of life. Nevertheless, deadly encounters with man and beast on an American frontier had not made a monster of this man. When he was only sixteen he fell in love; and his idolatrous worship of a girl three years older had softened him and led him to seek a gentler life. At seventeen he took the bit in his teeth and married her. A year later he entered the Methodist church. Under the influence of his wife, he devoted his next years to farming and to a study of theology; and at last became acquainted with Mormon missionaries who journeyed back and forth over the road by which he lived. Persecution of the saints in Missouri again awakened the hunger nearest his heart; and one night he slipped away to chastise in his own fashion three brutal rowdies, and then cast his lot with Joseph Smith.

He became a Mormon not because he was a mystic in need of a personal god, or was troubled about his own soul: no, but because he liked to fight for the underdog and preferred an adventurous life to any other. He met Joseph and talked with him and liked the man. He did not understand the burning quest in the blue eyes or the eloquence of the lips; but he believed in him and found him good.

One day, hearing that mobs were on the march, he had ridden to Far West to find the prophet. "If you ever need me, call me," he said. "I'm not a bad hand with a gun."

Joseph never called him, and the bold young man who offered his services lived in the ways of peace. He heard of the Danites, those avenging bands among the saints, and was eager to join them, but his wife persuaded him to remain on the farm. He loved his wife and children, but again and again he stared at the useless guns that hung on the walls of his home. He did not like peace. He did not like the monotonous routine of a homestead and all its deadly chores. For most men, the earth was something to be tilled, but for him it was a vast empire in which adventure waited on every hilltop, at every turn in the road, in every grog shop and tavern from coast to coast. He hungered to use his guns; and more frequently as the dull years passed he took them down from the wall and fondled them and polished them and wished he had an enemy to shoot at.

"You aren't happy with me," his wife would say.

"Oh, yes, I am." But he would sigh like a most unhappy fellow. "I don't have much to do around here." Thinking of the road and the open spaces, he added: "I hear there's trouble up in Nauvoo. I reckon they might need me there."

"But we need you here."

"I could run up and look around me. If the prophet needs me, then I could send for you."

But he did not go then. He cut cordwood for the coming winter, plowed his fields and planted his crops. When, two months later, he heard that Joseph had been murdered, he was too stunned to speak. He went into a forest, wondering persistently, vainly what he could do to avenge that death. Very gravely he returned to the house and stood before his pistols and looked at them, and then took them down and cleaned and loaded them. He handled them as if they were very precious.

After a few minutes he polished the blade of his hunting knife until it had the brightness of a mirror.

"Where you going?" his wife asked.

"To Nauvoo."

"What for?"

Without looking at her he said quietly: "The prophet has been killed."

"Joseph! You mean him?"

"Yes, and Hyrum too. And John Taylor was almost killed."

"What are you going to do now?"

Again he said quietly: "I'm off for Nauvoo."

"To get yourself killed too, I guess."

He looked at her and smiled. "There's nobody quick enough with a gun to kill me. I'll be all right." He rose and stretched his arms, feeling the young and vigorous strength of his body. He buckled the knife and pistols to his waist. Then he went out and saddled his favorite horse, flung a knapsack behind him, and rode up to the door.

"I'll send for you," he said. "The church needs me now."

In the evening of the sixth day he paused on a hilltop to gaze at a city shining in the sun. He had never seen it before. He had heard that Joseph turned a swamp into the largest city in Illinois, but he had not known that Nauvoo was such a beautiful place. It had wide clean streets and many fine buildings; and on a hill in the distance stood a great temple. For several minutes he gazed across the tops of buildings and trees or at the broad river or across the river at the city of Montrose —remembering how Joseph had escaped from a dungeon and fled to this unwanted swamp to build upon it the most magnificent city in the state. And for that he had been murdered.

Who, he wondered, would be the leader now? Many would strive for leadership, including Sidney Rigdon, Lyman Wight, Emma, and a host of others; but he hoped the leadership would fall to Brigham Young. It would be a pleasure to serve so brave and resourceful a man. He had watched Brigham gather the scattered and terrified saints five years ago and lead them over frozen prairie to the river and to a new home. He had offered his services to Brigham, but Brigham had not wanted avengers then. He wanted peace. "The best way to handle an enemy," he had said, "is to put yourself a thousand miles away from him."

There were other ways too, the man on the hilltop reflected, especially when the enemies were bandits and brigands who burned and raped and murdered. If the saints were to build God's kingdom on earth, there was no reason, as Lyman Wight had often declared, to allow scoundrels out of hell to stand in the way. A man could move a thousand miles from them but they would follow. They could be taught, not with sermons and precepts from the Bible, but with a blow in the teeth and a knife or a gun. That was the way this man saw the matter as he sat on his horse and watched the sun sink in golden splendor behind the purple reefs beyond Montrose. He hoped Brigham Young would no longer turn the other cheek.

For another half-hour he sat and pondered; and then, armed and ready, young Bill Hickman rode into Nauvoo.

CHAPTER II

BRIGHAM ARRIVED THE NEXT DAY. HE WAS IN NEW ENGLAND WHEN HE learned that Joseph had been murdered, and for hours he was too overwhelmed to think clearly or to wonder who the new leader would be. When at last this great question entered his mind, he hastened westward at all possible speed; but the news had traveled so slowly and his return journey consumed so much time that he did not arrive in Nauvoo until nearly six weeks after the prophet's death. He found a strangely silent world in Illinois, and the Hancock Prairie as hushed as a tomb. Hyrum had been slain with his brother, and a month later, Samuel had died from a brutal beating by a mob; and now the towns of Carthage and Warsaw were deserted by terrified gentiles who expected the Nauvoo Legion to march in with sword and fire. So many of the saints in Nauvoo were in hiding that it too looked to Brigham like an abandoned city.

After finding and talking with a few leaders whom he trusted, Brigham realized that he had not arrived a moment too soon. Sidney Rigdon for two years had been sulking in Pittsburgh; but upon learning of Joseph's death he had gone pell-mell to Nauvoo and with impassioned oratory had been pleading his own cause. He had enlisted a large and enthusiastic following.

"He's called a public meeting for day after tomorrow," said Brigham's old friend, Heber Kimball. "He expects to become president and prophet."

"Does he?" asked Brigham, wishing Rigdon had perished in the Missouri dungeon. "Well, between you and me, Heber, I intend to lead the church myself."

"You're the man for it."

"That's what I think. I'll be at that meeting—but don't tell Rigdon. Are there any more around here plotting to be the prophet?"

"Any more! At least a dozen, Brigham."

"Who are they?"

"Jim Strang——"

"That long-haired lunatic!"

"—and Lyman Wight and Emma. Emma says her older son is to be the leader when he grows up. Sister Lucy says that now Joseph and Hyrum and Samuel are dead, William is to be the leader."

"I'll see Emma first. You help me get the lay of the land. You're to be my chief counselor."

Brigham found Emma in the gloomy Nauvoo House, sole queen of it now and ready for battle. As soon as she saw Brigham, her thin lips tightened and her black eyes shone like jewels.

"What do you want?"

"Sister Emma, we have to choose a leader. I came to see you ——"

"We do not. When my son Joseph grows up, he'll be president. That's the way his father said it was to be."

"No, Sister. Joseph said Hyrum was to succeed him, but Hyrum is dead."

"And my son is to be the new prophet."

"No," said Brigham, a little impatiently. "We must have a man to lead us, not a child."

"My son is the new prophet. Remember that, and don't try any foxy tricks."

"We'll have to all talk it over. I'll see the other members of the Twelve."

Brigham did not intend to be a fox. He intended to be a lion, but first he would be very sure of his ground. The other pretenders had to be taken care of. The shaggy half-crazed Jim Strang was already calling himself prophet and president, and offering a forged letter to prove it. The letter, purporting to be from Joseph, declared that Strang was to be the leader; that the saints were to move to Voree in Wisconsin; that the apostles were all to obey the orders of James J. Strang. Furthermore, Strang said, an angel had appeared to him and thundered: "James J. Strang, thou art to be prophet of the church and successor to Joseph Smith!" Among Strang's supporters were William, Joseph's violent and blasphemous brother, as well as the crafty John Bennett whom the prophet had thrown out of the church.

Brigham decided to see Strang next.

"Brother Jim, I understand Joseph wrote you a letter."

"He did," said Jim, looking at Brigham with insane eyes.

"Let me see it."

"To hell with you. I'm the president now."

"But I," said Brigham gently, "am president of the twelve apostles."

"Joseph told you apostles to obey me. If you don't——"

"Shut up that nonsense, Jim. We won't obey you at all."

"Then," said Jim, wagging his wild dark head, "I'll excommunicate you."

Brigham smiled. He advanced and tapped the long black hair that hung across Jim's shoulders. "Listen, Jim, I don't want to see you send your soul to hell. You take my advice and shut up before someone shuts you up."

"God damn!" roared Jim, exasperated. "I'm president and prophet, I tell you! And I'm going to be king!"

"No, Jim, you're going to run right bang into a lot of trouble."

"What do you mean?"

"I'm president of the Twelve. I'm leader until a leader is chosen."

"Oh, no, you're not," said Jim, grinning cunningly as if to say, "I've found you out now!"

Brigham tapped the man again. "Brother James, I want you to save your soul and live to a ripe old age. And you will if you don't cause too much trouble."

Brigham turned away from the long-maned fellow with his delusions of grandeur. He would recruit a bunch of rogues and go off somewhere to fancy himself a king; or he would stay here and kick up so much strife that Porter or another would teach him a lesson. He was not dangerous, but Lyman Wight was. That hotheaded man had never given fealty to or obeyed anyone except Joseph; and now that the prophet was dead, Lyman was following his violent whims. He was enlisting saints in a company which he intended to lead to Wisconsin. Brigham did not wish to talk with him. He was not afraid of Lyman— he was not afraid of any man; but he did not want to argue with one who was all hot temper and curses.

"We won't pay any attention to Lyman Wight," he said to Heber. "He'll lead a bunch into the wilderness and they'll come crawling back or stay there to feed the wolves. But there's something else that worries me."

"Sister Emma?"

"No. I'll take care of Emma. It's all these damned crack-brained prophets around here. There's a man named Bickerton in Pennsylvania who says he's prophet and revelator now. And there's Jim Brewster. You remember back in Kirtland when he was a plain damn fool kid. Now he's a prophet. There's a fellow named Hedrick. He's a prophet too and has appointed a whole batch of apostles. Dave Whitmer says he's the prophet now. By the God of Israel, Heber, prophets are thicker around here than babies."

"We can excommunicate them."

"Yes, but every one would take a bunch of followers. We'd be left here with our wives."

"Maybe not all our wives," said Heber, grinning. "There's a lot of talk. No matter how hard we try to keep it a secret, celestial marriage is leaking out. One of my wives told her best friend and she told her best friend who also had a best friend who had a best friend; and so it goes. When all the best friends hear about it, then what'll we do?"

"Can't you shut your wives up?"

"Brigham, God Almighty Himself couldn't shut some women up. They just have to talk."

"I know. That's one of our problems. But we must keep celestial marriage a secret for a long while yet. Did you know Rigdon has half the saints believing in him? For a red cent I'd have Porter Rockwell send him in a canoe down the river."

"Just give him enough rope and he'll hang himself."

Brigham's smile was faint. "And hang a lot of us with him. Well, I'll see him tomorrow and damned if I won't have plenty to say, too."

"The whole thing will depend on what you say."

"I know it. If God is with me— Heber, you'd better pray for me tonight."

Sidney Rigdon had plenty to say. He stood in a wagon and talked across a park that overlooked the river; and for an hour and a half, his great voice rolled in thunder over his rhetoric. Thousands of saints had gathered to hear him, remembering in former addresses the man's timing, his dramatic change of tone, his wild histrionic gestures. After an hour of impassioned harangue, Rigdon began to act a little strangely: not one of those who heard him guessed that he had seen Brigham far back in the throng. Rigdon's voice began to shake. His whole body shook when he declared that back in Pittsburgh, God had appeared and commanded him to hasten to Nauvoo and offer himself as guardian of the people. For many years, he said, he had been Joseph's chief counselor; he had fought at his side in New York, in Ohio, and he had sat by him in dungeons in Missouri. He had more intimate knowledge of Joseph's mind and purpose than any other man alive. Suddenly his voice was petulantly shrill.

"God commanded me to come here and offer myself as your guardian! I have discharged my duty and done what God commanded me to do! You can please yourselves whether you accept me or not!"

That cry of doubt was a strange anticlimax to what the multitude had expected. For a few moments there was utter silence. Then a man cheered and others echoed him; but when it looked as if the thousands would acclaim Rigdon as leader, a great voice bellowed across the multitude. Ten thousand persons turned in amazement, for they had not known that Brigham was in Nauvoo. The effect of his sudden appearance and the sound of his booming voice were overwhelming. A woman shouted hysterically that the voice was the voice of Joseph. A man climbed to an eminence and roared: "Lo, the mantle of Elijah is falling upon Elisha!"

"Silence!" Brigham thundered.

And there was silence as he made his way through the multitude to the wagon where the abashed Rigdon stood. Rigdon, indeed, stepped down when he saw Brigham coming, and backed away as if in terror. Without looking at him, Brigham climbed to the wagon and swung to face his people.

"I do not care," he cried, "who leads this church, but one thing I must know, and that is what God says about it! I have the keys and the means of obtaining the mind of God on the subject! Joseph conferred upon our heads all the keys and powers belonging to the apostleship which he himself held before he was taken away, and no man or set of men can get between Joseph and the Twelve in this world or in the world to come!"

He paused. There was not a sound anywhere. Knowing that his next words would make or break him, Brigham waited for several moments and gazed down at the thousands of faces. His voice was gentler when he spoke again.

"You cannot fill the office of prophet, seer and revelator: God must do this. You are like children without a father and sheep without a shepherd. You must not appoint any man at our head: if you do, the Twelve must ordain him. You cannot appoint a man at our head, but if you do want any other man or men to lead you, take them and we will go our way to build up the kingdom in all the world."

Again he paused. There was not a person among the thousands who was not gazing at him earnestly and waiting for his next words. The next words, sudden and impassioned and final, came like thunder.

"I will tell you who your leaders or guardians will be! The Twelve— I at their head!"

There was no applause. There was not even a lone shout of approval or disapproval. Brigham waited. He wanted the multitude to look at him and feel in him, not a prophet, but the energetic and resourceful man who led them out of Missouri, and who could now gather them from their enemies and build them into an empire. He stepped down from the wagon and stood on the tongue.

"Brothers and Sisters, we will put it to a vote: whether you sustain the Twelve or whether you will not. All in favor of the Twelve, raise their hands!"

There was a sea of ten thousand hands.

"All those opposed?"

Brigham had won. The saints roared with joy and pressed around him; and when, a little later, he pushed his way through and turned toward his home, thousands of singing persons followed him up the street.

But he was too shrewd a judge of the human heart to believe, as Joseph had believed too many times, that a cheering multitude would cheer long. His fight was still ahead of him. He had inherited a leaderless and demoralized people, split into a dozen factions: to integrate these factions or to drive them out was his first task. In this he would be, as he would be in all necessary ways, a ruthless and, if possible, an invincible leader. There would be iron in his hand.

He had also inherited, he reflected, while going toward Nauvoo House, a hundred vengeful mobs that were now only abashed and waiting. They would strike again. Fools within the church he could handle; bandits were another matter. His strategy would be to maneuver and plot rather than to force (as Joseph had wished to) an open battle. To deal with mob leaders at their own level, he needed bold and loyal men —men who would use up the cowardly rascals and then keep their own mouths shut.

He was sitting in Joseph's study and thinking of his enemies, both in and out of the church, when a man entered who looked like a buccaneer from far places. Quick to size men up, Brigham observed the stranger's studded belt, his pistols, his knife.

"Hello, Brother Brigham Young."

"Hello," said Brigham, wondering where he had seen this man.

"I heard you talk a little while ago." The stranger advanced and offered a powerful hand. "I'm Bill Hickman."

"Oh, yes. I've met you before." Brigham was interested. Gray eyes met gray eyes as two men measured one another against the future. Then Brigham said: "Are you one of the saints?"

"Well, I don't feel very saintly but I've been a Mormon ever since I decided I wouldn't be a Methodist."

Again Brigham studied the man. "Why have you come to me?"

"Because," said Bill, going straight to the point, "I think you need me. As I figger it, you've got a tough job on your hands."

"How," asked Brigham cautiously, "do you think you can help?"

Bill's lips smiled under his handsome whiskers. "Well, this is how I see it. You've got a lot of enemies. Here in Nauvoo every third man on the street is your enemy. The prophet Joseph, they drove him out of New York and Ohio and Missouri, and then they murdered him. I think mebbe God might like a little vengeance for that murder." Bill paused, his gaze on Brigham's face.

"Go on," Brigham said.

"When you talked out there, I had my hands on my old smoke-poles. I figgered someone in that crowd would try to use you up. The way I see it, some men can be reasoned with and some have to be put out of sight. I guess the Lord won't mind if some of the sinners is found fast asleep. That's how I see it." He paused and waited but Brigham did not speak. "Or am I full of counterfeit talk?" asked Bill.

"Go ahead. I want to know how you see things."

"That's how. You have to build up the kingdom. God has commanded you to, hain't He? But you can't do it as long as you let masons and pukes and pot-soppers murder our prophets. Now me, I'm a peaceable man. I don't reckon to harm no one who obeys the Lord and lets us alone. But neither do I figger to let any sinful bandit out of hell touch a hair of your head."

That was forthright. That was within the understanding and intention of Brigham's mind and heart. He believed he could trust this man.

"Did you belong to the Danites down in Missouri?"

"All that," said Bill cannily, "was a long time ago. It would surprise me if I could remember."

"Brother Bill, are you afraid of anything?"

"Not that I ever set eyes on. I ain't never run yet, and dog on it, I'm too plumb old to begin now."

"Bill, I can use you but let me tell you something. I'm not afraid either but you can't fight the back of a porcupine with bare hands. I have a job to do. I am going to build the Lord's kingdom and I don't intend to let anything stop me. Nothing," said Brigham, looking at Bill.

"I understand you," Bill said.

"I need men like you. Right now, I want scouts to find out what the mobs are planning to do. Every day, I want to know what's going on. I want to know who my friends are and who my enemies are. Will that job suit you?"

"It fits me like my own skin."

"All right. But don't sock away any good men. Before you decide to sock any man away, tell me who he is and what sin he is guilty of. Then if he needs an operation just below the chin, I'll see about it. Those are orders."

"Yes," said Bill agreeably. "I always obey orders."

Brigham looked at him thoughtfully. "You married?"

"I been married twelve years."

"God revealed to the prophet Joseph a new principle. It's called celestial marriage. The leaders have the privilege of more than one wife so they can have more offspring to help them become gods in the next world. It's a secret. Never forget that."

"I've heard talk about it," said Bill.

"I know that. But it has to be a secret for a while. If anyone asks you if the leaders have more than one wife, say no. We have to lie about it until the time comes to make it known to the world. Would you like another wife?"

"God, I ain't thought about that. One has been about all I could manage."

"If you ever want another wife, tell me. Nobody can take more than one wife without my permission."

"I'll think about it," Bill said.

Brigham grasped the powerful hand again. "Now get on your job. Report to me daily."

"Fine and dandy. I will."

"And use your brains. If you get me and the church in trouble ——"

"I won't. That's part of my job."

"All right, find out what the damned gentiles are doing."

After Bill had gone, Brigham sat at his desk in thought. The Lord's kingdom had to be established throughout the world, and the Lord's enemies had to be converted—or rebuked. It was a big job. He reached for his tall hat and looked at himself in a mirror. It was about time, he remembered now, for him to take another wife. He had only five. Joseph when he died had twenty-seven—or more, because nobody quite knew how many there were. After Brigham's first wife had died in Kirtland, he had married Mary Ann Angel; and not until June, two years ago, had he taken a celestial wife. She was Lucy Ann Decker. A year ago he had wedded two women on the same day: Harriet Cook, a maid of nineteen, and Augusta Evans, a spinster of forty-one. Since then he had married Lucy's sister Clara.

While gazing at his strong handsome face, he thought of Clarissa Ross —as well as of wives whom Joseph had left. Emily Partridge was young and ladylike and healthy. He decided to drop around and see her for a moment, and give her a word of cheer.

Could the time come to make it known to the world. Would you like polygamy?

"Not I am not through above that. One has been about all I could manage."

"If you ever want another wife, tell me. Surely you will not take one without my permission."

CHAPTER III

BRIGHAM DID NOT HAVE JOSEPH'S SENSUOUS DELIGHT IN FAIR WOMEN. Polygamy for him was not now and was never to be a matter of carnal hunger: it was a commandment from God, and a great advantage in the world to come. For the most part, Joseph had taken young and attractive women; Brigham was content to mate with those of child-bearing age, even though they might be among the homeliest and most unloved of the saints. For he was not a lover. He did not woo his wives with soft caress and whispered endearment, or try to make of sexual embrace more than a simple physical union. His approach was unromantic; his mating was brief.

He was not interested in women except as wives and mothers of men. He was interested in building the Lord's kingdom, and in fulfilling the commandments which God had given to Joseph. His call on Emily was, therefore, only a cheerful greeting and a pat of his big rough hand. After that, he was off to his work, his mind busy with plans, his imagination shaping the architecture of his dream. Whether he would have to abandon this beautiful city, he did not know: it would depend on what the gentiles did. Perhaps they would be satisfied, now that they had murdered the prophet and two of his brothers. He sent other scouts into the unfriendly areas, read the newspapers, watched and waited.

Day by day he realized more clearly how enormous his task was. Among the newspaper editorials which he read, one declared him to be a counterfeiter, and all his followers chronic thieves; a second cried, "Every saint, mongrel or whole-blood, and everything that looks like a saint or talks and acts like a saint, should be compelled to leave!"; and a third editor wrote: "The Nauvoo charter has been repealed. We must now drive the brigands out of Illinois and scatter the adulterous whore-masters over the face of the earth. The time to strike is now while the scoundrels are leaderless and confused!"

After reading a score of such violent denunciations, Brigham told the young men and even the boys in Nauvoo to wear bowie knives. "If a stranger comes to this city, follow him and whittle on a stick or a shingle and whistle."

"Shall we tickle him with a knife?"

"Don't touch him. Just whittle and whistle. That ought to put ice in his blood."

Thereafter, when Brigham walked the streets, he saw anxious and harassed spies followed by a crowd of whittling and whistling men. If the stranger entered a tavern, the group entered also, and sat or stood around him, solemnly busy with their sharp knives, and whistling a doleful and tuneless ditty that was chilling. When the stranger went again to the street, the gang followed him. He was trailed remorselessly until he fled.

One afternoon a flabbergasted legislator burst into Brigham's office. He was covered with sweat.

"What kind of lawless city do you have here?" he howled. "Blood-thirsty hoodlums follow me everywhere!"

Brigham's face was grave. "Ain't you one of the legislators who repealed our charter?"

"Why, yes, I voted ——"

"That's the trouble. We used to have laws but you took them away. I can't protect you." Brigham's faint smile was sardonic. He was remembering the answer that President Van Buren gave to Joseph. He said: "Your cause is just but I can do nothing for you."

"I tell you my life is in danger! No matter where I go, these whistling stick-whittlers follow me. What's the meaning of it?"

"My life," said Brigham, "is in danger too. If I go out of the city, I see armed mobs. We came here from Missouri and built a beautiful city on what was a swamp. The man who built this city was murdered by men who helped elect you to office. You've repealed our charters. Your trial of the murderers of Joseph Smith has been a farce. Your cowardly governor will give us no protection. So we whittle and whistle to pass the time away." Brigham rose and bowed and opened the door. "I'm sorry," he said, "that I can do nothing for you." As the man turned to go, Brigham's eyes twinkled. "Perhaps," he suggested softly, "your life will be safer elsewhere."

He sank to his desk and chuckled. His simple plan of whittling and whistling was certainly curdling the blood of his enemies.

A man entered. Jedediah Grant, destined for high position in the church, was only twenty-eight in this year, but he had become one of Brigham's most trusted lieutenants. Humorless, hot-tempered, he was the most fanatically zealous of all the leaders. Under a high forehead, he had pale cold eyes that were too close together; a long thin blade of a nose that covered more than half the length of his face from his brows to the point of his chin; and a thin tight mouth.

"What is it, Brother Jedediah?"

"Sidney Rigdon is going to talk in the Park to his followers."

"I'll be there."

As Brigham strolled down the street, he wondered what to do with this stupendous fool. He did not like to throw him out—for Rigdon would take several hundred deluded persons with him. If Brigham were to cast every foolish prophet out, the ranks would be decimated by almost a third. Nevertheless, his patience was nearly exhausted—and it was completely exhausted after he listened to Rigdon's furious oratory.

"God," Rigdon howled at several hundred persons, "has given me a vision, and commanded me to lead the saints to Pittsburgh, the new promised land! The Almighty has promised me that I'll be the most powerful man on earth! I'll be so powerful that I'll cross the Atlantic, encounter the Queen's forces, and overcome them—and plant the American standard on English ground and then march to the palace of her Majesty and demand a portion of her riches and dominions; which if she refuse, I will take the little madam by the nose, and lead her out, and she shall have no power to help herself! If I do not do this, the Lord never spake by mortal! . . ."

Brigham groaned and turned away. The man was mad: that was the most charitable thing to be said of him. Of all his principal followers, Rigdon had made, not priests and bishops but kings; for in the kingdom of Sidney Rigdon, nobody was to be less than a duke or an earl; and Sidney himself was to be a potentate whose rule would be absolute.

When evening came, Brigham decided to go to Rigdon and try to argue with him.

"Brother Sidney——"

"I am President Rigdon!"

"Brother Sidney, I came to reason with you." Brigham looked at the man's eyes and knew there was no reason in him. "I don't like to throw you out of the church ——"

"*I* am the church!"

"If you continue your damned foolishness ——"

"Listen," said Rigdon, his eyes glittering under great shaggy brows, "if you persist in your usurpation, I'll tell the whole world about your wickedness, your abominable acts, your studhorse adulteries, your secret lecherous carnivals, your murderous Danites ——"

"Hold your tongue!"

"You're not fit to live! You're an abomination! You and all your followers are a gang of thieves and adulterers and whoremasters!"

Brigham flushed with rage. "Sidney, I'll ask the Twelve to excommunicate you tomorrow. So fall down, like Judas, and let your bowels burst out, and let the world see how much filth you had in you. Joseph once said he threw you off and we put you back on his shoulders. This time you're going out for good."

"You corrupt adulterer! You abominable apostate! You ——"

But Brigham had left the house.

The next day, the Twelve excommunicated Rigdon; and within forty-eight hours, that infuriated and wild-eyed prophet left for Pittsburgh, taking with him his loyal followers, of whom sixteen were kings, eleven were princes, and seven were dukes. With pleasure Brigham watched them go, reflecting that every last one of them would end in bedlam or in hell. He was sorry to see so many souls headed for Satan; and he wondered if it would not have been more merciful to have killed them before they were possessed by devils. It was better to die and go to heaven than to live a long life and go to hell.

That was a matter which he had pondered before. When in Missouri he saw apostates throwing their immortal souls away, he had said to Heber: "Sometimes I think it would be best to kill them while they can be saved. It's damned bad to let them give their souls to Satan." This theological point he had no time to settle now. His enemies, encouraged by violent newspaper editorials, were coming out of hiding and taking matters into their own hands. In Linn an army of bandits had just burned one hundred and seventy-five houses, and driven the saints like stampeded cattle into Nauvoo. As Brigham watched them pour in, some old and half-naked, some bloody from wounds, and others insane from grief and loss, he swore a great oath and sent for Bill Hickman.

"Bill, what's going on out there?"

"Murder, by God. If you stay in Nauvoo, the city will be sacked and burned. I heard the name of one of the gang leaders who killed Joseph and Hyrum. I went to his house over in Green Plains and asked for a night's lodging and told him I was from Missouri. So he kicked the wind in its face and told me the whole story. He says if the Mormons ain't chased out soon, they'll control Illinois just like they about controlled Missouri." Bill paused and considered. "I figgered I'd catch the old son-of-a-bitch alone and use him up. But you said to ask you first so he's still alive."

"Don't kill anybody. That would give the mobs an excuse."

"Well," said Bill, remembering, "I scouted everywhere. I seen several men who was in the black-face mob that murdered Joseph. I talked with them. They boast about it and how everyone was acquitted at the trial."

"Let them boast. Bill, do you think we should go west?"

"Well, the longer we stay here, the more trouble we'll have. What happened in Linn, it will happen everywhere."

"I guess we'll have to go west if we'n sell our property. All right, you move around and keep your eyes open."

Bill fingered a pistol. "If I run into any of them-there pukes who killed Joseph, you want me to sock them away?"

"No. I want no trouble." Suddenly Brigham smiled. "Governor Ford doesn't like our immoral practices because they differ from his own."

Bill grinned for a moment and then burst into loud guffaw. "Now if I caught him out alone——"

"For the last time I say no. Keep your guns in their holsters. Porter Rockwell gives me enough trouble. I hear he just killed a man over in Carthage."

"In self-defense," said Bill, but his grin was sly.

"It's ears and eyes and brains I want, not pistols."

"Just like you say. You're the general."

When Bill left, Brigham went to find his friend Heber. He told Heber the saints were whipped here.

"I know that," Heber said. "If we stay much longer, we'll be fleeing in our endowment garments. The sooner we go, the more property we can sell."

"You're right. Well, Heber, I'm taking the bull by the horns and spitting in both his eyes. We're going."

"Where?"

"To some valley outside of the United States. Lewis and Clark and Frémont have mapped several good places. So call all the saints in from the settlements. Just as soon as I can, I'll send the apostles across the river with two or three thousand. That will hold the mobs off until we can sell and get ready. If they see we mean to move, mebbe they'll stop burning and murdering us."

"But where," asked Heber again, "are we going to?"

"Anywhere, Heber, just so we get out of the United States. We'll go to a desert."

"A desert!"

"If we have a desert," said Brigham wisely, "then the saints will have to work. And besides, nobody else will want to come there."

"We want a place so bad nobody else will ever want it. Not even the United States."

"We'll find one." Brigham slapped Heber on his back. "Don't look so solemn! Only the Almighty God of Israel can whip us."

Brigham moved at once with all the energy he had. He summoned the saints to Nauvoo; and one by one the other towns and hamlets were emptied as thousands poured in afoot, on horse, in wagons, bringing their household goods and cattle, and settling on the outskirts of Nauvoo in shacks or tents or in nothing at all. Word went forth by a hundred riders that the saints were to gather and prepare for a great migration. To those who asked why he was going west, Brigham always gave the same answer: "To get away from Christians and out of the United States!"

He would go to some western desert and build the Lord's kingdom. He would have to cross fifteen hundred miles of wilderness, inhabited by Indians and wild beasts; cross a vast country almost without roads and trails; enter deserts upon which there would be little water or none at all; and ford mighty rivers that were unmapped and unbridged. He would have to fight hardship, starvation, disease. No other man here, perhaps no other man anywhere, would have dared to undertake so difficult an exodus; but Brigham dared, and he laid an iron hand upon the energy of his people.

Every home in Nauvoo was turned into a workshop. Laboring far into the nights, women knitted and sewed, fashioning warm and durable garments for a long journey. Men built wagons of all kinds, made harness for both horse and ox, coverings against wind and storm, compartments for food, barrels and casks for water. Labor was a mighty sound through the length and breadth of the city, and no hand was idle. All day, and sometimes all night, Brigham went from shop to shop, from group to group, cheering, advising, commanding. "That wagon ain't strong enough. Build you another." Again: "You don't want all that junk. You don't need it and your oxen can't pull it. Throw it away." And again: "Trade that ox off or shoot him. He can't stand the trip. And put a stronger axle in that wagon or you'll break down the first mile." He gave stern advice to the sisters too. "What you making all that damned folderol for? You ain't going to a ball, Sister. You're going through a wilderness of Indians and wolves."

He did much more than to advise or rebuke the thousands who toiled. Because he wanted all the saints to get out of the United States, he told Parley to instruct those in eastern states to embark by boat. He made an inventory of all the belongings, tried to sell the property of the church, and drove troublemakers out of Nauvoo. Haste was necessary now. Angry committees all over Illinois were clamoring for immediate expulsion of the Mormons, and the bold sheriff of Hancock County was working earnestly to keep peace. Matters came to a crisis when a furious committee in Quincy, declaring they represented sixty thousand gentiles, demanded that the saints leave the state at once.

"The hellhounds!" Brigham roared. "They won't even give us time to make wagons and sell our stuff!" He summoned Willard Richards, that fat jolly man who acted as his secretary and scribe. "Take an answer to that gang of Quincy hoodlums. Draw it up; say it's our desire to live in peace and to get out, but we want to take our old and sick with us, and sell our property."

The statement was sent and Brigham waited for a reply. He was enraged when the committee flatly rejected his proposition and returned word that the Mormons must leave at once. Brigham considered the matter and sent another message. He said at least a thousand families would leave Illinois immediately; and added that the saints had hundreds of farms, thousands of homes, as well as a temple and business establishments for sale. He asked for time to dispose of all these. Then he sent a letter to the President, and a letter to every governor except in Illinois and Missouri, inquiring in the name of God if there was in the United States anywhere an asylum for a persecuted people. "Exert your influence," he wrote, "to establish us in our civil and religious rights where we are now, or in some part of the United States, or at some place remote therefrom where we may colonize in peace." To this appeal he received only one answer. Governor Tom Drew of Arkansas wrote a thoughtful reply; but after pointing out that Arkansas would not undertake what Missouri and Illinois had rejected, he concluded: "Should the Latter-day Saints migrate to Oregon they will carry with them the goodwill of philanthropists and the blessings of every friend of humanity. If they are wrong, their wrongs will be abated with many degrees of allowance; and if right, migration will afford an opportunity to make it manifest in due season to the whole civilized world."

Brigham now realized that he would have to lead his people westward. He again went from group to group, urging them to greater effort, when he was accosted by John Taylor.

"Brigham, did you know there are warrants out for the arrest of you and me?"

Brigham had been examining a pile of yokes for oxen. He turned. "By Israel's God," he thundered, "we won't submit! We won't be dragged off and murdered like Joseph and Hyrum! They can all go to hell first!"

"But what shall we do?"

"We'll fight! John," he said, "you sleep too much. Help speed things up here. Four hours of sleep is enough for a while."

Winter was coming. The river was beginning to freeze, but Brigham knew that he and his people must leave Illinois soon or blood would run like water in every street in Nauvoo. He offered the temple for sale. He pushed at top speed the selling of land and homes. He appointed a leader to each unit of fifty persons, and told them to drive the workers to the last ounce of their strength. Preparations for the great migration went ahead at a sleepless pace; clothing and equipment grew into huge piles.

One afternoon while Brigham was talking in his office with John Taylor, a major from the United States army strode in.

"I have been sent by the governor," he said sternly. "There are warrants for the arrest of you two. How long do you intend to resist the majesty of the law?"

Brigham sank to a chair, overcome by the irony of the question. John lost his temper.

"You talk, sir, about the majesty of the law! Why, the law to us is mere farce! Majesty of the law! Where are the murderers of Joseph and Hyrum Smith? Have they been punished? No, sir, and you know they haven't. They're out now, burning our homes and killing our beasts, and you either won't or can't stop them!"

"Just a minute—" the major began, but Taylor swung to him in greater fury.

"Are we to sit still while marauders and house-burners come in and give us the hot iron? I tell you plainly, sir, I will not!"

"If you will listen——"

"Where is the spirit of 'seventy-six? If a man were not hardened and desperate, he would be ashamed to oppress a people already goaded beyond endurance! Talk about law! Sir, I stand before you, a victim of law! I have seen my best friends shot down! Was I not shot down too in the Carthage jail when two hundred murderers came upon us? Where is our governor, where are our generals, our judges? What are all these men but a pack of scoundrels? Are we beasts? I tell you, sir, hereafter I will protect myself, law or no law, judges or no judges, governor or no governor! I will not be murdered by scoundrels; and if I have to sell my life, I'll sell it for all I can! If you put me in jail, you will put me there dead!"

"If you would listen," said the major, somewhat abashed.

"We listened," said Brigham. "When Joseph and Hyrum submitted to arrest, the governor promised them protection and a fair trial. The governor was in Carthage with troops at his command when these men were butchered. If we submit to arrest, it will be the same old story." Brigham came around his desk. "Major, we will not submit."

"What, then, do you propose to do?"

"Leave Illinois as soon as we can. But we won't leave naked and without food in wintertime to journey fifteen hundred miles. That would be death. If we must die, we'll die here."

"I'm afraid, Mr. Young, that if you do not submit to arrest, the mobs will move in in spite of all I can do."

"Then we'll defend ourselves."

"Besides, the governor has lost patience. You promised months ago to leave ——"

"But not to leave naked and hungry. We'll leave next spring."

"If you wait until next spring——"

"Very well, sir. I'll see that two thousand families cross the river at once. Tell the governor that."

"I'll tell his Excellency but I can give you no assurance of what he will do."

"Tell him we're getting out as fast as we can. Tell him if he sends troops in here or lets the mobs come, we'll fight clear down to our boots and wade in blood to our necks."

"Do you mean that?"

"Major, do you doubt it?"

"No," said the major, looking at Brigham's eyes.

Knowing that neither the law nor the mobs would wait until he could move his people safely, Brigham ordered a thousand families to cross the Mississippi River. It was midwinter. The great stream was frozen over. The thousands crossed on the ice, herding their beasts with them, dragging a few household goods after them. It was a spectacle that made even Brigham pause to gaze at the straggling and desperate multitude. The weather was bitter cold, the mile of ice was now and then like polished glass; and all day long, persons and beasts slipped and skidded and fell on their way to the far bank. Brigham took command and moved with them; and when he reached the far shore, he turned to gaze at Nauvoo and to speak to the multitude.

"Our homes, gardens, orchards, farms, streets, bridges, mills, public halls, temple and all other improvements we leave as a monument to our patriotism, industry, uprightness of purpose and integrity of heart, and as a living testimony of the falsehood and wickedness of those who charge us with disloyalty to the Constitution of our country! Let us all kneel in prayer."

Upon the snow and ice, more than five thousand persons knelt and bowed their heads.

CHAPTER IV

RIGHAM TOOK THIS VANGUARD OF THE MIGRATION TO SUGAR CREEK, SEVEN miles from Nauvoo, and encamped there. He decided to complete preparations for the overland journey and push on with this multitude, and allow those in Nauvoo to follow as soon as they could. Some of his wisest leaders he left in the city, and some he brought with him. Many of those active in the early years of the church had died or had fled. Joseph's father had died five years before; the elder Whitmers had remained somewhere in Missouri; Newel Knight had vanished nobody knew where; and the embittered Emma had left the church, after denouncing it, after declaring that she had never believed a word of it, and had married a tavern keeper.

There was snow in the camp, there was a wild frozen storm overhead; and the temperature day after day stood close to zero. The suffering was intense. Brigham and his leaders had provisioned themselves for a journey of twelve months; but scores of families came into camp with no food for man or beast or with only a little, and soon all that Brigham brought with him he had given away. Daily men with hopeless eyes and gaunt bodies came to him to beg food for their oxen or their children.

"Damn it," Brigham roared at one, "you didn't show much sense! Why didn't you bring food?"

"Brother Brigham, I brought all I had. The mobs burned my crops."

"Well, go to my wagon and get a helping." A few minutes later he was looking into a wagon where a forlorn widow sat. "Sister, is this all you have?"

"Yes, Brother Brigham."

"Go to Heber Kimball and get something to eat."

There was no grass in this area; and after the corn was eaten, both horse and ox had to feed off the bark of trees. Brigham stared at the hundreds of beasts foraging for twigs, and drew his waistcoat around him. A year ago he had barely been able to fasten it but now it overlapped by twelve inches across his belly. His cheeks were sunken and his eyes had drawn back into his skull.

Day after day a blinding blizzard drove down from the north. All day and far into every night he went among the pilgrims, observing how some had leaned boards or poles against their wagons and were huddled under the rude shelter, with snow sifting between cracks and powdering their hair and bedding; how some crouched within small tents, without warmth of any kind, and sat there half-frozen, blowing breath on their red hands; and how others at night slept without shelter on the cold ground while the snow buried them under white mounds. To everyone he spoke a word of courage and hope but he knew that the morale of his camp needed more than his voice.

So he brought from Nauvoo a brass band, the members of which had been converted in England. On the fourth day, when the north wind was like a sheet of ice, and the snow was gray desolation upon wagon and tent and tree, Brigham ordered the band to play; and a Scotch reel sounded gaily from end to end of the camp. Persons came, stooped and shivering, out of their tents; men went eagerly in search of wood; and after a few minutes the band played a minuet while a great blazing fire laid its golden warmth on the wind. A woman began to sing.

> Come, ye disconsolate! Where'er ye languish,
> Come to the mercy seat, fervently kneel!
> Here bring your wounded hearts, here tell your anguish!
> Earth has no sorrow that heaven cannot heal! . . .

Hearing the high mournful voice, hundreds came to the fire; and presently the voices of men, women and children took up the song.

> Here see the bread of life, see waters flowing
> Forth from the throne of God, pure from above!
> Come to the feast of love, come ever knowing
> Earth has no sorrow but heaven can remove! . . .

Brigham stood apart and studied his people. Nothing, he reflected, could defeat saints who sang, or defeat him as long as he could persuade them to sing. It was one of his tasks to urge them not only to pray but also to sing and dance.

This task was impossible in the next week. The snow softened and rain fell—a cold and persistent and terrible rain that soaked everything in camp. It seeped through the covers and ran under beds; it dripped steadily between the cracks of pole-and-board shelters; it formed a sheath of ice upon wagon and harness and beast. Remembering their warm homes only seven miles away, empty now, abandoned to the mobs, the wanderers huddled in abject wretchedness of body and soul, no longer trying to keep their fires burning or their beds dry, and caring little whether they lived or died. Tirelessly, Brigham moved from wagon to tent, from group to group.

Late one night he was attracted by an object under a wind-swept tree. He went over and saw five women huddled above a sixth who lay on a wet blanket on the earth; and when he stooped to peer more closely, he saw that the prostrate woman was in the agony of childbirth. The other women were holding pots and pans above her to catch the rain, and making awnings of their skirts to protect her from the wind. The sick woman was moaning; the others were chanting in so mournful a way that Brigham felt chilled. He observed next that the woman's wet hair was matted around her skull, and that rain was luminous little rivers down her up-turned shoes.

Feeling a little sick, he went on but suddenly stopped. He had heard sounds of anguish, low, monotonous, terrible. These, he perceived, came from a lean-to against a wagon; and upon drawing near, he saw several persons in a dark wet group under the boards.

"What's the trouble here?"

A man looked up. "My wife is very sick, Brother Brigham. I think she's dying."

"Call a doctor."

"All the doctors in camp are busy."

Brigham fell to hands and knees and crawled under the shelter to look at the woman. She was wet through and chilled to her bones. She was dying. Four small children, shivering like beasts in a storm, were quietly weeping and clutching their mother's hands. Brigham felt of the children and saw that they also were wet to their skins. He put an ear to the woman's heart and a hand to her cold brow and then turned to her husband. The man, too, looked as if he were at the point of death.

"Carry her over to the fire in my tent. Take your children to Brother Heber."

"Yes, Brother Brigham."

All night Brigham searched through the camp, having fires built around the sick and dying, giving his own bedding to an old woman shaking with chills, speaking cheerfully to those who were numbed by cold and despair. Looking into sagging wet tents, he saw whole families crowded together in one wet bed, the children lying at the feet of their parents and trembling like a newborn colt in a winter morning. It was a gloomy and terrible place, this Camp of Israel—for that is the name Brigham had given to it. Even the horses and oxen, scattered everywhere, were humped up as if frozen rigid in the darkness and the rain.

Back and forth Brigham prowled, his mind busy with many things; his mind thinking of a nation founded on principles of freedom that had allowed thousands to be driven from their homes in midwinter; of mobs waiting over in Illinois to plunder and possess; of a noble temple that was standing in the rain this night, soon to be used for nobody knew what. Across the river were twenty thousand saints, among them the feeble and old and sick, making preparations to follow; and in many cities and hamlets in the eastern states, other thousands were getting ready to move. An entire people was on the march.

He smelled something that was like burning leather. He sniffed the wind, trying to tell whence the odor came; and saw a tent, set far back, that had a golden glow in the sagging canvas. Going to it he looked in and was astonished. A foolhardy man had built a fire close by his bed in the tent, and was now snoring soundly with his whole family while his boots burned at the fire's edge. Flame was smoking and hissing along the wet bedding.

Brigham stooped and shook the man. "Wake up!"

Full of sleepy alarm, the man sat up and reached for a gun.

"You trying to set a funeral pyre? Look what you done to your boots!"

"By God!" the man said. He snatched a frying boot and struck it on the earth.

"What's the matter?" asked the wife.

"We're burning up." In consternation he added: "By the God of Israel, look at my shoes!"

This night was only one of many in which a desperate multitude fought against rain and cold. For two weeks Brigham remained here, waiting for the rain to stop, preparing for the long journey, and receiving daily reports from Nauvoo. During the day, the men repaired or strengthened their wagons and harness, or went into Iowa countryside to buy provisions, or remained in camp to nurse their sick. From outlying regions, many curious gentiles came. They were surprised by what they saw. They were amazed when told that this camp of pilgrims was headed for the Rocky Mountains.

"Why didn't you wait till spring?"

"Because," said Brigham, "the damned Christians drove us out."

"Why didn't you stay and fight until the last dog was hung?"

"Because we would have been hung with the dog."

The inquisitor looked at Brigham and pondered. "How far is it to the Rocky Mountains?"

"About fifteen hundred miles more or less."

The man turned gravely to a companion. "By hell, I've got a notion to go too. I don't want to stay around such neighbors."

"Better join us," said Brigham. "I'll baptize you right now in Sugar Creek."

"Wait till I ask my wife."

When possible in the mornings or afternoons or evenings, Brigham had the band play. Stirring music did much to cheer the saints, even though the musicians stood under naked trees in the rain, with water running from their clothes and instruments. Always before the band played Brigham climbed to a wagon and led the multitude in prayer; and then said: "Sing songs of faith and hope. If you keep your faith, God will be with you."

After a week, a part of each day was spent in listening to complaints. Men came to him and said their supplies were being stolen—and stolen not by pilfering gentiles from the countryside but by saints in the camp.

"Someone stole all my harness," said a man, looking bleakly at Brigham. "I can't budge a mile without it."

"When did this happen?"

"When I was away working to get some corn."

"Why didn't your wife watch it?"

"She was too busy nursing the sick."

"Well, watch your stuff. They're not all saints in this camp. We have damned hellhounds among us. Now get busy and make yourself some more harness."

Brigham's chief assistants were Heber, Parley and John Taylor. Parley Pratt was a very sober man: he had lost most of his zest, his laughter, his appetites; for his first wife, Mary Ann, had learned that he had other wives and had abused him savagely and walked out. Where she had gone he did not know.

When Brigham entered Parley's tent one morning, he found that strong man bowed in grief. "What's the trouble?"

"Oh," said Parley, grinning feebly, "no more than usual."

"You still thinking about Mary Ann?"

"I guess so. After all, she was my wife many a long year."

"Straighten up," said Brigham, his face touched by sardonic amusement. "Some of the sisters don't have the spirit of the Lord in them. It's better to let them go. Besides, Parley, some of us have to keep whistling or this whole camp will lie down and die like a bunch of sheep."

"I know it."

"Did you know we have thieves among us?"

"Yes, I've heard that."

"Find out who they are if you can. If we catch them, we'll leave them in a tree with a rope necktie."

Parley squared his heavy shoulders. He felt a little better. "I'll see if I can catch the scoundrels."

Brigham went next to Heber's tent and looked in. "Heber, how are you this fine morning?"

"Fine morning!" cried Heber, and looked out at a drizzling rain and a dead sky. "In the name of God, is this ever going to stop?"

"We're moving in the morning. There's no use to stay here and freeze to death."

"You think we can get to the Rocky Mountains? I think we'll all die on the way."

Brigham entered the tent and put a hand on Heber's broad shoulders. "Of course we'll get there. Indians and wilderness are less dangerous than Christians. Besides, we'll be out of the United States."

Heber clenched his big hands. "I'm ashamed of myself," he said, "but all this infernal rain and snow and sickness and dying gets a man down. Three babies were born dead last night. And under the boards over there one of the mothers is dying."

"We all have to die," said Brigham.

As Brigham turned away, he saw the Bigelow sisters, Mary Jane and Lucy: they were healthy attractive girls and for a few moments he watched them as they walked arm in arm in the rain. It had been a month since he had taken a wife. He had nineteen wives but he was living with only seventeen and they were all back in Nauvoo. Just before leaving the city he had married four women in one day; and they were, he admitted to himself, a strange quartet: one was thirty years old, one was only seventeen; the third was one of Joseph's widows, and the fourth was a Quakeress by birth.

After considering the matter, he decided he was too busy now to propose to the Bigelow sisters. It would be better to wait until the camp was moving, but he might stroll over and pass the time of day.

"Sisters, how are you?"

"All right," said Lucy, a lass of sixteen.

"The rain hasn't broken your spirits?"

"No, Brother Brigham."

"Do you have a dry place to sleep?"

Mary Jane's blue eyes were looking at him curiously. She was twenty. She had a sweet mouth, an aquiline nose, and rich dark brown hair.

"It isn't bad," said Lucy. "When we get soaked we get up and dry out."

"Do you have food? Mebbe you'd like to eat at my wagon tonight. I have wild turkey."

"I don't know," said Lucy doubtfully, and looked at her sister.

"Of course we will," said Mary Jane.

Several persons ate by the fire at Brigham's tent, but he sat by the sisters and quietly studied them. They were ill at ease under his gaze. Lucy dropped a turkey wing in her lap and then giggled and flushed a rosy red. They were attractive girls. Brigham had observed them in the ballroom in Nauvoo, but he was not sure what they would be like in the nursery and the kitchen. By the time the meal was finished he had resolved to offer them marriage; and he rose and walked with them among the naked trees. The rain had stopped but the sky was chilled and dark: it was no evening for romance but Brigham was not a romantic man. He went straight to the point. After explaining celestial marriage and pledging them to secrecy, he asked:

"Sisters, will you marry me?"

Mary Jane turned startled blue eyes on Lucy whom she regarded as a child.

"Your glory in the next life," said Brigham, "will be much greater, and your happiness will be much greater, if you marry me."

"Yes," said Lucy demurely, "we can understand that."

Mary Jane's voice was tart. "How many wives are you allowed to have?"

"As many as I can take care of—if the Lord is willing."

"Is the Lord willing for you to marry us?"

"I'd not ask you if He wasn't."

Lucy turned to her sister. "It would be nice to marry the same man. Then we wouldn't have to be separated."

"That's true," said Mary Jane dubiously. She looked Brigham up and down as if to see how handsome and strong he was. A little maliciously she asked: "How many wives do you have now?"

"That," said Brigham, "is a secret."

"Would you," asked Mary Jane boldly, "love us as much as the others? Do you love all your wives just the same?"

"Just the same. I have no favorites."

"When we get to the Rocky Mountains," said Lucy, "will we all live in the same house? I mean could we have a little house of our own?"

"We'll see when we get there." He smiled. "We might all have to live in tents or dugouts and eat grasshoppers and roots."

"Well," persisted Lucy, "we want a little tent by ourselves. Or—or a dugout."

"You mustn't think of frivolous things."

"Oh, it isn't so frivolous. Women, you know, don't get along together very well. We wouldn't want to be quarreling all the time with your other wives. I think it's very sensible for us to want to live alone. Don't you, Mary Jane?"

"Yes," Mary Jane said.

"We'll see about it," said Brigham.

They had come to a hill and now stood together, looking across a drenched landscape to black clouds in the west.

"Somewhere out there," said Brigham, "we'll build the Lord's kingdom for His chosen people. We'll start tomorrow."

"Tomorrow!" cried Mary Jane.

"Yes. Meanwhile, you think this matter over. I want you to marry me, but you must also keep it a secret and tell nobody or the Lord will be very angry with you."

"But a lot of the saints," said Lucy, "know about celestial marriage. I've heard about it for years."

"They don't know about it, Sister Lucy. They just think they do." Shyly, awkwardly, he patted her shoulder. "Well, you talk it over and let me know."

"We will," Lucy said.

Brigham went down the hill and came face to face with Moroni and Tim McBride. He looked at them closely. Tim looked shrunken and sallow and half-starved and his eyes were cold and unfriendly.

"Brother Tim, haven't you forgiven me yet for marrying your girl?"

"I never will," Tim said.

"There's no sense in holding a grudge. Celestial marriage is still a secret, but if you or your father wants another wife, I'll let you take one. I'm letting only the leaders take wives but you two can if you want to."

"I don't want to," Tim said.

Brigham looked at Moroni and envied his soft brown beard. It looked almost as fine as silk. "Brother Moroni, do you want another wife?"

"I been thinking about it," said Moroni, his bright eyes twinkling humorously. "I know a sister named Maggie Williams that I might marry. But she has a friend, Agatha Thornberg, and they don't want to be separated."

"All right, marry both of them. It's sometimes better not to separate families and friends." Brigham considered a moment and smiled broadly. "When we get settled in our new home I think I'll advise the brethren to marry their mothers-in-law too. That's the best way I know to take care of that problem."

Moroni grinned, but there was no mirth in his son's eyes.

CHAPTER V

THE NEXT MORNING WHEN THE THOUSANDS OF EXILES STARTED ON their journey, the camp was a picture of overwhelming confusion. Brigham had assigned the men to companies, with a leader to each; and the captains ran around like wild men, trying to get their divisions together. They were angry, because every captain had among his men a few who were lazy and shiftless, and unable or unwilling to harness a horse or yoke an ox. The weather was intensely cold, with dry hard snow riding on a stinging wind. Some of the men hugged tiny fires or jumped around the fires, rubbing their hands and beating their breasts and watching other men labor. Some of the women, more energetic and eager than their husbands, led beasts in from the countryside and strove to hitch them to wagons. Children ran everywhere, frozen and frightened. Brigham went from company to company, cheering and advising and commanding; and by noon the first division moved out and took the road.

It was an amazing spectacle. The wagons in this camp were of every kind known to frontiersmen. Those able to afford them had large prairie schooners with thick canvas stretched tightly over the bows; and in each of these, drawn by two or four horses or oxen or in some instances by both horses and oxen in mixed teams, were women and children with bedding and provisions heaped around them. Men and children afoot drove the loose cattle, blowing on their cold hands and hallooing. Behind a huge schooner, as likely as not, went a rattling cart, or a two-wheeled trundle large enough only for a sack of flour, a pile of bacon and a child. Division by division, with wagon and cart and trundle, with oxen lowing and horses whinnying, with men and women shouting above the howling of infants and the cries of the beasts, the Camp of Israel moved out and took the deep mud of the road.

Company by company it fell in until a thousand wagons and carts stretched out in a long thin line. Some of the saints had chickens with them which they had in crates roped to the rear end of the wagons; and as the wheels jolted and squealed, a hen or a rooster would thrust a head up between slats, look around, and then vanish as if appalled. Some of the women—and even a few who were elderly—preferred to walk, so damp and cold were the wagons; and they trudged in snow and mud on either side, or went afield to assist in driving the cattle. Hundreds of men also walked, with little to do except to sink low into their coats and beat their breasts against the wind.

When every division was on the move, the caravan was two miles long.

During this bitter day, the first of his long and desperate exodus, Brigham rode a horse, going up and down the line and helping one person and another out of trouble. Many of the overloaded wagons sank in mud to their axles and held fast. Exasperated teamsters cursed and flogged their beasts. Now and then one would furiously climb down from his wagon and kick his horses or oxen and then blow on his hands and consider; whereupon with renewed anger he would smite his gaunt creatures again and cuff their ears.

"Stop that!" Brigham roared at an angry man who was flogging an ox with a piece of wet frozen rope. "You can't pull that out."

"Then what in hell," asked the man, looking around him, "am I to do?"

"Double up with the team behind you."

"If I do that every time I get in a mudhole I'll never get anywhere."

"Man, don't you realize those beasts are half-starved? It doesn't do any good to beat them to death."

"They ain't no hungrier than I am."

"Double up. And don't let me see you beating your teams again."

And to another: "Why do you set up there like a donkey on a throne? Get down and lighten your load."

The man grinned. "I wouldn't lighten a load much. I'm just skin and bones."

"So are your horses. Here," said Brigham to the teamster behind, "double up."

"Yes, Brother Brigham."

All of the animals were gaunt and underfed and shamelessly over-burdened—and none more than William Clayton's teams. Clayton was clerk of the multitude. He was a small and tidy man with soft dimpled hands, expensive jewelry and clothes. Because the passion of Clayton's life was order and precision, Brigham had not only made him clerk but had also given to him the task of freighting a large part of the church property, and of acting as its custodian. Clayton had several wagons that were heaped chiefly with flour and bacon and seed.

When Brigham rode up, he found one of the wagons sunk to the hubs. Clayton stood aside, gazing dolefully at the teams which stood with closed eyes as if they had frozen or turned to stone.

"Why," asked Brigham impatiently, "don't you double up?"

"Brother Brigham, as soon as I get out of this hole I'll be in another. I need bigger and stronger teams if I am to freight all this stuff."

"Brother William," said Brigham, his eyes twinkling, "life is a matter of getting into holes and out of them. The last hole is three feet wide and six feet long, but we'll get out of that one too if we are faithful."

"It's not that hole I'm worried about. It's this one."

Brigham rode ahead to another teamster whose wagon had sunk. "Didn't you see that mudhole or were you asleep?"

"Asleep, hell! The wagon before me got through all right."

"Double up with Brother William."

The teamster crawled down, moving as if he wore garments of ice. He limped ahead and gazed at his oxen. "By God, these oxes is stuck clear to their knees. If I was to take them out they'd fall over, they're that weak."

Up and down the long line rode this man whom neither cold nor mudholes, starvation nor exile could make falter or turn aside. He was never heard to laugh but often he smiled, so great was his amusement at the trivial or ineffectual or sad-hearted efforts of some of his people. Among the men were giants who did not have the push and courage of schoolboys: they wanted to sit down and blow breath on their hands when the job was to get a bogged wagon out or lift a fallen beast.

"What in hell is the matter? You think you'll get to the Rocky Mountains by setting up there on your hindend?"

The man addressed rose to his feet. Behind him, his wife and children poked their heads out to look at Brigham. "I think I'm stuck right here until the Lord comes."

"Look at me," said Brigham, and drew his coat around him. "I've lost a foot of belly in the last year but I'll lose another foot before I set down and whine. Didn't the mobs burn your house and corn and hay?"

"They sure did."

"Then I'd think you'd want to get away from the Christians."

"I got a notion," the man said, "to pull off to the side and build me a house and stay here."

"All right, if that's how you see it. Then get out of the way so the faithful can pass."

In this day of driven snow, of mud, of burning wind, the caravan made four and a half miles and pitched camp on a hillside. The wagons were drawn into a great semicircle; and within, a hundred men shoveled and swept the snow away and built a fire. Most of the pilgrims were too numbed, too sick at heart, to warm their suppers, and so ate frozen bread and meat; but others gathered to the fire and roasted wild turkey or chicken which they had killed on the way, or held bacon and bread to the flame to thaw them out. After supper was done, the band played; and a few of the men chose partners and danced. A few of them sang.

> Strong are your foes, but His arm will subdue them,
> And scatter their armies to regions afar!
> Then they will flee from the scourge that pursues them,
> For vain are their strength and their chariots of war! . . .

On the second day, after making five miles the caravan had taken on the appearance of a column of mud. All day gaunt beasts fell in their harness and struggled to their feet, blowing mud and water from their nostrils; or sank in mudholes to their bellies. When evening came, their legs were sheathed and their ribbed sides were streaked with earth. Their tails were ropes of water and mud. Short of provisions, many of the campers went to outlying settlements, seeking work; and while their wives drove their teams, they split rails, plowed land, and traded their labor for corn and bacon. Others, unable to find work, hunted for turkey and prairie chicken, or now and then shot a deer and rode triumphantly into camp. Those families without food received rations from Clayton's wagons.

"We'll all support one another," Brigham said. "As long as one eats, we'll all eat, and we'll all starve together."

The hungry inroads on provisions worried him, and very early in the journey he realized that he would have to be infinitely resourceful or his people would starve to death. Bitter weather made for ravenous appetites. When persons came from villages along the way and asked him to send the band over, Brigham eagerly assented; and the money or food collected in payment was stored in the general fund. All this added to little when divided among thousands; but all this, too, was only incidental. Brigham had up his sleeve a farseeing plan. Even before leaving Nauvoo, he had decided to stop now and then when he came to fertile untilled land, and to plant crops which the next caravan would reap. To this end he had brought machinery and seed. It was a wise and resourceful plan, this conversion of his vanguard into a marching industrial column that would plant and sometimes harvest and store for the thousands who were to follow.

He had not foreseen the remorseless cold, the depth of the mud, the swollen streams; and in spite of all his cheerful urging or thundering commands, in spite of the combined efforts of man and beast, the camp moved very slowly, covering only five or six miles in each day. During the evenings, and even while the camp crawled hour by hour, he organized his people, appointing a captain to every hundred families, and asking these in turn to name a leader for each group of fifty and each group of ten, together with clerks and guards. Under such supervision there was less scattering: the camp went forward in compact units, and did not always rest in one body, but spread over a large area to find grazing for the beasts.

After journeying a week, Brigham was forced to halt because of heavy rains and impassable streams. The storm came in such an avalanche that tents were blown down, boards propped against wagons were hurled down the wind, and schooner tops whipped wildly upon the bows and let the driving storm in. The first night in this camp on Chequest Creek in Iowa was one of continuous downpour; and when morning came, not a person was dry. Many of them were soaked to their hides. Beds were scattered everywhere with fallen tents upon them, and from under the tents, when daylight came, crawled men and women and children, looking like half-drowned creatures emerging from burrows. Nor did those in the schooners fare much better. Because their position was higher and less protected, rain drove in from front and rear and drenched them.

It was a forlorn and half-frozen multitude that faced this wild March morning. Preferring falling rain to wet beds, they came out, with garments clinging to them like their skins, for most of them had slept in their clothes. A few of the hardier men jested about troubles. Porter Rockwell, with his long black hair hanging like a matted cape, fetched an armful of wood and knelt in the rain to build a fire; but the wood was water-soaked, and after vain effort, Porter rose to his feet and laughed.

"By the Almighty God, what we need is an ark!"

"Yes," said another. "This is the second flood."

"If we had canoes, we could get to the Rocky Mountains. We need boats under our wagon wheels."

"Brother Brigham, we should make us some boats."

Brigham came over. He was wet too and looked unhappy.

"I feel like laying down here," he said, "and waiting for the resurrection. All this damned rain will raise the Gulf of Mexico an inch but it don't do us any good."

"You think the Lord always intends a rain to do good?"

"I don't see any sense in it otherwise."

"Mebbe," said Porter, "He intends to drown our enemies. I guess He figgered we should ought to have sense enough to go west in boats."

The men looked around them. Women with infants at their breasts were walking up and down in the rain, trying to hush their cries while husbands set the tents up. When a tent was ready, women and children entered it, but they could not sit on wet earth and they came out, or stood in the tent doors and stared around them. One man, laughing a little madly, seized a woman and danced up and down in the rain.

"If I could keep that up," he said, "I'd dry my clothes out. But I'm too gol-damned hungry." He pawed into a wet roll and fetched out a hunk of stale bread.

"It's breaking in the east," said Porter cheerfully. "Soon we'll be nice and dry."

Brigham, looking as if his God had deserted him, gazed at the water running from his hands and down his clothes; but when Heber came up, as wet as any other, Brigham smiled.

"Heber, in comparison with the way the Lord tested His people in the old days, this ain't nothing at all."

"Nothing at all," Heber said.

"I'd think," said Porter, "the Lord has tested us enough. Ain't that what He's been doing for years?"

"Call the band over," said Brigham. "We need music."

The members of the band came over, walking as if they had ice in their shoes and wore underwear of frost. From tent and wagon came the pilgrims to listen. A group of men gathered in a circle with arms around one another and sang.

> Children of Zion, awake from your sadness,
> For soon all your foes shall oppress you no more!
> Bright over yon hills dawns the day-star of gladness;
> Arise, for the night of your sorrows is o'er! . . .

After a few minutes, nearly the entire multitude took up the song.

> Children of Zion, His power will save you!
> O loudly extol it o'er land and o'er sea!
> Shout, for the foe will be slain that enslaved you!
> Oppression shall vanish, and Zion be free! . . .

Even while they sang, the black sky broke and sunlight fell upon a golden cloud. In a half-hour the sun was shining, though rain still fell, and the appearance and warmth of it transformed the camp. Men scurried for wood and returned with arms laden. Porter fetched a piece of dry board from his wagon and whittled shavings, and knelt to shelter a reluctant fire. Soon the flames were leaping in yellow heat and other fires were built; and hundreds gathered around to dry clothes and bedding, or to prepare a hot meal. When the rain stopped and the sun shone in full glory, the Camp of Israel hummed like an enormous hive of bees. Aroma of bacon and venison and biscuits filled the air.

"You don't want to lay down now till resurrection, do you?" Porter asked slyly of Brigham. "Wouldn't you like to fill your old belly first?"

"I'm plumb ashamed of myself," said Brigham, and accepted a plate of venison.

For twelve days the saints remained in this camp; for every day, every night, it rained. But they were busy. They laid bridges across swollen streams, repaired and reloaded wagons, nursed the sore shoulders of their beasts, and went to the scattered ranches to exchange labor for corn. On the sixth day, Brigham was surprised and angered to see a large company pull in from Nauvoo. It came in creaking old rattletrap wagons and carts that looked as if they were made of mud.

"Why in hell," Brigham demanded of the leader, "are you here?"

"Well," said the man, "we didn't want a-be left behind." He looked like one who had not slept or eaten for days. "Back in Nauvoo, they all intend to come."

"Damned foolishness!" Brigham roared. "We haven't enough food in the camp now. I told you to stay back there and provision yourselves."

"I know it." The ragged fellow looked sheepish but obstinate. "Brother Brigham, we just felt lost without you. We couldn't stay."

Brigham went from wagon to wagon to learn who had come. When he saw Eliza Burgess he was startled. A small woman, with large dark eyes that now gazed at him worshipfully, Eliza was a servant girl who had migrated from England. When she saw Brigham in Nauvoo she fell in love with him. She had read in the Old Testament that persons sometimes served seven years for what they wanted; whereupon, she had gone to Brigham's Mary Ann Angel, known to everyone as Mother Young, and asked if she could serve seven years in her house and then become one of Brigham's wives. How Eliza had learned that plural marriage existed in Nauvoo, Brigham did not know, nor would Eliza tell him. He told Eliza that if she wanted to serve, by all means to do so.

And here she was, humbly gazing at him, and with five years of servitude ahead of her.

"What," he said, "did you come for?"

"I want to be near you."

"Even if you starve to death?"

"Yes, Brother Brigham."

"Well, you probably will."

After inspecting the company that had moved in, he summoned Porter. "Go to Nauvoo and fetch the mail. Tell the rest of the saints to stay there until I order them to come. Tell Dan Wells that is my command and I want no more damned foolishness. Tell him we're all freezing and starving to death out here."

"I'll tell him."

"And make him understand that I mean it."

"I will. But you know Dan Wells is pigheaded."

It was not the pigheadedness of Dan Wells. The saints in Nauvoo felt deserted and terrified; and by thousands they were loading their few belongings into anything they could find on wheels and were setting out desperately to overtake Brigham. Porter said the road from Nauvoo to

Brigham's camp was lined with them. Company by company, they were pushing forward through the rain and the mud.

When he learned that fifteen thousand of his people were on the way to overtake him or soon would be, Brigham was speechless. Anger was his first emotion; but after a few minutes, Porter saw in Brigham's eyes something that was like a mist of tears. Then, suddenly, and still without having said a word, Brigham turned away.

He realized now what a stupendous task he had on his hands.

CHAPTER VI

IT WAS THE MEASURE OF THE MAN THAT HE DID NOT FLINCH. ON THE CONtrary, he moved with twice his customary vigor, realizing that he must push forward at once before the oncoming horde could overtake his camp. For four days with superhuman effort he went ahead, but on Chariton River he was again forced to halt: the road was so deep with water and mud that the teams floundered and sank and some of the smaller carts all but disappeared. Streams were so dangerous that when fording was attempted, several of the beasts were drowned.

For a week Brigham remained on the bank of the Chariton, thinking of his problems and wondering how many bridges he would have to build. He wanted a water route, but the reports of Lewis and Clark and others declared there was none. After a week, he had a bridge across the Chariton and pushed forward to Locust River and stopped again. Provisions were low. Every person in camp looked emaciated; some were too weakened for labor. Knowing that his whole camp would die of famine if he did not act quickly, he sent scouts in all directions; and Porter returned with good news. Thirty miles westward, he said, there was fertile land adjacent to a beautiful campsite. This the camp reached after wallowing in mudholes for another week. For two months it had been on the road and was still less than one hundred and fifty miles from Nauvoo. That, Clayton solemnly observed in his journal, made an average of two and one-half miles a day.

To Brigham he said: "We'll be ten years reaching the Rocky Mountains!" And he gazed at the fine cloth of his trousers which water and mud had ruined.

"How long was Abraham on the road?"

"Not ten years, I hope."

"Cheer up, Brother William. We'll be there in five."

Clayton gazed toward Nauvoo where his favorite wife was soon to have a child. "Five years?" he said. "You don't mean it."

"I mean," said Brigham, "we'll get there if it takes us forever."

The new site was so beautiful that the saints called it Garden Grove. On all sides grassy and flowered hills rolled away in thousands of untilled acres. Right here, Brigham said, they would plow the sod and plant crops; and within a week the area had been transformed. The divisions moved to different sites over a breadth of eight miles; and everywhere ox teams drew plows through the rich earth, while other teams dragged harrows behind men who sowed seed from their hands. Five thousand exiles were converted into an agricultural camp. While hundreds planted, others gathered and hewed timbers and built storehouses; and some, chosen for their skill with rifles, went out daily to hunt wild game. Women repaired garments, nursed the sick and cooked the meals; and children scattered in search of edible roots and wild fruits. One man set up a shop to mend shoes, another a forge and blacksmith shop, and a third tanned deer hides and made moccasins and gloves. No one except the sick was idle. If a man did not work, Brigham said he would not eat; and his word was absolute law.

Almost daily he sat as counselor and judge to hear tales of theft, of ill will, of petty woes. One of the brothers, said Parley, had challenged another to a duel.

"For what?" asked Brigham.

"Oh, they had a quarrel. He wants vengeance."

"Nobody fights duels in this camp. Send him here."

The challenger came, sulking and obstinate, with the light of murder in his eyes.

"What in hell," demanded Brigham, "are you up to? Can't you mind your own damned business?"

"I do. But no man can call me a lousy bastard and live."

Brigham gazed at the man: he was hulking and evil-tempered, and had an old scar above his left eye. "No man in this camp can challenge another to a duel. You go at once and apologize."

"To hell with it."

"What did you say?" asked Brigham. "Do you know I'm the law in this camp?"

"I don't give a damn what you are. He is going to fight me with pistols or I'll scalp him alive."

Brigham was angered. He faced the man and tapped him with an emphatic finger. "Forget this quarrel right now or I'll throw you out of camp."

"Oh, I guess you won't."

"You have two hours to apologize or get out."

"And if I say no?"

"I'll find a way to take care of that."

"You mean Porter Rockwell?"

"It's none of your business what I mean. Make up your mind and be quick about it."

"I won't apologize."

"Then get out."

"I won't get out."

"We'll see about that." Brigham called the members of his High Council and told them to discharge the man at once.

An hour later, the sullen challenger had a slip of paper laid before him. It said he had been discharged from the camp forever, and would leave immediately. He read the note twice and looked up: Porter Rockwell with hands on his pistols was gazing at him.

"All right," said the man. "I'll go."

"And the sooner," said Porter softly, "the better."

Other men felt the same swift discipline. When a prowling saint stole a beaver from the set of a trapper, Brigham gave him thirty minutes to return the beast and apologize. When another passed counterfeit coin, Brigham had the man summoned to his wagon. "This time you are forgiven. If you do it again, you'll be thrown out of camp and out of the church, and all your damned bogus money will be thrown in your teeth as you leave." When several men in a body were accused of theft, Brigham called every division to a meeting and climbed to his wagon.

"I won't tolerate thieves in this camp!" he roared—and his people knew he was violently angry. "I want to tell you this right here and now, if there are thieves among us, we'll find a way to take care of them!" Nobody misunderstood that. They had heard him speak many times of men who needed an operation just below their chins.

"And I want to tell you this: the hand of God will rest heavy upon thieves and adulterers and rascals of all kinds! Brothers and Sisters, I'd rather die by the hand of the meanest of all men than live among thieves. I tell you by the God of Israel that if there are thieves in this camp and I catch them, they'll wish they had been born in China of heathen parents and had worshiped idols and lived on rice! This is the only warning I will give you. If you can't follow the commandments of God in this camp, then go back to the Christians in Illinois!"

That was enough: he heard no more of thieves. He did hear of adulteries, but he was too wise to believe that thousands of persons could live in such primitive conditions, with whole families crowding into one bed, and not yield to sexual vices. Adultery was next to murder as a crime against God. He loathed it. He kept his eyes open and cocked a listening ear, but he knew that adulterers were too sly and skulking to be apprehended.

It was more important right now to plant crops and store food. He had a hundred men splitting rails, ten building fences, fifty building houses, twelve digging wells, ten laying bridges, and hundreds tilling the fields. Within a month, this virgin land had been turned into a huge settlement. The planted seed was coming through and spreading a pale green over the plowed lands. The crops were fenced. Cabins and storehouses and wells were ready for the thousands who were upon the road behind him.

When the work was done here, the camp pushed forward again; again paused in a fertile area to plant and build; and again moved into the west. Brigham had planned to pitch winter headquarters on the bank of the Missouri River where Council Bluffs now stands. There he would get ready for the long journey overland. But many of his plans were destroyed by his impatient or frightened people. Instead of remaining in Nauvoo, instead of waiting until crops were harvested and granaries filled, they had set out in their makeshift wagons and rattletrap carts; and when Brigham reached the Missouri, the road behind him clear across Iowa was an almost unbroken line of exiles. Into the camp at Garden Grove, and again at Mount Pisgah, they came by starved and ragged hundreds, and announced cheerfully that thousands were on their way.

Though worried sick, Brigham could not rebuke them: too many eyes filled with tears when they saw him, too many strong men clasped his hand and wept. "We couldn't stay behind," they said, with tears running down their wasted cheeks. "The mobs moved into Nauvoo."

"All right," said Brigham, again and again. "As long as I have a biscuit, you will share it. What belongs to one belongs to all."

Day by day, week by week, the multitudes came in. They did not stop to reap the crops at Garden Grove and Mount Pisgah. They were too eager to see Brigham and to go with him to the Rocky Mountains. By the time he reached the Missouri River, he had been overtaken by three thousand wagons and carts, thirty thousand head of cattle, hundreds of mules and horses, great flocks of sheep, and fifteen thousand persons. He had set out with a vanguard, and even with so small a number he had faced insurmountable problems. Now he had nearly twenty thousand persons on his hands, other thousands on the way, and winter just ahead of him.

"By the God of Israel," he said to Heber, "we'll all starve to death this winter. Next spring there'll just be our bones." He gazed gloomily out over the saints, scattered for miles up and down the river.

"It did a lot of good to plant crops along the way!"

"We'll send men back and harvest them. I guess we'll have to build a city right here. Heber, probably the job is too big for me."

"No job," said Heber, "is too big for you."

Working day and night, Brigham and his assistants organized the multitude, until every man in camp knew what his task was. Within a month, the settlement amazed the few gentiles who came from Iowa hamlets to see it. Even Brigham now and then stood on a high bluff and stared in wonder at his busy empire. The country itself was beautiful, with alternating reaches of prairie and woodland: from the picturesque bluffs high above the stream, the landscape fell away on all sides, and down to eight miles of rich alluvial bottomland running south. This bottom was crowded with carts and wagons, it was white with schooner tops and tents; and in clear blue mornings it was a valley of a thousand tiny fires. Many of the saints had crossed the river and pitched their camps there. Other thousands were in white villages north of the bluffs.

Standing on an eminence, Brigham could see his people for miles south, west and north; and below to the right or left on the river's meadows, he could see cattle grazing, with sometimes as many as five thousand in one herd. Most of the men were busy cutting and hauling timber and erecting cabins against the coming of winter, though some were content with dugouts in the bluffs or along the banks, roofed with willows or earth. Nearly all of the cabins were twelve by eighteen feet in size, made of cottonwood logs, and roofed with oak timbers split into boards and covered with dirt. Chimneys were made of prairie sod; doors were of shakes with wooden hinges and a string latch; the inside walls were daubed with clay. Very few of them had stoves. Those content with dugouts built them of willows and straw in puncheon style and cut a fireplace at the upper end. None of the cabins or dugouts had any floor except the earth, though a few of the more resourceful men gathered hard clay and tried to lay a plaster over the floor to make it hard and dustless.

Public buildings were also set up: workshops of various kinds, a grist-mill on the river powered by water, a house for public worship, and a stockade. A blockhouse was built for protection against marauding Indians, as well as flanking fortifications that could be manned by guns. Most of the saints had never seen Indians and very few were afraid of them, even though the men carried guns to their work and kept them always within reach. The Lamanites, offspring of one of the Lost Tribes of Israel, were only a degraded and unfortunate people who were to be pitied and redeemed and not slaughtered. Very few of the saints looked upon them as blood-thirsty savages or gave much thought to them. Brigham expected no serious trouble from Indians here because the saints overwhelmingly outnumbered them.

While groups of men built, others plowed and planted for the next year, mowed wild hay and stacked and fenced it, and herded the droves of stock. A few made willow baskets, washboards and half-bushel measures to be sold to Iowans the next spring. The women did much more than wash and cook: many of them labored with their husbands in building and planting; and others sat in tents to spin and knit and make garments for the journey. Within two months it looked as if an entire county, with all its people and improvements, had been transplanted unbroken to this land.

Everywhere throughout the vast settlement went the guiding hand of Brigham Young. He divided the camp into groups and subdivided the groups; laid out streets and trails; personally chose the site for every mill and workshop; established regular mail service between the camp and Nauvoo; and urged his people to sing at their work, and to dance in the evening when work was done. No person was idle except the sick and old. No person dared be.

"Listen," said Brigham one morning to a man sitting by a tent. "Are you sick?"

"No," said the man, turning a sour face. "Do I look sick?"

"You look well to me. Why ain't you busy?"

"Mebbe I don't want to be."

"Those in this camp who don't work don't eat. That's the law."

"Whose law?"

"My law. Get busy or get out."

"I don't like it here."

"All right: there's a road east, a road west: take your choice."

Brigham despised laziness. He tolerated no opposition of any kind. A few of the men strove to oppose him, and some, indeed, plotted against his life; but he had loyal spies everywhere, and a few hours after a plot was hatched, he had all the details.

One day Porter Rockwell came to him. "Bishop Miller is mad at you. He wants to go to Texas."

"Then why in hell doesn't he go to Texas! That man has caused me trouble all the way from Nauvoo. How many followers does he have?"

"About a hundred."

"Keep your eyes on him. If he makes a crooked move, I'll throw him out and kick his hinder as he goes."

And within a week, the ambitious and stubborn Miller was thrown out, and departed with a few followers to join the hotheaded Lyman Wight. In Nauvoo, Lyman had cursed everything under the sun and set out for Texas, taking with him a handful of persons who believed he was the new prophet. There was no use, Brigham had often said, to argue with a mule: you would get kicked for your pains, and it was best to do the kicking first. He knew that an iron fist was the only law that could govern a camp of homeless pilgrims. He reached decisions quickly and he never backtracked.

"You say Brother Ben stole a horse from the Indians? Porter, take the horse back and put Ben in irons for a week. Feed him bread and water."

If some of the men were afraid of Brigham, it was only the loafers, the skulking thieves, the ambitious. Such men he rebuked, not with a sermon, not by trying to appeal, as Joseph would have done, to reason and justice, but with a body blow that laid them out.

"You say Brother Cyrus stole all your bacon?"

"Yes," said a gaunt man who looked as if he had never eaten bacon in his life.

"Can you prove it?"

"Brother Parley knows he did."

"Parley would not lie. How many head of cattle does Cyrus have?"

"Seven or eight."

Brigham turned to his secretary. "Turn the cattle of Brother Cyrus into the church herd. Tell Cyrus when he gets hungry to come to me."

But suddenly Brigham was called from petty grievances to attend to a grave matter. There rode into camp one James Allen, a captain in the United States Army; and for a few hours there was tremendous excitement. Couriers ran everywhere, saying that an army was marching against the saints; and men ran for their guns. But Allen had come only to say that the country was at war with Mexico, and wanted a battalion of five hundred Mormons to serve in California. The incredible gall of that request left Brigham speechless.

"By God," he said at last to Heber, "can you match it? The government kicks us out and now wants us to fight for it! Here we are in a wilderness, homeless, facing starvation, and not knowing if we'll live or die; and the United States has the infernal brass to ask for five hundred men! What will the future say about that? They want us to fight for a flag that allowed mobs to burn our homes, rape our wives, and murder our leaders!"

"Tell them to go to hell," Heber said.

"I will—and I hope I can make my words blister like a hot iron."

But after considering the matter, Brigham changed his mind. Here was an opportunity and he was a statesman: he could have five hundred men transported to the west coast without expense to the church; and besides, they would be paid a wage, most of which would return to him for the care of the sick and old. He talked with his leaders and they approved; whereupon he called the saints into meeting and laid the proposition before them.

"After our persecutions," he said, "you may feel it is an insolence for our government to call on us now. Here we are, driven into a wilderness to starve. But we must distinguish between the central government, and the states of Missouri and Illinois."

"But what," called a voice, "did the central government do about it?"

"Absolutely nothing. That's all right: we're on our way out of the United States. But if a battalion goes, Captain Allen assures me that we can, while we're in the United States, camp where we please and as long as is necessary on our way to the Rocky Mountains——"

"The United States couldn't stop us!"

Another voice cried: "I thought we was out of the damned country!"

"Silence!" Brigham roared. "It is my belief that we should help our country in its time of need. We still love the Constitution and the flag, even though they did not protect us. Furthermore, we have a chance to get five hundred men to the coast without costing us a cent. I propose that five hundred men volunteer. I'll see to it that their families are taken to the Rocky Mountains. I pledge myself that they will eat as long as I have a crust myself."

There was silence. Brigham stood in a wagon overlooking the multitude; behind him on the ground stood Captain Allen and his aides. A voice shouted: "We don't want to go!"

Brigham grinned. "Well, if we can't get enough young men, we'll call on the old men; and if we can't get enough old men, we'll take the women!"

"I'll go!" said a woman. "Any way to get out west."

"You see? Here's a sister willing to go. If the men are afraid, we'll send a battalion of sisters."

"I'll go," said a man, and stepped forward. He was joined by a dozen others.

Nevertheless, it took Brigham three days to persuade five hundred men to leave. Five hundred wagons and teams, he knew, would be left standing on the prairies of the Pottawatomie and Omaha nations; five hundred families would be left without guardian or head. Just the same, it seemed wise to him to grasp this opportunity. Five hundred men were induced to go to Leavenworth; and from that fort a few days later they marched into the southwest.

In the Camp of Israel, there were five hundred fewer mouths to feed. Soon there would be a flow of gold from the marching soldiers. Brigham was feeling proud of this piece of statesmanship when Porter Rockwell rode in from Nauvoo. He came with a pack mule loaded with mail, and a mind full of unhappy matters. The mobs had entered Nauvoo, looting and burning, raping and murdering; and the saints who were there had fled across the river, departing so hastily that they took nothing with them. Now they were starving and dying on the Montrose side.

"The saints got ready to fight," said Porter, wishing he had been there. "They took a old steamboat shaft and made balls for a cannon. They stuffed barrels with powder and hunks of iron and buried them. They reckoned they'd blow the city sky-high and all the devils with it, but I guess the devils heard about it for they never come near enough to get blowed up. They brung cannon too. They set it right up by Boscow's store on Winchester Street, and then they fired in Barlow's old barn just like in Missouri they done in Haun's Mill." Porter pulled at his long dirty beard.

"How many of the saints were killed?"

"I never did learn. Brother Dan, he didn't know. Bill Hickman says a lot of them was shot and wounded."

"I left Bill there to watch the mobs."

"There was too damn many mobs to watch. Bill, he was busy, all right. They throwed him in jail but he socked them away and got out. One man was shot plumb in the forehead but it didn't kill him. The mayor of Quincy, Bill says, watched the battle. He was up in the temple tower. Well, another man was hotfootun it across a field and fell down and a cannon blowed one ear off."

"Have all the saints left the city?"

"Just about all. You should see them. It was rainun pitchforks when I left and the only tents they had was blankets over poles. All the women and children was sick, and there wasn't enough food in the whole camp to feed a dead baby. Most of the men was gone and the sisters was settun in the rain."

"Christians!" cried Brigham contemptuously. "Their mouths full of what they preach and their pockets full of what they practice. I guess the state of Illinois is satisfied now."

"They ought to be," said Porter. "They got a lot of property for nothun."

"Heber, we must send a company to fetch them over. Send bedding. They'll have to pick up their food on the way."

"Yes, Brigham."

"Get it off at once. How many are there, Porter?"

"About a thousand."

"How many wagons and teams?"

"I don't reckon they got a single wagon in camp."

"Send fifty wagons. Porter, you go along. By God, if we don't hurry, they'll all be dead."

While worrying about the destitute exiles, Brigham learned that he had a more terrible disaster right in his own camp. The long journey across Iowa in rain and cold and hunger had so weakened the pilgrims that thousands of them now sank under a dread disease which Brigham called black canker. It seemed to be a combination of fever and scurvy: it caused swelling in legs and arms until, in extreme cases, the limbs turned black and produced intolerable agony. Some said the disease was from want of vegetables; others thought it came from the miasmatic stench along the river bottoms; and a few said it was a punishment from God. The streams feeding the river were sluggish in early fall and as impure as open sewers; and the southwest wind brought to the camp a foul odor as if it came across a prairie of unburied dead.

Brigham had known there was sickness in camp and that a few persons had died; but not until he rode out in a late September day did he learn how much disease there was. The prevalence of it left him appalled. In a large camp west of the river, nearly half the saints were down; and as he went from tent to cabin, from cabin to dugout, he felt as if he too were ill. In every one of them, a man or woman or child, or sometimes several in one bed, were stretched out, their naked arms and legs swollen hideously and turning black, their faces hopeless and terrible. He went to other camps and learned before his inspection was done that thousands were ill; and he knew that if a remedy was not quickly found, the whole body of emigrants would be wiped out.

"Have we no medicine for this?" he asked a doctor. "Great God, do you realize half the camp is sick?"

"Yes, Brigham, I know it, but I know of no remedy. We are trying everything. In an old fort up north we found some horse-radish and we're trying that. Potatoes seem good in checking but not in curing it. You'd better send wagons back to the settlers east of us and buy all the potatoes you can."

"Are we to flee from Christians and die of scurvy! Is the God of Israel going to desert us now?"

"You answer," said the weary doctor. "You're the leader. Have you tried laying on of hands and prayer?"

Brigham turned away. Prayer was all right, but for his practical mind medicine was much better. If Joseph were here, he would say the Lord was punishing the saints for their sins; he would say the dread plague was a rebuke from an angry God. For Brigham, sniffing the southwest breeze, it was plain ancient sickness from the bogs and marshes and foul streams. He could lay hands on until he was exhausted, pray until he was purple in the face, but he could not by such methods arrest the inroads of blackleg. God would expect him to use his brains and not his hands.

Nevertheless, there was little he could do except to travel from camp to camp, see and hear the agony, touch fevered brows, and hope that cold weather would soon come. Within two weeks, he was horrified to learn that the sick were dying faster than the able-bodied could bury them. He thought he would break under the strain. No matter where he went—on prairie, river bottom or hillside—he saw fresh graves marked by boards on which were scrawled the name and the day of death; open graves waiting; or men digging graves, their mouths tight and their eyes bleak. Even more terrible, almost too terrible to endure, were the pictures of desolate agonies in the cabins and tents. . . .

In one he saw an old woman, alone on an unclean bed, her gray hair spilled around her face and over the pillow; her arms, almost fleshless a month ago, now swollen to the size of an axle tree, and as black as coal. His hand on her heart told him she still breathed but he knew she would be dead soon. In a second tent he found two children and learned from a neighbor that the parents were out burying the third. These two were far gone in disease: they looked like Negro babies, bloated with plague even in their throats and faces. One of them smiled at Brigham and tried to raise a swollen hand.

When he looked into the third tent, Brigham stopped in his tracks, too horrified to move. A mother, insane with grief, was sitting by her dead child and crooning to herself and brushing flies away. The child had been dead for some time: the awful smell of it filled the tent; and he knew that the mother, wholly out of her mind, had been sitting here day after day and night after night, crooning in madness and keeping the flies away. He found so many mothers keeping flies away from dead children that for the first time in his life he vomited from nausea.

He could not summon men to bury these children. Every man in the camp able to move was busy, digging graves and carting the dead to the cemeteries, or going from tent to cabin with food and water for those who lived. The droves of cattle were shepherdless now. Fences around stacked hay had been broken, and beasts laid waste to the winter's fodder. Where there had been a thousand fires in a morning, there was now only a handful; and in the public squares where men and women had danced and sung, there was silence.

Finding a shovel, but feeling weak in his knees, Brigham dug a grave and took a dead baby from its mother. To Heber he said: "Have Brother John tell the grave-diggers not to bother about coffins. Wrap the bodies in something and get them underground."

"How many have died?"

"God knows. Five or six hundred anyway." Brigham squared his shoulders. "Heber, how are you feeling?"

"I felt funny last night but I guess it was my imagination."

"Take care of yourself. I need you."

"Need *me*!" cried Heber. A dry smile warmed his pale face. "It's you we need, Brigham. You should go back to Pisgah."

"Not me. I'll always stay with my people."

"But if you get sick——"

"No, Heber, don't talk about it. Right now," said Brigham with a wan smile, "I have four more children to bury. They're rotten. Do you want to help me?"

"I'll always go where you go."

Brigham picked up his shovel. "Over here," he said. "Sister Ansey is out of her mind. You'll have to hold her when I take the baby away."

CHAPTER VII

E ARLY IN NOVEMBER, COLD WEATHER STRUCK THE CAMP. WHEN BRIGHAM arose one morning to find an icy northern wind, full of sleet, howling wildly over the tents and graveyards, he believed that the ravaging plague would be stopped. He was right: freezing weather was a better medicine than potatoes and horse-radish and herbs. The thousands who were ill began to recover. The gravest danger was past.

Nevertheless, it was a most desolate camp. Wives had lost husbands, husbands had buried wives, and in a few families the children had lost both parents; but the orphans were at once adopted into other homes. A committee was appointed to care for the destitute, and another to supervise the placing and housing of exiles who were arriving daily from the east. The crops planted at Garden Grove and elsewhere had been harvested. It would be another bitter winter of cold and want, even though there were hundreds fewer to feed than there had been three months ago.

When Sister Ansey came to him, Brigham realized that he had other problems besides want of food. She appeared like a frail ghost of a woman, with uncombed hair framing the fleshless whiteness of her face.

"Good morning, Sister."

She did not speak at once. She came timidly forward, her sunken eyes beseeching him.

"Are you in trouble?" he asked, distressed by her tragic appearance.

"Brother Brigham, where is my child?"

"Your child?" he said, but he knew what she meant. "You mean the one who died?"

"Where is his grave?"

"Sister, does it matter? Your boy is at peace now."

She approached him with supplicating hands, with the horror of the last weeks still in her eyes. "Where is the grave?"

"You want to see it? Come, I'll show you."

He went with her down the bluffs and to the river bottom, with an arm supporting her as they went; for she was so weak she could barely stand. They went through a grove of cottonwood trees and came to a small clearing; and between two rose bushes he showed her a small mound.

She stared at the cold unmarked grave, and Brigham looked around him, wondering if she would lose her mind again. With a choked cry that was even more terrible than her eyes, she threw herself face downward and hugged the mound, her thin arms reaching around and over it, her lips kissing the sod. She was not weeping. She was trying to hug the mound to her breast as if to draw her dead baby from its tomb.

Unable to endure her grief, Brigham turned away, going like an old man. After he had climbed to a bluff and looked back, he saw other mothers at graves along the river. He was amazed by the number of them; for they seemed to be everywhere, standing or kneeling by the cold graves. He realized then how lost in grief many of his people were and he knew he would have to bring them back to courage and hope. They could not survive a winter of starvation if they grieved over the dead. For him, death was unimportant: those who had died were at peace now and would rise to glory in the next life. But it was important, with a severe winter setting in, to arouse these thousands from their sadness and make them sing again.

After talking the matter over with Heber, he asked for several loads of wood to be delivered close by the stockade; and he sent messengers to the captains, telling them to summon the saints to Headquarters this evening. At sunset, Brigham stood on an eminence where he lived and saw the thousands coming singly or in groups from all directions. They came afoot and on horse and in carts, a steady stream from the north, the west, the south. Meanwhile, he had men building a great bonfire on a bluff near the stockade. After darkness fell, this fire was a light and a beacon to the whole camp.

Mounting a wagon in full view of his people, Brigham spoke to them, his strong voice carrying clearly to the farthest ear. "My brothers and sisters, there has been suffering in the Camp of Israel, but I ask you to remember that our concern is with the living, not with the dead. Those who have died are at rest in the arms of the Lord. They will come forth at the resurrection and we shall see them all again and live with them in glory. Do not grieve for them. We have a hard winter ahead of us and only half as much food for ourselves or our stock as we need. We must

« 358 »

have courage and faith. We must not yield to despair. We must all stand together as one man and support one another; and if we do that, we will pull through in spite of enemies and death and all the woes from here to hell.

"I want you to join me in prayer and then we will have the band play; and I want you to gather around this big fire and some others we'll start soon and sing and dance and forget your troubles." He paused and looked around him. Then he raised his right hand and bowed his head.

"O God, our eternal Father, we ask thee to watch over and protect us and keep us in the ways of righteousness, that our hearts may be full of thy spirit, that we may live in thy commandments and do thy bidding. Comfort those who have lost their dear ones and give them courage to face the future and assist in building thy church; heal those who are now sick and make them well again; and bless all of us and keep us safe through this winter, that we may resume our journey in the spring and establish thy church where we shall be beyond the reach of persecution and hatred. Bless us and keep us, O God, our Father, in the name of the Lord, Jesus Christ. Amen."

A solemn amen ran through the multitude.

"Now," said Brigham, turning, "let's hear some music."

The band was waiting; and as soon as it began, a thousand voices picked up the melody and sang the words. The pale cold sky was now lighted by a dozen fires.

> Zion, arise! Lo, the dark clouds are falling,
> The dawn of thy triumph doth joyously beam!
> Victory beckons and glory is calling!
> Soon all thy woes shall be only a dream! . . .

After a half-dozen hymns, Brigham told the band to play waltzes and polkas and quadrilles; and in separate groups, many of the saints danced in the firelight. In the square dances, old men called the turns, and younger men sought girls and danced for all they were worth, their faces eager in the glow of burning cottonwood and juniper. Some sang as they danced, others whistled, and a few played mouth organs and harps, adding to the music and gayety.

Brigham stood apart, reflecting on what he saw. He wondered if anything like it had ever been known before: twenty thousand pilgrims driven from their homes into a wilderness, and now dancing by campfires upon great bluffs by a mighty river, with Indians and wild beasts doubtless watching them from the far hills. Twenty thousand citizens of a free nation, driven into a strange land to freeze and starve—yet singing and dancing now while thin snow fell on a hundred graveyards! Even for him, unsentimental and hardheaded, it was an overwhelming spectacle; and he turned to his friend Heber and wiped mist from his eyes.

"Heber, has the world ever known anything like this before?"

"Mebbe in the olden times. Under Abraham or Moses."

"The Jews would understand this. I wish our Christian enemies could see us now. They hope we'll all starve to death but we won't. We'll pull through."

"Of course we will," said Heber.

"Next summer we'll find a place where our enemies won't bother us. From what Frémont says of the Utah Basin, I think I'll go there."

"Is it in the United States?"

"No. The Rocky Mountains is the boundary of the United States." Brigham watched the dancers. "I guess I'll dance. Have you seen Lucy?"

Brigham had married the Bigelow sisters, Lucy and Mary Jane. He now went to a far fire, seeking the youngest of his wives, remembering that he had been married to her several months and had visited her only once. When Lucy saw him, she excused herself, smiling graciously at her partner, and came forward to meet her husband.

"Let's dance," he said.

"All right." It seemed to her that he behaved shyly; certainly he did not dance well. "Tell them," she said, "to play a waltz."

"No, the waltz is sinful."

"Oh, I don't think so."

"It is, Lucy." While dancing with her, he gazed at her youthful face and said: "I'll visit you tonight. Send Mary Ann over with Eliza."

"Yes," she said, and smiled to show her dimples.

Brigham danced on the frozen ground, feeling stiff and awkward with a girl so light on her feet, and gazing a little enviously at the nimble young men around him. Well, he reflected, he was only forty-six: a young man still, but by no means as young as he had been; dancing came rather sedately to men of his age.

"Did I step on your feet?" he asked, knowing that he had.

"Oh, no. You dance very well."

He did not believe that. He liked dancing but it was a bit frivolous and giddy for a man whose job was to build an empire, whose dream was not of fair women but of tilled prairies, factories and temples, and missions flung to the farthest reach of the world.

When the dance was finished he released her. "About ten," he said.

He returned to Heber, wondering if he should dance with all his other wives, but not wishing to. Some women were so jealous and unreasonable: his wife Susan Snively, for instance, whose chilled gaze he met as he passed a fire: she had no children and he was impatient with barren women. Besides, if he danced only with his wives, the saints watching might become suspicious and believe that he had more wives than one.

"Heber, how many jealous wives do you have?"

"Most of them," said Heber, grinning. "No matter how a man behaves, it seems that some women have to be jealous."

"I get tired of jealous women. If I marry any more, I intend to be sure they won't cause any trouble."

"Likely as not," said Heber jestingly, "you'll marry the most jealous one in Zion."

That statement amused Brigham. When he remembered it twenty years later, he was not amused. "Is there much suspicion about celestial marriage?"

"I don't think very much since we left Nauvoo."

"It's mighty hard to keep it a secret. If all my wives was like Mary Ann," said Brigham, thinking of his Mary Ann Angel, a quiet and patient woman who gave him no trouble.

"Now and then," said Heber, "I could murder some of mine. If one has a new hat, they all must have a new hat just like it. If one has a baby, the others blame me because they don't have a baby. If I smile at one of them, another one says she's my favorite." Heber looked at Brigham. "My wives say Emmeline is your favorite."

"Foolishness!" Brigham cried. "I have no favorites."

"It's sort of hard not to," said Heber.

Standing by a wagon at some distance from the fires, Brigham could see all the groups. Only a few hundred were dancing. The thousands stood back and watched, with mothers and fathers holding babes to their breasts, and other children clinging to their hands or clothes. From time to time, men in groups broke away and dragged fresh logs to the fires; and constellations of sparks shot upward in great golden showers.

Knowing they would dance and sing until the wood was gone, Brigham said good night to Heber and slipped discreetly to Lucy's cabin. He entered softly but with no sense of guilt or shame: celestial marriage was as holy in his mind as charity or love. He found Lucy in the pale gloom of an oil lamp. A small wood stove was red with heat and the cabin was cozily warm, with firelight from an open grate dancing on the bed and walls.

"How are you tonight?" he asked, convinced that health was the most precious of earth's good things.

"All right," she said. There was mischief in her blue eyes.

He sat on the bed and began to take off his shoes. She did not like that: she wanted him to sit by the fire with her and listen to the gay music of the band. If he had been an ordinary husband, she would have known what to do; but he was prophet and judge in a great camp, now that Joseph was dead. And besides, he was so big and strong and stern: she hardly knew what to do with such a man, or whether she could do anything at all. She was almost paralyzed when she looked at the firmness and strength of his wide jaws and straight mouth.

She sighed and looked unhappily coquettish. After his second shoe fell and he began to pull off his big thick socks, she rose, still wondering how to soften him, and went over, summoning all the boldness she had. She stood before him for a moment and then obeyed an impulse and fell to his lap, her arms seeking his neck. Her soft red mouth touched his hard firm lips; and finding no kiss there, no response at all, she pressed her lips to his tanned cheek. His big strong arms went around her for a moment and drew her to him; whereupon, as if that one brief caress should be enough, he lifted her off his lap and set her on the bed.

She sighed again and looked at his weather-beaten profile. How many wives he had, she did not know; but she did know that none of them had softened him to tenderness. She was very young and very pretty: she had always been popular with men; she liked to coquette and make dimples in her cheeks and show how sweetly she could smile. But he paid no attention to all that and she was baffled.

With his socks off, Brigham unbuttoned his trousers and shirt and drew them off and then sat in his heavy endowment garments. Lucy did not like them. They were, she knew, symbolic in some way: they were worn by those who had partaken of the temple rites and had received the gift of the Holy Ghost. Nobody who wore these garments was supposed ever to take them off completely, but always to keep one foot or hand in them while bathing, or changing to clean underwear. Brigham, she reflected next, did not smell very sweet, but nobody did or could in this camp: there was too much labor and sweat, too few places to bathe. Suspenders had made a dirty cross on the back of his underwear.

"It's bedtime," he said, observing that she had made no move to undress.

"I don't want to go to bed yet."

"I must visit you and go get my sleep."

"Why do you always sleep alone?"

"It is good for a man. Every man should sleep alone in solitude."

"But don't you ever sleep all night with one of your wives?"

"Never."

She considered a moment. "I want you to hold me by the fire and kiss me."

"Nonsense," he said. "This is no time for romance."

"I don't want romance. I just want you to love me a little. You're my husband, you know."

"You are vain," said Brigham. "The Camp of Israel is no place for vain women."

Lucy flushed with anger. "Is it vain to want my husband to love me?"

"You're a coquette, Lucy. Remember all the graves on which the snow is falling now."

"But we are still alive. Brigham, don't you ever kiss any of your wives? Do you treat them all as cold as you've treated me?"

"You are being foolish. Come to bed."

Lucy drew a foot to her knee and removed a heavy shoe. She had beautiful legs and one calf was now exposed; but a sly glance at him told her that he could live with her fifty years and never know what pretty legs she had. She removed her other shoe and then her stockings; and fumbled with her dress. Without removing his underwear, he turned

the cover of the bed back and crawled in, and then lay with eyes closed
waiting for her.

She crossed the room and blew out the light. The fire was sorcerou
on the walls and ceiling, but there was no sorcery in this man: if onl
he would leave the bed and come to her and hold her on his lap by th
fire, and listen with her to the gay music of a quadrille! She wanted t
speak to him but she dared not call him Brigham again; and it would b
silly to call him Brother Brigham.

"Honey?" she said, standing by the fire.

"What?" asked Brigham. "Lucy, come to bed."

"Yes," she said meekly, and went softly to the bed and lay at his side

CHAPTER VIII

FINDING NOTHING FOR HIM TO DO IN ILLINOIS, BILL HICKMAN FOLLOWED the last of the exiles to the Missouri River and reported to his chief. Brigham had told him not to kill except in self-defense and Bill had not done so, though he had been tempted many times. He bashed a jailer's skull to escape; and when the mobs marched on Nauvoo, he shot five of the rascals from ambush and felt pleased with his afternoon's work. When he saw haystacks and homes burning, he skulked through the countryside, trying to surprise some of the men who set the fires; but all in all he had rendered small account of himself and felt chagrined.

It was midwinter before Brigham summoned Bill to his cabin. Brigham had never worried much about Indians, nor had his people, because they did not share the customary American fear of them. Indians for the saints were not bloodthirsty redskins but the descendants of Laman and the Lost Tribes. They had had a desperate and unhappy past, having long ago been slaughtered, enslaved, and driven into a wilderness; but for all that they were not savages but human beings with souls to be saved. Curses from both man and God had made nomads of them; and for the Mormons, they were to be converted and saved and not murdered.

Nevertheless, Brigham, who had seen little of them, discovered that they could be a persistent nuisance; for more and more they came to his settlement to beg or to steal.

"The Indians," he said to Bill, "are giving me some trouble. I think it's better to feed the lazy villains than to fight them but I haven't enough food. There's one, a half-breed, named Antoine Michet. You ever seen him?"

"I reckon I never have."

"He joined the church, but I might a-known he was a skipjack. Anyhow, he's turned plain damn sinner and swears he intends to scalp me. That ain't the worst of it. He plans to go ahead of me next spring and get all the tribes together and ambush my train. That's what I've been told."

"I guess," said Bill calmly, "you want me to sock him away."

"Well, what would you do with an enemy like that?"

"I'd use him up."

"Find out first if he means it. Then if he does, don't let anyone know what you do. And there's a horse thief around here who has sworn to murder Brother Orson."

"What's the villain's name?"

"I don't know. Get a description of him from Orson Hyde."

"All right," said Bill. "Just figger on two enemies less."

"Bill," said Brigham, looking into the man's cold eyes, "I expect you to use commonsense. I don't want the gentiles after me for murder. But I don't intend to let half-breeds and horse thieves destroy God's church."

"Count on me," said Bill, still speaking as if he took such desperate assignments in a day's stride. "I'll sock them away so there won't be no stories."

"Report to me when you're through. And Bill, how many of the saints are talking about celestial marriage? Is it leaking out?"

"A few talk about it. But I guess they don't really believe it's true."

"We must keep it a close secret. Do you want another wife?"

"Not yet," said Bill, grinning. "I took another one in Nauvoo, but I don't want to fool with any more."

"All right. Take care of those two villians."

"I sure will."

Here were two jobs after Bill's own heart. Two cowardly rascals were threatening the progress of God's church and had to be sent back to the Devil where they belonged. He was as pleased as a small boy. Sometimes, it is true, he felt that Brigham was unfair in not providing him with food and clothes and a house; for it seemed to him that he should not have to bother with those matters if he were to be a special emissary of death. Brigham had never given him anything—not even ammunition or a choice of ponies or a single piece of clothing. In later years he was to grow bitter over the neglect, but now he was happy as he went into his tent to clean and load his pistols and test the edge of his long hunting knife. So the half-breed blackguard had sworn to have Brigham's scalp, had he? Well now, Bill Hickman would see about that.

He mounted the fastest horse he could borrow and rode through the settlement, smelling out the trail of Antoine Michet, though pretending all the while that he was looking up his old friends. Finding no sign of the rascal in camp, Bill rode northward to the Indian agency and nosed around there; whereupon, having learned nothing, he went up the river to visit the friendly Omaha Indians.

It was on a clear day in January that he first laid eyes on Antoine. The man was tall and straight and looked more Indian than French, though he had a trimmed beard and carefully kept hands and clothes. Bill did not like the look of him: he was a scoundrel, all right, as anybody could tell by his stealthy movements and furtive eyes. Bill shadowed Antoine to learn where he lived and then rode back home to ponder and to wait.

Thereafter he went daily into Antoine's neighborhood up the river, declaring he was seeking stock which had strayed from the herds. Antoine rode a great deal too, though for what reason Bill could not determine; and one day the two men met on a hill.

"Hello," Bill said. "You seen any stray cattle?"

"What brand?" asked Antoine. His voice was soft and modulated. Brigham had said that to the wiles of the Lamanite, Antoine had added the cunning advantages of a formal education.

"A horse with a fleur-de-lis on the left thigh; and two ox OP on the right ribs. That's the ones I'm after today."

"I haven't seen them," said Antoine.

"You seen any stray cattle of any kind?"

"Not a single one."

"Do you ride around here a lot? If you do, you might keep your eyes open. For cattle, I mean."

For a moment Antoine considered that. "I ride only for pleasure," he said.

"I guess," said Bill dryly, "it must be a lot of fun."

"You a Mormon?" asked Antoine casually.

"Kind of a jack-Mormon," said Bill, pretending to be a somewhat stupid fellow. "Are you?"

"No," said Antoine, politely ignoring the question, "I haven't seen any cattle with those brands."

The next day while Bill was riding, Antoine unexpectedly joined him; but it was not until their third day together that Bill, still affecting to be stupid and unobservant, became confidential. Pretending to be weary of searching for cattle, he suddenly cried with impatience:

"To hell with them! Why should I work for the damned church?"

Antoine looked twice as crafty as a coyote. "You don't seem to like the church," he said softly.

"By God, I don't."

"Why not?"

"Well, I'll tell you if you won't say anything."

"Of course not," said Antoine. His handsome dark face was smiling.

Bill looked around him as if for spies. Lowering his voice, he said: "It's old Brigham Young. By God, I don't think he's any prophet at all."

Antoine considered that. From time to time as they rode along, he looked craftily at Bill, but Bill pretended not to know it. He affected a sulking fury and swore that Brigham was a scoundrel and a fraud. At last Antoine said:

"I don't like him myself."

"Who does?" demanded Bill vehemently. "I guess the old pod has tried to deacon a calf for you. But he does for everybody."

"He wouldn't let me take any more wives," said Antoine with spirit.

"The hell he wouldn't!" said Bill, affecting astonishment. "God knows he has plenty."

"How many?" asked Antoine.

"Who knows? About a hundred. That's what the hickory Mormons say."

Again Antoine rode in silence but Bill knew what was going on in the man's mind. He was not surprised when the half-breed asked:

"Why do we put up with him?"

"What else can we do? He has all the power."

"Don't you think there might be a way?"

"I've tried to figger out one. I know a lot of the Mormons would like to see him used up. I would, but I don't darst try it alone."

"I would," said Antoine.

Bill glanced at the dark face and was surprised by the hatred in it. "Alone?" he asked innocently.

"I know a better way," said Antoine. His voice suggested that he was beginning to trust this man. "When Brigham goes west next spring, we can set the Sioux and the Pawnees on him before he reaches Fort Laramie. They could ambush him and wipe out the whole camp."

"By God, they could," said Bill. He was thinking swiftly now. He had learned all that he needed to know.

"When Brigham wouldn't let me have another wife," said Antoine, growing very confidential, "I told him I'd dance over his scalp. I intend to."

"I don't blame you," said Bill. They were in a deep gully far from the camps, both Indian and white. The spot was all right, Bill decided, but he wanted to ask one more question. "How much money do you want to sock him away?"

"How much," asked Antoine softly, "am I offered?"

"This much," said Bill. His right hand had slipped suddenly to his pistol and the amazed Antoine found himself gazing into the unwavering barrel. "So you aimed to dance over Brigham's scalp, did you?" Bill's voice was as hard and his eyes were as cold as the pistol in his grasp. He looked at the half-breed's face: it had turned a sickly white and the eyes were yellow with fear. "Brigham," Bill went on, speaking calmly, "is the Lord's servant in building up the true church. I don't allow the Devil's jack-nasties to get in the way."

His finger pressed the trigger. Antoine spun halfway around in his saddle and clutched at the horn, but in the next moment he gurgled and pitched headlong to the earth. Bill dismounted and tied his horse to a bush. Unless he had erred in judgment, he had shot the villain through the heart; and he now bent over to see. Yes, it was through the heart, all right. Drawing his knife, and reflecting with a grim smile that he had never scalped a man before, he grasped Antoine's long black hair and pressed the sharp blade to the skull. After making an incision clear around the head just above the ears, he pulled at the scalp and skinned it off. For a moment he gazed curiously at the red and bleeding skull and then washed the scalp with snow and thrust it into the pocket of his coat.

After he had mounted and ridden a short distance, he stopped to look back: if the rascal were found, it would be supposed that Indians had done the job. As likely as not, though, he would be drifted under and eaten by wolves in the spring. Bill rode on, feeling that he had acquitted himself well. After all, Brigham was a prophet and knew what he was doing; and if sinners threatened to murder him, then the sinners had to be socked away and sent back to hell. That was the way Bill looked at it; and that, he was convinced, must have been the way the saints had looked at the matter in the days of the Old Testament when the enemies of God almost exterminated the righteous.

For the half-breed lying back there in the snow with a naked skull, he cared nothing at all, nor even thought of him, except to reflect that one enemy of the Lord would make threats no more. When he entered Brigham's cabin, he was so pleased that he grinned.

"Hello," said Brigham. "How are things going?"

"They could be worse. You told me that half-breed said he'd hold a war dance over your scalp."

"That's what he told me."

"That's what he told me. He got my dander up."

"He's a dangerous man."

"Not now," said Bill. "Now you can dance over his scalp." And Bill, still grinning, dragged the hide and hair from his pocket. "There it is."

"What's that?" asked Brigham, startled.

"It's the forelock of that half-breed."

"Is he dead?"

"If he ain't he sure fooled me. He looked dead as a last year's snow-flake when I seen him last."

Brigham looked curiously at the scalp which Bill was holding by the long black hair. "You sure you got the right man?"

"Sure, Brother Brigham. I don't go around sockun good people out of the way."

"Damn it, you didn't have to scalp him, did you?"

"Well, he aimed to scalp you so I thought I'd show him how it feels. Except he was dead as a doornail and never found out."

"Stick that out of sight. Someone might come in."

Bill thrust the scalp into his pocket. Brigham looked at the pocket to be sure the horrible thing was hidden; and then said:

"How about that horse thief who swore to kill Brother Orson?"

"I'm on his trail."

"Where did you leave this half-breed?"

"Away up north in a gully. He'll be snowed under and then the wolves will eat him."

"Don't get reckless. The enemies of the Lord have to be seen to but I don't want any trouble."

"Don't worry," said Bill. "I make sure before I act. Why, I even got that half-breed to tell me his plans. He aimed to ambush you next spring and wipe you out."

"That's what I heard."

"When he told me that, it was an open and shut proposition and I just used him up. He wasn't worth a red cent anyhow."

"Bury that thing in your pocket."

"I will. I wanted you to know one of the Lord's enemies was socked away."

Brigham smiled faintly. "After this I'll take your word for it. Leave the evidence outside. Have you taken another wife yet?"

"Just the one I told you about."

"Take another if you want one."

"Thanks," Bill said. "Two's about all I can take care of."

"All right. Now go brush-whip that horse thief."

Bill was on the trail of the horse thief but he was resolved to be sure the man was villainous. He had little reason to doubt it. Orson Hyde had pointed the man out to him and a more desperate-looking brigand Bill had never seen. The man was tall and lean and sly, with the plotting look of a coyote who had been starved seven winters. He rode a sleek pony around the encampment, boasting of his prowess with a gun, of his friendship with Indians, and of his murder of two men one winter when he trapped on a tributary of the Missouri.

When the fellow laughed, he showed ugly uneven teeth and narrowed his eyes in devilish cunning. Nobody seemed to like him or trust him. Moreover, he always had money and wore expensive clothing, though he was never known to work. So far as Bill could learn, the man gambled with the more sinful saints and stole from the Indians. Bill did not gamble and he despised gamblers; nor did he drink, for he was determined to keep himself pure in the sight of God.

The braggart's name was Heb Sudworth. Bill sized him up one afternoon and wondered how he could get the loud-mouthed cutthroat off alone. It was February before an opportunity came.

Heb was full of bad whiskey which he had bought nobody knew where; and his boasting was unusually loud and insolent. "There ain't a Mormon in camp," he said, "I can't whip with fists, knives, guns or giant powder. Not a ringtail roarer in the whole outfit!"

"How about Porter Rockwell?" asked Bill solemnly.

"Him?" asked Heb, and slapped his breast. "Tell him to come with his old shootun irons! I'll set him a lareover for meddlers! I'll make him a nice little funeral three feet by six!"

"I reckon you would," said Bill.

"You know Jim Bridger? I made his eyes turn as yellow as a sunflower. He went off on his ear but when I yanked the old smoke-iron out, his bravery was about as fat as a hen's forehead. He just grouted down and shut up his head."

"The damn coward," said Bill.

An hour later Bill caught Heb alone. "There ain't any brave men in this camp," he said, "but I know a redskin down the river who'd sock you away in a twinkle."

"A Indian?" asked Heb in amazement. "A Indian who'll fight me fair and free?"

"Yes. At least he said he would."

"In the name of the lick-spittun Christ, show him to me!"

"Come," said Bill, and they rode away.

"I guess you don't go in much for fightun," said Heb, leering at Bill.

"No, I'm sort of timid. I like to watch a good fight, though."

"Dodrot your skin and bones, you'll see one." Suddenly Heb gazed at the pistols at Bill's waist. "What do you carry them smoke-irons for?"

"Oh," said Bill, trying to look very sheepish, "they make me feel braver."

Heb slapped his saddle horn and roared. "I guess you'd jump right out of your skin if one went off."

"Like as not," said Bill. After a moment he added: "I hear you're sort of mad at Orson Hyde."

That made Heb almost fall out of his saddle with rage. He reached back and yanked a bottle of whiskey from a saddlebag and drank and wiped his mouth. "Who told you?"

"I don't know. I heard it somewhere."

"Listen," said Heb, leaning over. "That yellow-livered little pot-gutted son-of-a-she-wolf! You want a-know what I aim to do with him? I aim to skin his face off and stand on the hide!"

"Why?" asked Bill softly.

Heb drank again. "I'll tell you why. He told me I was a horse thief. He said I stole horses from the Mormons and sold them to the Indians."

"Did you?"

"What I do," said Heb, "ain't no man's business but my own. No gallows-faced swag-bellied Mormon can call me a horse thief and live."

Bill glanced around them. They were several miles down the river. Pretty soon now, Bill said to himself, I'll sock this sinner away.

"Where is this Indian who wants to meet Heb Sudworth?"

"Not much farther. You better get yourself ready."

Heb took another drink from his bottle. "I'm ready for anyone, even the Devil himself. Didn't I tell you I scart Jim Bridger yellow in the face?"

Bill wondered if he should not give this braggart a sportsman's chance. After all, it was no fun to draw a bead on a man and bore him through the heart: any sort of greenhorn could do that. If there was a quicker or more deadly shot in this whole country than Bill Hickman, then Bill wanted to know it. Gently he said:

"So there ain't a Mormon in camp who will stand up to the rack with you. Is that what you told me?"

"Not a one," said Heb. "The pack of cowards! No wonder they was chased out of Illinois."

"Now me," said Bill, "I'm a Mormon."

"Sure you are, you lily-kidneyed coyote. You carry smoke-irons around to make you feel brave." Heb roared with glee and slapped his bottle "You need a drink to give you some courage. Here."

"No, you drink it. You need the courage."

"What do you mean?" asked Heb.

"I mean I'm the Indian buck I told you about."

Heb did not understand that. He stared. "You're no Indian," he said.

"Well, suppose I take the place of the Indian." Bill stopped his horse. "I'll tell you. You see that grove of cottonwoods down there? All right: you dash down there and turn as quick as hell and see if you'n put a bullet anywhere inside my clothes."

"What?" asked Heb. "You mean that?"

"Sure I mean it."

"But you said you was afraid." Heb looked around him, unable to make sense of this.

"I don't think you can shoot," said Bill. "I think you'll miss me a mile."

Heb grinned. "You must be crazy," he said. "God damn it, I'll just murder you."

"Take another drink of whiskey," said Bill. "You'll need it to keep you warm. You'll be lying in the cold snow in a minute."

"You serious?" asked Heb. This unexpected turn of events had sobered him.

"Dead serious," said Bill, his voice changing. "You drunken horse thief, I'm giving you a fifty-fifty chance. You'd better ride."

Heb was flabbergasted. He looked at Bill and then gazed down the river at the grove of cottonwoods. "You must want a-die," he said. "I'll just murder you."

"Ride!" said Bill.

Heb drew a pistol and galloped away. At thirty yards he wheeled and fired, and Bill waited until he saw smoke from the gun. In the next instant he sent a bullet into the man's breast. Heb clung to the saddle and strove to fire again but after a desperate effort he fell, and his horse vanished in a cloud of snow. Bill rode over and dismounted. Upon seeing that Heb still breathed, he fired into the man's brain and then with his toe rolled the body over. Replacing his pistol, he seized Heb by the heels and dragged him to the river and threw him in. He returned and covered the blood with snow.

Three hours later he reported to Brigham.

"What is it?" asked Brigham.

"You remember the horse thief who swore to kill Brother Orson?"

"Yes."

"I thought you'd like to know he's changed his mind."

BILL WAS INVITED OVER TO TAKE SUPPER WITH BRIGHAM. THE TWO OF THEM sat to a roast of venison, boiled potatoes and bake-oven bread.

"It tastes darned good," said Bill. "In the last year I ain't always had enough to eat."

"Nor me," said Brigham, drawing his coat around him. "I've lost forty pounds in a year." After a moment he added: "Bill, I asked you over tonight because I want you to understand some things. You know I'm not a man who minces matters. God commanded the prophet Joseph to build up the true church, but the world is full of sinful people who will stop it if they can. I don't intend to let them stop me. Life is holy if it is lived in righteousness. If it's lived for the Devil, then it's worth no more than the coyotes out on the prairie."

"I know that," said Bill earnestly. "I want to work for the Lord."

"If I let scoundrels out of hell stop me in building the true church, I wouldn't be worth a red cent. Somewhere out in the Rocky Mountains I'm going to establish a kingdom for the saints. Now and then there'll be a devil in human form who will try to destroy us. Such hell-begotten rascals have to be sent back to hell."

"You can always depend on me."

"When I leave next spring I'll take Porter Rockwell and some others with me."

"Porter is mighty handy with a gun. I don't know I'm any better myself."

"I'll leave you here to take care of the horse thieves and counterfeiters. But don't make any mistakes. If you should kill a righteous man, you will burn in hell forever."

Bill grinned. "The Lord doesn't forgive mistakes so I don't intend to make any."

"It's not a sin to kill a devil, but it is a sin to kill any person whose soul can be saved. Always remember that. Some persons have lost their souls and they're better off dead than alive."

"You've got a big job on your hands," said Bill, looking with admiration at his chief. "All those thousands, I mean, and all the enemies. But you can always depend on Bill Hickman."

Nobody knew as well as Brigham what a job he had on his hands. Provisions were so scarce that he had ordered the captains to ration them to both man and beast; and adultery and gambling were so persistently reported that he had divided the camp into twenty-two wards and commanded the bishops to hold church services in each. He encouraged singing and dancing and every other innocent pastime he could think of to take the minds of his people off sinful thoughts. He tried to keep everyone busy.

Some cared for the stock; some fished and trapped and hunted for wild game; and others repaired wagons and harnesses and tents or made clothes or cut and hauled wood. He often wondered if epidemics of sin would break out among his people after he had left them here to seek a route westward and find a home; and as spring approached, he played with the idea of a revelation. He had never taken himself seriously as a prophet, knowing that his talents lay elsewhere and never feeling impelled to speak directly for the Lord. Nevertheless, with his hazardous journey drawing near, it seemed best to him to place himself in communion with the Almighty and lay down certain principles for the guidance of his people.

How Joseph had known when the Lord was speaking through him, Brigham had never understood; nor in regard to himself had he been able to tell which were his own practical notions and which came from God. He spent an evening alone in earnest prayer. It seemed to him that a divine spirit was moving him, and he sat at a rude table with paper and pen. It was a long document which he wrote; it was the only revelation which he was ever to give to the saints. Though he called it "The Word and Will of the Lord," it had none of the mysticism and exhortation and angry eloquence of the revelations which Joseph had received. It was plain common sense right out of the mind of Brigham.

It declared that the camp was to be organized into companies, each with its own captains, wagons and beasts; that the ablest from each company should prepare for the migration and take with them implements and seed for the planting of crops in the new Zion; and that the poor, the widows, the orphans and the sick should be provided for. The saints were to keep their pledges to one another, abhor evil, adjure drunkenness, pay their debts, and humble themselves and be unafraid; for God had delivered them from their enemies. In regard to Joseph: "Many have marveled because of his death, but it was needful that he should seal his testimony with his blood, that he might be honored, and the wicked might be condemned."

When this revelation was read in the Sunday gatherings, the saints realized that the great adventure now lay before them. In their homes, in their meetings, in groups while at work, they talked only of their forthcoming journey to a new land. But not all of them—indeed, only a few—were to leave this spring. Brigham was too astute, even if he had had provisions, to set out with twenty thousand persons across a desert and a wilderness. A picked company was to go ahead and choose a site and plant crops; and then the mighty exodus could begin.

For the exploring vanguard he chose a hundred and forty-four of the most fearless men. Hundreds begged to go, but Brigham went from company to company, his gaze seeking the ones on whom he could depend. "You—and you—and you. Get ready." He had decided to take a hundred and forty-four because that number symbolically represented in his mind the Twelve Tribes of Israel. He had not foreseen that many women would want to go; and day after day he was distressed and annoyed by those who came to plead with him, some in tears, some on their knees.

"No, Sister. We're going to an unknown land. Mebbe we'll have to fight Indians and wild beasts, and mebbe we'll all starve. It's no trip for a woman."

"But, Brother Brigham, I'n drive a team. I'n cook and I'll sleep on the ground. I won't be any trouble and you'll have to have cooks."

"No."

"I can mend and wash the clothes. Then the men will have time ——"
"Sister, no!"

He did relent for three women, including his own wife Clara, and Heber's wife Ellen; but after he had yielded to these, he would not budge, no matter how wildly hysterical a woman became in her desire to follow her husband.

The advance guard was to be a small marching army, with Brigham as general, with others as colonels and majors. There were divisions over each of which he appointed a captain. In camp was a small cannon and he decided to take that. Every man was ordered to have with him at all times a loaded gun, and never without permission to leave it for an instant. At five in the morning a bugle would sound, and the men were to pray before leaving their tents or wagons; whereupon they were to feed their beasts and themselves and be ready to march at the sound of a bugle at seven. At eight-thirty in the evenings, the bugle would sound again; and after prayer every man was to retire to his bed.

Early in April there was great excitement in the camp as one by one the chosen men pulled out with their wagons, while thousands gathered on hilltops to watch them go. There were few tears and little grief. A picked company was blazing a trail to the new Zion; and those left behind would wait patiently, plant and reap, and be ready to march when Brigham returned.

"Be careful!" said mothers to their sons, wives to their husbands. Sons and husbands swaggered a little and said they would scalp every Indian between Missouri and the Pacific Ocean.

"Have a little house ready for us if you can!"

"I'll have a mansion as big as Buckingham Palace."

"Don't forget to fence the crops!"

"If there's lots of venison, jerk some. Oh, did you get the sweater I knitted for you?"

Multitudes followed the wagons and then stood on the last hilltop to watch them vanish into the gray distance of the prairies.

There were seventy-two wagons, more than two hundred horses, mules and oxen, nineteen cows, seventeen dogs, and a few chickens. Each wagon had a teamster as well as a man who walked at its side, carrying a musket. The wagons fell into line; and upon looking back after a little while the marchers could see no sign except smoke of the world they had left.

Sitting in one of the wagons with Heber, and following the Oregon Trail that dipped into ravines and rose over hills, Brigham fixed his gaze on the west and wondered what adventures lay before him. Into that vast uninhabited country beyond the plains, explorers had gone, trappers and missionaries had followed; and stories had come back of Indian massacres, of deadly encounters with wild beasts; but there had been tales too of fertile valleys, enormous forests, and fields of wild flowers that covered whole areas. He had with him some rough maps, as well as some instruments which Orson Pratt had brought from England. The Oregon Trail reached almost to the coast, but Brigham did not intend to follow it when his scouts reported more favorable routes. He would leave it and return to it as seemed to him best. The course he had in mind lay across the present states of Nebraska, Wyoming and eastern Utah: how far it was to the Utah Basin, which he had in mind, he did not know—but he suspected it was considerably more than a thousand miles. He asked William Clayton and Orson Pratt to devise some kind of instrument to measure the distance.

Almost at once the spirit of his men, most of whom were young, displeased him: they whooped and sang and cursed as if they were setting out for the Garden of Eden. The worries, he reflected, were all his own. He had so little feed for man and beast that when, on the third day, he came to a grove of cottonwood trees by a small lake, he ordered the men to fell trees for their cattle, and to hoard their corn. Hundreds of trees were chopped down and the beasts fed on the leaves. One man misjudged the wind and allowed a tree to fall across the back of an ox and knock the animal as flat as a fallen tent.

"What in hell," Brigham roared, "are you doing there?"

"The wind got the best of me," said the man, stooping to peer at the beast.

Men rushed to the scene and dragged the tree away. They set the dazed ox on his legs. "Look!" one cried. "By God, it knocked his eye out!"

Brigham came over and saw that one eye had been driven back into the skull and apparently turned around. There was only a sightless ball in the socket.

"Pound him on his head," said a man.

"Leave him be!" said Brigham. "After this, watch what you're doing."

The animal shook all over while his one good eye turned mournfully upon his beholders. Then suddenly, as if released by a spring, the other eye popped out and turned around and seemed to be none the worse off.

"I'll be damned!" cried one. "You think he'n see now?"

"Sure," said another, brushing a hat in the beast's face.

"Now what are you doing?" yelled Brigham.

"He's all right now. The eye jumped back."

"Give him some corn and leave him alone."

Such were the problems that Brigham faced daily. On the fourth morning, a man rose from his bed, coughing and spitting blood.

"What is wrong with you?"

"I guess I'm sick, Brother Brigham." The man was seized by a spasm. Blood ran from his nose.

"You'll have to go back. Heber, tell any of the men who want to write letters to get them ready. This might be their last chance."

Covering sometimes ten, sometimes fifteen or twenty miles in a day, the caravan steadily approached the lands of the Pawnee and Sioux; but the men were unconcerned, never having fought Indians, and not taking very seriously the tales of massacres. A hundred miles from the Missouri, they came upon the site of a village, occupied a year ago by Pawnee and Tappas Indians. The fierce Sioux had burned it to the ground. Brigham was more concerned than his men. He knew that in this area there were at least five thousand warriors, and he expected trouble: again he told his men to keep their weapons always within reach, and to double the guard at night. Before they reached the Platte River, Shefmolan, flamboyant and arrogant chief of the Pawnees, rode into camp.

Brigham saw him and his retinue the moment they arrived; and one glance told him that the chief looked as suspicious and unfriendly as any Lamanite could. Summoning an interpreter, Brigham hastened over, going more swiftly than was his custom; and with a great flourish of his headdress, Shefmolan drew forth papers and proffered them with a contemptuous gesture.

Brigham read them. Statements from white men who had journeyed through, they declared that the Grand Chief would be friendly if given presents, but the very Devil himself if ignored.

"Ask him," said Brigham to the interpreter, "what in hell he wants?"

The interpreter spoke and the haughty chief answered. "He says he wants a lot of gifts."

"We can't afford a lot of gifts. Heber, fetch some tobacco and salt." When these were brought, Shefmolan looked down at them with incredulous disdain. "What does he say?"

"He says this isn't enough."

"Oh, the hell it ain't! Fetch him some powder and lead and flour."

When those were offered, the wily Indian's face softened a little; but he looked around him at the wagons and beasts and spoke again.

"He says he wants more. He wants a lot of gifts and then he says we must turn back because he doesn't want us to go west. He says we will kill all the buffalo or drive them away."

"Tell the fool we don't like buffalo meat."

That statement made Shefmolan look twice as incredulous as before. His gaze rested on Brigham.

"He says that's a lie. He says all men like buffalo meat."

Brigham was annoyed. "Tell him we want to live in peace but we are going west. By the God of Israel, mebbe he'd like to have a squint at our cannon! Have it wheeled over here."

Several men brought the cannon over. Shefmolan's attention was called to it, and for a moment he gazed curiously at the weapon but he did not seem to be impressed. He rode around it and then ignored it. Quite clearly, Brigham reflected, the resplendent brigand was not frightened at all.

"He says he wants more presents."

"Tell him we'll set the Sioux on him."

When that statement was made to Shefmolan, he looked at Brigham again. Then he spoke.

"He says the Sioux don't worry him at all."

"Tell him our provisions are scarce and if we're not to eat his buffalo meat we'll need all we have."

Upon receiving this word, Shefmolan signaled to his warriors. They gathered the tobacco and salt, ammunition and flour. Brigham advanced and offered his hand in friendliness, but the disdainful pirate only looked at him and grunted with scorn. Without shaking hands, he wheeled abruptly and rode away.

At once Brigham called his men together. "The Pawnees will attack. I want a hundred volunteers, fifty to stand guard until one, and fifty during the rest of the night. It's said mules don't like Indians, so stake some mules away out. Have the cannon ready to fire. One blast from that ought to scare them right out of their feathers. Understand that we're in grave danger and might be wiped out."

"I thought," said a man, "the Indians were cowards and won't fight."

"Even a coyote will fight," said Brigham impatiently. "Now to your guns."

Brigham himself stood among the first guard. As he paced back and forth, a rifle on his shoulder, he saw Indian fires on a hilltop a half-mile away. Before midnight, there was a ring of fires entirely around the camp. He could see Indians by the fires but he could not tell what they were doing; and from time to time he had men fire a gun, or two or three at once, to warn the redskins that the camp was prepared and alert. He observed that his men had lost their arrogant contempt: that circle of bright fires had sobered them and made them feel for the first time that this adventure into the west was no holiday.

After Brigham went to bed he was awakened several times by the firing of guns, but the night passed without attack. Early the next morning, the wagons moved forward, two abreast, with all of them in a compact body. Brigham did not expect to be attacked now but he did believe that the skulking rascals would try to steal horses and provisions; and in spite of alert vigilance, two of the best horses disappeared.

"They got my best one," said a man. And another added: "My best one too."

"Damn it," said Brigham, "we'll have to find them. We can't pull wagons with dogs."

He chose several parties of ten men each and sent them scouting. All day they searched, riding north, south and west into the land of the Pawnees; and the next day a dozen of the boldest men, led by Porter Rockwell, retraced the line of march. They had ridden about twenty miles when one of them saw an object moving in tall grass by the Platte River.

"I see something," he said.

"Let's go after it," said Porter.

When the horsemen were within a few rods of the crawling objects, one of them raised his gun to fire; whereupon, with startling suddenness, fifteen almost naked Indians leapt to their feet. Armed with rifles as well as bows and arrows, they boldly approached. Their gestures were so menacing that Porter's men all raised their guns.

"Stay where you are!" Porter cried. "If you come any nearer, we'll blow daylight through you." To his men he added: "I'll bet the sons-of-bitches don't understand a word."

But the Indians stopped and spoke among themselves. Then one of them turned. " 'Bacco," he said.

" 'Bacco, hell, you horse thief! We'll give you lead!"

Cautiously, as if ready to fight or flee at a moment's notice, the Indians advanced again, coming stealthily, a little anxiously step by step until their leader could almost touch one of the horses. He looked at the horse, and then with sly cunning at the rider; whereupon, with amazing boldness, he seized the bridle.

"Damn you!" yelled the man on the horse, unprepared for that move. He thrust a cocked pistol in the redskin's face. "Let go before I blow your skull off!"

The Indians retreated, stepping backward as softly as they had come, their bodies crouched and bent forward, their gaze fixed with solemn craftiness on the men. One of them, with signs and monosyllables, asked the horsemen to come down to the river.

"To be ambushed!" cried Porter in disgust. "Don't shoot. There might be a thousand in the brush."

"I think," said one, "we'd better hit the grit."

The horsemen swung and rode away. They had not gone far when the Indians yelled as if standing on hot embers and fired shots after them. When a bullet sang close to his head, Porter swore an oath and turned.

"No damn Lamanite can use me for a target! Come!"

Back the horsemen went at full gallop, but the Indians fled like rabbits and vanished. Halting, the men looked at the brush and waited.

"I'd like one shot," said Porter.

But there was no sign of Indians now: everything along the river was as motionless and silent as a tomb.

When this incident was reported to Brigham, he decided to leave the stolen beasts and get out of this country as fast as he could.

"I'll bet," said Porter, "a thousand Indians are watching us right now."

"I wouldn't doubt it. Go ahead, Porter, and find a route that isn't close to trees or bluffs or boxed gullies."

The caravan halted at four to allow the men to practice in use of the cannon. When darkness came, Orson Pratt, an academic man more interested in science than in pioneering, fetched his telescope out and peered at Jupiter's moons. Men gathered around him. One by one they were squinting and exclaiming when Brigham saw them.

"What in hell," he cried, "are you doing?"

"Looking at Jupiter's moons," said the abashed Orson.

"Damn Jupiter's moons! Bloodthirsty savages are all around us and you men bunch up to look at a moon! Where are your guns? Didn't I tell you never to leave them?"

The men scattered to their rifles. Brigham gazed at Orson, wondering about this quiet man who was so unlike his brother. He did not understand him. He did not like the flowery rhetoric and bombast of his sermons, his insatiable interest in gadgets and orbits, moons and stars and tides. He needed scientists, but he would have preferred a man whose beard was not so uselessly luxuriant, and who could shoot a rifle well enough to hit a barn at twenty paces.

"Put that thing away," Brigham said. "You'll be squinting through it some night and an Indian will put a telescope through your skull."

"The moons are very interesting."

"Put it away!"

"All right, Brother Brigham."

At three in the morning, Brigham was suddenly awakened and sat bolt upright, his flesh crawling. He was sure he had heard a hideous and triumphant yell.

"Heber! I think we're attacked!"

Yanking their trousers on, they seized their guns and leapt out. At the eastern end of the camp, they saw dark objects moving. They went over and found Porter and several men there.

"What's the trouble?"

"Well," said Porter, "I thought it was wolves. I seen something crawling along in the grass and so I took a shot at it; and up jumped a dozen Indians, yelling like crazy men and running like hell. Then I took another shot, but by God, I guess I missed." He sighed. "I should be killed to miss a shot like that."

"What time is it?"

"Almost daylight."

"Heber, get all the men up to stand guard. Tell them we'll move an hour earlier."

When daylight came, it was learned that a horse, tethered at the southern edge of the camp, had been frightened and had tangled in his rope and choked to death. One of the guards, in moving too anxiously, had accidentally fired his gun, and the bullet had lodged in the shoulder of another beast. And Orson Pratt's favorite horse was sick with bots.

"Damn!" said Brigham. "Before we get to the Rocky Mountains, we'll be dragging the wagons ourselves. Shoot that horse and let's be off."

For a week the caravan traveled early and late, eager to get beyond reach of the thieving Pawnees and to find better grazing for the beasts. Piles of dung foretold the approach to buffalo country; and the men began to whistle and sing, and boast of the great hunks of flesh they would eat. They were all half-starved. The dried dung (which Clayton said with a leer was politely called buffalo chips) was used to build the fires; and in evenings now a man played a violin, and other men danced with the three women or with one another. Or they sat apart from the women and told tales, the vulgarity of which angered Brigham, though he held his tongue. After all, he reflected, he had chosen the lustiest of the men, and it was pretty hard for them to travel week after week without women. It was difficult for them not to look at the three women present as Brigham had seen them looking.

It was just before the camp arrived in the Grand Island country of what is today Nebraska that the first herd of buffalo was seen. Uncontrollable excitement swept the train. Porter and two other men mounted the fastest horses and set out to give chase; and Clayton danced excitedly in his wagon and said he could see seventy-two animals on a bluff in the northwest. Brigham sent three more hunters to this herd. An hour later, he saw hundreds of buffalo far in the west and dispatched a dozen hunters in pursuit, telling them not to kill the tough old bulls, or more than the camp could eat. The other men now stopped to watch the hunting parties; and Heber, after jumping up and down like an excited lad, seized his rifle and set out afoot and alone. Most of the men who remained behind danced and yelled as if out of their minds.

"Look!" one shouted. "Porter is right in the middle of a herd!"

"By God!" cried another. "See, seven of them chasun one old cow!"

"Wait, I can't see Porter now! I think the herd run over him. . . . No, there he is, runnun the whole lickety-splittun bunch to hell and gone! By Julius Caesar, look at him go!"

"Look, Heber shot one!"

"Holy smoke!" yelled a man, appalled. "Here comes a herd right on top of us!"

It was true, but it was only a small herd. Unable to restrain themselves, men in the wagons grasped their rifles and went afoot, scattering over the prairie and running for all they were worth. The herd bearing down was a half-mile away but it was coming at full speed. As it drew near, the men shouted at the oncoming beasts and waved their guns.

"The damn fools," said Brigham, standing in a wagon. "It won't surprise me if they all get run over."

The next few minutes filled the camp with loud laughter. The small herd came furiously with heads down and clouds of dust pouring away behind. The foot hunters were still running to meet it. Suddenly an old bull plowed the sod in an effort to stop, looked at the men and snorted, and then swung to the right and vanished over a hill, with half a hundred shaggy forms thundering after him. The foot hunters, exhausted now, and astonished by the sudden disappearance of their prey, waved their guns in despair and sank to the earth.

Porter, meanwhile, having heard that a bullet would not penetrate a buffalo skull, rode close to an old bull, determined to find out. He leaned over and fired point blank at the forehead. The only effect was to cause the skull to smoke a little, and to make the old fellow shake with rage.

Some calves, separated from the herds, came in blind speed toward the wagons, with all the foot hunters in wild pursuit. One was shot. The dogs pounced upon it and brought it to earth.

Wondering if they had meat enough, Brigham turned to a captain. "We'll pull down to the river and camp. Go out with wagons and fetch the dead ones."

When the slain beasts were all brought in, the men saw that they had a bull, three cows and six calves. Within the circle of wagons the animals were skinned and quartered and the flesh laid upon the hides; and men gathered around to look at the heads and wonder how the creatures could carry such huge skulls.

"That's why they run with their heads down," said one. "They can't lift them."

The ferocious appearance of the heads fetched exclamations from nearly everyone who looked at them—the great shaggy manes, the bulging brows, the eyes that seemed tameless even in death. It was not long that the men stood and marveled. They were hungry. The smell of the clean meat watered their mouths, and they pitched in to load the fires and prepare for a feast.

Such appetites, such gluttonous gorging, Brigham had never seen: the men seized dripping chunks and almost buried their faces, or lifted their faces, smeared from forehead to chin, to grunt and laugh as they wolfed it down. Out of a mouthful one would murmur with joy; another wiped his greasy face and grinned; and others turned to gaze at the hunks roasting on the fire.

"It's good," said a man, and those words declared all that he could say. "It's the first meal I've had since we left Nauvoo."

"What in God's name was that?" asked another. He stopped chewing, his mouth crammed full, his eyes clouding with distress. He had heard the sound of disgorging.

A few yards from the camp were the parts of the beasts which the men did not want; and there the dogs, gaunt and starved and drooling, had been feeding like wolves. One had eaten so much and so rapidly that he had turned sick on his gluttony and was now vomiting. Hearing him, the men paused, their faces comical with distress. One laid his hunk of flesh in a pan and staggered to his feet. Men looked up at him and then at one another, their eyes anxious.

"What's the matter?" asked Porter scornfully, and filled his mouth. His wide black beard was shining with grease. "It's as tender as chicken. Me, I aim to eat so much I can't budge for a week."

"Don't you hear that sound?"

"What if I do? That don't bother me a tinker's hoot."

A man sighed and patted his belly. Another chewed softly, experimentally, as if to learn what his appetite thought of it. A woman laughed.

"I'll take the dogs away," said one, rising. "I don't intend to let them spoil this banquet."

"They don't spoil it for me," said Porter, and heaped his plate. "I'd be ashamed to be a dog if I couldn't eat without a-pukun."

"I feel all right," said a giant, and buried his face in a chunk of thigh. "I guess you fellers would like a lettuce salad and a cracker."

"A glass of buttermilk," said one scornfully who had never for a moment paused. He wiped his mouth on the back of his hand and roared with laughter. "What I wonder is have we cooked enough."

A tall thin man unexpectedly choked and hastily left the camp.

"What's the matter with such men? By God, wait till they have to eat rattlesnakes and gopher hide."

"Or a nice skunk stew. By heaven, I could eat the tongue right out of that old bull. Why didn't I cook that tongue, I want to know."

Most of the men fell to eating again; but a few, looking shame-faced, sat back and stared at their lustier companions.

"I kallate," said Porter, "I've eat about ten pounds now. But I feel good for at least another shoulder. Brother Brigham, what you figger we'll eat out in the Rocky Mountains?"

"Venison," said one.

"Coyotes, most likely."

"Crickets, according to Frémont."

"Brother Brigham, what do you say?"

"In a few years," said Brigham, "we'll eat anything we want."

"Some of the brothers," said Porter thickly, his mouth so full that his eyes bulged, "should have to eat coyote soup out of an old hide. Like Bill."

"What's the matter, Bill? You sick?"

"A little," said William Clayton.

Men turned to gaze at him. He was everlastingly catching colds and coughing and blowing his nose. At this moment he looked pale and ready to vomit, though he was gazing enviously at the gluttons.

"How far we come?"

"About two hundred miles," said Clayton.

"By God, is that all? How far we got left?"

"About a thousand, I guess."

"Holy smoke! In that case, I guess I'll eat another buffalo right now."

"Tim McBride," said Porter, looking at that tall handsome Irishman, "how much have you et?"

"Oh, about a calf," said Tim.

Porter looked at him curiously, remembering that Tim was still a little angry because Brigham had married his girl years ago. Very few men in camp knew that, Porter reflected, glancing around him; very few knew indeed that Brigham had more than one wife. He hardly knew what to make of Tim: the man had turned very studious in recent years and was studying books. For Porter, who could not even write his own name, that was a bunch of damned foolishness.

"Let's cook some more," he said, staggering to his feet.

A group of men rose and laid more flesh on the fire.

CHAPTER X

Having entered the buffalo country, Brigham knew that food would be abundant for his men but scarce for his beasts. Every year the Indians burned the prairies so that the grass the next season would be plentiful and tender; and already the desolated country was coming into view. Soon the rolling hills were black, with now and then a green oasis like an island where the fire had missed. Wind gathered the ashes and drove them in choking clouds over the wagons until the faces of the men were almost as black as the hills. When they shook themselves or beat their clothes, they were like hens emerging from a dust bath. Fire dust got into their throats, rimmed their parched lips, sifted down their backs, and made their eyes look inflamed and terrible.

Brigham sent scouts ahead to find the green islands and told his hunters not to kill more animals than the camp could eat. It was a question now not of too few buffalo but of too many: one day the men stood in wagons and with glasses and estimated that in one herd they could see a hundred thousand; for on all sides the prairie was black with them. They were so tame that it was difficult to keep the domestic beasts out of the wild herds. Shaggy old bulls often came within a hundred yards of the caravan and paused to stare, their eyes red and running from dust and wind; and then snorted and went thundering away. During the nights too it was a task to keep the cows and oxen from getting lost. Buffalo calves even entered the camp; and the men roped and examined them, and then butchered the choicest ones to roast over the fires.

Brigham knew from the first that he would have to make haste through this country; and when both horses and oxen grew so weak from hunger they could barely move, he sent scouts ahead to look for trees that could be felled for browsing. It was Porter who saved the camp. After riding far and hard for several days, he learned that upon islands in the river there was still grass and foliage. Buffalo, he reported, did not seem to swim out to the islands; but perhaps the gaunt oxen could.

Clayton, meanwhile, faithfully posted signs as he had done from the beginning. They were intended to guide the great exodus the following year.

From Winter Quarters 295 Miles
May 8, '47. Camp all well
W. Clayton

Brigham had asked him and Orson Pratt to invent an instrument to measure distance, but in the beginning, Clayton had tied a red cloth on a wagon wheel and patiently counted the revolutions and computed the miles covered. After a while he had devised, with the assistance of Orson, what he called a roadometer, and this crude instrument now reckoned the mileage for him. When Clayton set a sign on a post or a tree, he invariably said all was well, even though famished beasts were falling in the harness, and a black prairie stretched endlessly ahead. But in his journal he recorded every quarrel and feud.

Nobody after a few days tried to count the buffalo, or had much interest in them. They were like a dark moving landscape in all directions, or sudden clouds of dust when they rushed in stampedes that shook the earth. On the islands which Porter found, the horses and oxen were fed, and day by day the caravan crawled slowly until it came to greener land. The country was now yielding to alkaline desert, the buffalo to wolves. Men found a den of cubs one morning and brought them into camp, intending to make pets of them. They were only as large as an English hare, but they were ferocious little beasts, arching their backs and hissing until the dismayed dogs fell to their haunches and howled dismally.

"What'd you bring them in for?" demanded Brigham.

"We're going to make pets out of them."

"Kill them! Damn it, you'll get enough of wolves."

He had been increasingly annoyed and harassed. Some of his men, with awakened zest and hilarity, had been taking the journey as a huge romantic adventure in spite of Indians and hunger. They had become more vulgar and profane and disobedient, often roaring in camp with such loud joy that they could be heard for a mile. One morning several of them leapt up from prayer and dashed to the river where, gleamingly naked, they bathed and wrestled until Brigham marched down in anger. One evening, after the bugle had sounded for prayer, one of them made such obscene racket that his captain had him put in irons for the night. The next morning the disciplined man was purple with rage.

"I'll whip him!" he bellowed. "I'll smash his long nose flat on his chin!"

"You'll mind your business," said Brigham. "Do you want to be hauled in irons?"

"What do you mean?"

"You swore around last night instead of saying your prayers."

"Oh, to hell with prayers!"

Brigham turned a shade redder. "Do you want me to slap you in irons for the rest of the journey?"

"Of course not."

"Then obey orders."

At others Brigham was angry because they refused to eat anything but the hind quarters of the slain beasts, or wasted their ammunition shooting rattlesnakes and wolves, or mounted after breakfast and scattered over the hills, intent only on adventure. Some of them, when rebuked, sulked for days; others took the bit in their teeth and cursed like the very devil, or made jest of their prayers by saying simply, "God, I thank you." During the evenings they wanted to dance with the three women who were always worn out by their day's travel; and upon being refused danced with one another, whooping insanely and contorting themselves suggestively. Or they told vulgar yarns, played cards, and held mock trials, with one attorney prosecuting and another defending a man for murder. Even the pious Clayton enjoyed the horseplay but Brigham sat apart and scowled.

Too, the men were everlastingly demanding to know if they had left the United States. After the caravan left the desolate illimitable sameness of the prairies and entered the foothills of the Rocky Mountains, where bluffs were beautiful in their colors and vegetation was lush along the way, Brigham admitted, but dubiously, that perhaps they had entered Mexican territory, and the men behaved like half-crazed hoodlums. Finding wild cherry in bloom, they fetched it into camp by the armfuls, hugging it to them and breathing of it. They went pell-mell to groves of cottonwood and juniper, pine and willow and box elder; gathered enormous bouquets of wild flowers and left them scattered and trampled, and sent up a chilling yell when they first saw the beauty of moonlight on Chimney Rock. This country was fragrant. The streams were as clear and pure as the mornings. After choked hot weeks upon the prairie, after sand and saleratus and sagebush, sluggish foul rivers, ashes and dust and buffalo dung, the men gazed at the forests and howled with glee.

"So mebbe we're out of the United States! Well, by God, this looks better."

"A hundred times better. Look at those mountains! Who ever saw such mountains before?"

"Or streams. That water tastes like it was out of heaven."

Their profanity and noise were only an attempt to vocalize their happiness. But Brigham was angered. He was afraid the men would throw all discipline to the winds and take matters into their own unruly hands. Late in May he climbed to a wagon and let his anger speak.

"This morning I take for my text these words: I'm about to revolt from traveling with this camp any further with the spirit they now possess. I'd rather take a handful of men of faith and risk my life among savages than be with this camp when it turns its heart from God to folly and wickedness. I'd rather be alone. And I'm resolved not to go any farther unless you humble yourselves before the Lord and quit your folly. This camp has been card playing and falling in the wicked ways of checkers and dominoes and dancing. It's time to quit. There have been trials on every nonsensical thing. If these things are allowed to go on, soon you'll be fighting and knocking one another down and taking life.

"It's high time it was all stopped."

The men listened. They had, Brigham added, been driven from their homes and they were embarked on a great adventure; but they had forgotten the holiness of their mission. Instead of seeking a site for Zion, they were playing with the Devil and behaving no better than the gentiles whose ways they had spurned. He asked his fellow apostles present if they would humble themselves and covenant to serve God; and if so to raise their hands. The apostles raised their hands. He then put the question to the other men.

"All right, you have agreed to humble yourselves, and I will continue to lead you to the spot that will be our home. Tomorrow is Sunday. We will spend the day in fasting and prayer so that the Lord will watch over us and guide us; for without His guidance we are lost."

The next day the men did kneel in prayer, first as a group, and then singly and alone. But while engaged in humble thanksgiving, the man who had been put in irons looked over at his captain and thumbed his nose.

"I wasn't never much good at prayer," he said later to Porter. "I always figgered it was for the leaders."

"It gives you a good feelun inside," said Porter. "I never reasoned it done a man any harm."

"Or any good. Not if you ain't no better at it than I be."

Some of the more faithful left the camp to humble themselves and commune with God. Heber went, and was followed by Orson Pratt, Clayton and others; and when afternoon came, it was a depressed and spiritless camp. Looking at the beautiful country around them, the younger men could not feel that God had frowned on their fun. They were chastened, nevertheless, save for one here and there who sulked and scowled; for they looked at Brigham and remembered that they were alone in a wilderness. Wolves gazed at them from every hilltop, and both horses and men had felt the fangs of rattlesnakes. It was no time now to scorn Brigham's bold and resourceful leadership.

"Brother Brigham," said the man who had lain in irons, "I guess I'm sorry. I don't always act like I should."

"We're alone against the world. We must fight together."

"I know it. I won't cause no more trouble."

"Are you two men friends now?"

"Not exactly," he said, making a face at the thought. "But I guess we can patch it up."

Seeing Clayton passing, Brigham summoned him. "How far are we now from Headquarters?"

"Over five hundred miles."

"Fort Laramie must be getting close." Brigham gazed at Clayton, observing that he still strove to keep himself clean and shaven. He did not like dandies. Looking around him, he saw a man who was brutal to his horses. "Brother George, come here."

George came over, his large coarse face troubled by the summons. "What do you want?" he asked.

"I saw you beating your horses over the head. Did you ever stop to think that horses have feelings too?"

"They wouldn't pull."

"Couldn't, you mean. Don't you let me see you beating them again."

The man's eyes darkened. "Yes, Brother Brigham."

"And didn't I see you making faces in prayer meeting this morning?"

"Me? Why, I prayed like the very dickens. I never prayed harder in my life and that's a fact."

Brigham smiled faintly. Looking at the man, he asked: "What did you pray for?"

"Because you made me."

"No, I mean what did you ask God to do for you?"

"Well," said the man, wrinkling his brow in thought, "I just don't remember now. But it was a good prayer. I know that."

Brigham turned away. He was grinning broadly.

Because he planned to build stockades on the new site, Brigham paused to have a look at Fort Laramie, a famous refuge in a wasteland of Indians. It was, he perceived, an enormous structure, with dried brick walls fifteen feet high, and bastions at the corners. He liked the notion of a double gateway, with an intervening arched passage between: invaders could be allowed to enter the first gate, and from a high window in a wall, those inside the fort could look out and question them.

He did not like what he saw inside. The dirty bearded soldiers were permitted to keep squaws as mistresses; and the male Indian relatives of the kept women loafed inside, with nothing to do except to enjoy the privilege of idleness. The whole fort, so far as Brigham could see, was a huge adulterous nest; and after observing how it was built and which features he wished to copy, he turned to go, but the soldiers present were curious. Upon learning that these emigrants were Mormons, they gathered around and stared as if they were looking at men resurrected from ancient harems. Then they smirked and jabbed one another and pressed forward to ask questions.

"How many wives you got?" asked a big fellow who looked as if he slept in a cave.

"One," said Brigham impatiently. "How many do you have?"

That made the soldier guffaw. "No wives," he said. "I got a bunch of squaws. But we heared out here you fellers all have a lot of women."

Another soldier said: "Who are the three women down in the camp? They your wives?"

Heber answered. "You've heard lies about us. We are the most lied about people in the world."

"That right?" asked the big dirty fellow; but he was unconvinced. "Where in hell you going to?"

"We don't know. Are we still in the United States?"

"Holy Christ, yes. But you won't be if you go much farther. You headed for California?"

"We don't know," said Brigham. "Come," he said to the men with him.

He was eager to find a new home and plant crops; and besides, he had heard that an emigrant train of two thousand persons was on the Oregon Trail behind him. He wanted to keep ahead of it, not knowing how many enemies from Ohio, Missouri and Illinois might be en route. But the journeying was difficult now: there were steep hills to climb, dangerous streams to cross, and thousands of rattlesnakes and wolves on the line of march. The view was increasingly impressive: the blue and purple backbones of the Rocky Mountains lay across the western sky. Grass for the cattle was plentiful; the streams were full of trout. The hills roundabout were beautifully forested, and from them the hunters brought deer and antelope and wild fowl, and now and then a grizzly bear.

The men were alternately elated by the scenery or depressed by old graves along the Trail. Almost daily they gathered to look at boards stuck in the earth and to read the homely legends.

Matilda Crowley
B. July 16th, 1830, and D. July 7, 1846

"Only a year ago," said one.

"And just sweet sixteen!"

"How many graves have we saw?"

"God knows."

"I wonder why the wolves ain't dug her up."

"Looks like they tried," said Porter. "Mebbe they put rocks on her."

The next day, on coming to the Sweetwater River in what is now south central Wyoming, they were happy again. Back in their homelands they had never seen rivers pouring in cascading foam down a deep gorge, with the sheer walls rising hundreds of feet on either side. The streams of their boyhood had been sluggish and gentle and often foul; but here the water was as pure as sunlight, and the sculpturing of the canyons so picturesque that sometimes the caravan paused to allow the men to gaze at the wonder around them.

"I hope our new home is as beautiful as this."

"Yes," said Heber. "A man could really worship the Almighty here."

Brigham was affected too, but he seldom betrayed his gentler emotions. He noted the approaching grandeur and was pleased; but he was seeking a valley that would be mountain-walled and inaccessible to his enemies. At Fort Laramie he had learned that he would soon be in the country of Jim Bridger, famous throughout the West, and in other parts of the continent too, as an Indian scout, trapper, and adventurous blazer of trails. Brigham wanted to meet him.

Unexpectedly one morning, as if he had dropped out of the blue sky, Bridger appeared.

"I'm Jim Bridger," he said, speaking as if he expected that statement to knock a man down.

"I'm Brigham Young."

"Oh, you're the Mormons!" Jim gazed around him and Brigham looked at Jim. He was a crafty man, Brigham decided; there was cruelty and cunning in his eyes and mouth. "I've heard about you fellers. Where you headed for?"

"To get away from Christians," said Brigham slyly.

"Away from Christians! For God sake."

"You know a good place with plenty of land and water and timber?" The saints had gathered around to listen.

"God damn it, I know all the places in the West. But there ain't no good one this side of Oregon or California."

"How about the Utah Basin?"

"Nope, God no. There ain't no timber in it. Why, it's just a desert and a dead sea. In Bear Valley north of it——"

"Is there water in the Basin?"

"Water? A few trickles. I tell you it's a desert of horned toads and crickets and wolves. By the livun God, you'll wade in grasshoppers to your crotch. Down south, below Utah Lake, it ain't so bad. The Injuns there raise corn and wheat—and pumpkins as big as the state of Rhode Island. Wild fruit, you'n get a hundred bushels offen a tree. Timber too. And by God, there's a mountain of copper as big as Europe. Why don't you go to California? You'n get oak and walnut and hickory there, and water till you'll all drown. You'n grow anything."

"Can't we raise corn around Salt Lake?"

Jim spit a juiceless quid and bit deep into his plug. "Man, I tell you not in a million years. How'n you raise corn in salt? If you ever raise a bushel of corn there, I'll give you a thousand dollars for it."

"I'll collect that thousand, Mr. Bridger, next summer."

While Jim stared at the wagons and men, Brigham reflected that he did not want mountains of copper, or trees on which grew a hundred bushels of fruit. He wanted a barren and forbidding land that would drive his people to their best efforts and discourage gentiles from moving in.

"Around Salt Lake," said Jim, grinning, "you'n raise crickets. The Injuns live on them all winter and eat them by the schoonerful. You like crickets?"

"If there's water we'll raise corn. We'll raise anything that will grow in this latitude."

Jim smiled pityingly. "You'll just have a desert and a sea that don't have no water runnun out of it. Go to a good country. Go to Oregon. What in hell do you want to go to a desert for?"

Some of the saints were asking that question too, but Brigham kept his own counsel. He knew what he wanted. "Now tell me about the road after we leave the Oregon Trail."

A few days later he met another western scout, Miles Goodyear, who was guiding a small party on their way back east. Goodyear said also that the Utah Basin was a God-forsaken land of crickets, dust, hard winters and wolves. He did not offer a thousand dollars for a bushel of corn, but he did declare that no grain could be grown in the entire Rocky Mountain area.

"Go to California or Oregon. You'll starve to death anywhere else."

But Brigham had made up his mind, even though other scouts told him that coyotes and jack rabbits perished from hunger in the land he was headed for. His men were alarmed; the women wept. They all saw twenty thousand persons delivered to a desert and a dead sea; and when, a few days later, Brigham fell desperately ill with fever, they wondered if God was not warning him.

This sudden and terrible sickness they called mountain fever. It struck suddenly, and for no reason known to them; and the persons attacked fell into cold sweats, fever and delirium. After the caravan passed Green River, several of the men were laid low, but none was so sick as Brigham.

All one night he rolled in his wagon and muttered; and when morning came he was raving like a madman. Some thought his gibberish was probably the gift of tongues, a few wondered if he was possessed by a devil, but Heber knew that his friend was a very sick man. Heber knew also that the entire camp was half-paralyzed with dread and a sense of impending doom. "If he dies," the men said, almost whispering, "what will we do?"

The leaders gathered around Brigham and laid hands on him and prayed, asking God to save him for the leadership of twenty thousand saints. But their efforts were unavailing. So overcome by grief and fear that they acted a little mad, they climbed to the highest peaks and prayed there, as if they were trying to get nearer heaven so that God would hear. After prayer they looked westward at a stupendous empire of ranges and summits. White peaks, deep canyons, and long blue crests filled the landscape as far as vision could reach. The men felt insignificant and lost in such mighty sculpturing; and looked down into the canyon where their leader, the one man who could shape their destiny and their future, lay close to death. Under the blue sky, here on the zenith of a new and strange world, they knelt in prayer again; and when Heber turned downward, his eyes were blind with tears.

He hastened to learn if Brigham was better.

But Brigham was not: he was still out of his mind; and after considering, Heber said most of the camp would have to go on without him. A few would remain with Brigham, and give him pills and alcohol, and kneel in prayer.

"If God takes him," said Heber, pale and anxious, "we are all lost!"

"We might as well turn back," said another.

"Not me," said Porter Rockwell, but he looked as if about to weep. "Mebbe this means we're to turn back."

"No," said Heber. "God would never return us to the Christians."

In silent groups the men waited. Now and then one would go off alone to kneel in prayer and then come back, looking more shaken than before. After a few hours, a man ran through the camp, crying that Brigham was in his right mind; and there was a stampede toward his wagon.

"Brigham," Heber cried, "are you better?"

"Of course," said Brigham weakly. "Where in hell are we?" He saw the three women sitting together on the earth and weeping, and for a long moment he regarded them thoughtfully. "Sisters, dry your tears!" Looking at Heber he asked again: "I say where in hell are we?"

"Here in the Rocky Mountains."

"What day is it?"

"The thirteenth of July."

"Send the camp on ahead."

But now the men all crowded in, protesting, tearfully cursing, and begging him to let them wait until he was well.

"Brother Brigham, we want to stay right here!"

"Yes. By God, we won't budge without you. You led us this far and if we go a step farther, you must still lead the way."

"Nonsense," said Brigham. He gazed at the anxious faces around him, never having known until now how deeply these men loved him. He felt his own eyes growing misty, but he shrugged feebly and asked: "Who is in command here?"

"You, Brother Brigham."

"All right. I command the camp to go on." There were cries of protest again. Brigham struggled to sit up. "Heber, you heard the order. A few of you and the sisters will stay with me. Move the rest on!"

"Yes, Brigham."

Reluctantly, like disobedient lads, the men hitched beasts to the wagons and prepared to move; but one by one as they pulled out, they stopped to gaze back where Brigham lay. When the main caravan had gone two hundred yards down the canyon, Porter came to Brigham and said the men begged not to be sent ahead until he was well.

"Damn it!" cried Brigham, and sank, exhausted. He closed his eyes and breathed heavily for a few moments. Then weakly he spoke. "Heber, this is foolishness. Tell them to go on."

"Tell them to go on," Heber said to Porter.

"We'll go," said Porter, "but not without we can send messengers twice a day to learn how he is."

"All right," said Heber, "do that. Now go."

"Wait," said Brigham, still lying with his eyes closed. "Tell them to find a passage through the mountains. Tell them to emerge from the mountains to the Basin, and then bear northward to a place to put in seed. As God lets me see it, that is right. Now go."

Porter moved in to clasp Brigham's hand and squeeze it. Brigham opened his eyes. His white face smiled.

"Damn it, Porter, I ain't going to die or anything. Now hit the grit."

When the caravan had disappeared, Brigham again sat up to look around him. "Heber, I must go too. At once."

Still weeping, the women came over and protested, saying that he must not move until well. Brigham told them to come close; and when they did so, he patted their hands. By turns he took their hands in his big palms, and told the women they must not worry about him. He would soon be all right, he said. "You have been brave sisters," he said, "and I must not stay behind like a weakling. Let's go."

Brigham's wagon moved ahead, the women riding with him, Heber walking at the side, his anxious gaze on his leader. When they overtook the main camp, Brigham sank again and muttered that he could go no farther now. He was fighting to keep his mind clear, but the jolting of the wagon filled him with awful sickness; and he closed his eyes and breathed like a dying man. The women sat around him to keep away the hordes of mosquitoes. Heber sent scouts ahead, as well as wagons filled with picked men to build a road: it was not much farther to the goal they sought, but a range of mountains and many wild streams were across their path.

Toward evening, Brigham rallied again and sat up. Clayton brought him an armful of wild flax, and Brigham smelled the lovely blue flowers and said he would be well soon. He asked if any of the men were sick.

"One is very sick," said his wife Clara. "The others are all better now."

"Did anyone die?"

"No, Brigham."

"Are you sisters all right?"

"Yes."

"That's good," he said, and stroked the dainty flowers. Observing that the flax seemed to cheer him, the women went to a hillside and gathered armfuls of lupine and gilias and pentstemon, and almost buried him under them. "Let me see out," he said, aroused by the fragrance. The wagon cover was drawn back and he looked out to see grass knee-deep, a forested canyon, a beautiful stream, and gardens of wild flowers in all directions. "I'll soon be well. Don't worry about me at all."

His strength returned very slowly. Twice daily messengers came back to learn how he was; and they reported that scouts had found a pass through the mountains, and timber to build bridges. As soon as he saw their new home, he said, he would be as fit as a fiddle. Talk of their new home flushed his pale face, and enhanced the excitement that had been for days growing in the others, in the entire camp. As soon as he was able to move again, he saw much through the canyon to restore his health. He saw endless acres of wild flowers; and one afternoon, while journeying in a brisk rain, with the rain singing on the canvas above him and making music in the trees on either side, he marveled at the freshness and purity of the fragrance that came to him. It was the smell of flowers, evergreens, and ledges of stone under a cleansing downpour. Clara, sitting by him, thrust bouquets of flowers out into the storm to drench them, and then let him see how sweet they smelled.

And for unbroken miles he saw gardens of wild currant and gooseberry, and of elderberry in full bloom; acres of hop vines, of alder and birch; and then a mountain of red rock that rose above him in a sheer gleaming wall for a thousand feet. In this beautiful canyon (which the saints named Echo), the rattling of the wagons sounded like the hammers of a thousand carpenters. The lowing of a cow was taken up and amplified until it rolled down the ledges like the tones of a great organ; and the whistling of a man became the music of a dozen flutes. Brigham was so pleased that he asked the women to roll the cover back.

He overtook the main caravan again. When evening came, he left his wagon to walk a little; and the men, seeing him, hardly knew whether to sing or pray. Not until he lay near death and their journey looked purposeless had they realized how much they needed him, or with what painstaking care he had managed every step of their way. They followed him now to inquire how he felt; and Brigham grinned and said he felt like a two-year-old colt in a clover pasture.

"We'll soon be there, Brother Brigham!"

"Yes," he said, and his voice also trembled with excitement.

For several days he followed the caravan down gorges, over passes and across swift streams, impatient to see the country ahead. Only a few men were with him. The others, with eagerness mounting almost to frenzy, had pushed rapidly forward to enter the valley. With the cover of his wagon back, Brigham daily gazed to right or left in search of water and timber, or ahead of him for a glimpse of the Basin. It was on the twenty-third of July in the year 1847 that the mountains suddenly fell away and he found himself looking across a hundred miles of distance. With a cry he rose to his feet, and every person with him leapt too, as if after a journey of twelve hundred miles they were looking into heaven. Shaking all over, and unable to speak, they gathered around Brigham; and for several minutes not a person stirred.

They were gazing at one of the most magnificent views in North America, where Italy and Switzerland, as Sir Richard Burton later put it, lay side by side. Below was a vast plain, stretching almost as far as they could see, and surrounded on all sides by a great semicircle of mountains whose blue and misty shoulders were topped with white crowns. Far in the west was a gleaming expanse of water that in sunlight looked like a huge floor of silver upon the valley. The first thought that came to Brigham was this: "It is mountain-walled!"; the second, "It looks as if God built this place for His people!" His gaze swept the stupendous natural defenses against invasion, and then fell.

The broad valley running north and south had green patches upon its gently rolling length, and these, it seemed to him, indicated fertility of the soil. There seemed to be streams coming from the eastern mountains, as well as rivers and sloughs in the valley itself. The mountains seemed rather barren, but there would be forests in the wetter canyons: timber, water, rich soil and a protected valley—these were all he had hoped for! For these he could kneel humbly and thank God—after one hundred and two days of bold journeying beyond his native land and into the unknown! His breath entered him in a long sigh of joy and slowly he sank to his knees and bowed his head; and those with him obeyed his silent injunction to prayer. But it was prayer in which no word was uttered aloud. The pilgrims knelt for several minutes, with hands clasped to their breasts and heads bowed to their God, while each in his own way gave thanks for this home.

Then Brigham rose and the others with him, and again they looked at the new Zion. In Brigham's mind, while he noted point by point the great expanse, was a confused and clouded but glorious picture, in all its shining details, of the kingdom which he would build—the orchards and vineyards and gardens, the hamlets and fields, the cities and temples, and the broad clean streets. He would never turn the thriftless upon the granaries of the thrifty—men could not be robbed of initiative and ambition or they would cease to be men; but he would found here the United Order, a huge communal society, a mighty enterprise of labor and love and fellowship; and as he gazed at the valley, the water, the mountains and hills, the kingdom of his dream lay upon and became almost one with the empire he looked at, until in the misty wonder of it the fabulous hope and the unfulfilled achievement became for him almost as real as the plain below him. Like mirages that came and went were clean cities and beautiful temples, villages trembling against the purple haze of the far mountains, burgeoned orchards where the fruit hung in ripe and golden clusters, gardens with the trimmed and tended perfection of those he had seen abroad, wide highways across the valley's floor—the whole vision of which he had dreamed for a year now moved in upon him, and laid its shining magnitude from end to end of the Basin. Mountains and landscape became so blurred, and images and phantasms of his reverie swam so elusively upon the gray and golden distance, that he could no longer tell what before him was real and what was taking form out of thought.

He did not know that his eyes were wet.

Once before in his life, Brigham had been moved to tears: upon that terrible day when Joseph announced to him the plan of celestial marriage. Surprised by himself now, he turned abruptly away and went a few paces down the mountain; and there he sat with his arms on his knees and his forehead on his arms. The others, with emotion frankly making blindness of their eyes, looked down through tears at their leader; but only Heber knew that the stern and iron-hearted Brigham was weeping.

They waited, the men trembling and the women shaking uncontrollably, until Brigham came back; and when he came, his eyes were clear, and his mouth was set in its customary straight line.

"This is the place," he said. He swallowed twice before he spoke again. And then in a low voice he added: "We'll build our home down there."

CHAPTER XI

B RIGHAM CAMPED AT THE FOOT OF THE MOUNTAIN. WHEN HE ENTERED TH▸ valley the next morning, the main camp had been told of his coming and now rushed in a body to meet him, a few of them wildly enthusiastic but most of them depressed and dismayed. They had preceded Brigham by three days and had already begun to dam creeks, dig trenches, and make small reservoirs; but this country appalled them. The earth, they said, was so dry that it had to be watered before it could be plowed; they had seen only one tree since entering the valley; the bottomlands westward were beds of alkali; and no matter where they went, they stepped on big ugly crickets that swarmed in millions. Bridger, declared one, had been right: this land had been abandoned by God to drouth and crickets and wolves, prickly pear and cheat grass and thistles, to time and desolation.

"Is this our new home?"

"Yes," said Brigham. "We'll build here."

"We can't. We'll all starve to death."

"Nonsense." Brigham looked westward across the valley and waved a hand. "We'll make that desert blossom like a rose."

He was still pale and weak from his sickness, but he walked through the camp, praising those who had labored, rebuking those who had not, and giving to all of them his vision of what this country would be like in ten years. Nobody had ever been able to resist his enthusiasm; nobody was able now. The men came to life as he strode among them. They seized shovels, harnessed teams, set plows to the earth, and brought forth the seed which they had hoarded on the long journey.

"You think this land will grow things?"

"Damn it," said Brigham, "I know it. We'll turn this valley into a garden. We'll make it one of the wonder spots of the world."

The one who had asked the question now gazed out over the alkali wastes. He looked around him at the sagebrush, the withered grass, the black crickets crawling up every stem and shrub.

"Will corn grow here?" asked another, who had set up his blacksmith shop and was busy.

"Anything will grow here that will grow in this latitude."

Some of the men looked dubious, but little by little they caught the dauntless spirit of their leader; and a week after Brigham walked into it, the camp was transformed. The men were singing again. Most of them were like lads in a strange playground: they set out in exploring parties, some entering the canyons to search for timber, others going up and down the valley or to the dead sea. This inland lake amazed them. The water was heavy with salt, the shores were salt beaches, and the islands in it seemed to be bird sanctuaries. Day by day the explorers returned to report their discoveries. There were dozens of excellent hot springs; there was a slow meandering river which they named the Jordan; there was a little timber in some of the canyons, as well as a fine quality of building stone; there seemed to be ample water for irrigation; and the soil was not so worthless as they had supposed.

Around campfires in the evenings they caught Brigham's faith, and planned and dreamed, though now and then one gazed solemnly at the eastern mountains, trying to realize that his family was twelve hundred miles away. Brigham called the camp together and laid down the law. "The law of this valley," he said, standing in a wagon, "shall be the law of God, and no person will live here who does not obey that law. You will not work or hunt or fish on Sunday, but will keep that day holy. Anyone who does not like the law here may dwell where he pleases but he shall not dwell among us. No man shall buy or sell land, for all land will be held in common. Every man shall have land measured off to him, both in the city and for farming. He may have as much as he can till and may till as much as he pleases, but he must till all that he uses and take care of it. If he refuses to till his land, it shall be taken from him.

"All wood and timber and water will belong to the community, and all other natural resources: there will be no monopoly in this valley by any man of any such resources for his own wealth and power. Only dead timber is to be used now, for we must let the living timber grow for future use and carefully conserve it. All ditches, canals, reservoirs and other irrigation channels will be the common property of all; and any person trying to take greedy advantage of the materials which we must all use for our common welfare will be driven out of this valley. . . ."

Those bold and farsighted pronouncements flabbergasted some of the men: they had already explored and had intended to take this grove of timber, this stream, this land for their exclusive use. Brigham had said he intended to establish United Orders throughout the valley, and to make of the church a huge society of community enterprise, ownership and management.

"By God," said one, "how can a man get rich here?"

But Tim McBride was fired by this dream of socialism. "God gave the revelations to Joseph," he said. "We must obey them."

"You mean about the United Orders?"

"Yes. We are to own and share everything in common and work for one another. Then we'll have no rich men, no poor men, but will all be brothers in the gospel."

"I don't know about that. But will it work?"

"Of course it will," said Tim, "if we have love in our hearts."

When Brigham chose the site for the city at the foot of the eastern mountains, he took a block for his own use and another for the temple. He walked ahead with Orson Pratt, his engineer, and the crowd followed, going through sagebrush, crushing under feet the big black crickets, scaring up clouds of grasshoppers, and smelling the beds where wolves and catamounts had lain. The City of Great Salt Lake, Brigham said, would be in blocks of ten acres each, with streets eight rods wide and with twenty feet on either side given to sidewalks. There would be gardens and lawns, and every kind of shade and fruit tree and flowering shrub that would grow here. There would be no filth in this city, no petty shops, no ugliness of any sort; nor would any man be allowed to divide his property into lots for speculation. The temple and its grounds would cover forty acres, and would be beautified with trees and shrubs, beds of flowers, fountains and ponds.

As the men heard these statements one by one, they alternately stared at Brigham and at the desolation around them; and a few wondered if fever had affected his mind. They were all astonished by his audacity. Here they were, a handful of pilgrims in a desert of dust and insects and wild beasts; and yet he was talking of a city that would be more beautiful than any they had ever seen. He was talking of flowers and gardens and fountains upon this barren mountainside where they could see only sagebrush and sand.

"Holy hell," said one. "The crickets will eat all the gardens up."

"And mice and rats will march in armies down the streets."

"Mice, good God. There was a thousand in my tent last night. They crawled over me like lice."

"Yes, and when I woke up, my bed was full of crickets. They was smashed all over the quilts."

"I think Brother Brigham is out of his mind."

"Well, Joseph made a beautiful city out of a swamp. Mebbe Brigham sees things we don't see."

"But imagine a city here!"

Crickets and mice and rats, rattlesnakes and wolves were not worrying Brigham. He sent one body of men to build a road up a canyon, another to cut dead timber, and a third to erect a spacious but tentative building for church services. This he called the Bowery. A fourth group went with wagons to the dead sea and returned with hundreds of bushels of salt. He called for carpenters, lime burners and masons. He rode everywhere to urge the men to greater effort; and within ten days after he entered the Basin, adobe and log houses were being set up. Within three weeks, the Bowery was ready, and a huge stockade for defense against Indians had been begun. He had read in Frémont and others that the Utah Indians were cowardly and degenerate thieves who lived chiefly on crickets and roots; and though he expected little trouble from them, he was taking no chances. As the building progressed, he was the least amazed person in camp. Others now and then paused to gaze at what had been done and to marvel at the transformation taking place. It was incredible, it was a miracle, they said, little realizing that a great organizer was co-ordinating their efforts and driving them at top speed.

While many built, others plowed and planted, or dug canals to water the crops. A few under Porter Rockwell hunted wild game—for the daily fare now was chiefly of flesh. Blacksmiths hammered all day long, putting shoes on oxen, repairing axles and setting wagon tires. It was little wonder that the men were astonished. They looked around them and saw lime kilns smoking, houses, a great bowery, piles of timber, and row on row of wagons ready for the return journey—they saw, indeed, a teeming village where only three weeks ago there had been nothing but sagebrush.

Soon Utah Indians, seeing the smoke of fires and hearing the industry, came to the settlement to trade or steal. They were dwarfed and ragged and half-naked creatures who looked craftily at everything in sight and tried to make off with anything they could get their dirty hands on. Shoshonis came too, with whom the Utahans seemed to be at war; and one afternoon Brigham saw a terrific fight between two painted braves. One of the Utah rascals had stolen a horse from a Shoshoni buck and then traded it for a rifle. Discovered in the theft, he was unwilling to yield the rifle or return the horse; whereupon his exasperated foe broke a gun over the Utahan's skull.

Brigham expected the blow to lay the fellow out. It did stagger him and make him grunt but it did not by any means vanquish him. With blood streaming down his face, he went for his enemy like a wild beast. While the two warriors fought, an old Indian came up with a whip and laid it impartially over the heads of both. A stinging lash across the Utahan's face made him turn from his foe to strike the old man. That made the old warrior mad. With murder in his eye, he seized a pole and broke it over the Utahan's head.

Did all Indians, Brigham wondered, have skulls as thick as that? The old man now turned to the other warrior, who was his own son, and knocked him down; and then he lectured both of them and told them to do their trading away from camp. The Utahan looked abashed but he still plotted. When, a few minutes later, he saw a horse belonging to the Shoshonis, he leapt to its back and set off into the mountains as if a hundred devils were after him. With a howl of astonishment and rage, four Shoshoni warriors went in pursuit. A few hours later they returned with the horse and with blood on one of their rifles.

Satisfied with that vengeance, they built a fire and made ready for supper. When word of it went through the camp, all the men came to stare in amazement; for these Indian warriors, sitting imperturbably around their fire, were catching the big-bellied crickets and roasting them alive. They ate them from their fingers, and licked their fingers and palms after each mouthful.

"By the God of Israel!" cried Porter. "I wonder what they taste like."

"I don't think," said another, "I could ever make the riffle with one of them things. Look how they wizzle up when they fry! My old stomach would come up and stick right out of my mouth."

A few of the men turned away, sickened; but most of them stared, fascinated, while the warriors, indifferent to curious eyes, thrust sharp twigs through the writhing black bodies and held them above the flame. After roasting a wriggling insect and shoving it into his mouth, a buck would turn calmly and pick another off the sagebrush.

"By God, I'd eat roots first."

"Me, I'd eat my harness tugs."

"They might taste fine," said Porter. "We might be eatun some ourselves before a year rolls by."

"Are they too dodgasted lazy to hunt deer or do they like them things?"

"The way they waller them down I'd say they like them."

"Look, you see him over there? By God, he's et seventeen since I been standun here and watchun him."

The Indians preferred sugar and bacon and flour. After midnight, they would creep stealthily through the camp, intent on stealing not only food but ammunition and guns; and they became such a pest that Brigham told his men not to admit them to wagons or tents or houses. Foreseeing possible trouble in the months ahead, he rushed the building of the stockade. It was true, he reflected, that the Lamanites were, as the Book of Mormon said, a degenerate people.

His chief concern now, his greatest worry, was the journey back to the Missouri before winter set in, as well as what would happen to those who remained here while he was gone. They had arrived too late to plant crops that could be harvested this fall. The men could, of course, exist on roots and wild flesh; but during his absence they might be ambushed by Indians and wiped out. He might return to find bowery, stockade and every house burned to the ground. But he had to go, no matter what happened here; and on the seventeenth of August, less than a month after his arrival, he sent the first company on its way. He would take with him half the men, most of the wagons and teams, but no provisions except salt; because the little he had would be needed by those who remained. Those returning, he said, would live on fish and meat.

To those commanded to remain in the valley, he spoke from a wagon one morning as if they were his children, telling them to guard against Indians and disease, to be industrious and frugal, to love one another and to remember their God. Full of grief and fear, they listened to him;

and when he had finished they crowded around him, many of them with tears in their eyes.

"Brother Brigham, if you leave us a year you'll find just bones when you come back."

"God will watch over you."

"But you're the one who has been watching over us."

"Brigham, let us go with you."

Brigham looked at the tears in the eyes of strong men. He turned away for a moment a little overcome; and then he said: "Men, we have to build a kingdom here. This is no time to be afraid. I *must* go back; and you must stay here and plant and reap next summer so that we'll have food the next winter."

Suddenly a man broke under awful grief and fear and loneliness and left the group; and the other men stared at him, and then at Brigham.

"You know," said one, speaking more calmly than the others, "that we don't amount to much without your leadership. I guess we can try it; but don't be surprised when you come if you find us all dead."

"If you put your faith in God, you will all be alive when I return. I promise that."

"Has God told you that?"

"The spirit of God is in me this morning. I speak for Him when I say you will all live until I return."

Brigham had not gone far in his wagon when a white-faced man came running after him.

"What is it?"

"Brother Brigham, do you have all our letters?"

Brigham turned to Clayton. "Do we?"

"Yes, Brother Brigham."

The man turned away and went back to the camp where the other men were standing like children, eager to gaze at their leader as long as he was in sight. Brigham's eyes were misty when, dropping over a hill, he could no longer see those he was leaving. "I know," he said to Heber, "they will be all right. God has made me feel it." But he was deeply troubled and he was silent for a long while.

His journey was uneventful until he had covered several hundred miles. Then, unexpectedly one morning, he saw Porter riding back down the canyon at full speed, waving his hat and shouting. Brigham rose in alarm, knowing that Porter had unwelcome news.

"Hell and damnation!" roared Porter, galloping up to the wagon. "What is it?"

"You won't believe it! Parley Pratt and John Taylor are up there! They set out with sixteen hundred saints and there they be!"

For a long moment Brigham was too amazed to speak. Then he said, "My God!" in a voice that choked. Heber whipped his team and drove at a trot up the canyon; and Brigham, jolting around in the wagon, felt rage and despair. He had left these apostles on the Missouri to watch over the thousands: if the blockheads had disobeyed orders—and they had: when Brigham came up, he found them with sixteen hundred men, women and children, headed for the Utah Basin.

So furious that he shook all over, Brigham climbed down from the wagon and went over to face Parley. "By the God of Israel," he thundered, "what does this mean!"

"Why?" asked Parley.

"You blockhead! You incredible feeble-minded fool! What in the name of God do you think you are going to do in a desert in wintertime with this multitude? Are you out of your mind?"

"Why——"

Brigham turned to Heber. "We'll hold council at once. Call Parley and John in."

Heber saw that Brigham's face was violently red with anger. It was still red when he faced the other apostles.

"I don't like what I see!" he roared, looking at Parley and John. "The affairs of this church are managed by the Twelve, with me at their head. We work out plans for the good of all of us and then some pig-headed person upsets the whole damned works. When one of this quorum interferes with the plans of this quorum, he does wrong and God will punish him.

"Brother Parley, what right had you to set out into a wilderness with all these people? By what commonsense do you set out with sixteen hundred men, women and children into a huge unknown land with winter coming on?"

Parley's face was red too. His eyes flashed with anger.

"What under the heavens," Brigham demanded, "do you think all these saints will eat this coming winter? Where are the houses for women and children? What did you know of the land we'd find, or whether there would be wood to make fires, and flour and meat to fill hungry mouths? In Iowa you had fields, crops to harvest, houses to live in. Yet you set out on a long journey with women and children, not knowing where you're going or what you'll find when you get there! I will not tolerate such interference and such insubordination! If I am the leader of this church, then I am the leader, and I will not have my plans upset by men who refuse to act as God has commanded us. If I am not the leader—" He turned to other members of the Twelve. "Do you sustain me?"

"Yes," said Heber, speaking for them.

"If you sustain me, raise your hands." All of those present except Parley and John raised their hands. "All right, then. I will chastise Brother Parley or any other member of the Twelve as much as I please when they do wrong. I do it for your good and by the power of God invested in me."

"If," said Heber, "I or any of the brethren do wrong, tell us and we will repent."

"I chastise you," said Brigham, "that you might be saved and love me and stick to me. You are all exiles in a wilderness now. I am proud of the men who are helping me. There isn't a finer or braver set of men on earth. I love every one of you and I will stick by you and fight for you; but we have to stick together and fight as one man, not as individuals. It is us against the world now. We are going away into a desert to build our homes and our kingdom. We have been driven out of the Christian world. That's all right with me. To hell with the Christians. But I know we have a job on our hands, and if I am to be your leader, you will have to have faith in me and obey me. We left seventy men back there in a desert, not knowing if they will be dead when I return; and here you are with sixteen hundred saints, headed for a desert in wintertime. I tell you it is madness! It is damnable folly!"

Brigham turned and left the group. Taylor moved forward quickly and took his arm. "I have a terrible surprise for you," he said in a sepulchral voice. "I hope you can stand the shock."

"After the shock I've just had, nothing can surprise me."

"It is terrible. Don't be overcome by what you see."

"Is it mountain fever?"

"Much worse."

Brigham was surprised by what he saw. While he had been rebuking Parley and John, the women of the camp had prepared a great feast; and Brigham now gazed upon rows of improvised tables, laid with snowy white linens and burdened with fish and wild meats, fruits and jellies and relishes, white bread and cakes. John took him to the head of a long table and asked him to sit. Brigham sank weakly to a box, wondering if this was actually a banquet for him and his men, or a mirage of the kind he had seen when crossing the desert. He was unable to twinkle humorously as he usually did when outwitted; for he was thinking of this multitude headed for the Utah valley and per-haps starvation. This feast looked like the last irony in a foolhardy undertaking. Having eaten nothing for days except fish, he stared at the heaped food, the spotless napkin by his earthen plate, the silver-ware, the great roasts of venison and antelope. Still thinking of the desperate winter ahead of these sixteen hundred men, women and chil-dren, he found himself unable to eat.

This feast was for the men returning with him; and they now filed in, speechless with amazement, and took their places at the tables. As flushed and excited as schoolgirls, the younger women in Parley's caravan stood behind the men and served, urging them to try this roast, that boiled tongue, this stuffed heart; and the men, hungry for both food and women, so divided their attention between the girls and the table that they upset their plates on the white linen, spilled broth in their laps, and swore by heaven and earth that not even the Romans ever tasted anything as good. The women had seen starved men, but never such zestful gluttons as these. The smacking and gurgling and loud laughter could be heard in the quiet evening for half a mile.

"You sure took the soles off of my shoes," said one, and accepted an-other huge helping of venison.

"I'll have a misery in my belly for a week," said Porter, and made such a racket gulping a bowl of broth that another man slapped his shoulder and knocked his face into the bowl clear to his eyes. Porter set the bowl down and tongued his lips. He had crumbs of flesh hanging to his eyebrows, and grease glistening on his black beard. A woman stepped forward and wiped his face with a napkin. "Thanks," he said, and looked at a plate heaped with antelope tenderloin. "I feel all set to tackle it again." Then he looked over and observed that Brigham was not eating. "Brother Brigham, what's the matter with your appetite?"

"I don't feel hungry," Brigham said.

"You better get a good fillun. This is our last one till we reach the Missouri."

"Look," said another, "at all them-there delicacies on Brother Brigham's table. That's why he can't eat."

"I guess so," said Porter. But Heber looked over at his friend and knew what was in his mind.

"I don't feel very hungry either," he said.

Porter patted his belly and groaned. "There ain't no sense in my stoppun now. Sister, just load my dish with a pile of that elk heart. I intend to eat enough to last me clean to Headquarters."

"It's fish tomorrow," said another. "I aim to set here and stuff till daylight comes."

When the feast was done, the men walked around solemnly, bloated with food and pain. One of the men called for music and dancing, recitations and songs. A full moon was up now, and moonlight and firelight flooded the cove where the saints had gathered. The musicians struck up a quadrille, and the men scurried for partners, seeking the loveliest women and not caring whether they were married or not. One of them climbed to a wagon and shouted the turns; and a hundred men and women curtsied and whirled and pranced for all they were worth. A French four was next, and then a Scotch reel. Some of the dancers were barefooted, some were in rags.

Brigham sat in a wagon, still thinking of the winter ahead of these people, and frowning on the dancing. On the banks of the Missouri there had been shameful sins, and there had been adulteries among the converts on boats from England. The full moon, the music and laughter, and the strangeness of the country put wicked notions into the heads of the men here. He saw a girl slap a man's face. He saw another man try to seduce his partner into a thicket along the stream. So he rose and strolled through the brush and around the camp, his eyes and ears alert.

"Brother Brigham," said Parley, overtaking him, "I'm sorry for my disobedience. I have humbled myself before the Lord."

"It's high time."

"I want forgiveness."

"Parley, you may all starve to death this winter. There's no food in the valley, no crops to harvest. And if you all perish this winter, do you think God will forgive you for that?"

"I guess not," said Parley, humbled.

"It's the most damn fool thing I ever heard of. Another thing: I'm told you took two more wives while I been gone. Haven't I said that none of the leaders can take wives without my permission?"

"Yes."

"Then why did you? You waited until I got out of sight and then married two women."

"I converted them in England——"

"What if you did! Are you going to marry every woman you convert?"

"They loved me, Brother Brigham."

"Parley, I'm the leader. I cannot allow the brethren to marry every time they take a notion."

"But you," said Parley with spunk, "usually do. And Heber has more wives than I have. I have only eight."

"Take no more wives without my permission. How is the Trail from here to Headquarters?"

"Bad."

"Any big emigrant trains on it?"

"None that I know of."

"Did you have any trouble with Indians?"

"Nothing serious."

"How is the grass through the buffalo country?"

"There isn't any."

"It is good from here to the valley." Brigham gazed at him, his eyes cold with displeasure. "God knows, Parley, what you'll all live on this winter. If all these people starve to death, the sin will be on your head and God will never forgive you. Humble yourself after this."

"Yes," Parley said.

After the feast, a hush had fallen on the camp and the dancing and singing suddenly stopped. Word had gone from tongue to tongue that Brigham was very angry; and after much excited talk, the saints understood why. When the horrible realization came to them of what they had done, they were appalled and many were overcome by dread. They had set out on a gay adventure; and here they were, sixteen hundred of them, with little food and insufficient clothing and bedding, headed for a desolate valley and a hard winter. From tongue to tongue, too, went the rumor that Brigham had said they would all freeze and starve to death; and that when he returned, he would find only their bones in the nests of the wolves.

There was no more singing or dancing. Except in whispers, hardly a word was spoken. A terrified people went to their wagons and tents and sat in silent groups, thinking only of what lay ahead of them, of what indiscreet and shortsighted fools they had been. And when morning came, they loaded their wagons and hitched their teams, but they moved as if all life and hope had gone out of them. They looked at the stern face of Brigham, the anger and pain in his eyes, the tightness of his mouth, and could think of nothing to say, nothing to do except to move forward and accept their fate.

"You have to go on now," he said to Parley and the other leaders of the caravan. "There is nothing I can do to help you. You will need great courage and resourcefulness or you will all die. I urge you to put your faith in God and be faithful in your prayers, and perhaps He will watch and protect you; but even the Almighty can do nothing when His children disobey orders, upset plans, and act like fools. We'll all pray for you and hope for the best."

The faces of Parley and John and of others were very pale when they turned away. They sought their wagons, going like old men; and the huge caravan moved westward down the canyon. A thousand pairs of anxious eyes looked backward to Brigham and Heber who stood apart, in silence, as the last wagon disappeared.

Brigham drew a long breath. "Heber, I doubt we ever see them alive again."

Heber put an arm across Brigham's shoulders, and they turned to face the east.

CHAPTER XII

IT WAS A SADDENED AND WORRIED BRIGHAM WHO RESUMED THE JOURNEY. Riding day after day with Heber, he spoke often of the matter, saying that God had not made known to him what would be the fate of the pilgrims. But he felt that if they did not fall into sinful ways, if they finished the stockade, if they were mutually helpful and shared everything in common, then perhaps they would survive. If Brigham were there, Heber said, matters would be all right; but would they have sense enough to kill all the wild game they could find and jerk it before winter set in, gather wild fruit, seek edible roots and foliage?

"I don't know, Heber. Only time will tell."

When, after a journey of nine weeks and three days, Brigham arrived on the banks of the Missouri, his people dropped their work, poured out of dugout and shack and stockade, and lined the streets to greet him. Men bellowed until hoarse; women and children wept. Guns were fired, whistles blown, drums beaten until the hullabaloo was maddening; for a wilder welcome than this not even Joseph had received when he returned from the dungeon. Looking around him at the frenzied joy, Brigham knew the time was ripe to settle a matter in his mind.

Soon after arriving, he summoned all the apostles who were here, and met them in a soundproof cabin, covered and insulated with sod; and he said it was high time that he was elected president of the church. If he was to be leader and shoulder the responsibilities, then he should be invested with more power. "For see what has just happened! Parley and John, the damn fools, set out with sixteen hundred saints to starve this winter and be eaten by wolves. And when I rebuked them, they said they were apostles too, that I was only an apostle; and I tell you the church won't survive if every apostle is to be allowed to go his own way. I want authority to plan and build and command, or I will refuse to accept the responsibilities for what is done. . . ."

Without argument, the apostles assented; and a few days later in open meeting, the thousands voted to sustain the choice. Brigham Young was president of the church! That was what he had been plotting for ever since the day when he squelched the embattled Emma, dismissed Lyman Wight, and threw Rigdon out: now, responsible only to God, he could go ahead as dictator and build a kingdom.

He lost no time. His success, he well knew, would depend largely on the wisdom with which he chose his assistants; on the integration of his people into units which would function smoothly as a whole; and on stern discipline and swift punishment. There would be none of Joseph's tearful lamentation and indecision. He would rule with a hand of iron; and if enemies reared their heads, he would sock them away one by one. For he would have to be now, and perhaps to the end of his life, an absolute dictator over these thousands of exiles. That he would be misunderstood and persecuted and hated, he did not doubt; but his enemies would learn that they were not dealing with Joseph now.

During this long winter, one thought was constantly in his mind: what was happening to the seventy men he had left, and the sixteen hundred persons who had arrived, in the Utah Basin? They were out there twelve hundred miles in the most primitive conditions—and perhaps were dying of cold and hunger or going insane or setting out desperately for Oregon or California. But he could not spend all his time thinking of them. He had work to do here; and so eager was he to move these thousands next summer, to dream and plan and direct, that he paid little attention to his wives—except when he had to face their petty jealous nagging. They reproached him with favoritism, though he had no favorite so far as he could tell. They said he had deserted them. He had left them without food or clothes and had gone prowling into a wilderness; and had he not married several girls in Parley's company?

"No!" he roared, staring at the sad-eyed woman who rebuked him.

"Brigham, do you know I haven't a child yet?"

"Is it my fault if you're barren?"

"Barren! How do I know I am? Lucy isn't, or Clarissa or Emily or Emmeline. Laura isn't, Margaret Maria isn't. How do you expect me to have a child if you never come to see me?"

"I suppose," he said impatiently, "you expected me to fly back over the Rocky Mountains!"

"Well," she said sagely, "you should have taken a childless wife with you. But no: you took Clara because she is young and pretty. Why didn't you take Maria or Susan or Martha or me?"

"Mebbe," he said, "you're too old to have children."

"Too old!" she cried scornfully. "I don't have any chance. Do you realize you never visited me one single time last winter?"

"Didn't I?" he said, unable to remember. "I was busy. I have much to do besides visit my wives."

"Then you shouldn't have so many wives. You shouldn't marry a woman if you can't be a husband to her. And you should expect there'll be adultery."

He gazed at this wife and pondered. She was gaunt and homely but it did not seem to him that he had ever been partial. At any rate, he tried not to be. It was rumored among his wives that Emmeline was his favorite, but that gossip he regarded as so much nonsense. He had often been unlucky in his choices: it looked as if a dozen of his wives would never have children. A childless wife was an abomination.

"Tell me," said his wife tragically, "why Naamah always signs herself Naamah Kendel Jenkins Carter Twiss Young?"

"I suppose those are her names."

"She's stuck-up, the freckled thing! It makes her feel more important."

"The spirit of Satan is in you," said Brigham wearily.

"I want a child. You think I want to live forever and ever in the next world without children? I sure will if I have to count on you."

"What cabin are you in?"

"Two cabins north of Lucy—and I guess you know she's going to have a baby. And Emmeline too. And Clarissa, I guess, and Laura."

For a moment Brigham was appalled by the imminence of so many babies before he had his wives settled in the new homeland. "I'll visit you this evening. But I want you to understand that my mind is busy with something besides women. When we reach the Salt Lake Basin, we'll probably find the bones of seventeen hundred saints. That means nothing to you. But understand that I have problems and be patient."

"This evening?" she said brightly. "What time?"

"When I'm through with my work."

He turned away, reflecting that most women were more interested in admiring glances and murmured endearments or in devotion to trivial things than they were in serving the Lord. It had been good to be absent for seven months. As soon as he returned, here were his wives, fighting for an advantage, wondering which of them would be visited first, charging him with neglect. They distressed him. As a matter of fact, all the brethren who had more wives than one were distressed. Heber, poor fellow, was badgered incessantly; Clayton looked as if he wanted to flee to the North Pole; and Parley and Orson and John Taylor had had enough trouble for a thousand men. The sisters seemed unable to understand that their husbands had much to do besides curling their beards and trimming their hair, or giving their hours to romantic lollygagging. It was enough to get a man's dander up. And perhaps it was best, when all was said and done, to leave them to their gossip and knitting and see them as little as possible.

He had much to do this winter. He had to appoint heads to missions in eastern states and in England where the church had twenty thousand converts; as well as in China and the East Indies, Australia and the South Seas—because Joseph had sent missionaries to those lands. The saints in England he commanded to emigrate as soon as they could and to bring with them choice seeds of grain, vegetables, fruits, shrubs and trees; the finest machinery they could buy for spinning and weaving; the best of their animals and fowls. He wrote them to bring corn shellers, grain threshers and cleaners, machines and mills—and every other implement and article that would promote health and prosperity.

Nearer home he had many problems. It was, he said again and again, the duty of the well-to-do to assist the poor, to give them employment, to watch over their happiness and health. It was the duty of parents to be for their children examples of righteous living. When Heber observed slyly that Brigham had better stop chewing tobacco, Brigham's eyes twinkled but his lips did not smile.

"It's a nasty habit. I hope the saints have too much sense to imitate their leaders in all things."

He pointed out the need of printing presses and a museum in the new Zion; of all kinds of scientific instruments and equipment; of education in all fields. In the Utah Basin he expected to be, he wanted to be, isolated from the world; and he wished to have there everything necessary in the building of a model society. He did not intend to import anything, or want or need anything from the world which he was leaving.

"Not even tobacco," he said. "If the saints must use the vile stuff, we'll grow it."

Such was the larger dream to which he gave his resourceful mind. Here in the settlement were many things to be done before the great migration could begin: wagons to be repaired, oxen to be shod, crates and carrying racks and boxes to be made, clothing to make or mend, herbs and roots to be gathered for medicine, and all the companies to be organized. It was, he wryly admitted to himself, the most preposterous assortment of people and goods ever to embark on a long journey. Nothing was to be left behind; and in consequence they had seed and shovels and tongs, bureaus and secretaries, sideboards and sofas and pianos, chairs and carpets and stoves. They had broken-down horses, some with fistula or ringbone or pole evil, some that were spavined or fallen-hipped. They had cows with only one or two teats, oxen with three legs. They had pigs and chickens, cats and dogs and goats and geese, ducks and doves and beehives, and even pet squirrels.

He planned to leave very early in May. Preparations were almost completed in April when news came from the East that almost laid Brigham out. It was Heber who came to Brigham's cabin.

"Brigham," he said, his voice shaking with excitement, "do you know what has happened?"

"What?" asked Brigham, perceiving that Heber was very upset.

"The war with Mexico is ended."

"Well," said Brigham, not understanding, "all wars end sometime."

"My God, Brigham! I see you don't understand. Do you realize that the Utah Basin now belongs to the United States?"

That statement fetched Brigham to his feet. He looked as if he had been struck a blow; and slowly, as if it were being syphoned, all the blood left his florid face. He could only stare at Heber while the full realization of it came to life in his eyes.

"You sure?" he asked in a strange voice.

"Yes, Brigham. That territory has been ceded by Mexico. Porter just brought the newspapers."

"Great God," said Brigham, but not with anger, not with emotion of any kind. He said "Great God" because he was still trying helplessly to understand. For another long moment he stood and gazed at Heber, and then sank to a chair as if all the strength and emotion had been drawn out of him.

When evening came he was still dazed. He sought the cabin of his first living wife, Mary Ann Angel, accepted by most of the saints as his only wife, and by all of them as Mother Young. She was a quiet woman of great patience and sympathy. When she saw Brigham enter, she knew he had suffered a great blow, a bitter disappointment; because he went to the bed and sank slowly to it and rested his face in his hands. After watching him several moments, she went over and sat by him, and placed a hand on his bowed head.

"Brigham, what is the trouble?"

Without raising his face, he said: "Our new home now belongs to the United States."

"No!"

"Yes, Mary."

"Brigham, how did this happen?"

"The result of war." He lifted a haggard face. "Mary," he said, speaking like a defeated lad, "let me put my head in your lap a while. I'm so full of grief I want to die."

But he squared his shoulders the next day and went ahead. When the multitude heard the news, they were overwhelmed by consternation and anger; but in meeting Brigham told them to keep stout hearts and their faith in God. "It's our home," he said. "We'll defend it this time. If enemies march on us, we'll exterminate them. . . ."

And in May Brigham moved off in charge of the first train of three hundred and ninety-seven wagons and twelve hundred and twenty-nine persons. In his company were seventy-four horses, nineteen mules, twelve hundred and seventy-five oxen, eight hundred and eighty-three head of cattle, four hundred and eleven sheep, one hundred and forty-one pigs, six hundred and five chickens, thirty-seven cats, eighty-two dogs, three goats, ten geese, two beehives and eight doves. Falling in behind was Heber's huge division; and behind him came another ungainly caravan. Others were to come a little later.

They set out over the vast and lonely prairies, over the interminable distance to their new home, not knowing if they would find those in the Basin alive or dead, and with the bitterness of journeying in a country which they had tried to leave. Under leadership less wise and energetic than Brigham's, the motley pilgrimage would have ended in disaster during the first weeks; but under his firm and watchful guidance it moved slowly ahead, day after day, with every person among the thousands knowing his task, with every captain at his post. Messengers traveled daily from division to division; and Brigham knew of every woe and disobedience, apprehension and dread in every camp. Some of those whose relatives had gone with Parley were convinced that only the bones would be found of those sixteen hundred; and they would be bones now in a United States graveyard. That was the galling ignominy which they found it hard to take.

"To think we went twelve hundred miles to get away and now find ourselves governed by our enemies again! I can't understand why God allowed that to happen."

"Mebbe it's to test our faith."

"Hasn't it been tested enough? And I guess He will test it again by showing us seventeen hundred skeletons!"

"You're too gloomy. Most of them will be alive."

"What did they have to eat last winter? Brother Brigham doesn't think they'll be alive. You'n see it in his eyes."

"Brother Brigham has lots of worries we don't know about."

"Since he heard the Utah country is in the United States, don't you think he's aged faster?"

"Some. He looks awful full of trouble."

"But he never says much."

Another in the group spoke. "He says plenty to the complainers."

"We all complain too much," said a woman. "Let us pray and hope. Mebbe God has saved their lives."

"It's nice to say mebbe," said a second woman. "But none of us really believes it in his heart."

"Well, let's not complain. Brother Brigham will be hearing about it."

When Brigham heard of the loafers, troublemakers and complainers, he rebuked them with thoroughness that made their heads swim.

"Brother Philo says he won't go no farther without he has a better team." It was Porter speaking.

"Tell Brother Willard to lay the law down. If he don't come to his senses, throw him out."

"And Sister Betsy won't walk. She's barefooted and she says she won't drive pigs."

"Tell Sister Betsy if she don't take her pigs, she'll never have any in Zion."

"In Brother Heber's company, there's a man Hesekiah says he's afraid."

"Afraid! Tell Heber to send him back to the Christians."

"And a man named Arnold," said Porter, grinning, "he hit Brother Albert."

"Tell Heber I said to put him in irons."

To these thousands of wayfarers, the journey came overwhelmingly through all five senses. In appearance there had never been anything like it, Brigham declared, since the Israelites fled from their enemies. The oxen yoked to the schooners were weary and rawboned: under fleshless hides, their ribs rose like washboards as they breathed; their bellies were raw from the traces; their dull tired eyes blinked solemnly in the dust. Team by team, wagon by wagon, the caravan stretched in an unbroken chain for miles, lying over the hills and down and across the hollows, with the crawling progress of it so slow that it seemed hardly to move at all. Though superficially much alike, the hundreds of wagons were all different in their heaped cargo of persons and goods. One was loaded with flour and bacon and seed; visible on the next was only a teamster; the third was freighted with sofa and sideboard, tubs and kettles, axes and tongs and shovels; and the fourth was piled high with chicken crates and cats and a beehive, above which a cage holding two doves swung from a bow. In some the canvas framed a half-dozen heads of women and children.

On either side were the loose cattle, the dogs and cows, sheep and goats and pigs, herded together and driven by men, women and children, some of them barefooted and most of them in rags. Farther out were horsemen, the scouts who watched for Indians and wild beasts, the hunters alert for game. Dust rolled in low lazy clouds that sometimes completely hid the train, that filled the sky, that so obscured the sun that it shone dimly like a disc of gold. Out of the fog the riders appeared and into it they vanished.

The ungainly appearance was less vivid than the sounds; for there was every jangle and discord known to the human ear. The great and steady undertone came from the chugging and rumbling of the wagons as the wheels dropped into ruts, shook over hummocks of tough grass, or howled across streams bedded with cobbles. There was a continuous squealing in the hubs, squeaking of dried beds, flapping of schooner canvas in the wind. Above the maddening rumbling was the bleating of sheep, the lowing of cows, the goaded and persistent squealing of pigs, the barking of dogs, the dismal wailing of sick babies, the profane yelping of the herdsmen, the excited gabbling of geese and chickens, and the sudden and terrible braying of mules. Scouts declared that in a quiet afternoon, they could hear the confused thunder ten miles away. If they put ears to the earth, it sounded like the mighty stampede of a buffalo herd, except that above it, sharp and clear, came the squealings and cries. At first the infernal din almost drove some of the people insane: they could not sleep because the night was full of grunts and bleats and barks and the blood-chilling racket of the mules; but after a while they became used to the infernal uproar and would have felt lost without it.

They became used to the odors too: the sweating stink of plodding beasts, the dank breath of oxen that had the smell of warm intestines thrown in the sun, the strong stench of the hogs and the sickening smell of the sheep. When a breeze was blowing, a sensitive nose could, in the beginning of the journey, identify a score of different odors. It might be the smell of hot axle grease, the foul air from a crate of chicken feathers and dung, the clean fragrance of salt bacon, apples or flour. It might be the smell of bedding full of human sweat or the dry heat of the vast prairies; the scent of wild flowers trampled under the feet of the beasts or the stink of dogs that had rolled in an old carcass and then swum a creek. It might be the smell of diapers hanging from schooner bows. After journeying a few days, the pilgrims could not tell one odor from another: everything was blended in one offensive and omnipresent smell and they became as used to it as to their own breath.

On tongues also, the journey laid its earthy tang. In hot days, when no breeze was blowing, the wheels, turning felly-deep in white loam or sand, rolled up clouds of dust that spilled like fountains of flour or bellied upward in blinding density till sun and sky were hidden. Dust lay in powdered depth on canvas top, on the goods within, and like melting snow on the sweating beasts. It rimmed the eyes and mouths of both beast and person and made them look red and raw. The travelers breathed it and tasted it until the flavor of hot prairie was more familiar than that of the food they ate. They tasted also the strong wet smells of the teams and the milling herds; as when, again and again, a teamster or a drover cracked his whip, sheathed with dung, and filled the air with brown particles that floated in the dust and settled and melted on human tongues. Hogs cooled themselves in wallows and emerged looking like grotesque monsters of mud; and in the hot sun the mud dried and scaled off and mingled in floating particles with dried manure, with seared vegetation powdered under the marching feet, with hair and wool.

They felt this journey in every aching muscle and bone. Women and children, crowded into wagons among crates and boxes and bedding, were hardly able to move a limb all day long. Cramped and suffering, but complaining rarely, they fought off mosquitoes, closed their eyes against the heat and dust, and rode the jolting and squealing wagons over the endless miles. Other women and children helped to drive the beasts, some barefooted, others in ragged shoes that admitted the sand and grit; and the feet of all of them were gouged and abraded into bleeding sores. For the sick and the very old, the chugging of the wagons was almost unendurable; for the shuddering drop of a wheel into a deep rut shot excruciating pains through them; and the rumbling monotony so beat upon their senses that they were more dead than alive.

Some of them did die, and some babies were born dead or died soon after birth. These were buried in the vast loneliness of the prairies. Throughout the long journey, there were graves to the right or left of those who had died in former pilgrimages. Into most of the graves wolves had dug and scattered the bones; but if a woman turned faint at thought of leaving a loved one to be exhumed by wild beasts, Brigham scowled and declared that the dead were safe with God. If their bones were bleached by prairie wind, it mattered little: they would be gathered in the Resurrection and made whole again.

"It's the living who need us. The dead are at peace."

The women, nevertheless, gazed back across the miles, remembering the graves left one by one. Some of them almost lost their minds: nearly every day they saw desolate graves or now and then a tiny graveyard upon the prairie, with only Indians and wolves to keep watch. When, one evening, a woman threw herself on a mound and said she would never leave her child, Brigham called two men and had her forcibly borne away. This was no time for grief. This was a time for courage; and never once, no matter how terrible the scene he witnessed, did Brigham's stern face soften. His goal was the Utah Basin and he would get there with as many live persons as he could. If the sick or the old or the babies died, they would have to be wrapped in a blanket and left to their God.

He reflected, indeed, that the saints would be lucky if they were not attacked by Indians or some dread scourge and wiped out entirely. He kept the boldest scouts busy and every man close to his gun; he watched his camp like a hawk for signs of malaria or other fevers and for dysentery, tirelessly urging them to be calm and cheerful, to sleep soundly, to be careful of what they ate, and not to worry about the saints in the Basin. It was only to his unrelaxed and stern vigilance that the caravan owed its life.

Through it all, awake and asleep, Brigham was impelled by a great vision. He felt that this journey fed from the eager and searching millenniums in the remote background of human striving: it was more than desperate flight from enemies: it was a pilgrimage toward freedom, toward a fuller and richer destiny for the entire human race. In all its suffering and patience and courage, it was a mighty symbol of that struggle for perfection and peace that had been the heritage of humanity for centuries. He was fighting for a society that would be charitable and righteous and free.

His problems now were many. Having been told of Shefmolan's stealthy warriors a year ago, the saints were fearful of Indians; but Brigham cried with an oath that they were only the Lamanites, a degenerate offshoot of one of the Lost Tribes, and cowardly rascals every one of them. Nor did Indians show their faces while the divisions moved through the Sioux and Pawnee land. Brigham had not expected them to. When, he said, their scouts saw several thousand men on the march, all armed and alert, the dastardly redskins would flee to the hills—and apparently they did.

Brigham thought little about them, so pressing was his search for feed.

Expanses of prairie had again been swept clean by fire and buffalo; and after camp was pitched in late afternoon, it was necessary to scatter the animals far out. Herdsmen watched them until the beasts fed and lay down; and then the men drew a blanket or a coat over themselves, placed a gun within reach, and slept back to back against the oxen. The sheep and hogs foraged during the day, the former eating weeds and every stray blade of grass, the latter rooting in the earth and devouring anything they could find. Sometimes they came upon old carcasses and made a feast of withered hide and bleached bones; sometimes they tried to eat buffalo skulls. They were fed a little grain daily; the cats and dogs received the leftovers from meals; but all the other animals had to take what they could. As the prairies became more barren and desolate, the oxen and horses and mules looked like skeletons set upon legs. A few of the cows were milked night and morning, and the cream was put in jars and churned daily by the jolting wagons.

It was a busy camp each evening after the simple meals were done. Blacksmiths set up their forges and made music with hammer and tongs as they shod limping oxen, reset rattling wagon tires, repaired axletrees, crates and tongues. The women patched clothes or attended the sick; or now and then one withdrew to the shelter of a schooner to give birth to a child. There was not the music and song and dancing of the rain-drenched journey from Nauvoo to the Missouri: too many were ill, too many were dying, and too many, thinking of the pilgrims out in Utah, were overwhelmed by the desolation around them. These were not the reckless men who journeyed with Brigham a year ago. For the most part they were men with families, some of whom filled two or three wagons; and they were pressing into an unknown land and toward nobody knew what eventual doom. When they asked Brigham what the new home was like, he always gave the same answer: it would do well enough.

"But doesn't Frémont say it's a desert?"

"The soil is all right. There's water."

"But you say there ain't any timber."

"We'll build adobe houses."

"Will fruit and vegetables grow there?"

"Anything will grow there."

The men were not sure of that. In the faces of some was a fixed and anguished hopelessness; but others, with more faith in Brigham, strove to cheer their companions.

"At least we'll have freedom until the United States drives us out. Human beings can starve, they can suffer, but if they don't have freedom they are only beasts."

"But what about Indians?"

"Brother Brigham will scare them right out of their war paint."

"Porter says the valley is full of wolves, so why in hell are we taking sheep?"

"Well," said a man, grinning, "we're leaving one kind of a wolf for another. The wolves out there don't pretend to believe in God."

"I'll deacon a calf if we don't all starve to death!"

The journey was enough to bring fear to the boldest heart. When a man's spirit was lifting, he turned to behold graves that seemed fresh, or to see his own people carry a burden to a hillside. There were the abandoned articles of former migrations: broken wagons, yokes, cast-iron stoves, bones of horses and oxen that had been slain or had starved to death. There were the ruts of the Trail where wheels turned as if in six inches of dirty flour; dust in stifling clouds until children could barely see out of red and inflamed eyes; sheets of earth upon the wagons ahead, behind, until the plodding teams were lost in the dry blind pall of it. A day of this, or even a week or two, would have been tolerable; but to go endlessly, exhausted by thirst and heat, choked by dust, and to flay gaunt beasts that fell in the harness—to plod hour after hour westward, expecting to find seventeen hundred skeletons at journey's end: that was enough to break the spirit of any man.

When a wind came to drive the dust in gray mountains upward, then the landscape ahead, shimmering in hot air, was a vast garden of beautiful lakes, of forests, of soft blue hillsides, with the mirage lying upon distance as far as eyes could see. Often women wept to see such fresh loveliness and thought they were approaching their new home; and some did not learn for many days that they were gazing only at the tantalizing sorcery of desert heat.

There was much sickness in the divisions, but cholera was the scourge Brigham feared. The plague on the Missouri had taught him a lesson; and now in central Nebraska he had men dig wells when river and creek did not look good to him. Tirelessly, day after day, he moved through his own camp, watching for signs of scurvy and blackleg, rebuking the strong who behaved like weaklings, cheering the sick and old.

"Why do you set there on your hinder? You have a wagon tire about to fall off."

"I know it," said the man, and looked at the wheel, twisted by heat and dust. "I guess you'll have to leave me behind."

"Get busy. Repair that wagon before you go to bed."

"It's busted."

"Sister," said Brigham, turning to another wagon, "are you going to make it all right?"

"I don't guess so," said a woman whose face was gray with fatigue and age. "You'll have to bury me and go on."

"You ride in one of my wagons tomorrow and rest."

Porter came up, knocking dust out of his beard and clothes. "I see about twenty buffalo today."

"Then let's have fresh meat tomorrow."

New life possessed the camp when, next morning, the first shaggy beasts were seen coming over a western hill. Women gasped in amazement; children stared in solemn red-eyed wonder. Nearly every man in camp wanted to give chase, but Brigham chose a few hunters and ordered the others back to their posts. After the caravan entered the buffalo country, and herds raced like a low dark storm over the hills, there was terrible confusion. Hogs ran in circles, squealing and terrified, as if thunder and lightning were imminent; and one night the camp narrowly missed extermination under flying hooves.

When Brigham sat up, aroused suddenly from sleep, he heard a sound like that of approaching wind. Leaping to the earth, he saw at once that the camp was loud with terror: dogs were howling dismally, pigs were woofing and scurrying in the darkness, and mules were braying as if goaded with hot irons. Brigham listened to the ominous roar: it reminded him of a deep and distant storm upon an ocean.

Hundreds of persons were leaving their beds.

"Porter, what is it?"

"Sounds like a buffalo stampede. It's headed this way."

"Listen." The sound now reminded Brigham of the heavy muffled roar of a river down a gorge. "Quick, Heber, have the men bring the animals in—all the sheep and cattle and pigs right here in the inner circle." Soon, squads of men vanished into darkness. "Have a hundred fires built," he said, turning to captains. "Move quick, everyone!"

The excited cattle were now being driven in. They came hunched up, heads down, in terror, blowing from their nostrils.

"It's gettun closer," said Porter.

"Yes." Brigham ran from captain to captain to urge haste and then listened again. There could no longer be any doubt of it: the mighty journey of thousands of terrified beasts was bearing down upon them. A full moon was up; and in a few moments Brigham saw the vanguard come into view like a low dark wall. Then it was a moving tide of darkness that flowed over a hill and down, and breasted the next hill, with the black expanse of it pouring over hill and into hollow like a thundering sea.

"It's headed straight for us," said Porter. His voice was calm.

The tide had vanished now, but the thunder of it beat into the earth until the wagons trembled. Brigham knew that the vast herd was crossing a ravine; and while it was out of sight, he looked around at groups of women and children, clinging to one another and screaming; at the hundreds of men setting the fires; at the milling terror of cattle and hogs. He stared northward again; and after a moment, a wall of shaggy heads and shoulders came suddenly into view, and the tide poured up and spread in a flowing avalanche. It was a dense mass that seemed to unroll like an enormous blanket. Then heads appeared, obscured but certain, and the vanguard became visible as a thousand thundering beasts, with an unbroken depth of moving flesh behind.

The fires were burning brightly and made a reef of flame across the northern edge of the camp. In the next few minutes, Brigham realized, his people would be mangled and gutted, or the sight and smell of the fires would turn the hordes. He was unafraid but he was shaking all over. The women and children behind him sounded as if they had all gone mad; and the men around him were so appalled that they fell over one another in gathering dung for the fires, or ran in circles, not knowing what they did.

"Look!" a man cried. "They're turning!"

It was so. Swerving, as if turned by a huge rudder in the rear, the wild breast of the stampede swung in an arc to the northeast. The earth shook under the roaring feet. Such a stupendous spectacle these people were never to see again. Women still screamed and hid their faces, but all the men now gathered by the fires and shouted hideously, with fright ringing madly in their cries. When the vanguard swerved, it was no more than three hundred yards from the camp; and now every person who watched could clearly see the magnificent wild journey, the low heads and the flashing horns, the shaggy manes pouring backward on the wind, as the stampede like a dark and heaving landscape rolled by.

How many there were, nobody could guess; but several minutes passed after the first heads snorted and turned before the last of them came even with the camp. Some afterward said that for ten minutes, some for an hour, the seething ocean swept past them in rolling tide upon tide. When the last of it vanished, the thunder grew fainter and fainter; and except for the milling of the stock and the weeping of women and children, the night was silent again.

"By God," said Porter, biting off a quid of tobacco, "that's as close as I want to come to death."

"The fires done it! May God bless Brother Brigham."

"Go over," said Brigham to the captains, "and tell the sisters to stop their damned infernal yelling. They'll scare all our animals to death." Brigham looked down at his hands; they were still trembling.

After this horrible experience, the saints wanted to hasten through the buffalo country, but Brigham said they must kill and jerk all the flesh they could haul, as well as fatten all the meat-eating beasts, including the pigs. Tons of meat were jerked. After leaving the prairies and approaching the foothills, hunters fetched in deer and antelope, and sometimes sheep and goat and bear. Sight of the first brown bluffs of the Rocky Mountains made some of the men think they had almost arrived, and they wanted to push forward to learn the fate of the colony.

"Calm yourselves!" cried Brigham. "You've still got over six hundred miles."

They were now in the land of wolves and rattlesnakes. Almost daily the reptiles buried their fangs in stray cattle; and during the night, herdsmen had to keep watch against wolves. There were, nevertheless, a few amusing stories to cheer the heartsick wanderers. A man was hammering one evening when Brigham asked him if he had had poor luck.

"Dodgast it, yes. One of them varmints made a jump at my right ox yesterday and set his old tongs in my wagon tongue. It swole and swole until I had to unhitch."

"You mean the tongue or the snake?"

"The tongue. It swole up until I chopped six cords of wood out of it." Brigham made a face. "I've heard that story before," he said.

That story and others went through the camps. Legends were also told of the sheep: the rattlers struck at them and got their fangs entangled in wool, whereupon they were yanked along like ropes, with their rattles fraying out and their hides peeling off. Herdsmen then seized the snakes by their throats and used them for whips. It was said too that the hogs, and especially a big savage boar, despised rattlesnakes and pursued them with snorting fury. This boar also hated wolves; and when during the night he heard the skulking creatures, he charged like a small buffalo and almost frightened the other pigs to death. Every day some tale was told that brought a smile to tired and dusty faces.

"You should a-seen President Martin Van Buren. That's our big ram. He stumbled into a nest of rattlers and got so gad-danged mad that he thought his own horns was snakes. He romped around all afternoon a-tryun to shake them offen his head. He even thought the tail of a mule was a snake, and durned if he didn't bust old Gudget a blow that knocked his hinder right up even with his short ribs!"

The days were cooler now, the streams fresh; and day by day the westward view became more beautiful. Brigham rode in the lead wagon, with his division stretched out for two miles behind him, or he advanced on horseback, seeking camping spots and food. Because so few of the pilgrims actually knew that polygamy was practiced by their leaders, he discreetly rode and slept with Mary Ann Angel, and had little to do with the others who followed in wagons behind. The time was coming when he would have to make public announcement of plural marriage— and coming soon if gossiping women did not keep their tongues still; but he was not ready yet. He wished first to establish his people beyond the reach of persecution.

How he would do that, he did not know. It was a tremendous irony that he should lead them beyond the United States and then find himself returned to the nation he had left. But he would be far from his enemies, and federal authorities would leave him alone for a long while. He would build an army, as Joseph had done; but this time it would be a fighting army, and snoops and fools and other breeds of the ungodly would find their hides warmed if they came to the Utah Valley. Of this, of a hundred other matters, he thought as he rode along; but as he steadily approached the goal, he thought chiefly of the colony which he would soon find. In spite of his belief that God had watched over them during the past winter, he could not deny or hide his apprehension, or quiet the growing fear of his people.

Most of them were convinced that they would find only seventeen hundred skeletons. Daily men begged Brigham for permission to ride ahead of the caravan and learn the truth; but he said no. If they were all dead, then they were dead, and that was that.

"But if they are, Brother Brigham, we cannot stay there. We'd all go mad."

"Of course we'll stay there. If God has called them home, we'll bury the skeletons."

"We couldn't! We couldn't stand to look at them!"

"Be quiet," he said.

"But think," said a woman who had overheard, "think if they died and the wolves have gnawed all the flesh off— Oh, Brother Brigham, let's find out, and if they're dead, let's not go there!"

"That is our home," said Brigham. "And in the name of the God of Israel, calm yourselves! We need courage, not whining."

He was calmer than his people; but his face became whiter and more drawn as he approached the Basin, and his nights were troubled. He did not believe that God would desert him now. He remembered, nevertheless, the severity of winters in the valley—for explorers and trappers had told of them; and he remembered that the huge colony had entered in the fall of the year, and almost without food. He was still ten days from journey's end when he called Porter to him.

"Porter, in the morning take the best and fastest horse and go at top speed to Zion. Find out what happened. Come back just as fast as you went."

"Yes, Brother Brigham."

"Don't let anyone know you're going. And if they're all dead, just tell me when you come back."

In spite of excited pleas, Brigham now held the caravan to a few miles a day. He wanted the truth before he entered the valley: if the colony was dead, he would have to go on, of course, even though his people became delirious with grief and terror. While Porter was gone, he prayed often and earnestly, but always alone; and he was lying awake in his wagon an hour before daylight when Porter returned. Brigham felt a hand on his arm. "Yes?" he said, raising the canvas to look out.

"It's me, Brother Brigham."

"Well?" said Brigham, trying to speak calmly.

In a voice shaken by deep feeling, Porter said: "They're all right."

"Thank God!" said Brigham, and rose to kneel in prayer.

When, the next morning, he called his people into meeting, he could tell by their faces that they expected dread news. A part of the anxiety left their eyes when they saw their leader smile. "Brethren and sisters, I want to tell you something that will make you happy. The colony in Zion is alive and well." Without saying more, Brigham sank to his knees, and the multitude knelt with him; and for several minutes, not a head rose from prayer. Then, rising, Brigham said: "It's time you sang again!"

A deep voice started in song and hundreds followed:

> Let Zion in her beauty rise, her light begins to shine!
> Ere long the King will rend the skies, majestic and divine!
> Ye heralds sound the golden trump to earth's remotest bound!
> Go spread the news from pole to pole in all the nations round! . . .

Brigham stood apart and gazed at his people. There were tears in the eyes even of men.

CHAPTER XIII

WHEN, A FEW DAYS LATER, BRIGHAM'S DIVISION PULLED INTO THE valley, he rose in astonishment at what he saw. The colony had sent scouts to learn when Brigham would arrive; and now the whole multitude, looking like a people in desperate flight, was coming across the sagebrush mountainside toward him. Nearly everyone was running: fathers were carrying infants or dragging children by their hands; children were scattering in flocks and leaping the brush and bushes; women were frantically chasing after husbands and families, their hair streaming like scarves behind them; and dogs were yapping and howling their lungs out. More than sixteen hundred of them came in such mad breathless haste that they reminded Brigham of the buffalo stampede. They surrounded his wagon and climbed upon it and almost poured over him, fighting to grasp his hand and to greet him—weeping, laughing, yelling as if they were all out of their minds. Then in a frantic line on each side of the caravan, they went wildly from wagon to wagon, seeking relatives and friends, kissing one another, crying out of laughter and tears; and Brigham stood in his wagon and gazed at the frenzied reunion. With his heart warmed, he looked down at Mary Ann and smiled.

"Who ever saw the likes of this before!"

Mary Ann did not speak. She was weeping—and so were all the other women whom Brigham could see.

"Go on," he said to Heber.

Brigham lost no time in looking around him to see what had been done during his absence and how the colony had survived. His amazement grew as he went exploringly through the settlement. The men had built four hundred and fifty houses, a flour mill and three sawmills; they had fenced five thousand acres, two thousand of which were seeded to winter wheat. The remainder was plowed and ready for spring planting. They had dug long ditches and canals. Standing among the houses of adobe, brick or log, Brigham could gaze down to the south and west and see a huge field of plowed land where, a year ago, there had been only sagebrush and crickets; he could see a whole network of ditches and canals; and around him he could see signs of industry, no matter where he looked. The stockade looked as if it was finished. The houses, even though roofed and floored with dirt, seemed to be substantial and well-built. He was pleased.

But later, when he heard the story of famine and cold, he was horrified.

"We fattened up a little this summer," said Parley, laughing with his old zest. "But by the God of Israel, John Taylor and me wore the same trousers at the same time. A baby's diaper would have made a skirt for any woman here."

"It's true," said John. "He doesn't exaggerate much."

"As for our troubles, I don't know which was worst."

"Crickets," said a man.

"You remember them, Brother Brigham? The Indians ate them like they were venison tenderloin but there was too many for the Lamanites. Our crops just looked fine. The wheat and corn planted when you were here, it grew like the weeds and everything was dandy for a while. Then something happened. The crickets came by millions, by billions, hopping down from the hills. They came in armies so thick you couldn't see the ground. Every time we killed one, two came to bury him. Our fields turned brown, then black.

"And how we did struggle! Every man, woman and child worked day and night. We dug holes and herded them in by millions and buried them, bushels at a time. We plowed ditches around the fields and turned water in them and then drove the crickets in and drowned them by the tons. The more we killed, the more we had to kill. We tried fire and burned them by the shipload. Since the days of Egypt's locusts, I'll bet there ain't ever been anything like it. Fire and water and burial didn't make a mark on them."

Parley put a hand to his high broad forehead. "Well, we knew if they destroyed our crops we'd all die of starvation. Just the same, we gave up all hope. We figgered you'd just find skeletons when you got here."

"That," said Brigham, "is what most of the saints thought. Well, what did you do?"

"You'n thank the Lord for saving us. He came to our aid. We fought till we dropped in our tracks, too weak to move. We killed them by the acres and they came down in whole prairies. We killed them day and night and night and day but we might just as well have tried to brush the ocean back with a broom."

"Stop building up your story," said Brigham, "and tell what happened."

"The Lord saved us."

"That's true," said another.

"But *how*?"

"Well, the gulls came. First we saw a few of them and thought nothing about it. Then we saw hundreds and noticed they was eating the crickets, but we still didn't pay much attention. Then we saw them by the tens of thousands. They came in by the skyful and covered our fields like snow. And the appetite of a gull," said Parley, "has mine beat ten ways from Sunday. You wouldn't believe what they did. They eat all they could hold and then went to the ditches and drunk water and vomited and come back to eat again. Back and forth they went all day from the fields to the ditches, from the ditches to the fields, to eat and vomit and eat. They vomited so many crickets that they clogged our ditches and we had to keep busy and shovel them out so the water would run. Crickets was piled along the ditch banks three feet deep. And over at Salt Lake, there was a sight. Because the water looked like green vegetation, the grasshoppers come down in billions; and the shores was lined with them waist-deep."

"It sounds like the Lord is watching His people. Did the gulls save the crops?"

"A part of them. If they hadn't, we'd all be dead now."

"I'll tell you," said another, "what I did. When our food was all gone, I traded some oxen for a steer. After we ate all the flesh and boiled the bones, then we scraped the hide and boiled it. The soup from that hide was all we had for six days."

"It was the sego lily," said Parley, "that really saved us. The Indians eat the root, so we dug tons and tons of it. That's all some of us had to live on for weeks. Some of the saints," he added sadly, "died. Wild parsnip poisoned them."

"How many babies were born last winter?"

"Two hundred and fifty."

"How are the crops this year?"

"They could be a lot better. If it's a hard winter, mebbe we will all die this time."

"Were the saints righteous last year?"

"So far as I know," Parley said.

"How many more," asked John Taylor, "are coming?"

"Two divisions now and more later."

John shook his head. "It looks like another hard winter."

It looked like a hard winter to Brigham. It looked like famine with five thousand persons here and a lean harvest to feed them. Taking complete charge of the settlement and of every person in it, he moved at once to fight against extermination. The best hunters he sent to the far mountains to kill all the wild beasts they could find. Men, women and children were dispatched in all directions to dig and store the bulb of the lily and the edible roots of other plants. Some fished or searched for wild fruits; and others explored far in the south and the west for anything that could be eaten.

Winter came early, and it was the severest winter Brigham was to know in this valley. He placed the huge camp on rations, and said that by the God of Israel, any person caught thieving would be slain on the spot. In public meeting he shook gnarled fists at his people.

"If you want to know what to do with a thief, I say kill him on the spot! That is what I expect I will do. If I catch a man stealing, I'll be apt to send him *straight home*, and that is what I wish every man to do. Place all thieves in the line of a cannon loaded with chain shot. I will not tolerate thieves here! I will not tolerate adulterers or whores or swindlers or scoundrels of any kind; and I will know what to do with them if they show their sneaking faces in this valley. Such words might send a thrill of horror through you. But brothers and sisters, we are fighting to live, we are fighting for freedom and godliness, and we are fighting right now with our backs to a desert, against the world! The ungodly are our enemies and we'll know how to take care of them if they come here! . . ."

The thrust of his chin and the glint in his cold gray eyes chilled his people as they listened; and if any of them stole during this terrible winter, they did it with such cunning that nobody knew of it. The thousands came within his indomitable will as frightened chickens to a shelter; and even more than on the banks of the Missouri, his word was law.

One day Clayton told him about John Pack. On the journey a year ago, the beady-eyed unruly John had a store of bacon and flour, sugar and salt. After camp was made, he waited until the men had gone to bed; whereupon he slyly drew forth his provisions and cooked his supper. While listening to the story, Brigham reflected that there were several greedy and pigheaded and ungodly men in his city; but he felt a little more kindly toward them today because pilgrims arriving late in the fall had told him a strange story. Oliver Cowdery had returned. He had come to the Kanesville, Iowa branch of the church—and he had come as an abject and penitent man, looking as if he had been horsewhipped, and begging to be admitted again to fellowship. He was admitted, and immediately accepted a mission abroad.

Remembering Oliver, Brigham said: "Well, keep your eyes open. Nobody will ever live in luxury in this valley while others starve. Never —and God help those who try it. As for Brother John Pack, he always looked to me like an emissary of the Devil."

Nobody tried to live in luxury during this winter. Nobody dared. Every granary and storehouse and every home were open to Brigham's searching gaze. He spent nearly all his time visiting mothers and babies to see if they were nourished, looking into the meanest huts, watching more prosperous saints to learn if they were hoarding. The hovels that he and his people lived in, made for the most part of adobe, were small and windowless, with roofs of willows, rushes and earth through which the rains leaked. Beds were soaked. The floors were often ankle-deep with mud. Sometimes, when peering in, Brigham would see a woman holding a parasol or piece of canvas above her stove to protect it from dripping water. Not many of them had the luxury of a stove.

One day when the weather was thirty below zero he made his daily round, his hands and face and ears freezing as he went. Beasts in back yards were hunched up until they made a rainbow from their tail to their nose: their hair was spires of frost, their nostrils were rimmed with tiny icicles. Any one of them looked as if, pushed over, it would never rise again, but would lie rigid like an animal made of wood. Dogs at doorsteps seemed to be only frozen hair and doleful eyes and shivers. In a hencoop, to which out of curiosity he went, Brigham saw that the chickens had frozen dead on the roosts and dropped to the floor.

He stopped by a shack and looked in, having smelled food. "Sister, is it good?"

A woman rubbed at the smoke in her eyes—for her fire was an open one on the earth floor of the cabin. "Not very, Brother Brigham. I'm just boiling some roots."

Over against the wall were six shivering children: they could not endure the smoke and had withdrawn and sat in a row against adobe bricks upon which the melting frost was gray and wet. They were all barefooted: their toes, thrust up and motionless, looked as if frozen as hard as the walls.

Ordinary people, he decided, turning away, would perish under such conditions in a winter like this—but his people were not ordinary. They had endured weeks of rain across Iowa, plague and hunger on the banks of the Missouri, and months of hardship in the westward trek. God had prepared them for this ordeal.

Feeling chilled through and through, numbed to his marrow, with his bones turning brittle and his blood to ice, Brigham stopped at another hut and looked in. It was full of smoke but there was a fire on the earth floor and he went in. He had a stove in his own cabin, and in a moment he was coughing and choking and going to the door for air.

"You get used to it," a woman said.

Brigham returned, and in the gloom saw two small children, undernourished and pinched, shivering in a wet bed. He went over and put a cold palm to a cold cheek.

"Sister, do your babies have milk?"

"No."

"They must have. We have fresh cows. I'll see that you get some." He warmed his hands at the fire—which was less fire than smoke because of soggy wood and no draft—and peered at a kettle. "What you have in that?"

"Just some bones. We've eat all our cattle. I boil and boil the bones and try and make some soup."

"Is that all you have—bones?"

"Yes, Brother Brigham."

"I'll send you some sego roots. Put in a little salt bacon and it makes a fair dish. Go to Mother Young and she'll give you a little flour and bacon and sugar. Where's your husband?"

"Out huntun for something. He killed a wolf and wants to eat it but I can't stand the thought."

"Of course, eat it. Our job is to get through the winter. We'd eat crickets if we had them."

And so it was, week after week, during the long bitter winter. Every hut in the settlement, every wagon and tool and woodpile, looked as if frozen so hard that a blow would shatter it. During the days, men emerged from smoking shacks to the bitter air and sought wood, or mounted half-frozen horses and went in search of wild life. Brigham's wives also lived in dismal wet huts; but when they complained he told them sternly they had enough to eat and wear. If the childless ones looked at him with reproachful eyes, he strove to remember which were pregnant and which he should visit, eager to do his duty by all of them. He slept alone in a hut, shivering all night, no matter how much bedding he piled upon him; but he visited his wives daily, inquiring about their health, their food and fuel.

Many of the saints died this winter but they were the sickly infants or the old. Almost every day, men went out with spades and axes to the cemetery on a hillside and chopped graves in the hard earth. The next year, Brigham predicted, would be happier: they would have an abundant harvest, they would build homes for those now living in tents—and he never knew before looking into a tent whether he would find the occupants still breathing, or all frozen as stiff as wagon tongues. In one of them, late in January, he saw parents and four children piled together in all the bedding they had, with their freezing bodies shaking the covering; and he was so depressed that he stopped at the cabin where several of his wives lived, including Lucy and Mary Jane Bigelow, the girls he married while crossing Iowa.

Lucy was alone with her infant.

"Hello," he said, entering the warmth. The stove was redhot.

"Hello," said Lucy, rising to meet him. She was only eighteen, and still saucy and coquettish. "My husband looks frozen stiff."

"I am, Lucy. By the God of Israel, what a night! You can hear the air freezing into icicles while you walk through it." He went to the stove and warmed his hands. "Where are the others?"

"All visiting or helping the sick."

Brigham looked around him and saw a cradle and his child. "The babe well? Lucy, do you have a hunk of fried meat or a bowl of soup or anything?"

Lucy smiled and went to boxes where she had provisions stored. "A piece of meat? I have some jerked venison."

"That will do. Not much—I'm as hungry as a wolf but just give me a small piece." Brigham sat by the fire and ate the dry tough flesh. "You know," he said, turning a wry smile upon her, "I'd like to stay here tonight. I damn near freeze to death sleeping alone in weather like this." He looked around speculatively, remembering that four of his wives shared this cabin.

"Well," said Lucy archly, "I could slip out and tell them. I guess they could sleep somewhere else tonight."

"No," he said. "How are they? All well?"

"Yes, Brigham. But Mary Jane is awfully mad at you."

"Why?" he asked, chewing on meat as tough as shoe leather.

"Well, she's about decided she never will have a baby. Do you know you have several wives who have never had a baby yet? There's Martha and Maria and Susan and Ellen and Augusta and—and my sister."

"But that isn't my fault," he said, wondering why he had so many barren wives.

"Some of them think it is. Augusta——"

"She was too old when I married her."

"Well—maybe. Anyhow, some of them think it's funny they don't have children and Emmeline and Clara and others have so many. Besides, they're saying Clara is your favorite now. You let her come west with you the first time and you made all the rest of us stay back at Headquarters."

Brigham found the subject distasteful. He rose and filled the stove with wood and went over to look for a moment at his sleeping child. "I must get some sleep now," he said.

"But you'll freeze to death tonight. Brigham, stay with me and they can sleep in the other houses."

"No," he said, and went to the door.

Lucy rose quickly and came to him. "Kiss me good night," she said. "You've kissed me only twice since I married you."

"Have I?" he asked, wondering why women cared so much about kissing. It seemed to him to be a lot of foolishness. He bowed to Lucy and she pressed soft lips against his hard stern mouth. "Good night," he said, and quickly closed the door behind him.

In the small hut where he kept an office and slept alone, one of his older sons usually had a fire going but there was no fire tonight. The room was paralyzingly cold. The adobe walls were mantled with frost, frost was like glass hair and moss along the roof poles, and frost was a thin gleaming sheath upon the iron framework of his bed. Taking only his shoes off, he crawled in; and it was like entering a bed of ice. In nights like these, it made little difference how much bedding a man had under him or over him: he shook until morning and arose chilled and aching in every muscle and bone. Brigham lay on his back, looking at his clouds of breath that flowed away like steam, hearing the bitter cold snap in the roof logs. But he was thinking not of the weather, not of his wives, but of all the work to be done as soon as spring opened.

And as soon as the spring of 1849 came, men set plows to the earth and hauled timber from the canyons, built new channels for irrigation, and went in groups to colonize the valley north and south. The soaked huts dried out, and in warmer days the city became cheerful and busy. Every week saw unbelievable expansion in the settlement and in the plowed fields. One man had already colonized a village named Farmington; another bought the Ogden site from Miles Goodyear, the scout and explorer, and founded a colony there; and thirty men went south to settle on Provo River and build a fort.

For protection against both Indians and gentiles, but especially the latter, Brigham reorganized the Nauvoo Legion, calling to it every able-bodied male between the ages of fourteen and seventy-five. There were to be several regiments, with two battalions and ten companies in each. It was the army of the State of Deseret—and it was an amazing army when the companies gathered to drill: lads and gray old men marched side by side, some dressed in the remnants of their Legion uniform, some in rags; some carrying muskets or huge swords, some having only sticks to represent a gun. Some wore polished boots and some marched barefooted.

Remembering next that he was, in spite of his long exodus, under the American flag again, Brigham called a convention of delegates from all colonies in the Basin, and established the territorial government of Deseret under a constitution that granted unqualified religious freedom. Before May passed he was governor of the new territory. Federal authorities, he said grimly to Heber, were too damned far away to bother him now; and if they marched in, he would be ready for them. He would do as he pleased; for if Joseph Smith had been right, there would be civil war soon and the scoundrels back east would have their hands full.

But leading his people across a wilderness and seeing them through a winter of famine was, Brigham soon realized, only a small task in comparison with the one ahead of him. It was not the great migrations that had him worried. The saints who had remained on the Missouri, as well as thousands who had come from England, poured into the valley this summer; but at once they settled north or south and built homes. His gravest problem, indeed, he had not for a moment foreseen; and when he understood the enormity of it and its threat of ruin, he was overwhelmed.

A wild-eyed man rode into the settlement one morning, crying that gold had been discovered in California near Sutter's Fort, and tens of thousands of frantic men were leaving the eastern states to seek their fortune. Some were going by boat, but hordes were coming overland by wagon and cart, on horse or ox or afoot; and the first of them would soon arrive.

"Great God!" said Brigham, and for a while he could say no more. He could only remember that he had traveled sixteen hundred miles to get away from his enemies, and soon by the thousands they would be under his nose and up to their old tricks. When his people heard of the advancing goldseekers, they were furious. They gathered in angry groups and swore they would shoot the rascals as fast as they appeared and throw their bodies into the dead sea.

"Think of it!" said one. "By God, we come clear out here to a desert. We damn near freeze and starve to death. And now here they come, thousands of them!"

"Yes, Brigham says they'll come without food. He says they'll pour in here with only rags on their backs."

"That ain't the worst of it. They'll try to seduce our women. They'll be as thick as the mice and rats in every house we have. We'll find them in our beds and under our beds, eating our grub, making love to our wives and daughters."

"Why don't we take our army and drive them out?"

"Brother Brigham says they'll keep coming like the crickets."

Brigham said more than that. In public meeting he addressed his people, and they could see that he was angry again. "By the God of Israel," he roared, "I guess we'll never get away from the Christians! We move sixteen hundred miles to a desert and find ourselves in the United States again! I thought we'd be isolated here and away from our enemies; but gold—that abomination among metals—has been found in California, and thousands of rascals of all kinds will soon be pouring through here. I don't want any trouble. I want the saints to behave themselves and be peaceable, and we'll get rid of the scoundrels as fast as we can. . . ."

In July the first feverish companies arrived—and they were an amazing horde of frenzied men. They poured down the canyon and into the valley as if they had been delivered by a landslide in the mountains: scattered over the sagebrush plain, they came whooping and yelling as soon as they saw the Mormons, some of them running afoot, rifles in hand; some of them galloping on horses and leading pack animals; some of them riding oxen and flogging the beasts in an attempt to keep up with horsemen in the lead. Behind them came droves of wagons and carts in which men stood, waving hats and guns and howling with all their might, or clubbing their teams to make them gallop. They came, it seemed to Brigham, like an avalanche and a pestilence, bringing with them their sinful ways, their diseases, their blasphemy and cursing—as if a horde of devils had been let loose from hell.

And at once, without permission and almost without greeting, they overran the settlement, scattering like brigands intent on pillage, and swearing as they went. They pastured their beasts right in the wheat and corn fields, tore fences down, stole everything they could get their hands on, and left their offal wherever they went. Bolder men lost no time in trying to seduce the women; because they believed, like most persons back east, that the Mormons lived in horrible debauchery, with sexual orgies as the meaning and gospel of their lives.

One of them thrust his insolent face into the cabin where Brigham's Lucy lived. He grinned almost from ear to ear and stared at her. "Hey, why don't you ask me in?"

"Get out of here!" Lucy cried.

"You all alone?"

"Not as long as you keep your ugly face in the doorway!"

The man looked behind him and then softly stepped inside. Lucy was ready. She seized a stove iron in one hand and a sadiron in the other.

"What's the matter?" asked the man, still grinning. "Don't you like me?"

"Go, before I knock your brains out!"

"Say," asked the man, backing out, "is it true Brigham Young has a thousand wives?"

Lucy went over and slammed the door and bolted it.

Unabashed, this man, like his fellows, prowled through the settlement in search of women. They hardly knew what to make of girls who slammed doors in their faces: from all that they had heard, the Mormon women were easy of virtue, and indifferent to the number or kind of men they entertained at one time.

"By God!" cried one to another. Then, seeing a Mormon, he turned to him. "Say, how many concubines you got? Will you loan or rent me one for tonight?"

The other asked: "You got any squaws yet?"

The Mormon did not speak. Brigham had said to ignore these rowdies and they would leave soon. They did leave after two days, after stealing all they could, after deciding that Mormon women had been misrepresented; but other companies poured in, and before long Porter came to Brigham to tell him there would be a lot of half-breeds in the valley next year.

"You mean they're seducing the squaws?"

"Right and left. When the sisters said no, they went lickety-split to the Indians. I don't like what I seen."

"I don't like it either."

"Why don't we run them out? I'm just achun to sock away a few."

"No, Porter, I want no trouble."

Brigham went to find Heber.

"Heber, do you know those scoundrels out of hell have slept with all the squaws they could? That means trouble. That means they've given disease to the Indians and they'll take it out on us. By the God of Israel, gold-seekers ain't enough trouble! It'll be Indians too before long."

"Down south the Indians are already on the warpath. I hear they intend to destroy the Provo settlement."

"And four hundred more hoodlums arrived last night. Gold!" said Brigham contemptuously, gazing toward California. "Of what use is it, except to pave streets or make skillets? I'll never allow mining in this valley. I don't want to see shacks and gamblers and whores everywhere I look."

"Brigham, did you know some of the sisters want to marry these villains and go to California with them?"

"If they prefer gold to God, let them go. We have too many women here. I think pretty soon I'll have to announce plural marriage and let some saints besides the few leaders take more wives. We must do something for the unmarried sisters."

"That's the way I feel. Besides, they're all getting suspicious of us."

"I know it. Well, right now we have to see about the Indians. These cricket-eaters around us don't matter; but Frémont says the Indians down south are dangerous. Big Elk is the chief down around Provo: we'll have to sock him away." For a long moment Brigham pondered. "If I had a hundred men like Porter Rockwell, I could take care of all my enemies, red and white."

For several minutes, Brigham paced up and down, thinking of his problems. Then he swung to Heber and asked: "Where in hell is Bill Hickman? Hasn't he come yet?"

BILL HAD COME BUT HE WAS HAVING TROUBLE OF HIS OWN. ACTING ON Brigham's suggestion, he had taken another wife while on the Missouri, and had sent her ahead with a company. When he arrived in the valley and found her, he was amazed to learn that she had a baby a week old; for he knew it was not his child.

"By all the mouth-almighty pukes in Missouri," he roared, "don't have the gall to tell me that baby is mine!"

His wife turned pale and caught her breath. "Now, Bill——"

"Don't Bill me! You got cold, did you, and cottoned up to a man! You found you a good-lookun spoops in a white bang-up and fair-top boots!"

"Bill, it is your child."

"You horse-faced liar! I haven't been with you since a year ago. How could it be my child? Did I send it to you in a letter?" He walked over and stared at her and then turned to gaze at the infant. "Do you know adultery is next to murder in cold blood? That's what Brigham says. He says if a man finds a rip-staver with his wife just to try a sharp knife on him an inch below his chin. Where is its father?"

"I won't tell you!" Her eyes were full of terror now. She rose and backed away from him, and slowly, very slowly, he followed. "You wouldn't kill him! You wouldn't make the little thing an orphunt!"

That was too much for Bill. He fell to a chair, howling with mirth. "God no, I wouldn't. You're both headed for hell: that's punishment enough, I reckon." He rose. "There I was, workun like hell back on the Missouri, just strainun my old tendons to make a fortune for Bet and Baby. And you were bub and sis with some old hog-in-togs." He went to the door. "You'n have him. Just don't introduce him to me when my hand is itching in my old smoke-pole."

"Bill, you ain't going to leave me!"

"Excuse me, honey. I'm workun for the Lord. I hear Brigham wants to talk with me."

She followed him through the doorway. "Bill, you won't tell Brother Brigham."

"Go back to your dodgasted spoops. I got me a good wife and no whore like you. Go back to your sinful pop-squirt."

"Please don't tell on me!"

Bill grinned as he headed for Brigham's office. Well, it served him right he had no time to lollygag. His wife was dedicated to the Lord, and not if Brigham told him he could have a hundred wives would he ever marry again. He was grinning when he entered Brigham's office.

"Hello, Bill. You seem in good humor today."

"Not exactly. I want to work for the Lord. I'm so soft I'll soon be using a silk handkerchief to wipe my nose."

"I have plenty to toughen you up. Down around Provo the Indians are on the warpath. And I'm told, Bill, that somewhere on the southern route to California our colonists have found terrible evidence of massacres two or three years ago. Anyway, the saints down there are scared stiff."

"You want me to fight the Indians?"

"Well, as a rule I think it's better to feed them than fight them, but mebbe we've fed them too much. First, I want you to act as scout for a colony I'm sending down the valley. Then come back and report to George Grant and learn the Indians around Provo a lesson."

"When you want me to leave?"

"Right away."

"Well, count on me to use up a few."

Brigham followed him to the door and laid a hand on his shoulder. "As soon as you fill these two assignments, come back. I'll need you around here."

Bill was happy. He had been afraid he would have to settle again to the monotonous life of a farm. Sometimes he felt resentful, believing that Brigham was not fair with him; because for all the time he had spent and the risks he had run, he had not been given a single bushel of corn, a horse or an ox, or a red cent. It seemed to him the church ought to support his family and equip and provision him when he was fighting for the Lord. But today he did not give much time to thinking of Brigham's neglect. He was reflecting that the Provo Indians were said to be very brave, though for him all Indians were cowardly sneaks. These

Lamanites had been calling white men petticoats and saying they were afraid to fight.

He joined the colonists and pushed with them to a southern valley; and after several days of journeying he was appalled by what he saw. Two or three years ago, a body of emigrants, apparently headed for California, had been massacred. The wagons had been burned. Skeletons of men, women and children lay everywhere, all of them scalped, and their bones gnawed clean by wolves. Scalps of women had been hung on bushes along the way, with the long hair hanging in beautiful manes to the ground. The children had been scalped only on their crowns. Scattered around their bleached skulls or down their skeletons were sheaves of dark or golden hair. The bones of all were scarred by wolf teeth. Tough shreds of tendon clung to knees and thighs like dark twisted leather.

The colonists were paralyzed with dread. The women huddled by the wagons, unable to look at the gruesome record; and children clung to them and wept. The men paced back and forth as if half out of their minds and wanted to turn back to the northern settlements.

"No," Bill said. "Brigham told you to colonize in this valley. As for the Indians, in a few days they'll all be dead or chased plumb to hell and gone over the eastern mountains. You just set to work here and don't worry."

And at top speed Bill rode back to equip himself for the fight. He had a great broadsword at his side, a rifle in a saddle sheath, two pistols at his belt, and a long hunting knife. He joined his companions in the Provo area and learned that they were frightened too. They said a hundred and fifty soldiers were not enough.

"Not enough!" Give me ten men like Jim Hirons and Port Rockwell and I'll sock away every redskin in the Basin. I intend to get Big Elk himself."

"You talk pretty mouth-almighty," said a pale young man.

"Well, watch me when I uncork my old yauger."

A man named George Grant had been appointed captain; and three miles from the Indian camp, he organized companies, named officers, and put Bill in charge of the scouts. Then, around a campfire, a council of war was held, and canteens of whiskey passed from hand to hand. Grant's plan of attack disgusted Bill. He sulked, and in his breath cursed the man for a fool; and observing his scowling silence, Grant at last turned to him.

"Bill, I ain't heard you say what you think."

"I think you have a good plan to sock us all away. The only way to fight Indians is to slip up on them and let them have both barrels right in their eye."

Grant smiled. He fancied himself as a shrewd strategist. "You must be down at the heel. Here, wipe off your chin."

Grant passed the canteen but Bill did not drink. He cared little for whiskey, and not at all when his task was to sock away a bunch of crafty warriors. "You can't fight Indians if you march out in the open and bang away. They'll hide behind trees and pick us off. We should sneak up at daylight and ride like hell into their camp and blow their heads off before they know we're there."

"No," said Grant, shaking his head. "You don't know much about Indian warfare. We'll place the cannon on the south side the river and two companies on the north side, one above and one below. You choose twenty horsemen, good horses, good sabers and pistols. We'll chase the Indians out and you dash in and chop them up."

That, Bill, reflected, was the stupidest plan he had ever heard of. A man must be full of whiskey to think he could chase Indians out of their hiding place by shooting at them with a cannon. "You're the general," said Bill, "but all the Indians you chase out I'll eat for supper tomorrow night."

"By gad, you'll have a bellyful."

The next morning the cannon was put in place and the companies took their position across from it. Then the barrage began. The Indians were down on the river in a thicket of willows and cottonwood, but there was no sign of them except a little smoke from their fires. The cannon roared and shook the hillside; the muskets from the opposite hill poured a steady stream of lead into the brush. Bill with his men watched from an eminence some distance to the west. Now and then he saw a soldier fall, and men rush up to carry the wounded man away; for there they were, the stupid blockheads, right out in the open with the redskins sniping at them. If he had ever seen a worse piece of folly, Bill could not remember it. The cannon roared again and again, the muskets blazed all morning and afternoon; but except for the puffs of smoke from hidden guns down by the river, there was no sign of an Indian anywhere. Grant had believed that by firing from both sides into the thicket, he would scare the Indians out like a nest of rabbits. He had even said that the cannon balls crashing through the trees would drive them out in such haste that they would forget their rifles.

"Did you," asked Bill of Jim Hirons, "ever see such dumbness?"

"Nope," said Jim, a quiet heavy man who for hours had pulled calmly at his pipe and waited. "I reckon Grant don't know much about redskins."

"How many of our men is dead now, you figger?"

"I see them carry five away."

"And all they've done is trim off the twigs and blow the tops off of a couple of cottonwoods."

When sunset drew near, Bill turned to his twenty picked men. "Boys, it ain't orders but let's dash up to that Indian camp and give them a blast or two."

"Sure," said Jim, and put his pipe away.

"You all ready?"

"Let's go."

And down the hill they went at full speed. A hundred yards from the camp they stopped and fired and then rode furiously away. Bill heard bullets whistling near him but none of his men was touched. A few minutes later, Grant's bugler sounded retreat, and the Indians set up a howl of victory as if a thousand devils had been turned loose. Bill grinned. In camp he went among the men and learned that several had been killed or wounded.

After supper, Grant called his officers around him and stared solemnly at Bill. "My plan didn't seem to work. What do you advise?"

"Advise, hell! The plan I had won't work now. We should a-surprised them and socked them away. Now they know we mean fight."

"Do you think we wiped out a part of them?"

"I don't think all your chained lightnun hit a single hair of their heads."

"All day long," said Grant sadly, "I didn't see a gol-darned Indian. I almost decided there wasn't any."

"I guess you heard their yells."

"God, yes. It sounded like a million of them. Well, Bill, what is your plan?"

"I'n see only one way now. Choose five captains and let them pick ten men each. Just before daylight, let them crawl up as close as they'n get and hide in the grass and pick off the redskins as fast as they show their feathers. You stay with the other men out of gunshot where you'n watch; and when it looks like the right time dash in and we'll mop them up."

"You think that will work, Jim?"

"It's the only way I'n see."

"All right, we'll try it. I'll choose the captains and you pick your men."

Early the next morning, Bill and his ten men crawled foot by foot on their bellies over the earth until they were within eighty yards of the camp. Looking out cautiously, Bill could see the camp stirring, and a big Indian peering from behind a cottonwood tree. Whispering to his men, Bill told them to crawl forward until they all lay in a line; and to rest their rifles and choose something that looked like an Indian. To Jim he said: "I'll take that big scoundrel behind the tree. I figger to shoot his left eye out." He looked right and left at his men. "Get ready," he whispered. "Fire!"

Eleven muskets roared. The Indian at whom Bill fired pitched forward with a hideous yell and sprawled on his face. The other squads were firing now; and after the first volley, there was not a sound or a movement in the camp. One of Bill's men, losing his nerve, suddenly leapt up and yelped as if he had been knifed. For a moment he looked around him wildly and then dashed blindly into a tree. The impact knocked him down but almost at once he was on his feet again and going like the wind, with a dozen Indians shooting at him.

"I'll be dusted out!" said Bill in disgust. "I didn't know I had such a brave man in my company."

"He must a-seen an Indian," whispered Jim.

"Mebbe a muskeeter bit him. Look, see that face in the leaves over there?"

"No," said Jim.

"I think it's a face. I'll find out." Bill fired. There was a terrific yell as an Indian leapt four feet into the air and came down as if diving into a pool.

Until late afternoon the five squads lay behind their mounds and fired at everything in the camp that moved. There was no sound of a bugle. There was no order from Grant to charge. Bill knew that many of the Indians must be dead or wounded, because a most dismal wailing came from the brush as if every squaw were kneeling by a dead warrior. Toward evening the bugle sounded retreat and the squads turned around on their bellies and crawled away.

By God!" said Bill, getting to his feet. "A breakfast spell of Indians and
hain't socked them away yet."

im filled his pipe. "I think Brother George should ought to go back to
wives."

The next day was Sunday and Grant said there would be prayer and
rship instead of fighting. But Bill was curious. He was restless. He per-
ded Grant to choose fifty men and ride around the camp to learn how
ngs looked. Bill had not gazed long at the brush by the river before he
cided that the Indians were all dead or gone.

'Jim, let's dash in and see."

"Suits me," said Jim.

The two men rode down the hill and into the camp, firing their pistols
d yelling with all their might. There was no need to fire. Except the
ad and wounded and a few sick children, the camp was deserted. As
e men rode in, a warrior with a broken back tried to crawl into hiding,
hands clutching shrubs to drag himself along; and another, who had
ost of his face shot away, reached for a bow and arrow. Bill fired with
pistol into the Indian's skull.

There were eleven dead warriors in one pile. The sick and frightened
ildren were huddled together, moaning desolately; and almost within
ach of them lay two dead squaws. Everything in the camp had been
rned except the sick and wounded and dead. When Grant rode in, the
pelessly wounded were shot, and the others were sent to the City of
eat Salt Lake for treatment.

"Now what can we do?" asked Bill a few hours later.

"Well, down on Spanish Fork is another gang on the warpath. Pick
ur men and scout their position."

"Suits me dandy. Lot and Jim and John, let's go."

Mounted on fast horses, the four men rode south, only to discover that
e Indians on Spanish Fork had fled. They had, Bill soon learned, left
ies here; for an arrow came so close to his face that he felt the wind of it.
Iell!" he roared, and looked around him. He saw his foe, a big buck in a
icket fifty yards away; and with a furious yell he dug spurs in his horse
d bore down. The Indian left the brush and set off at full speed across a
earing. Deciding he would rather clout the rascal than shoot him, Bill
lloped alongside, leaning forward with his big sword ready, and hit
e terrified fellow a terrific blow across his skull. The Indian fell; and

Bill, unseated by the force of the blow and the weight of the sword, went down with him. In the next instant he leapt to his feet and buried the sword in the dazed man from his breast bone to his crotch. When he drew the wet blade out he did not wipe it.

"An old man in the city gave me this sword," he said, speaking to his men who had ridden up and were staring at him. "He said he wanted to wipe it off when I got back."

Jim looked at the dead Indian. "It looks like you just about gutted him."

"He made me mad," said Bill.

The scouts returned to camp and reported, and then rode westward in vain search of Indians. Bill said he thought they ought to finish the band they started with. They were only three miles up the canyon. He set off with Jim and now and then climbed the canyon wall to look ahead but they saw no sign of Indians. Bill was almost convinced they had disappeared over the eastern range when, upon looking down, he saw them in a ravine. He ducked with Jim behind a pile of rocks.

"They ain't seen us yet."

"They don't act like it," said Jim.

"What'll we do?"

"Let's give them a shot apiece."

"Then what?"

"By God, if they don't run, we will."

"All right. Pick your man."

They both fired and two Indians fell. The others scattered and fled, with the two scouts firing at them as fast as they could load their guns. As far as Bill could see the frightened Indians, they were going up the canyon at full speed. Turning, he waved his hat at Grant to advance with the company, and then went with Jim to the warriors they had slain.

"By God," said Jim, "you shot Big Elk!"

"Big Elk? I guess I did," said Bill, looking at the dead chieftain. "Jim Bridger has offered a hundred dollars for his head."

"You better whack it off."

Bill seized Big Elk by his heels and dragged him across a fallen tree, with the neck on the trunk, and then drew his sword. "I scalped a half-breed once," he said, "but I never whacked off a head before." Jim stared up the canyon to see if the Indians were returning and then watched the bloody severing of the head. Bill had cut through the throat to the bone.

He rolled the body over and cut across the back of the neck and around on either side.

"He's got a lot of blood in him."

"He sure has," said Jim. "Looks like you shot him through the heart."

"Looks like it," said Bill, pulling a buckskin shirt aside to look at the wound. "This sword won't have no edge on it when I get through this bone."

"Find a joint," said Jim.

Bill grasped the long hair and twisted the head around, probing meanwhile with the point of the sword.

"He's a big bastard," said Jim. "He's about the best-lookun Indian I ever did see."

"He won't have any head on him in a minute." With one hand Bill jounced the head up and down on the log and with the other he probed and cut. In a few moments he lifted the severed head by its hair. "Ain't that a blanket?"

"Yes," Jim said.

"I'll wrap it up in that. I want to see George's brave soldiers when they find it." He wrapped the head in the blanket and laid the bundle on a huge stone. Then by its heels he dragged the body to a clump of bushes and thrust the neck out of sight so that Grant's men would not see that it was decapitated. Big Elk's gun and bow and arrows he hid. Then he went with Jim a little way up the canyon and lay behind a pile of rocks and waited.

For most of Grant's soldiers he had contempt. When facing redskins in battle they turned pale and shook all over, but around the campfire afterward they boasted of the Indians they had slain. They were eager to possess bows and arrows and other trifles to carry home as evidence of their prowess as warriors; and Bill knew they would be curious to learn what was in the blanket.

He was right. When the soldiers came to the scene and saw the two dead Indians, they ran around like children, looking for souvenirs. Three of them saw the blanket and grabbed for it. When the head rolled out, they leapt back, aghast, with their eyes almost popping out of their skulls. Other soldiers came up and the whole lot of them jabbered like excited monkeys.

"Brave men," said Bill.

"Danged if they ain't," said Jim.

Bill rose and approached the men. "Any of you boys want that as a little relic of your bravery?"

"That head?" asked one, and shuddered.

"It's Big Elk's head. If you took it back to the city you'd be a hero."

"You killed Big Elk?" asked George Grant.

"Well, he looks dead to me."

"Then," said Grant, "I guess this war is over for good and all."

Bill mounted his horse and Jim handed him the head, now wrapped securely in the blanket, and Bill set off for home. On arriving there, he put the head in a big can and buried it to await the coming of Jim Bridger. He doubted that Bridger would ever come. That crafty scout had been inciting the Indians to attack the saints and he knew better than to come within Brigham Young's dominion.

CHAPTER XV

S O YOU THINK," SAID BRIGHAM, "THAT JIM BRIDGER HAD A HAND IN THIS? All right, Bill, keep your eye peeled for him, and if he shows his face around here, we'll run him out."

"I think he was at the bottom of it. I never liked that man's eyes. If he pokes his sneakun face around here, I'll make him hungry for a long journey."

Brigham gazed at his fearless scout. "So you think our Indian troubles are ended."

"For a while anyway."

"Well, we have plenty of other troubles. A lot of the saints are getting the gold fever. A lot of the sisters want to marry the scoundrels who come through here. If we don't do something about it, our city will be nothing but disease and whorehouses."

"What you want me to do?"

"Nothing right now, Bill—except to keep your eyes open and report to me daily. I want to know every single thing that's going on."

"You'n count on me."

Brigham also spoke to Heber of the matter, and Heber gloomily admitted that things looked bad. The thousands of men pouring through had brought venereal infections with them. Hundreds of them paused to seduce or marry the Mormon girls. Hundreds arrived too late to continue their journey and saw that they would have to winter here; and though a few were sincerely converted to the new faith, a great many only pretended to be. Back in Illinois they had heard from John Bennett and others that the Mormons were polygamous; and they wanted several wives while sojourning in Zion. Dozens of them, embracing the new religion and submitting to baptism and blessings, married girls and then deserted them, leaving pregnant and destitute, and sometimes diseased, women for the church to take care of.

"We warned the sisters," Heber said.

"Yes, God yes, a thousand times! Still they marry the villains, unable to tell the genuine from the counterfeit. If it keeps up much longer, I'll have a few of the ungodly rascals socked away. That will be a service to humanity and to God."

"We have bold men who will do the job."

"Yes. Heber, if the leaders would do their duty and marry all these unmarried women. . . . And there's another problem now. All these scoundrels have been talking about polygamy and they have the saints suspicious again. Just when I got them to work and forgetting their gossip, this had to happen. Little by little, the truth is leaking out."

"Why not announce plural marriage now?"

"I'm afraid to, Heber. A lot of the saints will take it just as hard as we did. I wanted to establish them in homes first and make them feel happy and secure. But the time is coming when we must tell. How many wives do you have?"

"More than thirty."

"I could support a few more," said Brigham, "but the ones I have are driving me crazy with their damned complaints."

"It's the truth," said Heber, and sighed. "Sometimes I want to tell mine to go to hell across lots. Their faith is as shallow as water in a tin plate."

"But a lot of the leaders ain't doing their duty. Parley has only eight wives. They hang back."

"I can understand that," said Heber. He smiled. "Some of the brothers say they don't understand women."

"Damn it, sometimes I think I don't. They set their minds on clothes and spangles and gewgaws. Well, Heber, see about the temple plans. And did you know all our beet sugar equipment smashed down out of Leavenworth?"

"It takes strong wagons to haul fifty tons of machinery across a desert." Heber rose. He looked at Brigham's face, thinking that the last few years had aged it, had bleached and furrowed it; but there was the same unconquerable will in the gray eyes. "I'll see about the plans," he said.

"And keep your eyes open. We won't marry the sisters to any more of these men until we know the men are sincerely converted. We should have them all examined for disease, too."

As Heber left the office, he saw several persons waiting to see Brigham; for Brigham had become oracle, guardian and godfather to thirty thousand souls. They came for encouragement, for money or food, for advice in the most trivial matters. One woman wanted to know if it was better to wear red or yellow flannel next to her skin. "Yellow," Brigham had said, but his eyes had twinkled. Another asked if she ought to give her sick baby sagebrush tea or a physic. A third wanted to know if it was more healthful to eat fried or boiled meat. All questions, no matter how silly, Brigham answered gravely and hid his mirth.

The woman who came in now looked as if she had lost all her friends. She was poorly clothed and undernourished. Her eyes were red from weeping; her nose was full of dead sniffles and sobs. She was pregnant.

"I am Minnie Harris."

"Yes, Sister Minnie. What can I do for you?"

Minnie blew her nose into an old stocking. "President Young, I'm in trouble."

"I can see that. What is it?"

"I married Thad Gosser."

"You mean one of the rascals headed for the gold mines?"

"I didn't know he was a rascal. He's deserted me."

"Did he become a member of our church?"

"Oh, yes. He went to church every Sunday." Minnie began to weep.

"Are you the only woman he married?"

"No. I thought I was for a while."

"How many did he marry?"

"Three that I know about. That is, besides me."

"Are they all going to have babies?"

"Two of them. But that ain't the worst," she said, and blew her pale nose again. "Just before he left, he told me he had a wife back in the States."

Brigham's tired face burned with anger. "Sister Minnie, you heard me in public meeting tell you again and again to leave these men alone. Why didn't you?"

"Because," she said, meeting his gaze, "I wanted a husband. There's a lot more women here than men. The saints who come from England and other places, they're mostly women."

"I know that. But I told you to leave these damned scoundrels alone."

"I know you did. But I'm twenty-nine, President Young. I couldn't wait forever to have babies."

"Nonsense! Some of the sisters never got married till they were past forty. It's better to have no babies than to have them in sin."

"You ain't fair!" she cried. The pale trembling creature rose to her feet. "How was I to know Thad didn't mean it? He was baptized. He went to church."

"He ought to have his throat cut from ear to ear."

"No!"

"Well, Sister, mebbe one of the brothers will marry you. I'll see."

He walked over and opened the door for her. Shaking with grief and fear, she went abjectly, clasping hands to her belly as if to protect the child. Though other persons were waiting to see him, Brigham sat in thought for half an hour, wondering how many of the women had been betrayed and deserted. Some of them, too ashamed or too proud, were hiding their guilt.

An agitated woman entered. She was tall and slender, with a tiny birthmark on one cheek, ugly teeth, and drooping lower eyelids. She said her name was Biddy Fox.

"Set down, Sister. What's your trouble?"

"My husband."

"All right: tell me about it."

"Well," she said, pulling her long upper lip over her misshapen teeth, "he don't treat me fair. Take last night. He got mad at me. He told me to go to hell."

Brigham's smile was barely perceptible. "Don't go," he said gravely.

"What?"

"Stay right here." Brigham never knew what to advise in a case of this kind. Even Heber had told some of his wives to go to hell. Biddy reminded him of a few whom he had married: gaunt women with determined chins who raised Cain over a thousand trifling matters. "We all speak with temper sometimes. Go back to your house and your work. As long as you are righteous you have nothing to worry about."

"No man can tell me to go to hell."

"It seems that one did. But I say again, *don't go.*"

The next visitor was a man. He was tall and rugged but he seemed to have a disposition that had soured. He blurted out his story: he had fallen in love with a girl but Heber Kimball was determined to marry her. "In fact," said the man, "he did."

"Nonsense! Heber has a wife."

"Yes, by God—several wives. You leaders ain't foolun all of us. It's about time you told the truth. Take my girl: Heber told her she'd have more glory in the next world if she married him. Me, what can I offer? In the next life, Heber will be up in the highest glory and I'll be down in the cellar. Why should any woman marry me?"

Brigham had been thinking fast. It would do no good to lie to this man about plural marriage: Heber had told the girl and the girl had told him. "It is true," said Brigham, "that God gave a revelation on plural marriage, and that a few of us have more than one wife. But that is a secret yet for a while." Brigham's gaze narrowed as he came forward. "Do you understand me?"

"I guess you mean I'm to keep my mouth shut. But, by God, I tell you a lot of them know. This girl of mine, she told more than me."

"I'll see her. I'll shut her mouth. And as for you, a lot of the sisters want husbands. Find another girl."

"I won't marry just any homely old horse. I pick me a girl and I don't want Heber or anyone to cotton up to her. I'm gettun damned tired of it."

"Cut out the profanity."

"Oh, the hell I will! Why, you cuss right in your sermons."

Brigham smiled faintly. "I save all my cussing for my sermons. That's where I need emphasis."

"Well, I need some emp—empasis," the man said. "I had another girl but one of them-there hellhounders grabbed her. I should a-blowed that son-of-a-bitch's brains out."

"It might have been a good thing," said Brigham gently. "Well, what do you ask me to do?"

"See that the next time I find a girl I marry her."

"What if she don't want you?"

"She'll want me if you big celestial glory fellers don't shine up."

Brigham's face broke into one of his rare smiles. "All right, pick your girl and I'll see that you get her."

"You mean that?"

"I always mean what I say. I'n never find time to say what I don't mean. And I mean it when I say you'd better watch your tongue and not say anything about plural marriage."

"Well, if I don't get the girl ——"

"Don't make any threats. It gets my Yankee dander up."

The next person who entered was one of the wives of John Lee, a handsome, fearless man who was one of Brigham's chief colonizers. When Brigham saw this woman, he could think only of the word thin: her face was long and thin, with a sharp misshapen blade of a nose, with pale thin hide drawn tightly over her sunken cheeks to the aggressive bone of her chin. Her forearms looked like brown withered tendons; her hands were only bone and skin and bluish nails.

"President Young, I need help." Even her voice was thin and nasal.

"How?"

"John ain't fair to me."

"In what way?" he asked, reflecting that her eyes resembled those of a flesh-eating bird.

"As I understand it, plural marriage means a man treats all his wives alike. It ain't right," she said, her eyes chilled by memories, "to love some wives more than others."

"Of course not."

"It ain't right to love some and beat the others."

"Does John beat you?"

"You couldn't call it love. Not if a man slaps you and calls you names."

"Mebbe you bother too much about love. If you have children and bring them up in righteousness ——"

"But a woman can't have children all by herself."

"No," he said, remembering that some of his wives had told him that. Just the same, many of the sisters seemed to think a man had nothing to do except to love them. They were avid, they were insatiable, in their hunger for silly trifling gestures of devotion. This woman was growing old; and doubtless John was spending his energy on the younger women in his household. Some women became intolerably greedy for affection when middle age closed around them.

"Doesn't he ever visit you any more?"

"Never!" Her vehemence startled him. "If I ask why, he says he's busy. Oh, he's busy all right—with the young girls he's married. And how much longer do we have to pretend one of us is a wife and all the others sisters or something? We can't keep that up forever."

"No," Brigham admitted, "we can't. Well, Sister, you have children. Some of my wives have none."

"That's your fault," she said.

The boldness of that statement nonplussed him. He felt anger but his voice was quiet when he spoke. "Not all women seem endowed to have children. As for you, I can see no reason to complain."

"I could have more children. It's my right. I just as well be an old maid as the way I live now. He spends all his time with his young wives and the Lord never meant plural marriage to be that way."

Brigham was bored. For a moment he played with the thought that the most unfortunate and pitiable man in the world was he who took more wives than one. Their demands wore you out. No matter what you did, they felt neglected and cheated and shoved out of the sun of their husband's affection. They were so earthy, so much of the flesh and so little of the spirit, so vain and soulless and petulant, that he sometimes wondered if they understood the new gospel in which they lived. If a man kissed and hugged a wife, she dimpled and turned playful like a kitten, and wanted to know if he loved her better than the others; and if he said no, he loved them all equally, then she thought he was a liar or a fool. The benevolently impartial devotion of a man to a score of women, they could not understand or believe in.

Meanwhile, this gaunt and unhappy woman had been gazing at him. "Sister, I often think that all women must despise one another. They are so vain and petty and spiteful that I doubt they have the spirit of the Lord in them."

"I suppose," she said acidly, "you're talking about your wives now."

"I'm talking," he said sharply, "about all of you. Most of you want only this dress or that bauble, this stick of furniture, that string of beads. You are slaves to style. You think your husbands have nothing to do but dance around you and bow and fawn and kiss your hands and tell you how sweet and charming you are." He rose and faced her. "The men here—and the women too," he said, his voice turning cold, "have a job. They have a kingdom to build, a gospel to spread throughout the world. There is no time, no place, no need for nagging and complaints. You go back to your home and work and children, and do not displease the Almighty who is watching over us."

The woman rose too and looked at him with distaste that was pale and sharp. But she had no will to oppose a man who seemed to be made of granite from his firm feet to his cold eyes. "You'n say it's all for the best but God doesn't."

"Good day," he said, and opened the door for her.

Brigham sat at his desk, feeling anger running through him in a mighty current. Half his time was wasted by saints whose interest lay less in serving the Lord, in building His kingdom, than in ministering to the petty wants of their flesh. Not often did he lose patience with them; but today this spiteful woman annoyed him, perhaps because she reminded him of some of his wives who fought for trivial advantages, for cheap personal triumphs. Some of them candidly hated one another. Some of them he wanted to turn over his knees and spank until their teeth rattled.

The next persons to enter were Tim McBride and his father Moroni. Brigham was a little startled: he had in Nauvoo married Tim's girl and had not learned whether the hotheaded Irishman had forgiven him. Moroni he had seen many times since coming across the Plains.

"We wanted to talk to you a minute," said Tim.

"All right. What about?"

"About the United Orders. It's our understanding you're going to establish them here in Zion. Is that right?"

"Yes," said Brigham. "But I'll have to wait, Brother Timothy, until some other things are out of the way."

"Well, my father and me, we want to go south a few miles and start a colony. We wondered if you'd let us go ahead with an Order there. Everybody wants one. We plan to share everything in common, just like God told Joseph we should. We'll be equal in management and ownership and profits."

"Don't you think we should wait until we've settled some other problems? We have to take care of these scoundrels coming through; and now I have Federal appointees on my hands."

"You're the boss," said Tim—and Brigham felt that he was forgiven. "Father, he thinks it was the greatest revelation ever given to Joseph, and we want to work it out. That's all."

"It was a great revelation. But we must wait a while."

Moroni was tugging thoughtfully at a handsome beard. "When you'll let us begin," he said, "tell us. We can line up a colony and move south. We plan to have stores, mills, shops and even farms and vegetable gardens all in common."

"That," said Brigham, "is the way the Lord wants it." He looked searchingly at the two men. "You remember I gave you permission to take more wives?"

"Yes," said Moroni calmly.

"We have a lot of sisters in Zion who can't find husbands. Celestial marriage is still a secret, but if you brethren want more wives——"

"I have three," said Moroni. "I married Agatha and Maggie that I spoke about back in Iowa. They didn't have any home, so I gave them one. I could support another wife or two, I guess."

"Brother Timothy?"

"I have two now."

"Are any of the brethren taking wives without my permission?"

"None that I know of."

"If you hear of any, let me know. No brother is privileged to take a wife without my permission. And I don't want any brethren taking wives except those who will keep it a secret."

"You can't keep it a secret much longer. All the saints talk about it and wonder if it's true or not."

"Brother Timothy, can't you support more than two wives? I want the sisters taken care of."

"I'm more interested in the United Orders," said Tim with dignity, "than I am in wives."

Brigham turned his cold gaze on Tim. "Didn't you belong to the Danites in Missouri?"

"I did."

"Aren't you one of the survivors of the Haun's Mill butchery?"

"I am—and so is my father. My mother too."

"I was thinking," said Brigham, "I might need you—if my enemies get too thick. Would you accept a dangerous assignment?"

"If the Lord asks me to. I'd much rather establish a United Order."

"We'll get to that a little later."

After they left, Jedediah Grant strode in. Brigham admired the burning zeal of this man but he did not love him; for nobody, it seemed to him, could love a man who looked like a hybrid of saint and fox, whose eyes were so close together and humorously cunning, whose mouth was so thin and piously severe—as if it had bitten deep into the ungodliness of the world and found that the core was a lemon. Jedediah was the firebrand of the church and loved his job. No matter where his pale eyes looked, they saw sin, the voluptuous and the carnal—until he roared with fury in his sermons, and screwed his lips into a pronouncement of doom.

"Brother Jedediah, you look upset."

"I am. Matters are going from bad to worse. If they keep on, you'll have another stinking Babylon or Rome right under your nose."

"What have you seen now?"

Jedediah pushed his chair forward. He drew his thin lips into a characteristic pucker. "Brigham, no matter where I go, I see sin. There's thieving, lying, blasphemy, bad habits. But worst of all," he added, tightening his hands, "is adultery. I think the time has come for a reformation."

"You said that last year and the year before."

"I say it again. You won't listen. You'll let sin flower here until you have another Garden of Eden."

That declaration startled Brigham. It seemed silly to speak of evil and a garden in the same breath. "The time might come when we have to purge the church. I don't think it has come yet."

"I know it has," said Jedediah, looking as if he had just come from a seraglio. "If you don't drive the sinners out, God will strike us down. There'll be plague and famine and pestilence. He'll send the locusts again."

"Is there really so much wickedness?"

"It's everywhere. Last night," he said, lowering his voice and looking preposterously secretive, "I was walking along South Temple Street. What did I see? I saw a brother sneaking out of the house where one of the sisters lives alone. That's not the only case. It's everywhere. After midnight there are orgies that would make you and me as red as a painted Indian."

Brigham smiled. He knew there were thieves and adulterers, but he did not believe matters were as dark and terrible as Jedediah declared. "Right now we have more serious troubles. We have the babies and disease left by the gold-seekers. We have something that might prove to be worse than that."

"What?" asked Jedediah.

"These Federal officers. So you watch the saints and tell me what you see while I take care of these damned jackasses President Fillmore is dumping on our doorsteps. Then we'll talk about a purge."

"I tell you, Brigham, a reformation is imperative!"

"All right, all right. But let me take care of the jackasses first."

CHAPTER XVI

CONGRESS HAD MADE SHORT WORK OF DESERET AND HAD ORGANIZED THE Territory of Utah. Brigham's people had elected him governor, but he soon learned that a man could be governor in name only. He had thought he and his people would be left alone in this valley; and he was angry when he learned that Federal officers were being sent out to tell him what he could or could not do. That was not the worst of it: the men who were sent had no knowledge of the temper of the saints or their conditions, and no sympathy for them. Why, Brigham thundered from the pulpit, should he tolerate the asses? And his people knew that he was girding for a fight.

He would have been less belligerent if Fillmore had sent men of tolerance and principle instead of the sorriest lot of petty shysters Brigham had seen since he left Illinois. Because their salaries were small, he suspected that these men were coming as adventurers or spies. He was convinced of it the moment he laid eyes on Perry Brocchus, the man sent out to be Federal judge.

"You are Mr. Young?" asked Brocchus, walking unexpectedly into Brigham's office.

"I am."

For a long moment the two men gazed at one another. Brigham's snap judgment was later sustained by men who wrote about Brocchus: he was vain and egocentric, a corrupt and vengeful hypocrite full of petty intrigues. In appearance he was slovenly. His clothes were untidy and soiled, his ragged mustaches still wore the grease and crumbs from his breakfast, his nails were black with filth. He had crafty eyes that were incongruous above the well-fed and placid expanse of plump cheeks and jowls. He was a fine chief justice, Brigham reflected sourly; but he was determined to live at peace with him as well as with the other pompous simpletons if they were impartial and minded their own business.

"I see you're sizing me up," the plump fox said.

"Yes, Judge. I hear that you're politically ambitious. You want to be delegate to Congress from this Territory."

A flush dyed his fat cheeks and enhanced by contrast the cunning of his pale eyes. "Why yes, Mr. Young, I had some such thought." He recovered quickly and added: "I am a receptive candidate."

Brigham barely restrained a smile. Could anyone be sillier, he wondered, than this fatuous gentile who fancied that Mormons would send him as their delegate to Congress? "I suppose you'd like to address my people in public meeting."

"Yes, that would please me very much. Right now, though, I came to ask you about one of your leaders named Daniel Wells. Didn't he say publicly the other day that the purpose of the United States is to exterminate the Mormons?"

"He did," said Brigham, wishing the hotheaded Dan would keep his mouth shut. "You will have to distinguish, Judge, between those who speak with authority here and those who don't. Remember that we were driven out of the United States."

"Yes, I know," said Brocchus, and fingered his soiled whiskers.

"The guarantee of freedom in the Constitution we have never had. Mobs drove us out of New York, Ohio, Missouri, Illinois."

"Yes," said the judge impatiently, "I know about all that."

"Then you should understand why some of the saints feel bitter about it."

"Saints," said Brocchus, as if tasting the word. His eyes were slyly alert. "You call all your people saints?"

"We are the latter-day saints. You may recall, Judge, that Jesus was the Son of God but they crucified Him."

"Yes," said Brocchus, not missing the innuendo.

"We were driven out here to a desert. We——"

"You are doing remarkably well," said Brocchus, looking out a window. "You are going to have a very fine city."

"We came to a desert," Brigham resumed, frowning at the interruption, "of sagebrush and coyotes and Indians and wolves. It might interest you to know that my brother set poison on his doorstep one night right here in the city and found thirteen dead wolves there the next morning. We have fought against rats and mice and bedbugs by the millions; against crickets and grasshoppers by the thousands of tons; against famine, disease, Indians and cold."

"But why are you telling me all this?"

Brigham's eyes turned cold. "I do not understand why the Federal government which allowed us to be driven out cannot assume now that we can appoint our own officers. If you came out here to spy on us and send reports to Washington, say that we're fighting for our lives and will not run this time. Do you understand me?"

"Yes," said Brocchus uneasily. "Governor, is it true that you have a secret body of avengers called Danites?"

That was a bold question. For a moment Brigham looked at the judge and wondered how long it would be before he chased him out or had him socked away. "All pioneer communities, Judge, have vigilantes when necessary to preserve law and order. We do not tolerate thieves and whoremasters in our midst."

That made Brocchus stiffen. "But if you have judges and courts, I see no need of vigilantes."

"That depends on the judges and the courts. Some of them are as corrupt as the scoundrels who come before them for trial."

"I see," said the judge, wagging his head. "Well, Mr. Young, I'll be very glad to speak to your people."

"May I ask what you wish to say?"

"Oh," said Brocchus evasively, "just some general remarks. In my official capacity, you know."

Brigham looked at him sharply. "All right, Judge. I'll let you speak at the general conference."

A few days later, the bowery was jammed to the doors, with thousands outside, eager to hear what the new judge had to say. What he had to say was, for the most part, innocuous enough: he was glad to be here, he hoped he would be of service, he had found the valley peaceful and prosperous. He said he did not seek to be delegate from the Territory; but if elected he would strive for the good of the persons he represented. After these casual remarks, his next words made Brigham and his leaders sit up.

Brocchus declared flatly that the United States had not been responsible for the persecutions in Missouri and elsewhere; and that he and all other respectable citizens had boiled with rage. "I have heard," he went on, "that some of you here declared that the United States is a stink in your nostrils, and is going to hell as fast as it can. I have heard that your leader on the death of our dear President Zachary Taylor said that Taylor was dead and gone to hell and he was glad of it. I regret to say that such remarks make me suspect your loyalty. But perhaps we can adjust these matters. Perhaps you will realize in time the obligations you owe to your constitution and your flag."

From that rebuke he stepped boldly to dangerous ground. He said he would now address the women; and he praised their thrift, the neat appearance of their homes, their happy and healthy children. It was the next statement that brought blood to thousands of faces. "To the women of this community I address myself with solemn regard for their welfare when I urge them to make every possible effort to become virtuous."

To the thousands for whom celestial marriage was only so much gossip, a calumnious charge of their enemies, a barefaced lie, the judge's statement was a monstrous insult. For those who knew the truth it was no less damnable because it hinted of vice in a holy covenant from God. A dozen men leapt to their feet to answer him; a thousand voices hissed and jeered. When Brigham rose he was trembling with fury—and all the more because Brocchus had alluded to a matter which he was trying desperately to keep secret. Brigham shouted for silence; and when he had calmed the howling multitude, he spoke clearly and slowly, but his voice shook with anger which he could not control.

"Judge Brocchus is either ignorant or wicked, one of the two. If I were to let some of the men here take the stand, there would be yanking of hair and cutting of throats. I do not want any trouble of that kind. But I do want to say to the judge that the whole civilized world knows that the United States saw us robbed and raped and murdered and driven out and did nothing about it. Hundreds of our men, hundreds of our women and children, are in their graves now, with their spilled blood crying to the Almighty for vengeance. I love the Constitution of the United States and I love my country, but I don't love the damned dirty rascals who administer its government.

"I know Zachary Taylor, he is dead and damned and I cannot help it. And I have no time for such corrupt fellows as Judge Brocchus who comes here to lecture us on morality and virtue. We do not have thieves and scoundrels, self-seeking politicians, murderers or adulterers in our communities. *We do not have whores!* It is an insult to our women for Judge

Brocchus to throw out such a damnable insinuation. I say it is an insult, and I will say no more."

Purple with fury, Brigham strode out, and his leaders and his people followed him.

The judge was angry too, but he was too frightened to do anything about it. He was remembering how Heber Kimball had stepped up to him and tapped him significantly. "Don't doubt that Zachary Taylor is in hell. You'll see him when you get there." Brocchus went off alone and wrote a letter of protest to Brigham, declaring that he intended no insults. Brigham's answer was like the blade of a sword. "Sir, let your good sense, if you have a spark left, answer—could you, had you mustered all the force hell could lend you—could you have committed a greater indignity and outrage on the feelings of the most virtuous and sensible assemblage of ladies that your eyes ever beheld? If you could, tell me how. Shall such insults remain unatoned for?"

That was not the only threat Perry Brocchus received. Of the meeting Brigham had said: "If I had crooked my little finger, he would have been used up. Why, even the sisters would have chopped him to pieces."

That was too much for the judge. Scared out of his wits, he packed his belongings and fled, and the other Federal appointees fled with him. They left the valley as if devils were after them. Brigham's scouts reported that the men rode like mad and never even dared to look back for a hundred miles. When last seen, they were still going at top speed.

Brigham was glad to see them go but he was not unaware that they would raise a great hullabaloo back East. It was not long in coming. Nearly every newspaper and preacher in the nation took up the matter, and amazement and rage poured from the pulpits and the editorial columns. Then something strange happened. The foolish judge, hot-footing it back east to raise a great hue and cry in his defense, damned himself with one statement that turned into a tremendous boomerang. In his report he wrote: "Polygamy monopolized all the women, which made it very inconvenient for the Federal officers there."

That strange confession amazed the country more than the judge's flight. Caustic editors took it up and demanded to know what in the name of hell and heaven Brocchus meant. Did he mean that Mormon women were so chaste that he could find no concubine? Had he been erotically starved? Alas, did the poor fellow's complaint boil down to this, that he had fled the Territory because he could find no mistress?

Reading the eastern papers as they came in, Brigham chuckled with delight. To Heber he said: "It looks like the good judge has done us a favor. The whole country is laughing at him."

Heber smiled and read with gusto an editorial that heaped a thousand words of withering sarcasm upon the judge's head. "I thought he'd cause us a lot of trouble."

"So did I. It shows what was in his mind after all. I'm told he did his best to seduce some of the sisters."

"I know he did. I know one who slapped his face so hard he spun around."

"He thought he was coming to a big seraglio and he couldn't find himself a single concubine." Brigham chuckled and read another editorial. Then he said: "Heber, the time has come to announce the principle of celestial marriage. We've been lying about it too long. John Taylor is lying about it in Paris right now. We just as well come out in the open and let the world know."

Heber was dubious. He fingered his chin whiskers and looked thoughtful. "I ain't so sure," he said.

"We just as well admit what the whole world is accusing us of."

"But a lot of the saints don't know. They've heard all the stories and had suspicions but the authorities have denied them. What will they think now about all our lies in the past?"

"How many do you think really know the truth?"

"Just the leaders including all the bishops. Mebbe a few more who have been let into the secret."

"Well, we'll publish Joseph's revelation. It's been nearly ten years since God revealed it to him."

"You know, Brigham, I'll do anything you want. Just the same, I'm afraid if we announce celestial marriage to the world we'll be in for a lot of trouble."

"Trouble is what we've always had. We just as well take it all in one dose and get it over with."

"What if the Federal government tries to stop us?"

Brigham considered for a moment. "In that case we'll fight."

"Well, just as you say. I kind of wish we had announced it in Nauvoo and got it over with then."

Brigham did not foresee what a violent storm the announcement would bring, both at home and abroad. When on Sunday morning, August 29, 1852, he spoke of the matter in a huge public meeting, and read the revelation which God gave to Joseph, the audience was stunned—or at least that part of it was which had regarded stories of polygamy as monstrous lies. Nor was its astonishment softened by Orson Pratt's long and scholarly preamble in which he explained the meaning of marriage, spoke of Abraham and Sarah and Hagar and cited other instances from the scriptures. All of the saints had long heard rumors of polygamy, but the great mass of them, without important positions in the church and with only one wife, had believed the stories were nothing but gentile rumors. Now the truth was before them. Now they realized that the Nauvoo stories about Joseph had been true. Brigham and Heber and Parley, Orson and John and all the other leaders had more than one wife. Such knowledge was overwhelming—and Brigham knew it when he looked at the faces. He saw anger and dismay, disgust and horror as singly or in groups the majority of the audience rose and left the hall.

In the weeks that followed, scores of them renounced their faith. Some packed their belongings and went to California; others remained to plot against their leaders whom they now looked upon as devils turned out of hell. The local newspaper published the revelation. Eastern editors read it with loud amazement and at once filled their columns with denunciation and abuse; while preachers, choked with rage, thundered from their pulpits. Many congressmen were angry too, and clamored for an army that would march out and exterminate the Mormons. Politicians running for office promised if elected to wipe out the "loathsome lecherous libertines" and the "concupiscent concubinage."

Brigham saw the mighty storm gathering back East but he had little time to think about it. He had too many grave problems among his own people. Among those who plotted against him, Gladden Bishop was the leader, a skulking sinful rogue who had been kicked out of the church and readmitted to it thirteen times. It was not a matter of revulsion with Gladden: he had always lain with as many women as he could. It was ambition. He thought he could overthrow Brigham and take possession of the church; and he set to work recruiting the malcontents and soon had a following of several hundred.

"By God," said Heber one day, "ain't you going to do anything with that scurvy scoundrel Gladden Bishop?"

"What's he up to now?"

"You know. He plans to chase you out. Why don't you stop him?"

"I'll hang him to a tree!"

"Denounce him in meeting next Sunday. Drive him out."

When Brigham rose to denounce Bishop, he was almost as angry as he had been when he answered Brocchus. Why, he roared, did the saints pay any attention to a man who had been thrown out thirteen times for his sinful habits? If they did not like it here, why in hell did they not hit the grit for California and hobnob with gentiles? "Don't stay here and invite persecutions, lest you get more than you know what to do with!"

Nobody missed the threat in that.

His voice rose in anger when he spoke again. "We have known Gladden Bishop for more than twenty years, and know him to be a poor dirty curse! Who broke the roads to this valley? Did these nasty little apostates? No, they stayed in St. Louis while we did it, peddling ribbons and kissing gentiles! I know what they have done here—they have asked exorbitant prices for their stinking little ribbons! We broke the roads. Now you Gladdenites, keep your tongues still, lest destruction come upon you!

"I'll tell you a dream I had. Two murderers crept into bed where one of my wives and children were. I said, 'You that call yourselves brethren, tell me, is this the fashion among you?' They said, oh, they are good men, they are gentlemen! With that I took my large bowie knife and cut one of their throats from ear to ear, saying, 'Go to hell across lots!' The other one said, 'You dare not serve me so.' I instantly sprang at him, grabbed him by the hair of the head, and, bringing him down, cut his throat and sent him after his comrade.

"I say that rather than apostates should flourish here, I will unsheathe my bowie knife and conquer or die!"

Thunderous cheering shook the bowery. Brigham mopped his brow and waited. Then: "You nasty apostates, clear out, or judgment will be put to the line and righteousness to the plummet!"

"Go to it!" a voice yelled. And others: "Go it, go it!"

"If," Brigham said, "you say it is right, raise your hands." Every hand in the audience was raised.

When Gladden Bishop heard of this fiery speech, of this veiled threat against his life, he shook in his boots and fled the city. Others followed him, for they knew that Brigham never made idle threats. They knew too well that if they remained, they would find the shaggy-haired Porter Rockwell or the softly ruthless Bill Hickman on their trail. Besides, they had heard rumors of blood atonement, though they knew of no instances, nor did any of their friends.

Blood atonement was a matter which Brigham had pondered for years. In his practical mind, the Bible was as unmistakably clear as two times two: Jesus had not atoned by His death for at least three sins: murder, adultery, and offense against the Holy Ghost. Did not the twentieth chapter of Leviticus say that the adulterer should be put to death? Did not the ninth chapter of Genesis declare that whoso sheddeth man's blood, by man shall his blood be shed? Did not the sixth chapter of Hebrews make it clear that those who receive and then repudiate the Holy Ghost could never atone by repentance only? Matthew said that those who spoke against the Son of Man could be forgiven, but those who spoke against the Holy Ghost should not be forgiven, neither in this world nor in the world to come. Indeed, the whole doctrine of salvation was founded on blood atonement, and without it there could be no remission of sins.

"The life of the flesh is in the blood," Brigham had said in conference, "and it requires the shedding of blood to make atonement for the soul." He believed that. The twenty-second verse of the ninth chapter of Hebrews declared that all things are purged by the shedding of blood; the seventeenth chapter of Leviticus said the life of the flesh is in the blood and only the blood could atone for the soul; and Jesus Himself cried out that those cast into prison should not come out again until they had paid the uttermost farthing.

That anyone should question biblical laws so explicit seemed to Brigham both stupid and sinful. There was the doctrine from Genesis to Mark. In language a child could understand, there was the statement, a hundred times repeated, that for the remission of the most damnable sins, blood had to be shed. He had preached this doctrine in the pulpit. He had told the saints they were headed for hell if they did not atone in the only way atonement could be achieved. Some of them had followed his advice.

When a man named Alred returned from a mission and learned that his wife had been adulterous, he went to Brigham. "She's awful sorry," he said, looking as if he had not slept for days. "She wants to save her soul."

"Then she'll have to shed her blood."

"That's what I told her."

"That's what the holy book says. There's no argument about it."

Alred went back and explained the matter to his wife; and with her consent, he took her on his lap and kissed her fondly and cut her throat from ear to ear. It was terrible. Nobody knew better than he how terrible it was when her warm blood drenched him; but her soul was saved and he would be with her in the next life. Other men had stabbed or shot their adulterous wives. They preferred privacy in the atonement, even though Jedediah Grant had shouted in public meeting:

"I say that there are men and women that I would advise to go to the President immediately, and ask him to appoint a committee to attend to their case; and then let a place be selected, and let the committee shed their blood!"

And Brigham, following Jedediah, had said: "Let us suppose a case. Suppose you found your brother in bed with your wife, and put a javelin through both of them, you would be justified, and they would atone for their sins, and be received into the kingdom of God. I would at once do so in such a case. I have no wife I love so well that I would not put a javelin through her heart, and I would do it with clean hands."

He believed in such atonement with all his heart, and he called upon the Holy Bible as his covenant and law. Apostates who had received their endowments, who upon accepting that sacred symbolic garment had been blessed by the spirit of the Holy Ghost, were as damned as the lowest thing in hell if they did not shed their blood and make their peace with God. If they had not the courage to do it, then it was merciful for another to do it for them. Brigham was worried by these hundreds of apostates who were throwing their souls to the Devil; but he did not want to send executioners out to save so many.

Jedediah did. "It's terrible!" he cried. "Hundreds of them are going straight to hell and haven't sense enough to know it!"

"That's true. They won't accept Joseph's revelation on celestial marriage. Some of them say it's a forgery."

"Well, you should appoint committees to take care of them. They won't do it themselves. If we don't save them, they will be lost forever."

"There are too many, Brother Jedediah. We can't shed the blood of hundreds."

"I don't see why we can't!" cried Jedediah, his burning gaze on Brigham's face. "We could handle them one by one."

Brigham shook his head sadly. "No. Persons back East are already howling like lunatics and demanding our extermination. If they ever heard of blood atonement— No, Jedediah, we'll have to let them go to hell."

"But what," demanded Jedediah fiercely, "are we to do with all the adulterers? I tell you we'll have a community of bastards."

"What would you do?"

"What you said in meeting. Put a javelin through every one of them."

Brigham grinned. "We haven't enough javelins. Are there so many of them?"

"Dozens of them. A lot of them seem to think celestial marriage just means adultery."

"Well, leave me now, Brother Jedediah. I want to be alone to think about it."

CHAPTER XVII

BRIGHAM HAD HAD THE SAINTS BUILD FOR HIM TWO LARGE HOMES, FRONTing South Temple Street, with two smaller buildings between them, one the tithing office of the church, and the other his own business office. The building farthest west, an imposing structure with many chimneys and gables, was called the Lion House, not only because among his people Brigham was generally known as the Lion of the Lord, but also because there was the figure of a crouching lion over the portico. This long building had sleeping apartments for children on the upper floor; and on the lower floor were the dining room, weaving room, laundry room, as well as chambers for several of his wives. The large home on the east, with two large porches supported by several columns, was called the Beehive House, because the honey bee had been accepted by the saints as a symbol of their thrift and frugality. In this building, known as his official residence, was his own bedroom, as well as the sleeping chambers of many of his wives.

After Jedediah left him, Brigham emerged from the small office between his two homes and went to the street and stood for a long moment in thought. He had intended to enter the Beehive House and seek his room to be alone; but he changed his mind and climbed northward to an eminence where he could sit and gaze at his city. He was proud of it, proud of all that had been done here in a few years. Below and to the right, within the great wall of sandstone that had been erected around the temple grounds, was the tabernacle, a miracle in itself; for under the arched ceiling of this place of worship, there was not a single pillar or column in the hundred and twenty-six feet of length or breadth. The acoustics had amazed every visitor who had entered it. Northeast of the tabernacle, a magnificent temple was being built. It would take a long time to complete it; but when it was done, it would be, Brigham had no doubt, one of the noblest structures in the world. Trees and shrubs had been planted in the grounds and along the streets; and from where he sat he could see flowers blooming.

Some day, perhaps after he was dead, this walled area devoted to God would be visited by millions of persons; and they would marvel at the industry and genius of a people who, herded like cattle into a wilderness, had erected here such a splendid monument to their faith. A block southeast beyond the temple wall was a large adobe structure used for theatricals and balls and feasts. He would build a theater soon, a great university, as well as co-operative banks and shops and stores. Entirely around the city he was having a wall built now: of gravel and mud and straw, it would be twelve feet high and nearly ten miles long. Just why he was building so tremendous a wall he did not know—unless it was to give employment to destitute converts from foreign lands.

Yes, he was proud of what had been accomplished in a few years. The desert *was* blossoming like a rose: south and west was the green of vegetables, the fragrance of orchards, the clean settlements with their broad streets. North and south in the valley were dozens of hamlets; for his empire now lay a hundred and fifty miles across the Basin. Soon he would have colonies far west, south and north—because exploring parties had reported the existence of fertile valleys in all those areas. He would have colonies north as far as Canada, west as far as California, and south to the Mexican border.

In the city at his feet, there was not, so far as he knew, a single gambler or prostitute; and he thought of the hypocritical gentiles back east who howled angrily about celestial marriage—and allowed harlots to swarm in their streets! In a recent sermon he had said: "If you tell a Christian a Mormon has two wives, he is shocked, even though he takes a fresh woman every night! Christian nations license women to open their doors and windows and carry on this abominable practice! New York City alone has fifteen thousand prostitutes and we haven't a single one here, yet they yelp to God of our immoral conduct. The miserable nasty hypocrites!"

Today he was worried by the adulterers in his kingdom. They would be driven out, and the saints would be warned again of the unpardonable consequences of such sinful practice. He would have other speakers address them, though he hardly knew whom to choose: he and Heber and Orson Pratt had spoken so often on the subject; Jedediah Grant was too fanatically violent; but there was Orson Hyde. That good man had once been kicked out of the church, but like Oliver Cowdery he had been readmitted and had been working faithfully and hard. Perhaps he would let Orson speak.

Again Brigham fell to thinking of prostitutes, and of Joseph's resolve, and his own likewise, to have none in the Mormon cities. In Christian nations there were hundreds of thousands of whores, every one of them a woman who could have had children and fulfilled the purpose for which God intended her; but now they were dark and unclean outcasts who sold their bodies to Christian men. During the last twenty centuries there had been millions of such women, burning their souls out in sinful practice, selling themselves to lecherous hypocrites who bought them for a trinket or a coin, slipped with them into a foul place, and returned to their wives and children, to their fawning lip-service to God in whose nostrils they were a stink and a rot.

In his empire, every woman could have a husband and a home. Every woman who needed food and shelter was taken care of. No woman had to slink along dark streets and hawk her soul to the Devil and lie in shame under the guilty breast of a Christian. Yet such were the men now, the preachers and judges back east, the congressmen and editors, who were clamoring for an army to destroy a community that gave to every woman the right of motherhood. He knew their kind. For after Brocchus fled, had he not been replaced by a gambler and a bully who sat on the bench half-drunk, with the harlot at his side whom he had brought with him! He boasted of his mistress in one hour, and penned lurid accounts to the President in the next. He sent his bodyguard to southern Utah to flog a Jew who had spoken disparagingly of a judge who sat on the bench with a prostitute. When Bill Hickman made the same remarks, the judge sent a warrant for his arrest, and Bill returned it with a note saying he would come up and horsewhip him on the bench.

Yes, Brigham knew the souls of the hypocrites who were determined to destroy him. He knew their blatant preachments and their secret practices, and he hated the whole lot of them as he hated hell. If an army was sent against him, he would chop it into pieces; he would teach a nation founded on principles of freedom that a persecuted people would not always flee.

As for polygamy, he was reflecting now, did not the Bible approve it? Orson Hyde in a sermon had argued that Jesus had several wives. If He were to pass through a Christian nation, with women following Him, fondling Him, combing His hair, washing His feet and drying them with the hair of their heads, what would the Christians do? Why, in the name of the God of Israel, they would tar and feather Him, and ride Him out on a rail. Jedediah had argued that Jesus was persecuted because He had several wives. Did not Celsus say so? It seemed to Brigham that Adam was God when he entered the Garden; and he was convinced that Adam was the temporal father of Jesus. To say, as so many did, that the Holy Ghost was the father of Jesus was so much nonsense; because the Holy Ghost was the spirit of the Lord and without flesh and could not beget children. Most theologians were so lost in the fogs of their conceit that they missed the simple truths in the Bible.

There were other proofs of the holiness of polygamy, one of which Heber had mentioned in a sermon. Heber had noticed that a man with only one wife was inclined to wither and dry up, whereas a man with many wives looked young and fresh. Remembering that statement, Brigham smiled, though believing it nevertheless to be true. Heber had more wives than any other saint, and he had the strength and vigor of a giant. Men with only one wife looked sallow and unhappy, like flowers trying to bloom in shaded areas.

He had not come here to inquire if celestial marriage was right. He knew it was. He had come to think about Jedediah's wish for a reformation and a purge. That there was sin in the city below him, Brigham knew well: his spies had told him, as well as his own eyes. There were women who, erotically stupid, chased any man who smiled at them; and men who, unable to understand that polygamy and adultery were as far apart as the Poles, looked upon celestial marriage as a license to lust. There were apostates headed for hell. He did not want to shed the blood of hundreds, even though convinced that it would be better so. He did not mind sending Bill or Porter or another out to kill his enemies—for he was fighting for the life of his people and plotting gentiles knew they were not welcome. Rather than cut the throats of several hundred stupid sinners, he preferred to drive them out and let them settle the score with God. He had thundered warnings year after year; he had exhorted, argued, threatened.

He rose now, feeling a little weary and old, not knowing what was the wisest thing to do, but resolved to speak boldly again in next Sunday's meeting. As he descended the mountain, he thought it would be well to let Orson Hyde speak; for that rugged and somewhat slow-witted fellow was a terrifying orator after he warmed to his subject. He had the passion and ten times the thunder of Jedediah.

In the Sunday meeting, Brigham's sermon did not have the scathing sarcasm or the profane vigor of many of his talks. He gazed upon the thousands and wondered what he could say that he had not said a thousand times. "Brethren and sisters, how odious it was last winter, in the sight of certain men who were here, to think that we had more lawful wives than one; yet they would creep into your houses, and try to coax your wives and daughters away from you. What for? Was it to give them a better character in the midst of the inhabitants of the earth? No—they wanted to prostitute them, to ruin them.

"I do not know what I shall say next winter if such men make their appearance here. I know what I think I'll say if they play the same game again. Let the women be ever so bad, so God help me, we will slay them. If any of you wish to go to California to whore it, we will send a company of them off; that is my mind, and perhaps some few ought to go for they are indeed bad enough. When I was in the southern settlements, there were girls weeping all the time, and they are perhaps in their graves now. The men who coaxed them away did not intend to take them to California. If such happens again, judgment shall be laid to the line, and they say that Brigham does not lie."

He paused. Far down in the audience he saw a grinning scornful face. It angered him. "Listen," he roared, "if there are any damned gentiles or hickory Mormons here, let them write down what I say and send it to Washington! Let them send soldiers here and by the God of Israel, right here on the spot we'll give them the due reward of their crimes! Write that down, you spies, and send it back East!"

Brigham's anger warmed Orson Hyde who had been waiting. He was a thick heavy man, with small eyes and a corrugated brow. When he rose to speak, he was angry too. He smote his left palm with his right fist and wasted no time in preambles.

"What have I to say concerning women that will come into the church and the Kingdom of God, and bring dishonor upon themselves, and endeavor to bring it upon the whole church, by cohabiting with these cursed scapegraces who are passing through here? I'll tell you! I'm going to say something upon those who dishonor the church in this way. I will tell ou what will happen to those men and women who commit lewdness, and go and boast of it, and laugh in the face of heaven.

"The day shall come when their flesh shall rot upon their bones, and as they are walking it shall drop, and become a nauseous stink upon the highway. Now go and boast that you can get all you want for a dress pattern, or a yard of ribbon; go and boast of it, and the Lord Almighty shall curse you all the day long! And when you step, chunks of flesh shall drop from your bones, and stink enough to sicken a dog! And let these contemptible wretches feel the Mormon spirit! I say with Brother Brigham, if such persons come among us and defile our women and our homes, then we'll put righteousness to the plummet and send them straight to hell!

"Do you know what happens to those who persecute us and sin amongst us? I'll tell you. I'll tell you about two of the Missouri mob that Brother Parley saw in Sacramento. One of these men was a colonel in the army that helped plunder and murder the saints. How did he die? I'll tell you. He died with worms in him. He was alive with big black-headed maggots that crawled through him, that went through him a pint and a quart at a time. Before he died, maggots were crawling out of this man's nose and mouth. He rotted alive and died in his rot. The flesh on his legs and arms and chest busted open and fell off his bones. That's how he died. And when he was dead, he was so rotten that nobody would touch him. They raked him into a blanket and carried him off, with the maggots falling out all over him. That, brethren and sisters, is what happens to those sinful devils who persecute the saints!"

The audience was horrified. A few of the women, sickened by such graphic retribution, rose and left the hall. Orson was pleased by the effect of his words; but he was not done.

"How did the other man die, that bloodthirsty mobster who helped drive us out of Missouri and burn our homes? He died of rot, too. The flesh of his face rotted and fell off, and one eye rotted out, and his nose fell off, and all the flesh fell off his jaws, and then the bones of his mouth and jaws fell apart! This man was full of worms, too. They ate through the flesh of his throat and bit into his jugular vein and he bled to death. He stunk so bad that no one could be in the same room with him. No one could stand it to brush the flies away, and they kept depositing more fly blows on him and these hatched into new swarms of maggots; and before the man bled to death he was actually crawling.

"Brethren and sisters, that's how two of our enemies died in Sacramento. That's the curse God put upon them; and that's the curse God will put upon you if you don't turn from your sinful ways and stop denying the spirit of the Holy Ghost!"

It was a shamed and silent people when they left the hall. Jedediah came to Orson and clasped his hand. "It was a fine talk," he said. "Maybe they'll think twice about their sinful ways now. Brother Brigham, did you notice how affected they were?"

"Yes," said Brigham, remembering the horrified faces.

"The time is ripe," said Jedediah. He was eager to reprove and exhort and baptize.

But the reformation had only begun when a major disaster struck the valley.

Brigham had many problems besides the sinfulness among his people. He had pushed colonization beyond the Territory of Utah—northward beyond Snake River in a valley he had named Limhi, and southward to the great canyon of the Colorado River; and in these far-flung settlements, Indians were murdering and scalping. There was the problem also of emigration. From England and elsewhere, the converts were coming by the hundreds; and because he could not spare men and wagons to fetch them across the Plains, he had sent word to the leaders to come by handcart. The saints, he wrote, could drive their beasts, load their few belongings in handcarts and draw or push these small vehicles by hand. Reports were coming to him of terrible sickness and hardship among the people who, inexperienced and without resourceful leaders, had set out in huge handcart migrations.

But all these problems were dwarfed by the disaster which he suddenly and unexpectedly faced. It was a plague and a famine. Since that barren summer when crickets hopped in millions over the earth, there had been drouth, there had been minor plagues of locusts and horseflies and other pests; but there had never been more than a partial loss of the crops. This summer of 1855 had given portents of great severity. There had been no rains since the planting; and because snowfall in the previous winter had been light, there had not been enough water to irrigate the tilled lands.

By the end of June, there were reports of extreme drouth up and down the valley, as well as incredible hordes of young locusts. When July came, Brigham knew that only a miracle could save the crops; and he summoned his carriage and some of his leaders and set out to visit the settlements. What he saw was enough to weaken a stouter heart than his own. No matter where he went, north or south, he saw the desolation of burned fields, dry chunks of earth like disintegrating slag, dust ankle deep in the roads and trails, vegetation seared and whispering in the hot breeze. Wheat fields had been stricken as with yellow fever. Hay fields were crisp brown areas, with the foliage withered and gone, and the stiff dead stalks of alfalfa taking on the toughness of maple twigs. He saw vegetables, drouth-killed and dust-laden, looking like hard moistureless fragments out of ancient graveyards; dry canals and ditches in which no water had run for weeks; piles of manure in farmyards, now sucked dry of all dampness and turned into mounds of brown flakes.

And everywhere in roads, along fences and over fields, were grasshoppers by the billions. They clung like some kind of awful fruit to the wires of the fences. They filled bush and tree with rustling life. They had eaten all the heads off the wheat and oats and barley, all the leaves off the hay, and now clung in rows up and down the dead dry stalks. Over the white dust of the road, they hopped in shifting and bewildering patterns ahead of the carriage, or took to their wings and clouded the sky.

The overwhelming number of them was not perceived until later, after their wings were grown. Then, still ravenous, they flew in armies so dense and enormous that everyone who beheld them was amazed. At full noon on a clear day they hid the sun and filled the earth with dusk; for a swarm of them in flight reached for miles across the valley, and was sometimes two miles in depth. Some of the men, returning from journeys of exploration, told of what they had seen. Standing on a peak twelve thousand feet above the sea and seven thousand feet above the valley, they were completely lost in a vast cloud of locusts. Above their heads they could see them as far as vision could reach; and upon descending they learned that the swarm through which they walked reached clear to the valley floor.

"They were so thick I couldn't see Jim a hundred feet away. All around us the sky was dark. The sound of them passing us was like that of a herd of buffalo a half a mile away."

The saints had seen crickets in huge armies but these did not fly. They had seen flights of grasshoppers but nothing comparable with what they saw now. From a distance, the stupendous migrations looked like a heavy thunderstorm, like sheets of rain, or like the dense smoke of a prairie fire. When standing in a cloud of them, there was only steady murmuring sound, and darkness everywhere.

Their presence became a vivid pestilence in more than sight and sound. Persons caught in the winged migrations were covered. Upon a woman's long hair, falling down her back, the locusts would settle three or four deep, until they hung in great wriggling clusters and she could feel the weight of them upon her. They settled upon clothes in unbroken layers; along arms as deep as they could gather and cling; and upon faces and hands where their rough feet were like living sandpaper. They clung to eyebrows until pulled off. They clung in writhing bunches to Orson Pratt's long beard until he said their weight was like that of a sadiron; for they buried his beard and then piled deep upon one another, hanging in great clots from his chin. They crawled or tumbled from hair to the naked flesh of throats and then wriggled or fell downward under clothes. Women screamed and fought blindly against them; and some of the men said they thought they would go mad from scratching feet and fluttering wings.

Driven to flight in their search for food, the pests went everywhere, and countless tons of them came down on the green water of Salt Lake. Washed ashore, they were knee-deep on the beaches. Other migrations struck the city. When persons saw the storm of them coming, they fled into buildings and closed windows and doors; and when the deluge came, they stood by windows and gazed at the incredible darkness of wings and hunger outside. Every roof and wall, every tree and shrub and sidewalk crawled as if alive. They struck the panes and sank scratching to the sills and gathered there until they were three or four inches deep. After a migration had passed over and the sky was clear again, persons rushed out with brooms and shovels and attacked the millions that had settled in the city. They swept them from walls, from doorways and windows; from lawns and sidewalks, from streets. Along the sidewalks ran streams of mountain water, and into these the locusts were swept; or they were heaped into piles and burned.

It was more than a plague. It was a nightmare—and many a saint saw in the dreadful visitation a warning and a punishment from God. Even Brigham felt it to be so.

"I told you we need a reformation," said Jedediah, standing by a window to look for the coming of gulls.

"Yes," Brigham said, staring at a roof where locusts lay in an exhausted sheet.

"The Almighty isn't sending any gulls this time."

"A few."

There had been, in fact, thousands of gulls, coming from Great Salt Lake and other lakes south; but their hunger was no match for such hordes. It hardly mattered whether gulls came or not: the crops were gone and winter lay ahead. When the last great flight had vanished into the mountains and the valley was clear again, fields looked as if they had been swept by fire and drenched with yellow heat. There was not a blade of grass, not a sign of foliage upon a million acres.

Knowing that he faced another crisis, Brigham ordered all families with stores from former harvests to put themselves on rations and give liberally to those who had none. He laid plans to build huge community granaries in which to store provisions for the lean years. He visited the more impoverished settlements to give encouragement and advice. Though he knew a deep winter would aggravate the famine and suffering, he prayed for abundant snow so there would be water for the next season's crops.

A deep winter came. Snow fell early on the brown and desolate valley and continued to fall; and by January it was from five to eight feet deep. The city was an uneven landscape of great white mounds. Doors to unused buildings were banked over and lost; and doors of dwellings stood at the end of white unroofed tunnels, with the snow piled ten feet deep on either side. As in a former terrible winter, he labored almost night and day, visiting the saints who had the least to eat and the most wretched hovels in which to live.

On an evening late in January, he looked into one of the shacks and saw the McBrides. How many persons were crowded into the two rooms, he could not tell, because for most of the saints, candles or kerosene lamps were a luxury they could not afford, and this cabin had only firelight. But when he looked in, he saw Moroni, whose long patriarchal beard was already turning gray, and Tim and several women and children.

Entering the damp barren place, Brigham warmed his hands at the fire and looked around him.

"Brother Tim, do you have enough to eat?"

"No, Brother Brigham."

"Why don't you?"

"Because," said Tim sourly, "the locusts ate all our crops."

"Where is your grub box?"

"Over there."

Brigham moved toward the box but was stopped by the picture of a lad of eight, sitting on the cold floor and gnawing at a bone. The boy looked up with gray eyes that were wide and solemn under his mop of dark hair.

"What is your name, my boy?"

"Nephi, Brother Brigham. Nephi McBride."

"Stand up, son." Nephi rose, and Brigham laid hands on the boy's thin shoulders. He looked at the sunken eyes and emaciated face. Then he gazed at the bone. "What do you have there?"

"Just a bone," said Nephi, and he held up a part of the thigh bone of a dog. The bone was almost as clean as polished marble—for the lad had gnawed off it even the scraps of tendon and sinew and had dug out the marrow.

"What is this the bone of?"

"A dog," said Nephi gravely.

"A dog!"

"It's all we have," said Tim. "We had to eat our horses and then we had to kill our two dogs." He gave Brigham a dry smile. "We have a cat left—and a few roots."

Brigham took the bone and turned it over and over in his hands. He patted the lad's dark hair. "I suppose you're pretty hungry, ain't you?"

"Yes, sir."

"Do you say your prayers every night?"

"Yes, sir."

"Brother Nephi, what are you going to be when you grow up?"

"I don't know, Brother Brigham. My grandfather wants to start a United Order; and if he does, I want to help him."

"Fine!" said Brigham, who liked the grave intelligence of this lad. "We'll start some Orders later and you can help. Right now, you had better go with your father to my home and tell Sister Emmeline to give you some food." Brigham turned to the two men. "Brother Moroni, is everybody well?"

"We are well, Brother Brigham. Just starved, that's all." His beard parted in a jovial Irish grin. "A dog doesn't make much soup."

"Well, go to my home and get a part of what I have."

The plague, and the almost fatal famine that followed it, Brigham accepted as a clear warning from God; and while tramping from shack to shack to learn how many of his people were eating their dogs and cats and roots, he pondered and laid his plans. In his office, he spent many hours with his counselors, agreeing with what they said but deciding that not a single one of them looked far enough into the future. A plague was one thing, a reformation was another: the one was ominous, the second was necessary—but a graver trouble lay beyond both. That a crisis was coming, that he would soon have to fight or flee, he never doubted for a moment. He had only to read the journals and newspapers sent to him by his missionaries in the States.

A part of his people were starving; and at the same moment nationally famous women were declaring that the Mormons gave wine to young girls to inflame their passions. In such stupid falsehoods, Brigham saw the handwriting on the wall. Clergymen, women's societies, journalists and editors were filling both pulpit and press with slanderous charges. Ministers were saying that "polygamy" would have to be driven out of Utah at the point of a bayonet; that the entire church ought to be dynamited; that all the missionaries back East were spies. Besides the falsehoods in newspapers, there were hundreds of lurid cartoons: one represented the Endowment House—that holy place of the Lord in which men and women were married for eternity—as a seraglio of lecherous persons—of lustful men who had ravished terrified girls. A second cartoon showed Brigham with eight hundred concubines and looking around with a sly leer for more. The whole Mormon empire was drawn in word and picture as a land of insatiable lusts and incredible debaucheries, where all men were horrible satyrs and all women were deflorated virgins. The denunciation and rage even came from persons in high places; for the Vice-President of the United States had written to a cousin in Utah to express his anger and disgust.

And meanwhile, thousands of persons were digging roots out of deep snow on the hillsides or eating their pets to keep from starving to death!

Yes, the handwriting was on the wall and Brigham knew that soon he would have to fight. It little mattered that he had fled to a desert, or that the Constitution guaranteed to him and his people freedom of conscience: pious hypocrites who lay with harlots, bigoted club women who were spinsterish with malice and envy, would force Congress to act.

He was thinking of the matter one afternoon and wondering what the outcome would be when his wife Emmeline entered. It was said in Zion that she was his favorite and she seemed to believe it. He was tired of her nagging.

"What do you want?" he asked impatiently.

She came over coquettishly and peered at him. "I want to curl your hair and make you look nice and handsome."

"Oh, curl my hair and be damned! You think of folderols right in the middle of a famine!"

"We'll get along just as well if you let me make you look nice."

"I'll have none of your fribbles. Go to the weaving room and make some warm garments for the poor."

"Let me curl your hair around your neck."

"No! I'm busy."

"But you're always busy."

"Listen, Emmeline. Do you realize some of the saints are eating their dogs? Go over to the McBride cabin and look around. Do you realize the United States is getting ready to exterminate us? And here you come with damned nonsense about curling my hair!"

Emmeline went to the door and looked at him archly and blew a kiss. He scowled for a long while after she had gone. He loved her, of course; but he despised her persistent efforts to curl his hair, to make him wear broadcloth instead of homespun, to trim his beard. He went to a window and looked out. Snow was falling. Emerging from the storm were the mantled figures of Heber and Jedediah.

They entered, shaking snow from their garments and blowing on their hands.

"We want to talk to you," Jedediah said.

"All right," said Brigham, wishing the man had a sense of humor "What is the trouble now?"

"Very serious," said Jedediah. His long pinched face looked frozen. It's adultery again."

"Who now?" asked Brigham impatiently.

Sensing that his leader was annoyed, Heber spoke. "Brother Jedediah as a plan he wants you to try."

"What is it?"

"This," said Jedediah eagerly. "I want you to call most of the bishops ogether and ask them if they have been adulterous."

Brigham considered. Joseph had divided the church into stakes, each of which covered a large area, and the stakes into wards, each of which vas presided over by a bishop. There were more than a dozen bishops in he city, and many more in the hamlets north and south.

"Have they been adulterous?"

"I think they have."

"If the brethren would take wives and stop dodging their responsibili- es!"

"But nobody can take a wife without your approval, and some of them ay you want them to marry the homely sisters first. Others say they an't support more than one wife."

"It's unfortunate," said Heber, "that most of the converts coming in are vomen. They outnumber the men four to one."

"That would be all right if the men would do their duty." Brigham irned to Jedediah. "All right. Summon the bishops and I'll meet them."

Brigham met them and was astounded. When he said bluntly that all 10se who had committed adultery were to stand, half the men rose to 1eir feet.

"What in hell!" Brigham cried. He stared at them and considered. You didn't understand me. I mean since you joined the church." he men gazed at him but they did not sit. "You mean to tell me," righam thundered, "you have all committed adultery and sold your)uls to the Devil! Is that true?"

"Well," said one of the abashed men, "women are women, Brother righam. Are we to let the miners and gamblers and whoremongers ave them? Now me, I have eleven wives and I can't support any more. he sisters want men. You have to realize there's hundreds of unmarried sters in the city."

"I know that!" Brigham snapped. He turned to another man among those standing. "How many wives do you have?"

"Six."

"Six! Can't you support more than that?"

"To tell the truth, I don't seem able to support that many."

To another: "How many have you?"

"Three."

"Three! Damn it, Brother Heber here has forty." After a moment Brigham added scathingly: "So you brothers are taking pity on the unmarried sisters, are you? You've given your immortal souls to Satan, that's what you've done!" He turned to Jedediah. "You're right. We need a reformation."

In the office, Heber said: "Don't blame them too much. If their wives cause them as much trouble as mine, I know how they feel."

"That's not the point," said Jedediah, whose grief with his wives was also severe. "The church is headed for hell the way it's going."

"Yes," said Brigham, "that's the point. We'll clean it out and mop it up. If we can't keep the saints righteous, we'll drive them to the gold fields where they belong."

"When shall we start?" asked Jedediah.

"Right away."

After the two men left, Brigham sat in his small office, brooding over the matter until darkness came; whereupon, deciding that he wanted no supper, he entered the Beehive House to seek his room. Usually, but not always, he indicated the wife whom he would seek in the evening by making a chalk mark on her bedchamber door; and while climbing the stairs now, he remembered that hours earlier he had marked Lucy Ann Decker's room. He went to her door and was not surprised to learn that the mark had been erased. Some of his bolder wives, whom he visited infrequently, were everlastingly rubbing the mark off a sister's door and putting it on their own, hoping that he would be absentmindedly inveigled in.

He stood quietly before Lucy Ann's door and grinned, wondering which one of the jealous wretches had erased the mark. He would know soon, of course—for there would be a chalkline on the guilty one's chamber. He entered his own room and took off his shoes; and then softly he went up and down the long corridor, peering at one door and another.

While he was engaged in sleuthing and grinning to himself, a door was opened, and the tall, fair-haired, blue-eyed Harriet Cook poked her head out.

"The mark," she said dryly, "is on my door."

Brigham stared at her. She was, he knew, perhaps the most intelligent wife he had; but he almost despised her because of her violent temper, her scorn for Mormonism, and the contempt in which she held the other wives.

"Who put a mark on your door?"

"Oh, didn't you? You haven't visited me in more than six months. I thought perhaps you had relented."

"You vain jealous woman."

"Yes, I know. You intended to visit that fat dumpy Lucy Ann this evening—but you visited her last week. Am I no longer one of your wives?"

"You're an ungodly and malicious woman——"

"Oh, never mind the lecture!" cried Harriet. Seeing another door open down the hall, she advanced quickly and grasped Brigham's coat and drew him inside. She knew that a moment later a dozen other doors had opened and a dozen women were peering out. It all seemed to her very stupid and silly and vulgar; but in her sweetest voice she said: "Brigham, you might visit me at least twice a year."

"Don't I?" he asked, looking at this tall slender woman who frightened most of his other wives to death.

"You know you don't. I think you're the unfairest man in the city. That poor little snub-nosed homely Martha—why don't you ever visit her? Why don't you ever visit Susan and Margaret Alley and Lucy Bigelow? Once you were very fond of Lucy but now the Lucy you like is Lucy Ann Decker. Why are you so mean to Clara Chase? You're driving her crazy."

"Did you drag me in here to deliver a sermon?"

"Drag you in here! Well, my dear husband, you don't have to stay. In fact, I wouldn't let you. But you're not going to Lucy Ann Decker's room. You're going to that poor faithful homely Martha—and if you don't I'll scream until the roof flies off."

Brigham shrugged. A few of his wives had always baffled him—and none more than this woman whose power of invective exceeded his own.

"All right," he said, wondering why he had taken so many wives—or so many of the wrong kind. He left Harriet's chamber and went down the hall and knocked gently on Martha's door. When he looked back, feeling henpecked and foolish and a little angry, Harriet lifted her brows and gave him a smile that was all malice and ice.

CHAPTER XVIII

How to purge the church of its sinners, Brigham hardly knew. Since the drouth of last summer there were thieves, but thieves were of little concern in comparison with the adulterers and apostates. The departure of apostates to other lands had filled him with angry misgivings; because it had been apostates in Illinois, in Missouri, in Nauvoo who fled and told their lies and stirred up trouble. Rather than let the ungodly wretches go back East and plot with the gentiles, he was of a mind to cut their throats; but there were, he reflected, too damned many of them.

The problem of adultery he would have to solve by finding husbands for the unmarried women. To this end he summoned to his office one man and another, and left to Jedediah and Orson the fiery task of preaching to the sinners and making them understand that they were headed for hell.

"Brother Alonzo," he said to a bishop who answered his summons, "why have you only two wives?"

Alonzo grinned. "Well, I can't afford any more."

"Afford!" Brigham cried. "It's your duty, man. How are we to root adultery out of here if the sisters can't find husbands?"

"I know that. But to tell the truth, I have a heck of a time getting along with the two I have. They quarrel until I want to take to shank's ponies and hit the grit. Women are too danged possessive, Brother Brigham."

"Yes, yes, I know. There isn't much of the Lord's spirit in a lot of them. How many children have you?"

"Five."

"Five! Where do you expect to get in the next world with only five children?"

"I've thought about it. But unless I can find some wives who ain't so danged jealous, I guess I'll have to do without much glory."

"Nonsense. Where will you be in comparison with the brethren who have a lot of children, and a lot of wives so they can have a lot more children in the next life? It's offspring that will advance you toward godhood."

"I know it. I've thought about it a lot."

"It's time you did something about it. Some of the brothers are doing their duty and some ain't. I've just married Harriet Barney and she makes the twenty-fourth wife for me. And you have two! It's shameful."

"I know it," said Alonzo, looking very silly.

"Let me show you something," said Brigham, drawing paper and pen toward him. "Brother Heber figgered it out. Now suppose a man marries one woman and she has a son at the age of twenty, a daughter at twenty-two, another son at twenty-four, and so on until she has ten children. Suppose the sons marry at nineteen and have ten children each like their father. When the first father is seventy-eight, how many offspring will he have? Only a hundred and fifty-two.

"Now suppose a man marries forty wives and each wife bears him ten children. Suppose his sons marry at nineteen, each taking forty wives and each wife having ten children. When the father is seventy-eight, how many offspring will he have? Three million, five hundred and eighty thousand, four hundred and forty-one!"

"What?" said Alonzo, his eyes popping.

"It's true. One will have a hundred and one will have millions. It's just as Heber said. When Heber is an old man he'll have more offspring than there are persons in Utah Territory today."

Alonzo's eyes were still popping with amazement. "Good Lord, how many wives does Brother Heber have?"

"About forty."

Alonzo shook his head. "I don't see how he gets along with them. Two drive me crazy."

"He gets along, Brother Alonzo, and think of the offspring he'll have in the next life. Tens of millions of them. He'll become a god while you're down in celestial glory with a handful."

Alonzo considered. "Then why don't you take a lot more wives?"

Brigham's smile was barely perceptible. "I'm too busy."

"I guess," said Alonzo, thoroughly rebuked by a vision of Heber's offspring, "I can afford one or two more."

"Ten," said Brigham. "Twenty will be better."

After Alonzo had gone, Brigham sat in thought. It looked as if Heber's increase would exceed his own by millions; and he resented his barren wives, of whom he had several, as well as a dozen others who were not very fruitful. Emmeline had borne him ten children; Lucy Ann and Emily had seven each; but he had only forty-nine children, an absurdly small number from twenty-three women. He was thinking that perhaps he ought to take a few more wives when another man entered.

"Brother Luke, I understand you have only one wife."

"Yes, by God, and one's enough."

"I say one isn't enough."

"If you had to live with her you'd say she was."

"I live with all sorts of women: tall and short, dark and fair, fat and lean, calm and hot-tempered, patient and flighty. I know all about women."

"You ought to," said Luke, grinning.

"I do. I get along with them. When I can't stand their damned complaints or love of fiddle-faddles I walk off."

"In a sermon last Sunday, Brother Heber told his to go to hell."

"Sometimes they make a man feel that way. But it's no harder to live with fifty than with one."

"Just fifty times as hard," said Luke.

"You're prosperous. You can support as many wives as I can. Besides, if you have only one, she'll be taken away from you in the next life and given to a man who obeyed the Lord's commandment."

"Well, I can't say I'd object to that."

"You'd better go read the apostle Paul. No man can be saved without a wife at his side—and the more the better."

"Brother Brigham," said Luke gravely, "I've listened to your sermons and to Heber's and Jedediah's and others. I've watched my neighbors. Some men seem to get along mighty nice with several wives, but some fight like the devil. Take Amos Broder: the old roof flies off of his house every morning. He has only four but you'n hear them for ten miles. I have a temper too. I wouldn't want wives if I had to sock them in the eye every day or two; and I wouldn't want to come back from a mission and not know if the children was mine or not. I wouldn't want to put up with all their fuss about new styles."

"It's true they're crazy about styles. It's just as I said in a sermon.

If a female angel came here, she wouldn't have a bushel of flax done up on the back of her head, or a dress dragging ten feet behind her, or hoops that let her petticoats fly over her head, or walk the streets with her spanker jib flying."

"It ain't only their styles. They fight like cats."

"I know it. Every woman, young and old, homely and pretty wants one man all to herself. If a husband leaves the house, her eyes follow him and she wants him to love nobody else. But I refuse to make a queen of one of them and peasants of the rest. I try to love them all the same.

"And, Brother Luke, there's another thing to consider. It's men like you who are causing all the adulteries. If you'd do your duty, the sisters wouldn't be sneaking off with the dirty curses who come through here."

"Well, that might be true."

"It is true. I want you to take more wives—at least eight or ten."

"If I see any I think I'n live with, I will. But not to save my ornery soul will I quarrel all the time with women."

"Think it over. I expect you to marry some of the sisters soon."

"I'll see."

After Luke had gone, Brigham left the office. One of his firebrands was addressing a multitude this afternoon and he wanted to hear the sermon. On his way down the street, he passed Heber's big house, and he saw Heber on the porch, calling his children. "Isaac, Jacob, Abraham! Joseph, Hyrum, Brigham, John! . . ." How many children Heber had, Brigham did not know.

"How are you?" he said, waving to his friend.

"If you see any of my children down the street, send them home."

Brigham was smiling. He had too lively a sense of irony not to be amused now and then. It was true that he did not always recognize his own children, and had once asked a lad, "Whose little boy are you?" only to learn that he had been speaking to his nineteenth son. Nor could he remember all their names. It was quite a task to name so many children; and one day, in looking over the list, he had been surprised to learn that he had three sons named Brigham, two sons named Hyrum, and two daughters named Mary. Some of the names, such as Moriancumur, Shemira, Alfales, and Feramorz, he hardly knew how to pronounce.

While listening to Jedediah's impassioned castigation of the sinners, Brigham was remembering that editors and ministers, as well as congressmen, were saying that all the Mormon wives would desert their husbands if given a chance. To silence such criticism, and to silence the complaining wives also, he resolved suddenly on a bold move. When the exhausted Jedediah sat down, Brigham stepped forward.

"I have a proposition to make to the sisters. Everywhere the brethren tell me they can hardly get along with their wives. Men will say, 'My wife, though a most excellent woman, has not seen a happy day since I took my second wife.' 'No, not a happy day for a year,' says one; and another has not seen a happy day for five years. It is said the sisters do not have the liberty they ought to have, that they are wading through a perfect flood of tears.

"I wish my own women to understand that what I am going to say is for them as well as others, and I want those who are here to tell their sisters, yes, all the women of this community, and then write it back to the States. I am going to give you two weeks to reflect, that you may determine whether you wish to remain with your husbands or not; and then I am going to set every woman at liberty and say to them, Now go your way, my women with the rest, go your way. And my wives here have got to do one of two things: either round up their shoulders and endure the afflictions of this world and live their religion, or they may leave, for I will not have them about me. I will go into heaven alone, rather than have scratching and fighting around me.

"I will set all at liberty. Tell the gentiles that I will free every woman at the next Conference, and let them take the children and the property. I want to do something to get rid of the whiners."

This unexpected announcement was a thunderbolt. After he ceased speaking, the hundreds of women in the audience stared at him, not knowing whether he was angry or out of his mind. He was not angry. He was sardonically amused, and he was calling all bluffs, both at home and abroad. Let them make of his proposition what they could; and let them go if they wanted to, his wives among the rest; and then perhaps the men could get down to the job of building the Lord's kingdom.

Brigham's words were published in the local newspaper and carried from tongue to tongue. The women were flabbergasted. And from tongue to tongue went his statement a few days later: that the brethren, by refusing to take wives, were making harlots of the sisters. Jedediah and Orson, meanwhile, were thundering their denunciations. Even the most placid saints realized that their leaders were angry, and they trooped to Brigham's office by the scores.

One of the first to come was a pale and frightened young man who had decided that he had better take another wife before the wrath of God descended on him. His name was Uriah Stiles. He brought three women with him: two sisters, Anne and Emma, and their mother Becky.

"What is the trouble?" asked Brigham, observing that Anne was a handsome girl but that Emma was as homely as a mud fence.

"Well," said Uriah, looking very foolish, "I hear you think we should take more wives. I got one wife," he added, looking quickly at Anne, though she very well knew that he had a wife.

"Can you support another wife?" asked Brigham, glancing at the sour face of the mother.

"I guess so. One, at least."

"You see," said Anne, smiling brightly, "if he marries me, I want him to marry my sister and mother."

"What?" asked Brigham, a little startled.

"That's it," said Uriah solemnly. "But danged if I know if I'n support that many."

"Are you a widow?" asked Brigham of the mother.

"Yes, Brother Brigham. My husband was killed by Indians two years ago."

Brigham looked from face to face and considered. Many of the saints had married sisters: he had done so himself. Some had married as many as three or four sisters, and a few had married the mothers also.

"We don't want to be separated," said Anne, putting an arm around Emma.

Brigham surmised that the shrewd girl was bargaining, knowing well that her mother and sister could never find husbands. "How much property do you have?"

"A good farm and thirty-two head of cattle and six horses. But I don't know if I'n support four wives."

"What does your present wife think about it?"

"Oh, she don't like it so well but she says she guesses it's all right if you say it is."

"I've always felt," said Brigham, his eyes twinkling, "that the best way to handle mothers-in-law is to marry them. Sister Becky, how do you feel?"

Becky turned her tired eyes on Uriah. "I don't want to leave my daughters."

"There's another daughter," said Uriah. "Ellen, she's fourteen. I guess mebbe I could marry her later."

"Then," said Anne happily, "we'd all be one family."

"If you're all willing," said Brigham, "you have my permission."

Uriah's face sagged a little. Clearly enough he wanted to marry Anne, but the homely sister and graying mother appalled him. "Then you think I should?"

"Yes. You ready to be married now?"

Uriah looked anxiously around him. "If I have to, then I guess now's as good as any time."

Brigham called his secretary. Anne hugged her homely sister and looked very happy, but Uriah still gazed around him apprehensively.

"Willard, marry Brother Uriah to these sisters."

"Yes," said Willard. His large plump face showed no astonishment at all. "Come with me."

Uriah followed with alacrity as if planning to flee as soon as he could. Anne put arms around her sister and mother and rubbed her cheek against Emma's shoulder. "Now we'll all be one family," she said, looking back at Brigham and smiling.

The next person to enter was Dan Wells, a large man with a deep gruff voice and the sternest face in the city. His eyes were far apart under great shaggy brows; a straight but very long nose lay down his face and almost across his wide upper lip; his broad hard mouth was framed by a stiff hedge of beard. Ever since his brave defense of the saints in Nauvoo, after Brigham's flight, he had steadily advanced in power until he was now fourth among the leaders. Dan Wells rarely smiled, but when he did, his stern face softened amazingly.

"How is the reformation going?" asked Brigham.

"Very good," said Dan, his voice coming like thunder out of his broad chest. "They're all confessing and being baptized again."

"There'll probably be more confessing than renouncing."

"A lot of them are scared." Dan's long face turned very grave. "Have you heard what happened to the last handcart expedition?"

"Yes," said Brigham, looking very unhappy. "What have you heard?"

"One of the brethren just got in. He says they're dying like stuck hogs."

"Where are they now?"

"On the Sweetwater. Fourteen of them froze to death in one bunch. They all huddled together in a clump of willows and were stone dead the next morning. Dozens are starving or dying from dysentery."

Brigham pulled at his brown beard. "Well, it was damned nonsense for them to start so late. Last summer they came through all right; and every woman who hiked across the Plains with a handcart got a husband that fall. That shows the exercise must be good for them."

"Yes, but this last expedition has got trapped."

"Send a rescue company. Get it off at once."

"Who'll I put in charge of it?"

"George Grant or Lot Smith. If they can't go, see if Tim McBride can."

"There's still another bunch on the way."

"I know it. They'll all freeze to death if we don't save them. Send the best teams and strong wagons and all the food we can spare."

"Doesn't George Grant need some scouts?"

"Tell John Flack or Lew Meacham to go as scouts; or Sam Bateman or Hosea Stout. Or Bill Hickman. No," said Brigham, pacing the room, "I might need those men here. But send some good scouts."

Brigham paced his office for a long while. Handcart migrations were all right, he still believed, if the fools did not set forth too late in the summer. The long walk toughened the saints. Weaklings were thinned out and only the hardy pioneers finished the journey. Nevertheless, he could not abandon hundreds to snowstorms and death. After coming to this valley, he had learned of the Donner Party, that brave and foolhardy group who had preceded him by a year. Taking the Hastings Cut-Off and getting bogged in the Salt Lake flats, they arrived too late to cross the Sierra Nevada and were winter-bound there; and from all that Brigham had heard, half of them had eaten the other half. He did not want the saints devouring one another; but even so, even if they all froze to death and were eaten by wolves, they would be more fortunate than many here. Their souls would be saved. Considering it from that angle, he put on his stovepipe hat and went over to the Endowment House to learn how Jedediah was getting along.

He found that zealous crusader standing in water to his waist and baptizing for all he was worth. Around him, awaiting their turn, were weeping women and solemn men, some of whom knelt in prayer. Jedediah looked pale and exhausted.

"Brother Jedediah, you mustn't stay in that water too long."

"It's the Lord's work," said Jedediah, and shoved a gasping woman under. She fought and floundered and was not wholly immersed; whereupon, Jedediah angrily seized her and thrust her out of sight. She came up choked and wild-eyed.

"You got her under that time," said Brigham, grinning.

"Some of them resist to the last minute. It's so hard to duck them you'd think the devil in them was a rubber balloon full of air."

"You better rest a while now."

"There is no rest in doing the Lord's work."

"There will be if you catch a cold in there. You'll be resting for a long time."

"I'm all right," said Jedediah. He laid hands on a burly man who went under like a sea beast.

"I wasn't ready!" the man roared.

"Had you confessed everything?"

"Every danged thing I could think of."

"I'd better put you under again. You look full of sin to me."

"All right."

"In the name of the Father, the Son and the Holy Ghost, I baptize you for the remission of sins. Now under you go again."

"How many have you baptized today?" asked Brigham.

"About two hundred."

"How many more do you have?"

"In the name of Israel's God, I don't know. Thousands, maybe."

"You better come out of that water. You look chilled through."

"I'm all right," said Jedediah, turning a pallid and frozen face to Brigham. "I am happy in doing the Lord's work."

A month later, Jedediah Grant was dead.

RIGHAM ACCEPTED THE NEWS CALMLY WHEN HE HEARD THAT HIS ZEALOUS firebrand had died of pneumonia; for death was only a temporary and unimportant interruption of life. Of greater moment was the last handcart disaster: the starved and almost naked survivors left half their number dead in the mountains, and those who reached the city were more dead than alive. Brigham decided he would have to send wagons for the next overland journey. While he was considering the matter, news came that staggered him—news that made the death of Jedediah or the handcart tragedy look very trivial indeed.

It was on Pioneer Day, the 24th of July in 1857. Brigham and thousands of his people had gone to Cottonwood Canyon for a huge picnic, and for a little while his mind had been free of worries. Suddenly a voice cried, "Look!" and Brigham turned to see Porter Rockwell coming at full speed like a wild man. His long black hair was streaming behind him in the wind as he urged his lathered and almost exhausted horse to gallop up the canyon. He rode straight to Brigham and leapt to the earth.

"Brother Porter, what is wrong?"

"Plenty, Brother Brigham! The government is sending an army to wipe us out! It's on its way!"

"An army! How do you know?"

"I saw it. I've changed horses and rode five hundred miles in five days!"

"You must be hungry," said Brigham quietly. "Go over and ask the sisters to feed you."

He spoke quietly but inside he could feel his heart pounding against his broad chest. He could feel a mighty anger rising within him. For a little while he went off alone to collect his thoughts and quiet his emotions; and his people, knowing that their leader was angry, forgot their gaiety and gathered in groups to look at him. In a few minutes he returned and mounted a wagon.

"Listen!" he roared. "I have very bad news for you. Brother Porter has just come and says a big army is on its way to wipe us out. It is only a few hundred miles from here now. But I don't want anyone to get excited or to act like crazy persons just because the United States is determined to destroy us. We'll have something to say about it. We will not be destroyed.

"God Almighty will give the United States a pill that will puke them to death, and it will be worse than lobelia! I said when we left the Missouri River to found our home in these mountains that if the mob would let us alone ten years, we would ask no odds of them. The ten years are past, and I say in the name of Israel's God we ask no odds now! We are ready to defend ourselves! Let the army come!

"And now, brethren and sisters, go back to your homes."

Brigham hastened to his office and summoned his boldest scouts, including Bill Hickman, Porter Rockwell and Lot Smith. These and a dozen more were, Brigham believed, the most fearless group of men who ever sat together in one room and offered their services to the Lord. In comparison with any of them, Jim Bridger, or most of the other scouts who were becoming legendary heroes, made Brigham smile with pity; for against a half-dozen Bridgers, he would have pitted any man in his office. He was proud of them. He needed them now.

"Boys," he said, looking at their bold bearded faces, "we have been through a lot of trouble. We have fled from place to place; fought Christians and Indians, drouth and plague and famine; but right now I guess we have a bigger job than we ever faced before. In sending an army to wipe us out, the United States means business. But we mean business too." He gazed at them a long moment before adding: "That army must never reach this city."

"The job suits us," said Lot Smith.

"That army, Porter says, is being led by Harney, the Indian fighter who is known as the Squaw Killer. When they put Harney in charge, you know what we can expect if he gets here. Three thousand soldiers are on their way. They're bringing a governor to replace me, and judges to say what we must do. That's President Buchanan for you, the dirty curse!"

The men looked at one another. If Brigham said that army must not reach the city, then by all the gods it never would.

"Porter says," Brigham went on, "that Harney boasts there are thirty men here he'll hang on sight. He must never cross the South Pass; and if he does, we'll chop him to pieces in Echo Canyon. We'll have enough boulders on the ledges ready to roll down to kill a hundred thousand men. But first, we'll stampede their stock and we will burn their trains. We'll stop them if it takes every last man of us to do it."

"Why," asked Bill, "are they sendun an army against us?"

"Because Judge Drummond, that nasty scoundrel who sat on the bench with a prostitute at his side, went back and lied about us. He told the President we drive all Federal officers out or murder them. He told that we have a secret oath-bound society called the Destroying Angels."

The men looked at one another. Bill Hickman smiled but the others were as sober as men could be.

"They have other excuses," Brigham resumed. "That renegade cur, Stephen A. Douglas, said in a speech that we're all bound by oath to avenge the murder of Joseph, that we are a band of villains who rob and murder every gentile who enters this valley. All these reasons are only damned excuses. The real reason for sending an army against us is to sidetrack the issue of slavery. The new Republican party last year was very bitter against us. John Frémont pledged if elected to exterminate us. The Republican platform promised to destroy what it called the twin relics of barbarism, slavery and polygamy. Now Buchanan is trying to save his face.

"Drummond's lies are only an excuse to stir up hatred against us. Remember that Joseph predicted a war between the North and the South. That war is coming. In fact, some of the states are threatening to secede now. So what is that dirty curse Buchanan going to do? Send an army to wipe us out and so scare the southern states out of their threats of secession. He probably also has a lot of friends who want to graft in army supplies.

"Remember this. You will be scouts and spies, but I don't want you to kill any soldiers except in absolute self-defense. Burn their trains. Burn their forts and bridges. Stampede their stock and chase them into this valley. Make things so damned miserable that they'll go back home and mind their business. But kill no one."

"You say three thousand soldiers are on their way?"

"That's what I'm told."

"Our army could use them up in a hurry . . ."

"That's not the plan. Do as I say and we won't have to fight soldiers. We'll starve them to death."

"That suits us," said Bill, looking forward with pleasure to his assignment.

Brigham followed the men to the door. "Always remember," he said, "what the attitude of the saints is. Dan Wells said it better than it has ever been said before. I'll read it to you." He went to his desk and returned with a copy of the local newspaper. The scouts gathered around him. "Listen to what Brother Dan says. 'As the good never wish for war, and the wise are always ready for it, let us continually seek that our weapons may be made bright and ready by our industry, and preserved so by a continued peace.' That," said Brigham gravely, "is our motto. Always remember it."

Brigham placed a man named Burton in command of several companies, and ordered him to prepare to proceed eastward at a moment's notice. Bill knew there was no need for him to go now: the soldiers would be a long while reaching the Rocky Mountains, and there would be no sense in his going to South Pass two hundred and fifty miles away to wait there week after week. He organized a group of scouts under his leadership, put guns, horses and supplies in readiness, and waited. It was while waiting that he heard of a matter even more exciting than the approach of an army.

In July a small emigrant train came out of the mountains and passed through the city. It was the best-equipped and most prosperous train that the saints had ever seen: the wagons were loaded with choice supplies, there was a herd of nearly a thousand cattle, and a hundred and thirty-six men, women and children were well-dressed and well-fed. These emigrants, on their way to California, had come from Arkansas, Missouri and Illinois.

Close by the City of Great Salt Lake they camped. Some of the men entered the city, and a few of them indiscreetly boasted not only that an army was coming to chastise the Mormons, but also that they had done some chastising themselves a few years ago. News of the boasting spread like a prairie fire. From home to home went the story that emigrants were passing through who had been a part of the Missouri mobs. The rumors, fed angrily from tongue to tongue, became full-bodied legends; and soon it was told that among these emigrants were the murderers of Joseph Smith.

The whole city was in an uproar. After the emigrants passed southward Brigham sent word that the saints were not to give any aid to the train: they were not to sell provisions or show friendliness; and in every way possible they were to be hostile without being overt.

Having nothing better to do at the moment, Bill decided to follow the emigrants southward to Dixie, the name the Mormons had given to the valley of Virgin River. Day after day he watched them, entered the camp and talked with them, but heard no boasting and saw nothing suspicious until the train encamped at Fillmore. In this settlement the wanderers were a hundred and fifty miles from Brigham Young and seemed to feel safe from attack. Eager to learn the truth, Bill drew the captain, a man named Fancher, into conversation.

After speaking in approval of the train, its discipline and equipment, he asked boldly: "Captain, is it true that some of the men with you helped drive the saints out of Missouri?"

"Saints? Are you speaking of the Mormons?"

"Yes," said Bill, grinning. "They call themselves saints."

"Are you a Mormon?"

"God, no. I'm a government scout."

"It might be true," said Fancher. "Anyway, we intend to help drive them out of this valley."

"How?" asked Bill, showing his friendliest smile.

"Well, for one thing an army is coming."

"Yes, I heard about that."

"There's another army coming from California. It's coming up over the Frémont Trail and join the army from the East. The two will wipe the Mormons out of here."

Bill looked down his nose at that. "Is it true," he asked gravely, "there's men in your outfit who helped sock Joseph Smith away?"

Fancher eyed him a little suspiciously but Bill's smile was that of a government scout. "I don't know. And by the way, what's your name?"

"Dave Hines."

"I don't know, Mr. Hines. I think the men are just boasting."

"But ain't you got some men here from Illinois?"

"A few. Most of us are from Arkansas."

"One of your men," persisted Bill, looking around him, "said you brung all this beef along for the army that's to come. He said you intend to stop in Utah and fatten them up."

"Just boasting," said Fancher. "These are our stock."

The story that four hundred dragons were coming over the Frémont Trail to destroy the southern settlements was carried by messenger from hamlet to hamlet ahead of the train. It was also said that the emigrants intended to halt when they found lush meadow and fatten the cattle and wait for the army. Bill looked upon all the tales as so much boasting; but many of the saints were alarmed and angry, and their leaders swung into action. Isaac Haight, military commander of the southern settlements, was a tall, gaunt, sallow man with a black square-cut spade beard and cunning avaricious eyes. John Lee, Indian agent at Cedar City, was a tall, broad and handsome fellow, with a quick smile that hid his cruelty, and a heart as bold as any in Zion. After hearing of what happened on Corn Creek, these two men decided that boasting had gone far enough.

There, it was said, an ox died, and ten Indians died after eating the flesh. At once another rumor spread like wild fire: the emigrants were putting arsenic in the springs and watering holes along the way. Upon hearing that other beasts had died, and that two Mormons had died after handling the poisoned animals, Bill rode over to investigate. It seemed to him that the cattle had probably died of poisonous weeds after bloating themselves with water; but Haight was convinced that the emigrants were spreading death. At least he said he was convinced—though Bill suspected the man had his greedy eye on the property of the emigrants.

Haight summoned a council of war. It was a secret meeting, but Bill was admitted because he was known as one of Brigham's most trusted scouts. He did not intend to talk or offer advice. He was content to listen while Haight cried that the braggarts and murderers had to be taken care of—and that the Indians could do the job.

"But how do we know," asked a man, "they ain't just boastun?"

"Well, it's not time to boast. I'm told they say they killed Joseph Smith."

"And claim they have the pistol they shot him with."

"And I've heard," said Haight, looking around him in the gloom of a cabin lit only by firelight, "that they raped some of the sisters on their way down here. They burned crops and poisoned water and tore down fences. They intend to come back with an army and kill all of us. And there's a big army coming the other way. It's time to fight and not sit and talk about it."

"That might all be boasting," said a quiet man named Haslem.

"No," said another. "Didn't I see them stick a knife in a ox and pour poison in the wound?"

"How do you know it was poison?"

"What you think it was? Water or lard?"

"If we let them go to California," said Haight, looking, it seemed to Bill, like Satan himself, "they'll come back with an army. There isn't any doubt about it. We'll be between two armies then. Besides, I'm convinced the vile curses who killed our Prophet are right here under our noses."

"And boastun about it!"

"By God, yes. Are we men if we let them get away? Brother John, what is your judgment?"

"I agree with you," said John Lee. "But mebbe we ought to see first what Brigham has to say."

"Brigham is three hundred miles from here. We haven't any time to ask his advice. Anyhow, I'm the commander in this district. My word is law here."

"That's right," said a man who was the bishop in Cedar City.

"Bill Hickman, what do you say?"

"Nothing," said Bill. "I'm just one of Brigham's scouts and Indian fighters. I have nothing to do with this."

Haight looked around him again. There was something about the man that made Bill want to sock him away. It was a cold-blooded calculating cruelty that was almost chilling. It was the blue-black spade beard that gave a ghostly pallor to his sunken cheeks, and the craftiness of the Devil himself to the narrowed eyes.

"I still think," said Haslem, "we ought to send a messenger to Brigham Young and ask what he thinks."

"Never mind what he thinks. We have to act right now before they get away from us. I vote to sock them away at once."

"How?"

"Arm the Indians and turn them loose."

"But what will Brigham Young say about it?"

"Yes, we'll have to ask him."

"In fact," said Haight, looking at the men, "I've had John already arm the Indians. They're all set."

"I wouldn't do anything till I'd asked Brother Brigham."

"By that time they'll be out of here and gone. Do we intend to let them go down and stir up California against us? We know what they're like. They intend to come back and use us up."

"That's true. We don't have no time to ask Brigham."

"We know what he'd say. He'd say to wipe them out."

"I don't think so," said Haslem quietly. "He told us not to kill anyone if we'n help it. He said to leave emigrants alone."

"We'll let the Indians do it."

"I think," Haslem persisted, "we'd better send a messenger to Brigham. I'll go. It's three hundred miles. I can make it in four days."

"You'll have to ride like hell."

"I will. I'll go right now."

The emigrants had camped in a small valley that was called Mountain Meadows. There was a fine cold spring and excellent feed for the beasts; and here, they declared, they intended to rest a few days before crossing the southern watershed. Haight did not intend to let them rest at all. He commanded Lee to turn the Indians loose; and one morning the emigrants were amazed to find themselves surrounded by redskins, and twenty of their members killed or wounded before they knew they were attacked.

Hidden in timber on the northern side of the valley, Bill sat on his horse and watched. He was convinced that Brigham would never approve this slaughter of a train, and he was resolved to have no part in it. Haslem hadn't had time to reach Brigham yet; but there the Indians were, yelling like devils and firing for all they were worth. The men in camp were not long in seizing their rifles; and after Indians began to tumble from ponies, the warriors withdrew beyond gunshot and sent frantic scouts to summon reinforcements. The emigrants meanwhile converted their wagons into a fortress and prepared for a siege.

For four days and nights they huddled among their wagons and watched the Indians pour in from all directions and build a circle of fires around the camp. In the third night, Bill learned, two men slipped out to seek help and got past the Indian sentinels. Bill groaned to think of what their amazement must have been when they were suddenly attacked by three white men. One of them was slain; the other ran in horror back to his people. The camp, Bill reflected, was doomed.

He knew it was doomed when he heard the plot of Haight and Lee. Now, Haight said, the camp would surely have to be wiped out; because they had learned that white men as well as Indians were seeking their death, and if any of them escaped to California they would tell a terrible tale.

"What," a man asked, "is the plan? To march on them?"

"God, no!" said Lee. He was agitated. He was frightened by the devils he had turned loose.

"But we have to wipe them all out now."

"Of course," said Haight. "We'll ambush them. We'll send someone with a white flag and we'll lead them out and chop them down."

Bill shuddered a little. He had socked many men away. He cared nothing about death and was ready to kill again for the Lord; but such cold-blooded butchery was a little too much for him.

"You intend to kill the little children too?" asked a man.

"We have to kill everyone old enough to remember—everyone more than six years old."

"Don't you think we should wait till Haslem comes?"

"Great God, we can't wait now! The first thing we know the Indians will chop us down. We're in too deep. We must all stick together in this and finish it just as soon as we can. To the end of our lives we must swear the Indians did it and we couldn't stop them."

"Yes," a voice said.

The men were sitting in firelight. Back in the shadows, Bill watched them and reflected: the whole thing had been a wretched blunder: scared out of their wits, Haight and his men could think only of wiping out the train and destroying the evidence of their guilt. They behaved like addle-witted schoolboys.

"We'll ambush them tomorrow," Haight was saying. "All you men fetch your wagons."

"Yes," the men said, and went alone into darkness.

The next morning the wagons assembled a half-mile from the camp, and a man was sent with a flag of truce. His flag was a white cloth which he held high above his head. After he had gone a little way, a man left the emigrant camp and approached him. They talked a few moments, and then the one with the flag waved to Lee, and the wagons moved toward the camp.

Watching from a distance, Bill did not see clearly what happened in the camp when the wagons entered. In the small enclosure was the agony of the wounded, the awful thirst of persons who had not drunk water in five days, the terrified faces of women and children. Believing that Lee and his men were their saviors, the emigrants crowded forward to touch their garments and to bless them. Some, with tears on their pale faces, knelt in prayer and asked God to watch over these brave men who were saving them from Indians; and all of them obeyed orders with the credulity of a child.

"There's only one way to save you," said Lee, gazing at the men. "We'll put the smallest children in the lead wagon, then the women and wounded in the next wagons. No, we'll put the wounded in the next wagons, then the women will march in single file, and behind them, the men. We'll lead you out of here."

"God bless you!" a woman cried.

Lee looked at her but his face did not soften. "You have to give up all your arms," he said.

"Why?" a man asked.

"Because if Indians see you armed you are doomed."

"I guess it's all right," said Captain Fancher. "Mr. Lee is saving our lives. We will place ourselves in his hands."

"We'll load your guns in a wagon. Get your wounded ready."

If anybody wondered why the youngest children were to go in a wagon by themselves, he asked no questions about it. While Lee and his men stacked the arms in a wagon, the men of the camp loaded the wounded. When Lee asked Fancher if he was ready, Fancher said he was, and Lee took his position in a wagon with the wounded.

"Go ahead," he said, speaking to the other drivers.

The teams moved away, taking the small children and the wounded; and behind came the women and larger children in single file, and behind them came the men. Lee was in the second wagon of the caravan, with wounded persons heaped all around him. As the train advanced, it passed between two lines of Mormon militia, the men standing solemnly ready, hands on their guns. Lee observed that the marching emigrants did not glance anxiously around them or seem to be alarmed.

After the caravan had gone three hundred yards, the lead wagon stopped, and Lee in the second wagon rose to his feet. The marching men and women and larger children were completely between two lines of Mormon soldiers. Bill, watching from a clump of bushes on the south, had his gaze on Lee who stood for several moments in the wagon and waited. Then, suddenly, Lee raised his hat.

In the next moment, Bill heard the roar of a hundred rifles, and saw a red barrage of flame. Seventy men, women and children dropped under that first deadly chain of fire. The guns roared again and twenty more fell. There was a third belch of flame. Meanwhile, Lee and his comrades in the wagons of the wounded were engaging in butchery still more horrible. Shooting, clubbing and knifing, they were murdering the wounded; and for a moment Bill clapped his hands to his ears to shut out the awful cries.

The next moment he saw something that made him stand. Unexpectedly, two men, coming to their senses and realizing the horrible treachery, took to their heels and fled like deer. Bill had never seen men run at such speed. Almost at once they vanished over the hillside; and then he saw Lee and Haight howling at their men and sending a dozen horsemen in pursuit. A few moments later, all the Mormons had fled the scene, and signaled to the Indians who had been waiting in ambush.

Yelling like assassins pouring out of bedlam, the Indians came out of hiding and swarmed over the dead and dying. One group raced to the wagons and carried the provisions away; a second made a bonfire of the emigrant fort; a third seized the small children and raced over the hills with them; but most of the redskins gave their energy to scalping and butchering where the Mormon militia had shot down more than a hundred and ten men, women and children.

One wounded man, hearing the yells, staggered to his feet and set off; but even while he went, blind with fear and pain, an Indian grasped his hair and scalped him. For a long moment the man wavered, his skull bright red in the sunlight; and then sank under a tomahawk in his brain. Others, writhing like desperate beasts, strove to escape by crawling, but the Indians leapt upon them with hideous yells and gutted them from breast bone to pelvis.

Feeling both anger and horror, Bill quietly looked at the scene and wondered what Brigham would say about it. He did not intend to tell

« 516 »

Brigham himself. For thirteen years he had served Brigham faithfully, but in all that time Brigham had never given him a cent for his labor, or even saddle horses and provisions, or food for his children and wife. Bill was growing tired of such neglect. If he killed a man and found five hundred dollars on him, Brigham took the money and put it in the church coffers. If he spent months fighting Indians and risking his life, he came home to learn that little or nothing had been done for his family while he was away. No, he would let Brigham find out about this in any way he could.

After the Indians had sated their lust for slaughter and blood and had fled, Bill went to the awful scene and looked around him. He had seen dead persons before, but never, he reflected, such a mangled gutted mess as he now beheld. Among those slaughtered and mutilated were about thirty children, ranging in age from seven or eight to sixteen. Like their parents, they had been scalped and tomahawked and disemboweled.

Westward the wagons were a smoking ruin of twisted iron and steel.

CHAPTER XX

B RIGHAM, MEANWHILE, KNOWING NOTHING OF THE INDIAN AND MORMON massacre, had been laying plans against the coming of an army, and reflecting on the wanton murder of Parley Pratt. The indiscreet Parley had fallen in love with the wife of a gentile in San Francisco. He had converted her and brought her to Salt Lake City; but the woman, grieving over the loss of her children who remained with their father, set out to recover them; and Parley had agreed to meet her in Arkansas to which the husband and father had gone. He had not met her there. He had been set upon, while attempting to flee, by the enraged husband and a few thugs, and had been shot and stabbed and left to bleed to death on an Arkansas highway.

Several weeks later, Brigham was thinking of the matter when John Lee strode into his office.

"What's this story," demanded Brigham, "about a massacre by Indians?"

"It's true," said John gravely. "The Indians wiped out that whole train. I tried my best to stop them but they got out of control."

"Go on! Tell me about it."

"Well," said Lee, "it was this way. This company from Arkansas and Missouri was a bad lot. All the way from here to Mountain Meadows they damned you and the church and said Joseph should a-been shot long before he was. They poisoned our cattle and fed the meat to the Indians, and several Indians took sick and died. That's when the trouble started."

"But I sent a letter by Haslem to Brother Isaac, telling him to protect that train."

"Yes, but it was all over when Haslem got back. Besides," said Lee, looking around him, "you said in your letter you guessed the Indians would do as they pleased. Well, they did."

"Why didn't you stop them? What are you Indian agent for?"

"I tried. But after some of them was poisoned, not even the Almighty could a-stopped them. You know how the Lamanites are."

"All right, tell me what happened."

"The Indians got mad and sent riders to all their tribes. Then they ttacked."

"Where were the emigrants?"

"On Mountain Meadows. When the Indians swooped down, the whites nade a circle of their wagons and dug holes and sunk the wheels. I tried o get the Indians to let them go to California but their blood was up. I ust as well a-talked to lunatics. Brother Isaac and me, we sent Haslem to ou and told him to ride like hell, but the Indians wouldn't wait. For five lays they yelled and rode around the camp until they had killed everyone."

"How many?"

"About sixty or seventy then."

"How many altogether?"

"Well, then they rode in and cut the throats of the women and children. They stripped them naked and scalped them and butchered them hor- ible. Then they left them to rot in the sun."

"How many?" Brigham roared.

"Over a hundred all told."

"My God! Wasn't anyone saved?"

"Just a few small children. They run off with the children and then etched them back and sold them to us."

"How old were these children?"

"Oh, very young. None of them more than seven or eight."

For a long moment Brigham gazed at Lee. "You mean they didn't kill he small children? I never heard of Indians saving small children before."

"Neither did I," said John, gazing steadily at his chief. "But they did his time."

"Why?"

"Well, I guess they figgered we'd buy them."

"I never heard of anything like that." Brigham was looking very sus- iciously at his Indian agent. "Well, what else?"

"Nothing much."

"Did you bury the bodies?"

"My God, we couldn't. You could smell them a mile away."

"You mean they're still rotting out in the sun?"

"By the Lord, you don't know how they stink. One reason is because hey were all rotten with syphilis before the Indians killed them."

"How do you know that?" asked Brigham sharply.

"Ask Brother Isaac. In fact, they was part of that Missouri mob. They boasted how they run us out of Missouri; and one of them swore he had the gun that they killed Joseph with."

"That was probably just boasting."

"I tell you they was a tough outfit. They were right out of hell."

"But how do you know they had syphilis?"

"If they didn't," asked Lee solemnly, "why would they stink so? You couldn't go within a half a mile of them three days later."

Brigham went to a window and looked out. "This," he said at last, speaking with emotion, "is the most horrible thing I ever heard of."

"But I tell you," Lee persisted, "they was a pack of hellhounds. Why, even the little children, they won't pray. I have two of them in my home, and when I get one of them to kneel to pray, the other one laughs at her. They swear like pirates."

"How old are they?"

"About five. They're just little savages. Honest to the Almighty, I never knowed a grown person who could cuss such a blue streak."

Brigham gazed at Lee and considered. How much of this story to believe, he did not know, nor did he know what to do about it. If Lee and Haight were guilty, to punish them would be to destroy all colonization in Dixie. If Mormons had a part in this crime, admission of it would arouse a wrath over the nation that would be mightier than any he had faced before—too mighty at the present moment, with an army marching against him.

"Did you know Brother Parley was murdered in Arkansas?"

"Yes, I heard about it."

"He was chopped down by a bunch of dirty curses. Joseph said we would see so much blood it would make our hearts sick. It's coming. The Federal army has reached the Rocky Mountains."

"Yes, I'd heard that too. Do you aim to let them through South Pass?"

"I don't know. I don't aim to let them through Echo Canyon."

"I feel bad," Lee said, "that I couldn't control them Indians."

"You ought to." Lee did not, it seemed to Brigham, look very remorseful. "It will cause more bitterness against us. If any more trains come through, I'll send soldiers to protect them against the Indians. It's your job to see that the Indians behave."

"That's a hard job," said Lee blandly, "especially when some of them gets poisoned."

Again Brigham gazed at the man, wondering how much of his story was true, how much was false. "Control the Indians after this," he said, and dismissed him.

A few days later, Brigham summoned all the scouts who were in the city and sent them to the eastern mountains. Under no circumstances, he said, was the Federal army to be allowed to cross South Pass. Bill rode side by side with Hosea Stout, a dirty, bearded roustabout whom he admired for his courage and his deadliness with a gun.

"We got a real job this time," said Bill.

"By the God of Israel, yes." Hosea bit off a huge quid of tobacco. "Brigham says there's some spies loose that we're to sock away. Richard Yates is one."

"We'll find him," said Bill.

While riding up Echo Canyon, Bill saw two scouts who were returning to report. They were Charles Decker and Jesse Earl, and Bill knew them as bold and resourceful men. "Howdy?" he said. "How's the war?"

"Not a gun fired yet," said Earl. "Ain't you been over?"

"Just on our way. We want a-know what's happened."

Earl assured him that a great deal had happened. Last August, Bob Burton had left the city with seventy-five men and had sent scouts as far east as the Platte; and when the vanguard of the army came in sight, it had been watched constantly and a daily express had reported to Brigham. For some reason, the Squaw Killer was not in command now.

"Who is?" asked Bill.

"Colonel Albert Sidney Johnston."

"Never heard of him. Can he fight?"

"We don't know. The way he handles his army don't scare us none."

"How big is the army?"

"God knows. It's scattered from hell to breakfast. The soldiers desert by the hundreds. Five hundred walked off in one bunch."

"Where is the damned army now?"

"All the way from Ham's Fork clear to hell and gone back East. The supply train is strung out a hundred miles. Charlie and me, we pretended to be Mormon haters and we entered the army and talked with the soldiers. You should hear what the bastards say. When we asked what they aimed to do, they all said the same thing. They intend to scalp old Brigham. They say when they get in the valley, each soldier will pick out a house for himself and a bunch of women. They all think they're going to have a harem and a lot of servants. They aim to hang the leaders and make the rest of us wait on them."

Bill grinned. "Ain't they countun their women a little soon? Where do they think we'll be?"

"They've heard about you. They figger you'll be hanging to a tree with the crows picking off your sidemeat."

"What do the officers say?"

"They won't talk. Since they captured Major Taylor and found a copy of the orders, they won't even grunt."

"Which orders?" asked Bill.

"From General Dan Wells. We're to stampede their animals, burn their trains, burn the whole country—but Port Rockwell has already been doing that. We're to keep them awake all night, fall trees across the road, destroy bridges, and just drive them crazy."

"Are the forts burned yet?"

"God, yes. Fort Bridger, that is."

"Who's burnun the trains?"

"That's Lot Smith's job."

"And our job," said Bill, looking around at his men. "Well, let's be off."

In a few days he came to Lot's small company, and Lot said he was mighty glad to see him. Bill was glad to see Lot Smith and to work under his command; for he had never known a more fearless man, or one more calmly and deliberately ruthless.

For the most part, Lot's company traveled during the night, and posted scouts during the day and took turns sleeping. Bill was usually sent ahead to look for approaching supply trains.

"Ox train a mile ahead," he reported at daylight one morning.

"Guards alert?"

"No. I think the whole damn outfit is asleep."

"Fine and dandy," said Lot, and with his men he dashed into the camp. The sentinel was caught napping. The teamsters were still in bed. "Who's in charge here?" Lot asked of a man.

"Captain Rankin," said a sleepy fellow, rubbing at his eyes.

Hearing the voices, Rankin came forward, walking angrily on short emphatic legs. "What's the meaning of this?"

"Are you in command here?"

"I am!"

"I'm Major Lot Smith. Turn your train around and head back for the States."

"By whose orders, sir?" asked Rankin, his eyes bulging with amazement.

"My orders, Captain."

"But on whose authority?"

"You see a part of the authority right here," said Lot, looking at his men. "The rest of it is back there in the brush."

"I'll do nothing of the sort, by God!" Rankin gazed back at the brush, evidently wondering how many men were concealed there. "This is insolence, sir!"

"It's orders," said Lot calmly. "Are you going or shall I burn your train?"

"How many men do you have back there?"

"About six hundred," said Lot, all of whose men were visible around him.

"Then, sir, I suppose I'll have to head back."

Rankin strode away, a short and thick and very indignant man. Within an hour his train headed eastward and pulled out; and Lot sent Bill to scout its movement. The next day, Bill reported that Rankin had turned westward again and was making haste.

"I guess," said Lot quietly, "I'll have to burn all the trains. It don't do any good to tell them to go back home."

He sent a captain and nineteen men to stampede the mules of the tenth regiment; and with twenty-three men he set out to intercept the supply trains moving in from South Pass. On the Big Sandy, Bill reported that he found a train of twenty-six large freight wagons on the old Mormon Trail.

"Good," said Lot. "We won't be so kind this time. We'll burn it."

His scouts watched the train's journey until nightfall; and a little before daylight, Lot and his men rode into the camp. The teamsters were awake but most of them were drunk. As Lot rode in, he had his men strung out behind him for a mile so that his force would seem to be much greater than it was.

"Who is commander here?" he roared.

"I am," said a large man, coming forward.

"What is your name?"

"I am Captain Dawson. And what is your name, sir?"

"I am Major Smith of the Army of Deseret. I'm going to burn your train."

"What? For God's sake, man, don't do that!"

"It's for His sake that I'm doing it. Tell your men to take from the wagons their private property but to be quick about it." Turning in his saddle, Lot signaled to his men and they galloped in. "Take their arms and put all the men under guard."

"You don't mean to burn the train?" asked Dawson. He was now behaving like a man half-scared out of his wits.

"Captain Dawson, you're part of an army sent out to exterminate us. This is war. Tell your men to move quickly, sir, or we won't wait."

Most of the teamsters were too drunk to understand orders, much less to recover their personal belongings; and they staggered around the camp, groaning and cursing, and threatening to shoot everyone in sight. They searched for their arms, but their arms had all been seized and stacked. Twenty rifles were trained upon them.

At this moment a man rode furiously into the camp, crying that he was from Colonel Alexander and had a message for the captain. Dawson sprang forward but Lot rode between the two men. "I'll hear the message," he said.

The rider gazed at him and then at Dawson. "What?"

"Captain Dawson, tell him to deliver the message." To the rider, Lot said: "And tell the truth. If you don't, I'll hang you to that tree."

"What?" said the man witlessly.

"We're prisoners," said Dawson. "Give the message."

"Colonel Alexander said to tell you the Mormons have armies in the field, and that you mustn't go to sleep at all, but keep guards all night. He said four companies with artillery will come tomorrow to escort you."

The irony of that was too much for Dawson. He shrugged and turned with a grin to the messenger. "Too late. You see what's happened."

Lot also grinned. "Too bad, Captain. Better luck next time. And now get all your men away from the wagons." Dawson summoned his men and led them a hundred yards up the creek. Lot sent a dozen of his men to guard them. "You got any powder in the wagons?"

The chagrined and drooping Dawson stared at his bills of lading. "No powder, Major Smith, but a lot of saltpeter and sulphur."

"In that case, Captain, I don't want to risk my men. I'll have to ask you to set the wagons afire."

"My God, no, Major!"

"Of course, Captain. It would be foolish for me to risk my men. I need them." Dawson had turned white. Still speaking very gravely, Lot asked: "Will you fire the wagons, Captain, or must I shoot you?"

Dawson clasped his hands in gawky and abject terror. "Major, I'm a sick man! I've been sick for months——"

Lot interrupted him by yelling: "Big Jim!"

"Yes, sir?" said a huge Irishman.

"You afraid of saltpeter and sulphur?"

"Major, I ain't afraid of the Devil hisself."

"All right, find some kerosene and drench the wagons and set them afire. Captain Dawson, you'd better get back with your men. It would break my heart to see you hurt."

When the kerosene had been spread, Lot seized a torch and ran with Big Jim from wagon to wagon until the whole train was a reef of flame. He then mounted his horse and rode off a hundred yards to watch. The burning of a train was, he decided, quite an odorous spectacle: the smell of bacon and dried fruits, of coffee and tea drenched the earth and seemed to make of the whole countryside an enormous kitchen. Suddenly, like a thousand hissing cats, a wagon exploded in sheets of blue flame, and the air was saturated with an odor that was overwhelming. Coughing and sneezing, Lot and his men rode farther back, and turned to gaze in wonder at the pale lovely gauze of burning sulphur.

A moment later, a horseman dashed upon the scene. After looking around him, he was so agog with amazement that he could only sit his horse and gape like an idiot at the fifty-seven flaming wagons. Riding over to him, Lot asked who he was and what he wanted; and the man stammered that he was a guard from another train and had come over to see what in the name of heaven was going on.

"That's fine," said Lot. "We'll burn your train next." He summoned

Dawson and took him and the messenger as prisoners. The other train he set afire while the astounded teamsters, retreating in a group under guard, stared at the bonfire of their wagons. One of Lot's scouts rode in and said there was a third train over on Big Sandy.

"Good. We just as well make it three in a row."

And off he went, leaving the second train in flame and smoke. Upon riding into the third camp, he asked a teamster where the captain was.

"Out after the cattle."

"Which way?"

"Out there down the hollow."

"Bill and Big Jim, come with me. You men disarm the camp."

A few hundred yards down a ravine, Lot found the captain. "Are you," he asked, "captain of this train?"

"I am."

"What's your name?"

"Simpson."

"Captain Simpson, I'm here on business."

"What kind of business?" asked Simpson, looking up at the scowling face of Big Jim.

"I'll take your pistols, if you don't mind."

"My pistols!" cried Simpson, turning red with anger. "By God, sir, no man ever took them yet! If you think you can, try it!"

"Captain Simpson, I'm engaged in the business of war—and so are you, if I'm not mistaken. I don't like bloodshed. It would take only a minute to kill you but I'd rather not."

Simpson looked at Bill, who was grinning; at Big Jim, who was still scowling, and resting a hand on a pistol. He turned with the men and went toward his camp; and a few moments later, seeing that his men were disarmed and under guard, he handed his weapons to Lot. "You have me at a disadvantage. We can't fight without arms."

Lot gazed at the man and considered. After such a craven fellow as Dawson, it was good to find a man who really wanted to fight. "Captain, in this war we don't need advantages and don't want them. If I give your men their arms, what will you do?"

"By God, we'll fight!"

"That suits us, Captain." Lot wheeled and faced the prisoners and his men. "Listen, Captain Simpson wants the guns restored. Then we'll fight it out ——"

"To hell with that!" cried one of the prisoners. "I'm a bull-whacker. I come to whack bulls and not to fight."

"Me, too," said another. "If Captain Simpson wants to fight, all right, but not us."

"What do you say to that, Simpson?"

"I say a damned dirty bunch of cowards!" He was red with fury. "You miserable yellow rats! If I'd been here while you were armed and you'd refused to fight, I'd have shot every one of you!"

"We're going to burn your train, Captain. I guess you'll have to take it with a grin."

Simpson was so enraged he looked strangled. He stared at his men, hating them, despising them. He turned to Lot. "And what kind of report can I make to the commander? You'll burn my train and leave these cowardly fellows to starve! What excuse will I have?"

"You were taken by surprise, Captain. That often happens in war. But we won't starve these brave fellows who were sent out to exterminate us. Load a wagon with food and pull it out."

"Two wagons," said Simpson. "Won't you give me two?"

Lot grinned. "All right, two. We'll need some provisions also. You see, the Federal government is boarding us while we burn your trains."

"A fine God-damned mess!" cried the captain, looking around him.

"See yonder smoke? That's from two of your supply trains."

Simpson gazed at the smoke and then at Lot. After a few moments he turned with scowling distaste to his men. "I ask one favor," he said to Lot. "Don't burn the train while I'm in sight. It will ruin me."

"Don't be squeamish, Captain. The trains burn nicely. They make a gorgeous fire. Besides, I haven't any time for ceremonies. You fellows came out for war, didn't you? And that's what you've run into."

"I don't know why we came out," said Simpson. "I came because I was ordered to."

"You came to scalp old Brigham Young. It'll take more than a Federal army to do that job. All right, you men, move fast and get your wagons out of here. Bill, take a dozen men and get us some food. Big Jim, get ready to fire them."

After this train was burned, Lot sent scouts in all directions but they could find no more; and thereupon he decided to stampede the cattle. His first effort rounded up five hundred head, and these he sent with three herdsmen into Salt Lake Valley. Soon after this exploit, he learned from one of his scouts that a captain named Marcy had been assigned to capture him, and was now hot on his trail.

Doubling back, Lot fell in behind Marcy and his troops; and just at daylight the next morning, he caught the camp off guard. When he and his men rode in, Marcy's soldiers scattered like hares, vainly seeking their rifles. A tall man in a captain's uniform strode out.

"I'm Captain Marcy," he said stiffly. "I presume I'm addressing Captain Smith."

"Major Smith, sir, though it makes little difference."

"I'm in command of United States troops. May I ask what armed force you command?"

"We are from Utah."

"What is your business here?"

"What is *your* business here?"

"I am looking for a new and shorter route to the coast."

"Nonsense!" Lot cried. "You've left the main road. It passes through Echo Canyon, as you know as well as anyone."

Lot's contempt made Marcy smile. "You seem to misunderstand my intent. We do not wish to fight the people of Utah——"

"No, I suppose the Federal army is just taking a little vacation!"

Marcy smiled again. He seemed determined to keep his temper. "I am sorry for the difficulties in Utah, but we are not out here to make war."

"Like hell you aren't. You're out here with a knife in your hand to cut our throats, but we've got a pretty good hold on that hand and we intend to keep it."

"You still misunderstand," said Marcy patiently. "I have with me letters of introduction to your leaders."

"Really, Captain? Then I suggest you *send* them in for you'll never get there yourself."

"Why not, Major?"

"Because if you try to enter the valley we'll chop you to pieces. If you had an army a hundred times as big as this one, there'd still be nothing but hide and hair left of it when it hit Echo Canyon."

"But we can take other routes, Major. There's a northern way."

"We are ready there, too."

For a long moment Marcy gazed at Lot and considered; and Lot, in glancing around, saw that the captain's men were now armed and waiting.

"Major, will you take my letters of introduction to Governor Young?"

"No, Captain. I don't expect to return this winter. I expect to remain here and see that you fellows have a nice comfortable time of it when the snow is ten feet deep."

Marcy looked at Bill, at Irish Jim. "Very well, Major, if that's the way you see it."

"Come," said Lot, and with his men he galloped off. He had not gone far when he saw that he had been stealthily surrounded. "This way!" he shouted, and dashed down a steep bank and plunged into Ham's Fork. He was barely in time. No sooner had he and his men crossed the river and gained the opposite bank than a body of cavalry came into sight and ordered his surrender.

"Go to hell!" Lot roared.

The troops quickly dismounted and fired, and two of Lot's horses fell. "Don't shoot," he said. "Let's be off."

At full speed he and his men rode away and out of sight.

CHAPTER XXI

A FEW WEEKS LATER, BRIGHAM'S GRIN WAS BROADER THAN IT HAD BEEN IN many months. Johnston and his army were snowed in upon the ruins of Fort Bridger; and around him in all directions his frozen beasts lay dead for thirty miles. Scouts reported that the animals which had perished numbered hundreds, perhaps thousands; and that there was no feed for the living, no shelter for the men. The soldiers, with only sage-brush for fuel, were huddled in tents under clumps of willows; and all avenues of escape were buried under ten feet of snow.

Brigham was ginning at more than that. Cumming, the new governor, whom a Federal army had escorted to the burned ruins of the fort, had had a hole dug in the frozen earth and roofed with logs; and this hut he called the capital of Utah Territory. The new judge was holding court there, and a grand jury was indicting the Mormons right and left. That was too much for Brigham's sense of irony. The United States, doubtless for reasons of politics or graft, had sent an army at huge expense to ex-terminate the Mormons; and there it was, high in the mountains, snow-bound and frozen and scared to death. There Cumming, the incredible dolt, was sending proclamations to "ex-Governor Young," declaring that he, Alfred Cumming, shivering in a dugout, was the new governor—though Brigham had never been removed by the President. There a new judge, sent to replace the loutish Drummond who had fled his harlot, was presiding over a grand jury in a hole in the earth, and indicting the Mor-mons for treason.

It was all too much for Brigham. He laughed until tears ran down his cheeks, hugged his portly belly, and meditated on ironic gestures. A white mule belonging to the army had wandered into the city. Remembering this, Brigham drew a sheet of paper to him and wrote a letter to Johnston, offering to return the beast or to care for it; and concluding: "But should you prefer leaving it in my care during the winter, it will probably be in better plight for you upon your return to the East in the spring."

"When he reads that," he said to Heber, "he will die of apoplexy."

"I hope," said Heber, "he does."

Brigham gave his energy to more than ironic thrusts at his snowbound and flabbergasted foe. He sent a memorial to Congress, asking for fair play. "Please let us know what you want of us before you prepare your halters to hang, or apply the knife 'to cut out the loathsome, disgusting ulcer.' Do you wish us to deny our God and renounce our religion? That we shall not do."

Knowing that his petitions and memorials achieved little, Brigham waited for indignant voices in the East; and when he read the fiery words of Sam Houston, the Texas hero who was now a Senator, he was so pleased that he chuckled. If he had a dozen Houstons in the eastern states, his troubles would be done with.

"The more men you send to the Mormon war," Houston had said on the Senate floor, "the more you increase the difficulty. They have to be fed. For sixteen hundred miles you have to transport provisions. The regiments sent there have found Fort Bridger and other places heaps of ashes. They will find Salt Lake City if they ever reach it a heap of ashes. Whoever goes there will meet the fate of Napoleon's army; for these people if they fight will fight desperately. They are defending their homes. They are fighting to prevent the execution of threats that touch their hearths and their families; and depend upon it that they will fight until every man perishes."

Brigham pondered what he had read. It might be better, he reflected, to burn the city and flee, rather than to chop an army to pieces in Echo Canyon. That would be smart strategy. That would arouse the sympathy of the world. Finding the notion more and more engaging as he considered it, Brigham read again.

"As for troops to conquer the Mormons, fifty thousand would be as insufficient as two or three thousand. I say your men will never return, but their bones will whiten the valley of Salt Lake. Mr. President, if you will find out what the Mormons are willing to do, we may have peace. But so sure as the troops advance, so sure they will be annihilated. These people expect nothing but extermination. . . ."

It seemed to Brigham to be a fine speech from a great champion of freedom; and as he reread passages which pleased him, he decided not to chop the army to pieces in the canyon but to burn the city and flee. He would desolate every settlement in the entire valley and take his people to Mexico if he must. Houston was right: he could destroy an army of a million men, but if he did, the States would howl with infernal wrath and send another army, routing it in from Oregon and California. It would be better to burn and withdraw. That he would eventually have to do so, he did not doubt, for he had been told that Albert Sidney Johnston was a very stubborn man.

During the next weeks, Brigham kept scouts posted to watch the snowbound army, and sent word over the earth to summon home all the apostles and other leaders in foreign lands. He called his people in from many of the colonies north, west and south, and laid plans for another great migration, sending vast stores of food southward to be ready when the saints burned their cities and marched again.

"Freedom," he said to his leaders, "is the thing we're fighting for. We'll fight until we find it, or until we are all murdered. There should be no fear in our hearts. I want to see no fear in any man; and if I do, I'll throw him out of here."

Above the watchfulness and anxieties, this winter of 1858 was a gay one, with many festivals and dances, parties and theatricals and banquets; for Brigham was determined to keep the morale of his people at a high level and be ready for any crisis. He wrote Johnston that if he entered the valley when spring came, he would find the city in ashes and the people gone. "You may have the valley; but you will find it as we found it ten years ago: the home of rattlesnakes and crickets and coyotes and wolves."

Late in February, a person unexpectedly arrived. He was Colonel Thomas Kane, a man who had often spoken in defense of the saints, especially in Washington. Joseph had known him. Brigham had seen him years ago. Sick, with only one companion, Kane had gone to the Isthmus of Panama and thence to Los Angeles, and from there overland to Salt Lake City. He had come as peacemaker and friend. "I want to see Brigham alone," he said.

"Colonel," said Brigham, smiling, "I know what's on your mind. Your mission is hopeless."

"No, Governor, not hopeless. I am a sick man——"

"Of course you are. You look sick and scrawny and starved. You look like you'd come through a hundred fevers."

"I'm a sick man and I'm ready to go when God calls me. But I don't want bloodshed here. I've come thousands of miles at my own expense. I've always been friendly toward the Mormons."

"I believe that, Colonel."

"I want peace here, Governor. I'm an army man and I know if Johnston comes down Echo Canyon next spring, you can chop him to pieces and never lose a man. But that is not the Christian way."

"Christian way, Colonel! Do you talk to me of Christians? For twenty years we've been trying to get away from them."

"Yes, I know. But we can iron out the difficulties——"

"No, Colonel. I'm proud of your friendship and I trust you. But I know better. I know how we have been driven like cattle for thirty years—from place to place until we fled to a desert. I know our enemies will never stop until they have exterminated us or driven us out of the country. You can't tell me anything else."

"You miss some important aspects of the matter. Why, back East they're already calling this expedition Buchanan's Blunder. The European press is up in arms about a nation founded on principles of liberty that is, as you say, driving a part of its people to their death. And that's the point. Public opinion is turning your way. Buchanan would never dare send another army. It's being found out that his Secretary of War is a grafter. Contractors have made millions on this expedition. Don't you see that you have them whipped? But not if you destroy the army——"

"I'll not, Colonel. We're going to burn our homes and flee again."

"Burn your homes! Destroy all that you've built up in ten years?"

"Didn't we build in Ohio and have to leave it? In Missouri? Didn't we build a city in a swamp in Illinois and have to give it to our enemies? We're used to it, Colonel."

"Not that," said Kane, shaking his sick gray head. "In God's name, don't burn your homes!"

"That's exactly what we'll do. We're ready to leave. Every man knows his job. When Johnston resumes his march, a hundred men will turn this city into a bonfire."

"God, no, no! Let's not do that! Let's find a peaceful way out."

"There is no peaceful way." Brigham brought a fist angrily to his desk. "Colonel, we tried peace again and again. They murdered us. They raped our women, burned our homes. Well, by the God of Israel, this time we'll burn them ourselves!"

"No," Kane repeated, shaking his head. "Not that, not that."

"What do you propose?"

"Let them march in. Give them your hospitality and friendship. Then you'll shame your enemies back East until they'll hang their heads."

Brigham smiled. "Colonel, I'm afraid you have a child's belief in the prevalence of shame. Nothing can shame them. Even burning our homes and fleeing into another desert won't shame them. No, you're wrong. If I let the soldiers in here, in a few weeks they'll own us. They'll seduce our women, bring disease among us, gambling, drinking, whoring, thieving. No, Colonel, I won't have them among us. That's final."

"But if they give pledges——"

"And besides, Johnston is setting the Indians against us. I have scouts out. I know what he's doing. Indians are chasing our stock off and tell us a white chief at Fort Bridger told them to."

"Well," said Kane, "I'll go over and see Cumming and Johnston and try to reason with them."

"If you want to. But it will amount to nothing."

It did not amount to much. While Brigham was busy with plans to burn the city, word came that Cumming would enter unescorted. Early in April he did. Dan Wells said he didn't want Cumming in the city at all, but Brigham said not to bother about it; for the feeling of the saints, he declared, would be cold enough to freeze peaches.

On his journey down Echo Canyon, Cumming was overawed: he saw such huge bonfires that the entire gorge was illuminated during the night when he came through. He was met by an army that saluted him and listened to his quavering speech; whereupon the soldiers hurried down the canyon and met him again, pretending to be a second army, and met him a third and a fourth time—until Cumming decided that the mountains were alive with armed men. Along the canyon walls, and upon the peaks on both sides, he saw great fires in the darkness, heard the reverberations of rifles, the weird echoes of mules and men. In Weber Canyon he was met by other armed companies; and in the village of Farmington, a band turned out to play national anthems. Cumming was confused by all this. He was flabbergasted the next day when, upon finding the roads choked with throngs moving southward, he asked who the people were and where they were going and was told that they were the Mormons fleeing to another desert. Every home, he was grimly assured by those who accompanied him, would be burned; every shrub and tree would be cut down; and the whole area of Utah would be a blackened and treeless desolation.

When lodged in the city, he asked Brigham to come and visit him; and Brigham went, accompanied by Heber Kimball and George Smith. He found a large and very fat man whose big face looked like that of a stupid sulking woman. The corners of the mouth turned down sharply. The gray eyes, too close together, seemed to have gathered habitual petulance that looked all the more foolish because of the enormous roll of fat under the weak chin.

"Mr. Young," he said, "you have a beautiful valley here. Your fruit has excellent flavor."

"We like it," said Brigham, grimly amused. "If you had come in last fall, we could have made you more comfortable."

That veiled remark made Cumming look startled. "My winter hasn't been pleasant. I have a crow to pick with you on account of that."

"Very well," said Brigham, smiling faintly. "You preach a sermon about it. For your text I suggest, 'The people who know me best love me best.'"

Kane had entered and now spoke up quickly. "That, Brigham, is not only a text. It is a sermon in itself."

After the innocuous visit was terminated, there was earnest discussion of Cumming. George Smith swore to the Lord that at first he thought the man was a drunkard. "But when I examined him with my glasses, I could see he's only a moderate drinker. But he's a glutton. He must weigh two hundred and fifty pounds."

"Well," said Kane, "I caught the fish, Brigham. Now you cook him as you please."

The next day, while Brigham was wondering what to do with his fish, word came to him of what Cumming had said after the visit. Cumming had declared that Brigham was as mild as a lamb and not a fighter; but Heber Kimball, he said, was a fierce rogue who needed hanging if a man ever did. They were not bad fellows, all in all. He thought he would like them.

In the next interview, Brigham almost lost his temper. Cumming wanted his mansion. He had not, he admitted, been able to learn where it was, and he wanted to know at once. Scowling like a great sulking boy, he said: "Ex-Governor Young, I want my office."

Kane spoke up quickly. "The office you speak of, Governor Cumming, is part of Mr. Young's private residence."

"Then where is my office?"

"That question," said Brigham sharply, "you will address to the man who sent you here."

"Do you mean to say I'm here as governor and don't even have an office?"

"That's just about it. And I'd like to ask, Governor, why you have set the Indians upon us. We have lived at peace with them. Now they come into our homes and say we are squaws and won't fight, and that the soldiers will come in and help them murder us."

"That ain't possible," said Cumming, and choked a little. The fat on his throat turned crimson.

"You'll have a hard time making us believe anything else. Perhaps I may see your private instructions?"

"Why, yes. But not right now."

Brigham placed no faith in this man or in Kane's efforts. Day after day the streets of the city were crowded with the saints from northern settlements who were on their way south. The plant of the newspaper was moved to a southern town; church records were boxed and shipped to Provo; stores of supplies moved steadily southward by wagon and pack train. Cumming was annoyed. If the Mormons moved out, then, he said, he would find himself governor of a burned area, peopled by Indians and soldiers. To his protests, Brigham always gave the same answer.

"When the soldiers march in, we burn the city and leave."

"Then what will I do?"

"Ask the man who sent you."

When, one day, Cumming demanded to know where the Territory's safe was, Brigham took him over two high fences to a vacant lot. "There it is."

"But why do you keep it here?"

"Because, Governor, we intend to burn the city but we don't want to burn any Federal property."

Cumming was a bewildered man. In one public meeting after another, he addressed the saints, declaring that he had come to rule fairly and calmly; but a man would shout: "Didn't your grand jury indict President Young for treason last winter?" Then Cumming would burn with anger and confusion. When he opened his mouth again, a voice would roar: "Didn't you say Heber Kimball should be hanged?" Then, sweating and panting and rosy with anger, he would waddle like a great duck out of the building and go to his room to meditate.

The exodus southward gathered such volume that Cumming went out to the road to Provo to investigate. He counted eight hundred wagons in one train. Accosting the leaders, he urged them to return to their homes; but they ignored him or gave him short answer.

"Send the soldiers back and we will."

In desperation he went again to Brigham. "Isn't there any way to stop all this moving?"

"Yes, Governor. Send the soldiers back and we'll accept you as governor and return to our homes. As it is now, the Federal government is sending six thousand more soldiers. You know that."

"Yes, I know it and I'm doing all I can to stop it. By God, if I can't stop it, then I say to protect yourselves if the soldiers come!"

Cumming's outburst brought a sly twinkle to Brigham's eyes. "In that case, Governor, you might as well join us. If we choose, we could use them up in a hurry."

"No," said Cumming, looking red and foolish, "I couldn't very well join you."

"Then which side would you be on? The middle wouldn't be very safe."

"I'll do this," said Cumming desperately. "I'm going to Johnston and tell him to stay where he is until I order him to move. If he doesn't, then I'm going to call on your army to make him do it."

"Then you'd better hurry. The roads will soon be open."

"I'll go at once."

"By all means. When Johnston moves this way, we set the fires."

Whether the fires would ever be started, Brigham did not know— for matters were turning in his favor. On the floor of the Senate there had recently been scathing indictment of Buchanan's expedition. The New York *Times* had declared that it "would puzzle ordinary men why a hostile army was sent against Utah. If the whole business does not end in open and bloody rebellion, it is not likely to be saved from that issue by any special wisdom on the part of the general government." Sam Houston called the expedition an intolerable evil; and a few days later the *Times* said witheringly that the Mormon issue offered all that was needed for the glory of statesmen. "Impudent imposture, murders, rapes, polygamy, treason, defiance to the government—nothing is wanting to convert our venerable president into a glorious crusader. An army was sent to chastise rebels before it was ascertained whether there were any rebels to chastise!"

Brigham smiled with quiet satisfaction as there came to him the damning editorials from the eastern press. One outburst he liked especially. "Whatever our opinion may be of Mormon morals, there can be no question that this voluntary and even cheerful abandonment by forty thousand people of homes created by wonderful industry, in the midst of trackless wastes, after years of hardship and persecution, is something from which no one can withhold his admiration. Such sincerity is not to be sneered at."

Brigham had been right in his judgment that desertion of homes would excite anger and sympathy throughout the civilized world; and day by day he waited to learn what the final result would be. He did not wait long. Word came that a peace commission was on its way at full speed; and early in June, a Major McCulloch of Texas, and L. W. Powell, a senator-elect from Kentucky, rode into the city. They entered a city that was deserted save for a handful of men who waited to apply the torches. Upon learning of their arrival, Brigham summoned his leaders from their tents and shanties south of Provo and held a meeting in the Council House.

Powell announced pompously that he had brought a pardon from the President. Annoyed, Brigham rose to his feet and spoke calmly of the settlement of the Basin, the coming of Federal officials, the troubles which ensued. "The Federal government," he said, turning to Powell, "has sent us the worst shysters it could find: cowardly politicians, drunkards, and judges who sat on the bench with a whore at their side."

McCulloch leapt to his feet. "It's not agreeable to me," he roared, "to hear the government spoken against!"

"I'm not speaking against the government," said Brigham sharply. "I'm speaking against the scoundrels in high office. I'll thank you, Major, if you'll correct me when I speak against the *government* of the United States."

"We're not interested in the past," said Powell. "As for President Buchanan, I believe him to be a wise and patriotic man."

That angered Brigham. "Then what do you want of us? Why are you here?"

"We want you to submit to the laws and let the government send in troops."

"I suppose, Mr. Powell, you justify Missouri in the treatment it gave us?"

"I don't know the facts in that case."

"I suppose you justify Illinois?"

"I'm sorry, President Young, but I'm ignorant of those matters."

"Mr. Powell, we want security for our safety. That's what we want."

"The only security we can offer you is the President's proclamation."

Brigham took the document and looked at it again. "Gentlemen, allow me to read from it. The President says this is no crusade against our religion. He says: 'The Constitution and laws of this country can take no notice of your creed, whether it is true or false. That is a question between your God and yourselves, in which I disclaim all right to interfere. If you obey the laws, keep the peace and respect the rights of others, you will be perfectly secure, and may live on in your present faith.'" Brigham looked at Powell. "Do you mean to tell me we can count on that?"

"Absolutely. The President would not say it if he did not mean it."

"The President," said Brigham, his lips curling, "has pardoned us for forty-three crimes, and we're guilty of only one of them."

"Which one is that?"

"Burning the supply trains."

"We are not here to investigate. We are here for peace."

"If we allow the soldiers to come in, will you keep them out of our cities?"

"I pledge you we will."

Brigham frowned. He did not believe it, but he was weary of bickering. He asked his leaders present if they wished to speak. George Smith rose. He said he accepted the pardon because he did not want bloodshed. Looking down his nose at McCulloch, he declared he did not think Buchanan would violate his pledge unless it was to his political advantage to do so. Right now, added George scathingly, a depleted treasury would not allow him to repudiate a promise.

Heber then rose and said he was for peace. Other leaders echoed Heber but Brigham was unconvinced. "Gentlemen," he said wearily, "it is one thing to make a pledge, another to keep it. It is my personal conviction that the soldiers will demoralize what we have labored ten years to build. You have heard my counselors speak: they want peace, and so do I, but I am not as credulous as they are. I have little faith in these pledges. Just the same, if Governor Cumming will promise to maintain law and order in this valley, you may tell Johnston to march in."

"I'll do everything in my power," Cumming said.

"Will you sustain our police against the lawless elements in our cities?"

"Most emphatically I will."

Brigham shrugged. For a moment his gaze rested on Cumming, then on Powell and McCulloch, and then on his own leaders. When he spoke, his voice seemed to Heber to be weary and without hope.

"All right," he said, "tell Johnston to come."

CHAPTER XXII

BRIGHAM KNEW THE HUMAN HEART TOO WELL TO BELIEVE IN PLEDGES born of political expediency; and the fact that the army behaved itself while marching through the silent and deserted city did not reassure him at all. He sent word to his people to return to their homes. He himself went into retirement, unable to believe that his enemies would not eventually whip him or that an attempt would not be made on his life. The entrances to his homes were locked and bolted and guards were placed outside. There would be no public meetings, he said; and no visitors would be admitted to his presence whom he did not wish to see.

The army marched south and established itself in Cedar Valley, the largest regular force ever concentrated upon the soil of the United States in a time of peace. There Fort Floyd was built. It was named for the Secretary of War who soon proved himself to have been the most execrable traitor in the Union; because, sympathizing with the southern states, he had sent a part of the army as far away as he could. Near the fort was Frog Town where whiskey was offered at ten dollars a gallon. A score of harlots entered the valley.

Editors back East were now declaring that the Mormons ought to be reformed, and that the officers, both civil and military, should prove to be exemplary. Brigham was bored by such naive statements. He turned to Heber.

"How are things going?"

"The reformers are behaving as you expected. Last week a justice of the supreme court got so drunk he fell into a gutter. He swore like a brigand and said he would shoot Craig, the Indian agent. He yanked out a pistol and Craig yanked out a knife but they were too drunk to get on their feet. So they laid in the gutter and swore at one another."

"What is this story about Chief Justice Eckles?"

"Oh, him," said Heber, and scowled. "Why, it's true, I guess. We found a letter he dropped. It was to a lieutenant named Bennett. Eckles wrote he was damned sorry he hadn't been able to find a mistress for Bennett."

"Is it true some of the officers have induced a few of the sisters to go to Camp Floyd?"

"I guess so, Brigham. At least a dozen went. Did you hear of the officer who went through Nephi? He offered one of Sam Ostrom's wives three hundred dollars to go with him. But over at Camp Scott, that's the worst. The soldiers are raping the squaws. They slip into the tents when the bucks are away. The bucks rent their squaws out for money to buy whiskey. The worst is that the soldiers have syphilis. Chief Yampants the other day burned six squaws because they had syphilis."

Brigham groaned. "The Indians will all be demoralized by syphilitic half-breeds. How many whores are there in this city now?"

"It's hard to find out. Porter says he knows of about twenty. By the way, did you see this article in the *Atlantic Monthly?*" Heber drew the magazine from a pocket. "Read this paragraph."

Brigham read: "The unruly crowd of camp followers which is the inseparable attendant of an army has concentrated in Salt Lake City, and is in constant contact and conflict with the Mormon population. An apprehension prevails, day after day, that the presence of the army may be demanded there to prevent bloodshed. The judges are probably on their way to the States to resign their commissions."

Brigham sighed. "I knew it would be this way. How many police do we have now?"

"We've added two hundred. That makes four times as many as we had."

"Well, we'll let matters take their course for a while. Keep me advised."

A week later, Alexander Wilson, the United States attorney for Utah, called on Brigham to say good-bye. His wife's health was poor, he said; but Brigham knew that this tall thin man was sick of the conditions here. He faced Wilson and smiled.

"When you get back to the States, you will be asked many questions about me. Tell them that I am here, watching the progress of civilization."

Wilson's pale face grinned. "I will, President Young. I'll tell the truth."

"The truth," said Brigham, "ought to be enough."

After Wilson left the office, Brigham sat for a long while in thought. In a crisis like this, he knew of nothing to be done. Gambling and drunkenness, prostitution and murder were rampant; but there was a new governor now, unfriendly judges, and an army to enforce their will. He would have to wait. Unless he was mistaken, there was a war brewing between the northern and southern states; and if it came, he would again take control of his people. Until then, he would rest and read, and let civilization be as sinful as it wished to be.

One day Heber told him the story of the grafters. When Johnston arrived a year ago with his army, he learned to his amazement that he had three thousand bedsacks, of use in summer picnics but worthless for soldiers wintering seven thousand feet above the sea. He had only seven hundred and twenty-three blankets for twenty-five hundred men, but he had nearly two thousand pairs of epaulets. He had only eight hundred pairs of boots, only nine hundred and thirty-eight coats; but he had nearly twelve hundred military stocks, as well as huge stores of other gadgets for which he had no use. The Secretary of War had allowed his friends to sell the army large quantities of worthless goods. More than that: one of Secretary Floyd's friends was paid ten cents a pound to transport across the plains tons of flour which he actually bought in Utah. Such, said Heber, were the shameless grafters who were going to civilize the Mormons.

Brigham's laughter was sardonic. He was still chuckling a half-hour later when one of his wives entered. He scowled when he saw her—for she was one of the worst pests in his household. One week she wanted a dress, the next, jewels or furs; she coaxed and wheedled, and if she failed in these, she flew into tantrums.

"Brigham," she said silkily, "have you seen what Europe is saying about you?"

"What?" he asked, disliking the coquettish way she stroked his hair.

"They're calling you the new Prince of Orange. They say your threat to burn the city is equal to that of the Dutch when they flooded Holland to save it from France. You proud?"

"What is it you want?"

"Aren't you proud to be called the Prince of Orange?"

"Clothes or jewels?"

"I need a fur coat."

"A fur coat!" he bellowed. "Do you know how much a fur coat costs?"

"But you have lots of money. Besides, my old coat is falling to pieces."

Yes, he reflected, he was a wealthy man—but only because he had been a shrewd one. He had bought parcels of real estate, or had taken for himself choice pieces in the new colonies; he had a few mills and shops of his own; he drew a salary from the church coffers. But he had to make a lot of money to support a family like his.

"Fashions, fashions, that's all you women think about!"

"Now don't get vulgar the way you did in a sermon."

"How?" he asked, squaring around to look at her.

"Why, you said—you said right in meeting that if a woman walked down the street with a—a ——"

"A what?"

"With a cob stuck in her—oh, it makes me blush to think of it!"

"I despise your damnable fashions!" he roared. "I can't walk the streets without seeing your legs. If a wind blows, I see clear to your rumps."

"Brigham!" she cried, pretending to be shocked.

"If you must wear hoops, why don't you tie them down with weights so your petticoat won't blow over your head? You show one end as much as the other."

"Brigham, you embarrass me."

"Nothing embarrasses a woman if she's in style."

"Just the same, you've noticed at dances the men go after the women who are well-dressed."

"A pile of folderols! Fine feathers don't make a lady."

"They make her look better."

"If you saw an angel, do you think she'd have three yards of dress dragging in the dirt? No. She would be neat and simple. If it was the fashion for men to go unbuttoned, do you think I would?"

"Of course."

He rose and faced her. "You frivolous person! I don't like your damned nasty fashions. Did you ever see me with hermaphrodite pantaloons on?"

"Fornication pantaloons. That's what they're called now."

"Rather than be a slave to such giddy nonsensical——"

"But a fur coat isn't giddy."

"It costs too much. If I bought furs for all my wives and daughters, I'd not have a cent left. Go on, make a coat for yourself. Run along."

After she had left, Brigham sank to his desk and put a hand to his brow. The frivolous interests of women filled him with anger and grief —and even with shame; for the best of them set their hearts on peacock frills, tinseled ornaments, superfluous masses of silk and satin. Besides his wives, he had nearly a score of daughters whose heads were turned by every new fashion that came with the wind. Money was needed to keep missionaries in the field, to build temples, to care for the sick and the poor; yet the giddy-headed creatures clamored for fur coats when there were persons without enough bread to eat. Formerly they had made their clothes. They had sewed and spun and washed, but now they wanted to buy every new thing they saw in the stores.

There were his daughters. A dozen of them were receiving young men in the huge parlor; and every week, almost every day, they begged him for this dress, that hat; for silk stockings, jewels, trinkets; for candy and flowers, and silly adornments for their hair. He had told the young men to leave the house by ten o'clock, but of late he suspected that they were not doing so. He suspected they turned the lights down and sat in darkness and lollygagged. He resolved one evening to investigate.

When, with candle in hand, he peeked in, he found matters as he had expected them to be. The lamp had a pile of books in front of it to dim the light; and off among sofas and pillows were the girls, tightly clasped in strong young arms of men who murmured nonsense in giddy ears. He entered softly, and then marched from couple to couple, thrusting the candle into their red and guilty faces and regarding them with a terrible scowl. He went to the lamp and knocked the books aside and turned the light to its fullest brilliance. Then he gazed around him for several moments during which the fall of a pin would have sounded like a bombshell. Still without speaking, he entered the hallway and returned with a great armful of hats and coats.

"It's after ten o'clock," he said. "You gentlemen will identify your wraps."

The abashed young men came forward and pawed in the heap of

clothes. One by one they found their coats and hats and quietly left the house.

Brigham turned to his daughters. They were, he admitted, an attractive group of wenches. Some were blue-eyed and fair, some were tall and dark and stately; and all of them were full-bosomed and warm-lipped. Their cheeks were flushed now with shame but their eyes were cold.

"How many times do I have to tell you that your young men must leave by ten o'clock? How many times must I tell you to keep the light as it should be?"

A tall queen with black hair and eyes came over and faced him. "You don't seem to trust your daughters very much."

"I know the world. I know men and I know women."

"At least you think you do."

"Silence!" he thundered. Barefooted and with his candle he entered the hallway and climbed the stairs. He felt rather old and foolish tonight.

Month after month he remained in hiding, with guards at his doors, with enemies doubtless plotting his death; with his empire disintegrating around him; with gamblers and harlots and fraudulent officials making a jest of all that he had built and fought for. It seemed to him that his wives and daughters ought to realize how grave the situation was and to put frivolous thoughts from their minds. It was little enough to ask. But with Federal troops almost in their dooryard, with the whole future dark and uncertain, they persisted in thinking of guilty wooing in unlit corners, of every foolish change in styles.

As a matter of fact, Brigham sank more and more under silence and bitterness during these two years of self-imposed imprisonment. He continued to direct the affairs of his people, to colonize north and south, to establish the church in far lands; but as yet he could see no way out of the dilemma here. The soldiers, it appeared, would remain forever. Other harlots came to the valley, other gamblers, other shysters of a dozen breeds; and daily reports came to him of violence and sinful doings among his own people as well as the gentiles. Editors and preachers in the eastern states were again denouncing polygamy and the Mormons; and visitors of all kinds were coming to the city.

Brigham was bored by most of the visitors but it was no part of his plan to refuse to see them. He was bored by Horace Greeley. As soon as he looked at the famous editor of the New York *Tribune*, with his great mound of forehead, his long loose beard that hung under his chin like a half-sheared fleece, his narrow eyes and tight lips, he knew that Greeley was too pompously sure of his own greatness. Brigham surmised, too, that the man's grotesque clothes were chosen to impress and not out of disregard of appearance.

Clasping hands over his huge belly, Greeley gazed serenely at Brigham as if he were studying something out of a jungle. "I'd like to ask you some questions," he said.

"All right," said Brigham.

"Is it true you Mormons believe in a personal devil?"

"We do."

"Why?" asked Greeley, his fat face as solemn as an owl's.

"Because we believe in a God with body, parts and passions, not in a spirit that moves around in the universe like a piece of fog. We believe the Devil is a person and not an evil force in the atmosphere."

"Isn't that a rather primitive belief?"

"All truth is primitive after you've panned the ore down to the gold."

Greeley heaved a great sigh. "You also believe in polygamy?"

"In celestial marriage," said Brigham gently.

"Isn't it the same thing?"

"Not at all. Celestial marriage is a covenant from God. Polygamy in itself may be only a vice."

"I see," said Greeley. His Scotch eyes twinkled.

"It may interest you to know, Mr. Greeley, that we don't believe in prostitutes and that we try to keep them out of our communities. Most Christians believe in the good women they marry, and the bad women they sneak off to bed with. We believe all women have a holy function in life."

"And what is that?"

"To have children and a home to put them in. All the women in our communities have husbands."

"Even the homely ones?"

"We attach no great importance to a lovely face. Righteousness and not beauty makes the good mother."

"Do you find that your—your celestial marriage, as you call it, takes care of the problem of adultery?"

"We have adultery, but not as much as in your cities back East. Adultery for us is one of the three worst crimes."

"What, may I ask, are the others?"

"Murder, and sinning against the Holy Ghost."

Greeley hitched around in his chair. "I suppose you believe the Holy Ghost is a real person too."

"Yes."

Greeley looked a little flabbergasted. "Is it true, President Young, that you believe in marriage for the dead?"

"It is true."

"Will you explain what you mean by that?"

"There is marriage for this life and for the life to come. If a person dies without being married for the life to come, we marry them so they'll have mates in the next world."

"I've heard you believe in propagation in the next world."

"We do."

"You mean—you mean actually, as in this life?"

"Yes. At the resurrection, we'll take up our bodies again ——"

"And your passions?"

"Certainly. We'll be human beings like we are now, only more glorified and pure."

"As I look around me," said Greeley, his eyes full of quiet humor, "I see no need of an army here."

"Neither do we."

"I may as well tell you in confidence that I expect to run for president of the United States. If I win, there won't be any army here."

Brigham did not miss that indirect appeal for political support. He said: "We agree to that."

"President Young, what is your attitude toward slavery?"

"We don't believe in it. We don't believe in degrading human beings. And I'm aware, of course, of your fight against slavery."

"What do you think the outcome will be?"

"War."

"Oh, I doubt that. Why do you think so?"

"Our prophet Joseph predicted war between the northern and southern states."

Greeley smiled. "Have all his predictions come true?"

"They have."

"When do you think that war will come?"

"Any day now."

"I hope not," said Greeley, and rose to take his leave.

Though regarding him as too pompous and ambitious, too foxily curious, Brigham did not dislike Greeley. Toward another famous visitor he felt less friendliness. When the name was announced, he told the guard to wait a while, and went to his library where he kept everything that had been published about him. Artemus Ward had written an imaginary conversation with Brigham and had concluded: "I girded up my Lions and fled the Seen. I packt up my duds & left Salt Lake which is a 2nd Soddum & Germorrer, inhabited by as theavin & onprincipled a set of retchis as ever drew Breth in eny spot on the Globe."

The malicious article Brigham now reread to refresh his memory. For a moment he stood in thought before turning to the guard. "Send him in," he said.

There entered a tall, loose-jointed and gawky young man who seemed to Brigham to be the most utter greenhorn he had ever seen. Ward's long coarse hair was yellow; his eyes were green and morbidly sunken and full of sly malice; and his preposterous clothes hung to his gaunt frame as if they had been slept in for weeks.

"Mr. Ward?"

"Yes," said a voice that matched the personality.

"Sit down."

Ward almost fell to his chair and then sprawled, with his lean legs sagging as if paralyzed. His sly eyes were studying Brigham's face.

"I read your article about me," said Brigham. "You seem to have a most extensive knowledge of us."

Ward's sallow face flushed. "I was afraid I might not be welcome."

"Everybody is welcome here. Unlike the persons you live among, we have nothing to hide." Ward's green eyes were now looking furtively around him. "I suppose," Brigham went on, "you're here to gather information for more articles. I want you to investigate everything, but if you're looking for Sodom, I'm afraid you'll have to go down to Camp Floyd."

Ward turned uneasily and grinned. "I guess I wasn't very fair to you."

"We're used to it." Brigham rose. He was bored by this gawky youth who fancied himself as a humorist. "Make yourself at home in our city. If I can be of any help to you, let me know."

Ward rose to his ungainly legs and mumbled a few words of thanks. His eyes were still searching. He went out, shuffling awkwardly; and from a window, Brigham saw him gazing at the Beehive House and up and down the street, as if wondering where all the wives and children were.

Brigham did not like him but he sent word to his leaders to treat Ward with every possible kindness. The gaunt and vindictive humorist was treated to more kindness than he had ever known before. He came down with mountain fever and would have died if several women had not waited on him day and night. Not many weeks passed before Brigham reflected that his judgment of the man had been unerring; for as soon as Ward was able to walk he hunted through the city and made notes, and upon returning to the States his malice was unabated. He made a small fortune lecturing about the Mormons, holding them up to the ridicule of the world, calling their society petticoatism and plunder, and declaring that seventeen women begged to marry him.

For another of his many visitors, Brigham felt only admiration. He had heard of Richard Francis Burton's journey to Tanganyika, of his twenty-one attacks of fever in his attempt to find the source of the Nile; but he was not prepared for the ghoulish figure that strode in. This emaciated person had sunken cheeks, lips shrunk back from the teeth, a yellowish skin, and a cruel mouth half-hidden by long drooping mustaches. He looked like the sort of man who would go down the Darb-al-Sharki, the coast road through the Nejd Desert over which no European had traveled before him; the kind who would take any risk to see the holy hillock of Ohod and the Tomb Chamber. Looking half-devil and half-human, nevertheless he had the quiet air of one who had observed all the follies of the human race and had found them much alike in all places.

"I've heard of you, Captain," said Brigham, grasping the hard lean hand.

"And I have heard of you. Indeed, I have journeyed seven thousand miles to join a colony that is sensible enough to allow polygamy."

That statement nonplussed Brigham. "What do you mean?"

"I apply for admission to your church."

Brigham smiled. "Captain, I think you've done that sort of thing before."

Burton grinned, but he did not take his keen probing gaze off Brigham's face. "I have," he said. "That's my profession."

"And what have you learned from all your joining of churches?"

"President Young, although every Moslem thinks Mohammed's remains are interred in the Hujrah at Al Madinah, the matter seems as doubtful to me as that of the Holy Sepulcher at Jerusalem."

Brigham's smile broadened. He had never before seen such a person as this civilized skeptic who poked his nose into all the holy spots of earth and wrote of them all with urbane and erudite scorn. Burton was saying:

"I've visited the Five Mosques of the Prophet, the Mosques of Kuba, the cemetery of Al Bakia, and Hamyah's tomb at the foot of Mount Ohod. I've seen the burial place at Medina, the Ka'bah at Mecca. In the Tomb Chamber there lay Fatima, Omar and abu-Bekr. But none of it interested me more than your colony out here in a wilderness. I have heard much about you but discarded all of it. I came to see for myself."

"It was a long journey," said Brigham, looking at the big scar on Burton's left cheek.

"I am going to write a book about you. First, though, I ought to join your church."

"I'm afraid, Captain, this is one church you'll have to write about without joining."

"You are very sensible," Burton declared. Whether he was speaking with grave irony, Brigham could not tell. "Polygamy is an ancient and honorable custom."

"Not polygamy, Captain. We call it celestial marriage."

The yellow lids fell for a moment across Burton's black eyes. "For the student of these matters," he said quietly, "it makes little difference what you call it."

This strange wanderer, looking as if he were made of bone and buckskin and fire, remained in the city a month, observing the Mormons and taking notes. Then he left to write his book; and when a copy of the book came to Brigham, it pleased him more than anything else that had been written about him by a gentile. Burton declared flatly that all stories about the Mormons, published by anti-Mormons and apostates, were venomous. Brigham liked that. He liked what Burton wrote about him

"Altogether the prophet's appearance was that of a gentleman farmer in New England—in fact, such as he is. He is a well-preserved man, a fact attributed to his habit of sleeping, as the Citizen Proudhon so strongly advises, in solitude. His manner is at once affable and impressive, simple and courteous: his want of pretension contrasts favorably with certain pseudo-prophets that I have seen, each of whom holds himself to be a 'Logos' without other claim save a semi-maniacal self-esteem. He shows no sign of dogmatism, bigotry, or fanaticism. His manner is cold—in fact, like his face, somewhat bloodless."

Brigham laid the book down and went to a mirror. He looked first at his handsome brown beard and then at his cheeks: they did look rather pale, he reflected, and wondered if he should change his diet. He returned to the book.

"His powers of observation are intuitively strong, and his friends declare him to be a perfect judge of character. If he dislikes a stranger at the first interview, he never sees him again."

That was not true, Brigham decided, looking back across the years. He did not like Artemus Ward but he had gone to see the dolt when he was ill, and he had taken to him some rare old wine. He had seen many persons whom he would rather have set adrift on a raft in the Pacific.

"Of his temperance and sobriety there is but one opinion. His life is ascetic: his favorite food is baked potatoes with a little buttermilk, and his drink, water. Of his education I cannot speak: 'Men, not books—deeds, not words,' has ever been his motto; he probably has, as Mr Randolph said of Mr. Johnston, 'a mind uncorrupted by books.' Yet he converses with ease and correctness, has neither snuffle nor pompousness. He has been called hypocrite, swindler, forger, murderer. No one looks it less. He is the St. Paul of the New Dispensation: true and sincere, he gave point, and energy, and consistency to the somewhat disjointed, turbulent, and unforeseeing fanaticism of Mr. Joseph Smith. There is total absence of pretension in his manner, and he has been so long used to power that he cares nothing for its display. The arts by which he rules the heterogeneous mass of conflicting elements are indomitable will, profound secrecy, and uncommon astuteness."

Brigham paused to reflect on the charge of profound secrecy. It was true, he supposed, but how, he wondered, could it have been otherwise

No man could govern sixty thousand persecuted persons if he made a public record of his methods. He sighed and read again.

"He is no common man, and he has none of the weakness and vanity which characterize the common uncommon man. A desultory conversation cannot be expected to draw out a master spirit, but a truly distinguished character exercises most often an instinctive—some would call it a mesmeric—effect upon those who come in contact with it. It is observable that, although every gentile writer has represented Mr. Joseph Smith as a heartless imposter, few have ventured to apply the term to Mr. Brigham Young. . . ."

Brigham laid the book aside. He was glad that so worldly and civilized a man had written about him, and he hoped the book would have a large audience. It could do much to correct the malicious and often venomous misrepresentations of other writers, including the sallow Artemus Ward who was now filling his pockets with the pay of his adolescent wit. He wished a thousand Captain Burtons would visit the city.

CHAPTER XXIII

RIGHAM WAS PREACHING A SUNDAY SERMON WHEN THE HUGE AUDIENCE was startled by the sudden appearance at the tabernacle door of Porter Rockwell. That dirty long-haired giant looked like a wild man as he strode up an aisle to speak to his chief; and Brigham, who saw him coming, knew there was an important matter on his scout's mind. Looking neither to right nor left, Porter crossed the great building, climbed the steps to the amphitheater, and went straight to his chief. Nine thousand persons watched him and waited. The moment Porter whispered in Brigham's ear, the audience knew that he had imparted grave news; because Brigham suddenly straightened and clenched his hands. For several moments Porter whispered to him and then went to a chair and sat.

"Brethren and sisters," said Brigham, looking at the hushed multitude before him, "Brother Porter has been riding day and night to fetch us tremendous news. And still, it is nothing that will surprise any of us. Our prophet Joseph predicted it long years ago; and like his other prophecies, it has been fulfilled. This nation has gone to war!"

There was utter silence. If a pin had been dropped in this huge tabernacle, its fall could have been distinctly heard from end to end of the building. The saints gazed at Brigham, or turned softly to look at one another: the northern and southern states had gone to war, but Joseph long ago had known they would. Brigham was speaking again.

"This is sad news, brethren and sisters, because now there will be blood and suffering upon this land. And yet, for us in a way, it is good news. Our enemies will now be so damned busy killing one another that maybe for a while they will leave us alone. Maybe for a while we can build again, and kick these gamblers and whores out of this valley. There is so much ungodliness and sin in the world that it is not strange to us if brother fights against brother and blood runs like water; for Joseph predicted that it would be so. Joseph looked into the future and saw the time would come when men could no longer make slaves of men, and grind them down and exploit them to put filthy gold in their own purse.

"Brethren and sisters, we hate their damnable ungodliness, but I ask you to pray for them. I ask God to lead them back into the ways of righteousness and fellowship. But while they are murdering in the name of Jesus, let us live humbly in the ways of the Lord and rebuild our kingdom. Abraham Lincoln is president now. I hope he will be so damned busy he will leave us alone!"

This was the opportunity for which Brigham had been waiting. He came out of retirement and prepared to consolidate his kingdom; for Lincoln soon recalled the army and sent a letter to Brigham, declaring that he would leave the Mormons alone if they would leave him alone. That was what Brigham wanted. He could now establish United Orders and weld his people into one invulnerable unit.

Putting on a broadcloth coat and a tall hat, he went out one morning to stroll through the city and to plan. There were thousands of young trees growing along the streets now; shrubs in full and fragrant bloom; and the smell of the green valley in the air. A theater was nearly completed, and when ready, it would be the finest in the West. The temple was climbing skyward, stone by stone. He wanted every saint to have a beautiful home and yard and garden. There would always be thriftless and lazy persons, even in Zion, but he would tolerate no poverty, no wealthy tyrants, and none of the vices which had corrupted great civilizations in the past. He wanted every man and woman to work and have work to do.

He had been ridiculed for building a wall around the city. He had been asked the sense of it, and in a sermon he had given his answer. Walls were built, he said, and ditches were dug, bridges were made to give the unemployed work to do. Every year he spent hundreds of thousands of dollars out of church funds to provide work for those who needed it. And why? Because there was an abundance of potatoes and flour and beef for everyone but he did not believe in the dole. It was best for a man to work for his living and find joy in his labor. In that sermon he had thundered:

"I say to all grunters, whiners, hypocrites and sycophants who snivel, crouch and crawl around the most contemptible of all creatures for a favor, should it enter my mind to dig down the Twin Peaks and I set men to work to do so, it is none of the business of all earth and hell, provided I pay the laborers their wages!"

Nevertheless, it was hard to make some men understand that neither God nor the soil nor the government owed them a living. It was difficult to put ambition and pride into a sloth. Just the same, he would not *give* money or food to those in need, except the old and the sick: he would make them work for these things, and understand the nobility of labor. Some of the brethren—and often they were big strong fellows—were so lacking in pride and self-respect that they would accept charity, they would beg, they would sit on their lazy hinders and starve before they would take a shovel or a trowel in their hands. Some of the sisters whined endlessly, saying they did not have this or that; and what did they want when it was all summed up? They wanted clothes in the brightest and latest styles, and time to strut down the streets to make other women envy them. They were too lazy and vain to sew and weave, to make simple homespun things, to beautify their homes and cultivate flowers on their lawns.

There would always be, he reflected, looking at a shack and wondering who lived in it—there would always be inequalities: some would have more and some less, because some were more intelligent and ambitious. There could never be a utopia in this world. But there could be united effort, with every person serving in the common plan; and there could be an abundance of goods for all. The selfish and the greedy, vain for power, hungry for more than they needed, would have to be restrained; and the timid and inefficient would have to be encouraged. As long as he lived, nobody need starve or wear rags; for there would always be work for those unafraid of it.

After he was dead—and he was getting to be an old man—perhaps disaster would overtake his people. Possibly the church would fall into the hands of greedy men who would exploit it for their own ends. To safeguard against that, he wanted to establish an Order in every community, and to found a tradition of mutual sharing and aid. A railroad was coming and with it would come a horde of gentiles. Mines would eventually be opened in the West, and possibly in Zion after he was dead; and in the industrial world to come there would be the brutality and greed that made animals of men. It was his task to preach against the sins of wealth and social position, to make home manufacture of home products mandatory, and to see that every working man shared in community effort and the distribution of goods. If all the saints became partners in a vast enterprise, then they would feel pride in their endeavor and would resist the barbarous philosophy of every man for himself.

That was Brigham's dream. When he returned to his office, he was glad to find the McBrides there. He liked the idealism of Moroni, and the bold quick temper of his son.

"Brethren, what can I do for you?"

"Brother Brigham," said Moroni, "in our little settlement south of here, we want to establish a United Order. You remember that Joseph——"

"Yes, yes, I've just been walking and thinking of that."

"We've named our settlement Josephville. Do you approve?"

"Why, yes," said Brigham. "I don't think it's a good thing to name too many towns after the authorities of the church. Up north we have a Brigham City. If we have a Brigham City, we certainly ought to have a Josephville."

With Moroni and Tim was a youth of fifteen, a tall, straight youngster with dark hair, dark gray eyes and a frank spontaneous smile. Brigham now looked at him. "Whose son?"

"Mine," said Tim. "His name is Nephi."

"Oh, yes, I remember. Ain't you the boy who was gnawing the thigh-bone of the dog years ago?"

"Yes, Brother Brigham."

"We dang near starved to death that winter," said Moroni.

"Most of us did. Brother Nephi, didn't you tell me then you wanted to grow up and help establish an Order?"

"Yes, Brother Brigham."

"Well, young man, you hop right into it. You can help your father and grandfather."

"I intend to," said Nephi, grinning broadly.

"An Order is being founded in Brigham City. I suppose you know how to go about it? If you don't, drive up and look at that one."

"I think we understand," said Moroni. "We're to own and share everything in common. We plan to have our own mills and shops and our community store. Everyone will work and take pride in his work."

"That's the important thing," said Brigham quickly. "The happiest people in this world are the people who keep busy. The very happiest are the people who take pride in the work they do. You'll want to see to it that each man has the job he can do best: some in the mills and shops, some on the farms, some in the gardens and orchards."

"Yes, Brother Brigham."

"I don't want anyone hogging it all. Give them all work and plenty to eat and wear and pride in their work. That's all it takes to make a happy world. You must all be brothers and sisters in the gospel and all socially equal."

"That's the way we see it."

"Brother Tim, how many wives do you have?"

"Two, Brother Brigham."

"Only two? Why don't you take some more? I'm thinking of taking another myself if I can find the right woman."

"That's the trouble. It's not easy to find sisters who will live with other women."

"No. But we have to realize that women must hate and quarrel with one another or they wouldn't be happy. God seems to have made them that way. Tim, you are not doing your duty to the Lord. Find you some more wives."

"I will if I can. I found one but she wanted me to build her a house by herself."

"Some of them feel that way—but they don't have the spirit of God in them. Well, you go ahead and establish the Order. If you need any help or advice, come to me."

When the men rose to leave, Brigham walked over and ruffled Nephi's dark curly hair. "You'll probably be the leader of the Order some day, so learn all you can about it."

"Yes, Brother Brigham."

"Well, let me know if you have any problems."

After the men had gone, Brigham sat in thought. He was thinking of the Order, and of finding another wife, and of Bill Hickman—because Bill Hickman, for some reason, had turned sour. Brigham decided to send for the man and learn what the trouble was.

The next day, Bill walked in. Brigham knew at once that the man was in a sulking mood.

"Brother Bill, what has happened to you?"

"Why?"

"I've been told you don't like me any more."

Bill pulled a chair up and looked at his chief. "Brigham, if you want to know, I'll tell you. I don't think you've been fair with me."

"Oh, you don't? In what ways?"

"Well, for just about twenty years I've done what you told me to do. I've murdered for you——"

"Not so loud," said Brigham.

"By God, I don't care who hears me! I say I've socked your enemies away for twenty years. What have I got for it?"

"The Lord will reward you."

"Yes, and you too. But you and Heber and Dan and all the other authorities, you've feathered your old nests pretty well. What do I have? By the God of Israel, not a thing. When I was off chopping them up for you, my family about starved to death. You didn't pay me no wages like the apostles. You didn't even feed my kids."

"Brother Bill," said Brigham softly, "I wouldn't get too mouth-almighty about this. I've had a lot of things on my mind."

"You don't scare me none," said Bill—and his gray eyes were colder than Brigham's. "I ain't afraid of any man, alive or dead. I say you never treated me fair and I don't know as I'd help you again, even if you ordered me to."

For a long moment Brigham gazed at his avenger. "What," he asked impatiently, "do you want? You're not trying to threaten me, are you?"

"No, Brigham. But from now on I guess I'll accumulate some property like you. I'm not a young man any more. I won't always be able to work."

"I always thought you were happy serving the Lord."

"I was. But I ain't happy to see my family starve while I'm off socking some scoundrel away."

"Don't get funny notions in your head," said Brigham. His voice was gentle but Bill sensed the threat behind it. "I say the spirit of God isn't in you today. Property in this life means very little; storing up treasures in heaven means a great deal. You had better think it over."

Calmly, in the way of a man who had faced many dangers and had been afraid of none, Bill rose to his feet and gazed soberly at his leader. "I still say you ain't been fair to me. You better think that over."

Brigham flushed with anger. "Bill, if you want to go and accumulate some property, do so; but I say again, don't get any funny notions in your head."

For a long moment two fearless and ruthless men gazed at one another—and neither gaze faltered. They understood one another well.

"All right," Bill said, and abruptly left the office.

For a little while, Brigham thought of the matter. He did not like
the look in Bill's eyes when the man turned to leave; but Porter Rockwell
and others were still faithful to him, and there was nothing to worry
about. If Bill got funny notions in his head . . . Brigham decided to go
for a walk and try to put Bill Hickman out of his mind.

He was sauntering down a street when his gaze fell on a woman. She
was tall and fair, with an excellent figure and a proud lift of her head
and throat. Quickening his stride, he came abreast of her and raised his
tall hat and spoke.

"I think I haven't met you before. Are you one of the sisters?"

"Yes," she said, glancing at him fearfully.

"I am Brigham Young," he said.

"I know that," said the tall girl. Her gaze noted that he was portly,
that his soft brown hair was getting thin. Quietly she added: "I am Harriet
Amelia Folsom."

"You have not been here long?"

"Not very."

"Are your people recent converts?"

"Yes," she said, and walked more quickly, as if afraid of him.

Brigham was not to be outdistanced; but he did become aware, with
surprise that grew to astonishment, that his heart was beating more
rapidly. "Sister Harriet, are you trying to run away from me?"

"I have to go," she said. Her clear gray eyes looked at him and again
she quickened her pace.

"I won't hurt you. Am I somebody to be afraid of?"

"No," she said, still walking briskly. "I am late."

"Are you going home?"

"Yes."

"Then I'll escort you home. I'll protect you," he said dryly. "There are
hoodlums in the city."

"Thank you, but I need no protection."

He kept at her side, though he was panting a little, for she walked
with the quick lightness of a bird. He did not speak again until she came

to the adobe house where her parents were staying. "Will you ask me in?" he said, a little amused.

"I—I don't know." She had turned to the gate and was looking at him as no woman, so far as he could remember, had ever looked before. Most of the sisters were eager for his attention but this tall queen acted as if she wanted to see the last of him.

"I'd like to meet your parents. I haven't, have I?"

"No."

"Then I'll go in with you."

She almost fled from the gate to the house; and Brigham followed, a little annoyed. Her parents he liked at once. They were devout, he perceived; and they were overawed. The mother caught her breath when she spoke; for that Brigham, the president and prophet, should call at her humble home was hardly less than a miracle. The father stumbled about, seeking chairs.

"I met your daughter," Brigham said, "and I liked her so well I wanted to meet her parents."

Harriet's eyes widened. She started to speak but decided not to, and then turned with a quick nervous movement and bit her lip.

"We're mighty proud to have you visit us," the father said; and the mother, recovering her wits, added: "We feel highly honored, President Young."

"Sister Harriet seems afraid of me. Do I look like a brigand?"

Harriet flushed and her lids fell. The mother said quickly: "She is hard to get acquainted with."

"She'll like you," said the father cheerfully, "when she knows you better."

"If I have my way she is going to know me better."

They hardly knew what to make of that. The parents looked at their daughter whose fair face was still flushed. She caught her breath sharply and glanced at Brigham and then looked away.

"Harriet," said the mother, with gentle pride in her voice, "is quite accomplished. Would you like to hear her play or sing?"

Brigham turned to look at the small piano. Before he could speak, Harriet said: "Mama, please. I don't care to."

"But you would for President Young, wouldn't you?"

"Of course," said the father. "Sing for him."

"No," said Harriet, a little angrily. "I do not wish to."

The mother sighed and gazed at her daughter as she might have looked at any riddle. "I think she will, President Young, if you'll come again."

"Mama! I will not."

"Then I'll come again," said Brigham, and rose. The parents rose too, but Harriet sat stubbornly and gazed through a window. "Sister Harriet, will you sing for me next time I come?"

She did not answer. "Harriet," said the father sternly, "will you answer President Young's question?"

"I don't care to sing," said Harriet icily.

"But won't you next time?"

"I do not promise."

"I'm sure she will," said the mother, unhappy with chagrin.

Brigham's stern face broke into a rare smile. "Anyway, we'll ask her to."

He went up the street feeling twenty years younger, feeling almost giddy, with his heart pounding absurdly like that of any boy in love. For the first time in his sixty-one years something had happened to him— a strange and adventurous emotion of the kind he had never felt before. This girl went to his head like the whiskey he had drunk when he had mountain fever: memory of her was a glorious warmth in his whole being; and his step was so awake, his manner so gay and carefree, that when he met Heber the good man was startled.

"You act like you had good news," said Heber, his shrewd eyes searching Brigham's face.

"Heber, I think I'm falling in love."

"What!" cried Heber, astounded. Never in forty years had he seen Brigham look this way. "In love at your age!"

"Better late than never," said Brigham, his eyes twinkling.

"You mean you've never been in love before?"

"Not like this. I guess I've always been too busy to fall in love."

Heber was alarmed. If the great leader started falling in love at his age, then God alone knew what would happen to the church. "Who is she?"

"Harriet Folsom."

"I don't know her."

"I didn't two hours ago."

That giddy statement left Heber speechless. He peered at Brigham as if he were seeing him for the first time; and at last he asked: "You mean you're falling in love with a girl you've just met?"

"I know it, Heber."

"In my opinion," said Heber sternly, "it is more important for you to find out what Governor Dawson is doing. Things look bad."

"I'll attend to that later. Right now I'm going to change this suit of homespun for broadcloth."

"And how about the United Orders?"

"They can wait."

"I'll be damned," said Heber, and watched his friend go up the street.

Brigham went to his office and gave himself critical attention, wondering meanwhile why Harriet had been so unimpressed. Formerly, women had been glad to marry him: he had said in sermons that he could find more wives in a week than younger men could find in a year: it was strange that a young woman should snub him now. Perhaps it was because of his age. He was stout, but he was still vigorous and healthy, and he did not feel like an old man. As Burton said, he was well-preserved. It was true, he admitted, gazing in a mirror, that his hair was thin, that his beard needed trimming.

Going to his room, he changed his homespun suit for one of excellent broadcloth; put on a stiff white shirt with a high collar; and chose a dark cravat. He wore no mustaches and no whiskers on his lower lip, preferring to have his strong mouth fully exposed; but his beard was six inches long and came down his cheeks in soft luxuriant growth. His brown hair, almost as fine as silk, fell in tangled curls over his ears. Perhaps he looked too stern: he peered at himself, noting the heavy ragged brows, the cold gray eyes, the long nose that rather flattened out at the base. Nevertheless, he was a handsome man, even at sixty-one. His legs were thick but they still could dance. His belly was full, his torso was heavy and thick, but he doubted that there was a handsomer man in the city.

Not vain, and given little to thoughts of himself, he now gave time to the most thorough self-searching of his life. He would call on Harriet this evening and learn if she liked him better in fine clothes. He wanted to marry her. He intended to.

Harriet could not restrain a smile when she observed that he had gone home and groomed himself. He looked like a statesman, all right—but not like a lover. He looked as if a tender word or a clinging kiss would be as alien to him as to a statue of granite. The parents after a few moments excused themselves, saying they must call on a neighbor; and Brigham gave them a statesmanlike smile for their courtesy and tact. When he was alone with Harriet, he gazed at her a little sheepishly and asked: "Do you like me better now?"

She did like him in that moment: he was almost boyishly gawky. She felt that there was tenderness and passion in the man. Nevertheless, she said with soft malice: "You look like President Young."

"This is a fine suit," he said. "I suppose it's still true that feathers make the bird."

"At least they look better with their feathers on."

He chuckled softly. Then he gazed at her so unwaveringly that she blushed. "Harriet, why don't you like me?"

"I haven't said I don't."

He rose and sat by her and leaned forward. She turned away. "Do I scare you?"

"No."

"I scare a lot of people." His voice sounded as if the matter worried him. For a long moment he considered while his eyes studied the color in her fair cheeks and throat. Then he went straight to the point. "Sister Harriet, I want you to marry me."

She caught her breath with sudden swift resentment.

"Will you?"

"No."

"Why not?"

"President Young, haven't you wives enough?"

That question angered him a little. He scowled. "Not until I have you."

She turned and looked at him curiously. There was scorn in the curve of her lips. "How many wives do you have?"

"I have had twenty-four. They are not all living."

"I'd think that many would be enough even for a prophet."

He was not used to such rebukes. For a moment he considered giving her a lecture, but he decided that a lecture would only make his suit more difficult. So he was silent, hardly knowing what to say, or whether to speak at all. If he were to speak as president and prophet, she would only look at him scornfully; and if he were to speak as man and lover, doubtless she would think him old and foolish. He was baffled.

"Will you play or sing for me?"

"I'd rather not."

"I love music, Harriet. I'd like to hear you sing."

"Please, not now."

"Would you rather have me go?"

"Don't you usually do what you want to do?"

Again he was nonplussed. She had looked at him with eyes a little frightened. He wished he could be more gentle. "Harriet, I've fallen in love."

"Is that anything new? You've fallen in love twenty-four times."

"No," he said. "I've always been too busy. I love my wives but I don't think I ever really fell in love before."

"It hasn't taken you very long."

"I always do things in a hurry," he said, smiling. "Will you marry me?"

"Of course not."

"Are you in love with another man?"

"No."

"Then I want you to love me. In the next world you will share my glory."

She moved quickly as if to rise and leave him but he caught her hand. Angrily, she drew her hand away. Still baffled, and not knowing what to say or do, Brigham rose and took his hat.

"Sister Harriet, you think it over."

"Think what over?"

"I want you to be my wife. You pray to God for light and see if He does not tell you to marry me."

Her lips curled. "In such matters, I consult my heart and not God."

He felt again that a lecture would do her a lot of good; but he went to the door and stood there, looking back. "You think it over," he said. "Good night."

Within a few days the whole city knew that Brigham was wooing the tall and queenly Harriet Folsom. Tongues wagged. Wagers were laid. Would she or would she not marry him? Would she dare say no? And if she did, what would Brigham do? Some of the leaders were annoyed and troubled, for it seemed to them that Brigham had more important matters to attend to. But most of the saints were as excited as children and watched his carriage draw up to her door and observed how long it remained there.

Brigham never doubted that the haughty lady would yield. Soon, however, he found his hands full of trouble, and for a little while he was too busy to make his daily call.

CHAPTER XXIV

LINCOLN DID NOT KEEP HIS PLEDGE TO LEAVE THE MORMONS ALONE. HE allowed Congress to ram through an anti-bigamy act which was aimed at the saints, even though it did not mention them by name. Then he appointed as governor of the Territory a bigot who arrived with blood in his eye and bitter words in his mouth. On the third day after he landed in the city, Governor Dawson declared to the legislature that the Mormons were disloyal; and within a week he asked a woman to be his mistress, a circumstance that brought swift vengeance upon his head. Threats against his life sent him into hiding; and soon thereafter, Brigham was told that Dawson had become a raving lunatic who delivered patriotic harangues at the walls and ceiling of his room, and shouted through his open window that he had landed right in the middle of Sodom. After recovering his senses he decided to flee and secretly left in the night; but eight furious men trailed him and overtook him and almost beat him to death.

When Brigham learned of this he was so angry he choked. "By the God of Israel," he thundered, "who did it?"

"We haven't learned yet," Heber said.

"This is a fine kettle of fish! Just when we get a little peace and the persecution against us is dying down, the governor is almost flogged to death! Heber, we must find the scoundrels and bring them to trial. This will make a terrible stink back East."

"I know it," said Heber, shaking his head sadly.

"I won't stand this damned lawlessness! The police must find those culprits and find them at once."

Brigham paced the floor, wishing that the men who flogged the governor were buried deep in hell. Enemies back East magnified a flogging into a rebellion, a murder into an armed insurrection. As soon as one ghost had been laid, a dozen new ones leapt to the scene. Never could he build a peaceful kingdom here as long as stupid fanatics among his own people behaved like the brutal hoodlums which easterners believed all Mormons to be. It was one thing after another: a Mountain Meadows massacre, an unauthorized murder by one of his avengers, or the chasing of governors right out of the Territory.

Heber came the next day to tell him that three of the guilty men had started for California but had been overtaken by the sheriff and a posse. One of them, resisting arrest, had been killed; and the other two after arriving in the city had tried to escape and had been shot down.

"I don't know if they really tried to escape or not," Heber said.

"It don't matter. They got what they deserved. Where are the others?"

"In jail."

"I want a quick trial. I want them to get the limit. Who are they?"

"Isaac Heibaur, Wood Reynolds, Jason, John and Wilford Luce, John Smith, Moroni Clawson and Lot Huntington."

"Which ones were shot?"

"Huntington and Smith and Clawson."

"I won't have rowdies beating up the governors, even if they are scoundrels who try to seduce the sisters. See that they are tried at once."

"All right. Have you seen Joe Morris yet?"

"No. What is he up to now?"

Joseph Morris up in Weber County fancied himself as a prophet and had several hundred followers. Brigham hardly knew what to do with him. Joseph had been plagued by false prophets, but this was the first one to rear his head in Brigham's kingdom. While wondering what to do with the fool, Brigham was startled one morning to find his door kicked open and to behold a shaggy-haired man on the threshold.

"I come to see you," said the stranger, marching uninvited to Brigham's desk.

Brigham looked at the man's glittering eyes and decided that he was faced by a madman. "What do you want to see me about?"

"I have two letters from God," said Morris solemnly.

Brigham was about to say, "To hell with you and your letters from God," when he was stopped by something the man did. Morris leaned across the desk and thrust a dirty bearded face at Brigham and grinned. The grin was so terrible that Brigham shuddered.

"What do your letters from God say?"

"They say you got a-reform or you'll be damned. You're all wrong." Still grinning, Morris tapped the desk with a foul finger.

"How am I wrong?"

"About the second coming of Christ. He'll come any day now."

"All right," said Brigham impatiently, "let Him come."

"But what'll happen to you?" asked Morris earnestly. "I'll tell you. Unless you reform and follow me, you'll be damned. You know what it says in the Bible? It says an angel come down from heaven with the keys of the bottomless pit and a chain in his hand. He laid hold on the dragon, that old serpent which is the Devil, and Satan, and bound him a thousand years. You know who that angel is?"

"Who is he?"

"Your humble servant, Joseph Morris."

"Oh, to hell with all that!"

"Now wait," said Morris with comic solemnity. "Don't you make me angry. I'm the latter-day Moses, that's who I am, and God tells me what to do. Why," he declared, drawing to his full height, "you don't receive no revelations. You never did. You ain't no prophet. Now me, I get so many revelations I got six clerks writing them down. For behold, I am he that shuts and no one opens, and that opens and no one shuts, even Jesus Christ; and I am about to speak unto you again——"

"That's enough," Brigham said. "I don't care about all your damned opening and shutting. What do you want?"

"I come to tell you that you're a failure and I am the speedy Moses. You're to stop sending missionaries out and give all your time to get Israel ready for my coming. I can't tell you many things today, but when I'm head of the church I'll make all things plain to you and to all men; for I am he that opens and he that shuts——"

"Never mind all that opening! Brother Joseph, how many followers do you have?"

"Only a thousand now but I'll have the wide world when I enter my kingdom." He smiled and again Brigham was startled. When the man was earnest, he wagged his shaggy beard and his eyes shone with the zeal of a fanatic; but when he grinned he was a picture of diabolic cunning. Slowly the grin faded and he said: "I am the greatest prophet who ever lived except Jesus."

Brigham remembered the false prophets whom he had known—and especially J. J. Strang, that black-bearded fool who went with his followers to Beaver Island and was slain six years ago. He remembered the deluded Sidney Rigdon.

"You," said Morris, thumping the desk again, "are a fraud. My people share everything in common and I give all my time to revelations. I've already got six big volumes and God says He's just begun to tell me things. But I tell you one thing: Christ is coming again this month."

"This month?" said Brigham, wondering what to do with the man.

"This month! That don't give you sinners much time to repent."

"I understand you've thrown some of the brethren into prison."

"They are sinners! If Christ wants to let them out, all right. I won't."

"I understand you have an army too."

"I have. And when I get a big enough army I'll march down here and blow you right over the Twin Peaks. That is," he said, remembering, "if Christ don't do it Himself."

"Well, Brother Joseph, when Jesus comes, tell Him about me."

"I will," said Morris eagerly. "But you still got enough time to repent and join me. For I am he that opens and he that shuts——"

"All right," said Brigham, leading him to the door. "Just go right on opening and shutting and let me know when Jesus comes."

"I will," said Morris gravely, and allowed himself to be pushed out of the office. He turned. "You still have time. I come down to warn you."

Brigham decided to leave this madman to the new governor. He did not want eastern editors to say that he was exterminating rival prophets; and besides, he was busy with other matters, including his wooing of the cold and unyielding Harriet. He felt so bogged down with troubles this morning that he resolved to put on his best clothes and go over to visit her. More and more, as he had persisted, Harriet had refused to talk to him at all. Perhaps she would sing to him today.

He strode in as usual and greeted the parents cheerfully and inquired about their health; whereupon he turned to the daughter who as usual refused to look at him.

"Sister Harriet, how are you today?"

"Well, thank you."

"Will you sing for me?"

"I'd rather not."

"Harriet," said her distressed father, "you're very foolish. I'm ashamed of you."

The awe the parents felt around Brigham had not diminished. That their accomplished daughter should refuse to play or sing for the president and prophet was the most intolerable grief in their lives. That she should refuse to marry him was incredible.

"Harriet," said the mother, "why are you so obstinate?"

Harriet was annoyed. She rose and entered another room and closed the door.

The mother shook her head sadly and looked at Brigham. "We've talked to her, President Young. We've tried to make her see the light."

"Yes," said the father, "we've argued and argued."

"Does she pray?"

"Yes. But she says God doesn't tell her to marry you."

"She must humble herself. She does not pray earnestly enough."

"She never did humble herself much. She's a very stubborn girl."

Brigham looked at the closed door. Even if she would not sing for him, he wanted her in the room.

"If she prays and humbles herself, God will show her what is right."

"We tell her that, but she gets that proud look on her face and sulks."

"Is she in love with another man?"

"Not that we know of. One used to call now and then."

Brigham reflected that he would have to learn the name of the man and call him to a mission and get him out of the way. "Has she read the revelation on celestial marriage?"

"Yes, we're sure she has."

Brigham sighed like a lovesick lad and gazed at the door through which Harriet had passed. He was on the point of going over and asking her to return when his friend Heber appeared from the street. Heber framed his big body against an October sky and peered into the room.

"Brigham, is that you?"

"Yes," said Brigham, rising.

"You'd better get out here. Colonel Connor is marching into the city."

"What!" Brigham cried. "I told him to stay out of here with his damned army."

"He sent word he'd march in if hell yawned beneath him."

"Excuse me," Brigham said to the parents, and left the house. "Where is he?"

"Entering down there. I guess he's coming to enforce that anti-bigamy law." Heber pointed to the southwest. Then he looked at Brigham, wondering why, when so many grave matters impended, he should spend his time wooing a girl. There was a change in the Lion of the Lord.

Brigham was not thinking of Harriet now. He was striding briskly down the street to have a look at Connor's army. And there it was, all right, coming up State Street with fixed bayonets, and a band playing for all it was worth. It marched up State to First South and turned eastward and stopped before the residence of the governor.

"This looks like war," Heber said.

"No, I won't have war."

"Are you going to let armies march in and camp right in our city?"

"He won't camp in it."

"Almost in it. He intends to build a fort right up there against the mountain, between Red Butte and Emigration. We'll be right in the dooryard of an armed fort!"

The soldiers were listening now to the new governor's harangue. Brigham could not hear Governor Harding, the man who had replaced Dawson, but he knew well enough what he was saying: that the Mormons were disloyal to the Constitution and the flag and would have to be brought to their senses; that the soldiers were here to enforce the laws. While Brigham gazed calmly at this amazing spectacle of an army right in his city, Heber worked himself into a towering rage. He stared at the soldiers and then at Brigham, and at last he spoke frankly.

"Brigham, it seems to me there's a change in you since you met this girl. Are you going to let these damned soldiers camp right next to our city and build a fort? Don't you realize that this anti-bigamy law will make hell pop all around us soon? Don't you realize if you marry again now you'll make matters worse back East?"

"We'll see about that," he said calmly.

And he remained calm later when, in addressing the legislature, Governor Harding was so insulting that many of the church leaders were furious. In years gone by, Brigham had thundered from the pulpit and threatened war; but now he seemed unmoved. The governor was limiting the probate courts to such innocuous matters as the probating of wills; he was authorizing marshals to summon as jurors such persons as were known to be unfriendly to the saints; and he was taking complete command of the militia.

He sent a posse northward, and it brought Morris and his followers to an unhappy end. The shaggy prophet was in his fort when his surrender was demanded; and when he did not come out, a cannon was fired. It killed two women and knocked the chin off a young girl. Then the posse bore down. Morris threw his arms skyward and yelled, "All who are for me and my God, in life or in death follow me!" In the next moment he was shot dead.

For Heber and others, such matters were ominous, and the future looked blacker than it had looked in a long while; but Brigham refused to be alarmed. Soldiers were building Fort Douglas right by the city; the governor was swearing by everything under the flag that he would clean up this lawless valley; and soldiers and hoodlums, gamblers and harlots swarmed in the streets. As a matter of fact, Brigham was done with armed opposition. He wanted to integrate his people into a huge socialistic body that could resist any kind of invasion. He wanted to give Federal appointees enough rope to hang themselves. But above all right now, even while it was rumored that his arrest was imminent, he wanted to make the cold and haughty Harriet Folsom marry him.

In a bitter evening of December, when snow was driving over the city, he called on the young lady, resolved to accept only yes as an answer. The parents observed that he looked more determined as he laid his hat and coat on a chair and turned to the fire. He rubbed his heavy hands in the warmth.

"Is Connor still at Fort Douglas?" the father asked.

"No," said Brigham. "He has gone up on Bear River to murder a few hundred frozen Indians."

"Is he coming back here?"

"Oh, yes. As soon as he has slaughtered the Lamanites."

"Why don't you stop him?" asked Harriet unreasonably.

"Why," he asked, turning to her, "don't you marry me?"

The mother spoke up quickly. "We've talked to Harriet about it. We've explained how foolish she is. For it's the Lord's will," she said, speaking to her daughter.

Harriet's lips curled.

"It's the Lord's will," the father said.

Harriet rose and went to a window to gaze at the storm. The parents looked at one another and then rose, saying they had a visit to make; and in a few moments they left the house. For a little while Brigham warmed himself by the fire and Harriet looked at the gray blizzard. Then she came over and sat by the fireplace and Brigham drew a chair up and faced her.

"Sister Harriet, are you going to marry me?"

She did not look at him. She was gazing at the flame of a cedar log. "President Young," she said at last, "if I marry you it will be on certain conditions."

"What are they?"

"I mean you will have to make promises."

"What promises?"

"In the first place, I must have a home of my own. I won't live in those big ugly houses with your other wives."

"Ugly houses?"

"Yes, with their silly old dormer windows. I must have a home of my own."

"All right, I'll build you a house." He considered a moment and added: "I'll build you a palace."

"In the second place," she went on, still gazing at the fire, "I won't sit around and spin and sew and knit and wash and iron. I'll go with you. When you visit the settlements, I'll go with you."

She was driving, it seemed to Brigham, a pretty stiff bargain. "I guess you can go along if you want to. But it isn't very nice riding hundreds of miles in a carriage over dusty roads."

"I must go," she said firmly. "In the third place, don't expect me to try and be friendly with all your wives. If I like some of them, all right, and if I don't, that will have to be all right too. I think some of them are nice, but some of them are just terrible."

He looked at her and considered that. Some of them, it was true, were jealous and shrewish; but it seemed to him, nevertheless, that Harriet was not properly humble. "If you can't like all of them," he said, "I suppose you can't. Anything else?"

"Yes. In the fourth place," she said, speaking as if she had arranged all these demands, one by one, "I must occupy first place in public. I mean if you take more than me to a dance or the theater, I must dance with you first and I must always sit on your right."

That demand annoyed him. It had often been said that he had favorites: if he yielded to Harriet in this, it would be said that he had a new favorite, and he would not like that. "You insist on that?"

"I do."

"Anything else?"

"Yes. This might not seem important to you but I want it. You already have wives named Harriet, so I must be known as Amelia."

"That is easy to grant. I wish the other requests was as reasonable."

"They are all reasonable. You are not a woman."

"Well, is that all?"

"No. I must have some nice clothes. Some of your wives look outlandish in public. I won't wear old homespun things that look like they came across in a handcart. And out in public I won't act like I love your other wives, as some of them do, making little smiles and saying sweet things they don't mean. I won't be a hypocrite because you say God likes it better that way."

Brigham was chuckling within. He looked at her full brow, her intelligent eyes, her firm chin—and realized that he was offering marriage to an uncommon woman. Just the same, her demands were most unreasonable. He rubbed his hands and said: "That all?"

"You'll have to spend a lot of time with me. You can't come to my house once in six months and kiss my hair and say hello and then disappear for another six months. And another thing: if I have to eat in the big dining room, I will sit at the head of the table with you. If that makes the others jealous, then you'll have to settle it with them. I'm going to be more than just wife number twenty-five."

"It looks like it," he said, smiling faintly. "Well, if I promise all those things, will you marry me?"

"Yes."

"Will you marry me if I don't promise them?"

"No."

"Then I guess I'll have to promise them."

"You don't have to marry me. There are other women."

"But I intend to marry you. Have you thought of everything?"

"If you keep those promises you'll have your hands full."

"I don't doubt it," he said. "It sounds like I'll be busy."

She turned to look at him, her gaze coldly steady. "Do you promise?"

"Harriet, I think you're unreasonable."

"As I said, you're not a woman. In celestial marriage, it seems to me God didn't pay much attention to the woman's side of it."

Brigham looked at the fire and pondered. "I promise," he said.

BRIGHAM SET MEN TO WORK AT ONCE TO BUILD A MAGNIFICENT PALACE for Amelia. It was to be a huge and ornate mansion of many rooms; and meanwhile, after the marriage, she took a little cottage by herself. Often she ate with Brigham in the large dining room of the Lion House, and he kept his promise to sit with her alone. They shared a small table at the head of the room; and the other wives and many of the daughters were flanked on either side of a long table. Amelia had lovely clothes, jewels, and a carriage of her own; and in the theater she sat with her husband in his box, and the other wives sat in a special row of chairs in the parquet. She was, as she knew she would be, both envied and feared. She stepped into the great household as queen, and she held her position as queen, no matter how bitter the gossip behind her back.

Her first dinner in the dining room was an adventure that would have paralyzed a girl with less spirit and courage. She entered on Brigham's arm and went to the small table reserved for them, allowing him to assist her to her chair. The other wives were already seated. Amelia appraised them with swift glances, but swift glances were enough. They were a most unusual group. In age they varied so widely that among them there seemed to be daughters, mothers and grandmothers; and they ranged through every conceivable size. Some were tall and some were very short; some were as gaunt as a starved ox, and some were great mounds of flesh and fat. Some sat bolt upright; some spread in their chairs as if boneless. Some looked as if dressed for the nursery, some for parties, some for the kitchen. All of them watched her with friendly or jaundiced or vindictive eyes; for none of them had ever sat apart with Brigham, or enjoyed such favors as the new bride received.

Amelia ate gravely, quietly, but she was all eyes and ears; and one by one she sized them up. Nearest to her, and on her right, was a large and shapeless woman who looked very old: her gray hair was parted severely and combed down, her gray eyes were rheumy and tired, he mouth, without bitterness, was two thin and wrinkled lips. Amelia liked her—for her face was kind. On this woman's right was a small elderly person with a small pinched face. Her eyes were too close together but not cunning or spiteful; her nose was absurdly snubbed; the corners of her mouth turned sharply down and ran in furrows down her chin. This woman looked as if her disposition, while not mean, was cramped within a few axioms and prejudices and content to rest there.

Across from her was one of the queerest in the whole lot. She had a huge horse face, long and gaunt and bony, with a high forehead that formed a sharp corner at her graying hair, shaggy brows that seemed lifted in perpetual amazement, large pale gray eyes with abnormally wide lids. Her long arched nose reached down to a broad upper lip that was like a tiny bleak plateau above a wide straight mouth. Her chin was so huge that it seemed to fill a third of her face. The woman on her left was as unlike her as a woman could be. She was dainty and feminine. She looked scared. She had her hair combed, like so many of the others, in a topknot—but with a difference: there were two parts that made a T of clean white scalp on this woman's head. Younger than most of them, she was, it seemed to Amelia, the only shy and self-conscious one in the entire lot.

Next to her was one of two women who looked venomous. This wife's hair, though done in a braided knot high on her head, was skinned back so tight that it drew all the wrinkles out of her forehead and slightly lifted the brows above the small and malicious eyes. Her mouth was a sharp little arc. Perhaps she was one of the barren wives—else why, Amelia wondered, should she look so soured. Across from her sat a sweet grandmotherly old soul who wore a quaint starched bonnet, with the ties of it laid back over her thin shoulders. At her throat a fine old broach held a bit of lovely lace. Her faded eyes were full of kindness and soft humor; her hair was snow-white. When Amelia entered, this wife had looked at her and smiled in welcome.

The woman on the same side of the table and two seats down had not smiled. She had a long oval head and a face slightly dished, so that in profile it resembled a huge lima bean; but she was one of the handsomest women here. She seemed fond of jewelry; for besides the large bar pin that held the high lace collar, she wore rings in her ears, and a rope of beads knotted at her bosom. It was obvious that this wife felt aloof and tolerant pity for most of the others.

Some of the women kept looking Amelia's way, either to stare at her or at the food she and Brigham were eating; for on Amelia's table, she admitted with more chagrin than triumph, were delicacies denied the rest of them. The food on the long table was abundant but plain. On Amelia's table were choice preserves and jellies and pickles, though she did not touch them. She was not hungry. The resentment in many of the faces had stolen her appetite.

She was, she admitted to herself, almost morbidly curious—for a stranger assortment of women she had never beheld. Halfway down the table was the largest hulk of all, a woman middle-aged, with sleek dark hair plastered in shallow waves to her big round skull and roped in an immaculate braided knot. She gazed at Amelia with eyes serenely stupid in her full smooth face. There was nothing serene in the wife two seats beyond her. As a matter of fact, Amelia wondered at first if this person was a woman. She looked like a man, like a fierce Italian patriot. She had a fine dark moustache; and it looked also as if she had a fuzzy beard over her strong jaws and chin. The broach at her throat and the big artificial flower in her dark hair made her look preposterous: a pipe over her ear and two pistols at her waist would have seemed more appropriate.

After studying all of them, Amelia decided that only two could, even by stretching the truth, be called lovely; and in them it was less perfection of feature than womanly softness. They were younger. Their hair was not done up in grandmotherly knots. Their mouths looked as if they had been kissed—and that was more than Amelia could say of the other lips here. At least seven of the others looked like hellcats who would blow the roof off any house; and gazing at her husband now, Amelia wondered why he had chosen so many wives who were unwomanly. Perhaps it was true, as he had said, that he had been too busy to fall in love, and had been interested only in intelligent mothers and healthy children. Among his fifty offspring, there had been none deformed, feeble-minded, or physically weak.

Nevertheless, it made Amelia shiver to think of the courage a husband must have to embrace so many wives with such stubborn chins, such cold eyes. He was a brave man, she decided, and smiled within—or a most obtuse one. Amelia fell to thinking next of the countless rumors about these women. Of Harriet Cook, a tall woman with light hair and blue eyes, it was said that she caused Brigham more trouble than Buchanan's army; for she often denounced Mormonism, heaped scorn upon celestial marriage, and frightened Brigham right out of the house. Of Martha Bowker, a quiet little woman with piercing dark eyes, it was declared that Brigham had forgotten her, and that Martha lived alone like any spinster. Susan Snively, gossip said, spun and dyed and passed unnoticed from year to year; Ellen Rockwood, in poor health, was visited once in every six months; Twiss, childless, waited on Brigham with faithfulness that neglect only whetted; and Clara Chase, ignored during her fourth confinement, was driven insane. It was now being said that Emmeline, long Brigham's favorite, was dying of a broken heart since he married Amelia.

How much truth there was in the many rumors, Amelia did not know; nor did she know whether she would ever learn the names of all these wives and children. Among the wives there had been, she remembered, a Mary Ann and a Lucy Ann, several Harriets, an Augusta, an Emily, a Clara, Margaret and Louisa, Susan and Ellen and Maria, Martha, Zina and Naamah, Mary and Miriam and Eliza. It was all very confusing; for among the daughters were Elizabeths and Marys and Emmelines, Zinas and Miriams and Louisas. She sighed, thinking that perhaps it would be best not to try. Brigham himself hardly knew the names of all his children, especially now that grandchildren were multiplying around him; and sometimes he mixed the names of his wives. She knew by sight the tall, graceful Emmeline, the round, sandy-haired, blue-eyed Twiss, the tall sharp-nosed Harriet Cook. But most of them were only unfriendly faces, and she thought it would be best if they remained so.

"Are you through?" asked Brigham.

"Yes," she said, and rose from the table.

Every gaze was upon them as they passed out; and she knew that as soon as the door closed behind them, there would be a deluge of gossip.

"I want to go home now," she said.

Brigham fetched her coat, for the time was January and it was bitter cold outside. They went to the cottage where she stayed, and she found it cosy and warm, with a great log burning in the fireplace.

"Are you happy?" Brigham asked.

She smiled, wondering if he had ever asked that question of a wife before. "I am all right," she said. "Most of your wives do not like me."

"You imagine it."

"No. A woman senses these things."

"Well," he said, removing his coat, "do women ever like one another anyhow? I sometimes doubt it."

"Some of them will like me and I'll like some of them. But I say again, don't expect me to be around them."

"That was a promise," he said, and warmed his hands.

She thought he looked old and tired tonight; he was a little stooped, and his face was pale and drawn. It was hard to think of him as husband and lover. It was hard to imagine herself in his embrace. Drawing a chair close, she sat by him and laid a soft hand on his knee. She felt compassion and tenderness. He had never known love—not really, not deeply; for all his life he had been too busy plotting against enemies and building his kingdom. Only now did she realize how lonely he was and how alone he had always been. It had not mattered much perhaps when he was young; but now that he was growing old, now that most of his work was done, he was turning without knowing it to gentler things and seeking tenderness. She hoped she could be what he needed and what none of his other wives had been. For none of them really loved him, it seemed to her; and how could they be expected to? He had been with them so little. Perhaps Emmeline loved him; but that most of them did not was as clear to her as the topknots on their heads. They had married him for the celestial glory and because he was president and prophet; and he had married them because it was a duty; he wanted many children in the next life. That was all very well; but he would have been a greater man, with more pity and tolerance and vision, if a wise woman had softened him.

"Brigham," she said, "do you love your other wives?"

"Of course," he said, gazing at the fire.

"What does love mean to you?"

He looked at her. "What does it mean to you?"

"Oh, tenderness chiefly. A wish to help my husband be a greater man. But you have always lived alone. Your closest friend is Heber Kimball but you really have no close friends. Not your wives, certainly. Haven't you ever needed friends?"

"I guess I've always been too busy."

"Haven't you wanted friends?"

"I've never thought about it."

"You need friends now. That's why you thought you fell in love with me. But you're not in love with me really."

"Of course I am," he said.

"You've always been so fierce," she said, patting his big strong hands. "Now most of your work is behind you and you need something else."

"What?" he asked, a little amused.

"A woman perhaps. I think that's why you came to me but I don't think I can be what you need. I can try. That's why I want to go with you on your trips. You need softening."

"I don't have a job for a soft man."

"You've always wanted to fight your way through things—to burn supply trains and shoot your enemies. Don't you think gentleness and mercy are better weapons?"

"Not against bigots."

"They might be. You've never tried them."

"Soon," he said, speaking slowly, "I'll be arrested. I'll be tried for bigamy and jailed. What does gentleness have to do with that?"

"Don't let yourself be arrested."

"Then I'll have to fight. I'll have to march out with an army."

"Maybe not."

He shook his head. "I can see the handwriting on the wall."

For a little while they were silent. Then he said he was tired and guessed he had better go to bed; but she said he would do nothing of the kind.

"You're going to stay with me tonight."

"No," he said, frowning, "I always sleep alone. It's better for a man."

"You're alone too much. Tonight you stay with me."

And forthwith she began to undress him. He was amused. Most persons, even his friends, were afraid of him; but this woman seemed not to be. He admitted (to himself) that he liked her soft hands on him. He liked the gentle efficient hands that were unfastening his cravat and the buttons of his stiff white shirt.

"Lean forward," she said; and when he leaned forward, she drew his coat off. Then she sat on the floor and unfastened his boots and drew them off, and his stockings, and patted his strong white feet. Rising, she went to the bedroom and returned with a nightshirt.

"What's that?" he asked, looking at it.

"A nightshirt."

"But we saints sleep in our endowment garments."

"Oh," she said. She had forgotten about these holy garments, this underwear, which the saints were given after receiving the Holy Ghost in the temple or the Endowment House. They were supposed never to take a garment entirely off without first thrusting a foot or a leg into a clean garment; for as long as they wore their garment or kept one foot or one leg in it, neither weapons nor disease could harm them.

Brigham, meanwhile, was wondering about her. His other wives had urged him to curl his hair or trim his beard or wear more expensive clothes; but none had undressed him or told him where he was to sleep. His sense of humor was awake to this energetic and possessive caretaker.

"You don't think I'm going to sleep here all the time, do you?"

"Oh, no. Habits are too strong. Just tonight—and besides, you have other wives."

He went over in his underwear and sat by the fire while Amelia went to the bedroom to undress. After a few moments, she called out of darkness, telling him to come to bed; and he obeyed her, still amused and a little astonished. He knew little of the ways of women but he realized that Amelia did not want his embrace tonight. She wanted only to lie on one of his strong arms and reach up and twirl his soft hair or playfully pull at the handful of whiskers on his chin.

"Go to sleep," she said, and with gentle fingers closed his eyes. Then she cuddled against him and put her fair cheek to his face and slept.

IT WAS NOT KNOWN, EVEN BY THOSE CLOSEST TO BRIGHAM, WHAT HAD HAPpened to the rugged leader whose way until now had been that of the torch and sword. His enemies were moving in but he refused to be alarmed. Connor marched up to Bear River in Idaho Territory and murdered several hundred Indians, including women and children, and then marched back to establish a provost guard right in the city. He chose, indeed, a building belonging to the church—it stood across the street from the south gates of the temple square; and he announced that traitors had better seek a more "genial soil" or receive the punishment they deserved. The newspaper at Camp Floyd, the *Union Vendette*, trumpeted: "It should be distinctly understood that here or elsewhere, Uncle Sam will have what he wants—when he wants it—under all circumstances—from all people under the flag, and that, too, at his own estimate of what is a fair price."

That veiled allusion to the anti-bigamy law was for some of the church leaders a declaration of war. Brigham was in Provo when Connor marched in, but Heber went at full speed to tell him about it.

"He set up a guard by the temple gates?"

"And by the God of Israel, right in our own building!"

"I wonder what he wants now."

"War, Brigham. He intends to arrest you, and you'll get what Joseph got."

Brigham sighed. "If we were on a raft in the middle of the Pacific, our enemies would send an army after us."

"Don't go back unprotected. If you do, you'll spend tonight in jail."

"I guess so. But it's coming, Heber, sooner or later."

Gathering two hundred armed men as an escort, Brigham rode northward to the city. Heber said they must remove that guard, let it cost what it would; but Brigham said no.

"That would mean war, Heber."

"We can ask Edwin Stanton to move it."

"We might as well appeal to a stone monkey. We'll wall up the sou[ ]
gates."

"Brigham, now is the time to strike while Lincoln has his hands full."

"It would do no good. They would drive us into Mexico."

When Brigham arrived in the city, he found it full of armed men wh[o]
had poured in from the settlements to protect him. He sent them back [to]
their homes. He had the south gates walled up but he made no attem[pt]
to dislodge the guard. Hotheaded saints came to see him, to denoun[ce]
his meekness and to demand war.

"Are you going to leave these damned soldiers right under our nos[e]
and in our own building?"

"Yes."

"If they camp in the temple grounds, I guess you'll leave them the[re]
too!"

"I think they'll stay out of the temple grounds."

"Like hell they will! Give them an inch and they'll take the city."

"The anti-bigamy law gives them a stranglehold on us," said Brigha[m]
quietly. "Now that the soldiers are here, we cannot fight them. It is t[oo]
late."

"Of course we can fight them. Lincoln couldn't afford to send an arm[y]
now."

"But an army would come later."

At this moment an excited man dashed into Brigham's office. His ey[es]
and hair were wild. He was so agitated that for a moment he was unab[le]
to speak.

"What is it?" Brigham asked.

"They're going to arrest you!"

"Who?"

"Connor and Judge Waite!"

"How do you know that?"

"We heard them say so. The Judge, he said he wanted three of yo[u]
and Connor was to slip up and surprise you. And Connor said he would [ ]

"Are you sure of that?"

"You knew," said Heber impatiently, "that it would be this way."

"Yes," said Brigham. He turned to Dan Wells. "Brother Dan, give th[e]
signal."

Dan Wells left the office and gave the signal. The result was imm[ediate]

diate and overwhelming: within an hour, two thousand men in the city had leapt to arms and filled the streets. That, it seemed to Brigham, ought to make Connor think twice before he moved. Nevertheless, Brigham did not intend to wait for a military arrest. He summoned Isaac Gibbs, a marshal, and said he wanted to be arrested on a charge of violating the anti-bigamy law, and arraigned before Kinney, the only friendly judge in the city. And quietly, before Connor knew what was going on, Brigham was arrested and admitted to bail and held for the grand jury. He thought it was a shrewd move but some of his leaders were unconvinced.

"What if the charge is dismissed? You'll be arrested again. They'll keep after you until they've shot you down."

"I have no doubt that I'll be dismissed and arrested again."

"Then what's the sense of it? Are we going to be sheep until we are all murdered? While Lincoln has his hands full, we can drive Connor and his scoundrels out of here. If an army comes, we'll chop it to pieces in Echo Canyon."

"That time is past. Soldiers would come in from all sides."

"Well, at this rate, we'll all be in jail."

"If it is the Lord's will, then we'll all go to jail."

"Brigham," said Dan Wells, "I don't understand you. You've changed."

"We can't fight the United States. That's all."

"We did once."

"Yes, and it got us nothing."

"We'll have a repetition of Carthage."

Brigham fully realized that he might be murdered. His enemies were closing in and his troubles were multiplying. He knew that when the Union Pacific completed its line to Ogden, gentiles would pour in by the hundreds. He knew that the discovery of precious ore in Bingham Canyon was a threat to the security of his people and the integrity of his empire. But he did not intend to fight or even to resist arrest. He hoped that he could consolidate the saints into a unit that would stand as one man against the invading hordes, and preserve their heritage.

That seemed to him to be the only way now. For thirty-five years the saints had fought or fled by turn, but neither fighting nor fleeing had solved their problem or mitigated by one jot the bitterness of their enemies. He would be—as fundamentally he had always been—loyal to his country and its flag.

He soon had an opportunity to manifest that loyalty. When news came that Lincoln had been re-elected, Brigham saw the astute chance he had been waiting for. He summoned his leaders.

"Turn out the city," he said. "I want a demonstration of loyalty to the Union that will send Connor under a culvert to hide his face. I want dozens of patriotic speeches; but I don't want any allusions to that mouth-almighty grafter Floyd, or to that Benedict Arnold, Albert Sidney Johnston, who came out to punish us for disloyalty and then ran off to fight for Jeff Davis. I want all the bands out. I want a parade, and in it I want every man, woman and child in the city who can walk. When that's all over, I want a big banquet for Connor and his staff."

The demonstration did not send the hard-boiled Connor off to hide his face but it did amaze him. He saw a parade a mile long; he heard bands blaring every patriotic air he knew; he heard speeches to the glory of the Union, its armies and its flag. He saw thousands listening to those speeches, and he heard applause that shook the rafters. He saw streets filled with people, saw them in every window and doorway, and beheld flags no matter where he turned. At the banquet, he heard toasts to the President, the Union and its armies; and afterward he witnessed the most remarkable display of fireworks that he had ever seen.

Brigham gave a short address, but for the most part he sat back and observed the results of his statesmanship. He was at Social Hall where many of the saints were dancing when the hard-faced Connor came up to him and proffered his hand.

"President Young, this is the greatest display of loyalty I've ever beheld."

"I find it gratifying," said Brigham.

"I've erred in my judgment," said Connor, looking around him. "I thought you Mormons were disloyal. I see I've been mistaken."

"I'm glad, General, that you've changed your mind."

"I have. I propose that we live in peace hereafter. I also propose to abolish the *Union Vendette*. It serves no purpose."

"I agree with you. It stirs up trouble."

"We don't want trouble, President Young. Why, damn my hide, if there are more loyal Americans anywhere, I'd like to know where they are."

Brigham's face was inscrutable but he was pleased. This was statesmanship. This was getting what he wanted and making his enemies like it. When, a month and a half later, Lincoln was assassinated, Brigham turned the city out again and shook it from cellar to rafter with patriotic fervor. But even though he had made a friend of Connor, he did not deceive himself with the notion that his troubles were over. This was only a lull in the storm. The *Vendette* was abolished, but a newspaper at Fort Douglas took its place and it was twice as bitter. Preachers and editors back East had not changed their minds.

When Brigham came to trial for bigamy, he expected to be acquitted; because Judge Kinney, before whom he stood to plead not guilty, had a record in the Territory that was not very savory. Heber Kimball had once denounced him in public meeting as a man who took "unhallowed liberties with females"; and other saints had hinted that Kinney, like some other Federal appointees, had some nameless children by squaws. Brigham's eyes twinkled when he looked at the judge, and it was only with an effort that Kinney restrained a sly smile.

"President Young, is the court to understand that your plea is not guilty?"

"Not guilty, your honor."

Kinney looked around him. There was nobody present except a few of Brigham's friends.

"It looks as if no witnesses have appeared to testify against you."

Brigham looked around too, but his face was a solemn mask. Nobody—as he knew better than the judge—dared at this moment to appear against him.

"I see no witnesses, your honor."

"In that case, President Young, there is nothing for the court to do except to acquit you of the charge. You are free to go."

Brigham knew that he would be arrested again; and before the storm gathered fresh violence, he wanted to consolidate his people into an invulnerable unit. To this end he made frequent trips to the colonies where Orders had been established. An individualist himself, he believed in personal initiative and competitive practice; but he also believed in collective community enterprises. He was aware of the wide range in human intelligence, talent and ambition: there could never be a utopian society in which everyone could share equally; but there could be an order in which none needed to starve. The old, the sick and the poor must be taken care of. Above all, every person should have the right to work and to find work to do.

He had already built a remarkably integrated spiritual kingdom. From the president down to the lowliest deacon, every man knew his duties and was an inseparable part of the huge pattern. The empire was divided into areas called stakes, and over each there was a president with his counselors. The stakes were subdivided into wards over which the bishops presided. Brigham had knowledge of everything of importance that happened throughout the length and breadth of his kingdom. If a woman was ill up in Soda Springs, if a man was without food in Ogden, if a child refused to pray in Fillmore or a brother refused to pay his tithing in St. George, Brigham knew about it. He knew of nearly every petty quarrel, every feud, every meanness or unhappiness or complaint; because ward workers called regularly at the homes and spent evenings asking questions, giving advice and aid, and learning the nature of every problem; whereupon they reported to their bishops who in turn reported to their stake presidents who reported to Brigham. It was a smooth and efficient network that covered every hamlet and every home. It was, visitors said, the most remarkable social integration that had ever been achieved in the history of humankind.

But his people, Brigham well knew, needed more than that if they were to resist the inroads of gentiles. They needed industrial as well as spiritual fellowship. To achieve that, he wanted large enterprises that would be collectively owned and managed—so that every man could share not only in the profits but also in the pride of growth and accomplishment. It was for this reason that he founded Zion's Co-operative Mercantile Institution and invited all the saints to buy stock in it so that it would represent the commonwealth of his people. The huge parent wholesale store was built on Main Street in Salt Lake City, and thousands of the saints bought stock in it. Brigham wanted retail stores in every city, town and hamlet, to be fed from the central granary but to be locally owned and managed. He wanted his people to buy only from their own stores and to freeze the gentiles out, or at least to force them to trade only in institutions which they had built.

To distinguish the Mormon stores, he ordered placed above every door a sign on which there would be a picture of an all-seeing eye, and over it the words: HOLINESS TO THE LORD. "Then," he said, "a wayfaring man, even though a fool, will not err and get into the wrong store." He had spies everywhere; and if a saint deliberately entered a gentile store, he was tapped significantly on the shoulder and told not to err again. Before the gentile stores in Salt Lake City, his pickets marched back and forth all day long, observing those who entered and reporting the names of guilty saints to Brigham.

Other co-operative institutions were founded, and Zion closed its doors to the invasion of gentile merchants.

Still, that was not quite true. Brigham tried to close the doors—because this city and valley belonged to him and his people. They had built their homes in a desert and they had a right to shut their enemies out. But in spite of all he could do, enterprising gentiles, and even apostates, forced their way in and set up in business. When he laid down a boycott against all gentile merchants and marched pickets past their doors, he drove the smaller merchants to the wall; and one day an angry and perspiring man burst into his office.

"Look here!" he roared. "You're bankrupting me!"

"How?" asked Brigham, as if he did not understand.

"Why, by telling Mormons not to trade with me! I had a good business but now I don't sell a bolt of cloth in a week!"

"I'm sorry. We have our own stores and prefer to trade there."

"Then I'll have to sell out."

"As you please."

"Then buy me out and I'll leave Utah."

Brigham palmed his beard and considered that. He wanted gentile merchants to pack up and leave, but he was too shrewd a statesman to buy them out; for they would go to the eastern states and say that only Mormons could do business in Salt Lake City.

"No," he said calmly, "we don't want to buy you out. Any merchant has a right to do business here, be he Jew, Mohammedan or Christian. Anyone, so long as he is honest, is welcome here."

"But I'm going bankrupt! The Mormons traded with me until you told them not to. You march your pickets past my doors all day long and not a single Mormon has been in for months."

"It is our policy for Mormons to trade with Mormons. We do not object at all if gentiles want to trade only with gentiles."

"But you're forcing us out! Every one of your damned stores has that all-seeing eye and that holiness to the Lord over its door. We can't compete against anything like that."

"Then you had better go into some other business."

"Why won't you buy me out?"

"I don't want to. I invite competitors. It makes business more lively."

"Lively, hell! It has bankrupted me!"

"Well, I'm sorry—but it's your problem and not mine."

After this angry merchant left his office, Brigham drummed on his desk and pondered. He was bankrupting small merchants; but the four apostate Walker brothers were for a while almost too much for him. These four men, after having refused to pay their full tithing to the church, had been cut off, and thereupon had built the largest department store in the city. They were shrewd merchants and they prospered—until Brigham rose in public meeting and denounced them, set spies at their doors, and declared that he would excommunicate any saint caught entering their institution. He knocked the Walker sales of sixty thousand dollars a month down to five thousand; but they were four stubborn men and stuck by their guns. After a while, Brigham learned that his people were sneaking into the Walker store from the rear, and that small Mormon merchants were secretly buying their goods and restocking them.

That discovery made Brigham so furious that he kicked a dozen of the sinners out of the church and thoroughly frightened his people. He frightened the gentile merchants too. Some of them, when going to their homes after dark, walked in the middle of the street and carried loaded guns in their hands. All of them, a little later, offered to sell their holdings to the Mormons at seventy-five cents on the dollar and leave the city.

"I am sorry," Brigham wrote to their committee, "but we do not want to buy you out. We did not ask you to come here, and we do not ask you to leave. It is your privilege to stay as long as you wish to. . . ."

Two other apostates, a man named Godbe and another named Harrison, were also giving him trouble. They were vain and pompous fellows who announced that they had talked with God, and God had commanded them to open mines in Utah. Harrison said he had also talked with the ghost of Humboldt who would soon reveal to him truths that would knock Darwin's theories into a cocked hat. He then started a magazine the purpose of which was to organize opposition to the Mormons and work out a plan of attack. With Godbe he set to work to organize a mining company; and Brigham foresaw hundreds of tents and huts and shacks, and the coming of more gamblers and harlots.

Often during these years, he felt that he would be defeated in spite of all he could do. Formerly, he would have had Porter Rockwell tap Harrison on his shoulder, and advise him to seek his fortune and establish his magazines elsewhere. But Brigham was an old man now. He had foolishly taken two other brides; and one of them, a shrew named Eliza, was giving him more hell than all his wives together had given him before. She wanted expensive clothes and jewels and a mansion like Amelia's; and when she did not get them, she threatened to denounce him as a fraud, to write a book that would "expose" Mormonism, and to sue him for divorce and half a million dollars. During these troubles, his friend Heber died. When Heber fell from a carriage and injured himself, Brigham did not think the matter was serious; and he was astonished a little later to hear that Heber had caught pneumonia and died with startling suddenness. Other assistants had died or deserted. Bill Hickman had turned thoroughly sour and was hatching plots of his own; and Porter Rockwell did not seem to be as faithful as he once had been.

Yes, Brigham was growing old and feeble, but he still fought with all the strength he had. During the years after Lincoln's death, he struggled to integrate his empire, to make of it an industrial and spiritual unit that could withstand any kind of invasion—for such a solid front was the only weapon left to him. If his people stood together they could resist to the end.

More and more frequently, he summoned his carriage and visited northern and southern colonies to learn what they were doing. Often Amelia went with him. With him too went apostles and others, and especially Wilford Woodruff who, if he lived, would some day be president of the church. Brigham was proud of the Order in the city named for him: it had company stores, a woolen mill, a tannery, a hat factory, lumber mills, a large dairy, with every man sharing in ownership and management. There was no idleness, no poverty, no greedy struggle for privilege and wealth. "This," he said to Woodruff, "is the way the saints should live. We need such an Order in every city and hamlet in Zion."

"My conscience, yes," said Woodruff, but the wagging of his head was not emphatic.

"How is everything?" asked Brigham of one of the leaders here.

"All right, Brother Brigham."

"Is everyone satisfied?"

"Yes, I think so."

"That is good. That is the way it should be."

He was no less proud of the Order which the McBrides had founded in Josephville, six miles south of Salt Lake City. There was a fine and pervasive idealism in this colony, and an enthusiastic fellowship.

"Brother Moroni, is everything going well?"

"Yes, Brother Brigham. But my son is manager now. Like you, I'm an old man."

"Does every brother have a hand in the management?"

Tim had come up with his son Nephi. "Yes," he said.

Brigham looked at Nephi, a tall and handsome young man with frank eyes. "Is this the boy I saw gnawing that bone years ago?"

"Yes," said Nephi, remembering that year of famine.

"Brother Nephi, some day you'll probably be a leader here. Do you think you can keep the Order going after we are all gone?"

"I'll try my best."

"You must. It's the only chance we have to whip our enemies—build ourselves in and shut them out. All the brethren are happy here?"

"So far as I know," said Tim.

"I wish we had a thousand Orders like this. Then no power in hell could destroy us. Well, let's see what you've done."

They walked through the settlement and Brigham perceived that it was much like the one in the city named for him. It had the same clean new homes, spacious lawns, trees and shrubs and flowers; the same shining mills and shops; the same busy hum throughout the village. The common storehouse was piled deep with provisions. In the gristmill were hundreds of bags of flour, bran and grits.

"I don't see how we could have a famine now."

"Not here," said Moroni. "We could feed Noah through a hundred floods."

"My conscience," said Woodruff, gazing around him, "I should think you could."

Woodruff was also getting to be an old man. Most of his life he had spent in travel, both as missionary and as president of foreign missions; and in consequence he was not so well known to the saints as many of the apostles. This was the first time Nephi had ever seen him; and now he gazed curiously at Woodruff, observing that he was a plump and kindly man with mild blue eyes and a kindly smile.

"Well," said Brigham, "we must go. Keep up the good work, Brother Timothy. Have you taken any more wives yet?"

"One, Brother Brigham."

"Only one? Take some more."

"This one causes all the damned hell I can take care of."

Brigham glanced over at Amelia who was sitting in his carriage. He grinned. "I have a hellcat too, Brother Tim. My last wife is driving me crazy."

"We've heard about that," said Moroni. "She's divorcing you."

"Under the law," said Brigham dryly, "I don't see how she can divorce me."

He was pleased by what he saw in Provo and other southern towns. Industry was not so completely socialized as in Brigham City and Josephville; but the spirit was there, and the effort. The men were proudly building co-operative units. There was no poverty in these settlements, no social caste or arrogant pride, no attempt on the part of any man to exploit the labor of another.

As he rode through Dixie, he looked unhappily westward toward the Mountain Meadows area. The bones of the slaughtered emigrants had lain for two years before soldiers buried them. Today the Federal government was investigating that massacre and promising to bring the guilty persons to trial. It was a matter that Brigham wished to forget. He was more interested in stories told him about the Indians—the lazy and thriftless Lamanites whom his people had been trying to convert in this area— the stupid Shivwits who were almost too indolent to feed themselves, and the filthy Paiutes who liked to sit in the sun and pick lice off themselves.

When an Indian was converted, he was baptized and given another name, clothes and food. "But the lazy lubbers," said a Dixie saint, "eat their food and wear their clothes out and then come back to be baptized again. That was true of O-cak-kwit that we renamed Matthew and Pegara-rump that we renamed Abraham. Matthew and Abraham want to be baptized about every two weeks."

Brigham grinned. "The lazy scoundrels. I don't know how the Lord expects us to redeem the Lamanites."

"I don't either. That's all baptism means to them—just some more clothes and some more food. If we won't baptize them again, they say they'll join some other church."

Brigham looked over all the southern colonies that were founding Orders and set out for home. "That," he said to Amelia, "is the way the whole world should live—all brothers and all helping one another. The strong should help the weak, the well the sick. When resources and industries are all shared in common and every man is proud of the work he does, then we can build a Christian world; but as long as a few own everything and the others work for them, there will be poverty and sin and war, and all the ungodliness that stinks to high heaven."

"But some men are lazy, Brigham. Some men would never have anything, no matter what you did."

"Very few men are lazy if they have work they can be proud of. If they just get bed and board out of their labor, you can't expect them to be happy; but they'll be happy if you make them feel they're part of a wise plan."

"I'm not sure of that."

"I know it. Make a man proud of his work and you have a happy man."

Amelia was dubious but she liked his vision of an empire in which every man, woman and child would share abundantly in the comforts of life. It was poverty, Brigham said, that produced most of the ills of the world; it was a want of pride, a sense of meaninglessness, of futility, that drove men to crime. She hoped he could make his dream come true.

"But what will happen to the church after you're gone?"

"I don't know. I wish I did."

"Do you think these socialistic Orders will survive?"

"I don't know."

Amelia squeezed his arm. "Brigham, I didn't know you were such an idealist. I thought you were just a hard-headed business man."

"It's plain horse sense. If human beings are to be happy, they must be happy in the work they do. They must feel they're accomplishing more than three meals a day and a bed to sleep on. Is that idealism?"

"No, that isn't. But it's idealism to think some men won't grab everything if they can."

"They won't while I'm alive."

"But after you're gone, some will get richer and some poorer. Who will be the next president?"

Brigham hesitated. He had hoped that one of his sons would be the next president. "The President of the Twelve," he said. "Brother John Taylor."

"But he's not a strong man. He won't fight the way you have. The gentiles will chase him right out of here."

"I'm trying," said Brigham wearily, "to shut the gentiles out."

"But you can't." She squeezed his arm again. "You can't, Brigham, but just the same I hope you make your dream come true."

He might have made his dream come true if his most implacable enemy had not been sitting in the White House. As he rode along, observing how his people had turned a desert into green fields, into orchards and vineyards and prosperous homes, his mind was busy planning a kingdom that would endure after he was gone. He did not know that at this moment, President Grant was searching for men who could go to Utah and scatter the Mormon empire to the four winds. He did not know that the storm had gathered again and was ready to break.

CHAPTER XXVII

HE SENSED THE TROUBLE WHEN HE PICKED UP THE CHICAGO *Post* AND read what it had to say of the new governor whom President Grant was sending to Utah. "Vincent Vaughan," wrote the scathing editor, "is the new governor of Utah. His qualifications are as follows: he was a rebel throughout the war; engaged in a couple of duels after the war; his name is euphonious enough for a ten cent novel. . . ." So that was the kind of scapegoat Grant was sending to lord it over the Mormons!

But Vaughan, like so many governors before him, arrived in the Territory, looked around him and fled. Meanwhile, a newspaper, the *Tribune*, had been founded as a mouthpiece of the gentiles in the city who had organized themselves into a fighting league; and at once the editors were declaring that the Mormons were dupes and serfs and downtrodden geese, and that their leaders were theocratic frauds. It looked for a moment as if the streets would run with blood. There was a city election; and when Brigham saw the anger of his people, he gave orders that no saint was to draw a weapon, no matter what was said or done. Thereupon his leaders vented their rage in boos and hisses when listening to the political speeches of their opponents.

A minor crisis developed when Dan Wells, mayor of the city, was mobbed and beaten. His clothes were torn off. Some of the gentiles threatened to shoot him. Of this outrage, of rioting at the polls, of threats of lynching, Brigham calmly received reports in his office. To every angry person who came to him he said, "Under no provocation are the saints to draw weapons or do anything to precipitate a fight. I insist on peace." He realized, nevertheless, that matters were drawing to another major climax.

Above all, during these trying times, he wanted to keep the sympathy of powerful editors in the eastern states. He hoped for another Buchanan Blunder to save him. Many of the editors throughout the country were in lively sympathy with the Mormons and were indignant; and as fast as the principal newspapers came to him, Brigham eagerly read them in an attempt to gauge the drift of public opinion. The Omaha *Herald* was angry. President Grant's object, it declared, was to break the political power "of the people who conquered Utah from a desert waste into a beautiful garden. A conspiracy exists to destroy men and institutions in a territory whose civilizing and industrial achievements are the admiration of mankind."

The San Francisco *Examiner* was no less emphatic. "The whole thing is instigated by a 'ring' of Republican politicians who are looking to the speedy admission of Utah as one of the States of the Union. These small fry, popinjay politicians, and would-be statesmen know full well that they will have no show for promotion until the Mormon power is broken. Hence it is that they seek to create a civil war by packed juries, unprincipled judges and perjured witnesses. That a vile little clique of corrupt politicians should be permitted to use the power of the government to embroil a peaceable community in civil strife, to gratify their personal greed for place and plunder, is an outrage upon decency, humanity and justice! . . ."

Other great newspapers were no less vehement in their denunciation. For a while, Brigham thought the tide would turn in his favor, and that public indignation would cause the President to change his mind. But U. S. Grant was a stubborn man. He had resolved to destroy the Mormons and he paid little attention to angry editors. He boldly sent to Utah a judge with instructions to pack a jury and throw Brigham into jail.

Brigham did not see Judge McKean for some time after the man arrived. He did not want to. He was told that McKean was a bullet-headed and obstinate man who announced boldly what he had come to do. He was going to pick jurors who did not believe in polygamy; and if necessary he was going to arrest every Mormon in the Territory and send him to jail. For his first victim he chose a nobody named Tom Hawkins; and that astounded man was sent to prison for "lewdly and lasciviously cohabiting with women." With his test case out of the way and a picked jury ready, McKean set out for bigger game.

"He'll have us all in jail," said Dan Wells, his big face full of rage and woe. He had not forgotten how he had been flogged and almost lynched.

"It looks like it, Brother Dan."

"Well, by the God of Israel, why don't we stop them! Are we going to let this scoundrel choose juries from our enemies and send us up for ten years for our religious convictions?"

"We cannot fight the United States," said Brigham wearily. "If it's the Lord's will for us to die in jail, then we'll die in jail."

"But you used to say the Almighty helps those who help themselves. In the war——"

"No, Dan. We'll give them enough rope to hang themselves. That's our only chance now. If they hog it enough, the whole country will be on our side. That's the only strategy we have."

"But they won't stop at jails. We know what mobs are like. They'll murder you just like they murdered Joseph."

"That may be the Lord's will."

"Brigham," said Dan Wells angrily, "listen to me. They drove us out of place after place. They drove us into a wilderness where they thought we'd starve. We settled in a valley that nobody else wanted and it belongs to us. This is our home. We've fought and suffered to make it our home. Now we should protect it. If we fight for our rights, people back East will sympathize with us and say we are doing only what they would do——"

"No, Dan. Not now they wouldn't. The only way we can get sympathy is by not resisting."

Dan turned impatiently. A few years ago he was general of the Army of Deseret. He had stopped Johnston and his army dead in their tracks and made them freeze all winter in the mountains. Now—now he was only the mayor of the city, threatened by jail and lynching and not knowing when he would be shot down. He wanted to fight while there was still a chance.

"Then you intend to let McKean pack juries and send us all to jail!"

Brigham smiled. "They'll have to build a lot of jails. Our wives will join us. It will cost Grant three million dollars to lock us all up."

"But they'll lock you up. A week won't pass before you're arrested. They'll lock all the leaders up. Then what will the saints do? They'll be robbed and raped."

"Let's give them plenty of rope. That's our only way to whip them."

"Mark my word, Brigham. You'll be arrested next."

"I expect to be."

"And you'll be in jail the rest of your life."

"I think probably I will—unless public opinion comes to our aid."

Dan shook his head. "I'd rather fight," he declared, and left the office.

Dan was right. McKean's next move was to have Brigham arrested for lewd and lascivious cohabitation. When Brigham was arraigned, his counsel made a motion to quash the indictment, and McKean angrily overruled the motion and pounded his desk.

"The case at the bar," he said, flushed with rage, "is called The People versus Brigham Young, but its other and real title is Federal Authority versus Polygamic Theocracy! The government of the United States, founded upon a written Constitution, finds within its jurisdiction another government—claiming to come from God—imperiam in imperio—whose policy and practice, in grave particulars, are at variance with its own. A system is on trial in the person of Brigham Young. Let all concerned keep that fact steadily in view! Again I say the motion is overruled!"

Brigham's attorney was nonplussed. Some of the church leaders present were filled with angry consternation, but Brigham himself was as calm as a June morning. He listened quietly to the plea of his counsel, sometimes eloquent, sometimes scathing; but he knew that nothing the man could say had power to move this stern judge. McKean had been sent by President Grant to put the Mormons in jail, and that was precisely what he intended to do in any way that he could. He listened impatiently to the counsel's argument and then admitted Brigham to bail of five thousand dollars; and as soon as that was done, he had Dan Wells arrested, and George Cannon, editor of the Mormon newspaper, and admitted them to bail.

Most of the eastern press headlined the case in a way that Brigham had not expected. The New York *Herald* announced in huge words:

THE MORMONS ARMING!

and added in the next issue:

OPEN RESISTANCE TO THE LAWS!

Such foolish headlines made Brigham smile. There was no resistance. His enemies, beyond all question, were determined to make an end of him this time. It mattered little that he and his people had fled into a wilderness, had reclaimed a desert, or that the Constitution gave to them the right to worship God in their own way. He had been hailed into court like any common hoodlum, and he knew that he would be convicted and sentenced.

His health was very poor. He was getting to be an old and a feeble man. Upon learning that his case would not come up until the spring term of court, he decided to go to the southern colonies and a warmer clime to spend the winter. In his carriage, escorted by an armed guard, he set out for the Rio Virgin Valley, taking Amelia with him; but he had not gone far before a messenger overtook him. It was Porter Rockwell.

"What's the trouble, Porter?"

"By God, Judge McKean has ordered your case up."

"Now? I thought it was to be next spring."

"He won't wait."

"Then he can take the bond and arrest me again."

"But he won't forfeit the bond. He says you're runnun away."

"Oh, the hell I am! Well, my lawyers can fight it out with him. I'm not going back now. Tell them that, Porter."

Brigham resumed his journey but he had not spent much time in the southern settlements before some of his leaders came to him. They found him in St. George. He called a meeting in the town to decide what should be done.

"Now what do they want?" he asked, turning to John Taylor.

"The judge won't forfeit the bail. He says you must return at once."

"Why didn't he send officers to fetch me?"

"He will if you don't return."

"My conscience," said Wilford Woodruff, "I don't think you should!"

"Why not, Brother Wilford?"

"Because the judge intends to arrest you for murder."

"That is true," said Taylor.

"Whose murder?"

"Well," said Taylor, "it seems they've been digging up some things. Maybe they've been talking to Bill Hickman. Anyway, it's for some of our old enemies that were socked away."

"The judge is also angry about the Mountain Meadows affair."

Brigham looked around him. "Well, I guess I can stand a trial for murder. Remember how Joseph left Nauvoo and was brought back by a messenger?"

"Don't go back!" cried one of the saints of St. George. "They'll murder you. They'll do just what they did to Joseph."

"How are the saints behaving in Salt Lake City?"

"The city is very tense," said John Taylor. "There might be riots and fighting at any moment. They all seem to feel lost when you go away."

"Brother John, I'll soon be going away for good. You'll be president then."

"Yes, Brigham. I don't know what we'll do without you."

"You'll all go to jail, I hope. That's the only thing to do." For a long moment he considered. "Well, the Light says, 'Brigham, return.'"

Persons crowded around him, protesting, pleading. If he returned, they said he would be killed as Joseph was killed.

"I'm in the hands of the Lord. He will rule for the best good of Zion as long as we are faithful and unafraid."

"But He didn't save Joseph and He won't save you!"

"He didn't save His own Son, did He? In ways unknown to us, it was all for the best."

"You can go to Arizona—or to Mexico. There's no sense to go back just to be murdered."

"I won't desert my people. I won't run away. Get my carriage ready."

It was a long cold journey back to the city. On the second day, Brigham came to a village named Kanarra; and there old John Parker, one of Joseph's former bodyguard, burst from the crowd and threw himself at Brigham's feet. He was weeping like a child.

"Brother John, what is the trouble?"

"Don't go back!" John cried, clasping Brigham's legs. "In God's name, don't let them kill you!"

"Why not, John?"

"Because we all need you! If they kill you, we will all be murdered!"

"I won't run from my enemies."

"Please don't go!" Tears were running in the wrinkles of John's face. Other persons were weeping and urging Brigham to flee.

"No," he said. "Let's be off."

At Cedar City he was met by Porter Rockwell and two other men.

"What's the news, Porter?"

"Bad news. You'll be killed. The whole country is sayun you run from your enemies. The city is armed and ready for you."

"That's all right. I'll slip in after dark."

"Mobs will be ready," said Porter, shaking his long graying hair. "It won't be very safe."

"Just the same, Porter, I'll never desert my people. And after I am dead," he added, looking at John Taylor and Wilford Woodruff, "I hope the authorities stand by their guns."

"But you'll be killed," said Porter.

"I'm not afraid to die."

The time was December. The next day the party ran into a blinding snowstorm and for an hour was lost. Brigham said they had better take the mail stage, and in a wild gray wind they returned to Beaver. It was impossible to see more than two rods ahead of the carriages, but men went afoot, seeking the road and breaking paths for the horses. Brigham was wrapped in blankets with Amelia at his side.

"You cold?" he asked, reaching for a mittened hand.

"I'm all right."

"Are you afraid I'll be murdered?"

"Yes."

"Well, I'm an old man. Perhaps my time has come."

"John Taylor and Wilford Woodruff seem scared. If they're to be the leaders after you're gone——"

"Yes," he said quickly. "But John was shot down in the Carthage jail. He shouldn't be afraid of anything."

"I'll bet he runs away when he's president."

"If he does, then God help the church."

Upon arriving in Beaver, Brigham took the mail coach, leaving instructions to his party to follow as soon as the storm lifted. On the coach he was surprised to find General Connor.

"Hello there, General. How are you?"

Connor turned and clasped Brigham's hand. "How are you, President Young?"

"Old and feeble, General. I get weaker and weaker."

"This prosecution is a damned outrage. If McKean will admit you to bail, I'll sign bonds for a hundred thousand dollars."

"But McKean wants me in jail or dead."

"It's a damned outrage! President Grant must be insane."

Brigham smiled. "Mobs are waiting for me in Salt Lake City—in the city that I built, General. They want to murder me."

"It's outrageous!" shouted Connor, and clenched his big bare hands. "By God, if I can help you——"

"No, General. I'm afraid my enemies have me this time."

"Why don't you fight the scoundrels?"

"That would do no good. You're an army man and you know that. The United States would shoot us all down before the fighting was done with."

"As you decide, President Young. But if you should fight, I'll be there to help you."

"Thank you, General Connor. From a fighter like you, such an offer is very gratifying."

At Cove Fort Brigham left the stage and rejoined his own party. More than a foot of new snow had fallen in the Pine Valley Mountains on Wild Cat Pass; the telegraph wires were down; the road was buried. Men with fresh horses broke a road ahead; but through Dog Valley the storm was so heavy and blinding that the teamsters could barely see their horses. When, facing the stinging blizzard, the beasts refused to move, men went ahead of them, leading them with ropes and breaking a path. Sleet was like small shot against the windows of Brigham's carriage.

Sitting with only a part of her face showing out of the blankets, Amelia was thinking of this strange man at her side. Never, she supposed, had he ever wavered in his resolve to serve the Lord; never, she believed, had he ever been afraid. For thirty years he had ruled men with an iron hand and had unerringly read their hearts; but all that he knew about women could have been written in one short sentence. In spite of anti-bigamy laws, old age, and enemies who numbered millions, he had married twice since he married her. Mary Van Cott was all right—a slender, graceful and intelligent girl; but Eliza Ann was a shrew out of hell. She was suing Brigham for divorce and two hundred thousand dollars; and this scandalous affair had done nothing, here or back East, to soften the bitterness against him. Yet she had no doubt that he would marry again if he took the notion.

"Brigham, why did you ever marry Eliza Ann?"

"Damned if I know. To fulfill one of Heber Kimball's predictions, I guess. Once we were standing on the banks of the Missouri and Heber said he'd bet I some day married the worst shrew in Zion. He was right."

"But couldn't you tell by her face she was after your money?"

"I can't always read a woman's face."

"How is it you read men so well and can't read women at all?"

"I don't know. That's always puzzled me."

Amelia sighed and looked at the windows. They were lost here under a great wild storm, with the wind howling like lunacy across the hills. She thought it might be best if they perished here; for Brigham's face was yellow with age and weariness, and he hadn't the strength to go back and face a charge of murder. She took a mitten off and reached into his big glove to clasp his hand.

"Don't worry about me," he said. "I am in the Lord's hands. I have done my best to serve Him faithfully, and what He does with me now is for Him to say."

Just south of Salt Lake City, Brigham's party was met by Dan Wells and several men among whom Brigham saw the tall coated figure of Nephi McBride.

"Why in hell," roared Dan, "did you come back?"

"I don't run from my enemies, Brother Dan."

"Then God help you!"

"How is everything?"

"Bad, damned bad."

"I hear there's a charge of murder."

"There is. They caught Bill Hickman napping and arrested him. The dirty traitor broke down and confessed everything."

"I've been expecting him to. He turned sour on me years ago. What has he been confessing?"

"Why, all that he ever did, I guess. Back on the Missouri and here in Zion. They say he has confessed to about twenty murders, not counting all the Indians. By God, Brigham, we're all going to be tried for murder now."

"You too?"

"Yes—every last dog of us."

"You out on bail now?"

"Yes."

"How much?"

"Fifty thousand. The district attorney wanted five hundred thousand, but even McKean thought that was a little high. As for you, Brigham, they don't intend to let you out on bond at all."

"It doesn't matter. I been thinking on my way up here, Dan. I think the only way we can win is to all go to jail, every man, woman and child of us." Brigham pondered a moment and then saw the intent gaze of Nephi. "Brother Nephi, how is the Order in Josephville?"

"It's all right, President Brigham."

"That's good. Well, let's enter like thieves in the night into the city we built."

It was the day after Christmas. Under cover of darkness, Brigham slipped like a thief into the city and sought his home.

THE NEXT DAY HE WENT TO THE COURTROOM AND GAVE HIMSELF UP. HE was not admitted to bail, but McKean said he should choose as prison one of his own houses; and he became a prisoner in his own home with armed men on guard outside. He admitted that the future looked pretty dark. McKean could, with a packed jury, send him and his leaders to jail for life or even to the hangman's noose; and there was little that the saints could do about that. Nevertheless, Brigham believed that the God of Israel was protecting his people. He waited calmly, patiently, to see what would happen—and the thing that happened astonished even him.

One of McKean's cases had been carried to the Supreme Court of the United States, and that solemn body repudiated the judge and all that he had done. It said he had unlawfully drawn his juries, served invalid summonses; and in consequence quashed all his indictments and dismissed all his proceedings. Dan Wells and others were jubilant.

"Thank God," said Brigham, "for the Supreme Court. I don't know how democracy could survive without it."

He was a free man again, but he knew that this was only another lull in the storm. When spring came, he walked into a conference of his people.

"A word to the Latter-day saints," he said, facing the great audience. "Good morning!"

"Good morning!" cried the audience in one voice.

"How do you do?"

"Very well!"

"How is your faith this morning?"

"Strong in the Lord!"

"How do you think I look after my long confinement?"

"First rate!"

"I do not rise to preach a sermon but I will say a few words to you. Many would like to know how I have felt the past winter. I have enjoyed myself exceedingly well. I have been blessed with an opportunity to rest. I have no complaint to make, no reflection to cast, for all that has been done has been overruled by the wisdom of Him who knows all things. I have no reflections to cast upon these courts. They have disgraced themselves. I have nothing to say with regard to their conduct. It is before the world, it is before the heavens continually."

These few remarks exhausted him, but at the close of the meeting he came forward to offer a benediction. "I bless you, my brethren and sisters, and I bless you strangers, and I say unto you, peace be to you, as well as to the saints, in good words, in good actions, in a good life to serve the Lord our God. I crave blessings upon the good everywhere, among all the nations, kindreds, tongues, peoples, sects and parties, wherever the honest and the pure in heart are found. God bless them, and I say peace to you henceforth and forever."

When he left the building, leaning heavily on his cane, the saints saw for the first time how old and feeble he was. He knew himself that his days were short. He knew also that he would be persecuted to the very end, that his enemies would give him no peace. For the whole nation was in an uproar. One Federal judge had been rebuked by the Supreme Court; a second, it was now revealed, had bought his office; and a third had been exposed as a bigamist.

While prosecuting the saints for bigamy, McKean had mounted his bench one morning and had seen on his desk, right under his nose, a newspaper which declared that his associate, Judge Hawley, had more than one wife. In fury he leapt to his feet and told the marshal to bring in the grand jury; and after the jurors had taken their places, the judge looked at them and roared, "The Salt Lake *Herald* says Judge Hawley has more than one wife! It says he is guilty of adultery and fornication, and is a fraud and a hypocrite! You must indict Judge Hawley for bigamy or sue the paper for libel. Retire!"

It had been an incredible scene. "He was so damned mad," said Dan Wells, "he almost spit his teeth out. I thought he'd choke."

"Did they indict Hawley?"

"No. He resigned and hit the grit." Dan leaned back and laughed. "By the God of Israel, it's funny. President Grant sends judges to indict us for bigamy and the judges indict one another!"

Brigham chuckled. "All they need is enough rope."

"You seen this?" asked Dan, dragging a newspaper from his pocket. "Let me read you this from the New York *Sun*. 'Grant's administration carries its foul contagion into the judiciary. To Judge Sherman in Ohio, Judge Delahay in Kansas, and the drunken Judge Durell in Louisiana, is now to be added Judge Strickland in Utah.' Strickland," said Dan, "is the one who bought his office. I guess they haven't heard about Hawley yet."

"Grant has a nice mess on his hands. His administration has been corrupt from start to finish."

The two old men looked at one another, remembering forty years of persecution. Then Dan said:

"McKean has been dismissed."

"The next judge will be worse."

"They have a lot of bills before Congress now. Senator Logan of Illinois, Senator Frelinghuysen of New Jersey, even Merritt from Idaho up north. They're all out to destroy us." Dan's long face became very solemn. "Brigham, what will happen to the church after you are gone?"

"I don't know, Dan."

"John Taylor will not fight the way you have."

"We'll have to leave it in the hands of the Lord."

"Do you think we'll all be jailed again?"

"Yes, of course."

Soon after the new judge appeared, Brigham found himself a prisoner again in his own home. He was jailed this time because he would not pay alimony to Eliza Ann, his shrewish wife who was doing her best to ruin him. The government would not recognize her as one of his wives, yet demanded that he pay her alimony! Well, he expected to be a prisoner until he died: his health was very poor and he was rapidly sinking. His health, as a matter of fact, had been broken, but his spirit was as unconquerable as ever.

One morning Nephi McBride dropped in to see him.

"Brother Nephi, how is the Order in Josephville?"

"Very good. We are all working together."

"That is fine. Do you have a set of rules?"

"Yes, Brother Brigham. We are all working and sharing in common."

"That is as it should be."

Brigham sank back among pillows and closed his eyes. If his people helped one another and shared in common and were faithful to the Lord, then the Lord would protect them and see that all was well. In some places, as in the colony of Sunset in Arizona, the entire community lived as one family. This seemed also to be true in Orderville, in Kingston, and in Richfield where his son Joseph was the guiding spirit. He wished he had the health and energy to establish an Order in every settlement, including Salt Lake City.

Nephi had been gazing at Brigham's sick face. "Brother Brigham, you must get well. Until our troubles are settled, we cannot get along without you."

"I'll never be well again."

"If you die now, the church will go to pieces."

"Nephi, why do you say that?"

"Because I think our leaders will hide or run away."

"They mustn't do that. They must all go to jail. All the saints must go to jail for that is the only way now."

While a case was pending in the Supreme Court, Brigham was released again; and he dressed and entered his carriage to visit the southern colonies. He was so ill he could barely sit up and he felt deep in his heart that this would be his last journey. When he returned home, he stood for a little while, leaning on his cane and gazing across the green valley or over at the great temple which was now half-finished. Soon he would look upon all this no more.

He never looked upon it again. Feeling sick, and too weak to sit up, he went to bed; and his huge family and many friends, alarmed by his condition, softly entered his room to gaze at him anxiously or to kneel in prayer. They prayed for his recovery but Brigham looked at them and knew he was dying.

"Don't grieve for me," he said, his tired old eyes looking from face to face. "Death is a passing to a better world." Hearing sounds of grief, he rose a little and looked at a group of kneeling women. "Sisters, why do you weep?"

"For you, Brother Brigham."

"Do not weep for me. Dan, is that you?"

"It's me," said Dan Wells, looking as if he would weep too.

"Where is John Taylor?"

"Right here, Brigham."

"You will be president, John. Your troubles will be many. If the persecution keeps up, you must all go to jail. That is our only weapon now."

"Yes, Brigham."

"No matter what happens, we must be true to our principles."

"Yes."

On the sixth day, Brigham seemed to fall asleep. From person to person in the city went the news that Brigham slept, but those close by his bedside knew that he was falling into his last sleep. A doctor felt his pulse and looked at the bloodless face.

"The end is not far," he said.

Wives and children and friends filled the house and the sick chamber and waited. After a while, Brigham's lips moved, but those bending low could not understand what he said. For several minutes he was so quiet that some thought he had died. Then his lips moved again.

"Joseph," he said. "Joseph—Joseph."

Those were his last words.

By telegraph and by rider, news of his death went to every city and hamlet throughout the valley; and for three days the roads were alive in all directions. His people came by thousands on horse and afoot, by wagon and carriage and train. By thousands they filed through the tabernacle and past the bier to gaze for a last time upon their leader; and by thousands they fell into the mammoth procession that followed the body to its grave. Among them were Moroni and Tim and Nephi McBride—three very silent men in a hushed multitude that wept when it knelt in prayer. The man who had led them for thirty-three years, who had rebuked them and fought for them and cared for them, who had thundered at them as prophet and clasped their hand as friend—this man was dead. When they needed him most, when they faced a graver crisis than any they had ever faced, the Lord took the Great Pioneer from them; and none could say what would happen now.

Nephi looked at his grandfather and saw the same question in his eyes that was in the eyes of every man around him. He saw it in the eyes of John Taylor and Wilford Woodruff, of Joseph F. Smith and Dan Wells. In eyes red from weeping, or in eyes too dry to weep, there was only one question, one thought. It was a mighty and an overwhelming question that stood in the hearts and minds of twenty thousand persons. Nephi put it into words when the three men turned away.

"Grandfather, who will lead us now?"

PART THREE

EVENING

CHAPTER I

NEPHI, TIMOTHY AND MORONI MCBRIDE, SON, FATHER AND GRANDFATHER, paused at Eagle Gate to look across the wall at the temple. During the last years of Brigham's life, it had risen into the sky stone by stone, month after month and year after year, while scores of carpenters, masons and engineers labored, and other men with ox teams brought from a nearby canyon the great slabs of rock. For more than twenty years, this magnificent House of the Lord had been taking shape; and it was still unfinished. When completed it would be, these men believed, the noblest building that would ever stand between the Rocky Mountains and the Pacific Ocean.

"But after it's done," said Tim, "the damned gentiles will probably burn it like they did the one in Nauvoo."

"Or make a fortress of it," said Nephi. "They'll move the Fort Douglas artillery into it and shoot us from the windows and towers."

Moroni smiled. He was an old man now—he was eighty-seven; and though he could look back across a half-century of persecution, of rape and pillage and murder, of wandering and exile, his faith in the eventual triumph of Zion was undisturbed. Since Brigham died five years ago, Tim had become gloomy, almost morbid and sometimes violent, in his outlook; for he had reached the age of sixty-eight, and it seemed to him that the older he became, the more hopeless was the cause of the saints. He also could look back across fifty years—back to the time in Missouri when he was a hotheaded Danite; back to the slaughter at Haun's Mill, the destruction of Nauvoo, the long desperate migration to a new land. He had seen Brigham build an empire in a desert. And now this! Never before during his fifty years of labor and hope had the future looked so black for the chosen people of God. Perhaps the Almighty still watched over and protected them; but it seemed to him folly to believe, as his father did, that the church was not headed for disintegration and chaos. Because the Federal government had spoken again—and this time in such vigorous and ruthless terms that only the most sanguine optimist or inexperienced fool could hope for a way out.

"Yes," he said, still gazing at the beautiful structure that was laid to the foundation of the towers. "It will be fortified and used to house the soldiers. There'll be a brothel in the basement, and a saloon in the baptismal font."

"No," said Moroni, stroking his long white beard. "The God of Israel will never allow that."

"But what happened to our temple in Kirtland, in Nauvoo?"

"The one in Kirtland still stands."

"As a warehouse or something. The one in Nauvoo was burned to the ground. And where is the temple God commanded Joseph to build in Missouri?"

Nephi's thoughts and his father's words had filled him with deep anger. No matter where he looked in this city now, he could see gentiles. He could see cheap shops, gambling dens, houses of prostitution; and upon the streets, he could see every breed of scoundrel who had followed the great migrations westward. Pioneers had trailed the explorers into a wilderness, and had built homes and cities there; and all the rascals out of hell had followed to become a parasitic growth on every community. When he was a youth twenty years ago, he had never been accosted by women in this, the city of saints; but now if he walked at midnight, harlots met him at every corner, thrust their heads from the windows of cheap rooming houses, infested the dance halls, and sometimes even dogged men to their homes. And among them now and then was a woman who had once been a Mormon wife. If Brigham were alive . . .

"Let's go," he said, "and learn what President Taylor intends to do."

John Taylor received them cordially, but there was only hopelessness and pain in his tired old eyes. Only seventy-four in this summer of 1882, he looked much older: he was thin and stooped, his swarthy bloodless face bore a record of inner sickness, his hands trembled on his desk. But there was still about him that grave politeness, that somewhat cold dignity, which as a young man he had brought from England.

"What," he asked, "can I do for you?"

"What," asked Tim, "can anybody do for us now?"

"Things do look pretty black. The anti-bigamy law of 1862 was bad

nough. This new Edmunds law seems to seal our doom. You knew
bout it?"

"That is why we are here."

"What," asked Nephi, "are we going to do about it?"

"What," asked John Taylor wearily, "can we do? We'll all be arrested
nd jailed. That's as certain as the whores on our streets. We must desert
ur wives or face imprisonment; and no matter what we do, it looks as
f we'll have to desert them anyhow."

"President Taylor, is that what you intend to do?" It was Moroni speak-
ng.

"No, Brother Moroni. I'll never desert my wives. I imagine, though, that
many of the saints will."

"If they do, what will become of the sisters?"

Taylor's gray wrinkled face was lighted by ironic amusement. "I
lon't know. Year by year Congress has outlawed us. They gave suffrage
o the sisters, believing they'd rise in anger and vote their husbands into
ail. When our delegate spoke in favor of that bill, he astonished the
vhole world. Now they've passed a law to give us three years in jail and a
ig fine. The next step, I think, will be a law allowing husbands and
vives to testify against one another. They can't convict us unless they do.

"As to your question: what will the sisters do? Didn't you know the
overnment is going to build a big home, a kind of army barracks, on
ifth Street? It is believed that all our wives will flee to it for sanctuary.
t's to be called," said Taylor smiling, "a Refuge for Unloved Wives or
omething of the sort. How many of the sisters do you think will enter
t?"

"None," said Tim; but his wise old father wagged his head.

"A few, President Taylor. Tim has one who might."

"Are we," asked Nephi, "going to fight this Edmunds law?"

"Yes."

"How?"

"In various ways. We are going to present to Congress a mammoth
etition of protest. We are going to refuse to testify. In that case, we may
e jailed for contempt of court—but not for three years."

"But they can keep arresting and jailing us."

"And they probably will."

"Then, President Taylor," asked Nephi impatiently, "*how* are we going to fight it?"

"In every way we can except by force."

"Why not use some force?"

"It is too late for that."

"By God, they drove us out here to a desert—and now they march in to drive us into the ocean! Why run this time? Why not turn our back to the wall and fight until we are all dead? It's better to be dead if we can't live as free men."

John and Moroni gazed at Nephi, remembering that when much younger they had felt that way. But they were old men now: age took out of a man the fiery idealism of his youth, bled him of anger and impetuous resolves, as with one law and another his government slowly broke him to his knees.

Nephi spoke again. "They sent an army against Brigham and he stopped it. If we fight——"

"Yes, Brother Nephi, it could be done then. Now there's a railroad an army at Fort Douglas, and thousands of enemies all around us. Conditions have changed since Brigham stopped Buchanan's army. Peaceable resistance is the only weapon we have."

"We could," said Nephi, "form another Danite society. Bill Hickman is dead; Porter Rockwell and all the other Danites are dead; but there are men today just as bold as they were." Nephi rose and began to pace the office. "President Taylor, I've heard my father say that if Joseph had let them go, the Danites would have socked away all the mobs in Missouri. I say it's time to fight.

"You know as well as I do that all these fires are not accidental. Our co-operative stores are burning down. Our mills and factories are burning. Are we going to wait until the gentiles burn everything we have built? Are we going to sit around like old women or Lamanite squaws?"

Moroni sighed. "He reminds me of the old days, John. You and I felt that way a long time ago."

"And back East," Nephi went on, "what are they doing? They're murdering our missionaries. You can't pick up a newspaper without reading of a new horsewhipping or lynching. If the government lets scoundrels murder us, are we going to sit back and wait until our throats are cut?"

"I know," said John Taylor quietly, "how you feel. But forcible re sistance of any kind is too late now. It has been too late ever since Brigham let the army march into the valley. If we try to resist, we'll get what we got in Missouri. We'll be exterminated or driven out."

"No matter what we do, what'll we get except extermination? They'll put us all in jail and turn the soldiers loose on our wives. I tell you we have to make a stand or the church is doomed."

"Some of the leaders," said Taylor, speaking with the weariness of a man who had fought for fifty years, "want to make peace. They think we should give up plural marriage and the Orders and everything else the gentiles don't like."

"Who thinks that?"

"Wilford Woodruff for one."

"Why," asked Moroni, "don't they like the Orders?"

"I guess it's because they can't compete with them. They set up a store in Brigham City but it went bankrupt. It's the same everywhere we have an Order."

"You say," asked Nephi, "Woodruff wants to give up plural marriage? Who are the other Judases?"

John's pale old face reddened a little. "You speak too impulsively, Nephi. You are still young——"

"I am thirty-six."

"Hardly more than a boy. You haven't had fifty years of it. You weren't shot down in the Carthage jail. You weren't burned out in Nauvoo and driven into a wilderness to starve. You haven't known plague and famine and murder."

"Then let those who are young carry on the fight—but let's fight. Joseph and Brigham fought to the day of their death. They never gave up—and Brigham was old. If they had given up, there'd be no church today."

"But Brigham had nothing to fight such as we have now."

"Oh, no!" cried Nephi scornfully. "Just plagues and famines and armies! He was jailed but he never gave up his principles. If he was alive now, he would still be fighting."

"I knew Brigham well. It's true that he never gave up; but after he was an old man he became tired, just as I have. Youth can go on fighting —but age—age grows weary of the sword and the torch."

"But you don't mean that you are giving up?"

Taylor's lean old hand came down in an angry blow on his desk. "I'll never give up. I'll fight to the day of my death just as Brigham did. But I'm only one man in the leadership."

"You are president and prophet of the church."

John Taylor smiled sadly. "Yes, but I am not Brigham Young. Brigham *was* the leadership. I am only the president."

"You could be the whole leadership," said Nephi impatiently.

"No. There's only one Brigham Young in a century. I am only John Taylor who made the mistake of setting out with Parley Pratt at the head of sixteen hundred persons. If I had been a Brigham Young, I'd not have done that. As it is now, not all the leaders see things as I do—and God does not make it known to me who is right. Some think we should make peace with the gentiles on the best terms we can get. Some think we should oppose them at any cost."

"Some think we should give up plural marriage and the Orders?"

"Yes."

"You say Wilford Woodruff does. He is president of the Twelve—and if you should die, he will become president of the church."

Moroni smiled in his white beard. "He means, John, you should go on living."

"We are both old. Brother Wilford is seventy-four."

"The fact remains," said Nephi, "that Brigham would never have accepted peace on terms offered by his enemies. He never did."

"No, Brigham did not. But things have changed a little since he died. Some of the saints are beginning to marry among the gentiles. Some have gentile friends, do business with them, even enter into partnerships. I don't like what that will lead to. Brigham foresaw all that; and he often said to me that if the saints and gentiles mixed, the church would disintegrate. Brigham was a very wise man."

"But if we all stick together and refuse to mix ——"

"They won't, Brother Nephi. It is useless to talk about it. The saints and the gentiles will mix generation by generation; and for that reason, Brigham wanted to keep the gentiles out of this valley. But they are pouring in. No commandment that God Almighty ever laid down can prevent the slow modification of a religion that is in daily contact with its enemies. I see the time coming. I can't see any way to stop it."

"We intend," said Moroni, "to keep our United Order."

"I hope you do. I am only saying, Brother Moroni, that the handwriting seems to me to be on the wall. I think Brigham realized it in his last years. I think that's why on his deathbed he cried out to Joseph. If I had the power under heaven to fight off this curse from Washington —but what can I do? Soon we'll not be allowed to vote. We have no officers, no judges, no courts except those of our enemies. We have no rights as citizens. Our converts from foreign lands who come here can no longer be naturalized. We have all the status of felons, even though we have never been imprisoned. We are a people without a country, yet are punished by the laws of the nation in which we live—and have special laws enacted for our punishment alone. There are a thousand spies in this valley, and day and night they are busy gathering evidence. Every move I make is watched. I am shadowed if I go down the streets. Spies look through the windows of my home, prowl around my house all night, insult my wives when I am away, taunt my children with bastardy, steal my property, poison my beasts, pollute the well water in my back yard. It's a nightmare," said Taylor wearily. "I have no privacy, no peace, no rest. And I am old and sick. Under the Constitution, I am granted my religious conscience; but I have no freedom, no liberties."

"Nevertheless, I want you brethren to understand that I will never yield. I fought side by side with Brigham for more than forty years. I was with Joseph when they shot him down—and I was shot down. I'll die as I have lived by the principles which God revealed to Joseph. But I am only one man in the leadership. I cannot tell you what the other leaders will do, or what will happen to the church when I am gone." For a long moment Taylor was silent. "Perhaps," he added, "I'll feel in dying as I think Brigham felt. Perhaps the last darkness will be a terrible intimation of what is to come."

"If," said Nephi, "we repudiate the principles God gave to Joseph, then our church will be only another church. Then the Lord will have no church to represent Him on this earth."

"That is true."

"We'll be no different from any other Protestant sect."

"If it comes to that, then so it will be; but I have no power to stop it."

Nephi looked at his grandfather. "Some of us will fight," he said. "We'll fight them right in their teeth in any way we can and must."

"Very well," said John Taylor. "If I were younger, I'd join you."

At the door Nephi paused to look back at this tired old man. He returned and laid an arm across the bent shoulders. "President Taylor, I understand how you feel. But some of us will fight. The spirit of Joseph and Brigham is not yet dead among us."

CHAPTER II

THE MCBRIDE CLAN, IN ALL RESPECTS MUCH LIKE MANY OTHERS WHICH had grown up under plural marriage, occupied a compact unit of houses in the village, six miles south of Salt Lake City, which Moroni had named Josephville. In one large building, with many empty upstairs rooms, now that all his wives but three were dead and all his children married long ago, lived Moroni with Kate, Agatha and Maggie. Though a very old man with a bald head, Moroni was still handsome, chiefly because of his long white beard to which he gave scrupulous care, his snowy white mustaches which fell like curling foliage down over his whiskers, and his bright alert eyes.

His three living wives looked a little as if they had been transplanted from another and different world. Agatha was fat and shapeless, but Maggie was as lean and gaunt as any woman could be. Her hands were fleshless and terrible to look at, with long brittle nails, with veins like branched blue vegetation under her pale old skin. Her false teeth, which she always wore, made her face seem to be chiefly of bone; for when she smiled, she showed twenty-two teeth in her withered face, and an unclean expanse of artificial gums. Agatha had false teeth too, but most of the time she left them in a jar of water in her bedroom. Her face was too plump to be wrinkled except around her mouth: when she relaxed, her nose came down and almost rested on her chin, and her mouth looked like a pouch with the strings drawn tight. The eyes of both were still clear and intelligent. Maggie's eyes, indeed, looked much too young in her old yellow face. Agatha's eyes were calmly hazel and reflected an untroubled mind.

Kate, the wife with whom Moroni slept, not because she was a favorite but because he had married her before the other two, was more than eighty and looked much older. She was a small woman. She was hardly more than an armful of skin and bones, topped by a pile of beautiful gray hair. She moved with the softness of a shadow, never making a sound when she opened or closed a door, or entered the big living room to sink like a lapful of age to her chair. At the table she ate slowly, quietly, to keep her loose teeth from clicking.

When Moroni lodged food under one of his plates, he yanked the plate out with such anger that those watching him expected to see a jawbone come forth. Then he would hide the offending thing in a napkin and march out; and a little later he would return, his jaws munching experimentally. "The blamed dang things!" he would cry, speaking to nobody at all. For a few minutes he would stare thoughtfully at his plate, as if remembering the years when he had eaten without interruption; and then sigh and feed again. Maggie always watched him a little anxiously, but Kate ignored him, and Agatha smiled and gummed her food.

"Do they hurt?" Maggie would sometimes ask.

"If we don't have our own teeth in the next life, I hope the Almighty has some good dentists!"

Next to Moroni's house on the right were two houses belonging to his son Timothy. Tim had married only three women and they were all living. His first wife, and in many respects his favorite, was Fanny, a large woman of sixty-four whose bulk was muscle and not fat. She was the most aggressive and determined person in the entire clan. Her big red hands, her powerful arms, her stern mouth and searching gray eyes all declared that she knew what she wanted, and when and why. She did not say much, but when she spoke she meant what she said, and nobody was foolish enough to oppose her will. Not even her son Nephi had ever dared do that. To Moroni's long and windy harangues, to Kate's assortment of ailments, to Nephi's idealism she gave the same attention that she bestowed on the dog or the cat.

Tim lived with her many years before he took a second wife. Sarah was now fifty but she looked older: she was the kind of woman who had never looked young. When she came as a bride to Tim's home twenty-five years ago, Fanny had looked her over, had looked her up and down, quietly, critically, as she might have noted the good and bad points of an ox or a cow. "She's all right," she had said, and had accepted her; but she had never pretended to love her. Nevertheless, the two women had lived without meanness or quarrels; because Sarah was a quiet and somewhat timid woman, and had no wish to boss a household. Mother Young had been her ideal of what a plural wife should be. She had emulated that patient and kindly woman, and had been during all her married life an inoffensive and industrious shadow.

Tim's third wife was of another kind. He had taken Louisa when she was fifteen—she was now thirty-one—and he had always been sorry he ever laid eyes on her. Louisa was a shrew—and a most remorseless and energetic and violent shrew at that. She was tall and still slender, with flashing eyes, thin lips, and the most malicious tongue in Josephville. Intelligent and resourceful, she spent most of her time, it seemed to Tim, devising ways to goad her husband to fury, or to outrage the gentle Sarah, or to raise hell in the large family of Nephi. She raised such an infernal rumpus during her first year of married life that Tim had been driven to build a cottage for her, as Brigham had built a mansion for Amelia who in tradition was Louisa's notion of what a plural wife should be.

"Brigham Young had enough wives to populate a city!" the dark-eyed Louisa had cried at sixteen. "If he could afford that big mansion for Amelia, I guess you can build me a cottage."

And Louisa now lived by herself in a cottage back of the main house. Without children, without friends, she stormed around in her small kingdom like a person out of bedlam; or, tiring of that, strode into Moroni's or Nephi's house to raise the devil there.

Nephi had four wives and twenty-one children, all living in a large two-story building next to his father's. His wives gave him more trouble than Louisa with all her cunning had ever given Tim. Short-tempered and impatient, with the energy of his mother and the idealism of his grandfather, Nephi often looked at his wives, reflecting on their vanities and petty bickering, and sometimes wanting to strangle them. Often he wondered which he loved most, or if indeed he loved any of them; for they seemed to him to be the most impious and ungodly lot in the town. Sometimes, too, he remembered that he was regarded as the handsomest man in Josephville, and that other women had spoken with malicious astonishment of his taste in wives.

Genet, his first, was now thirty-five and had eight children. She gave him the least trouble. She had light brown hair, large and rather bulging gray eyes which she tried to roll coquettishly, a sallow tired skin, and a mouth that had always looked sick. When she caught a cold it erupted in sores on her mouth—and she seemed to have a cold most of the time.

She was not, Nephi had been forced to admit, a very intelligent woman —nor were all her children as bright as he wished they could have been. Toward the other wives, Genet was patronizing and maternal, with a quiet current of malice under her kindness. She pretended to love them— and patiently, almost tenderly, despised them.

The first of the three to invade her house had been Maude, now thirty-four and with eleven children. She was the most unattractive of the four. A stout and muscular and rather shapeless woman who looked when standing, walking or sitting as if she could not make up her mind where she was, she seemed to have grown without design or reason. Her eyes were extremely small and too close together. Her brow was low. The third wife had confided to the youngest that Maude looked like an over-fattened pig for which there was no sale. But it was not Maude's eyes or her heavy face or her small tight mouth that persons remembered best. It was her laugh. Her laugh was a hybrid of ha-ha and giggle that always preceded or followed everything she said. It was humorless and utterly without mirth, yet had a strange and inexplicable spontaneity. Half cough and half twitter, it came out of her in quick evenly spaced syllables that ran in a series of five or six. After laughing, she always looked around her with grotesquely awkward cautiousness as if determined to be aware of anyone who was amused. Her voice was quick and thin like her laugh.

It was Maude's habit to sit around and stare with comical gravity at the other wives and children, or to make remarks that were softly venomous but intended to be impersonal and searching; because she was, as nobody knew better than herself, the intellectual woman of this house. She had more formal training, had read a great number of books, and used better English. Those were her advantages and never for a moment did she lose sight of them.

The third wife was Ruth—and Genet still wondered persistently and a little impatiently why Nephi had married her. Ruth was now twenty-seven and had two children; but the woman's whole interest was in clothes and superficial appearances. Though men found her attractive, she was not lovely in any respect: she had blue eyes which, like Genet's, were too large and full, and seemed, when gazing ardently at a man, almost to stand out of her skull. She was horse-faced, with a high full brow, a large arched nose, a wide mouth that smiled over big teeth, and an aggressive chin. Her body was no more beautiful than her face. Her posture was bad because of a curvature of the spine that had rounded her shoulders. Her breast, even before nursing, was flat. Her legs were bowed and her ankles were thick.

But what Ruth lacked in physical beauty she strove to put on her in clothes and jewels. Her thick waist she tried to make wasplike; her stocky body she tried to slenderize and heighten by wearing tall bonnets and high shoes with curved heels. Her basque always fitted her like her skin from her neck to her hips, with the princess line acutely emphasized. She loved innumerable gores and darts and seams, steel or jet buttons the size of peas down front or back, and bodices trimmed with embroidery, and fur or ribbon garnitures. She affected big cuffs with ruching about the wrists; puffs at the shoulders; and high collars instead of V-necks because her breast was flat. She wore such large bustles that from the rear she somewhat resembled a centaur. For evening wear, she put on a train as long as Nephi would tolerate, and decorated herself with big bowed sashes and gaudy artificial flowers. Because her hair was abundant and therefore suitable to the latest styles, she afforded a great knot high on her head, bangs across her forehead, clusters of curls above her ears, and tendrils of hair against her neck. Sometimes she coiled and twisted braids into such intricate patterns and used so many combs and ornaments in the coiffure that the other wives looked at her in amazement. A high headdress made her seem taller and more slender. She chose and wore her bonnets so cunningly that they framed her face and made it appear to be less coarse and bold of feature, more piquant and feminine.

Formerly her persistent demands had almost driven Nephi out of his wits. Ruth wanted satin fans painted with flowers and landscapes; Chinese paper fans with bamboo handles; long kid gloves in delicate colors and of twenty-four button length; gay and dainty parasols; buckles and combs and belts set with cheap brilliants; cases of silver or tortoise shell for her calling cards (of which she had none); and earrings, bracelets, necklaces, beads and breastpins. She wanted oil to make her hair shine. Upon learning that actresses were using coloring to redden their lips, she begged for that.

Genet's response to Ruth's insatiable interest in clothes was unlike that of the other wives. Knowing herself to be plain and dowdy, she went to the other extremes, and refused to wear anything except simple aprons and skirts, and the homeliest shoes she could find. She neglected, with painstaking deliberateness, her skin and her hair, and almost never kept her pale mouth clean. Ruth wanted to buy in the gentile stores because articles, she said, were lovelier and more fashionable there. Genet trudged to the community store and pretended that everything in it was the best in the world.

Maude's intellectual advantages, and Ruth's vulgar taste in ornaments, bored Chloe, the youngest of the wives and by far the most attractive. She was only twenty-two and had been married only three years. She was still childless. Resolved to be gay and reckless, and dare the Devil wherever she found him, Chloe danced around the house, sang old songs that were sometimes a little lewd, and now and then ventured to tell a lewd tale. Nephi had converted her from a gentile uncle and aunt who had taken her as a child when her parents died; but Chloe had married Nephi only because he was tall and handsome and well-to-do. She loved his dark curly hair, his Irish eyes, and his clean firm mouth, even though it knew little of kissing. Young, fickle and vain, she had imagined it would be fun to live in a polygamous house—and especially to seduce the husband away from the other wives. Finding herself unable to do that, she had turned a little sour and twice as frivolous, and was bent on having a good time with Lura, Genet's oldest daughter.

Chloe was too thick in her legs and waist to be girlish, too awkward in her movements to be very supple and seductive; but most men found her charming, and particularly when she slipped away to the city and drank two or three cocktails on the sly. She had a mass of soft brown hair; a skin that looked sweet after she had bathed and powdered it, but porous and rough when uncared for; a pert upturned nose; a wide but ripe and sensuous mouth; and a firm chin. Her eyes were a pale cold blue that not all her coquetry could soften.

It was her manner that attracted men. When Chloe felt herself desired, and especially after a half-hour of well-chosen flattery, she yielded to warm bubbling spontaneity, and laughed and smiled and dimpled, using her brows and eyes and hands as devastatingly as she could. When aware of herself, she was too calculating to make men move suddenly toward her; but when caught off guard by a well-turned compliment from a handsome man, she was almost irresistible.

Lura, the daughter, was a thin pious girl, but she had a skin that all the wives envied, dark gray Irish eyes like her father's, and an impetuous love of life that her gawkiness did not hide. She had associated with gentiles; and already, like so many of her generation, was feeling shame because she had so many half-brothers and half-sisters, so many grandmothers and greatgrandmothers, so many impertinent questions to answer. Under Chloe's tutelage, she strove to take the doctrines of her church less seriously, and had been seen making a sly face at prayer, or winking when old Moroni solemnly intoned from one of Joseph's revelations. She was resolved not to be a plural wife for any man—and certainly not for old Abner Tuttle who had been hinting and peeping during the past year. Chloe told her she ought to marry a gentile. There was one in whom she was interested—but so, if she could read signs correctly, was Nephi's youngest wife.

Mark Browe, a frequent visitor at Nephi's home, was about thirty, and belonged to a prominent gentile family. He was a tall man with the kind of worldly politeness that Lura admired—and the kind of face that made her catch her breath when she looked at him. His hair was black and heavy, and, together with his long handsome sideburns and his black mustaches, set off the pallor of his face. His eyes were very dark and seemed always, at least when gazing at Chloe, to burn with hopeless ardor. His charming smile flashed across perfect white teeth. Lura stared at him with helpless wonder—but knew that Chloe was the woman whom Mark came to see.

Mark was present when Nephi, Tim and Moroni entered the house. Genet, the most pious of Nephi's wives, came forward anxiously, for never before had she seen his face so full of trouble. Even Moroni, she observed, was unusually solemn.

"Did you see President Taylor?"

"Yes." Nephi looked at Mark, wishing that gentiles would stay out of his house.

"What did he say?"

Nephi was still gazing at Mark. "We'll hold a meeting at grandfather's."

"Oh, don't bother about me," said Mark, rising. "I was going anyhow."

"Where," asked Nephi, "is Chloe?"

"In her room dressing." It was Maude who spoke. She was sitting by a window with two babies on her lap.

"Tell her to come," said Tim. "We want all the sisters there."

Mark smiled. When gentiles were present, Mormon men always spoke of their wives as the sisters.

Moroni led the way to his house, with Tim, Nephi and Genet following. Kate, Maggie and Agatha were sitting in their customary chairs when the men entered. Nephi had sent Genet to find all the women.

A few minutes later, the three men and their ten wives were gathered in grave council, even though Louisa smiled maliciously, and Ruth and Chloe looked bored.

"We have talked with President Taylor," said Nephi, acting as spokesman. "There can no longer be any doubt about it. The Federal government intends to break up every plural home in this valley and to jail us or drive us all out. Any of us can expect arrest at any moment. We are meeting now to decide on what we will do. Some of the brethren and sisters have gone into hiding since the Edmunds Act; some are planning to go to Mexico or Canada or the Hawaiian Islands. A few," he said scornfully, "will desert their wives and children. Father and Grandfather and I have talked it over while coming home. We don't intend to run or hide or desert. At the same time, we want to keep out of jail if we can."

"How?" asked Louisa, still smiling.

"This is no time to grin!" cried Nephi hotly. "I say here and now that if any woman among you expects to be a Judas, she had better get out. They can't convict us if we won't testify against one another."

"We're meeting now," said Tim, looking at his shrew, "to decide if we are going to stick together or go to jail."

"The women," said Louisa calmly, "won't go to jail. It's only the men."

"Change your tune!" cried Fanny. "If our husbands go to jail, we'll follow them."

"Let us," said Louisa, looking at the boss of Tim's household, "let us speak for ourselves."

"Do you mean——"

"Tush," said Moroni. "Do you remember what Brigham once said in a sermon? He said it would cost the Federal government three hundred million dollars to build a prison big enough to hold us. They would roof it over, he said, from the summit of the Rocky Mountains to the summit of the Sierra Nevada; and when they got us all inside, we'd dig out and go preaching over the world. He said there isn't a wife in Zion who would not follow her husband to jail."

"Brigham Young," said Louisa, staring at the huge topknot on Ruth's head, "was ignorant about a lot of things. One of them was women."

"If," said Nephi caustically, "Brigham was wrong, there will be a home for polygamous wives on Fifth Street. It will have the finest furnishings and private baths, and the handsomest gentile men to wait on you."

"Honestly?" asked Louisa.

"That would be fun," said Chloe.

"How many of you," asked Nephi, "will prefer that to jail? If you do, speak now."

"How long," asked Ruth, toying with a Chinese fan, "would we be in jail?"

"The rest of your lives!"

"Why don't we all go to Mexico?" asked Chloe.

"What," asked Louisa impatiently, "did you call us in here for? And could we have some fresh air in here?" She looked at the three old women.

"You ain't so smart," said Kate.

"Oh, no? I suppose I'll have to be as old as you before I'm smart."

"Never mind the fiddlesticks," said Moroni. "As Nephi says, we won't run and we won't hide. We'll stay right here and learn if Congress is mightier than God."

Nephi drew from a pocket an old copy of the *Atlantic Monthly*. "I don't know how many of you ever read an article in this. It says that out in the Rocky Mountains is a community that blends the voluptuousness of Bagdad with the economy of Cape Cod. In the Endowment House in Salt Lake City, secret rites are practiced similar to the mysteries of the Nile, and presided over with all the solemnity of priests of Isis and Osiris. That article is only one among ten thousand that have appeared since Brigham died. All through the States, it is said that our temple rites are sexual orgies, and that young girls come out of them raped and bleeding. When President Young died, the government seemed to think that we would all be leaderless and frightened, and give up plural marriage. Deciding that we won't, it has passed this infamous Edmunds Act, and now it intends to put us all in jail. It will have public opinion behind it."

"And poetry," said Louisa.

Nephi looked at her. "What do you mean?"

> "Oh-ho, there goes pa
> Back to Washington,
> But he won't take ma!"

Moroni grinned. He knew she was alluding to a territorial delegate who had been denied his seat by Congress.

"You know the rest of it?" Louisa asked Nephi.

> "Oh-ho, here comes pa
> Back from Washington!
> Too much ma."

Ruth and Chloe were giggling. Even toothless old Agatha smiled.

"Do you," Nephi asked Louisa, "think that's funny?"

"Of course. You would too if you had any sense of humor. I'll give you another one if you won't look so damned solemn."

"No, you won't," said Fanny. "Don't try to be so smart."

"I've never understood," said Tim, gazing at Louisa, "why you are so pleased by ungodliness."

"But it really *is* funny," said Chloe, trying to restrain her mirth. "After all, that's just the way it happened."

A smile had parted Moroni's white beard. After a moment the gentle Sarah smiled, and then Maggie, showing almost the whole expanse of her terrible teeth. Observing the amusement around her, Maude broke loose in brittle giggles. Nephi shrugged and then grinned.

"Too much ma!" Fanny cried contemptuously. "I don't see anything to grin about. I guess you think the Almighty finds it funny too!"

"Here's some more poetry," said the malicious Louisa.

"In the Mormon beds out West," said Louisa, humming the words to the tune of a Mormon hymn,

> "In the Mormon beds out West,
> There the concubines do rest,
> While their husband visits Emily and Jane!
> Oh, the babies do abound
> In tens of thousands all around,
> While the husband now slips in to see Elaine!"

Nephi suddenly lost his smile. He was about to speak when Chloe moved impulsively forward and said: "They're singing that over in the city now. And they're telling stories that would just split your old sides."

"You don't say!" cried Fanny.

"Well," said Moroni, composing his patriarchal face, "let's come back to the subject."

"We haven't left it," said Louisa. "It's still too much ma. That's what the government is mad about."

"Do you," asked Nephi, "intend to testify against father when he's arrested?"

Louisa looked at Tim. She did not answer, but her black eyes harbored secret notions.

"If any wife here," said Fanny, "testifies against her husband, I'll knock her head in with a meat cleaver."

"If we don't testify," asked Ruth blandly, "what will happen?"

"You'll go to jail for contempt of court."

"For how long?"

"As long as they can keep you there. When you're released, they'll throw you in jail again. They intend to keep doing it until they break us down."

"Then," said Chloe to her husband, "why don't we all hide for a while?"

"We'd have to hide forever."

"What," asked old Maggie, who had been gravely listening, "does President Taylor intend to do?"

"I don't know. When it gets too hot, I imagine he'll hide or run away. We're here to find out what we're going to do. If we have any wives who are traitors and intend to betray us ——"

"They won't," said Fanny. "Not as long as I'm around." She was looking at Louisa whom she despised.

Tim was looking at Louisa too. "Would you testify against me?"

Louisa's lips curled. "Wait and see."

"Now is the time to answer. Would you?"

"Well, you know what the poetry says.

> "The Mormon man delights to see
> His Mormon family all agree;
> His prattling infant on his knee,
> Crying, 'Daddy, I'm a Mormon!'

"Hey, the happy! Ho, the happy!
Hi, the happy Mormon!
I've never known what sorrow is
Since I became a Mormon!

Or," said Louisa, looking at Fanny, "since I married one."

"I think," said Tim a little angrily, "we've had enough of your nonsense. You still haven't answered. Some of the sisters have said they will send their husbands to jail if they can. Such women are not saints. They should be excommunicated. Shouldn't they?" he asked, turning to his father.

"Of course," said Moroni. "But they're just talking to hear their tongues wag."

"Oh, no, they're not."

"It seems to me," said Louisa tartly, "that you're not fair with the women. What are we expected to do? Our husbands will be in jail. According to the law, we're not even married women, so we can't get a divorce. Neither can we find a husband because we are already married. It all sounds pretty silly."

"And another thing," said Chloe, "gentile children are always asking in school how many brothers and sisters Mormon children have, how many grandparents, even how many mothers. It's one question after another all day long."

"You associate with gentiles too much," said Nephi, looking at his youngest wife.

"That's how I learn things."

"You learn nothing that we don't already know."

"Oh, is that true! Did you know before I told you who burned the academy in Provo?"

"Because Mark Browe says a Mormon did it, that doesn't make it so. Some gentile scoundrel did it. We all know that."

"Well," said Fanny in her hard voice, "let's get back to the subject. If any wife here doesn't intend to stand by her husband, let her speak now."

"We'll ask them one by one," said Nephi. He turned to the old women. "Grandmother?"

Kate had been huddled in a big chair, quietly listening. "I've always lived my religion," she said in a weak old voice. "I intend to till I die."

"Maggie?"

"I feel the way Kate does."

"Agatha?"

"I," said Agatha, smiling, "am only a sister. Nobody can prove anything else."

"I guess I don't have to ask my mother," said Nephi.

"Of course not!" said Louisa. "She's better than we are."

"All right. Mother?"

"If," said Fanny, "any snoops come here to arrest my husband, I'll send them home on crutches."

"Sarah?"

"I," said Sarah, her eyes fluttering, "will try and help Fanny send them home."

"Louisa?"

"I've told you I don't know. I guess if officers come to arrest us, they will. They have the law on their side."

"But will you testify or go to jail?"

"I can't say till that time comes."

"The law," said Fanny, looking with contempt at this wife who had a cottage of her own, "might be on their side; but God is on ours."

"I've never noticed that He paid much attention to our troubles."

"It seems clear to me," said Nephi sharply, "that Louisa intends to testify. I think Father might just as well expect it and be prepared."

"Tend to your own wives," said Louisa. "You'd better be prepared for Chloe and that nice-looking man shining up to her."

Chloe colored. After staring at her for a moment, Nephi resumed. "Genet?"

Genet also reddened when all eyes turned to her. "I'll go to jail." She choked a little, thinking of her loyalty. "You didn't have to ask me any more than your mother."

"Maude?" asked Nephi patiently.

"I guess I'll go to jail like Genet. But who'll take care of my children?"

"Who," asked Genet sharply, "will take care of mine?"

"They will be taken care of. Ruth?"

Ruth was still toying with her fan. "I think I'll go home before you're arrested. Do you expect us to swear to lies?"

"You don't have to swear to anything. Just keep your mouth shut."

"I'll try to do that. I'd rather go home."

"Chloe?"

Chloe had been trying to look charmingly bored. She had on a low bodice that revealed her fair throat and a hint of her breasts. She loved to wear a low bodice and show as much as she dared because then she could outrage the flat-chested Ruth. Before speaking, she put a hand archly to her throat and coughed gently.

"I think," she said, intending her words for a jest, "that I'll elope with some man and save you trouble."

"This is no time to be funny," said Nephi sternly. "Answer."

"She isn't being funny," said the malicious Louisa. "She means it."

"Did you?"

"Of course not. Louisa will do well to keep her cottage a little cleaner and stop passing judgments."

"It's a lot cleaner than your interest in Mark Browe."

"You lie if you say I'm interested in him!"

"Women," said Louisa wearily, "can fool men but not other women."

"Shut it up!" cried Nephi. "You still haven't answered."

"Oh, well," said Chloe impatiently, "I'll be as dumb as an ox. But what makes you think we're all going to be arrested? You've never been arrested in nineteen years of marriage. Mark says——"

"We don't care," Fanny cut in, "what that louse says."

"He isn't a louse! He's a nice man. Because he isn't a Mormon, that doesn't mean he isn't all right."

"He's a louse and a hypocrite. Nephi ought to spit in his face every time he sticks his long snooping nose in Josephville. He comes over here to spy and then run and tell the gentiles."

"He doesn't. He comes to see Lura."

"Lura, my eye! He comes to see you."

Nephi was staring curiously at Chloe. For years he had been too busy to pay much attention to the doings of his wives. This was the first hint he had had that Chloe was interested in Mark.

Under his gaze, Chloe's color deepened. "Why should he come to see me? I'm married."

"Well," said Nephi, still wondering about his youngest wife, "we'll all stick together. Then they can't convict us."

"Oh, bother!" cried Louisa, disgusted. "There's evidence everywhere. Everyone in Josephville knows."

"Nobody in Josephville will testify against us."

"I don't believe it. What about Alonzo Jackson? He hates the sight of you and always has. What about Abner Tuttle? He's sour because old Lucinda has never let him have another wife. He'd love to see you all in jail."

"If they don't keep their mouths shut, we can find ways to shut them."

"Oh, yes, of course! You forget that Brigham Young is dead. So is Porter Rockwell and all the others like him."

"But I'm still alive," said Nephi.

"You wouldn't hurt a rabbit."

Nephi pondered that remark. Moroni had once told him that he was a cross between Joseph and Brigham—and Nephi had said jestingly that he supposed he had the worst traits of both men. His mother had told him he was too idealistic; his wife Ruth had called him brutal. It was hard, he reflected, to make out what he was, but he felt that he could take care of a traitor if he had to.

"If my courage fails me," he said quietly, "my father can handle the job."

"Your father," said Louisa, "is an old man. And even when he was a Danite in Missouri, I don't think he ever scared anyone."

"You talk too much," said Tim, remembering the fate of John Lee and Bill Hickman.

Nephi rose. His dark gray eyes had turned cold. "I'm not worrying about Jackson," he said, gazing at Louisa. "I'm not worrying about Abner Tuttle. If our wives are faithful to their religion and their God, things will be all right. If they're not faithful, God will know what to do with them, even if I don't."

"Don't look at me, Nephi. I'm not interested in putting you in jail. But I know some persons who are."

"Who?"

"I'll keep that to myself."

Nephi stared again at Chloe, and then at Louisa. "Do you mean Mark Browe?"

"Why ask me? Find out for yourself."

"I will," said Nephi. "If it's that sneaking gentile, I'll break his neck the next time he comes here."

"Tush," said Moroni. "Louisa just likes to hear her tongue wag."

"Brigham Young," said Tim, looking hard at Louisa, "never did like barren women. I'm beginning to understand why."

CHAPTER III

A FEW DAYS LATER, NEPHI LEARNED THAT PRESIDENT TAYLOR AND HIS counselors had resolved to present to Congress a petition, signed by a hundred thousand Mormons, begging that a committee be sent to investigate affairs in the Territory before hostile action was taken. To him had been given the task of circulating the petition in Josephville. After the McBrides had signed, including Louisa who said it was a shame to waste good paper, Nephi went forth to visit all the members of the Order. He called first on the Frosts.

He liked Datus and Nabbie, though it seemed to him that they took their religion with too many quips and jests. Datus had refused, even under Brigham's urging, to take a second wife; and the fat jolly Nabbie had said, laughing in full-throated mirth, that if another wife entered her house, she would shove her into the oven and roast her as she might any other hen. Datus always smiled at that.

"I know," he had said, "that I'll have the lowest degree of glory; but, by dang, I look around at men with a lot of wives and it seems to me they got things backward. They are having their hell right here and now. I'd rather miss the hell and have less heaven."

When Nephi entered, the Frosts were preparing to eat; and the house smelled, as it always did, like a huge kitchen. The table was piled deep with rich foods: a brown and dripping roast, jellies and preserves, candied figs, thick yellow cream and a large cream pie that was two inches of mellow depth. Datus and Nabbie always fed like two happy plump hogs, with juices gushing in their mouths and running from their fingers and overflowing their dishes. Datus himself, it seemed to Nephi, ate enough for a dozen men, explaining that he had to make up for his father who nearly starved to death coming across with Brigham. Nephi had seen the man eat three fried chickens at one sitting, together with heaped plates of mashed potatoes, yams swimming in their syrup, ears of corn, golden and buttered and tender, and a whole mince pie.

"Hello, Nephi. You're just in time for dinner."

"It smells good."

"It is. Your old grandpap wants a good set of false teeth in the next life; but if Nabbie ain't going to cook for me, I hope the Lord sets a good table. Will it be as good as what we have here?"

"Better."

"You know, it's funny God never told Joseph anything about that. Well, pull up your chair."

Nephi fetched a chair. Datus and Nabbie, he remembered again, always breathed and smelled of food as if they were fat granaries of creams and syrups and spices. But everyone loved them. Their hearts were as big as pumpkins; no hungry person was ever turned away from their door.

"What you got there, Nephi?"

"A petition to Congress. We're going to fight the Edmunds Act."

"It won't do any good," said Datus, reaching for food, "it ain't worth a tinker's hoot. Plural marriage is doomed. I can't figger out how God thought it would work in this world."

"It has worked."

"Not by a jugful. You can't name a man who ain't in hot water with his wives all the time. Even you."

"What nonsense!" cried Nephi, but he winked at Nabbie. "I have no trouble."

"Like hell you don't."

"Even you and Nabbie quarrel once in a while."

"Yes, but as soon as I get through, I don't have to tighten my belt and begin all over with a fresh one. Nephi, it ain't none of my business, but sometimes I wonder if all the men are blind."

"How?"

"Why, take you. You know Mark Browe is shining up to Chloe."

"He comes to see Lura."

"No, Nephi, not if I'n see to the end of my nose. That slick scoundrel is after your wife. Of course, I never could see eye to eye with the Lord in marriage. I figger women have passions just as men do—and no man can keep a lot of wives satisfied. Can he, Nabbie?"

"He'd have to be a lot better man than you are."

"If," said Nephi, "the sisters would follow their religion, then things would be all right."

"No, Nephi—not as long as women are women and men are men.

Adultery for us is next to murder but there's always been a lot of it. There still is. I see what I see and I don't say much, but I ain't asleep. A lot of children in Zion today don't know their own fathers."

"Well, maybe so, Datus. The sisters know what is sinful, and if they send their souls to hell, nobody can stop them. I know there's adultery—even here in Josephville."

"Yes. We all know it."

"But there's adultery in families with only one wife."

"Not so much of it."

"Nephi is lucky," said Nabbie. "He's so darned good-looking that all his wives love him."

Datus grinned. "As to that, I don't want to say. But I tell you plural marriage is doomed. Pretty soon you'll be in jail. So will Tim, so will Moroni, and all the rest. Then what will happen to the church?"

"Nothing can destroy its principles."

"What good are they if you can't practice them? And I'll tell you another thing that is doomed. The United Orders. Right here I see signs of it all around me."

"In what way?"

"Every way. Some men seem to be getting greedy all the time. Take Alonzo Jackson. Just between us, he ain't satisfied. He says some work harder than others. That's true. Some of the saints around here is getting pretty danged lazy. They don't starve any more and their bellies is always full, and so they don't want to work as hard as they did. Then, besides that, some of the men in the fields want to work in town. They say they do all the dirty work while some just boss."

Nephi considered that. It was true that an experiment which began in idealism, in whole-hearted co-operation, in fellowship, was showing signs of jealousy and strife. All the men had been assigned to the work which they could do best: some on the farms, some in the orchards and gardens, others in the mills and forges and the store. They had all been given according to their needs. In the early years, everyone had been happy and satisfied and prosperous. None had stolen or had seemed to want to. None had complained. But as the community grew, as the storehouses were filled with good things to eat and wear, first one or two and then many had wanted a different kind of work, or had said that others had an unfair share of food and clothes.

"If anyone wants to leave the Order," said Nephi, "he may. If anyone is dissatisfied, let him go elsewhere."

"Well, if you keep it going, you'll have to be another Brigham. Some persons don't understand anything but a kick in their rump. Brigham Young knew that."

"Who besides Alonzo is dissatisfied?"

"I won't be tattletale. Look around you. You'll find out in a hurry that things ain't like they used to be."

"I'll go and see Brother Alonzo now."

Alonzo Jackson was the huge and rather surly fellow who managed the gristmill. He had only one wife but only because he could find no young women who would marry him. That circumstance, Nephi suspected, had helped turn the man sour—as well as his envy of men who had many wives. Whatever the reason, Alonzo for a long while had been growing more unhappy and belligerent; had been greedy for more power; had been asking for a louder voice in community planning. Leadership in the Order had descended from Moroni to Tim, and then to Nephi; and Alonzo had not only resented that, but had said it smelled too much of the divine right of kingship.

"Hello," said Alonzo when Nephi knocked on his door. "Come in."

Nephi entered, reflecting that Alonzo was one man who never addressed another as brother, or Nephi as bishop. Nephi explained the petition and Alonzo signed, giving to his signature big ostentatious loops and curves, and scrupulously placing a period after his last name, as well as two customary dashes across one of the loops.

"How," asked Nephi, "is the Order getting along lately?"

"How should I know? I'm busy."

"I've heard some of the men aren't satisfied. Is that true?"

"You better ask them. I ain't a snoop."

"Are the crops good this year?" asked Nephi cheerfully.

"I don't get out much to see. That ain't my job. I work instead of settun around on my hinder like a lot of them."

"Those who don't work, don't eat. That's what Brigham said."

"They pretend to work. They put in their time but they don't do anything."

"Do you have any loafers in the mill?"

"In the mill," said Alonzo, looking at Nephi with unfriendly eyes, "we all work. I see to that."

"Well, if any of the men are loafing, we should have them up before the Council."

"There's one thing," said Alonzo, deciding to speak his mind, "that I don't like."

"What is that?"

"It don't look fair to me for a man with a lot of wives and children to share just like us who don't have that many. Now me, I got only one wife and four children. I get food and clothes for them. That's all. I work like a dog but I don't get any more than a part of what I earn. Some men don't work any harder but they get a lot more. That ain't fair."

"It might not seem fair to you, Brother Alonzo; but in his revelations to the prophet, God said we are to share according to our needs."

"I still say it ain't fair."

"You are saying you don't think God is fair. He told us to establish a system in which there would be no poverty and no wealth, no rich, no poor. My father works as hard as any man, yet he has only three wives and four children at home."

"I know that. Just the same, I don't think the Almighty wants me to work to support other people. Why in hell should I?"

"For twenty years," said Nephi, still speaking quietly, "we have had this Order. In all that time, nobody has gone ragged or hungry. Nobody looks vainly for work. No little children are undernourished, no old people are homeless. That is what God intended. If you do more than your part in this world, you will be rewarded in the next. You have all you want to eat and to wear, and a good house to live in. It would do you no good to accumulate property that you can never take with you."

"I could leave it to my children."

"There's no need to. Your children will always have plenty."

"I got a different notion. The government ain't going to let us go on this way. I've heard they intend to take all our property away from us. Then what will I have for all my hard work and what will my children have?"

"I don't think the government will interfere with our Order."

"Like hell it won't." Alonzo grinned. "I suppose they ain't going to put you in jail either."

"Not if I can help it."

"Help it, my foot! What did some big preacher say back East? Why, that the Fort Douglas artillery will come over and shoot us all down."

"That was DeWitt Talmage, but that's only his opinion."

"I don't care what his name was. I say you'll be in jail and I won't have a single damn thing for twenty years' work. If I owned what I made, then my family could have it; but I don't even own the house I live in. I guess don't really own the clothes on my back."

"You're getting bitter," said Nephi, speaking a little sharply. "If we all stick together, the government can't whip us. If we don't, we are lost. Over in Salt Lake City there are five hundred positions which the gentiles want, and many of which they already have. Congress has passed a law that virtually disfranchises us and places us under the complete rule of the gentiles. This is no time to quarrel, Brother Alonzo, or fall down in the harness. It is a time to fight and fight hard. If, as you say, some of the brethren are not doing their part, bring their names to the next meeting."

Alonzo was unconvinced. He said good night curtly and closed the door.

Nephi called next on Abner Tuttle, a man even more soured than Alonzo. Abner, now sixty but still in vigorous health, had been embittered by his wife's attitude toward plural marriage: Lucinda had steadily refused to allow a second wife in her home. Years ago, Abner had pleaded and then threatened; he had gone to Brigham Young for advice; and he had covertly wooed every young woman who would listen to him. He had found several who would have married him, but Lucinda said no. She was a stately and educated woman who had come from New England; and though she devoutly believed in the tenets of her church, she said with a slyly ironic twinkle that one wife was enough for any man—and much more than most of them deserved.

Nephi found Abner reading in the *Doctrine and Covenants.* He had read the revelation on plural marriage until he knew it by heart, but almost daily he pored over it, remembering his loss, reflecting that in the next world he would have to live forever and ever with one woman. Other men would have many wives, and enough children to cover a planet. Lucinda had borne him only one child, and that child had died when young. What he was to do, how without offspring he was ever to become a god,

he could not for the life of him tell; and year by year he became more reti
cent and bitter.

"Hello, Brother Abner. How are you this evening?"

"About as usual, Nephi."

"How are you, Sister Lucinda?"

"Oh, still in the land of the living."

Abner took glasses off his nose and looked very stubborn and resentful
He stared at his wife without warmth or friendliness. While Nephi ex
plained the petition, Abner looked from him to Lucinda, thoughtfully
chewing at a mustache which he drew into his mouth until it lay fla
and combed down his lip.

"Why," he asked, "should I sign it? God knows they'll never arrest me."

"We should all sign it. The more signers we have, the more attention
Congress will pay to it."

Abner grunted and set the spectacles on his nose. "What would happer
to a man if he took more wives without his wife's consent? Would that b
sinful?"

"I don't know," said Nephi, smiling at the despair in Abner's face. ".
think not. Sister Lucinda has been very unreasonable."

"I have not," said Lucinda calmly. "Abner has had a hard time sup
porting one wife in this world. I don't want to live in poverty in th
next."

"But God would provide," said Abner. "What am I to do? I won't ever
have a grandchild. Lucinda won't have any more children if she lives til
Jesus comes again, so why should I go to heaven?"

"Perhaps if you talk with Sister Lucinda, you can change her mind."

"Change it, hell! I've talked till I feel like a pump that needs priming
If I take another wife she'll leave me."

"Is that true?"

"That is true."

"You are not obeying God's commandments if you refuse to let you
husband obey them."

"I've always reasoned," said Lucinda, "that God intended plural mar
riage for those with enough tolerance and charity to bless it. I'm a ver
jealous woman—and I don't like women. I know my failings and trus
that God will forgive them. Besides, I've observed that men don't show
much sense in choosing wives—and that the first wife never has muck

choice in the matter. If Abner were to marry other women, I should be allowed to choose them, because I'll have to live with them throughout eternity. But Abner is like all men. He takes a fancy to giddy young things with a Grecian bend walk in a brocaded bustle and tarletan underskirts. He likes a flaming red pelerine. Not even Brigham showed much sense in choosing wives. If a houseful quarrel all the time in this world, then I assume the presence of God will not keep them from quarreling in the next."

Nephi was smiling. He liked her spirit and intelligence. "Abner, would you let her choose your wives?"

"Her!" said Abner, grunting scornfully. "She'd choose old worn-out hacks with spavined hocks and green eyes."

"I'd choose women who could bear children. You say that's what you want. But what you really want is silly girls with rosettes on their slippers. All men are that way. Did you ever stop to think," she asked, turning to Nephi, "that in the next life plural wives will have to live together for millions of years? Then why shouldn't they be such women as can love and respect one another, instead of a houseful of cats such as Heber Kimball had? Surely God expected men to use their intelligence."

"Yes, He did. And it's true that most of us show bad judgment."

"Did you?"

"I'm afraid so," said Nephi, wagging his head sadly. "My wives don't get along."

"Abner wants young girls. I'm fifty-six. I'd look nice in a houseful of schoolgirls."

"I don't want young girls," said Abner, but his eyes lied.

"My dear, I've seen all the girls you wanted to marry—or at least as many as you'd let me see. They have all been vain simpletons who would spend time on their hair while I did the work. Men," she added, speaking again to Nephi, "run after that kind when they're old—and especially then. Abner even has his eye on your daughter Lura."

"I do not!" cried Abner. His eyes were guilty and secretive.

"If Abner wants to marry schoolgirls, he may, of course; but I'll leave."

"You want me to marry grandmothers."

"No, just women old enough to have some sense."

"Well," said Nephi, who had heard such arguments before, "I must make other calls. I hope you two can come to an understanding."

"We never will," said Abner, gazing at his wife. "She's selfish."

While walking to the next house, Nephi pondered the matter; and there was, he admitted, a lot of truth in what Lucinda said. The happiest plural family he had known was his grandfather's: Kate and Agatha and Maggie, and the other wives when living, had seldom quarreled. But most of the plural families were a hell on earth. The wives fought one another, abused the children of one another, and the children cultivated the feuds of their parents. It had been so in his father's home. He, the child of Fanny, had disliked some of Sarah's children; and he could not remember the time when the house had not shaken with family rows. His own family was no better. Genet softly despised his other wives; Ruth was aloof and tolerant; and Chloe, it seemed to him, hated all of them, wives and children alike.

When he came to the next house he stopped and listened. It was the home of a man who had nine wives and more children than Nephi had ever counted because he had never seen them all together. He knew of no family that fought more often or violently than this one; and inside now, so far as he could tell, was a terrific rumpus that was shaking the house from the rafters to the cellar. After listening a few moments, he smiled broadly, for this sort of thing was too much for his Irish sense of humor. Brigham Young used to castigate such warring groups and tell them they were outraging the Almighty; but Nephi could only grin at them and pass on, wondering how the Almighty would discipline them in the next life.

After visiting several more families to gather signatures, he went home feeling tired, and more humorless than he liked to feel. His house was dark. Upon entering, he lit a lamp and gazed around him, wondering if his own wives had been fighting, and if his children had said their prayers. He decided to spend the night with Chloe. She was a little giddy and her heart was too fondly set on a gay time; but he found her very charming and womanly. Genet and Maude had always frozen him; and Ruth, in spite of all her coquetry, her devotion to clothes and ornaments, was as frigid as ice.

He went softly to Chloe's door and knocked and listened. There was no answer. He rapped again, and then gently opened the door and looked in. Chloe was not there. Clothes were flung over the dresser, over the bed and floor, as if she had left in haste. For several moments he stood in the room, gazing around him, and wondering where she was; and then went out and quietly closed the door. He was still deliberating when he heard a voice at the head of the stairs. He looked up to see Maude, candle in hand, her hair a horrible mass of twisted curls and tiny topknots, her gown an old Indian blanket, her small eyes staring at him with coaxing intentness.

"Chloe has gone out," she said, "but I am very lonely tonight."

Nephi shrugged. "Oh, all right. I'll be up soon." He turned away to have a look at the daily newspaper, and to wonder why Brigham Young passed the age of sixty before realizing that among all his wives he had favorites.

CHAPTER IV

IN NEPHI'S CARRIAGE, A WHITE-TOPPED SURREY DRAWN BY TWO DAPPLED BAYS, Chloe and Lura had gone to the city. They told Genet they were going to shop for Nephi, having in mind a linen duster and an Ascot tie; and when Genet asked suspiciously why they did not buy in the Josephville store, Chloe said the ties were much prettier in the gentile store of the Walker Brothers, and the linen dusters much nicer in a Jewish shop on State Street. "In our store," she added, "there's nothing good enough for a man as handsome as Nephi"—and with a wry face Genet had admitted the truth of that.

Chloe did intend to purchase a duster and a tie, but those were not her chief reason for going. She had an appointment with Mark Browe. She did not know if she loved Mark, nor did she know while driving the six miles to the city how she would get rid of Lura. Mark had been stealthily wooing her for many months, not only by entering Nephi's home on one pretext and another, but also by sending anonymous flowers, and by secret messenger a heavily boned bodice with a Lillie Langtry waistline, as well as a pair of evening slippers with a silver rosette over the instep. Never before had she met the man in secret; and tonight she was thrilled and almost scared to death. She was afraid not of him but of her hotheaded husband who might be very violent if he caught her flirting with a gentile. And she intended, of course, to do nothing more than to flirt a little and show him how charmingly irresistible she could be. He was such a handsome and cynical infidel that he fascinated her; and besides, she liked his taste in gifts.

To Lura she said: "There's a play at the theater tonight. Would you like to go?"

"Oh, yes!" said the naive Lura.

"I can't go," said Chloe gravely, her blue gaze on the trotting team. "After I buy the things I have to call on a friend—and oh, dear, she'd be angry if I didn't! But," Chloe added, patting Lura's hand with gentle contempt, "you can go and then tell me about it on the way home."

It was nice to have a simpleton like Lura to hide behind. They drove p State Street to the theater; and an attendant stepped briskly down to ther the reins and hitch the team.

"I think you're just in time," Chloe whispered, again patting the happy ura. "Here is money for the ticket—and meet me here at the carriage." he watched Lura cross the walk and go up the steps; when at the door ura turned to wave at her, Chloe raised her fan and smiled.

Her smile vanished the moment Lura disappeared. Quickly leaving the rriage, she went north on State Street to South Temple, and then past melia's Palace and through Eagle Gate. Mark came out of shadows and ok her arm.

"Come, before we are seen." They walked northward and he stopped at small hotel. "The room is 207. You go up and I'll be there in a minute." Chloe felt stifled as she entered the hotel and climbed a narrow stairway the second floor. Seeing nothing clearly, and feeling more foolish than uilty, she went twice up and down the long corridor before she und the room; and after she entered it, she did not realize for several oments that a bottle of whiskey and two of wine stood on a small table. he looked next at the bed and saw that it had a gay cover of dotted Swiss uslin. Then she sank weakly to a chair.

Mark entered softly—so softly indeed that she almost screamed: this eeting had already gone beyond what she had expected. At once he nelt at her feet and covered her palms with kisses, and then kissed her rists and arms before looking up with dark ardent eyes. Although ewildered, and hardly aware of what the man was doing, Chloe did re- ect, nevertheless, that his eyes were not so handsome as Nephi's.

"I adore you!" he said, pressing her palms to his cheeks, and his lips the stiff satin of her dress.

"Do you?"

"You know I do."

Her blue eyes that looked at his dark hair were both terrified and nning. Her smile was that of a frightened girl—but also of a woman ho was wise in the gallantries of men.

"Why," he asked, "do you live in that preposterous house in Joseph- lle?"

"It's my home."

"No! It's just a polygamous harem. How do you tolerate it?"

"You forget that I'm a married woman."

"Married!" He looked up at her. "Did you say *married*?" He smiled. "You're no more married than I am. Darling, I hate to say it, but you're only a concubine, a mistress, a harlot."

She drew her hands away. Knowing that she was offended, even if only because so vain, he redoubled his ardor. He kissed her hands madly and then sat at her feet and clasped her legs. Between impassioned kisses on the satin over her knees, he said: "You're not a—harlot. You're an adorable foolish—woman who—believes in—a lot of—nonsense that—Joseph Smith pre—tended to receive—from God." Suddenly he rose, looking bored and very cynical. He grasped the bottle of whiskey. "Drink?"

"No. I've never tasted whiskey in my life."

"Chloe, I don't see how you live around those other women. They're such dull stupid old mares and you're so young and charming and beautiful. Are you afraid to drink with me?"

Though feeling weak and frightened, she said: "You know I'm not afraid of anything."

"Then you will drink with me."

"But the Word of Wisdom doesn't allow me to drink."

"Oh, the word of Joseph! Chloe, do you realize soon that all these Mormon frauds will be fleeing from their harems into a desert? In all directions you'll see them at a full gallop with their saintly hair standing up and their adulterous ears burning. They will crawl into badger holes and never poke their fornicating faces out; and if they do, we'll throw them into jail and keep them there. Are you going with them or with the few civilized persons in the city?"

"I don't know. I guess I'll go to jail with my husband."

"Won't that be a beautiful end for a beautiful woman! Here you are, an adorable and lovely girl intended by God to make some man happy; but you will sit in jail with the other concubines and eat bread and water and grow old and gray and play with the mice and wait for glory in the next world——"

"Don't!" she cried. "You just want to make me unhappy."

"You are unhappy—and I'm unhappy because you are. Chloe, I'm going to tell you some things tonight. Old Brigham tried to keep the gentiles out of this city but here we are and we are in control. In the next few years we'll chase all the Mormons into Mexico or the Pacific Ocean. We'll control the police, the judges, the courts, and every territorial office. We'll take the vote away from them; we'll disfranchise them; we'll jail them. All their children will be bastards. All their wives will be deserted concubines. I'm telling you all this because I know I can trust you, and because I want you to be happy and keep out of the mess. If I thought you'd run and tell Nephi——"

"I won't," she said.

"You'd be stupid if you did. I can help you when trouble comes. I can help you tonight and I'm going to. I'm going to help you by making you understand how intelligent gentiles look at Mormonism and what it is for them; and when you see it as I see it, as the whole civilized world sees it, you'll never have the gall again to say you're a Mormon. But first I want to make you comfortable." He went to the bed and made a back rest of the pillows and extra quilts, and then led the amused but not unwilling Chloe over and settled her snugly and comfortably. "There," he said, appraising her as if he had hung a picture on the wall. "If you want a drink while I'm talking, just ask for it."

Mark went to the big walnut rocker in which Chloe had been sitting, and sank and stretched lazily, filled and lit his pipe, put his feet on the table where they stood up alongside the wine and whiskey bottles, smiled across at Chloe and began.

"I don't know how to make you understand just how foolish and vicious this so-called religion is, and why it must be exterminated. I'm not going to talk about Joseph Smith, who was only an illiterate fanatic without any sense of humor but with plenty of carnal appetite; or about Brigham Young who in some ways was a great man but was, nevertheless, a bigoted dictator who had absolute control of the lives of a hundred thousand persons. Chloe, I think I can suggest the foolishness of the whole thing by two or three attitudes. One of them is this.

"Any good Mormon must be obedient to his prophet and seer—to the hierarchy of his church; and if he is, he may ignore all other laws, including those of the nation in which he lives. Joseph Smith was killed and for the Mormons that is proof that he was anointed of God. John Taylor was not killed, and that is proof that he was saved by God to be president now. When the Mormons left Nauvoo and journeyed across Iowa, some of the gentiles would not speak to them, and that was proof that all the wicked were against them; but some of the gentiles assisted them, and that was proof of Mormon holiness because the hearts of the wicked were melted to assist them. When Johnston came with an army, that proved the Mormon church was the true church because it was hated and persecuted by an evil nation; but when the army withdrew without a battle, that was proof God was protecting His people. In other words, no matter what happens, it proves to Mormons that Mormons are a chosen handful of God. The leaders can do no wrong; because if they refuse to do a thing, it is wrong to do it, and if they do a thing, then it is right.

"That," said Mark, smiling cynically through tobacco smoke, "is the way of it. It's just that simple. There is the story of a devout Mormon woman that will show you how nimble a Mormon conscience is. When it was told that a Mormon leader went to a prizefight, she was very angry and said it was a lie; but when it was proved to her that the man did go, then she said that if he went, it was all right, because if it had not been all right, he would not have been there. That's the kind of infallibility the Mormons place in their leaders.

"Chloe, have you ever been through the Endowment House rituals?"

"No, I refused. That's only for wives who are married for eternity and receive the Holy Ghost."

"Then you probably know less about them than I do—and what I know is only what apostates have told me. Let us suppose you and Nephi were going through. You would enter and put on flowing robes of linen or muslin. You would wear a white cap that would also serve as a veil; and he would wear a round piece of linen drawn up in front as a bow. Under the robe you would wear the endowment garment, a sort of combination jacket and trousers. Mormons, of course, believe nobody can be injured if he never entirely takes this garment off. They say Joseph Smith foolishly took his garment off the day he went to Carthage or the bullets could not have touched him.

"Listen with your sense of humor, Chloe. There you are, all dressed up, plus white stockings and white linen slippers. You then go into separate rooms, and you are washed by a woman, Nephi by a man. That purification ritual is supposed to cleanse you of all sin. After that, you are anointed with oil; and a little oil is put on your eyes to make them see more clearly on your ears to make them hear the Lord's warnings, on your mouth so you will speak with wisdom, and on your feet so you will be swift in obeying the commandments of your leaders. Then you're given a secret name that is to be your name in heaven.

"The Mormons have always been fiends for strange names. Joseph Smith started it; but did you know that years ago all the apostles were given titles? Brigham Young was the Lion of the Lord; Heber Kimball was the Herald of Grace; Parley Pratt was the Archer of Paradise; Orson Hyde was the Olive Branch of Israel; John Taylor was the Champion of Right. Someone else was the Keeper of the Rolls, another was the Patriarchal Staff of Jacob, another was the Banner of the Gospel, another was the Entablature of Truth, another was the Sun-Dial, another was the Gauge of Philosophy. Lyman Wight, the apostle who ran off to Texas, was the Wild Ram of the Mountains.

"It's all very pretty," said Mark, pouring himself a drink. "It's like the games little children play. Now to come back to the endowment. After you get a mysterious name, you go into another chamber and hear a voice say that those who haven't enough courage to belong to God's chosen people may withdraw, but those who go on must keep the secrets or they will have their throats cut from ear to ear. Those who have the courage now enter the third room.

"They now take part in a crude representation of the creation, temptation and fall as given in Genesis. You put on an apron of white linen on which is sewed a piece of green silk to represent a fig leaf. You put on a veil. All good Mormons are buried in their endowment robes and the woman's face is covered with the veil and that veil is never to be lifted until her husband gets ready to lift it in the next world. If he refuses," said Mark, grinning at her, "she can never look on God.

"Next you go in the fourth chamber and are tempted. Your temptations are chiefly the gospels of Baptists and Methodists and others—and you resist them, of course. You know they are all abominations. Then two good fellows represent St. James and St. John and proclaim the gospel of Mormonism. You accept it. If you accept it—and you wouldn't be there if you didn't intend to—you are given secret and mysterious handclasps and passwords that will help you along when you get to heaven. Then—" Mark paused and looked at her thoughtfully while he sipped whiskey. "Do you know what happens then?"

"No," she said, still gazing at him as if he were the Devil.

"Then you kneel and raise your hand and take a solemn and terrible oath to help avenge the death of Joseph Smith, to teach your children to do likewise, to obey without question all commands from your church authorities, and to keep forever secret what you have just seen and heard. Then you have certain marks cut on your endowment garments—though what in the name of hell they are supposed to symbolize, I don't know.

"I have told you only what happens in your Endowment House. A lot of persons think there are sexual orgies, horrible debaucheries, raping of little girls. I don't think anything of the sort. I think it is just a lot of masonic hocus-pocus and half-witted childlike foolishness. How intelligent persons like you can take it seriously— Does your sense of humor want a little drink?"

"Just a little one," said Chloe, smiling strangely. Whether this man was a devil, whether he was mocking her or trying to instruct her, and why he had met her here, she did not know. She was resolved to listen and remain sober and be as crafty as he was.

"As I have told you," said Mark, knocking his pipe out and refilling it, "Mormons assume that they have the only mortgage on heaven and that all the rest of us are damned. Their gall and arrogance are beyond all computation. I don't question the sincerity of most of them—nor their humorlessness either. They have to be a humorless and naive people to think they can set up polygamous harems in the United States and its territories, and to say that gentiles are persecuting them because they don't like it. They have to be childlike to imagine that lust can be disguised as religious principle. Part of the world is furious with them and part of it is laughing. Have you heard the latest stories about the Mormons?"

"I don't know," she said, toying with her drink. "I've heard some of them."

"Well, here is one I heard only yesterday. When the railroad first came through, a lot of persons back East wanted to see Brigham Young and his wives—because Brigham before he died was the most discussed man in the world. One time a society woman was riding through Nebraska when the train ran into a herd of buffalo. She ran to a window and looked out; and though she did not know it, what she saw was an old buffalo bull that had been cut to pieces and scattered up and down the track. She looked at a certain part of him and then threw up her hands and yelled, 'Great God, we've run over a Mormon bishop!'"

Chloe giggled but blood slowly dyed her face. "That's an awful story!" she cried, and laughed like a tortured child.

"It shows what the world thinks of polygamy—of all of these harem-keepers who look at a notebook and study the names and say to themselves, 'Now which one should I visit tonight?' That's the way Heber Kimball used to do. He had so damned many concubines he couldn't remember their names, much less tell which one he slept with last. Chloe, how often does Nephi visit you?"

Chloe's face turned as red as a ripe tomato. "Shame on you to ask such a question!"

"Why? I'm curious."

"I won't answer."

"All right. Just the same, there you are, a woman made to love and adore, living in a harem with that pale-faced Genet who never had a thought in her life; and Maude who breathes as if under her dress some invisible person was kneeling on her stomach; and Ruth who will never be happy until she has learned to walk gracefully with fifty pounds of ornaments on her head. There you are, living among harlots, and it's time you got out of it. Answer this question then: why don't you have children?"

"I don't want any."

"That's sensible. God knows what will happen to all these thousands of children after we get through with their fathers. They will be bastards— and that's the plain truth of it. Mormon women seem to be more fertile than gentile women—and that reminds me of another story I heard the other day. You know, back East your Mormon men are regarded somewhat in the light of bulls and rams and studs; and since Artemus Ward and others wrote of thousands of children in every dooryard, Mormon wives are made to litter like sows. Brigham Young, you know, was always patting some child on the head and saying, 'Whose little one are you?' only to learn that the little one belonged to his clan.

"Well, this is the story about the fertility of Mormon women—and the slowness of the train from Green River to Ogden. One day it was puffing along through the canyons when the fireman ran to the conductor and shouted, 'In the name of the Mormon God of Israel, you must hurry!' 'Why?' asked the conductor. 'Because one of Brigham Young's wives is about to have a baby!' The conductor frowned. 'If she's going to have a baby,' he said, 'why did President Young let her get on at Ogden?' The fireman wrung his hands in despair. 'You don't understand!' he roared. 'She wasn't that way when she got on!'"

Again Chloe giggled and colored. She drank from her glass and choked and then asked desperately: "Why do persons tell all these awful stories about Mormons?"

"Because," said Mark blandly, "that's the way they see you. There's more in that story than a slow train. A lot of polygamous babies in this valley don't have the fathers they think they have. I'll wager that not all of Brigham Young's children were Brigham's—and perhaps," said Mark with a dark cynical smile, "that's why he was always asking children who their father was."

For a long moment Chloe met his gaze and held it. There was passion in his face, but there was also violence and cruelty. There was much more than sardonic mirth in his dark eyes.

"Chloe," he said, "I've been trying to suggest to you how gentiles look at Mormonism. For us all you plural wives are living in adulterous and shameful concubinage. We are going to put all your husbands in jail; we are going to build a big home for their concubines; and we are going to drive the United Orders and all the other silly communism out of this territory. It's stupid of you to stay out in that brothel in Josephville and wait until the sky falls and you're helpless and have no place to turn. We are going to smash not only polygamy but also Mormonism in this city and in every town north and south; and we'll do it if we have to bring in an army."

"Give me," she said, "another small drink."

He rose and poured from the bottle for her; but when unexpectedly he bowed to kiss her lips, she turned away.

"Very well," he said, speaking gently because he knew she would eventually yield, "if you don't like me, you don't; but I urge you to save yourself from the chaos that is coming to Mormonism—and coming just as soon as all our plans are ready. All your polygamous Mormon men will be in jail—including the McBrides; and all you concubines will be glad to turn to any friend you can find. If you all flee, that is all right: go to Mexico or Canada or anywhere you please. But if you stay here and persist in your lecherous seraglios, your goatish zenanas, your lustful rookeries, your bawdy libidinous love nests that prostitute women and make an unclean thing of marriage and the home ——"

"Mark, please!"

"Then leave that nasty home and marry me."

"You don't," said Chloe wisely, "really want to marry me. You just want to seduce me."

He looked at her and very slowly he smiled—and it was a warm and engaging smile in spite of the mockery and cruelty and cunning in it. "All right," he said calmly, "would that outrage you? You've been sleeping with a man and you're not married to him."

Indignantly, Chloe leapt to her feet. She seized her hat and gloves and fan and went to the door, expecting him to follow, to beg her to remain, to kneel to her and murmur ardent phrases into the folds of her satin dress; but he did nothing of the kind. He sat imperturbably and looked at her, his smile more cynical now, his eyes unmistakably bored. Chloe tossed her hair and stamped her feet once, realizing furiously, murderously, that she had moved too soon, that her bluff had been called, and that she could do nothing except to go—or stand here like a penitent and absurd fool.

"Thanks for the drink!" she said, trying to make a rapier of her voice.

"Not at all," said Mark suavely. "You know you are always welcome to anything I have."

That made matters worse. That made her seem cheap and ungrateful and—and everything he said the Mormons were. "Well," said Chloe, drawing herself up haughtily and lifting her brows, "thanks for the lecture!"

"You're welcome," he said. His smile spread a little and made patterns at the corners of his eyes. "If you ever feel in need of a drink or a lecture again, uh—let me know."

That, so far as she could tell in her bewildered state of mind, in the clamor of outraged vanity, in the confusion of pity and hate and love that possessed her—that was an insult. She did not know whether it was or not, but she could not stand here like a—like a polygamous wife and try to figure it out; and so with a bang she slammed the door. Mark heard her going with angry quick steps down the corridor and then down the stairs; and with a sigh he filled his pipe and his glass.

CHAPTER V

FORMERLY, WHEN THE ORDER WAS YOUNG IN JOSEPHVILLE, THE MEMBERS had all eaten together in a community hall; and the women, divided into groups, had taken turns in cooking and serving. After several of the members took more wives and the children became numerous, larger homes were built and the families lived and ate separately. In Nephi's house, where twenty-six persons lived, five tables were placed end to end across the large dining room; and Nephi sat at one end and Genet at the other. Before breakfast, and again in the evening, there was prayer. Usually it was Nephi who offered thanksgiving or asked the Lord for guidance, though now and then he called on a wife or an older child, or on a neighbor if one was present. On the morning after Chloe and Lura visited in the city, he looked down the two rows of faces, and every member of his family except Chloe looked at him.

"Chloe, will you give thanks?"

Her glance at him was swift and startled. When she saw that everyone had closed his eyes and bowed his head, she put a hand to her mouth and coughed, and then in sudden panic tried to remember what to say. Her delay was so unexpectedly long that Nephi raised his head and looked at her; but gently he said:

"Chloe, did you hear me?"

"O God, our Father," she said, her voice shaken by emotion, "we ask thee to look down on us this morning and bless us, that we may be worthy of thy love and guidance, and strong and—and holy in thy sight. Bless this food that it may give us strength to obey thy commandments; bless us, our Father, and bless all the saints in Zion; and bless our—our enemies and lead them back into the ways of—of righteousness. These blessings we humbly ask in the name of thy Son, Jesus Christ. Amen."

After the amen, solemnly intoned by everyone, including the smallest children, Maude looked at Chloe, wondering why she had faltered at prayer. Tactlessly she asked: "What are you blushing for?"

"Oh—am I?" asked Chloe, glancing uneasily at her husband.

"It looks like it to me." Maude's small humorless eyes filled with suspicion. "You got home pretty late, didn't you?"

"Not very. Did we, Lura?"

"I never noticed," Lura said.

"Of course," said Chloe tartly, "it takes some time to drive to the city and back."

"Did you," asked the persistent Maude, "find what you went for? I mean the Ascot tie and the duster."

"I couldn't find anything I liked."

"She went to visit a friend," said the naive Lura. "I went to the theater."

That statement made Nephi look at Chloe. "I hope you are not visiting gentiles. This is no time to be doing that."

Chloe's blue eyes flashed. "And what if I did! Some gentiles are just as good as we are."

"That's true," he admitted quietly. "But now that we are facing worse troubles than ever, I think it would be best——"

Suddenly Chloe rose to her feet. She was angry and tearful—and she hated Genet and Maude for the way they were looking at her. "I get tired," she said, "of being treated like a child! If I step outside this house, somebody wants to know where I went, what I was doing, if I visited gentiles. I'm sick of it!" She stared at Nephi, hoping he would speak in her favor; and when he did not, she turned and ran to her room, sobbing as she went.

"Well!" said Genet, feeling a little angry. "What a tantrum."

"What time," asked Nephi of Lura, "did you get home?"

"Daddy, I don't know. It was after midnight."

"Do you know what friends she visited?"

"She didn't tell me."

"I didn't mean to upset her, but this is no time to be mingling with gentiles. They are all spies. I am watched no matter where I go."

"I think," said Maude, "that Mark Browe is a spy. The other day I saw him talking with Alonzo Jackson."

Genet cleared her throat. "I don't think," she said, looking self-conscious as she always did when differing from another, "that he's a spy. He's just shining up to Chloe."

On either side of the table, children were gravely listening and gazing in turn at the speakers. Maude looked at Ruth who had remained discreetly silent.

"Ruth, what do you think?"

"I think," said Ruth calmly, "that Chloe is listening."

Chloe's door was opened with a bang, and that tearful and furious woman looked out. "You're damned right I'm listening, you bunch of gossips! You're always talking behind my back!"

"That will do," said Nephi. He had turned a little pale. "None of us say anything we're not willing to have you hear."

"You're all dead set against me!" cried Chloe, stamping her feet. "You all think you're so pure and holy and I'm so wicked! I'm just as good as Nephi and I'm a lot better than his other wives."

Maude vented a brittle laugh and looked anxiously at her husband.

"We've had enough of this," said Nephi. "The spirit of the Lord does not seem to be with us this morning."

"Well, maybe it will be when you find out what the gentiles are going to do to you! If you knew what I know, you'd be packing up and leaving."

"What do you mean?"

"Find out for yourself. You're all so damned smart."

Full of dull and useless anger, Nephi rose and left the house. This was no time for quarrels—not with spies everywhere, not with a nation of gentiles again united in a crusade to drive the saints from their homes. It was a time for humility and prayer, and an undivided front against the foe. And besides, he was worried this morning about the Order in Joseph-ville: threatened by envies and feuds within, and an invasion of gentile persecution from without, it would have a troubled time surviving. On the surface it was as serene and efficient and brotherly as it had been in the beginning; but under the surface there was dark ominous unrest.

Nephi walked down the main street of the village, observing with pride the houses of the brethren, each with its lawn and trees and flowering shrubs, and its garden behind—for this town was a model of what Brigham had declared every town should be. In one part of it were the homes, and in another part were the mills and shops and granaries. The whole of it had been thoughtfully planned and landscaped: and nowhere in it was there an ugly shed or stable, a sign of discarded cans and bottles and rags, or unsightly weeds in gardens or along ditches or anywhere. Everything looked clean and cared for and in its place.

While walking he came to the community store—yet it was less a store than a granary of clothes and food. Owned in common by every member of the Order, it was their commissariat of the present and their storehouse against the future. To each family was given from it what the Council of the Order deemed fair: the allotment was determined by the number of persons in a family and by their age. There had been complaints, of course. Some of the brethren, some of the sisters, were twice as hard on clothes as others were, and in consequence often looked shabbier than their neighbors; but that was their fault. Some had more ravenous appetites. Some had distaste for certain foods, gluttonous fondness for certain delicacies. Yes, there had been problems, there had been feuds and envies, but none that patience and commonsense had not solved. No social order, it seemed to Nephi, could ever be worked out that would be happily adaptable to all the differences in humility and greed, ambition and laziness, and scorn of, or pride in, personal appearance.

When he entered the store, he was pleased to observe the great quantities of stuff piled everywhere. The small mills and shops flanking the storehouse poured most of their produce into this community larder; and here were hundreds of cases of canned fruits and vegetables; thousands of bottles of pickles, jellies, preserves; huge bins of sugar, salt and condiments; garments of all kinds hung in neat rows, mounds of lumber and brick, and shelves sagging with a community's wealth. Not all of the stuff was produced here. A part of the excess in fruit and vegetables and flour was sold, and with the money was bought those articles which the Order was unable to grow or make.

"We look prosperous," he said to the storehouse manager. "We could endure a long famine."

"We certainly could," said the man, gazing proudly around him.

"Are the crops good this year?"

"We have the biggest crops we've had since Brigham passed away."

"Is everything going all right?"

"So far as I know. Of course, some of the brethren always find fault, no matter what you do. Brother Alonzo was in yesterday and he was fighting mad. He seems to think he's the only one who ever finds a worm in his meal or clothes that wear out."

"Well, we have a meeting this afternoon and Brother Alonzo can shed his complaints. How much cash do we have in the bank?"

"I'd have to look at the books. We have several thousand dollars."

"We have to buy a lot of machinery next year. There'll be a meeting today at two."

"I'll be there. So will Alonzo, with blood in his eye."

"That's his privilege," said Nephi, smiling. "I want to settle a lot of matters today."

After leaving the store, he went to the shops, the cannery, the mills, looking in on each. In the gristmill were thousands of bags of flour, of oatmeal, of bran and grits. Nephi liked the clean fecund smell of this busy place. He liked to watch the belts and elevators, or the men at work, everyone of them gray with flour. He liked to look into a long low building where many of the sisters sat at their weaving and spinning, or into a shop where a half-dozen cobblers made shoes, or into a third where men made harnesses and yokes for the beasts. There was no factory yet for the production of farm implements but Nephi hoped to have one soon, as well as a large plant for the making of sugar and syrups, and another for furniture. It had been Brigham's dream to make Zion self-sustaining and to import nothing. That was his dream for Josephville, though Nephi knew the Order would always have to buy iron ore and other metals, tobacco for those who persisted in using it, spices and salt, and various other staples. But a self-sustaining community could not be built in two generations. Privately he dreamed also of a great hothouse so that living rooms at all seasons could smell of flowers; and possibly even a small temple some day—because temples were being erected in St. George, Manti, and Logan.

There were twelve men in the Council of the Order, and when Nephi arrived at the church house the other eleven were there, as well as many other persons, including Tim and Moroni and the sulking Alonzo. Nephi went to the altar and opened with prayer and then descended to the floor and spoke.

"Brethren, you all know as well as I do that the saints are again facing grave trouble. More than ever before, it is necessary for all of us to stick together as one man; because once again we are fighting with our backs to the wall. It is vitally necessary to defend and preserve our Order in Josephville. For twenty years it has been a common bond between us—a bond against rags and hunger, and a bond in fellowship. We have faced problems, but no problem that we haven't been able to solve.

"Lately, there has been more than the customary ill-feeling; and I think it has been caused chiefly because the gentiles are preparing to destroy us. Instead of allowing new persecutions to separate us, we should see that they draw us closer together. For seven years I have been your bishop and the general manager of our Order, and during those years I have always encouraged you to speak your minds. We don't get anywhere if dissatisfactions are buried, if we nurse grudges, if we want to get something off our chest and don't; so this afternoon if anyone has complaints, let him speak, or let him forever hold his tongue. That was the policy of Brigham, and that has been mine.

"I have heard reports of stealing, of quarrels, of petty feuds. I am told that some of the brethren think they are unfairly treated. In fact, one of them has told me so. Now is the time to speak. Most of you present helped my grandfather start this Order years ago. In the beginning, we were all determined to make it work in the ways that God commanded of our prophet. We did make it work. We all took pride in our labor, remembering Brigham Young's statement that the only labor which can make a man happy is that which is performed creatively and gives to him a deeper meaning. To that end, we all shared in the ownership and management and results.

"Brethren, I am proud of our record. Since Josephville was founded, nobody here has been hungry, nobody has wanted for clothes or a house to live in or work to do. Perhaps we have been too prosperous—because things are not what they were in the beginning. Then we were happy and glad to work, and we were building against the threat of famine and starvation in years to come. Now we have so much that famine seems out of the question; and so our minds are turned to other thoughts. Some now want positions of greater power. Some want the kind of food and clothes we do not grow or make here, or do not buy. Some seem no longer to make their labor a creative experience.

"We cannot prosper and be happy in such an atmosphere; so speak out and let's have your complaints and grudges and then we'll decide what to do about them."

For a long moment there was silence. Then Alonzo Jackson, looking around and seeing nobody ready to speak, rose from his chair and clasped with two great hairy hands the chairs in front of him. "Bishop McBride, I have some things on my mind."

"Brother Alonzo, speak straight out."

"Just rest your mind on that. I will. I always do. No man alive can say I ever minced words. I don't plan to mince things now."

"Very well, Brother Alonzo. Let's have them."

"I don't like the way things has been going for a long time, and the other night I told you some of the things I mean. I guess you was referring to me in your talk."

"I was," said Nephi agreeably. "Now tell them to the Council."

"Well, I've got a lot of things to say. I guess I just as well begin at the beginning. In the beginning, like we all know, we all had a say-so in things. Brother Moroni was sort of our leader, but we was all in on the management. It ain't that way any more. When Moroni stopped being our leader, then his son Tim was; and now it's you. It looks to me like a family affair. I mean the McBrides have always been the boss and still are. That don't look right to my way of thinking. I don't think God meant it to be that way. When Joseph died, it wasn't one of his sons who became president and prophet. It was Brigham. When Brigham died, it wasn't any of his sons. It was John Taylor. When Taylor dies, it won't be any of his sons either. So why should it be that way here?"

"Brother Alonzo, would you like to be bishop and general manager?"

"Well, I don't say as I would, but I know some who would like to be."

"It's true that the Council voted my father in, and then voted me in. If the Council wants to vote me out, that will be all right with me."

"Well," said Alonzo, "I ain't never liked the way it was done. And another thing I don't like. It might be true as you say that you're a kind of general manager; but what work do you ever do? What work did your father ever do? Now me, I labor like a dog all day in the mill; but you, you run over to the city or anywheres you please."

Another man rose. "I'd like to ask Brother Alonzo what *work* Brigham Young ever did. But where would we be today if we hadn't had him? He never worked in a mill or on a farm or in a factory; but he was busy all the time. As they used to say, he slept with one eye open and one foot out of bed. We all know there wouldn't be any church if Brigham had not been—well, our general manager. And I know there wouldn't be any Order in Josephville if it hadn't been for Moroni McBride."

Many turned to look at Moroni who was calmly stroking his white beard.

"Just the same," said Alonzo, "it don't look right to me for some of us to work all day and others to ride around in a buggy."

"Put it to a vote!" cried one.

"No," said another. "It isn't necessary to vote. Jesus never worked either in the way Brother Alonzo means. And if Alonzo hasn't any more on his mind than that, he'd better sit down and keep his mouth shut."

"Who around here can make me keep my mouth shut?"

"Brother Alonzo," said Nephi, "go on with your complaints. After we have heard them, we'll decide what to do."

"Well, don't think I'm finished yet. Them-there was two things on my mind. Now another thing is this: in the beginning we owned everything in common; but now we don't. Nowadays any man can work on the side for his own profit. If he has a lot of wives and children, some of them can raise garden stuff and sell it in the city to buy fancy clothes. Or they can raise fruit and sell it and buy what they want. I don't have any time to do that. I am busy all the time making flour for your bread and oatmeal for your mush and bran for your hogs."

"You should have more wives and children," said a man, grinning up at him.

"Never mind about me and more wives. By the God of Israel, I tell you I work all day long and all I get is enough to eat and wear. I don't have money to buy fancy stuff. Look at Nephi's wife Ruth. That-there woman has enough jewelry to stock a store. Where does she get it? Why, she buys it. Where does Nephi get the money?" Alonzo looked around him; and when nobody answered, he raised his voice and thundered: "Where does he get the money?"

"Brother Alonzo, are you accusing Brother Nephi of being a crook?"

"I don't accuse nobody of nothing. I asked a question."

"I'll answer it," said Nephi. "They do sell a little fruit and vegetables they raise. But I had some property in the city and sold it and that's where my money came from."

"Well, what about us who don't have anything to sell? My children would like fancy things too. They come home from school and tell about the fancy things others have; but I don't have money to buy stuff."

"Few of us do," said Nephi. "My grandfather has none. My father has very little."

"That reminds me," said Alonzo. "Now take Moroni over there. He don't work no more but he still has all he wants that the rest of us make."

"My God!" cried a man impatiently. "Haven't you ever read Joseph's revelations? The sick and the old are to be cared for. They're not expected to work."

"Just the same, I don't have no old relations around for other men to support."

"If you had any, we'd take care of them."

"But I don't!" cried Alonzo. "It ain't fair for me to work to help feed the relations of others."

"I guess Moroni earned all he gets. If it hadn't been for him, where would you be today?"

"By God," cried Alonzo angrily, "what do I have? Nothing I can call my own. Even the house I live in, it's not mine. I don't have a cent in the bank."

"That's all right. When you get too old to work, you'll eat just the same. We'll take care of you."

"But what," asked Alonzo, "if I should die first?"

That question brought scornful laughter. "If you die, you won't be worrying about eating."

"But what'll I have to leave to my children?"

"Confound it, man, they'll have plenty just as you have had."

"Well," said Alonzo, wagging his big skull, "I still say it ain't right. And another thing: how about tithing? I know it's a principle of our church that we give it ten per cent of what we make. But why should we? What does the church do for us? Not a danged infernal tarnation thing! Why should we give money to build temples in Manti or Logan, or pay fat salaries to the leaders?"

"Tithing," said Nephi, "also goes to feed the old and care for the sick, and to send missionaries over the world."

"Just the same, some of the authorities is getting wealthy while we work for them. Brigham said nobody was to be rich. It ain't right."

"Brother Alonzo, have you any other complaints?"

"He could complain all day."

"Alonzo, set down and shut up your jib."

"I'll speak my mind," said Alonzo, "and I ain't finished yet. There's crookedness in this Order. There's stealing. There's favorites. When I go to the store, I get the worst; but if members of the Council go, then things are picked over and they get the best there is."

"That's a lie," said the manager of the store.

"It ain't. It stands to reason the men with the best jobs gets the best food and clothes. It's always been that way in this world."

"I'll trade jobs with you. You run the store and I'll run the mill."

"You couldn't," said Alonzo. "You don't know how."

"Brother Alonzo, have you any more complaints?"

"Yes, but I've made enough for one day. I don't like how things is run in this Order and I ain't going to stay in it."

"You don't have to."

"But if I leave, what do I get?"

"I move," said Nephi, "that the Council decide what is a fair share in money and goods to give Brother Alonzo, and that it be given to him."

"But who says what is fair?"

"The Council will say, and you will take that or nothing!" Nephi was angry. Knowing that he was about to lose his hot temper, he paused for a long moment and gazed at his people; but when he spoke again, his voice shook with rage. "This is a hell of a time for the saints to be bellyaching! The other United Orders are going to pieces or have already been grabbed up by a handful of greedy men! I won't let that happen here. We'll continue to take care of the old and the sick and to be brothers in a gospel of love or I'll wash my hands of the whole damned thing and the selfish persons in Josephville can have it!"

Again he paused. When he spoke, his voice was calmer, but after a few moments it rose in thundering fury. "Again we are in grave danger from our enemies. The Federal government is determined to destroy us. There are spies everywhere. If you drive the roads you find United States marshals everywhere, some of them pretending to be farmers, or beggars walking from town to town. And here we are, our backs to the wall, and the Alonzo Jacksons can't think of anything better to do than to bellyache! Well, by the God of Israel, let them pack up and clear out! If they don't, we'll drive them out, and if they won't go, we'll make this place unsafe for them!

"Alonzo Jackson, we'll pay you and you had better hit the grit! This town is not safe for you now!" Nephi stopped, shaking with disgust and fury. "That's all I have to say. The meeting is adjourned."

CHAPTER VI

MONTH AFTER MONTH NEPHI FOUGHT TO KEEP THE JOSEPHVILLE ORDER from disintegrating, but he was making a losing fight and everyone but himself knew it. Moroni shook his wise old head, studied Joseph's revelations every evening, and looked around him at the signs of approaching chaos. After Alonzo Jackson was paid in money and goods, he left the village; and his defection touched off others who were unhappy and fearful, until, one by one, seven more families came to Nephi to claim their share.

It was less their ambition or greed within the Order than it was their restlessness, their fears and anxieties, their dread of arrest and imprisonment, their want of courage in the face of a new and mighty crusade against them. The Federal government was moving under the Edmunds Act. The number of arrests for unlawful cohabitation or polygamy was increasing; the espionage system of the gentiles was spreading to every hamlet in the valley; and street brawls between saints and gentiles were occurring almost daily in Salt Lake City. Press and pulpit in the States were again violent in denunciation, and clamored for extermination of the "Sodom in the Rocky Mountains." There was no Brigham Young to counsel and lead a terrified people; no iron man who had stopped an army in its tracks, who had threatened to burn a city to the ground, who had sent corrupt officials fleeing for their lives.

The uncertainty was all the more dreadful because nobody knew what to expect, or when or how the great blow would fall; but that overwhelming ruin was coming, very few of the saints doubted, here in Josephville or elsewhere. The apprehensive waiting had fallen like a blight on every home in Zion. It had, Nephi admitted to himself, entered like a gathering nightmare into his own home. His wives were more irritable; they quarreled incessantly and the children echoed them; they lived from day to day in gloom and doubt. That Nephi and Tim and Moroni would all be arrested they took for granted. They would be jailed.

"And what," asked Maude anxiously, "will we do then? When they put you in prison for several years, everything here will go to pieces like a straw shed in a cyclone."

"If nobody testifies against me, they can't put me in jail."

"Oh, you make us tired!" said Ruth. "There are many who will testify. Alonzo Jackson will. He told Datus Frost he intended to. And Louisa will. Mark Browe will. There will be dozens ready to testify when the time comes. Why don't we all go to Mexico? We have colonies on the Janos and Bavispe rivers. We could go to Colonia Morelos. I have relatives there."

"I won't run away."

"I know a family going to the Piedras Verdes River. They say there is a lot of fine land in the Colonia Pacheco. We could go there and be done with all this persecution from the United States."

"I tell you," said Nephi impatiently, "I won't run. Would you have all the saints pack up like cowards and leave this valley that belongs to us? God set this country aside as a home for His people. We will stay here."

"Yes, in jail," said Maude. "For fifty years we've been driven over the earth like the Jews. As Moroni says, the gentiles recognize two sides all right: their side and the wrong side. It will always be that way."

"My grandfather does not intend to run."

"But he admits we can't fight the government, now that Brigham is dead."

"We will fight," said Nephi with desperate patience. "It's all we can do. God will show us a way out."

"You make me tired," said Ruth, studying her jeweled hands. "Nephi, I don't like to say it but it seems to me you like to be blind."

"What do you mean?" he asked, looking at her with eyes weary from lack of sleep.

"I mean you're always howling about spies—but never see those right in your own house."

That indiscreet statement brought Nephi to his feet. He strode over and looked down at Ruth, his face turning dark red with anger. "Ruth, what are you saying?"

"The truth," she said, but his eyes frightened her. "If you don't believe me, ask Maude."

For a long moment he gazed at Ruth and then turned slowly to look at Maude. "What does she mean?"

"I guess she means Chloe."

For several moments Nephi looked at one wife and then the other, trying to understand what they meant. "Where," he asked at last, "is Genet?"

"Over at Tim's."

"Tell her to come here."

When a little later Genet entered with Ruth, her face was flushed by excitement. She knew why she had been summoned. When Nephi wanted the whole blunt truth of a matter he always turned to her.

"Genet," he said, "what is this gossip about Chloe?"

Genet was so overcome that she lost her voice. She could only stare helplessly at the angry face of her husband and make funny spasmodic movements of her lips.

"Speak!" Nephi thundered.

Genet coughed and sputtered and strove to speak.

Ruth said calmly: "You can see the truth in her face."

"What truth?" he demanded. "Why doesn't someone speak out? Must I go to my mother to learn what you're afraid to tell me?" Observing that Genet was still speechless, he swung to Ruth. "Well?"

"I'll tell you," said Maude, who had more courage than the other two. "Chloe has deceived you."

"Deceived me! How?"

"I should think you could guess that. Are you a blind man? Is your faith the faith of a little child? Can't you see a thing when it's right under your nose as broad as a house and as long as a river?"

Still in the dark, Nephi gazed from wife to wife, wondering what they were driving at. "Genet, how has she deceived me?"

"Oh, good Lord!" Maude cried. "Do you want us to write it down for you and draw it? We mean Mark Browe."

"Mark Browe," he said, staring at Maude. Then he swung to Genet. "What does she mean?"

"Well," said Genet, still flushed and agitated, but in control of a weak voice, "she means— I guess you know what she means. It looks like Chloe is going to have a child."

Nephi looked around him and saw a chair. He went to it and sank weakly, with a hand to his forehead. "A child? And what if she is?"

For a long moment he was silent, gazing at the floor; and his wives looked at him, Genet with compassion, Maude with wonder, and Ruth with gentle scorn. In a lost voice he asked: "Isn't it my child?" There was no answer. "Isn't it?" he asked again. He looked at Genet.

"We don't think so," Genet said.

Slowly, deliberately, in a way that chilled them, he rose to his feet. He looked around him as if unable to realize where he was. Then in a voice terrible in its quietness he asked: "Are you sure?"

"Pretty sure," said Genet.

He looked at Maude. "Are you sure?"

"As sure as I want to be."

And then to Ruth: "Are you sure?"

"Ask Chloe."

"Where is she?"

"As usual, over in the city."

With icy malice Maude said: "She's still looking for an Ascot tie and a linen duster. She thinks you'd look handsome in an Ascot tie."

"When will she be back?"

"It's hard to say. This afternoon, I guess."

Genet spoke. "Nephi, now don't lose your temper. That will do no good."

"Of course it won't," said Ruth. "If she wants that gentile, let her have him."

The three wives were gazing intently at their husband; and in the mind of all three was the thought that Chloe was his favorite. She was younger, prettier, more charming. In the minds of all three was also the thought that they would not want to be in Chloe's shoes this afternoon.

"It might be best," said Genet, "for you not to see her for a few days. It will do no good to lose your temper."

"What?" he said. He had not understood. He was thinking of Chloe and remembering all her journeys to the city. He had thought she went only because she was young and gay and liked to shop in the better stores. "What time is it?"

Ruth looked at a clock. "Two."

"Will Mark Browe be with her when she comes?"

"Sometimes he is," said Genet.

The tactless Maude spoke next. "Nephi, don't you think you've been awfully dumb? Why didn't you see this a long time ago?"

"Because," said Genet with humorless loyalty that infuriated Maude, "he is not suspicious. He has work to do besides watching lollygagging women."

That wifely defense fetched a sly smile to Ruth's long face.

Nephi went to the door. "I'm going to see grandfather. When Chloe comes, let me know."

While Nephi told his grandfather what had happened, the old patriarch stroked his armful of beard and gazed thoughtfully at his grandson. His bright old eyes twinkled. "I knew it all the time," he said.

"You knew it? You knew my wife was adulterous and never told me!"

"Nephi, there has always been a lot of adultery among the saints. I'm used to it. Plural marriage is kind of hard on the sisters. Did you ever think of that?"

"Hard on them how?"

"Well," said Moroni, smiling out of the wisdom of nearly a century, "I never did see eye to eye with Brigham in some things. He felt a wife should be patient and wait—even if she waited forever. Some of his, I think, did. Women are animals, Nephi, just like you and me. They have appetites too. If a man has forty-four wives, as Heber Kimball had, then he's in for a lot of trouble. Forty-four women," said Moroni sagely, "just about have to have forty-four men to keep them happy—and usually that many can't do it. I sometimes think the Lord doesn't know much about women." Still tugging at his long beard, Moroni asked: "How often did you visit Chloe?"

"I don't know. As often as I could."

"Well, she's young and full of life. Some women live for children, some for men, some for clothes, but mighty few of them live for the Lord. Chloe is a woman who lives for men. Do you love her very much?"

"Yes, I suppose I do."

"You'd better let her go. She'll never be happy until she has a man all by herself. And maybe," he added waggishly, "she won't be then."

"But I love her."

"I know. I loved a woman once but a gentile got her. In the Lord's plan, such things happen." Moroni reached out with his cane and thrust at his grandson. "And don't go and beat the living daylights out of Browe. It won't do any good."

"Just the same, that's what I intend to do."

Moroni chuckled. With bright twinkling eyes he gazed at his grandson. "If it will make you feel better, do it; but when you're as old as I am, you'll know it's plain damn foolishness."

"Tell me," said Nephi, "how you knew about this before I did."

"In Nauvoo and across the plains and here I've seen many things that I hope never get in history books. I've lived with women for more than sixty-five years. I know a lot about them, now that I'm too old for it to do me any good. Besides, my son, handsome men like Browe don't keep calling for the fun of it."

"He's a spy. I thought that's what he came for."

"I guess that was part of it."

"Grandfather, in our church, adultery is the worst sin next to murder. Chloe can't save her soul unless she sheds her own blood. You know that."

Moroni wagged his head owlishly, remembering the blood atonements of thirty years ago. "Just give her your blessing and let her have him. It's for God to punish—or forgive."

"But her soul——"

"No. I've never believed the Almighty is as unforgiving as Brigham did. I think He will find a way to bring the sinners into heaven." Moroni prodded again with his stick. "In fact, I think hell will be a pretty empty place when all is said and done. It wouldn't surprise me if Satan doesn't have a single tenant."

"I don't know," said Nephi, "what has happened to you. Grandfather, I think you're getting soft."

"Age," said Moroni. "When we're young we fight, and when we're old we forgive."

"But blood atonement is a part of our doctrine. If you throw that out——"

"Nephi, I'm an old man and I'll soon face my God. I expect to learn that I misunderstood Him in a lot of ways—especially when I was young."

"Well, I'll see what Father has to say."

The gloomy Tim was not so charitable as his philosophic father. His deeply lined face drew into a terrible scowl and his unhappy eyes darkened.

"All sinners should be punished," he said. "She has sinned."

"Of course she has. But how should she be punished?"

"If she was my wife I'd beat her head off. And as for that sneaking gentile spy, I hope you don't intend to let him get away."

Nephi felt anger rising again. His whimsical old grandfather had made the matter seem almost trivial; but his father placed it, as Brigham used to, in the category of the damnable.

"But if I beat the daylights out of Browe, it will give the gentiles an excuse to come out here and make trouble. He belongs to the most powerful faction in the city."

"Trouble is coming anyhow. Have things reached the point where the scurvy devils can seduce our wives and go off whistling?"

"I hope not."

"Then do your duty as a husband and a saint."

"You'll do nothing of the kind," said Fanny, entering from the kitchen. "You had no business to marry such a silly giggle-face. Let her go. We have enough worries without bothering about what happens to her soul."

"But we were speaking of Mark Browe," said Nephi stiffly.

"Let him go too. Brigham Young used to say a scared enemy was of more value than a thousand dead ones."

"I suppose," said her son caustically, "he'll be scared if I give him my wife and my blessing!"

"Much more than he will be if you beat him. Just let them both go and wash your hands of them."

"She's here," said a voice at the door, and Nephi turned to see Genet's red and anxious face. "They've come," she added, whispering hoarsely.

"Did he come with her?"

"Yes."

Nephi turned to his father. "You coming over?"

"Why should I? Do you need help to flog a scurvy cur like him?"

"No."

"Don't kill him," said Tim gravely. "Just put the fear of hell in him."

"Do nothing of the kind," said Fanny, going with her son to the door. "Tell her to pack her duds and get out—and let him go with her."

The moment Nephi entered his house, he knew by Chloe's face that she suspected the truth. She stood at the far side of the room as if prepared to flee; but Mark Browe, apparently unalarmed, was sitting, with one of Maude's children on his lap. With Genet behind him, peering around,

Nephi stood in the doorway and looked across the room at his youngest wife. She turned white under his stare and shrank away, her hands feeling along the wall for a door as she withdrew.

"Stay where you are!" said Nephi.

Hearing the voice, Mark looked up; and then, seeing the rage in Nephi's face, he rose slowly to his feet. For a long moment, nobody moved or spoke. Chloe cowered by the wall. Maude and Ruth sat nervously, affecting to be attentive to the children around them. Mark Browe gazed steadily at Nephi.

"Send all the children out," Nephi said.

Maude rose hastily and began to herd the children out, behaving as if she were driving geese. She led and shoved them through the rear door. In the yard they made noisy outcry; and after a moment one of them climbed to a window and flattened his nose, gazing in.

Nephi now advanced. "Come over here," he said to Chloe. She came fearfully, trembling from head to feet. Her face was white. Her pale blue eyes looked glazed with terror.

"What is the meaning of this?" asked Mark.

"Shut up!" Nephi did not look at him. He was gazing steadily at his wife as she slowly came forward to meet him. When they came face to face, Nephi laid hands on her trembling shoulders. "Look at me." Chloe strove to but her gaze fell; and then, hurt by his clutch on her flesh, she turned to escape. His hands closed on her shoulders and she stiffened. "Look at me." She raised eyes that were wide and terrified in her white face. "Is it true?" She did not speak. *"Is it true?"* he roared.

"What?" she asked, speaking as if his hands were on her throat.

"Have you been adulterous with this man?" She swung away with a cry of pain, but again his powerful hands turned her and shook her until she faced him. "Have you?"

Her answer was so low that he barely heard it. "Yes."

"Are you going to have a child?"

"Yes," she whispered. She was so weak now that she would have fallen if his hands had not supported her.

"Is it his child?"

"Yes." She was not looking at him. Her head had sunk to her breast as if she had fainted.

For a long moment Nephi held her in his powerful grasp, gazing at her, realizing the truth. Then, suddenly, he released her and she fell to the floor as if her legs were broken. Without looking down at her, he swung to face Browe.

"You low gentile spy! I give you the hospitality of my home—even to you, an enemy; and you sneak around——"

"Wait a minute!" cried Mark. His swarthy face had turned pale but he seemed unafraid. "Chloe and I love one another."

"You liar!"

"Ask her."

Nephi turned to look at his wife where she lay as if dead. "Chloe, is it true?"

"I think she has fainted," Maude said.

"Fetch me some water!" cried Nephi.

Both Genet and Ruth strove to move but were helpless. They were at the point of swooning too. Maude rose, feeling dizzy and half-blind, and went for a pail of water. She fetched the pail to Nephi; and in one terrible deluge he flung the entire contents into Chloe's face. She gasped and turned over. Her eyes fluttered and opened, and she tried to sit up. Observing that she was only partially restored, Nephi said:

"Fetch me another pail!"

Maude ran to the kitchen and brought a full bucket; but before Nephi could hurl it, Browe took his arm.

"I think," he said quietly, "she can answer now."

Nephi gazed at her. "Chloe, do you hear me?"

"What?" she said, and shook her drenched face and hair. "What is this?" she asked, and exploring fingers touched her wet breast.

Nephi set the bucket down and grasped her arms. He raised her to her feet. Then he saw that the fear in her eyes had yielded to insanity that was awful to look at.

"What is this?" she asked, and again her fingers plucked strangely at her breast.

"She's out of her mind," said Maude.

Nephi stared at Chloe to be sure she was not acting; whereupon, convinced that she was not, he swung again to Browe, resolved to flog that man within an inch of his life. But at this moment a calm voice said: "Don't be a fool, Nephi." Everyone but Chloe turned to the door. It was Moroni. He was standing there like a venerable patriarch, gently stroking his beard.

"Maybe," he said, slowly advancing, "they do love one another. That's the first thing to find out." He came up and looked at Browe. "Are you sure you love this woman?"

"I am."

"Or like a lot of the gentiles, did you just want to seduce a Mormon wife?"

"I answered your question."

"How long have you loved one another?"

"A long while."

"Why didn't you say so when you first found it out?"

Mark looked around him—at Chloe who was being walked by Maude and Ruth, at Genet who was weeping, at Nephi. Then his gaze met Moroni's. "Moroni McBride, you and I see life differently. We are enemies on that account. I am, as your grandson has said this afternoon, a spy—but we are all spies now in this fight to a finish. I kept coming here for reasons that will be clear to you when you are brought into court. Besides that, Chloe wanted it kept a secret because she was afraid of Nephi and because she argued she was already married."

"She is."

"But not according to the laws of the land."

"Never mind your gentile laws!" said Moroni sharply. "Do you intend to marry this woman?"

"If she will marry me."

"Or do you intend to desert her?"

"I answered you."

"Mark Browe, if this had happened thirty years ago——"

"Oh, yes!" cried Mark impatiently. "You needn't tell me! I'd be dead now. One of Brigham's avengers would have seen to that. But we have the whip hand now, Moroni McBride, and your destroying angels don't scare us. They all died with Brigham Young."

"Not all," said a voice.

They turned to see Tim in the doorway. He advanced, his gaze on Browe; but Moroni thrust at him with his cane and said:

"Stand back, son. I'll handle this." To Browe he said: "If you love this woman, take her. We do not tolerate adulterers among the McBrides."

"Adulterer!" cried Mark scornfully.

Moroni quietly tapped his arm. "I said never mind. We want to be rid of both of you as soon as possible—and don't ever show your face in Josephville again." Still speaking quietly, Moroni turned to Maude and asked: "Is she herself now?"

"I think so."

"Fetch her here."

They brought Chloe over. Moroni took her arm and brought her face to face with Browe. "Chloe, do you love this man?"

"Of course I love him!" With a cry she went to Mark and he put an arm around her. Then, her lips curling, her pale blue eyes flashing with scorn and contempt, she looked at Nephi, at Moroni, at Tim. "If you want to know what I think of you, I hate you! I despise you! You told me all gentiles were sinful and wicked and I believed your stuff until I met an intelligent man—not a man," she said, addressing Nephi, "who believes in golden plates and a Urim and Thummim and harems and bastards! He made me see all your silly religion for what it is. It's cheap and shoddy and contemptible and nasty——"

"That will do," said Moroni.

"Oh, shut up! I'm talking now! When we get you all in court for your adulterous carnal vices—vices!" she cried wildly, stamping her feet. "Then you can talk! Then you can tell your polygamous God all about it! Then——"

"Maude," Moroni said, "go pack her things. Nephi, hitch a team."

Nephi turned abruptly and left the house, and Maude went to Chloe's room. Genet was shaking terribly and moaning, her face bowed to her arms. Ruth was pale but in control of herself. Mark turned with his arm around Chloe and led her outside; but at the door she looked back and said to Moroni:

"Wait till we see all you adulterous sinners in court!"

When the carriage came, Moroni said he would drive them to the city; and he climbed to the front seat, and Mark and Chloe took the rear seat. Without farewell or another word spoken, the carriage drove away, while Nephi and Tim and Maude stood in the yard and watched it disappear. Then Maude looked at her husband and entered the house; but for several moments Nephi stood there, gazing in the direction the buggy had taken. Then, moving like a man suddenly old, he entered the house and stood for a little while, gazing around him. Genet still sat in shuddering grief. Maude and Ruth had gone upstairs.

A few minutes later, Nephi entered Chloe's room and softly closed the door. He looked at the bed, the windows, the walls, behaving like a man who had returned after long absence and was trying to recognize what he had formerly known. He turned to the closet where Chloe had kept her things. There was nothing in it except an old bonnet, a piece of dotted veil, a strip of blue ribbon. Still, he observed at last, there was something more.

On a high shelf above the nails was a small box, wrapped in pink paper and tied with green cord that had end tassels. He reached up and took the box in his hands and turned it over and over, wondering what it was; and then, deciding to open it, he gently unfastened the string and unwrapped the paper and took the lid off. What he saw made him stiffen. It was a handsome Ascot tie—a broad scarf of fine pale blue silk. In its folds was a lovely tie pin. For several minutes Nephi stood in the closet, holding the scarf in his hands and looking at it, softly touching it; then he returned it, wrapped and tied the box and set it on the shelf. He looked at the bonnet, the veil, the ribbon; and after touching the ribbon and hesitating, he smelled of it and recognized Chloe's powder. He folded it carefully and put it into a pocket of his vest.

CHAPTER VII

NEPHI'S HOUSE WAS NOT THE SAME AFTER CHLOE FLED WITH HER LOVER. Nobody was the same. Genet looked as if she had aged overnight. Ruth took her spite out on the furniture, declaring that they had to put up with the worst assortment of odds and ends in Josephville. Nephi had never thought much about the furnishings in a house: the pioneers had used what they could find and had made the most of what they had; and that which had been brought across the plains long years ago had been broken and mended and scarred until it looked almost as crude as that which the most unskilled craftsman had made with hammer and axe.

At one side of his huge living room stood a long case clock, decorated in green lacquer. On one side of it was a paneled oak settee, and on the other a block-front bureau. All three had been so battered and broken and misused that they were ugly to look at and of little service. The thirty chairs were a most ungainly assortment. Among those that were only homemade benches and stools were a rush bottom, a Windsor, and a Phyfe dog-foot, all as awkward and out of place as the lacquered clock had formerly been in a one-room log cabin. Yes, he admitted, looking at the relics of migration or crude tools, the room did look as if it had been furnished with second-hand junk.

"Right now," he said, "there are more important things than furniture."

"But you have money. Why don't you buy us some decent stuff? There is nice furniture in some of the gentile stores."

"To hell with the gentile stores!"

He left the house, having more important things on his mind. More than two years had passed since the Edmunds law was enacted, and during that time, matters in Zion had been ominously quiet. A few of the brethren had been arrested. A few had fled. There had been a few street fights in Salt Lake City and in southern towns. But Nephi knew—and his sagacious grandfather knew—that this quietness was only a lull before the storm. The gentiles were marshaling their forces, sending spies to gather evidence, preparing their grand juries; and before long they would close in. No power under heaven could stop them, or prolong the day when the blow would fall.

It fell in Josephville a little sooner than Nephi had expected. He was lying in bed early one morning, listening to birds in the trees outside, when he was fetched bolt upright by an infernal racket. At first he thought it came from his father's house, and then from Moroni's. He was holding his breath and listening when Genet thrust a white face into his room.

"Nephi, good God! Hurry!"

"What is it?"

"The officers! They're trying to arrest your father!"

Leaping from the bed, Nephi dressed in such haste that he put his shirt on wrongside out and forgot his socks. He seized a pistol and slipped it into a coat pocket and rushed downstairs. At full speed he left the house and ran toward his father's, but when almost at the door he stopped short. At this moment the door was flung open and a man was catapulted out, literally head over heels. He struck the earth on his face and shoulders and rolled, clawing and cursing, and a moment later sprang up. Blood was bursting from a wound in his forehead and drenching his face with crimson stain. That much Nephi had observed when a second man left the house in such haste that his knees buckled under him and he skidded and sprawled. In the doorway appeared the embattled Fanny, her clothes torn, her hair scattered like a gypsy's; and behind her was Tim.

Glancing at the two men, one of whom sat as if dazed while the other with an open palm mopped at his face, Nephi advanced and stared at his mother.

"What is the trouble?"

"Trouble!" snorted Fanny. "Those snoops and spies walked right in without knocking! The scurvy louses don't have a search warrant or any other kind!"

"What do they want?"

"Why don't you ask them?"

The man who had been sitting now rose to his feet. For a horrified moment he gazed at his companion who was half-blind from the blood that jetted out and gushed down his face. Then he turned to Nephi.

"We are officers!" he shouted furiously.

"What do you want?"

"We came to arrest Timothy McBride!"

"For what?"

"You damned well know what! Unlawful cohabitation and polygamy!"

"You infernal liar!" cried Fanny.

"Do you have a warrant?"

"We don't need a warrant!"

"You gentile louse, you'll need a warrant if you ever enter my house again!"

"What happened?" asked Nephi of the man who had spoken.

"What happened!" he howled, struggling between disgust and rage. "What does it look like? They threw us out!"

Nephi restrained a smile. "Well, you'd better go back where you came from and stop breaking into respectable homes."

"Breaking in! I tell you we're officers! You're resisting the law!"

"If you want to arrest anyone here, bring a warrant."

"We don't need a warrant," said the man, advancing. Unexpectedly he stopped and looked again at his bleeding companion. "Jim, you hurt much?"

"I guess I am," said Jim. "I'm bleeding like a stuck hog."

"What did she hit you with?"

"I don't know," said Jim, trying to stanch the flow of blood. "It felt like a sadiron or an axe. I'd better go to a doctor."

The other man took Jim by his arm. "We'll be back," he said. "We'll arrest the whole stinking caboodle of you."

"All right," said Nephi, "but bring warrants."

When the men had disappeared, he turned to his mother; and after staring at her for a moment, his sense of Irish fun got the best of him and he laughed. "What did you hit that fellow with?"

"A piece of stove wood."

"Did they enter without knocking?"

"Of course they did. They marched right in, as big as life and grinning all over. It didn't take me long to knock their grins off."

"I think you must have hit him with a kingbolt." Genet and Maude and Ruth, followed by children, had gathered round; and to Genet Nephi said: "Tell Grandfather to come here. We must decide what to do."

A few minutes later, the clan had gathered in secret meeting in Tim's house. "What are we to do?" asked Nephi. "Shall we submit?"

"We'll have to," said Moroni, pulling his beard more vigorously this morning. "They'll arrest Tim but I don't think they can convict him."

"Why not?" asked Tim.

"Because nobody will testify against you."

"Oh, like hell they won't! There'll be a whole mob ready to swear to lies."

"Nobody has to swear to lies," said Nephi. "A lot of persons know that we all practice plural marriage."

"Why," asked Ruth, "doesn't Tim go away somewhere?"

"Because," said Tim, "I won't run."

"We decided long ago that we won't run. Too many are running now."

"Then they'll arrest all of you."

"I think," said Moroni, "they'll arrest only Tim now. If they can convict him, then they'll come for Nephi and me."

"Why," asked Sarah, who had been weeping, "do they pick on Tim?"

"They have to pick on one of us."

"I think they're after Tim first," said Moroni, "because they know he was once a Danite." He looked around him. "Where is Louisa?"

Others looked around and realized that Louisa was not present.

"Genet, go to the cottage and fetch her."

"I think it best," said Ruth, "for us women to go away. I have some friends leaving for Mexico and I could go there. Maude can hide with her relatives up in Ogden. Genet could stay here."

"Just as you please," said Moroni. "My wives are staying with me. If I go to jail, they go too."

"But there's no sense in that."

"It's the way they want it."

Genet returned to say that Louisa was not in her cottage. They all looked at Tim.

"She isn't?" said Tim. "Then where in hell is she?"

"I don't know. Her bed wasn't slept in last night."

The members of the clan gazed at one another. "I smell a rat," said Moroni. "Tim, where's your wife?"

"Good God, I don't know. Fanny, where is she?"

"My idea," said Fanny, "is she's a spy, just as Chloe was. I imagine you'll find them together."

"Chloe," said Nephi impatiently, "was not a spy."

"Son, come to your senses. When you are tried, Chloe will be there to testify against you."

"I don't believe it."

"I do," said Ruth.

"When," said Fanny, "a man gets wrapped up in a woman, he can't see plain daylight. Louisa and Chloe were both spies. Let's not talk about them. Let's plan what to do. I won't let any more snoops in my house, not if they have a stack of warrants as big as Mount Ensign."

"I guess," said Moroni to Nephi, "you had better hide. When they come back they'll arrest all of us, wives included."

"Not me," said Fanny.

Ruth rose and came to Nephi's side. "Come over home. I want to talk to you."

Nephi looked at Maude and Genet. "All right, we'll go over and plan something. Grandfather, keep your eye peeled. Let me know the moment you see them coming."

When Nephi was alone with his wives, Ruth spoke her mind. "What's the sense," she asked indignantly, "for Maude and me to stay here? If we stay, you'll be arrested too. If we go, they can't arrest you if you have only one wife in the house. So we had better go—and go right now."

"Is that," asked Nephi, turning to Maude, "the way you feel?"

Maude was uneasy under his gaze. "Well——"

"I guess," said Genet, "you intend for me to take care of all your children."

"I," said Ruth acidly, "will take my children with me. Why should you complain? You'll have *our* husband all to yourself."

Genet reddened. "Of course, if you take your children——"

"Don't think I'd ever leave them with you. If you don't like that arrangement, you go and I'll stay."

"Oh, no, I won't. I married Nephi first. According to the law I'm his wife."

That crass statement made Ruth choke with fury. "By God, so you throw that in our faces! Well, I won't stay now! I wouldn't live around you!"

"But it's true," said Genet, quietly triumphant.

"And I say you lie!"

"Shut it up!" Nephi roared. "You are all my wives, one as much as the

« 682 »

other. You make the Lord ashamed of you. If Ruth and Maude want to go away——"

"I'm going," said Ruth. "I won't live with this nasty sour-face."

"If you go," said Nephi, frowning at the interruption, "I don't see how they could convict me—not if I was living with only one wife."

"Especially," interposed Genet, "if she was your lawful wife."

Nephi looked at her with angry disgust. "You're no more my lawful wife than Ruth and Maude are. Get that hellish notion out of your mind."

"But I am," said Genet stubbornly. "If they stay, you'll be arrested for adultery. If I stay——"

"And I say you're wrong! You sound like a damned gentile."

"I'm going," said Ruth. "If I ever come back, I'll have a house of my own. I wouldn't live with her another day to save my soul."

"By God!" Nephi roared, getting to his feet. "Do women ever have anything on their minds but their own vanities? The whole church could be falling to pieces, the gospel trampled under the feet of sinners, the temple burned to the ground—and you'd still be fighting one another! The spirit of God isn't in you. I say to shut up your infernal meanness or you can go to hell across lots and I'll be glad to see the last of you. This is no time for spite. It's a time to do what is best for all of us. If Ruth and Maude want to leave for a while, then pack your things in a hurry."

"If I tried," said Ruth, "I couldn't pack them half as fast as I want to."

"Or one-tenth as fast," said Genet, "as I want you to. And don't forget all your brass jewels and tin diamonds."

"You shrew," said Ruth, turning to look at her. "You homely shrew."

"I'm no homelier than you, you long horse-face!"

"Silence!" Nephi thundered. "Ruth, pack your things and shut up!"

Genet rocked quietly while the two women went to their rooms. A smile curved her unlovely mouth; there was a gleam of triumph in her large pale eyes.

Loading clothes and children into the carriage until it looked as if it would sink under the burden, Ruth and Maude drove out of Josephville, the former to join friends a few miles out, and the latter to drive to Ogden and return the carriage from there. They left hastily and without farewells. They had not been gone an hour when Lura dashed in to tell her father officers were coming. For a moment Nephi fingered the pistol in his coat, wondering if he should take it with him. After thinking of the matter, he decided to go unarmed; and he entered Chloe's room and laid the gun behind the package on the top shelf. Then he left by the back door and hastened to Moroni's.

Tim and Fanny were there; and Kate, Maggie and Agatha had come down from their rooms and now sat in their rockers, looking very old and unalarmed. Sarah had locked herself in Louisa's cottage. Nephi was excited and knew it. Tim scowled and nursed a dark anger that gave a dangerous gleam to his eyes. Fanny, still embattled and ready, folded great arms across her breast and waited.

Going to the window, Nephi saw the approaching men. They were coming in a buggy; and as far as he could make out, there were five of them, all heavily armed. It was well known that the McBride clan was one of the most fearless and hotheaded in the valley. Not for many years had gentiles molested them or invaded their privacy, with the exception of Mark Browe, a ubiquitous spy who prowled everywhere. These men approaching now did not seem to be in any hurry to fulfill their mission.

"They are going to father's place," said Nephi, reporting from the window. A few moments later he added: "This time they are knocking."

"I should have stayed there," said Fanny, "to cave their skulls in."

"Now," said Nephi, "they're looking around them. One of them is peeking through a window. He has a pistol in his hand."

Moroni chuckled. "Do they look scared?"

"They don't look very bold. But every man has three guns on him."

"What," asked Fanny, "are the sons-of-bitches doing now?" Her swearing made old Kate look at her.

"They're still knocking and peeking. Two of them, with a pistol in each hand, have gone to the back door. Can you hear them pounding?"

"Oh, yes, we'n hear their damned racket. If they pound on Louisa's door, Sarah will die. If I was there, I'd take the guns out of their hands and curry their dandruff with them."

"They're coming here," said Nephi, his voice gathering excitement. "Grandfather, you'd better meet them."

Moroni grasped his stick and rose. He went to the door and opened it before there was a knock; and five startled men faced him. Every one of them had a pistol in each hand as if ready to set upon a nest of brigands.

"Hello, gentlemen."

"Hello," said one. "Are you Moroni McBride?"

"I am. What can I do for you?"

"We're looking for your son Timothy. We have a warrant for his arrest."

"On what charge?"

"Unlawful cohabitation with women and lascivious polygamous practice."

"What," asked Moroni, "are you? A firing squad? You'd better put those guns away."

"We'll do as we please about that. Is your son in there?"

"Tim, are you here?"

A deeply angry voice replied: "Tell the sons-of-bitches I'm here all right."

"Yes, gentlemen, he seems to be here."

The leader stepped forward. "We've come to arrest him."

"Just a minute," said Moroni. "This is my home. I don't allow anyone to come in flourishing pistols at me. Put your guns up."

"By God, no," said another man. "You might have a whole bunch of armed men in there."

"If I have, your pistols wouldn't do you much good. But I haven't. There isn't a gun in the house. It looks like you have all the guns in Zion in your hands or strapped to your belts."

"Send your son out here and tell him to come with his hands up."

Tim rose and went over to the door. "To hell with you. I put my hands up for nobody—and least of all for a gang of infernal jack-nasties like you."

"Watch your tongue, Tim McBride. You're talking to officers of the law."

"To hoodlums out of hell. Let's see your warrant."

The leader produced a paper and Moroni looked at it. "Do you have a warrant for me?"

"Not today. We want Timothy McBride first. He used to belong to the Danites or Destroying Angels or Sons of Dan or Daughters of Gideon—or whatever they were called." The leader looked at Moroni and grinned. "We'll get you later. We can't prove yet that these old women aren't your sisters as you say; but we have the evidence on your son. All right, Timothy McBride, come out!"

"I'll come when you put those smoke irons away."

One of the men sheathed his pistols; and observing him, the leader and the others did likewise. Then Tim stepped past his father, and at once two men seized his arms.

"Stop that!" Tim cried furiously, shaking them off. "Don't put your gentile paws on me!"

"Oh, all right," said the leader agreeably. He turned to Moroni and grinned. "We'll be after you one of these-here days. And Nephi too. Tell him the good news."

As Tim was led to the buggy, the clan gathered at the door and windows to watch him go.

"Can't we get him out on bail?"

"They won't accept bail."

Believing that officers would return for him and his grandfather, Nephi left the house, resolved to hide until darkness came. He spent the afternoon in the basement of the Frost home, and a part of the time Datus sat in the cellar to talk with him.

"Danged if I'n see, Nephi, how they'n arrest you with only one wife now. You think Chloe would testify?"

"I don't know, Datus."

"Well, a lot of us will swear that one wife is all you have. If they can't find any more they'll be stuck. How you figger they arrested your pappy and not you or Moroni?"

"I guess they figure they can convict him. Besides, he used to belong to the Danites and they want to get all the old Danites first."

"That's to protect their own skins, I guess. Nephi, if they arrest you, what'll happen to the Order?"

"It's going to pieces anyway."

"Well, cheer up. Too many people look for the worst and then make the worst of it. How about a hunk of cream cake?"

"No thanks, Datus." Nephi smiled wanly at his friend. "I feel down at the heel today."

"It sort of took my appetite too. It ain't right for us to come out and make a desert blossom like a rose, as Brigham said we would, and then have to give in to our enemies again. If we went to the South Seas they'd follow us. Did you know some of the brethren are going to Canada or Mexico?"

"Yes. Ruth is going with some of them."

"They're all scared stiff. When they hear about Tim, Josephville will have a lot of empty houses."

"Their faith is weak, Datus."

"Well, mebbe. But, by darn, year after year of this would weaken any faith. I feel kind of wobbly myself. Why in hell does the Almighty let our enemies keep after us? Brigham used to say it was to test us like Job was tested. But it's been fifty years now and that seems a tolerable time to find out what He wants to know." Datus shook his head and took a quid of tobacco. "Have they arrested President Taylor yet?"

"I think he's hiding. Most of the leaders are hiding now."

"That won't do any good. They can't hide forever. Nephi, what is this segregation law I read about?"

"Oh, that. Well, Datus, they try us on two charges—unlawful cohabitation and polygamy. They can put us in jail longer by convicting us on two offenses."

"It sounds queer. That would be like trying a man for murdering another and then for killing him."

"Just about."

"And after they shoot him for murdering a man, I guess they'd prop him up and shoot him again for killing the man. First thing we know, they'll be trying the saints for every wife he has. If he has thirty, he'll get ninety years."

"Only eighty-seven," said Nephi dryly. "They'd accept the first."

When darkness came, Nephi went to seek his grandfather, entering quietly by the back door. Moroni was reading by the fireplace; and his three wives, sitting around him, had been lulled to sleep by his monotonous voice. But if nobody listened to him, he did not mind. He read to himself really, sometimes distinctly, but usually in unintelligible muttering as if he were almost asleep too. His wives sat around and nodded like old things in a wind and then slowly sank to rest.

When Nephi entered, Moroni looked up and took his steel-rimmed spectacles off his nose.

"Did they come back?" asked Nephi.

"No, but they will. Nephi, have you seen the speech one of our leaders made to Congress on the Edmunds law?"

"No."

"It is fine." Moroni set his glasses on his nose. "I want to read you one paragraph." Taking the *Deseret News* and peering over his glasses for a moment at his sleeping wives, the old man cleared his throat. "Listen to this. 'I am comforted, Mr. Speaker, by one reflection: that Christianity which has been so much vaunted upon this floor, and which has been held up in contradistinction to that system which many of my constituents believe in, was itself a persecuted sect, and its founder was crucified between two thieves. And from that day until the present, every man who has ever stood among his fellowmen to declare principles which came in conflict with popular ideas has, in almost every instance, had to lay down his life as proof of the sincerity of his convictions. There has been no end of false statements made on this floor concerning the people with whom I am connected; but while this flood of false statements has been pouring over the country concerning the people in Utah, scarcely a voice has been heard in their defense.'" Moroni removed his spectacles and gazed at his grandson. "Maybe our leaders back there will get some sense in their heads yet."

"Grandfather," said Nephi, drawing a chair close to the old man, "our leaders in Utah are all hiding. What can the saints do when their leaders hide? Why in hell don't they face the music and go to jail? That's what I'm willing to do."

"Joseph hid."

"But Brigham didn't."

"Oh, yes, he did. In Missouri."

"It's cowardly to hide. I think we have only one way to win—and that is for every last one of us to go to jail."

"We can never lose," said Moroni. "You should read in Joseph's revelations like I do and then you would feel stronger." He laid the newspaper down and turned for the *Doctrine and Covenants*. "Listen," he said, thumbing the pages. "'Verily, thus saith the Lord unto you my servant Joseph, that inasmuch as you have inquired of my hand to know and understand wherein I, the Lord, justified my servants Abraham, Isaac and Jacob, as also Moses, David and Solomon, my servants, as touching the principle and doctrine of their having many wives and concubines——'"

"Oh, but I've read it!" Nephi cried. "I know it by heart."

"But just listen. 'I reveal unto you a new and an everlasting covenant; and if ye abide not that covenant, then ye are damned; for no one can reject this covenant and be permitted to enter into my glory.'" A hundred or a thousand times, Moroni had read the 132nd revelation on plural or celestial marriage; and each rereading declared to him anew the folly and sin of those who now wanted to repudiate that covenant. "Nephi, no matter what persecution we suffer here, we must abide. If we do, we shall inherit thrones, kingdoms, principalities, powers and dominions to all heights and depths; for thus saith the Lord. If we do not abide in that covenant, then we are forever damned."

"Yes, I know that. You had better read it to Wilford Woodruff and some of the other apostles."

"If they give up that covenant, they will be damned. What if they do put me in jail? What if I die in jail? I will go home to the Lord and live in His glory."

"If we all went to jail, the gentiles would give up. That was Brigham's plan."

"Too many of the saints don't like jails."

Moroni was reading again and Nephi was thinking when a knock fell on the door. It was sudden and peremptory. Nephi rose, startled, but his grandfather said calmly:

"They have come. I was expecting them." He went to the door and opened it and saw two of the men who had taken Tim to jail. "Come in, gentlemen. I hope you bring good news."

"Good news! We have a warrant for your arrest."

"Well, come in. I can be ready soon."

A little abashed by such courtesy, the men entered. The three old women had been awakened, and now gazed at the intruders. Nephi stood by the fireplace. After finding the case for his spectacles, Moroni turned to the men.

"I should think," he said, twinkling at them, "the government would arrest persons it can convict."

One of the men came forward and looked at Agatha.-"Are you married to this man?"

"Of course not," she said calmly. "I'm his sister."

"Sister! Tell that to the grand jury!" He turned to Kate. "Are you married to this man?"

"Yes."

"What! Has one of you admitted she's married?" He swung to Maggie. "Are you?"

"No."

"Oh, you're another sister! Where were you born?"

"That's none of your business."

The man shrugged and turned to Moroni. "It's true," he said, "that we haven't been able to learn where these women were born, or even what their last name is. Kate, Agatha, Maggie," he said contemptuously. "That's all we know about them. But we have a warrant for you."

"Yes," said Moroni, "I understood that. Agatha, fetch my big coat. And let's see. I'll take the *Doctrine and Covenants* for I'll have a lot of time to read."

The man by the door was grinning at Nephi. "Do you," asked Nephi, "have a warrant for me?"

"Not yet. We will later."

The other man who had been staring at the old woman turned sharply to Nephi. "You!" he cried. "Where are your wives?"

"My wife is home."

"Yes, one of them. We were over there. Where are the others?"

"If you think I have others, you find them."

"You had four until Chloe left you. Where's Maude and Ruth?" When Nephi did not answer, the man said: "By God, we'll find them. We'll find them and then put you in jail too."

"Why don't you now? There are persons who will testify against me."

"Who are they? Chloe won't. And she's made Mark Browe promise that he won't. So who will?"

Nephi was astonished. So Chloe would not testify, and had asked Mark not to! "Keep hunting and you'll find witnesses."

"We'll find your other wives."

"Well, gentlemen," said Moroni, with his big coat on and books in his pockets, "I am at your service." He buttoned the coat over his long beard, stooped to kiss Kate's gray hair, and then grasped his stick and went firmly to the door.

CHAPTER VIII

ORONI WAS HELD ONLY A FEW DAYS AND THEN RELEASED, BUT TIM WAS brought to trial. Nephi wanted to find a good gentile lawyer to defend him; Moroni said it would be a waste of money and that Nephi should act as his father's attorney. Nephi decided he might as well. He had visited grand jury rooms and was familiar with the procedure; but the statement to the jury in Salt Lake City on this January day in 1885 seemed to him to set a record in bitterness.

Roger Hanson, the district attorney, said that every person tried under the Edmunds Act had been convicted. "Thirty-seven adulterous men are now in jail, and we're going to send ten thousand after them. This nation is outraged as never before by these unclean, foul, stinking harems under the American flag; these lecherous debauched nests in the name of religion and God; these innocent children born into bastardy, and these deluded women who degrade their bodies to the carnal appetites of ruttish men who insult everything decent in the civilized world!

"I say, gentlemen, that a mighty nation will exterminate with our courts if we can, with the sword if we must, this infamous blot upon American life. We have been patient too long. It has been half a century since a dissolute man named Joseph Smith took a harem and invited his henchmen to do likewise. Since then the Mormons have gone on in their whoredom, and they are taking more concubines right now, right today under our noses! They don't intend to give up these wanton pleasures, or stop skulking around like thieves to visit their shameless mistresses!

"Gentlemen, do you want your children to go on associating in the schoolroom with bastards? Do you want to realize that every second woman you meet on the streets is no better than a harlot? Do you want to apologize to visitors who come here? You do not! And today you have before you one Timothy McBride who belonged to the infamous murderous Danites in Missouri. . . ."

Nephi made no statement.

"Call," said Hanson, "Louisa Maynard."

When Tim's third wife came forward, neither Nephi nor Moroni was surprised; but Tim looked at her as if he wanted to wring her neck.

"Your name is Louisa Maynard?"

"It is."

"Is that your legal name?"

"It is."

"Are you married to Timothy McBride?"

"How could I be?" asked Louisa, looking at Tim. "He had a wife when I met him."

"Did you become one of his plural wives?"

"I did."

"Did you accept him as a husband and did he share your bed?"

"When he felt like it."

"Did you have any children by him?"

"No."

"Louisa, while you lived with him, did he live with other women also?"

"He lived with two women named Fanny and Sarah."

"As wives?"

"Of course. They both had children by him."

"Did you ever become ashamed of yourself? Didn't you feel degraded?"

"Yes, many times."

"Then why didn't you leave?"

"Because he wouldn't let me. He said my soul would be damned if I left him."

"Then he forced you to live in sin by threatening you. Did he force his other wives?"

Louisa did not like such questions or the look in Tim's eyes or the quiet meditative way in which Moroni pulled at his beard. She did not like the way Fanny was looking at her from the fourth row.

"You better ask them."

Realizing that he had forced his witness too far, Hanson turned. "I may recall this witness later. Summon the woman known as Sarah McBride."

When Sarah came forward, she looked as if she would faint at any moment. Her face was white. She went trembling to the chair and sank; and when asked to stand for the oath, she wavered and almost swooned.

"What is your name?"

"Sarah McBride," she said, speaking hardly above a whisper.

"How old are you?"

"Fifty-three."

"Are you one of the plural wives of Timothy McBride?"

"No."

"No? Then who are you?"

"I'm his sister."

"Oh, so you're his sister!" Hanson fixed her with a sardonic grin. "Are you married?"

"No."

"So you're not married! How many children do you have?"

"Four." Realizing the nature of her admission, Sarah gasped and started to leave the chair. "I meant——"

"We all know what you mean. You have four children, yet you are unmarried." Hanson turned and grinned at the jury. "Sarah McBride, who is the father of these children?"

"I—I don't know."

Nephi rose. "I object to examination of this witness. She is beside herself and in no condition to testify. She doesn't know what she's saying."

The judge frowned. "The examination will proceed."

Hanson now paced, hands behind his back, his shrewd eyes on Sarah's white face. Suddenly he swung toward her and shouted: "So you don't know who the father is!" Then in a voice softly menacing he asked: "Are you admitting that you have mothered four bastards? Are you telling us—" He broke off suddenly.

Sarah had fainted. With a sharp gasp as if too weary and frightened to live, she slumped forward and slid from her chair to the floor. Nephi sprang to her aid and carried her to Moroni's side, and Moroni put an arm around her as her head sank to his breast.

"I hope," said Nephi angrily, addressing Hanson, "that you are satisfied!"

"This isn't the first time," said Hanson blandly, "that truth has made persons faint in a courtroom. Nor is it the first time that Mormon women have told barefaced lies. Summon the woman known as Fanny McBride."

Fanny was glad to be called. She came forward, ready for battle; and when Hanson looked at her large stern face and the anger and contempt in her unwavering gaze, he was momentarily nonplussed. He realized that this time he had a fight on his hands.

"Your name, please," he said, after she had been sworn.

"Fanny McBride."

"Are you married to Timothy McBride, the defendant?"

"Of course I am."

"How long have you been married to him?"

"Forty-three years."

"That's quite a long time," said Hanson, smiling. "Where were you married?"

"That's none of your business."

The smile left Hanson's face as if it had been wiped off. He looked at the judge to learn what he thought of this huge belligerent woman.

"Are you the only wife Mr. McBride has?"

"No. He has three wives. And let me tell you something, Mr. Gentile Lawyer. He has three wives and he has been decent to all of them. The Mormons may be guilty of what you call polygamy but they don't sneak around and visit whores the way you gentiles do. They don't have just one wife that they lie to and a lot of harlots they go to bed with."

"Your honor——"

"Shut up!" Fanny cried. "I've been watching your satisfied grins this morning. You like to get some poor woman all upset in her mind and make a fool of her so that you and the judge and the jury can grin at her. Well, let me tell you something. The saints might have more than one wife; but there weren't any whores in this valley until you and your ilk came. You brought the harlots and gamblers and pimps and all the ungodly degenerate scum of the earth. Salt Lake City has a red light district now. And why? Because men like you want one. There wasn't any such disgrace when we first came to this desert and didn't have sinful gentiles to put up with. There wasn't a whore in the whole valley then. You've been running off this morning in mouth-almighty style about how sinful we are and how decent you are; but you'd better clean your own houses first and stop using women to satisfy your ungodly lusts."

"Your honor!" Hanson cried angrily. "Is the court going to allow this woman——"

"Shut up your infernal jib!" said Fanny. "I'm talking now. I'll tell you all your nasty suspicious gentile mind wants to know. Yes, Sarah is Tim's wife. She has four children and they are his children. You fine bunch of Christian gentlemen," she said, swinging to the jury, "put that down in your notebooks. Louisa is his wife too, but she's a vain cowardly woman and the McBrides are ashamed of her. Get this in your thick skull, Mr. Gentile Lawyer: Tim McBride is guilty of living up to the principles of his church and not being afraid to. Send him to jail for that. There's no need to go on with this trial. If you want to know the whole truth, why don't you call him to the stand instead of getting a scared woman to make fun of?"

"Your honor," said Hanson, now thoroughly angry, "will the court shut this woman up or find her in contempt?"

"Try to shut me up!" cried Fanny, turning to the flabbergasted judge. "I'm giving you the evidence you want so you can convict this man. I should think," she said, turning to Hanson, "you'd want me to talk. A lot of the saints come here and lie to try and keep out of jail. My husband isn't afraid of your damned old jails. You can't make us give up our principles if you put us in jail until we die. So stop dragging this trial out just to amuse yourselves and let the jury bring in a verdict of guilty."

Hanson was mopping his brow—for never before had he known a witness like this woman. The women usually evaded and lied, committed shameless perjury, denied the paternity of their children, repudiated their marriages, and did everything they could to keep their husbands out of jail. This incredible woman had the candor of a half-wit.

"Your honor, this witness is dismissed."

"Please step down," said the judge.

"So you don't like the truth!" said Fanny scornfully. "I thought you wanted all the evidence in the record in case this is appealed to the Supreme Court. Why don't you put it all in? Put in I said those old blatherskites on the Supreme Court have slept with harlots too. And our congressmen who passed this Edmunds law, how many of them have a clean conscience in their relations with women?"

"Please step down!" said the judge.

Fanny rose and stepped down but she turned to face the judge and to shake her fist at him. "Why don't you arrest me for cracking one of your snoops on the head when he sneaked into my home? If you're interested in decency in this city, why don't you arrest these gentiles for sneaking into bed with harlots? We could give you a lot of names. Do you call that decent? Do you call it civilized to make whores of women?"

"That will do!" said the judge angrily. "Go to your seat before I find you in contempt of court."

"I don't care. I'm not afraid of your stinking old jail."

"The prosecution will proceed," said the judge, looking as if he had narrowly escaped with his life. He looked over at the McBrides. Moroni was smiling and quietly stroking his beard.

"Call Timothy McBride."

Tim was still amazed by his wife's outburst. It would do no good, he reflected, to lie about the matter now; and when he was asked if he had more than one wife, he said:

"Yes, I have three."

"You admit you've been living with three women?"

"I do."

"Haven't you passed two of them off as sisters?"

"I don't remember."

"Oh, you don't remember! You don't remember if you have lied about it?"

"I've admitted," said Tim impatiently, "what you wish to prove. I won't answer arrogant questions."

"Well, you admit you've been living intimately with three women in defiance of the law. You admit you have a wife and two concubines——"

"I do not. I have three wives."

"Are you sealed to them?

"Your honor," said Hanson, turning to the judge, "for the benefit of those jurors who may not be familiar with it, I want to explain the Mormon system of temple marriage. The Mormons not only believe in polygamy. In their mysterious temple rites, a man can be sealed to his concubines for time and eternity. By sealing, as I understand it, they mean they are married for the next life as well as this one. But a man can be married to women for the next life and not for this one, or for this one and not for the next one. He can even be married to women he has never seen. Why, he can even get married for the next life to women who are dead.

"I don't," said Hanson, shrugging, "understand all this temple hocus-pocus. No gentile is admitted to temple ceremonies, but a few apostates have told what happens in those mysterious ritual chambers. When a man and a woman go to get married for eternity it seems they put on white gowns and smear one another with oil and go through a Garden of Eden scene, with the man pretending to be Adam and the woman, Eve. Someone else pretends to be God and someone else a serpent and so on. Don't ask me," said Hanson, grinning at the jury, "what all that foolishness is supposed to represent. Joseph Smith figured the business out; and when his own resourceful mind failed him he stole from the Masons. It is said that he was sealed to hundreds of women for the next world, and that Brigham Young was too. The more concubines, the merrier. It is said that in the Mormon temple there are sexual orgies more vile and lustful than any recorded in ancient history; but I don't know if that is true. The practices are kept secret.

"For the purpose of this trial it does not matter. But it is necessary to know how many wives the defendant has besides the three he admits. How many, Mr. McBride, have you?"

"I told you three."

"Are you sealed to them for the next life?"

"I can't see that that's any of your business."

"Here!" said the judge. "Defendant will show proper respect——"

"Then let him show some respect for the beliefs of a persecuted people!"

"Mr. McBride, how many women are sealed to you for the next life?"

"I refuse to answer."

"You see?" said Hanson to the jurors who had never taken their gaze off Tim. "His refusal to answer is an admission that he has been sealed to a lot of women. Mormon men grab as many concubines as they can in this life, and hunt around to find a thousand or two for the next life. If they can't find live ones, they go to the graveyards and find dead ones."

"This trial," said Nephi, rising, "is reaching a new depth in crass abusiveness."

The judge leaned forward. "How many women," he asked Tim, "have you been sealed to?"

"That is my business."

"Unless you answer, you will be found in contempt."

"What of it?" asked Tim hotly. "You'll give me the maximum for unlawful cohabitation and the maximum for polygamy. Does it matter if you add a few extra thirty- or sixty-day periods for contempt?"

The judge turned to the clerk. "The defendant is found in contempt. Make a note of it."

"Mr. McBride," said Hanson, "how many dead wives do you have?"

"Mr. Gentile Lawyer," said Tim, "I am guilty under the Edmunds law. Let the jury find me guilty. I refuse to answer any more questions."

"Dismissed. Summon Mark Browe. Just so the Mormons can't say they don't have a fair trial, I intend to prove all these cases to the hilt. Besides, your honor, more of these cases may be appealed to the Supreme Court, and it is well to have all the evidence in the record."

Mark Browe added to the record only what he saw in the McBride homes—and it was only what Fanny and Tim had already admitted. When Browe was dismissed, Nephi stepped forward, saying he would cross-examine; but he did not intend to cross-examine at all. He was very angry.

"I want it also in the record that this gentile was a spy and a seducer! Put it in the record that he was a scurvy underhanded cur, and that if I am ever brought to trial I'll sue him for stealing my wife and I'll hire the most brilliant gentile lawyers in the city!"

"Your honor, I move to strike everything he has said."

"It will be stricken."

"Why?" Nephi roared at the judge. "Don't you want the higher courts to know about the employment of contemptible seducers to sneak into respectable homes? Don't you—" Nephi stopped short. Moroni had come over and was whispering in his ear. Without saying another word, Nephi returned to his seat.

For a long moment Hanson stared at Nephi. Then he said: "Call Alonzo Jackson."

Alonzo looked as if he had been sulking and plotting insurrections ever since he left the Order. He crossed his legs, folded his arms, and scowled at Nephi who was still trembling with rage.

"Mr. Jackson, how long did you live in Josephville?"

"Nearly twenty years."

"Do you know Mr. Timothy McBride, the defendant?"

"Sure, I know him."

"Have you known him for twenty years?"

"Longer'n that."

"Were you ever in his home?"

"Many a time."

"Do you absolutely know that Mr. McBride lived with three women as his wives?"

"Sure. Everybody in Josephville knows that."

"Are you a Mormon?"

"I used to be. I ain't now."

"Why did you leave the church?"

"Oh, there's a lot of reasons. I never liked the way it was run. To tell the truth, I never took much stock in Joseph Smith's revelations—especially about polygamy. Besides, I never liked the way the McBride outfit run the United Order. They hogged it all and made the rest of us do the work."

"I see," said Hanson sympathetically. "Do you know if Moroni McBride has several wives?"

"Why, yes. Of course they're old now, and for a long time he's been callun two of them his sisters."

"What are the names of those two?"

"Agatha and Maggie."

"But you know that formerly he treated them as his wives?"

"As much as a man could know. I never saw him in bed with them but everybody knowed he did."

"Went to bed with them, you mean?"

"Sure, that's what I meant."

"Did you ever have more than one wife?"

"No. One woman was enough for me."

The judge smiled.

"Could you have had more if you had wanted them?"

"I guess I could."

"But you didn't think it was right to take more than one?"

"No, it never seemed right to me."

"That is all."

"I'll cross-examine," said Nephi, and went over to face Alonzo. "Alonzo Jackson, you just said you never took much stock in Joseph's revelation on plural marriage."

"That's what I said."

"And you just said you never wanted more than one wife. Have you forgotten all the young girls you tried to persuade to marry you—including two of my daughters? Have you forgotten the time you went to Brigham Young and asked him to help you find some wives? Have you forgotten how, ten years ago, you used to slip away from your wife and go over to Salt Lake City to the dances and try to find girls who would marry you? Have you forgotten how you complained to me one day and I said there were middle-aged women who would marry you, but you said you wanted young girls, even though at that time you were past fifty? Have you forgotten all that?"

"I don't remember nothun of the kind," said Alonzo, his eyes flickering wickedly.

"Isn't it true you left Josephville and the church because you couldn't find any girls of sixteen or eighteen who would marry you?"

"No, that ain't true."

"That's all."

"I rest the case," said Hanson, smiling at the judge. "Unless Mr. McBride intends to harangue the jury, I rest without further argument."

"Mr. McBride, do you wish to address the jury?"

"What's the use?" asked Nephi. "We rest on our rights under the Constitution, but this court recognizes no such rights. It is useless to plead to a picked jury and a prejudiced judge."

"Gentlemen," said the judge, "without leaving your seats you will arrive at a verdict." And when, a few minutes later, the foreman announced the verdict, the judge leaned across the bench and spoke to Tim.

"Mr. Timothy McBride, you have been found guilty of unlawful cohabitation and polygamous practice in defiance of the laws of this nation. The court again takes this opportunity to rebuke not only you but also that strange religious sect to which you belong; and to make clear the position of the United States in regard to the Mormon Church.

"For more than forty years the leaders of this church have disregarded those feelings of decency, those traditions of piety and righteous living, and that esteem for womanhood upon which civilization has been built. In their avowed beliefs and in their deliberate practice, they have reverted to a barbarous level of life which, no matter how widely entertained by certain ancient Jews, has for countless centuries been held in contempt by every right-thinking person. The love practices and cults of early and semi-civilized peoples constitute no sanction to deluded persons today; for if that were so, then sanction could be drawn from any pagan or barbarous custom for its emulation by any group in any period of history.

"With the so-called sanctions which Joseph Smith is supposed to have received from the Almighty God, this nation and this court have no concern except as they become a threat and a menace to the welfare of the citizens. The pagan and impious practices of the Mormon Church do now threaten the progress of this nation, do outrage cultivated sensibilities, and do furnish a vicious example to deluded or unregenerate citizens; and it has become necessary, therefore, to drive polygamy out of this city and valley. It will be driven out with all possible speed, and to that end every legitimate resource of this nation will be employed.

"It is the opinion of this court that if Joseph Smith had not used as a precedent to justify his own carnal appetite the half-civilized practices of the Jews, the Mormons would today be in possession of Nauvoo. If they had been less orthodox in their creed, less patriarchal in their practices, and less biblical in their tenets, then they would not today be rebuked by the outraged conscience of their countrymen. It is also the opinion of this court that most of the Mormon men guilty of the sin of concubinage are at heart law-abiding and decent citizens who have been deceived by a handful of leaders, among whom the most notorious and least defensible was Joseph Smith.

"The court can take note of your unfortunate delusion and of the problems which it has raised; but the office of this court is to punish and not to teach. It can express the hope that these Mormon men will come to their senses and repudiate their shameful doctrine before the agencies of the law send them all to prison. If they do not, then every polygamous person in this Territory will be arrested and jailed as fast as the officers and the courts can find and convict them.

"Mr. McBride, have you anything to say in your defense before judgment is passed upon you?"

"No, your honor."

"Then stand and hear the sentence." Tim rose to his feet. "You have been found guilty of unlawful cohabitation and of polygamous practice; and once you were found in contempt of court. On the first count your sentence is six months in jail, on the second it is three years, and on the third it is sixty days. You are therefore sentenced to three years and eight months in prison at hard labor; and in addition you are fined one thousand dollars. If the fine is not paid, you will serve one year in prison for each five hundred dollars thereof.

"The defendant is now remanded to prison to serve his sentence. Mr. Prosecutor, you will proceed with the next case."

CHAPTER IX

THE CONVICTION OF HIS FATHER PERSUADED NEPHI, AS NOTHING ELSE COULD have done, that his church was facing disintegration and defeat. It was clear now that the few arrests since Brigham's death had been intended as warnings. The government had been waiting for the saints to repudiate plural marriage; and now, with no such repudiation forthcoming, the ruthless Edmunds Act was to be enforced. There was no Brigham to solve this problem, no Nauvoo Legion, no army of Deseret under a vigorous Dan Wells. Early in 1885 President Taylor fled and was hiding somewhere north of the city. Other leaders were hiding or had left the country. A hundred thousand saints, scattered over a breadth of five hundred miles, were leaderless in the gravest crisis they had ever faced.

How swiftly disintegration was moving like invisible darkness through the church, Nephi had no way of knowing, but he could see signs of it all around him. Josephville, one of the most compact and indissoluble units in Zion, was thoroughly frightened by Tim's sentence. Under cover of night, a dozen of the men packed their belongings and slipped away, going nobody knew where. Perhaps they had set out on a journey of a thousand miles to the colonies in Mexico or Canada, or had taken boat to Hawaii, or had fled to the desolate and almost inaccessible desert of the San Juan upon the Colorado River. They had gone rather than face arrest and jail. In one week Nephi would ask a man if his heart was stout, his faith unshakable; and in the next he would learn that the man had fled.

"One by one," he said to Moroni, "they are going. They promise me they'll stay but as soon as my back is turned they hit the grit. Even the manager of the store has gone. He loaded a wagon with all he could pile on, locked the store, and disappeared. Some of the farmers are gone or are hiding. It will be a lean harvest this year."

"When they heard President Taylor is hiding, they lost their courage."

"Well, what can be expected when our president hides like a coyote!"

"Nothing. But you are safe."

"Why am I safe?"

"Because when you were talking to Mark in the courtroom you had the judge and district attorney scared. That's why I stopped you. If you had gone on they would have known you were bluffing."

"I was bluffing. Still, we might be able to prove they visit harlots."

"I think you'll be safe till the jails are full. So you'd better try to keep this community together and the Order going."

Nephi tried, but it was like standing on a shore and trying to hold the tides back. He spoke to his people in Sunday meetings, branding the leaders of the church as cowards, and urging those still in Josephville to stick by their principles if it cost them their lives. He had them sing their hymns of hope and courage. He asked them to bring testimonials of the goodness of God; and one grizzled old farmer told how he had been miraculously saved when a wagonload of logs fell upon him and knocked him unconscious. The oldest woman in the village spoke of that winter of famine, long ago, when she and her family were about to eat of poisonous roots and were stopped by an angel's voice which cried: "Throw that stuff out!"

But all these miracles had been told before and Nephi realized that it would take more than threadbare chronicles to save his people. It would take more than hymns about Deseret and the innocence of children's faces and the divinity of Joseph Smith. "There's only one thing to do," he said to Moroni. "We must all go to jail. Are we going to dally around until we are all disfranchised vassals, until we are a degraded and underprivileged minority like the Lamanites?"

"You are right, Nephi. We could save the church if we all died in jail."

"Then why in hell don't we? Imagine if a hundred thousand of us marched to jail! What would the world say to that? This nation was founded by pilgrims who fled to escape persecution. If a refuge for freedom of conscience put an entire people in jail, what would the world say to that?"

"It would raise such a rumpus that they'd have to let us out."

"Then why don't our leaders go to jail instead of hiding?"

"I don't know."

"Well, by the God of Israel, I'm going to find out!"

When Nephi went to the city, he knew that Taylor and other leaders were hiding or had fled the country; but he found Wilford Woodruff, president of the Twelve. He had seen little of Woodruff but he had always liked the man—and knew of nobody who did not like him. Seventy-eight in this spring of 1885, Woodruff was a stout and white-haired and kindly old gentleman whose tastes had run to scholarship. For fifty years he had faithfully kept a journal; and if he could have followed his wish, he would have written a history of the church, and biographies of Joseph and Brigham. But he had traveled a hundred and seventy thousand miles among the far-flung missions and had had little time to give to his studies. When a young man he had converted and baptized so many persons in England that an alarmed clergy had called the matter to the attention of Parliament.

When Nephi entered Woodruff's office, the tired old man did not rise but waved him to a chair.

"I am Bishop Nephi McBride of Josephville."

"Yes, Brother Nephi. I remember you now. Did you wish to see me?"

"Yes, Brother Wilford. Where is President Taylor?"

"My conscience, don't you know?"

Nephi smiled. Woodruff's exclaiming by his conscience had become a legend in Zion. "No, I don't. He's hiding—but where?"

"It's a secret," said Woodruff, gazing at Nephi with the mildest blue eyes in the world.

"I will keep the secret."

"He is hiding in the home of Brother Thomas Rouche in Kaysville."

"Who is with him?"

"Nobody at all, I guess."

"Where is his counselor, Joseph F. Smith?"

"He went to Hawaii."

"The coward! The son of Hyrum Smith flees halfway across an ocean!"

"You are very young," said Woodruff in his gentle and unworldly way. "John Taylor is like me. I don't sleep by nights and I am weary by day. Many of us are old men and we are tired. I envy Brother Dan Wells for he is in Europe."

"But you must know what the gentile leaders are saying—that the shepherds fled when the wolves appeared, and the sheepfold is deserted."

"My conscience, do they? Yes, I suppose they do; but the Lord will look after us."

"Do you know what the saints are saying about you and President

Taylor? That when you face a problem you always say the Lord will look after us. This is no time for our leaders to be running."

"But Jesus fled to escape the edicts of tyrants. All the shepherds in the Bible fled at one time or another. That is neither new nor disgraceful."

"But if the leaders flee, the church cannot survive."

"It would do no good for President Taylor to remain here and be imprisoned."

"It would do a world of good. It would give courage to the saints who don't know where to turn or what to do. Brigham Young did not run."

"Brigham faced great problems but none as difficult as we face. The government is going to take from us all our church property. We are deeply in debt. There are bounties on the heads of some of the authorities, and spies are hunting them for the rewards. I myself suffer from asthma until my life is a burden day and night. Brother Nephi, you are young and healthy and have energy; but when you are an old man you will not see all things as you do now."

"I'm sorry if I spoke too hastily. But President Woodruff, what are we going to do? My father is in jail. My grandfather was arrested. All my wives but one have gone away and I may be arrested any time. The Order in Josephville is falling to pieces ——"

"It already has in other places."

"Yes, even in Brigham City!"

"Even there. Well, we are doing our best. We have our shrewdest man in Washington to learn if there is no way toward peace; but I am afraid we will have to make compromises. If we were to give up plural marriage ——"

"We cannot! Do you intend to desert your wives?"

"No," said Woodruff mildly. "But I say if we were to give up plural marriage ——"

"President Woodruff, do you realize what you're saying? Have you forgotten that God told Joseph Smith this is a holy and everlasting covenant and that if we do not keep it we are damned?"

"I am familiar with all of God's revelations to Joseph."

"Then how can you consider repudiating a covenant that is necessary to our salvation? Are we to lose our souls to please our enemies?"

"I think God expects us to obey the laws of our country."

"Then why did we leave Nauvoo? Why did Joseph and Brigham resist to the end? Why didn't Joseph compromise? He knew if he did not he'd be murdered. Why didn't Brigham——"

"Brother Nephi, I haven't the strength to argue with you. I do well to live from day to day. I can see no way out, no solution of our problems, if we do not compromise. We are still fighting this Edmunds Act but it is a losing fight. In the tabernacle next month we are going to hold a huge protest meeting."

"What good do protest meetings and petitions and memorials do!"

"Very little, I guess. Some of the saints are fighting in other ways that we authorities do not approve. They are spying on gentile leaders and tracking them to brothels. They intend to try to scare them by publishing their names. It will do no good."

"It might. Brigham said to fight snakes and coyotes at their own level."

"No. Guerrilla tactics have always lost for us more than they have won. Anyway, old men must prefer diplomacy to the sword. Brother Nephi, you exhaust me. I wish you would leave me now."

"But what are the saints to do? Have the authorities no advice to give them? Are they to pack up one by one and pull out for Mexico or Canada?"

"I don't know. I feel that the Lord will take care of them."

"You know that isn't true."

"You have worn me out, Brother Nephi. Will you leave me now?"

"I'm sorry," said Nephi, looking at the sick old face. "I am sorry I upset you; but I leave as I entered with no advice, no plan, no hope to give to our people."

He left the office, feeling sorry for an old man who no longer had the strength to fight, but feeling more deeply sorry for a people who had no leaders. The church was now in the hands of a few old men who were weary of struggle. If an old man, Nephi reflected, had taken control after Joseph was murdered, the church would have perished then; and it was unfortunate now that Wells, Taylor, Woodruff and others were not forty years younger. Brigham during his vigorous years had been called the Lion of the Lord, but in old age he was more of a fox than a lion. Woodruff was right: the sword yielded to diplomacy, and righteous anger to persuasion and compromise when men entered the shadows of their last years. And even if Taylor and Woodruff were younger, matters might still be unchanged; for these men were not and had never been leaders in the way that Brigham was. They were Hamlets and not Caesars.

What to do, or whether anything at all could be done, Nephi did not know. He decided to spend the day walking through the city to observe the changes that were taking place. Salt Lake City had a population of thirty thousand now, about a third of whom were gentiles. It had modern comforts, including street railroads, libraries and theaters and clubs—and brothels and saloons! The broad streets, down which ran the clear mountain waters of City Creek, cooling and cleansing the air, were lined with hundreds of trees, deciduous and evergreen. There were many lovely lawns and flower beds; there were shrubs and bushes everywhere, showing the first signs of bloom.

The streets themselves had always been rather unsightly. During the dry seasons they were often ankle-deep with dust that winds lifted in clouds and spread over the city; and after a heavy rain they were pitted with ruts and mudholes, and covered with a thin dirty flood that washed against buildings, or gathered in torrents that cut a network of channels. Nevertheless, it was a beautiful city, lying on a gentle mountainside and facing a magnificent range in the west.

Nephi walked up and down South Temple, State and Main, stopping now and then to gaze at the more notable landmarks of Brigham's life. The temple, nearing completion, and costing several millions of dollars, was a splendid monument to the Lord. Of gray granite, it had a length of two hundred and a width and height of more than a hundred feet. It was intended to be, and it seemed to Nephi that it was, a marvel of beauty and strength. Of greater interest to visitors was the new tabernacle. Elliptical in shape, and seating nine thousand persons, its roof was an enormous dome of heavy lattice-work that rested on great sandstone pillars. Its acoustic quality amazed everyone: the human ear could hear a pin drop two hundred feet away; and a person who whispered in the east end of the gallery could be distinctly heard in the amphitheater in the opposite end.

The theater which Brigham built was by far the finest in the West. The Social Hall where he and his wives had danced was still standing; and so was the old tithing office which had been the first home of the *Deseret News*. It was a tall homely frame building with four columns in front that supported two porches. Amelia's Palace was as gaudily pretentious as ever; beyond it was the school which Brigham had built for his own children; and the Lion House and Beehive House, now occupied by members of his family, looked durable enough to stand forever. Yet Nephi had a feeling that most of these old buildings would eventually be torn down. For him, for thousands, they were buildings to love and cherish and preserve for all the generations to come; but if gentiles were to own the city, or even if Mormon leaders were to compromise, then perhaps every building of Brigham's time would be destroyed to make way for factories, banks, and stores.

Nephi looked at every one of them as if gazing on them for the last time. Back in Nauvoo, the temple had been destroyed and the stones of it were laid as doorsteps of gentile homes; but the Nauvoo House still stood, as well as the homes of Rigdon, Brigham, Parley Pratt and others. They were falling into ruins—for nobody seemed to care about them now. In Nephi's opinion, the church ought to buy and preserve them—as well as any early structures that remained in Palmyra, Kirtland and Far West. Years hence, after the frontiers were all conquered, and great-grandchildren knew of pioneering only what they read in books, the first homes of Joseph, the Kirtland temple, and the homely cabins from Palmyra to the Mississippi would be shrines to visit and touch. He had once seen a photograph of Joseph's Nauvoo home, and for an hour he had looked at it, trying to realize that the Prophet had lived in it; trying to realize all the fears and heartache and bitterness of which that building today stood as a silent and deserted symbol. He had felt the same emotion when looking at a photograph of the Kirtland temple. In its time it was the finest building in a huge area—but it had been much more than that. It had been a House of the Lord, built at great cost of labor and sacrifice, when the church and Joseph and the dream of a new and better order on earth were still young and fighting for their lives. If persons could go to the land of Jesus and actually touch the manger where He had been born, it would be an experience, a prayer, a sacrament that would restore strength and faith to the weak heart. Likewise, it seemed to him, if in years to come the saints could go to the birthplace of Joseph, to the houses in which he lived, the temples in which he knelt, the jail in which he was martyred, they could more deeply realize the meaning of their long and bitter heritage.

But perhaps everything would be destroyed. Perhaps in time there would be only a body of legends, a few scattered and fraudulent relics—as there was in regard to Jesus today. That would be all. There would be a faded daguerrotype of Joseph at which the saints would stare, trying to believe that he once lived. They might visit his birthplace and be told that under this bank or factory or in yonder plowed field had once stood the log hut in which he was born. They would go to Nauvoo and find a town there, but no sign of the great and beautiful city which legend said the Prophet had built on a swamp. They could go to Carthage but never be convinced that on any part of it there had once been a two-story stone jail, or that any spot of its earth had received a prophet's blood. Because even now, as a matter of fact, very few—if indeed any—of the saints knew where his body lay.

Perhaps, Nephi reflected, he was being too sentimental about it; but history, nevertheless, was full of parallels. Jerusalem and the shores of Galilee were still facts. Orson Pratt had told, after his return many years ago, of standing on the Mount of Olives, of humbly laving his hands in the Jordan, of gazing at what he was solemnly assured was the spot in Gethsemane where Jesus prayed; but in that entire land there was not today a single known thing that Jesus ever touched, nor a foot of ground on which He was known to have stood. His gospel remained but He had been swallowed by legends. The greatest of teachers were overtaken by oblivion and fables and buried deep under the centuries; and if Joseph was to remain with his people as a man who once lived and fought and suffered, and who sealed his ministry with his blood, then the homely survivals of his labors ought to be preserved. For was he not already passing into the shadows of legend? Was not the manner of his death disputed? Some said that after he fell he was propped against a well curb and riddled with bullets; some said a man approached with a bowie knife to sever his head and was struck blind by lightning; and some declared that his head had been severed and carried away. Some said he rose from his grave on the third day and ascended to heaven, attended by a celestial army. Some said he had twenty-eight wives, some a great many more, and some fewer; and his apostate relatives still swore that he had only one. And among the saints today, did not some declare that his revelation on celestial marriage was a forgery?

Yes, indeed: the legends were already overtaking and obscuring the facts; and with gentiles coming into power and the Mormon leaders abdicating, it was hard to tell what the future of the church would be. Nephi's vision of it did not make him happy. If the church of Peter had been lost, might this one not also go down into darkness? It seemed so to him. He was still thinking about it, still wondering what he or anybody could do, when he was fetched up by loud voices. He perceived then that he had come to a dark alley that led into an unused street; and down this alley he heard angry men in the dusk.

Without hesitating he ran toward them, and saw as he ran a group of about forty men who seemed violently excited. Whether they were saints or gentiles he did not know. Upon approaching, he saw that in the milling group was a terrified and half-naked Negro who had been roughly handled; for blood was running from wounds in his scalp, his body was lacerated and his clothes were almost torn off. For a moment Nephi stopped and looked at the mob. In the center of the group, several men were dragging the Negro, and other men, cursing loudly, pressed in.

"What is the trouble?" asked Nephi of the man nearest him.

The man turned a sour angry face. "Who are you?"

"Nephi McBride."

"Are you a Mormon?"

"Yes. I'm the bishop in Josephville."

"Well, this black son-of-a-bitch just murdered Brother Andrew Burt!"

"Why?" asked Nephi, walking at the man's side.

"Ask him! Ask the lousy gentiles!"

Nephi considered. Then: "Where are you taking him?"

"To the jailyard."

"What for?"

"To lynch him."

"No! My God, you mustn't do that!"

"God damn you! Are you a gentile?"

"I told you who I am."

"Then act like a saint and come along."

"But we mustn't do this! Don't you realize it will give the gentiles an excuse for violence?"

"Who cares? We can be violent too."

Nephi followed the mob to the yard, wondering meanwhile how he could prevent this atrocity. He had no time to get in touch with church authorities—but where were they! How could anyone get in touch with leaders who were hiding—the cowards, who should have been keeping their people from such brutality as this!

After entering the yard of a small jail, the mob did not pause in their angry stride. Nephi crowded in. The Negro was the most abject and cringing animal he had ever seen. Men on each side were dragging him by clutching his hair and flesh; and while the procession headed for a tree, other men leapt in and kicked him and smote him with fists. They all seemed to Nephi to be violently out of their minds; and whether he was more sickened by the Negro's terror or by the brutal rage in the faces of his captors, he did not know. The whole scene appalled him. It was incredible that his own people, the saints of God, should be dragging a fellow being to his death as if he were a wolf. This was a new revelation of the hearts of men, a terrible and revolting revelation.

When he saw a rope thrown over a high limb, he came to sudden and furious life and hurled men aside on his way to the inner circle. "Stop!" he thundered. "In the name of Israel's God, I forbid you to do this!"

The man with the rope in his hand turned to look at Nephi. His face looked bloated with ugly bestial ferocity. "In the name of Israel's God, who are you?"

"I am Bishop Nephi McBride!"

"Go on home!"

"Brethren, in God's name listen to me! I don't know what this man has done! I am told he murdered, but in that case, deliver him to the law!"

"Law!" the man roared. "God damn it, there is only gentile law! There is no law for us and you know it!"

"In the name of the God who is watching us, don't do this! Consider the consequences! You will only give to the gentiles an excuse for greater violence——"

"Shut up!" a man howled. "Are we going to listen to his bilking chin music? Nephi McBride, go off and hide your face with our church authorities!"

"Sure!" cried another. "Go off and hide with John Taylor and the apostles, the yellow-livered cowards!"

"Brothers, listen——"

"To hell with you! Put the rope around the black son-of-a-bitch's neck! What are you standing there for? Are you waiting for the gentiles to come?"

When the man with the rope moved toward the Negro, Nephi grasped his arm. "In the name of Joseph Smith, listen to me! Listen to me!" he shouted, turning to the angry group. "If you do this, blood will run like water in the streets of this city! All the hoodlums in Zion will use it as an excuse to burn our homes, rape our wives——"

"Oh, shut up!" said a big man. He advanced from the group and faced Nephi. "Bishop, listen to me. For years we've listened to our leaders who tell us to be peaceable and then sneak off to save their cowardly hides. But I'm not turning the other cheek any more. From this day on we are fighting; and if you're afraid to fight, go back to Josephville and crawl into a cellar. This scurvy gentile killed one of our brothers in cold blood. If we turn him over to the law it will be gentile law, and he will go scot free and be given a medal. So back out of the way, Nephi McBride, before we give you a dose of it."

"Back up!"

"Go crawl in bed with John Taylor!"

In this moment Nephi felt his heart leap. The Negro had moved a little toward him and had reached out with a shaking hand to touch him. The man's yellow eyes, rolling in terror and entreaty, were looking up at Nephi, while blood made a black-and-red patchwork of his face. In one swift moment Nephi saw the awful picture: a cowering bloody man supplicating him with one touch of his finger! In the next moment, two men grasped Nephi and hurled him back.

"We don't want to hurt you! But you had your mouth-almighty say and now shut your jib!"

Nephi struggled vainly in the clutch of four men. Finding himself helpless, he strained forward, staring at the horrible nightmare of the scene. He saw the shuddering black man yanked to his legs; saw around his neck a rope that fell in a long curve from the tree; saw men grasp the other end of the rope. He was looking at the Negro's face when the rope tightened. In that moment he saw such utter terror as he had never seen before, and heard a choked mad scream that went into him like a dagger. His eyes then were too obscured by mist to see clearly. He knew only that an almost naked man, bloody from his scalp to his feet, was kicking wildly and pitching from side to side, and then slowly turning round and round in the air. Nephi bowed his head. When he looked again, the black man was silent and limp, and a score of men were looking up at the lynched face and bulging eyes. Then the body came down and sprawled as the legs, like broken things, gave way. The bloody head sank to the breast.

Sick and furious, Nephi left the scene. He found his carriage and drove home at a gallop, not because he feared pursuers but because he wanted to get away from that dead creature in the jailyard. It seemed to him that this outrage would bring the gathering storm to a deluge, and give to the gentiles the excuse they had been waiting for. There could be no peace now.

"Yes," Moroni gravely admitted, after hearing the story, "it looks bad. Every newspaper and pulpit in the nation will take it up and magnify it into a rebellion and a massacre. But I know how the men felt. We have no courts and judges. We have no leaders any more."

"It's horrible," said Fanny, who with Genet and Sarah, Kate, Maggie and Agatha had heard the story. "No matter what he did, there's no excuse for lynching."

Moroni looked at her with wise old eyes. "Women don't understand the passions of men. The best of us can become lynchers. I learned that in Missouri long ago."

"I still say it's a shame!"

"I've seen too many men killed to worry about a dead Negro. It little matters whether he was hanged at once or after a long trial."

"There wouldn't have been any trial."

"No, there wouldn't. The important thing is what is going to happen now. Did you see any of the authorities today?"

"Only Wilford Woodruff. He's old and tired and whipped. I think he wants to make peace on any terms."

"Where is President Taylor?"

"Up in Kaysville. Joseph F. Smith fled to Hawaii. All the leaders but Woodruff are hiding or have gone."

Thoughtfully Moroni pulled at his beard. "Why does Woodruff stay?"

"I don't know. I think he feels he'll not be arrested. I can't say why."

"What will happen now?" asked Fanny.

"Only God knows."

"It's easy," said Moroni, "to predict what will happen now. The Federal government will move a hundred times as fast and with a thousand times as much power. With our leaders hiding, I see very little to hope for."

"We can stick by our principles," said Nephi.

"Yes," said Moroni, smiling at him. "Of course we can. But it takes buildings and leaders plus principles to make a church. We stuck by our principles when we left Nauvoo." He set his glasses on his nose and reached for a book. After peering at the pages and reading nothing, he looked down his nose at Nephi. "The Lord might show us a way out of this. I hope He does. I can see no way myself."

CHAPTER X

A S LONG AS THE LEADERS REMAINED IN HIDING OR SAFELY IN OTHER COUN-
tries, nothing could be done to avert wholesale apostasy, flight,
imprisonment and ruin. Nephi gave most of his time to the colony in
Josephville, urging the men to go ahead with their labor and to be unafraid. Moroni said there was nothing to do but wait and learn how drastic
the Federal government intended to be.

They did not have to wait long. The lynching, as well as other acts of
violence, aroused a mighty wrath in the nation; and pulpit and press cried
more loudly than ever for the extermination of Mormonism, even at the
point of a bayonet. Famous journalists like Kate Field joined the crusade
and strove to enlist the support of other writers, including a humorist
named Samuel Clemens. Senators on the floor of Congress demanded
immediate and ruthless prosecution. Sensing that the anger of a nation
was at last behind them, gentiles in Salt Lake City, including the editors
of the anti-Mormon newspaper, clamored for more arrests and convictions, and the confiscation of all property belonging to the church.

In a late April evening, Datus Frost came to see Nephi and Moroni.
He was excited.

"Do you know what has happened?"

"What?" asked Nephi, knowing it must be terrible or it would never
arouse the emotions of Datus.

"Good God, it's awful. It's what some of the saints have just done."

"Well," said Nephi impatiently, "what is it?"

Datus looked around him. He gazed at the three old women and said
it was hardly a matter to speak of in the presence of ladies.

"There's nothing," said Moroni, "they haven't heard by this time."

"Well, then I'll tell you. Of course, I don't know for certain it's the
saints doing this. It might be the damned gentiles, but the man who told
me says it's some of the brethren, all right. I'll tell you what they're doing."

"Tell it and stop humming and hawing."

"They're taking two-quart glass jars and filling them with stuff. Then they sneak up in the night and hurl them through windows."

"Whose windows?"

"Gentile windows. The homes of the district attorney and the commissioners."

"What do they put in the jars?"

Datus looked again at the women. Only Agatha was gazing at him. "Well, it's— Dodgast my hide, I don't know how to say it."

"Oh, say it!" cried Nephi.

"Well, it's human manure."

"What!" Nephi was so horrified that he rose to his feet; and old Moroni, usually so imperturbable, leaned forward to look at Datus. "You sure about this?"

"Absolutely sure. I was over in the city today, and some of the brethren, they were talking about it. A lot of bottles have been throwed through windows the last two nights."

"My God!" said Nephi. He looked at his grandfather. "Have the saints stooped to the level of hoodlums who scribble on privy walls!"

Moroni leaned back in his chair. "There have always been hoodlums among us."

"Imagine what will happen when that story gets back East! In the name of God, how are we going to fight against dung-throwers? The fools are playing us right into the hands of our enemies. First it was a lynching and now it is this!"

"It's the sort of thing," said Moroni, "the gentiles want the saints to do. It gives them an excuse to stop at nothing."

"It allows them to represent us as the degraded libertines the people back East want to believe we are."

"Yes."

"Another thing," said Datus, who liked to tell news that staggered persons, "Some of the brethren have been acting as detectives. They've tracked the attorneys and judges for weeks and say they can prove they visit prostitutes. At least some of them. They say some of the prostitutes will march right into court and swear it's true. That is, they will if they are paid to do it. So the brethren intend to make a great scandal out of it and chase the gentiles out of here."

"I knew they were doing that," said Nephi. "Damned if I blame them.

Some of those persecuting us do visit whores and the world ought to know it."

"It won't do any good," said Moroni. "They'll turn it against us some way."

"I guess you knew," said Datus, "there's to be a big protest meeting in the tabernacle next Sunday."

"Yes."

"Of course," said Moroni. "But that won't do any good either. Our leaders won't be there."

Very few of the leaders were there, having known well that officers would be at the temple gates to arrest them if they dared to show their faces. It was a mammoth meeting. The saints came by thousands and filled not only the huge tabernacle but the temple grounds as well. Sitting with Moroni far up in front, Nephi wondered what good anyone thought this meeting would do; but he was eager to hear what was said. When feeble old Wilford Woodruff appeared he received a wild ovation; and when he spoke, his weak voice was clearly heard at every point under the great dome. The church, he said, was still determined to fight the Edmunds Act; and he wished to read again a statement that had been prepared and published three years ago.

"We did not," he said, reading from a paper, "reveal celestial marriage. We cannot withdraw or renounce it. God revealed it, and He has promised to maintain it and bless those who obey it. Whatever fate, then, may threaten us, there is but one course for men of God to take; that is, to keep inviolate the holy covenants they have made in the presence of God and angels. For the remainder, whether it be life or death, freedom or imprisonment, prosperity or adversity, we must trust in God. If any man or woman expects to enter into the celestial kingdom of our God without making sacrifices and without being tested to the very uttermost, they have not understood the Gospel."

Nephi looked at his grandfather. "That's better! I thought he had given up but it doesn't sound that way."

"There is still hope," Moroni said.

After a few remarks Woodruff sat, returning to his chair as if he had exhausted his strength; and younger men, all of them minor officials in the church, delivered impassioned speeches, dwelling chiefly on the grievances. The purpose of this huge meeting, they said, was to make a statement of the injustices endured by the saints, and to protest to the President of the United States.

"I will read to you," said one, "the statement of our grievances, and then our protest. First, in regard to our grievances, it is to be noted that spotters dog our footsteps. Delators thrust themselves into bedchambers and watch at windows. Children are questioned upon the streets as to the marital relations of their parents. Families are dragged before commissions and grand juries, and on pain of punishment for contempt are compelled to testify against their fathers and husbands. Modest women are made to answer shamefully indecent questions as to the sexual relations of men and women. Attempts are made to bribe men to work up cases against their neighbors. Notoriously disreputable characters are employed to spy into men's family relations. Contrary to good law, persons accused of crime are held to be guilty until they prove themselves innocent. Trial by jury is no longer a safeguard against injustice to a Mormon accused of crime. Accusation is equivalent to conviction. Juries are picked to convict, and if they fail to find a verdict against the accused when he is a Mormon, insult and abuse are heaped upon them by the anti-Mormon press. Men, fearful of not obtaining justice in the courts, are avoiding arrests, are hiding, are fleeing, believing no fair and impartial trial can be had.

"That, brethren and sisters, is the statement which we shall submit to the President. With it we will send a protest, and I now wish to read it to you.

"We protest against unfair treatment on the part of the general government.

"We protest against a continuance of territorial bondage, subversive of the rights of free men and contrary to the spirit of American institutions.

"We protest against special legislation, the result of popular prejudice and religious interference.

"We protest against the conscience of one class of citizens being made the criterion by which to judge another.

"We protest against the tyranny of Federal officials, and the continuance in office of men who disgrace their positions and use their official power as a means of oppression.

"We protest the partial administration of the Edmunds law—the punishing of one class for practicing their religion, and exempting from prosecution the votaries of lust and crime.

"We protest against the breaking up of family relations formed previous to the passage of the Edmunds law, and the depriving of women and children the support and protection of their husbands and fathers.

"We protest the prosecution of persons, many of whom were infirm and aged, who entered into plural marriage before it was declared a crime.

"We respectfully ask for the appointment by the President of a commission to fairly and thoroughly investigate the Utah situation, and pending its report we solemnly protest against the continuance of this merciless crusade.

"Brethren and sisters, we will submit our statement and our protest to President Cleveland; but our dealings with the Federal government for fifty years do not encourage the belief that the President will listen in sympathy, any more than Van Buren and Taylor and Grant did. But we are again fighting with our backs to a wall—and there is nothing we can do except pray that the President and Congress will again read—if indeed they have ever read—the Constitution of this great nation, and discover for themselves that we have always lived within the rights granted us by that document. Our only crime, yesterday and today, has been and still is our belief that we are entitled to freedom of conscience in our religion. We have never asked for more than that, and we shall never ask for less.

"It is necessary today to sound a solemn warning. Some of the brethren, carried away by their tempers and goaded by injustices, have been guilty of vile and unpardonable conduct. I allude to matters that are too delicate for public discussion. On behalf of President Taylor and other authorities of the church, I want to say to you in most emphatic terms that we do not and will not countenance such dastardly affronts as have been made upon certain Federal officials. We will not countenance mob law and mob conduct. If the persons guilty of these atrocities are caught, it is hoped that they will be tried and punished. Such persons are not wanted in this church and will be excommunicated as fast as their names become known. . . ."

Moroni's beard was nodding in quiet approval. Nephi approved too; but what, he angrily asked of himself, did these speakers propose to do except to address another futile memorial to the President? How were the saints to protect themselves?

After the meeting, he learned that hundreds were asking the same questions. They gathered in angry groups on the temple grounds, in the streets; and Nephi went from group to group to learn the temper and mood of his people. Behind the tabernacle, a very furious man was speaking to about forty men and women.

"What in the name of hell and high heaven," he roared, "is the sense of such damned protest meetings? It's like a herd of sheep was surrounded by wolves and sent a plea for help to a bunch of jackals! That's all the good it will do us! That's all the good it ever did ever since Joseph was tarred and feathered in New York. By God, there's enough protests and petitions and memorials back in Washington to bury the President's desk six feet deep! Brigham Young never wasted time on petitions—or if he did, his petition was a sock in the eye and a kick in the pants!"

The speaker looked around to see if spies were listening. He lowered his voice. "Brigham had his own methods for taking care of enemies. He socked them away. Since he died we've been a damned bunch of bleating sheep without a leader, and the longer we wait the bigger our troubles get. There's only one way to handle gentiles." He paused and looked from face to face.

"What is that?" asked a man.

"Don't ask me. You know. But what did they tell us in meeting? Why, if we get in a fight, they hope we'll be tried and punished! By God, it's come to this: we turn the other cheek and get our skulls knocked in. We're to let them peek in windows, insult our wives, mock our children, arrest us, convict us on the testimony of liars, and jail us! That's it."

"But what," asked the man who had spoken, "can we do? As you say, we don't have any leaders now. We can't split up in small mobs and fight in the dark."

"Listen! You heard Woodruff say if we don't stick to celestial marriage we are damned. But how are we going to stick to it? In jail? Who'll support our families? Are we to let our wives and children starve to death? It sounds like that's what they expect. Well, by God, I won't. I'm going to sell out and pack my wagons and hit for Canada."

Nephi stepped forward. "But don't you realize that if we go to Canada, there'll soon be similar laws there?"

"Not where I'm going. I'm going to hell-and-gone back in the wilderness where the only law is a man's conscience and his gun."

"We came to a wilderness here. Gentiles and laws catch up with the wildernesses. It does no good to run away. We've been running for half a century."

"All right, you stay. Go to jail. When you get out, you'll find your children starved and your wives raped; and then they'll stick you in jail again."

"That's right," a woman said. "One of my neighbors, he's in jail, and one of his wives was raped. Then she married the man," the woman added humorlessly.

"You mean the man who raped her!"

"Yes. Well, she didn't have no way to make a living."

With Moroni at his side, Nephi went to another group. There a woman was laughing hysterically and pointing a derisive finger at a prosperous gentile. When Moroni took in the situation he grinned broadly; and Nephi, in spite of his contempt, had to smile. For a long while he had known that a few of the wealthier gentiles, unwilling to join the Mormon Church but eager for its sensuous privileges, had taken several wives to themselves; and here was a flabbergasted fellow who had been arrested and was out on bail.

"Look at him!" said the woman, shrieking wildly. "He has four concubines that he calls wives!"

"They are my wives. It's no worse for me than for you Mormons."

The man was so humorless and woebegone that he looked ridiculous. Why he had come here, none knew, unless it was to seek fellowship among the persecuted. That a polygamous gentile should fancy himself a blood brother of the Mormons was too much for these men and women; and they stared at him and howled with laughter.

"What's so funny?" he asked, getting very red. "Calling it celestial marriage doesn't change it. It's still polygamy."

"There now, don't you worry," said the woman soothingly. "Uncle Sam will pardon you. Polygamy as a matter of conscience is unforgivable, but as a matter of lust it has always been condoned. And just the same, you're not so bad as your lawyers and judges who visit harlots."

Gossip about spying on lustful gentiles, Nephi heard in other groups; and a few days later the city shook with apprehension as if an earthquake impended. The news had leaked out and had spread like fire. There was a statement of it in the anti-Mormon newspaper. In sweeping the city, the story took on the proportions of a legend: it was declared that six hundred gentiles, including all the leaders, had been trailed to dens of vice and were now to be exposed to the ridicule of the world. That many were guilty was soon made manifest. A few fled, a few went into hiding, and others barked with rage in public meetings. They denied the charge, but their blanched faces and shaking knees were observed by Mormon spies who heard them. Where, the gentiles wondered, would Mormon lightning strike next! This was too like the years when Brigham exposed Federal judges for the wanton rascals they were, and sent them out of the valley with their hair standing on end.

The lightning was not long in striking again. Some of the hotheaded young saints decided that Mormon grief could be symbolized by half-masting the flags; and on the Fourth of July an amazed city awoke to find the flags at half-mast on every Mormon building. Nephi had not heard of this plot. When he entered the city about noon, the streets seemed deserted, but two hours later, pandemonium broke loose. The gentiles had been busy, consulting among themselves and recruiting their forces; and like an army of vengeance they marched up Main Street to the Z.C.M.I. The Mormons had been busy too. Couriers bore word of the uprising to groups that had been hiding and waiting, and down South Temple they marched to meet the gentiles. The two bodies of men came together in front of the co-operative store, and it looked for a few minutes as if there would be a pitched battle. While the two groups faced one another, other hundreds joined the gentiles on the south, the saints on the north, until the broad street was jammed full a hundred yards in either direction. Nephi stood in the vanguard of the Mormon horde.

"Have we a David?" asked a saint. "If so, let's challenge their Goliath!"

Between the two lines, gentile leaders and officials from the city were working desperately to avoid a riot. From line to line threats and challenges were hurled; but policeman shoved warriors back into their groups, impartially cursing belligerents from both sides, and looking anxiously at several men in front of the store. Presently one of these men advanced and shouted for silence.

"We have not learned who is responsible for this dastardly insult to our flag! But we have sent a delegation to the city hall and we expect to know soon! Meanwhile, the first man on either side who starts a riot will be arrested for treason!"

Both armies broke into small groups that hastened over to the city hall;

but when Nephi arrived he learned that the crowd there had been dispersed. An hour later, the flags on the Z.C.M.I. and the theater were flying at the top of their staffs, but angry mobs still prowled in the streets or marched eight abreast from building to building. When at dusk Nephi left for home, the flags were still at half-mast on the courthouse, the tithing office and the plant of the *Deseret News*.

"What was the reason for it?" demanded Moroni.

"I don't know. Some of the men said it was to show the nation that we have gone into mourning."

"What foolishness!" said Moroni. "For years it has been said we're disloyal to our country; and now this happens! Back in the States they've been hoping for just such an incident. Lynchings, stinkpots, and half-masting of the flag! We can expect hell to break loose now."

In press and pulpit from coast to coast, hell did break loose in bitter furious denunciation. In Salt Lake City, the gentiles closed in and took a firmer hold on all public offices; and in their newspaper they declared that the Mormons had always been guilty of treason and ought to be driven from the nation.

MORMON TREASON!

> The rape of the flag on the Fourth of July is only the beginning. Every public-spirited citizen who loves his country and its glorious symbol, the stars and stripes, should take solemn warning from that unprecedented desecration. On the 24th of July, their Pioneer Day, it is expected that treasonable Mormons will half-mast the flag again. Every loyal person must be prepared to prevent such an atrocity, and to defend his flag with his life. . . .

The gentiles were prepared. As the fateful day approached, spies were busy everywhere, the police force was enlarged, and the Federal government was advised to be ready at a moment's notice to march an army in. It was a tense and anxious city. When toward evening of the 23rd, Nephi walked the streets, he saw persons, both Mormon and gentile, looking apprehensively at the flags to see if they were at full-mast. Every one of them was when he went home.

But on the morning of the 24th, every flag in the city was at half-mast. Nephi had gone to the city soon after daylight; and as soon as he learned what had happened, he galloped back to Josephville and burst in on his grandfather. He flung himself to a chair and laughed until tears rolled down his face. He left the chair and sprawled on the floor, howling with such uncontrollable joy that his mother heard him and came over, and stood and looked down at her son, wondering if he had gone mad. Moroni pounded the floor with his cane and demanded to know what had happened; but for several minutes Nephi could only roar out of agonized mirth that broke in a flood across the unhappiness of the last four years.

When he sat up he was exhausted. "The flags—" he gasped.

"Yes?" said Moroni. "What is it?"

"The flags are—all at half-mast—today!"

"What!" Moroni rose and marched over to his grandson. He poked him with his cane and cried: "Good God, boy, what are you laughing at!"

"Don't be alarmed," said Nephi, wiping at his eyes. "You don't understand."

"I understand that an army will march in now! And you laugh——"

"No, you don't understand. You see—you see, U. S. Grant died yesterday!"

CHAPTER XI

T HAT SUPERB IRONY THE GENTILES COULD NOT MISS, AND THEY RELAXED their vigilance. The tenseness in the city, the feeling that two armies would soon be at one another's throats, considerably abated, and the next few months were relatively quiet. Both factions had been frightened. But Nephi knew, and every thoughtful Mormon knew, that this was only the lull before the final and overwhelming storm. In the last half of this year and the first months of 1886, more persons were arrested and jailed than in all the previous years put together. Every Mormon leader of any importance had hidden or fled, but Federal spies were tirelessly busy trying to find their hiding places. The home for polygamous wives was nearing completion on Fifth Street. The press back East was demanding more drastic legislation, and many editors and preachers were boldly declaring that complete extermination of the Mormons was the only possible solution. "We must," one editor wrote, "march an army in and shoot them down as they shot the emigrants at Mountain Meadows."

In Salt Lake City, meanwhile, gentile leaders were preparing for the final struggle. Their public statements revealed that they no longer hoped to be able to drive all the Mormons out: too many of them preferred jail to flight, too many of the plural wives preferred imprisonment to perjury, and too many of the younger men were eager for battle. Realizing all this, the gentiles resolved to enlist in the crusade all groups and factions, religious and political, back in the States; and when they heard that the G.A.R. encampment was to be held in San Francisco, and that several companies would pass through the city en route, they saw the opportunity they had been waiting for.

When Nephi read the jubilant announcement that the Grand Army of the Republic would camp in the city for several days, he felt helpless with rage and despair. He strove to arouse Moroni to fury; but more and more as the weeks passed, Moroni had withdrawn to quiet contemplation of his books. There was nothing to be done, he said. With the leaders hiding or in jail, the saints scattered and unorganized, the church bankrupt, the whole nation up in arms, there was little use to talk about it.

"If we all said that, where would we be?"

"Right where we are now."

"Yes," said Nephi bitterly, "where we are now! And where am I? One of my wives is down in Mexico. Another is hiding in a cellar up in Ogden. A third married that scurvy spy Mark Browe. The Order has gone to pieces in spite of all I could do. So what do I have left to fight for?"

"The next life is important. This one we endure. Your father is in jail but does he complain? Not the last time I saw him. He sleeps on a stone floor, eats food that would starve a dog to death; but not all the scoundrels in hell could make him renounce his principles. We can only wait and see what happens. You're jumping at a stone wall when you try to fight the United States now."

"Are you going to hear the campfire speeches?"

"No. All that will be said I've heard a thousand times."

"I'm going. I might make a speech myself."

Moroni smiled and his upper plate fell. "The gad-danged thing!" he cried. "If the Almighty gives me a good set of teeth, I don't care what I suffer here."

"Then you won't go with me?"

"No, Nephi. I feel too tired."

"I'll see if Datus will go."

But Datus did not want to go. He said the church was whipped now, the saints scattered, and God would have to gather His children in His own time and way. "I realize now that when Brigham died we was all whipped to a frazzle. You better have a good meal and forget your worries."

"Datus, you'd better come with me. There might be bloodshed."

"That's all the more reason for me to stay right here."

Perhaps, Nephi reflected next, his mother would like to go and hear what was said.

"Me?" asked Fanny. "In God's name, son, we all know what that damned army of the republic will say."

"Well, let's go hear them."

"No. But if you're going, take a basket of food to your father. He gets thinner and thinner."

"I want you to go. I might give a speech."

Fanny looked at him as if he had said he might jump off a precipice. "You try any speechmaking and that mob will crack your head. You better sit like a good little boy and listen. Why don't you take Genet?"

"She's afraid. And besides, she's sick."

"She stews around too much. My husband's in jail but I don't fret and fume all the time."

Nephi went alone. The companies of the Grand Army had moved into a large skating-rink in the center of the city and built a circle of fires. When Nephi arrived, the fires were blazing, a great multitude had gathered, and upon a flag-draped platform a score of persons were waiting. Upon walls and strung from pole to pole were enormous banners, the most conspicuous of which declared:

OUR LOYAL PEOPLE WELCOME THE COUNTRY'S VETERANS!

The speeches bored him. A Federal judge asked the Grand Army to help exterminate the Mormons; a General Beaver of Pennsylvania pledged aid; and then the chaplain from Fort Douglas roared that he had worn the blue, as well as the holy raiment of God, and asked every one of the five hundred thousand veterans to "enlist in this war against whoredom!" When the district attorney spoke next and declared that "the purpose of Mormonism is the overthrow and destruction of the American home," Nephi left the meeting.

He found the McBride clan in conference. Moroni had read in the evening newspaper that the new governor, Caleb West, a Kentucky judge who had fought for the South, had just arrived in Salt Lake City; and that the Home for Polygamous Wives was ready to open its doors. He had also learned that John Taylor was sick abed.

"Sick?" said Nephi. "His conscience ought to make him sick!"

"When Governor West talks to Tim," said Moroni, "we must be there."

"I suppose—but what for? He'll tell my father he must give up his principles and become a good Christian gentleman. West will try to bribe the saints with a promise of pardons!"

"Did you know," asked Genet, "the officers were out to arrest Abner? He married a young girl three years ago and today Lucinda left him."

"Didn't she know about it?"

"Of course not," said Fanny. "She should have left that sly old fox long ago."

"Maybe she'll enter the Home now," said Genet.

"I want to see that damned whorehouse," said Fanny. "When you go over to see Tim, I'm going along."

But Governor West did not see Tim for many days. There were more important saints in jail and he talked with them first, though what he was talking about, only the prisoners knew. "We'll soon know," said Nephi one evening, because he had learned that West would talk with his father next. Fanny and Genet and Sarah said they would go to the city with the men. They were eager to see that big building which Fanny called A Home for Whores. No Mormon wife, she said, would ever enter it, but all the prostitutes of the city, pretending to be deserted wives, would move in for free board and room.

It was early one autumn morning when the five of them set out for the city. On each side along the way were small farms and orchards and gardens; and today the trees were deep with fruit, and the gardens were golden with melon and pumpkin still on the vine. The air was sweet with ripening and growth. Moroni gazed around him, remembering how this country had looked forty years ago. It was hard to believe that a desert of saleratus and sage, cactus and thistle and crickets, had been turned into a valley of green foliage and autumn colors. It was indeed true that Brigham had made a desert blossom as a rose. He had brought the magic of water to a land that Frémont and others had called worthless and God-forsaken; and here it was, a miracle for every easterner who saw it.

"All this," said Nephi, waving a hand at the valley, "will be taken from us. If we colonized the North Pole, the gentiles would move in and say we were monopolizing ice."

"They can't take our homes," said Fanny, "if we won't give them up."

"Of course they can. We'll be disfranchised vassals with no right to own property."

"I guess we need an island."

"Yes, with ten thousand miles of ocean all around it."

"They'd build boats," said Moroni, "and come."

"We'd sink their damned boats."

"They'd keep coming. It would be like Brigham said of the crickets. When we killed one, ten came to bury him."

"Are all these Mormon homes?" asked Genet, looking around her.

"Not all. A few gentiles are scattered along here. As soon as a saint packs up and leaves, a gentile rushes in."

As they drove up State Street, Nephi pointed out the new buildings, saying this was a gentile store, that a gentile bank——

"That was a Mormon store three years ago."

"Yes. Mark Browe's father bought it."

"It looks like half the buildings are owned by gentiles now."

"Almost half. See that bank over on Main, that big department store, that new hotel. They're all gentile."

"To say nothing," said Fanny, "of all the whorehouses!"

Nephi drew up on Fifth Street and they sat in the carriage to look at the Home. It was not an unattractive building. The main part of it was three stories high, and on each side was a large wing two stories high, the wings forming extensions toward the street. The grounds were landscaped. Trees and shrubs had been planted. Flowers were in bloom. The building as a whole looked like a huge family hotel or rooming-house.

Its official name was the Women's Industrial Home, but even the gentiles had from the first called it the Home for Polygamous Wives. It had been financed by prominent women in the States who accepted charitable donations and formed the Industrial Christian Home Association of Utah. Congress had been asked for a hundred thousand dollars but had given only forty thousand. Fifty thousand dollars had been spent in erecting the home, and several more thousand in furnishing it.

While they were gazing at this stupendous affront to the conscience of a free people, a man left the building and came forward. He smiled as he approached and then doffed his hat and bowed.

"Good morning," he said affably. "I see you're looking at our new industrial home." When nobody spoke, he asked: "Are you folks Mormons?"

"Yes," said Moroni, his eyes twinkling. "We fetched three of our wives for you. How many do you have in there now?"

"None yet," said the man, looking a bit foolish.

"Do you expect any?" asked Fanny.

"Oh, yes, indeed. A great many have come to ask about it. We've had thousands of visitors."

"I'm not talking about visitors. Have any Mormon wives come?"

"Well, just to see it. We don't have any applicants yet."

"You never will."

"Do you ladies wish to apply?"

"Yes, of course!" said Fanny.

"Does each room have a private bath?" asked Moroni.

"And a gentile lover?"

"Would you like to go in and see it?"

Moroni moved to climb down but Fanny grasped his shoulder. "Stay right where you are! I've said no Mormon will ever step inside the brothel, and if you do, we'll leave you there."

"I guess," said Moroni, "we won't go in."

"A fine waste of money!" Fanny cried. "Do you know what will happen to that big army barracks mess of lumber and brick? All the prostitutes of the city will move in so the lawyers and judges——"

"Mother!" said Nephi.

"Oh, all right. Let's go on. I've seen all I want to." She sat back indignantly, but while Nephi was gathering the reins she leaned across Sarah's lap and spoke again to the man. "If any Mormon wife ever enters that outlandish barn, be sure your scurvy Salt Lake *Tribune* publishes the news right across the front page. Because it will be news. Now," she said, sitting back again, "drive on. To think I left my work to come and see a bawdy house!"

Moroni chuckled. Nephi was grinning.

"I don't see anything funny," she said. "If Brigham was alive, that damned insult would be burned down."

"Yes," Moroni admitted, "it probably would."

The women intended to visit in the city while Moroni and Nephi went to the jail to hear what Governor West had to say to Tim. After the team was anchored at a hitching post, Moroni looked at Fanny and wagged his beard.

"If you aren't here when we come back, we'll look for you in the Home. But be sure you get nice rooms."

"Most of the time when you think you're funny you're only foolish."

Moroni chuckled and turned away.

A few minutes later, Nephi was alarmed by his father's appearance. Tim had been in jail less than three years but he looked very sallow and emaciated. He had not taken his imprisonment cheerfully. He had taken it in stubborn sullen anger and had spent a part of the hours nursing plots and thinking of vengeance.

"Father, you don't look well."

"I'm all right."

They were in the outer office where Tim was awaiting his interview with the governor.

"Have you seen Governor West?"

"He'll be along soon."

"What is he trying to persuade the saints to do?"

"To give up their principles."

"He has talked with most of them, hasn't he?"

"You ought to know. You're out where you can read newspapers."

"Son," said Moroni, patting Tim's stooped shoulders, "don't get bitter. We must endure persecution without complaint."

"It's all right for you to say that. If you lived month after month——"

"Joseph lived in a dungeon, chained to a stone floor. He did not complain. Jesus carried His own cross. Besides, soon you'll be out and Nephi and I will be in."

"Do you," asked Tim, looking at his father, "know where Louisa is?"

"No. We never see her."

"How's Fanny and Sarah?"

"Well and cheerful. We left them a few minutes ago."

"How is the Order?" asked Tim, looking at his son.

"Bad," said Nephi. "One by one they're pulling out."

Two men entered. Nephi guessed at once that the plump-cheeked gray man was Caleb West. He looked like a kindly and frustrated person who wished he had been left in his Kentucky judgeship.

"Is one of you Timothy McBride?"

"I am," said Tim. "This is my father and this is my son."

West shook hands with the three men. His gaze, Nephi observed, was direct and frank. "Do you," West asked of Nephi and Moroni, "also have more than one wife?"

"That, Governor," said Nephi, "is a question we prefer to ignore."

West looked at him and smiled. "Just the same, if you have, you might as well hear what I have to say to your father. Shall we draw up chairs and sit?"

After the men were seated, and the governor's secretary had laid writing materials in front of him on a table, West drew forth a sheet of paper.

"I have," he said, speaking as if interviews had worn him out, "talked with most of the imprisoned Mormons. I came out here unprejudiced and with the best of intentions, hoping I could effect some kind of compromise and adjust the difficulties. So far, I have had little success."

"None, really," observed the secretary blandly.

"Recently the Mormons in jail have drawn up a statement which they all say they intend to sign. If they do, then my labors will all have been useless. With your permission, I want to read the statement to you.

"It says: 'Of the members of the Church of Jesus Christ of Latter-day Saints now imprisoned for alleged violation of the Edmunds law, all but four had plural wives from its passage to thirty-five years prior to its passage. We were united to our wives for time and eternity by the most sacred covenants, and in many instances numerous children have been born as a result of our union, who are endeared to us by the strongest paternal ties. So far as compliance with your proposition requires the sacrifice of honor and manhood, the repudiation of our wives and children, the violation of sacred covenants, heaven forbid that we should be guilty of such perfidy. Perpetual imprisonment, with which we are threatened, or even death itself, would be preferable.'

"That, gentlemen, is the way they seem to feel."

"That," said Tim, "is the way I feel."

"What is the proposition you made them?"

"That they must give up their polygamous practices. I came out here to adjust the difficulties if I possibly can. So far, the Mormons have given me no co-operation whatever. There are two sides to every problem, and there are two sides to this one. I do not, like so many persons in the States, feel unfriendliness toward the Mormons. I do not agree with those fanatics who are demanding your extermination. At the same time, I am governor of this Territory, and I have taken an oath to support and enforce the laws of my country. That to the best of my ability I will do.

"Now since arriving, I have talked with nearly all the Mormons in jail, and with the leaders out of jail—that is," said West impatiently, "with those who aren't hiding or who haven't run away. Some of the minor leaders I have talked with are eager to reach a compromise. That spirit, I am sorry to say, has not been manifested by any Mormon who has been convicted under the Edmunds Act. Without exception they stubbornly resist all efforts to solve this grave problem."

"What do you expect?" asked Tim. "We are spied on, arrested, convicted by perjurers, jailed. We are felons in the opinion of the government which persecutes us. Because we will not give up our religion——"

"With your religion," West interrupted, "I am not concerned. I am concerned only with the laws of the nation which I serve. I will not even argue whether they are fair or unfair laws. They *are* laws, passed by the Congress and signed by the President. They are laws which every citizen of this country must obey, or he must take the consequences of disobedience. I am out here to enforce them. If the Mormons would co-operate with me——"

"In what way, Governor?" asked Moroni.

"Polygamy," said Caleb West, "must be abandoned. There is no if or uncertainty or doubt about it. Polygamists must give up all their wives except their first."

"But we are bound to our wives, Governor, by sacred covenants. We have children by them whom we love."

"I can understand that. The fact remains——"

"Governor West," said Nephi, "it is a solemn tenet of our church that those who abandon their wives will be forever damned. You are asking us——"

"Again I say I cannot be concerned with the principles of your religion. Those are not within my jurisdiction."

"But consider our position. I take it that you are a religious man. If it meant loss of your soul to give up that religion, would you do it—or would you go to jail?"

"That again is a question which it is not necessary to answer. Let me repeat. My only concern is the enforcement of the laws. If your religion is in disagreement with those laws, then you will have to give up your religion or leave the country."

"We left the country once!" cried Tim. "What good did it do us?"

"Our pilgrim forefathers," said Nephi, "once had to make the same choice. Rather than give up their religion, they left the countries of their birth and came over here to found a nation where every man could wor-

« 734 »

ship God as he pleased. It is that nation which is now trying to drive us out."

"That we need not discuss."

"No, Governor! But I wish those persecuted pilgrims could listen now!"

"I understand," said West impatiently, "that some of the Mormons are going to Mexico and Canada."

"They are cowards."

"I'd not say so. I'd say if your wives and children and religion mean so much to you, then you should go elsewhere."

Nephi had been fighting to control his anger. "Governor West," he said, "now listen to me for a minute. You came from Kentucky. Until you came here, the Mormons were only a people you had heard about. You came here; and you can stand on the capitol site and look out over a valley. What do you see? You see farms and homes and hamlets everywhere you look. You could see them for three hundred miles north or south. Thirty-nine years ago we were driven out of our country and we moved to a desert. We came——"

"I know——"

"Just a minute! We came to a desert, a God-forsaken wilderness where even the Indians were starving to death. We left that country which we loved. Our enemies drove us out in the middle of the winter; and if we hadn't had a Brigham Young to lead us, we'd not be talking to you now. Governor West, I say we came to the most desolate God-forsaken place we could find—a place that Brigham thought nobody else would ever want. We nearly died of plagues and famine. But we built our homes and lived in peace.

"Then what happened? Then the gentiles followed us, sent an army to destroy us. They brought whores and gamblers and all the breeds out of hell. Now they want what we built. After thirty-nine years of sacrifice and labor in this desert, now they want to drive us out again and take our homes as they did in Nauvoo. And you say blandly, Why don't we go to Mexico or Canada! We built in Ohio, in Missouri, in Illinois, and our enemies took it all away from us. With what we could carry we went to a desert and built, and you ask why we don't give that up too!"

"I say again," West cried, "that all this is not my concern! I am not here to discuss with you the misfortunes of your people in the past. I am here——"

"Governor West, you say you are here to enforce laws and that we are disobeying the laws. May I remind you that the Constitution of this country guarantees to us freedom of conscience? We are guilty of nothing except freedom of conscience. The Edmunds Act is unconstitutional."

"I am not the judge of that. The Supreme Court has found it constitutional."

"Would the Supreme Court go contrary to the intolerant prejudices of the majority? The plain truth is this: we are guaranteed our religious rights and you have been sent here to take them from us."

Governor West flushed with anger. "Gentlemen, it seems useless to prolong the discussion. I came out here to help you. If you refuse to co-operate——"

"You came to help us in the way the Federal government helps the Indians—by taking everything away from them and putting them on a worthless reservation under the pretext of civilizing them. If you mean by co-operating that we must deny our wives and children, renounce our religion, give our homes to the gentiles, then we'll stay in jail until we die."

"I assure you that you will all be in jail. In your schools, your churches, your newspaper you Mormons openly defy the laws of this land."

"But not the Constitution."

"You defy," cried West, "the laws of this land as upheld by the Supreme Court! And I am sorry, I am deeply sorry, that you persist in a folly that can mean only your eventual destruction. That is exactly what it will mean. If I knew where your President Taylor is, I'd talk with him; but I suppose he would say only what you have said. You leave me no alternative. I must use every agency and force at my command to wipe polygamy out of this Territory. That will be done. That will be done if I have to put every Mormon in jail. If imprisonment does not bring you to your senses, then an army will march in and you will all be driven out of the country or shot down if you resist."

"Is that final?" asked Nephi. "Is there no way by which we can keep both our principles and our home?"

"There is absolutely no way. You will give up polygamy or you will be exterminated."

"Then some of us will choose extermination."

"That is for you to decide. My patience is almost exhausted. If, as seems likely, I can hope for no co-operation from the Mormons, I shall ask the Congress for legislation that will pronounce your death sentence. I don't want to do that. I was sent here in a final desperate effort to settle this matter; but if I cannot settle it, I know very well what will be done. The first thing to be done is to put every one of you behind bars."

Governor West rose and his secretary rose, and they went to the door by which they had entered. "Good day, gentlemen," he said, and bowed and left the room.

"Well," said Tim, "that settles it. We'll all die in jail."

"No," said Moroni. "When they learn we're all willing to die in jail they'll change their policy. Well, Tim, keep cheerful. You'll soon be out and we'll be in."

Nephi soon learned that Governor West meant what he said. He announced in the *Tribune* that he had lost all patience with the Mormons and would make no more efforts to settle the problem by compromise. He wrote to the Secretary of the Interior and demanded a more drastic law than the Edmunds Act. He asked to have Fort Douglas strengthened by additional troops. And with all the power at his command, he moved vigorously to put every polygamous Mormon in jail.

In the McBride homes, officers were expected at any moment. Fanny spent half her time spying from the windows, declaring that if snoops came to her house again she would lay their skulls in two halves like a split watermelon. Sarah spent most of her time in Louisa's cottage. Genet wasted away.

It was not the women but the children who worried Nephi. He could remember when, a few years ago, he had a houseful of gay youngsters, but it was no longer so. All of Ruth's and Maude's children had gone to them; Genet's eight lived in sober thought, wondering why Maude and Ruth and Louisa had fled, why Tim was in jail, why their father was so anxious. Lura and her older sisters said they would never marry. "Why should we?" Lura demanded. "You say it's sinful to marry gentiles, and gentiles say it's sinful to marry Mormons. Marriage seems to be sinful no matter which way you look at it."

"You can marry," said Nephi, "when this trouble is settled."

"But when will it be settled? It's been going on for years now. Besides, every man who has asked me to marry him already has wives."

"She means old Abner Tuttle," said Genet.

"He's not the only one. There's others and they're all as old as the hills. Why do old men always want to marry young girls?"

Nephi was gazing at her, trying to think of a reasonable answer, when one of his sons, a lad of twelve, asked:

"Father, why do we have so many enemies?"

"Because," said Lura bitterly, "we don't live like other people."

"Well, why don't we?"

How, Nephi wondered, could this generation be made to understand? Those of Lura's age had been born into comfort and peace. He himself had been born in this valley; but from his grandfather he had heard as a child the story of Ohio, of Missouri, of Illinois. For Lura's generation, the mobs and corrupt officials, the plagues and famines, and the mighty migration were only legends—only the remote and unreal stories in books—like Washington's crossing the Delaware or Hannibal's crossing the Alps. These young men and women today did not have the wrath and zeal and the bitter memories that had made an unconquerable people of their grandparents. They had lost that single-mindedness of purpose which had driven an exiled horde across a continent to build an empire.

Nephi gazed at his sons and daughters and wondered what they and their children would be like in forty or fifty years. Often he had gathered his children around him and had told them of the past, of the incredible hardships of the pioneers, of his own sufferings during a winter of famine; but it was hard to make them understand who had never been hungry, or realize their heritage who had never been afraid. He might as well talk of Indian massacres or legends of the Civil War. Perhaps only a persecuted and desperate people could rise to the nobility of self-sacrifice and achieve great things.

If that were true, what would unite this and the next and the next generations in an invulnerable clan? Would the firm and single purpose of Joseph and Brigham be eroded like stone and scattered like shifting sand? Would the Mormons, like the Jews, become a wandering and outcast people; or would they mix with the gentiles and yield their principles and traditions one by one until their church was only another abomination in the sight of God? He did not know—or perhaps deep in his heart he knew too well.

CHAPTER XII

ONE MORNING NEPHI WAS WALKING IN THE VILLAGE, STARING AT WHAT was left of a once flourishing Order, when Lura came to tell him that his grandmother was very ill. He went over and looked at Kate's tired old face but he felt no grief. Death for him, for all the righteous saints, was not a terrible thing. It was only release from this life, this brief sojourn in which God tested the faith of His people before calling them to their punishments and rewards. He laid a hand on her withered brow.

"Grandmother, you sick?"

"No, Nephi. I'm just awfully tired."

"I'm tired too. I almost wish I were as old as you are."

He descended to talk with Moroni, but that old patriarch was reading his books and had nothing to say. Nephi was again walking through the village, looking at the idle gristmill, the empty shops, when he met Abner Tuttle. Abner had grown a ragged beard, streaked with gray, that made him look much older than his sixty-odd years.

"You heard the news?" he asked.

"What news?"

"Well, I just come from the city. They say President John Taylor is dying."

"President Taylor is dying." Nephi said the words without trying to realize what they meant. John Taylor was dying: that was unimportant: all men had to die. But what would his death mean? He had been hiding for three years but he had never been willing to compromise. "Are you sure?"

"That's what they told me." Abner's eyes had been quietly studying Nephi. "Bishop McBride, I wanted to speak to you about something."

"Yes, Brother Abner."

"You knowed that my wife Lucinda left me?"

"I heard she did. You should have told her about your other wife."

"I didn't want no quarrels." Abner hesitated, still gazing at Nephi. "Bishop McBride, I think I'll go to Mexico."

"Why? You'll not be arrested. You have only one wife now."

"That's what I wanted to speak about. If Lura will marry me, would you consent?"

"Lura!" Nephi cried. For a moment he felt anger. Then he saw how ironic it was: here was a saint asking for his daughter as a plural wife, and he, Bishop Nephi McBride, did not like it! "Does Lura want to marry you?"

"She says no, but a woman changes her mind if you keep after her."

"It doesn't seem to me, Brother Abner, that now is a time to be taking plural wives. Not as long as this persecution lasts."

"But I'd go to Mexico." Then very gravely Abner said: "Of course, I ain't so young as I used to be; but Brigham Young married when he was older than I am. I still feel pretty young."

Nephi still struggled between anger and a sense of the ridiculous. "Well, if Lura says yes, I won't oppose it. I think it would be better to wait a while."

"Would you speak a good word for me?"

"No, Abner. You'll have to persuade her yourself."

"But you won't discourage her?"

"I'll say nothing about it. Right now, the fact that President Taylor is dying seems to me much more important."

It seemed so important before the day was done that Nephi hitched a team to the carriage and set out for Kaysville. There seemed no good reason to go; but if John Taylor was still alive, he wanted to hear what he said. At the home of Thomas Rouche in Kaysville, there were no carriages outside; and sensing that the utmost secrecy was shrouding Taylor's death, Nephi drove to a hitching post in the town and then slipped to a rear door.

In the darkened house—only candles were burning—were several men, not all of whom Nephi recognized. He observed that the bearded long-faced Joseph F. Smith had returned from Hawaii; and that Taylor's other counselor had come out of hiding to bid his leader farewell. All of those present were hunted men. Every one of them had been dodging arrest for years; and when Nephi knocked softly and entered, they all came quickly forward and looked at him sharply, not knowing at first whether he was enemy or friend.

"It's Bishop McBride," said one. "Hello, Brother Nephi."

"Hello, Brother George. How is he?"

"Very low."

Nephi went to the bed and looked down at John. The large swarthy face had the pallor of death but Taylor was still conscious; and when he recognized Nephi, he smiled.

"Brother Nephi, how are you?"

"Well, President Taylor. I'm sorry to find you this way."

"It doesn't matter. God is calling me home. How are things in Joseph-ville?"

"Very bad. One by one they pack up and flee."

"The Order?"

"There's little left of it. All of the Orders are gone now."

"Yes, all of them."

Taylor closed his eyes. The other men sat on each side of the bed and looked gravely at his face. Nephi stood at the foot of the bed, remembering the time ten years ago when the mighty Brigham died. Brigham had known there were troubles ahead, but he could hardly have foreseen how in ten years the church would disintegrate; how all the principal leaders would be in jail or hiding; how thousands of the saints would be in flight. That had been a dark hour but not so dark as this one.

"Does he sleep?" one asked.

"Not yet," said Taylor, and opened his eyes. "Brother Joseph, what is going to happen to God's children?"

"Brother John, I don't know. This is the first time in three years that the president and his counselors have met together."

"Yes."

"They may never meet again."

"We must have faith and hope," said Taylor. His voice was so weak that they barely heard. "Wilford, as President of the Twelve, will be your president now."

"Yes, Brother John."

Taylor looked around him from face to face. "You must—go on fighting. We must never—give up—our principles."

The men did not answer. Taylor spoke again.

"Is—Dan Wells—still in Europe?"

"I think he's coming home."

"I wanted to see him—once more." Again Taylor's gray eyes, naturally deep-set and now looking sunken, slowly closed. White hair faintly touched with gray lay upon his broad high forehead. His thin hands were clasped on the coverlet over his breast.

For almost an hour nobody spoke. The other men present gazed steadily at their dying leader; and Nephi, watching their faces, wished he could read their minds. That they were facing the most difficult crisis of their lives, it seemed to him they were all fully aware. It was not that in John Taylor they were losing an empire builder, or even a man who had led aggressively and well. It was not that they needed him—because for two and a half years he had been hiding, and for all the good he had done he might as well have been dead. Nephi loved the man but had always felt gentle contempt for him. Most of the saints had loved John Taylor much more than they had loved Brigham—but it had been the ruthless and unsentimental Brigham who had saved them from ruin. It was, God knew, another Brigham whom they needed now; but there was not here, or anywhere in Zion, another dictator when a dictator was needed. Joseph F. Smith, so far as Nephi could size him up, was an unimaginative and humorless fanatic much like the Jedediah Grant of thirty-five years ago. The other counselor was an abler man but he would not be president. Woodruff would be president, and he was old and tired and would soon be dead.

Perhaps two hours passed in silence before John Taylor stirred again. His lips moved, and all heads bowed to hear him. After a great effort that seemed to draw upon all the strength he had, he spoke in a hoarse whisper. "I feel to thank the Lord," he said, and those were his last words.

Nephi had wanted to talk with the leaders here but they ignored him; and an hour after Taylor's death he was driving homeward. This visit to the bedside of a dying man had been utterly meaningless. John had said they would hope and fight and never give up their principles; but this was only the last feeble utterance of a man who had given up fighting years ago. Joseph F. Smith had been in Hawaii for nearly three years and would doubtless flee again; the other counselor, with a reward on his head, would seek his hole. There would be a secret meeting of the Twelve to sustain Woodruff as president; and then they would scatter and leave their people to the gentiles and the jails. If Brigham were alive, he would climb to the highest roof and defy his enemies. He would march at the head of his people and call on the Federal government to build enough jails to hold them. Yes, if Brigham were here, he would lead a hundred thousand saints to prison and stay in prison with them until the crack of doom.

Nephi looked around him in the darkness. The entire area through which he was driving was picketed, he well knew, with deputy marshals; and perhaps even now he was being followed. He gazed up at the mountain night, vast in its breadth, infinite in its distances, and reflected that this *was* a fitting home for God's people. But God's people were in a sorry mess now! Every Mormon leader was in prison or in hiding or in exile. Hundreds of women had left their homes, and often their children, and had fled; scores were in jail for contempt of court; and scores were hiding like outlaws in the homes of friends. Old men were coming out of prison, broken in health—as his own father would soon come. A few had killed themselves. A few of the younger wives, maddened by fear, had fled into the mountains with a baby in their arms; and one of them had wandered in the hills until her infant died and then had buried it under a pile of stones.

When Nephi arrived home the time was after midnight. He unhitched and cared for his team and was about to enter his house when he thought of his grandmother. There was no light in any of Moroni's rooms. He entered by a rear door, removed his shoes, and softly climbed the stairs to Kate's chamber. The shades were up and a full moon had risen. The light fell in paths and pools upon the floor and across the chairs and bed. It fell upon Kate's small face and upon her two bony arms that someone had folded across her fleshless breast.

For a moment Nephi thought his little old grandmother was dead: there was no sign of life, nor the faintest stir of cover as she breathed. After gazing down at her, he bent low and put an ear to her heart. Distinctly, unmistakably, he heard its tired beat. It was very slow—so slow that it seemed to pause and rest between one beat and the next. There was nothing else to suggest life in the shrunken form. The face was white with death; the hands and arms were those of a corpse.

Nephi tiptoed to other bedrooms, and in one saw a woman sleeping. In another chamber lay Moroni. Nephi quietly entered and saw that the tired old gentleman had chosen Maggie to share his bed. He lay on his side with one arm around her, with his face half-hidden in her mass of white hair. Moroni slept so quietly that he seemed to be dying too. Well, he would be dead soon, and Maggie and Agatha also; and they would be more fortunate than those who lived. The generation who fought and worked with Joseph was swiftly passing away; and with them, Nephi deeply felt, would go something—an unconquerable spirit, a single-minded zeal that would not live with the same strength in the generations to follow.

Moroni must be very tired tonight or he would be sitting by his first wife. And yet, Nephi reflected, returning to Kate's chamber, there was no reason why he should. Kate was slowly and peacefully dying; the weary old heart would grow fainter and fainter until at last it would pause on a half-beat and stop. There was something beautiful in death that came so naturally, so quietly, that it was only deeper sleep. The little old lady's work was done and she was entering a momentary darkness that lay between the sorrows of one life and the glory of the next. There was no reason for grief. There was no reason to sit by her and wait for the end.

But Nephi did sit here to think of her going, and of Taylor's; to remember that all of Joseph's generation would soon be gone. Dan Wells and Wilford Woodruff still lived. Bill Smith, the prophet's violent brother, was down in Springville, but nobody had seen much of him for a long while. The first generation of saints, zealous and faithful, had closed their records and gone to their reward. The second and third generations were not what their fathers and grandfathers had been. Of the present apostles, Nephi liked only two: the others were men of wealth, cunning politicians, plotting opportunists who would come out of hiding, make peace with the gentiles, and build larger fortunes.

Again he bowed to his grandmother and heard the heart beating but more faintly now. Its periods of rest were longer—so long indeed that he was surprised after an interval to hear it beat again. The face was so dead and at peace that it was difficult to believe there was life in the breast. The white hair, neatly parted, framed the pallor of the wrinkled forehead; the mouth without its teeth was sunken. For another hour he sat here, bowing now and again to listen—and realized at last with a pang of dismay that the tired heart had stopped. There was no sound now. He kissed her hair and drew a white coverlet in a shroud to her chin.

The next morning Moroni was cheerless and looked almost ready for the grave himself. He asked if President Taylor was dead, if his end had been peaceful, and if he had given any advice before he went.

"None," said Nephi. "Woodruff will be president now. Everything will be as it was before."

"Yes. Your grandmother also passed away last night."

"I know. Grandfather, when the gentiles hear Taylor is dead, they'll move twice as fast and hard. Now is the time when they'll strike the final blow."

"Yes, we can expect hell to break loose now."

"And there's nothing we can do," said Nephi, turning wearily to the door. "Nothing—nothing at all."

CHAPTER XIII

THE UNITED STATES MOVED WITH DRAMATIC SUDDENNESS THE DAY AFTER John Taylor was buried. The district attorney brought suit in the supreme court of the territory to take from the church all property in excess of fifty thousand dollars; and in this confiscatory move Nephi saw the end of all the co-operative stores and community enterprises. The only property not involved by the suit was burial grounds and places of actual worship. This was a blow at the communistic empire which Brigham had built, and it was intended to destroy that empire once and forever.

The move against co-operative industries was not the only one. In Idaho Territory there had been passed a Test Oath which disfranchised all persons believing in plural marriage; and this law had been upheld by the Supreme Court of the nation. A U. S. marshal in Idaho had just boasted in open court that he had a jury impaneled to try Mormons "that would convict Jesus Christ Himself if He were on trial." The gentiles in Utah now moved for a test oath here; and into Congress at almost the same moment was introduced the Cullom-Struble Bill to disfranchise every Mormon in the country and destroy the church. That it would be passed, nobody had any reason to doubt.

Nor were those the only vigorous moves that followed close on Taylor's death. Gentiles in Utah and over the nation cried that the time was ripe, as it had been when Brigham died, to wipe Mormonism out while it was leaderless. The officials in Salt Lake City moved toward that end with every agency at their command. Nephi had grown accustomed to news of arrest, but he was now appalled by the virulence of the crusade. Mormons were arrested by the scores, and soon, it seemed to him, by the hundreds. They were convicted and jailed as fast as witnesses could be summoned and evidence taken. Swiftly, summarily, they were marched before the grand juries as if an entire people were on trial—as indeed they were. The trials became briefer and more ridiculous. There were no acquittals—and nearly all of the sentences were for the maximum under the law.

Over the entire territory, hundreds of the saints were being rushed to the courtrooms, convicted, and jailed. It was at last, beyond all further question, a leaderless and terrified people. Nowhere under the Utah sky was there a ray of hope. Nowhere in the nation was a voice lifted in the defense of these pioneers who had colonized a desert. Nowhere was there a sign of organized resistance. More and more the saints hardly dared speak to one another, not knowing who were traitors, or where the spies were.

Nephi was yet unborn when the saints had been scattered and driven out of Missouri; but he had heard his father and grandfather tell of those terrible months, and what he saw now must be, it seemed to him, much like the bewildered exodus then. Because in this valley, and in all the valleys north, west and south, thousands were in desperate flight, and thousands were hiding, afraid to come out and flee. In despair, Moroni closed and locked the doors of his house. Tim had served his sentence and had been released, an old and broken and emaciated man; and he now sat day after day in bitter brooding, little caring whether he was arrested again. Fanny did not lock doors, but almost overnight she lost a part of her anger and energy and had little to say. Genet spent half her time weeping, with her children gathered around and weeping too.

Nephi did not yield all hope. He knew of little he could do to stop this swift and inexorable destruction of his church, but he was resolved to do what he could. He was resolved not to hide and not to run. Of the Order in Josephville, little was left, and the escheating of church property meant that the community buildings and mills and shops would soon belong to the United States. Perhaps he could give courage to the members who had not fled and persuade them to stand by their principles to the end.

Day after day, therefore, and week after week he labored among them. He was dismayed and angered and sometimes amused by what he found. Among the farmers of the Order, few had taken plural wives; but he learned that even those who could not be arrested and jailed were half scared to death and spent much of their time hiding. One of them Nephi found burrowing in a haystack.

"Brother John," he cried, pitching hay off and exposing the frightened man, "what in hell are you doing in there!"

"By God," said John, peering out, "I'm hiding."

"What are you hiding from? You have only one wife."

"I know that. But they're passing so damned many laws that all of us are guilty of something."

"What are you guilty of?"

"I don't know. But I hear they're going to arrest all of us."

"Come on out of that hole!"

John came forth and shook hay from his clothes. He looked at Nephi and grinned. "Can't they jail me for anything?"

"Not a thing. Brother John, look. See the fields out there you're supposed to till? Where are the crops? You haven't planted a single seed."

"Bishop Nephi, I don't dare to work in the fields."

"Nonsense!"

"And how is it you ain't arrested yet?"

"I guess they haven't got around to me."

"Is it true all your wives left you?"

"No. They're hiding. Never mind my wives. I ask what are we going to eat if you don't plant the crops?"

"I don't know," said John, looking out at the fields. "But if they put me in jail I won't do much farming."

"They won't put you in jail. They can't. Go ahead with your work."

"See Brother Wilbur's place," said John, pointing to a distant field. "He's gone. He had only one wife but he hit the grit."

"In God's name!" cried Nephi. "If the brethren are all going to run, what will become of the church?"

"If we're all in jail, there won't be no church. That's how Wilbur saw it. Now me, I hide and sleep a while and my wife watches for the bastards. Then she sleeps and I watch."

"For shame! They can't arrest you, so go ahead with your work."

"But if they're going to take all our property, why plant crops?"

That question, Nephi reflected, was unanswerable. "Well, plant enough for your own use. Keep busy. And don't be afraid of arrest. They're arresting only the brethren with plural wives."

Nephi went next to Wilbur's place. It was not only abandoned; obviously it had been left in great haste. In the silent house, clothes and food were scattered everywhere, as if the family had hastily snatched a few things and run. Dishes in the kitchen were unwashed. It looked to Nephi as if a meal had been interrupted. Perhaps a neighbor had come from the city, crying that all the saints were to be imprisoned; and Wilbur thereupon had quickly hitched a team to his old buggy, grabbed a few clothes and a little food, and set out for lands unknown. Hundreds of families up and down the valley had left in haste no less extreme. Hundreds of farms had been sold for a little or nothing or deserted outright by the men who had suffered privations to build them.

Josephville itself was a picture of desolation. Not a shop or a mill in it had been active for a long while. Windows in the stores had been broken by men who sought provisions before fleeing; and of the piles of clothes and foodstuffs there seven years ago, little remained. Beasts had been turned loose in the unplanted fields. In the church itself, once the center of the community's social life, there had been no services for weeks except Kate's funeral.

And what Nephi saw here, he realized was true in a thousand communities that were formerly prosperous and happy. How many of the saints had fled he did not know. Nobody knew. They had gone north, south and west, with only one thought in their minds: to get beyond the country that persecuted them. Their parents and grandparents fled from Missouri which was to have been Zion. Years later, Brigham had declared that Zion would be in this Basin; but look at it now!

"I don't know," Nephi said to his parents, "of anything I can do. Josephville looks as if its inhabitants had run from a pestilence or a flood."

"A pestilence," said Fanny. "It's the pestilence that started in Palmyra. It will never stop until we're chased into the ocean."

"Are you losing your faith?"

"No." Fanny sat and looked at her son. "I'll never lose my faith but I don't understand why God allows it. Hasn't He tested His children enough? You insist on hoping when there's nothing to hope for. After we are all in jail what will happen? There won't be any church. Not here. What will happen to our children? They won't even be citizens. They will be called bastards and will have the rights of felons. We'll never be allowed plural marriage in the United States and it does no good to pretend anything else."

"We must be true to the principles we believe in."

"I will be. I'm not afraid to die in jail. But I don't fool myself that all we have to suffer is a few years in jail and then everything will be all right. Jail isn't to get rid of us. It's to make us give up our religion. That's what your father thinks too. Don't you, Tim?"

"Of course," said Tim, raising his shaggy head.

"Well, sure, it's to make us give up our religion."

"Then stop pretending things will be all right. They never will be again. If we had Brigham Young— But that isn't true," she said impatiently. "Not even Brigham could get us out of this mess. Only God can and for His own reasons He won't. Is it true that hundreds of the saints are leaving the church?"

"I guess it is. That's because of this new test oath."

"Is a vote worth so much they become apostates?"

"With some of them."

"Well, I'll stick to my principles even if they kill me. But I won't fool myself any longer. When they put your father in jail, I thought there'd be some way out of this trouble; but now I know better. I'm expecting the worst."

"How is grandfather today?"

"He feels pretty bad. He was fooling himself too but not now. But he won't ever be arrested, so why should he worry?"

"He's worrying about the church. None of us are worrying about ourselves."

"I am," said Fanny. "If Sarah doesn't go away, your father will be arrested again; and I won't ask her to go away. I'm worrying about the children. What is there in the future for them? No matter where they go they'll be persecuted. They'll be taunted and made fun of. They'll feel degraded. And I worry about Genet. She'll be dead soon."

"We'll all be dead eventually."

"I wish to God I was. Kate was lucky to get out of it."

"You're losing your courage," said Nephi, smiling at his mother.

"Oh, courage! As long as Genet and Sarah sit around and bawl, I have all the work to do. You might try and straighten your wife up."

"I've tried."

When Nephi asked Genet to have courage and go ahead with her work, she sank to a chair and wept afresh. She looked as if she had done nothing but weep for months.

"There isn't any hope!" she cried. "That's what your mother says!"

"Never mind what my mother says. The saints in the past suffered worse things than this."

"I don't see what!"

"Famine and plague and murder!" cried Nephi. "We still have enough to eat. We're not sick—unless you persist in your damned weakness and get sick. God is trying your faith and you sit and bawl about it. Come to your senses."

"Even your grandfather doesn't think there's any hope!"

"But I do."

"No, Nephi," she said, looking at him. "Don't lie. You know you'll be in jail soon. Then what will I do?"

Nephi rose, wearily, and went to the door to look out. "We can be faithful to our principles; and if we must, we'll leave the rest to God."

"But God won't feed my children."

"I'll feed them!" he said, turning angrily.

"Yes, in jail!"

One morning a few days later, Nephi said he was going to drive through the valley north and south and learn anew what was happening. "I'll be gone several days; so fix me a grub box and a bed."

"Nephi!" Genet cried, her voice shaken by terrible fear. "You're leaving us!"

He was astonished. He went over and laid hands on her thin shoulders and looked into her pale swollen eyes. "Of course I'm not leaving you. I'm no coward."

"Don't lie to me. You don't intend to come back."

"Oh, in God's name, Genet! I just want to find out what is happening. I want to know how many are running away."

"Do you promise to come back?"

"Of course I'll come back. Now put a little food in a box and make a bedroll."

The number of saints who were running away amazed him. As a matter of fact, it seemed to him, as he drove north or south to the main roads, that the whole population of the valley was on the move. It was not, of course; but everywhere he looked in this summer of 1889, he saw pilgrims heading for Mexico or Canada. He saw persons in the hamlets, in farmyards, in the towns who were mending their harness and yokes, repairing wagons and buggies, trying to sell their property, and getting ready to go.

For several days he jogged over the valley, content to look and ponder, to feed his team at ditch banks and to sleep under the stars; but after he more fully understood the extent of the exodus, he wondered if he could not persuade these saints to remain. One morning, having camped at a roadside spot, he was preparing breakfast when he saw three wagons coming. Behind the wagons, men and boys were driving a small herd of cattle. Convinced that this was an emigrant train going south, Nephi went out to halt them.

"Good morning," he said to a desperate-looking man who was teamster in the lead-wagon. "Are you a Mormon?"

"Who are you?"

"I am Bishop Nephi McBride of Josephville."

"At least that's what you say."

"I am."

"You're probably a United States marshal." The man looked around at three women who sat behind him. The next move surprised Nephi. One of the women quickly thrust a rifle forward. The man seized it and turned the muzzle toward Nephi. "I don't know who you are. I don't want any trouble."

"I tell you I'm one of your brethren in the gospel."

"You might be and you might not be. We are leaving and we don't want any trouble; but no United States marshal is going to stop us."

"Where are you going?"

"That is our business."

"Brother, why don't you stay and go to jail with the rest of us? Why run away?"

Other men came up from the rear. "Who is this man?" asked one.

"He says he's a Mormon."

"He's probably an officer. What do you want?"

"I want you brethren to stay in Zion."

"What for?"

"Your principles."

"We'll take them with us."

"But what will happen to the church if you all leave?"

"The church," said the man on the wagon, "is where God's people are. Now stand back. We don't know who you are but we don't want any trouble."

Nephi drew a deep breath and stepped back. Well, he reflected, watching the emigrants go down the road, in this land of snoops and spies no saint could any longer tell whether he faced friend or enemy. He hitched his team and drove north; and in the days that followed he could no longer doubt that another tremendous migration was under way. By the thousands the saints were leaving. They were going south to Mexico, north to Canada; and a few with more means were going to coast ports and embarking for Hawaii and the South Seas. It did not matter: they were going, and they were going armed and desperate, resolved that no power under heaven would stop them. No power tried to—except a few earnest men like Nephi who were striving to keep communities together and prevent a mass flight. The Federal authorities were glad to see them go.

Everywhere Nephi went he saw deserted farms, deserted homes, and beasts turned to the fields to live as they could. Often he stopped to enter a house and look around him; but the emptiness and desolation dismayed him, and he was helpless between anger and grief. That a persecuted people, driven to a desert, should have built so nobly and well; that they should now be goaded into desertion of a half-century of suffering and toil—that seemed to him more unjust, more bitter and tragic, than any misfortune endured by the Jews. He liked to think of Brigham's amazement and wrath if the Great Pioneer could rise today and look around him. He had chosen a God-forsaken spot to which he thought the gentiles would never wish to come; yet here were the gentiles, twelve years after his death, again driving his people into a wilderness. If he could see his people setting out with a handful of possessions, again to seek a new home, again to place a thousand miles between them and their enemies, between the right of a free conscience and the intolerance of a free land— if he could rise and see all this, would his heart break, or would he clench his fist and defy all the forces of hell? Nephi could not answer that—but he felt that Brigham would mount the pulpit and hurl such a challenge as the world had never before heard.

Turning at last away from the country and its roads burdened with desperate pilgrims, Nephi drove to the city, eager to know if the saints there were fleeing too. He went first to Fifth Street to look at the ironic monstrosity called a Home for Polygamous Wives. Its charitable doors had been opened for nearly three years, but no Mormon wife had entered it. Not even among those who despised their husbands, nor among those who had left their husbands or whose husbands had deserted them, had there been a single admission. Only seven women in three years had accepted the sanctuary, and they were women who had been abandoned by gentiles.

But there the building stood—a monumental insult to the conscience of a free people. Rumor declared that it was to be sold, or converted into a post office, or made an adjunct of the Fort Douglas barracks. In any case, except for seven women and a few caretakers, it was a huge and expensive emptiness, a piece of smug and bigoted federal folly.

After driving slowly past and turning on the Home an ironic grin, Nephi went to a hitching post and left his team. He searched through the city but he was not able to learn how little or how much the saints here had been demoralized. President Woodruff's office was locked. He sought his friends in the city, but there was nobody home, though whether they had fled or were hiding inside or had been jailed he could not tell. He glanced into courtrooms and saw trials in progress. In Mormon establishments there was only a handful of shoppers, but gentile stores were thronged. The more he looked around him, the more deeply he felt that a blight had fallen on the city, and that the saints were now aliens within it.

He drove homeward, noting as he went the clouds of dust on the highways that marked the journey of his people. Unless something happened soon, the whole Mormon population would be in flight, going they hardly knew where but seeking a land friendly to their conscience. There was nothing anyone could do to stop them now. They had to flee or go to jail—and nine out of ten preferred to flee. For them flight was the only way out, as it had been in Nauvoo; and it was a pity that there was no aggressive and resourceful leader to guide them in mass migration and establish them as a unit in a foreign land. Perhaps, Nephi reflected, he could gather a hundred families and lead them to one of the Mexican colonies, or into the forested wilderness of the Canadian Northwest.

The notion took hold of him as he drove home; and when he arrived he laid the plan before Moroni to learn what the wise old pioneer thought.

"Why only a hundred families? Why not a thousand or ten thousand?"

"Well, the more, the better."

"If we set out from here with a hundred, by the time we reached St. George we should have a thousand."

"Perhaps—if they haven't all gone."

"They would join us in Provo, in Fillmore, in Beaver, in Cedar City, in Harmony—in every colony between here and the Mexican border."

"Then you like the plan?" asked Nephi eagerly.

"Yes. But it's too late to start this year. We could get ready this winter."

"If we had a big colony—the biggest anywhere—then we could build the church again. But would the saints go if we had none of the apostles with us?"

"I don't know. Some would, some wouldn't."

"But we don't want a schism. If all the authorities stay here——"

"We had better wait a while," Moroni said. "But we can keep it in mind and sort of be ready."

"Will you go?"

"I don't know if I'n stand another long journey. I'll try."

"Then we'll do it! In the name of Israel's God, we'll gather all the saints we can and lead them out of the United States!"

"But don't be too hasty. You see the brethren in Josephville and learn if they'll go. Nephi, I have an idea something is going to happen soon."

"What?"

"I don't know," said Moroni, wagging his long white beard. "But I have a feeling in my bones."

CHAPTER XIV

Moroni felt an important move was imminent because it was known that an influential Mormon was in Washington, or had been recently, trying to persuade congressmen to tolerate plural marriage; but Nephi had no such feelings in his bones. When spring opened, he set to work to convince the few families in Josephville that they should migrate to Mexico. Those like Datus Frost, who had only one wife, saw no reason to leave; but men with plural wives were eager to go. They began to repair wagons and harness, to make crates, to sell such personal belongings as they had no room for. They talked of the new Zion which they would found. Sarah and Genet stopped weeping and pitched in; and Fanny asked why in the name of all that was sensible they had not gone long ago.

Nephi labored almost day and night, seeking recruits in the country roundabout, advising and assisting them, furnishing them with such supplies as were left in the store, appointing captains as Brigham had done, and talking with Moroni who had been in two migrations and knew what to do. When summer came, Nephi wanted to go, but he was delayed by one rumor and another. Where the rumors came from, nobody knew, nor did anybody know if there was any truth in them. One rumor said the President was going to pardon all Mormons and restore them to their civil and religious rights. Another declared that Congress was going to repeal the Edmunds Act.

One morning Nephi was in his home, discussing plans with his captains, when Moroni entered. At once Nephi knew that the old man was overwhelmed. For a long moment he stood at the door, shaking a newspaper in his hand and staring at his grandson.

"What is the matter?" asked Nephi.

"We are betrayed," said Moroni, and sank to a chair.

Nephi seized the paper, a copy of the *Deseret News*; and as he read the story on the front page he also sank to a chair as if life were going out of him. "My God!" he said, and looked at his grandfather.

"What is it?" asked a captain.

"Woodruff has sold us out!"

"How?"

"Listen!" This is what Nephi read:

To Whom it May Concern:

Press dispatches having been sent for political purposes, from Salt Lake City, which have been widely published, to the effect that the Utah Commission, in their recent report to the secretary of the interior, allege that plural marriages are still being solemnized and that forty or more such marriages have been contracted in Utah during the past year; also that in public discourses the leaders of the Church have taught, encouraged and urged the continuance of the practice of polygamy ——

I, therefore, as president of the Church of Jesus Christ of Latter-day Saints, do hereby, in the most solemn manner, declare that these charges are false. We are not teaching polygamy, or plural marriage, nor permitting any person to enter into its practice, and I deny that either forty or any other number of plural marriages have, during that period, been solemnized in our temples or in any other place in the territory.

Inasmuch as laws have been enacted by Congress forbidding plural marriages, which laws have been pronounced constitutional by the court of last resort, I hereby declare my intention to submit to those laws, and to use my influence with the members of the church over which I preside to have them do likewise.

There is nothing in my teachings to the church or in those of my associates, during the time specified, which can reasonably be construed to include or encourage polygamy, and when any elder of the church has used language which appeared to convey such teaching he has been promptly reproved. And I now publicly declare that my advice to the Latter-day Saints is to refrain from contracting any marriage forbidden by the law of the land.

"The coward!" cried one.

"Worse than that," said Nephi. "He now calls it polygamy. He says he hasn't encouraged plural marriage, yet not long ago he said to all of us that we did not reveal plural marriage and could not therefore renounce it! He said no matter what happened, we must keep that covenant or be damned. But now—now to the whole world he calls celestial marriage polygamy!"

"He must be out of his mind."

"No," said Moroni. "He has just deliberately sold us out."

"And look!" said Nephi, who had turned a page. "He and his counselors have been hiding in San Francisco. No wonder nobody could find them! Well, I'm going over to see the Judas. Grandfather, you going?"

"Of course."

They found Woodruff alone in his office, an old and a very weary man who seemed to have been sitting in thought. His face brightened for a moment but then filled with alarm; for even to blurred old eyes like his, Nephi was an angry man.

"President Woodruff, what in hell do you mean by this?"

"Will you sit down, Brother Nephi?"

"I won't leave this office until I learn by what right you have sold us to our enemies."

"The last time you were here," said Woodruff, putting a hand to his wrinkled face, "you wore me out. I cannot stand argument at my age."

"I didn't come to argue. I came for an explanation. Did you receive a revelation from God authorizing this?"

"Well——"

"Did you? Answer plain yes or no."

"No."

"You did not?"

"I received no revelation but I did spend days in solitary thought. I prayed and after prayer I felt inspired. I felt the Lord was directing me."

"You *felt* it!"

"I felt inspired."

"You were willing to place the church and its people in jeopardy because you *felt* inspired? God's revelation to Joseph was a certainty. Yet because you *felt* something, you are willing to repudiate it! God spoke to Joseph and gave him a holy covenant; and you pray and throw it out!"

"I will not argue with you. My conscience, I am president of the church——"

"But Joseph was its prophet."

One of Woodruff's old hands thumped angrily. "I am president. I prayed and felt inspired and I am sure it is God's will."

"If it was God's will in so grave a matter, He would make it known to you. I also have felt inspired after praying. Every good person does. But a feeling is not a commandment from God. In plain language, President Woodruff, God told Joseph that if this covenant is not kept, those violating it would be forever damned and no atonement could save their souls. Yet you think you have the right to annul a covenant, break up thousands of homes, make bastards of thousands of children, harlots of thousands of wives. God will have no mercy on you for that! If Brigham were alive he'd throw you out of the church head over heels."

Woodruff drew a long breath and looked at Moroni. "Do you feel this way about it?"

"Only a revelation from God could justify you in this. Most of the saints will feel that way."

"What," asked Nephi, "did your counselors say about it?"

"Well, they took it very hard. Joseph F. Smith wept——"

"I should think he would! Do you remember how the apostles wept when Joseph revealed this commandment to them? Brigham said he wished he had never been born. Yet they endured persecution year after year——"

"If," said Woodruff, speaking with the patience of eighty-three years, "you will let me, I'll explain the matters that led me to this decision. But I have no strength to argue with you. I am old and sick. I'll soon face my God but my conscience is clear.

"Brother Nephi, it has been made plain to us after sixty years that we cannot fight the United States. We cannot make war on seventy million people, or defend ourselves against them. Our church is bankrupt. Our property has been escheated. I hope the government can be prevailed on to give back what it has taken from us."

"Is property so important?"

"My conscience, what would we do without it? We'd be ruined."

"In that way we have been ruined many times."

"But not so completely."

"We left Nauvoo," said Moroni, "with only the rags on our backs."

Woodruff raised a hand to silence him. "Well, that is one thing—bankruptcy. There are many others. The test oath has been upheld by the Supreme Court, and now there is a bill pending to disfranchise all of us. If we don't compromise, that bill will be passed. We have lost political and industrial control of this city and this territory, even though we outnumber the gentiles three to one. Our converts from other countries cannot be naturalized. In other words, we are a bankrupt people without a country and without any rights. Many of the saints are weary of the conflict——"

"Only the old men," said Nephi.

"They have urged on me the necessity of compromise."

"Such as your counselors who wept when they heard about it!"

"Brother Nephi, hundreds of the saints have left the church. Hundreds have fled."

"Just a minute! Weaklings have always left the church. Are you compromising to please the apostates? Those who fled did so to escape compromise. President Woodruff, face the facts. Those who urged compromise are business men who want the patronage and goodwill of the gentiles. Anyone who urged you to compromise did so because he is more interested in making money than in serving God. And as for fleeing, why shouldn't we all leave this valley? We fled three times before."

"But not you. You were born here. I tell you the brethren are weary of the struggle—of building and fleeing and building and fleeing."

"It's better to give up our property than our principles. It's better to give our enemies everything we have ——"

"But not all the saints feel that way."

"I'm not speaking of money-grabbers! President Woodruff, more than one thousand three hundred saints are in jail right now. They went to jail rather than compromise. They are willing to die in jail. You are not speaking for those in jail and the thousands ready to go to jail. You are speaking for a handful of merchants who talked you into compromise to save their unclean stinking pocketbooks.

"I'll face you with your own words. After Joseph was murdered and the saints were being driven out of Nauvoo, the apostles—and you were one of them—sent a message to our people throughout the world. Have you forgotten it? That message said that the saints were never to seek to save their lives or fortunes at the expense of truth and principle. It said we would all live in our religion or die together. And more recently you signed another statement that said we must be faithful to the holy covenant of plural marriage, even if it cost us our lives."

"I know it. I did say that."

"You have given your reasons for repudiating a covenant from God. I want to ask you some questions—and they are questions that thousands will want to ask you. Nearly fifty years ago, God gave us the covenant of plural marriage. As an omniscient being, He looked ahead and saw all the persecutions and trials that would be heaped upon us. If it is all right to renounce that covenant now, why did He give it to us, knowing it would be only fifty years of purgatory?"

"I cannot explain God's mind. I do not know His plans for His people."

"If God saw we would have to renounce that covenant in a few years, why did He not let Joseph compromise? Joseph and Hyrum died for that covenant. Why didn't God abolish it to save the prophet's life?"

"I cannot tell you."

"Answer this: why did you tell the world you have not approved or encouraged plural marriage?"

"I said in the last year or two."

"But it's only in the last few days that you prayed and felt inspired. What right did you have not to encourage it a year ago?"

"My conscience, I said I will not argue with you."

"No, you will not even answer questions. What are the thousands of saints to do who will not accept this cowardice? There are thousands. The McBrides will not accept this betrayal, not if we must die as Joseph died. Where is the leadership for those of us who will go to jail rather than be false to our principles? Are we to become wanderers on the earth like the Jews? Answer me, President Woodruff."

"I can say no more. I prayed and felt that God was directing me. The saints will have to accept the leadership of their president and apostles."

"We will not. We have been betrayed. Thirteen hundred men in jail have been betrayed. The thousands of sisters who would not enter the Home have been betrayed. Of what use has been all their sacrifice?"

"I have reason to know," said Woodruff, still patient, "that the President intends to pardon all the saints now in jail."

That statement brought Nephi to his feet. "Oh, so that is it! You have renounced a covenant to get a pardon for men who never asked for one! You made a political horse trade and told your conscience that God would bless you for it!"

"There is no need to get angry. If you get angry with me, I must ask you to leave."

"I'll go soon, but before I go I intend to speak my mind. I'm going to speak for the thousands in jail and out who would like to come here and tell you the same things. I will speak for those like Joseph and Hyrum who died, and like Brigham who went to jail. Will you listen?"

"Yes. But speak calmly if you can."

"Calmly! Would to God Brigham knew what you have done! Have you ever been in jail? No! Have your counselors been in jail?

"President Woodruff, let's face the facts. You have betrayed us—and there's no use to pretend you've done anything else. There's no use to pretend that the church in this valley will not go on in betrayal to the end of its days. The apostles have approved your action; and after you're dead, one of them will be president; and after he's dead, another much like him will take his place. Do you remember what one of your counselors said when Brigham was sick? He said, 'I thought of his death, if it should occur, and recoiled. It seemed to me that he was indispensable. What could we do without him? He was the brain, the eye, the ear, the mouth and hand for our people.' He should have added that Brigham was also the courage.

"What have we done, what can we do, without him? Why, go on and yield principle by principle until our church is only a wealthy corporation of special privilege and power! The covenant of plural marriage is gone. The Orders are destroyed. Those two were the blood and life of our religion. If there are any more principles which the gentiles dislike, they will be given up also. I am not a prophet; but I do pray and I too feel inspired after prayer. You felt inspired to destroy divine commandments. I feel inspired to tell you what the church will become for those of you who remain in this city and this valley.

"For more than sixty years, President Woodruff, the saints have been a persecuted people, driven from place to place. I hardly have to tell you that—for you were in Ohio, Missouri, Nauvoo. I hardly have to remind you that they endured arson, rape, murder, and saw again and again the destruction of all that they had built. Even when their prophet was slain, they had the courage to pack up and flee to a desert and build again.

"What I want to point out to you is this: they built on a desert under a leader who would not have compromised unless God Himself thundered the command from heaven. Not once in those sixty years was there compromise or any thought of it. Joseph never backtracked or made peace at the expense of his conscience; and if he ever considered doing such a thing, there is no record of it. In spite of plagues and famines and armies against him, Brigham never compromised by one jot. He was an old man too. He was jailed. So many threats were made against his life that in his last years he had a bodyguard, and never knew from day to day if he would live to see the next morning. But he never flinched, and you know it, I know it, and every man, woman and child in Zion knows it.

"But now what? Why, the end of all that Joseph and Brigham fought for! Don't tell me it isn't so or that you don't know it. Don't tell me that sixty years of hardship and persecution have not been sold for another piece of silver. Yes, hell yes, the church will get its property back; the saints will be pardoned; and you and the other leaders will go ahead making your shameful peace. You will make peace with the gentiles, you will make political trades, you will deny your wives and children; but you can never forget that two holy covenants are as dead as the message of Jesus in the heart of intolerance everywhere!

"The time is coming, President Woodruff—the first signs of it are already here—when the saints and gentiles will mix and marry, dance and love together, trade votes, perjure themselves, and worship the same god—and that god will be money. This church that was to establish a new gospel of brotherhood on earth will have bigger banks and factories, its millionaires and its beggars. Some will own factories—and some will own nothing but their self-respect. There will be the same wealth and poverty, luxury and starvation, snobbery and humility that are found all over the world. And our church, the one that began in a cabin in Palmyra and was driven across a continent, will be no different from churches anywhere!

"It will be no different, President Woodruff, because the covenants that made it different are now dead. It will be a church but it will no longer be God's church. It will be like the churches that have persecuted us for sixty years. God established His church more than eighteen centuries ago, and what happened to it? The leaders compromised too and chose to be wealthy instead of righteous. The leaders of this church will do likewise.

"Oh, they will keep the rituals! All churches have done that. They will go through all the empty sacraments. Even abominable churches do that. But they will not keep those few simple principles which God gave us to prevent whoredom, poverty, greed, starvation. I and many others will leave you this counterfeit of a church which the gentiles now smile on. The church that Joseph founded is dead. After sixty years, the sun has set upon God's church in this city and this valley!"

Woodruff turned to Moroni. "Do you feel such bitterness?"

"We have a right to feel bitter, Brother Wilford. There can be no church if our wives are to be whores and our children bastards."

"But they will not be. We'll keep them in any way we can—only we won't have any more plural marriage. That's all."

"That isn't all!" cried Nephi. "Now that marriage has been made shameful, are our people to be sneaks until they die? Have you thought of what all our children are going to have to face?"

"Yes, many times."

"You have made thousands of children illegitimate."

"I have thought of that too."

"The time will come when children and grandchildren will apologize for their parents. Plural marriage will be a shameful thing in their memories for generations. And do you realize that now there will never be any Orders, any pride in mutual ownership and management? Do you realize it is now every man for himself?"

"Yes, Brother Nephi. Are you brethren going to leave the church?"

"Where *is* the church? It's where its principles are. Because its principles are no longer in this valley, we are going to leave—and take as many with us as will go."

Woodruff rose, looking twice as old and tired as when they entered. He followed them to the door. Almost timidly he laid a hand on Moroni's shoulder.

"Good-bye," he said gently, wearily. "May God bless you and keep you."

CHAPTER XV

NEPHI SENT A CARRIAGE TO OGDEN TO BRING MAUDE AND HER CHILDREN; and on October 11, 1890, a caravan of forty-seven wagons and buggies pulled out of Josephville and headed south. In the first wagon sat Nephi, with Moroni at his side. Behind them was a carriage with Fanny and Tim in the front seat, and with Agatha and Maggie in the rear, lying on a huge bed of feather ticks and blankets. In the other vehicles was the remainder of the McBride clan, followed by persons from the Josephville colony and the surrounding farms. Several men rode mowing machines and hay rakes—because teams had been hitched to every implement that could be drawn on wheels. The strongest wagons were loaded with tons of machinery that had been torn from shops and mills, and with food, seed, clothes and furniture. In the rear was a herd of cattle, driven chiefly by children.

When a little way out, Nephi handed the reins to Moroni and rose to look back. His heart was full as he gazed at the ruins of what had been the most perfect community in Zion. All the mills and shops and homes, all the farms, all the shade trees and gardens and flower beds were being left to the saints who had placed property above principle.

"The church authorities," he said bitterly, "will take all that. All that we built in thirty years they'll now enrich themselves with."

"Of course," Moroni said.

"They'll own factories and banks, mines and railroads. They'll excommunicate us."

"Oh, no. We'll excommunicate them. We're taking the principles."

"Sit down!" Fanny cried, scowling at her son. "Quit gawking and making yourself feel bad."

"Set down," said Tim, "and forget it."

"This reminds me," said Moroni, after Nephi had sat, "of the time when we left Nauvoo. We looked back then but it didn't do us any good."

Nephi put an arm around the old man. "Well, we'll establish an Order in Mexico that will be just as good as the one we had."

As he urged his team forward, Nephi was thinking of the amazement and wrath which Woodruff's manifesto had aroused among the saints. Moroni remembered the anger and consternation which greeted Brigham when, twenty-seven years ago, he announced the doctrine of celestial marriage. The anger now, he said, was greater; the disillusionment was more overwhelming. Nephi had not traveled far or talked with many to learn that. Most of the men with only one wife had taken the matter calmly—for they did not care. Among those with more than one wife, a few had said it was all for the best. It was best, they said, to be done with a problem that had caused so much persecution and loss. But most of the saints were furious and heaped upon Woodruff their wild and abusive wrath; and some had been so enraged that they packed up overnight and set out for foreign lands.

On the march southward, several wagons were to join Nephi's train before he reached Provo; and beyond Provo and in the southern colonies, he hoped to induce many to go with him. He hoped to have a thousand by the time he crossed the Mexican border. They could then establish a big colony; and if driven out of Mexico, they would go to the South Seas.

Moroni said he felt tired and thought he should rest. Nephi piled quilts against a box of canned goods, and the old man stretched out, laid his long white beard down over his breast, and closed his eyes.

"I'm all right now," he said.

"You put him in a buggy!" Fanny cried. "You'll jolt his liver out."

"He wants to be up here."

"I'm all right," said Moroni, waving a thin old hand. "I guess I'm good for one more journey."

Sitting alone now, and watching sweat darken the flanks of his beasts, Nephi gave his thoughts to the days ahead. How far it was to the Mexican colonies, he did not know—but hardly more than nine hundred miles. If they averaged twenty miles a day, they would arrive long before Christmas. Ruth had written that there was plenty of fertile land on the Bavispe River; an abundance of water and timber; and the kind of climate that made houses unnecessary. The weather here was turning cold, with threat of rain; but before long they would be in the warmer clime of the Mormon Dixie, and then in Arizona . . .

"Grandfather, you all right?"

"Yes. On the last hilltop I want to look back."

"We all do."

On the last hill, beyond which they would forever drop from sight of Salt Lake City, Nephi brought his wagon to a halt; and the teamsters behind him, guessing what was in his mind, drew alongside. The herdsmen sent the cattle over the hill and down. Then all the emigrants, except Agatha and Maggie, left their wagons and buggies and gathered in a silent group in a drizzling rain to look northward at a beautiful city on a mountainside. With the same emotion, a few of them had once turned to gaze at Nauvoo. Terraced on the mountain flank they could see the homes, and down below it the great temple, clearly visible in its spires and the great angel with a trumpet.

"Was Nauvoo more beautiful than Salt Lake City?"

"Much like it," said Moroni. "Only there, the temple stood above the homes."

"This is the last time," said Nephi, "that we shall see all this. Let us kneel and I will lead you in prayer." Nephi knelt and the others knelt in a circle around him.

"O God, our heavenly Father, look down upon your children kneeling here and guide and protect us. Four times in the past your children were driven forth. Four times they have tried to find a land that would allow them freedom of conscience and religious rights. We are driven forth again, and in this hour of need may thy spirit be with us, and may we have the courage to be faithful to thy holy covenants.

"In the words of Joseph, we believe in being honest, benevolent, virtuous, and in doing good to all men; indeed, we may say we follow the admonition of Paul: 'We believe all things, we hope all things.' We have endured many things and we hope to be able to endure all things. If there is anything virtuous, lovely, or of good report, we seek after these things. Bless us, our Father; and bless our enemies who have driven us forth, and bring them into ways of charity and tolerance. Teach them to seek that human fellowship and that devotion to liberty which alone can establish thy kingdom on earth. For us and for them, we ask these blessings in the name of thy Son who died on a cross to set men free. Amen."

They all rose, and without speaking, without again looking back, entered their wagons and carriages and turned down the hill. Ahead of them the sky was gray and wet. Above them, after a little while, the whole vault

« 768 »

of heaven darkened and lowered; and they journeyed under a broad belt of fog and rain. Somewhere ahead of them, said Moroni, the sun was shining; but Nephi looked at the deepening shadows and the thick gloom down the valley and said the sun had set.

THE END

CHILDREN OF GOD

Set in Linotype Granjon type
Format by A. W. Rushmore
Manufactured by the Haddon Craftsmen
Published by
HARPER & BROTHERS
New York and London

The

Harper Prize Novel

Contest

Its History and Terms

THE
HARPER PRIZE NOVEL
CONTEST

The Harper Prize Novel Contest is held every other year. The purpose of the Contest is to give prominence and success to a writer whose real quality has not hitherto found a wide audience. Any author is eligible for the Prize who is a United States citizen and who has not published a novel in book form prior to a certain specified date (announced at the beginning of each contest). Only unpublished works may be submitted. The judges of the 1939 Contest are:

Louis Bromfield   Carl Van Doren

Josephine W. Johnson

Other eminent writers and critics who have served as judges for these contests include:

Harry Hansen	Dorothy Canfield
John Erskine	Thornton Wilder
Ellen Glasgow	Henry Seidel Canby
Stuart P. Sherman	Grant Overton
Jesse Lynch Williams	Bliss Perry

Sinclair Lewis

The first Harper Prize was awarded in 1923 to Margaret Wilson's *The Able McLaughlins*, which also received the Pulitzer Prize. The second winner was Anne Parrish's *The Perennial Bachelor*. The third was *The Grandmothers*, by Glenway Wescott, the fourth Julian Green's *The Dark Journey*, the fifth Robert Raynolds's *Brothers in the West*, and the sixth Paul Horgan's *The Fault of Angels*. The seventh award went to H. L. Davis's *Honey in the Horn*, which also won the Pulitzer Prize; the eighth to

Frederic Prokosch's *The Seven Who Fled*. To this distinguished list is now added *Children of God* by Vardis Fisher.

Comments of Noted Writers and Critics on the
HARPER PRIZE NOVEL CONTEST

"It seems to me to have been awarded consistently to novels of the highest merit."—*Sinclair Lewis*.

"The Harper Prize has had a singularly distinguished record . . . reflects the best that is being done in contemporary literature."—*Louis Bromfield*.

"All interested in contemporary literature should be grateful to Harper & Brothers for establishing a literary prize of such value."—*William Lyon Phelps*.

"I have come to look forward with eagerness to the announcement of the Harper Prize award."—*Harry Hansen*.

A circular containing full information as to terms of award and conditions for submission of manuscripts will gladly be supplied, on request, by Harper & Brothers.